the treasury of
science fiction classics

the treasury of
science fiction
classics

EDITED BY HAROLD W. KUEBLER

Hanover House
Garden City, New York

Library of Congress Catalog Card Number 55-5273

contents

introduction

—and suddenly there was the atom! They had worked and sweated all night long on that lonesome desert in New Mexico making last-minute adjustments and preparations. It was almost dawn when they were ready to begin the test. The men grouped about the instrument panel grew silent and tense. The time had finally come. One man began counting off the seconds: ten—nine—eight—seven—six—five—four—three—two—one —zero—and suddenly, on that morning in mid-July of 1945, the atomic age was born.

For centuries mankind had known of the atom. Every schoolboy learned that it is the smallest particle of an element. During that wartime summer of 1945, however, the atom took on a new meaning. Mere mention of the word brought instant fear into the minds of men. The fearsome picture of the horrible mushrooming cloud was forever implanted on the brain of every man and woman. The world had experienced a man-made cataclysm of undreamed violence. Total destruction became a real and ever-present possibility.

As time passed, however, the world became aware of the more pleasant side of the atom. Newspapers and magazines began painting glowing word-pictures of what the atom was capable of doing for the advancement of mankind. Science was going to harness the atom's power for man's benefit, as well as for his possible destruction. In this atmosphere of expectation, of mankind's pausing on the brink of a wonderful new world, man's mind was stimulated by the thoughts of the tremendous things to come. And science fiction came of age.

Contrary to common belief, science fiction is not a new product resulting from the atomic age. It is not at all stretching a point to say that it is as old as literature itself. As far back as the second century A.D., a Greek philosopher by the name of Lucian of Somasata amused himself by creating fictional trips to the moon. All through the history of literature one can find traces of the development of science fiction. Contributions toward its growth came from almost every civilized country in Europe. Early in the 1600s the famous German astronomer, Johannes Kepler, wrote *Somnium*, in which he vividly described an imaginary trip through space to the moon. Not many years later England's Bishop Francis Godwin wrote *The Man in the Moone*. In this same period France's legendary poet and soldier, Cyrano de Bergerac, composed his *Voyages to the Moon and Sun*. There are many more such examples that could be mentioned, but these few are sufficient to prove the point. Science fiction had its roots planted long, long before man ever dreamed of the possibility of an atom bomb. What is new about science fiction is its dramatic, booming growth in popularity during the post-war years.

It is interesting to note the effect which scientific discovery has had on the development of science fiction. In the 1600s, when the works of Kepler, Godwin, and De Bergerac were appearing on the literary scene, the world was in a state of shock and bewilderment resulting from the new theories of Copernicus. The very idea that the earth might not be the center of the universe, but rather only one of many planets revolving about the sun, was more than most people could bear. When Galileo's new telescope proved Copernicus to be correct, a wave of enlightened enthusiasm swept through Europe and stimulated the writing of some of the earliest-known science-fiction literature. At the time the stories appearing in this book were being written imaginations were once again being revitalized by a series of new scientific discoveries—such as Samuel Morse's telegraph, Thomas Alva Edison's electric light, Marconi's radio, and the Wright brothers' airplane. Whenever great scientific discoveries have been made science fiction seems to have experienced a corresponding advance in creative output and popularity.

While science fiction does go back to the Greeks, the selections chosen for this anthology have been restricted to the early period of the so-called "modern era" of science fiction. This period begins with the writings of Jules Verne and H. G. Wells and terminates shortly before World War II. It was at this time that science fiction became a distinct literary entity. Earlier efforts in the realm of science fiction were limited and were for the most part mere exercises in creative writing. Philosophers, scientists, clergymen, and statesmen sometimes used science fiction as a tool in order to dramatize more effectively their various theories on life, science, and nature. In this group are included such great names as Bacon, Voltaire, Erskine, More, and Swift. It was only with the advent of Jules Verne—and then of H. G. Wells—that the picture radically changed and science fiction became a major literary development. Gradually there appeared on the scene such fine writers as Sir Arthur Conan Doyle, Frank Stockton, Ambrose Bierce, Karel Capek, Aldous Huxley, S. Fowler Wright,

E. M. Forster, David Keller, Olaf Stapledon, Philip Wylie, and many others too numerous to mention. It is from this rich literary treasure that the selections in this anthology have been chosen.

To those readers who are new to science fiction and to those who are accustomed to thinking of it in terms of pot-boilers written by hack writers for pulp magazines with lurid covers, this anthology must come as a pleasant surprise. Collected here are exciting novels and stories that share a common distinction: all are classic works of science fiction that have stood and passed the test of time. Each selection has been chosen specifically for its acknowledged excellence and for the high literary reputation of its author. Each story is famous in its own light and is as stimulating and intriguing now as on the day it first appeared in print.

In selecting material for this anthology, variety as well as quality was a main consideration. In this big 704-page volume there are four novels —three complete and one slightly abridged, a reading version of a play, eight short stories, excerpts from three other novels, and the complete script of a famous radio broadcast. Two of the most unusual pieces to be found here are the play and the radio script. The play, *R. U. R.* (*Rossum's Universal Robots*), was produced on Broadway by the Theatre Guild in 1922 and is considered to be the first successful science-fiction play. An adaptation of *R. U. R.* was performed on television last year, and once again it proved to be an exciting play of great imaginativeness. No other work of science fiction has succeeded in duplicating the commotion and notoriety aroused by Orson Welles' electrifying radio broadcast, "The Invasion from Mars." Based on H. G. Wells' novel, *War of the Worlds*, this 1939 radio production threw thousands of listeners into panic as its stark realism led them to believe that New Jersey and New York were actually being attacked by creatures from Mars. Both of these pieces were ideal choices for this book of classics, as they remain supreme in their respective media.

Many readers will recognize H. G. Wells' *The Time Machine* as being perhaps the most anthologized piece of science fiction ever written. Any anthology purporting to be a volume of science-fiction classics must of necessity include this great masterpiece, for it was this short novel that inaugurated the science-fiction tradition as we know it today. Another selection of interest is the slightly abridged version of Garrett P. Serviss' novel, *Edison's Conquest of Mars*. When H. G. Wells failed to write a sequel to his famous *War of the Worlds*, Serviss, intrigued with the idea of interplanetary conflict, took up the story and brought the war to the planet of Mars. It is interesting to note the contrast in style between the two.

It was not my intent to comment on the selections in this book except where I thought an additional word or two, such as above, would be of interest. The main purpose of THE TREASURY OF SCIENCE FICTION CLASSICS is to give the newer generations of readers an opportunity to sample a few of the great classics that form the foundation upon which modern science fiction is built. The editor hopes that this short excursion into the past of science fiction will be informative as well as entertaining.

HAROLD W. KUEBLER

worlds

in collision

the conversation
of eiros and charmion

by EDGAR ALLAN POE

Πυρ σοι προσοιοω
I will bring fire to thee.

—Euripides—*Androm.*

EIROS: Why do you call me Eiros?

CHARMION: So henceforward will you always be called. You must forget, too, *my* earthly name, and speak to me as Charmion.

EIROS: This is indeed no dream!

CHARMION: Dreams are with us no more; but of these mysteries anon. I rejoice to see you looking life-like and rational. The film of the shadow has already passed from off your eyes. Be of heart, and fear nothing. Your allotted days of stupor have expired; and, to-morrow, I will myself induct you into the full joys and wonders of your novel existence.

EIROS: True, I feel no stupor, none at all. The wild sickness and the terrible darkness have left me, and I hear no longer that mad, rushing, horrible sound, like the "voice of many waters." Yet my senses are bewildered, Charmion, with the keenness of their perception of *the new*.

CHARMION: A few days will remove all this;—but I fully understand you, and feel for you. It is now ten earthly years since I underwent what you undergo, yet the remembrance of it hangs by me still. You have now suffered all of pain, however, which you will suffer in Aidenn.

EIROS: In Aidenn?

CHARMION: In Aidenn.

EIROS: Oh, God!—pity me, Charmion!—I am overburdened with the majesty of all things—of the unknown now known—of the speculative Future merged in the august and certain Present.

CHARMION: Grapple not now with such thoughts. To-morrow we will speak of this. Your mind wavers, and its agitation will find relief in the exercise of simple memories. Look not around, nor forward—but back. I am burning with anxiety to hear the details of that stupendous event which threw you among us. Tell me of it. Let us converse of familiar things, in the old familiar language of the world which has so fearfully perished.

EIROS: Most fearfully, fearfully!—this is indeed no dream.

CHARMION: Dreams are no more. Was I much mourned, my Eiros?

EIROS: Mourned, Charmion?—oh, deeply. To that last hour of all, there hung a cloud of intense gloom and devout sorrow over your household.

CHARMION: And that last hour—speak of it. Remember that, beyond the naked fact of the castastrophe itself, I know nothing. When, coming out from among mankind, I passed into Night through the Grave—at that period, if I remember aright, the calamity which overwhelmed you was utterly unanticipated. But, indeed, I knew little of the speculative philosophy of the day.

EIROS: The individual calamity was, as you say, entirely unanticipated; but analogous misfortunes had been long a subject of discussion with astronomers. I need scarce tell you, my friend, that, even when you left us, men had agreed to understand those passages in the most holy writings which speak of the final destruction of all things by fire, as having reference to the orb of the earth alone. But in regard to the immediate agency of the ruin, speculation had been at fault from that epoch in astronomical knowledge in which the comets were divested of the terrors of flame. The very moderate density of these bodies had been well established. They had been observed to pass among the satellites of Jupiter, without bringing about any sensible alteration either in the masses or in the orbits of these secondary planets. We had long regarded the wanderers as vapory creations of inconceivable tenuity, and as altogether incapable of doing injury to our substantial globe, even in the event of contact. But contact was not in any degree dreaded; for the elements of all the comets were accurately known. That among *them* we should look for the agency of the threatened fiery destruction had been for many years considered an inadmissible idea. But wonders and wild fancies had been, of late days, strangely rife among mankind; and although it was only with a few of the ignorant that actual apprehension prevailed, upon the announcement by astronomers of a *new* comet, yet this announcement was generally received with I know not what of agitation and mistrust.

The elements of the strange orb were immediately calculated, and it was at once conceded by all observers, that its path, at perihelion, would bring it into very close proximity with the earth. There were two or three astronomers, of secondary note, who resolutely maintained that a contact was inevitable. I cannot very well express to you the effect of this intelligence upon the people. For a few short days they would not believe an assertion which their intellect, so long employed among worldly considerations, could not in any manner grasp. But the truth of a vitally important fact soon makes its way into the understanding of even the most stolid. Finally, all men saw that astronomical knowledge lied not, and they awaited the comet. Its approach was not, at first, seemingly rapid; nor was its appearance of very unusual character. It was of a dull red, and had little perceptible train. For seven or eight days we saw no material increase in its apparent diameter, and but a partial alteration in its color. Meanwhile the ordinary affairs of men were discarded, and all interests absorbed in a growing discussion, instituted by the philosophic, in respect to the cometary nature. Even the grossly ignorant aroused their sluggish capacities to such considerations. The learned *now* gave their intellect—their soul—to no such points as the allaying of fear, or to the sustenance of loved theory. They sought—they panted for right views. They groaned for perfected knowledge. *Truth* arose in the purity of her strength and exceeding majesty, and the wise bowed down and adored.

That material injury to our globe or to its inhabitants would result from the apprehended contact, was an opinion which hourly lost ground among the wise; and the wise were now freely permitted to rule the reason and the fancy of the crowd. It was demonstrated, that the density of the comet's *nucleus* was far less than that of our rarest gas; and the harmless passage of a similar visitor among the satellites of Jupiter was a point strongly insisted upon, and which served greatly to allay terror. Theologists, with an earnestness fear-enkindled, dwelt upon the biblical prophecies, and expounded them to the people with a directness and simplicity of which no previous instance had been known. That the final destruction of the earth must be brought about by the agency of fire, was urged with a spirit that enforced everywhere conviction; and that the comets were of no fiery nature (as all men now knew) was a truth which relieved all, in a great measure, from the apprehension of the great calamity foretold. It is noticeable that the popular prejudices and vulgar errors in regard to pestilences and wars—errors which were wont to prevail upon every appearance of a comet—were now altogether unknown. As if by some sudden convulsive exertion, reason had at once hurled superstition from her throne. The feeblest intellect had derived vigor from excessive interest.

What minor evils might arise from the contact were points of elaborate question. The learned spoke of slight geological disturbances, of probable alterations in climate, and consequently in vegetation; of possible magnetic and electric influences. Many held that no visible or perceptible effect would in any manner be produced. While such discussions were going on, their subject gradually approached, growing larger in apparent diameter, and of a more brilliant lustre. Mankind grew paler as it came. All human operations were suspended.

There was an epoch in the course of the general sentiment when the comet had attained, at length, a size surpassing that of any previously recorded visitation. The people now, dismissing any lingering hope that the astronomers were wrong, experienced all the certainty of evil. The chimerical aspect of their terror was gone. The hearts of the stoutest of our race beat violently within their bosoms. A very few days sufficed, however, to merge even such feelings in sentiments more unendurable. We could no longer apply to the strange orb any *accustomed* thoughts. Its *historical* attributes had disappeared. It oppressed us with a hideous *novelty* of emotion. We saw it not as an astronomical phenomenon in the heavens, but as an incubus upon our hearts, and a shadow upon our brains. It had taken, with inconceivable rapidity, the character of a gigantic mantle of rare flame, extending from horizon to horizon.

Yet a day, and men breathed with greater freedom. It was clear that we were already within the influence of the comet; yet we lived. We even felt an unusual elasticity of frame and vivacity of mind. The exceeding tenuity of the object of our dread was apparent; for all heavenly objects were plainly visible through it. Meantime, our vegetation had perceptibly altered; and we gained faith, from this predicted circumstance, in the foresight of the wise. A wild luxuriance of foliage, utterly unknown before, burst out upon every vegetable thing.

Yet another day—and the evil was not altogether upon us. It was now evident that its nucleus would first reach us. A wild change had come over all men; and the first sense of *pain* was the wild signal for general lamentation and horror. This first sense of pain lay in a rigorous constriction of the breast and lungs, and an insufferable dryness of the skin. It could not be denied that our atmosphere was radically affected; the conformation of this atmosphere and the possible modifications to which it might be subjected, were now the topics of discussion. The result of investigation sent an electric thrill of the intensest terror through the universal heart of man.

It had been long known that the air which encircled us was a compound of oxygen and nitrogen gases, in the proportion of twenty-one measures of oxygen, and seventy-nine of nitrogen, in every one hundred of the atmosphere. Oxygen, which was the principle of combustion, and the vehicle of heat, was absolutely necessary to the support of animal life, and was the most powerful and energetic agent in nature. Nitrogen, on the contrary, was incapable of supporting either animal life or flame. An unnatural excess of oxygen would result, it had been ascertained, in just such an elevation of the animal spirits as we had latterly experienced. It was the pursuit, the extension of the idea, which had engendered awe. What would be the result of *a total extraction of the nitrogen?* A combustion irresistible, all-devouring, omni-prevalent, immediate;—the entire fulfilment, in all their minute and terrible details, of the fiery and horror-inspiring denunciations of the prophecies of the Holy Book.

Why need I paint, Charmion, the now disenchained frenzy of mankind? That tenuity in the comet which had previously inspired us with hope, was now the source of the bitterness of despair. In its impalpable gaseous character we clearly perceived the consummation of Fate. Meantime a day again passed, bearing away with it the last shadow of Hope. We gasped in the rapid modification of the air. The red blood bounded tumultuously through its strict channels. A furious delirium possessed all men; and, with arms rigidly outstretched toward the threatening heavens, they trembled and shrieked aloud. But the nucleus of the destroyer was now upon us; even here in Aidenn, I shudder while I speak. Let me be brief—brief as the ruin that overwhelmed. For a moment there was a wild lurid light alone, visiting and penetrating all things. Then—let us bow down, Charmion, before the excessive majesty of the great God!—then, there came a shouting and pervading sound, as if from the mouth itself of нiм; while the whole incumbent mass of ether in which we existed, burst at once into a species of intense flame, for whose surpassing brilliancy and all-fervid heat even the angels in the high Heaven of pure knowledge have no name. Thus ended all.

the star

by H. G. WELLS

It was on the first day of the new year that the announcement was made, almost simultaneously from three observatories, that the motion of the planet Neptune, the outermost of all the planets that wheel about the sun, had become very erratic. Ogilvy had already called attention to a suspected retardation in its velocity in December. Such a piece of news was scarcely calculated to interest a world the greater portion of whose inhabitants were unaware of the existence of the planet Neptune, nor outside the astronomical profession did the subsequent discovery of a faint, remote speck of light in the region of the perturbed planet cause any very great excitement. Scientific people, however, found the intelligence remarkable enough, even before it became known that the new body was rapidly growing larger and brighter, that its motion was quite different from the orderly progress of the planets, and that the deflection of Neptune and its satellite was becoming now of an unprecedented kind.

Few people without a training in science can realise the huge isolation of the solar system. The sun with its specks of planets, its dust of planetoids, and its impalpable comets, swims in a vacant immensity that almost defeats the imagination. Beyond the orbit of Neptune there is space, vacant so far as human observation has penetrated, without warmth or light or sound, blank emptiness, for twenty million times a million miles. That is the smallest estimate of the distance to be traversed before the very nearest of the stars is attained. And, saving a few comets more unsubstantial than the thinnest flame, no matter had ever to human knowledge crossed this gulf of space, until early in the twentieth century this strange wanderer appeared. A vast mass of matter it was, bulky, heavy,

Reprinted by permission of the Estate of H. G. Wells.

rushing without warning out of the black mystery of the sky into the radiance of the sun. By the second day it was clearly visible to any decent instrument, as a speck with a barely sensible diameter, in the constellation Leo near Regulus. In a little while an opera glass could attain it.

On the third day of the new year the newspaper readers of two hemispheres were made aware for the first time of the real importance of this unusual apparition in the heavens. "A Planetary Collision," one London paper headed the news, and proclaimed Duchaine's opinion that this strange new planet would probably collide with Neptune. The leader writers enlarged upon the topic. So that in most of the capitals of the world, on January 3rd, there was an expectation, however vague, of some imminent phenomenon in the sky; and as the night followed the sunset round the globe, thousands of men turned their eyes skyward to see— the old familiar stars just as they had always been.

Until it was dawn in London and Pollux setting and the stars overhead grown pale. The winter's dawn it was, a sickly filtering accumulation of daylight, and the light of gas and candles shone yellow in the windows to show where people were astir. But the yawning policeman saw the thing, the busy crowds in the markets stopped agape, workmen going to their work betimes, milkmen, the drivers of news-carts, dissipation going home jaded and pale, homeless wanderers, sentinels on their beats, and in the country, labourers trudging afield, poachers slinking home, all over the dusky quickening country it could be seen—and out at sea by seamen watching for the day—a great white star, come suddenly into the westward sky!

Brighter it was than any star in our skies; brighter than the evening star at its brightest. It still glowed out white and large, no mere twinkling spot of light, but a small round clear shining disc, an hour after the day had come. And where science has not reached, men stared and feared, telling one another of the wars and pestilences that are foreshadowed by these fiery signs in the Heavens. Sturdy Boers, dusky Hottentots, Gold Coast negroes, Frenchmen, Spaniards, Portuguese, stood in the warmth of the sunrise watching the setting of this strange new star.

And in a hundred observatories there had been suppressed excitement, rising almost to shouting pitch, as the two remote bodies had rushed together, and a hurrying to and fro to gather photographic apparatus and spectroscope, and this appliance and that, to record this novel astonishing sight, the destruction of a world. For it was a world, a sister planet of our earth, far greater than our earth indeed, that had so suddenly flashed into flaming death. Neptune it was had been struck, fairly and squarely, by the strange planet from outer space and the heat of the concussion had incontinently turned two solid globes into one vast mass of incandescence. Round the world that day, two hours before the dawn, went the pallid great white star, fading only as it sank westward and the sun mounted above it. Everywhere men marvelled at it, but of all those who saw it none could have marvelled more than those sailors, habitual watchers of the stars, who far away at sea had heard nothing of its advent and saw it now rise like a pigmy moon and climb zenithward and hang overhead and sink westward with the passing of the night.

And when next it rose over Europe everywhere were crowds of watchers on hilly slopes, on house-roofs, in open spaces, staring eastward for the rising of the great new star. It rose with a white glow in front of it, like the glare of a white fire, and those who had seen it come into existence the night before cried out at the sight of it. "It is larger," they cried. "It is brighter!" And, indeed the moon a quarter full and sinking in the west was in its apparent size beyond comparison, but scarcely in all its breadth had it as much brightness now as the little circle of the strange new star.

"It is brighter!" cried the people clustering in the streets. But in the dim observatories the watchers held their breath and peered at one another. "*It is nearer*," they said. "*Nearer!*"

And voice after voice repeated, "It is nearer," and the clicking telegraph took that up, and it trembled along telephone wires, and in a thousand cities grimy compositors fingered the type. "It is nearer." Men writing in offices, struck with a strange realisation, flung down their pens; men talking in a thousand places suddenly came upon a grotesque possibility in those words, "It is nearer." It hurried along awakening streets, it was shouted down the frost-stilled ways of quiet villages, men who had read these things from the throbbing tape stood in yellow-lit doorways shouting the news to the passers-by. "It is nearer." Pretty women, flushed and glittering, heard the news told jestingly between the dances, and feigned an intelligent interest they did not feel. "Nearer! Indeed. How curious! How very, very clever people must be to find out things like that!"

Lonely tramps faring through the wintry night murmured those words to comfort themselves—looking skyward. "It has need to be nearer, for the night's as cold as charity. Don't seem much warmth from it if it *is* nearer, all the same."

"What is a new star to me?" cried the weeping woman kneeling beside her dead.

The schoolboy, rising early for his examination work, puzzled it out for himself—with the great white star, shining broad and bright through the frost-flowers of his window. "Centrifugal, centripetal," he said, with his chin on his fist. "Stop a planet in its flight, rob it of its centrifugal force, what then? Centripetal has it, and down it falls into the sun! And this——!"

"Do *we* come in the way? I wonder——"

The light of that day went the way of its brethren, and with the later watchers of the frosty darkness rose the strange star again. And it was now so bright that the waxing moon seemed but a pale yellow ghost of itself, hanging huge in the sunset. In a South African city a great man had married, and the streets were alight to welcome his return with his bride. "Even the skies have illuminated," said the flatterer. Under Capricorn, two negro lovers, daring the wild beasts and evil spirits, for love of one another, crouched together in a cane brake where the fire-flies hovered. "That is our star," they whispered, and felt strangely comforted by the sweet brilliance of its light.

The master mathematician sat in his private room and pushed the papers from him. His calculations were already finished. In a small white phial there still remained a little of the drug that had kept him awake and active for four long nights. Each day, serene, explicit, patient as ever, he had given his lecture to his students, and then had come back at once to this momentous calculation. His face was grave, a little drawn and hectic from his drugged activity. For some time he seemed lost in thought. Then he went to the window, and the blind went up with a click. Halfway up the sky, over the clustering roofs, chimneys, and steeples of the city, hung the star.

He looked at it as one might look into the eyes of a brave enemy. "You may kill me," he said after a silence. "But I can hold you—and all the universe for that matter—in the grip of this little brain. I would not change. Even now."

He looked at the little phial. "There will be no need of sleep again," he said. The next day at noon, punctual to the minute, he entered his lecture theatre, put his hat on the end of the table as his habit was, and carefully selected a large piece of chalk. It was a joke among his students that he could not lecture without that piece of chalk to fumble in his fingers, and once he had been stricken to impotence by their hiding his supply. He came and looked under his grey eyebrows at the rising tiers of young fresh faces, and spoke with his accustomed studied commonness of phrasing. "Circumstances have risen—circumstances beyond my control," he said and paused, "which will debar me from completing the course I had designed. It would seem, gentlemen, if I may put the thing clearly and briefly, that—Man has lived in vain."

The students glanced at one another. Had they heard aright? Mad? Raised eyebrows and grinning lips there were, but one or two faces remained intent upon his calm grey-fringed face. "It will be interesting," he was saying, "to devote this morning to an exposition, so far as I can make it clear to you, of the calculations that have led me to this conclusion. Let us assume——"

He turned towards the blackboard, meditating a diagram in the way that was usual to him. "What was that about 'lived in vain'?" whispered one student to another. "Listen," said the other, nodding towards the lecturer.

And presently they began to understand.

That night the star rose later, for its proper eastward motion had carried it some way across Leo towards Virgo, and its brightness was so great that the sky became a luminous blue as it rose, and every star was hidden in its turn, save only Jupiter near the zenith, Capella, Aldebaran, Sirius, and the pointers of the Bear. It was very white and beautiful. In many parts of the world that night a pallid halo encircled it about. It was perceptibly larger; in the clear refractive sky of the tropics it seemed as if it were nearly a quarter the size of the moon. The frost was still on the ground in England, but the world was as brightly lit as if it were midsummer moonlight. One could see to read quite ordinary print by that cold clear light, and in the cities the lamps burnt yellow and wan.

And everywhere the world was awake that night, and throughout Christendom a sombre murmur hung in the keen air over the countryside like the belling of bees in the heather, and this murmurous tumult grew to a clangour in the cities. It was the tolling of the bells in a million belfry towers and steeples, summoning the people to sleep no more, to sin no more, but to gather in their churches and pray. And overhead, growing larger and brighter as the earth rolled on its way and the night passed, rose the dazzling star.

And the streets and houses were alight in all the cities, the shipyards glared, and whatever roads led to high country were lit and crowded all night long. And in all the seas about the civilised lands, ships with throbbing engines, and ships with belling sails, crowded with men and living creatures, were standing out to ocean and the north. For already the warning of the master mathematician had been telegraphed all over the world, and translated into a hundred tongues. The new planet and Neptune, locked in a fiery embrace, were whirling headlong, ever faster and faster towards the sun. Already every second this blazing mass flew a hundred miles, and every second its terrific velocity increased. As it flew now, indeed, it must pass a hundred million of miles wide of the earth and scarcely affect it. But near its destined path, as yet only slightly perturbed, spun the mighty planet Jupiter and his moons sweeping splendid round the sun. Every moment now the attraction between the fiery star and the greatest of the planets grew stronger. And the result of that attraction? Inevitably Jupiter would be deflected from his orbit into an elliptical path, and the burning star, swung by his attraction wide of its sunward rush, would "describe a curved path" and perhaps collide with, and certainly pass very close to, our earth. "Earthquakes, volcanic outbreaks, cyclones, sea waves, floods, and a steady rise in temperature to I know not what limit"—so prophesied the master mathematician.

And overhead, to carry out his words, lonely and cold and livid, blazed the star of the coming doom.

To many who stared at it that night until their eyes ached, it seemed that it was visibly approaching. And that night, too, the weather changed, and the frost that had gripped all Central Europe and France and England softened towards a thaw.

But you must not imagine because I have spoken of people praying through the night and people going aboard ships and people fleeing towards mountainous country that the whole world was already in a terror because of the star. As a matter of fact, use and wont still ruled the world, and save for the talk of idle moments and the splendour of the night, nine human beings out of ten were still busy at their common occupations. In all the cities the shops, save one here and there, opened and closed at their proper hours, the doctor and the undertaker plied their trades, the workers gathered in the factories, soldiers drilled, scholars studied, lovers sought one another, thieves lurked and fled, politicians planned their schemes. The presses of the newspapers roared through the nights, and many a priest of this church and that would not open his holy building to further what he considered a foolish panic. The newspapers insisted on the lesson of the year 1000—for then, too, people had anticipated the end. The star was no star—mere gas—a comet; and were it a star it could not possibly strike the earth. There was no precedent for such a thing. Common sense was sturdy everywhere, scornful, jesting, a little inclined to persecute the obdurate fearful. That night, at seven-fifteen by Greenwich time, the star would be at its nearest to Jupiter. Then the world would see the turn things would take. The master mathematician's grim warnings were treated by many as so much mere elaborate self-advertisement. Common sense at last, a little heated by argument, signified its unalterable convictions by going to bed. So, too, barbarism and savagery, already tired of the novelty, went about their mighty business, and save for a howling dog here and there, the beast world left the star unheeded.

And yet, when at last the watchers in the European States saw the star rise, an hour later it is true, but no larger than it had been the night before, there were still plenty awake to laugh at the master mathematician —to take the danger as if it had passed.

But hereafter the laughter ceased. The star grew—it grew with a terrible steadiness hour after hour, a little larger each hour, a little nearer the midnight zenith, and brighter and brighter, until it had turned night into a second day. Had it come straight to the earth instead of in a curved path, had it lost no velocity to Jupiter, it must have leapt the intervening gulf in a day, but as it was it took five days altogether to come by our planet. The next night it had become a third the size of the moon before it set to English eyes, and the thaw was assured. It rose over America near the size of the moon, but blinding white to look at, and *hot;* and a breath of hot wind blew now with its rising and gathering strength, and in Virginia, and Brazil, and down the St. Lawrence valley, it shone intermittently through a driving reek of thunder-clouds, flickering violet lightning and hail unprecedented. In Manitoba was a thaw and devastating floods. And upon all the mountains of the earth the snow and ice began to melt that night, and all the rivers coming out of high country flowed thick and turbid, and soon—in their upper reaches—with swirling trees and the bodies of beasts and men. They rose steadily, steadily in the ghostly brilliance, and came trickling over their banks at last, behind the flying population of their valleys.

And along the coast of Argentina and up the South Atlantic the tides were higher than had ever been in the memory of man, and the storms drove the waters in many cases scores of miles inland, drowning whole cities. And so great grew the heat during the night that the rising of the sun was like the coming of a shadow. The earthquakes began and grew until all down America from the Arctic Circle to Cape Horn, hillsides were sliding, fissures were opening, and houses and walls crumbling to destruction. The whole side of Cotopaxi slipped out in one vast convulsion, and a tumult of lava poured out so high and broad and swift and liquid that in one day it reached the sea.

So the star, with the wan moon in its wake, marched across the Pacific, trailed the thunderstorms like the hem of a robe, and the growing tidal wave that toiled behind it, frothing and eager, poured over island and island and swept them clear of men. Until that wave came at last—in a blinding light and with the breath of a furnace, swift and terrible it came —a wall of water, fifty feet high, roaring hungrily, upon the long coasts of Asia, and swept inland across the plains of China. For a space the star, hotter now and larger and brighter than the sun in its strength, showed with pitiless brilliance the wide and populous country; towns and villages with their pagodas and trees, roads, wide, cultivated fields, millions of sleepless people staring in helpless terror at the incandescent sky; and then, low and growing, came the murmur of the flood. And thus it was with millions of men that night—a flight nowhither, with limbs heavy with heat and breath fierce and scant, and the flood like a wall swift and white behind. And then death.

China was lit glowing white, but over Japan and Java and all the islands of Eastern Asia the great star was a ball of dull red fire because of the steam and smoke and ashes the volcanoes were spouting forth to salute its coming. Above was the lava, hot gases and ash, and below the seething floods, and the whole earth swayed and rumbled with the earthquake shocks. Soon the immemorial snows of Thibet and the Himalaya were melting and pouring down by ten million deepening converging channels upon the plains of Burmah and Hindostan. The tangled summits of the Indian jungles were aflame in a thousand places, and below the hurrying waters around the stems were dark objects that still struggled feebly and reflected the blood-red tongues of fire. And in a rudderless confusion a multitude of men and women fled down the broad riverways to that one last hope of men—the open sea.

Larger grew the star, and larger, hotter, and brighter with a terrible swiftness now. The tropical ocean had lost its phosphorescence, and the whirling steam rose in ghostly wreaths from the black waves that plunged incessantly, speckled with storm-tossed ships.

And then came a wonder. It seemed to those who in Europe watched for the rising of the star that the world must have ceased its rotation. In a thousand open spaces of down and upland the people who had fled thither from the floods and the falling houses and sliding slopes of hill watched for that rising in vain. Hour followed hour through a terrible suspense, and the star rose not. Once again men set their eyes upon the old constellations they had counted lost to them for ever. In England it was hot and clear overhead, though the ground quivered perpetually, but in the tropics, Sirius and Capella and Aldebaran showed through a veil of steam. And when at last the great star rose near ten hours late, the sun rose close upon it, and in the centre of its white heart was a disc of black.

Over Asia it was the star had begun to fall behind the movement of the sky, and then suddenly, as it hung over India, its light had been veiled. All the plain of India from the mouth of the Indus to the mouths of the Ganges was a shallow waste of shining water that night, out of which rose temples and palaces, mounds and hills, black with people. Every minaret was a clustering mass of people, who fell one by one into the turbid waters, as heat and terror overcame them. The whole land seemed a-wailing, and suddenly there swept a shadow across that furnace of despair, and a breath of cold wind, and a gathering of clouds, out of the cooling air. Men looking up, near blinded, at the star, saw that a black disc was creeping across the light. It was the moon, coming between the star and the earth. And even as men cried to God at this respite, out of the East with a strange inexplicable swiftness sprang the sun. And then star, sun, and moon rushed together across the heavens.

So it was that presently, to the European watchers, star and sun rose close upon each other, drove headlong for a space and then slower, and at last came to rest, star and sun merged into one glare of flame at the zenith of the sky. The moon no longer eclipsed the star but was lost to sight in the brilliance of the sky. And though those who were still alive regarded it for the most part with that dull stupidity that hunger, fatigue, heat, and despair engender, there were still men who could perceive the meaning of these signs. Star and earth had been at their nearest, had swung about one another, and the star had passed. Already it was receding, swifter and swifter, in the last stage of its headlong journey downward into the sun.

And then the clouds gathered, blotting out the vision of the sky, the thunder and lightning wove a garment round the world; all over the earth was such a downpour of rain as men had never before seen, and where the volcanoes flared red against the cloud canopy there descended torrents of mud. Everywhere the waters were pouring off the land, leaving mud-silted ruins, and the earth littered like a storm-worn beach with all that had floated, and the dead bodies of the men and brutes, its children. For days the water streamed off the land, sweeping away soil and trees and houses in the way, and piling huge dykes and scooping out Titanic gullies over the countryside. Those were the days of darkness that followed the star and the heat. All through them, and for many weeks and months, the earthquakes continued.

But the star had passed, and men, hunger-driven and gathering courage only slowly, might creep back to their ruined cities, buried granaries, and sodden fields. Such few ships as had escaped the storms of that time came stunned and shattered and sounding their way cautiously through the new marks and shoals of once-familiar ports. And as the storms subsided men perceived that everywhere the days were hotter than of yore, and the sun larger, and the moon, shrunk to a third of its former size, took now four-score days between its new and new.

But of the new brotherhood that grew presently among men, of the saving of laws and books and machines, of the strange change that had come over Iceland and Greenland and the shores of Baffin's Bay, so that the sailors coming there presently found them green and gracious, and could scarce believe their eyes, this story does not tell. Nor of the movement of mankind now that the earth was hotter, northward and southward towards the poles of the earth. It concerns itself only with the coming and the passing of the star.

The Martian astronomers—for there are astronomers on Mars, although they are very different beings from men—were naturally profoundly interested by these things. They saw them from their own standpoint, of course. "Considering the mass and temperature of the missile that was flung through our solar system into the sun," one wrote, "it is astonishing what a little damage the earth, which it missed so narrowly, has sustained. All the familiar continental markings and the masses of the seas remain intact, and indeed the only difference seems to be a shrinkage of the white discoloration (supposed to be frozen water) round either pole." Which only shows how small the vastest of human catastrophes may seem, at a distance of a few million miles.

when worlds collide

by EDWIN BALMER and PHILIP WYLIE

THE STRANGERS FROM SPACE: It was no tabloid but the *Times*—the staid, accurate, ultra-responsible New York *Times*—which spread the sensation before him in the morning.

The headlines lay black upon the page:

SCIENTISTS SAY WORLDS FROM ANOTHER STAR APPROACH THE EARTH

DR. COLE HENDRON MAKES ASTONISHING STATEMENT IN WHICH SIXTY OF THE GREATEST PHYSICISTS AND ASTRONOMERS CONCUR.

Tony was scarcely awake when Kyto had brought him the paper.

Kyto himself, it was plain, had been puzzling over the news, and did not understand it. Kyto, however, had comprehended enough to know that something was very different to-day; so he had carried in the coffee and the newspaper a bit earlier than customary; and he delayed, busying himself with the black, clear coffee, while Tony started up and stared.

"Dr. Cole Hendron, generally acknowledged to be the leading astrophysicist of America," Tony read, "early this morning gave to the press the following statement, on behalf of the sixty scientists named in an accompanying column."

Tony's eyes flashed to the column which carried the list of distinguished names, English, German, French, Italian, Swiss, American, South African, Australian and Japanese.

"Similar statements are being given to the press of all peoples at this same time.

" 'In order to allay alarms likely to rise from the increase of rumors based upon incorrect or misunderstood reports of the discovery made by Professor Bronson, of Capetown, South Africa, and in order to acquaint all people with the actual situation, as it is now viewed, we offer these facts.

" 'Eleven months ago, when examining a photographic plate of the region 15 (Eridanus) in the southern skies, Professor Bronson noticed the presence of two bodies then near the star Achernar, which had not been observed before.

" 'Both were exceedingly faint, and lying in the constellation Eridanus, which is one of the largest constellations in the sky, they were at first put down as probably long-period variable stars which had recently increased in brightness after having been too faint to affect the photographic plate.

" 'A month later, after photographing again the same locality, Professor Bronson looked for the two new stars and found that they had moved. No object of stellar distance could show displacement in so short a space of time. It was certain, therefore, that the newly observed bodies were not stars. They must be previously unobserved and unsuspected members of our solar system, or else objects, from outside our system, now approaching us.

" 'They must be new planets or comets—or strangers from space.

" 'All planets known to be associated with our sun move approximately in the plane described by the earth's orbit. This is true, whatever the size or distance of the planets, from Mercury to Pluto. The two Bronson Bodies were moving almost at right angles to the plane of the planetary orbits.

" 'Comets appear from all directions; but these two bodies did not resemble comets when viewed through the greater telescope. One of them, at the time of the second observation, showed a small but perceptible disk. Its spectrum exhibited the characteristic lines of reflected sunlight. Meanwhile, several observations of position and movement were made which made it plain that the two Bronson Bodies were objects of planetary dimensions and characteristics, approaching us from out of stellar distances—that is, from space.

" 'The two bodies have remained associated, approaching us together and at the same speed. Both now show disks which can be measured. It can now be estimated that, when first observed, they had approached within the distance from the sun of the planet Neptune. It must be remembered, however, that they lie in an entirely different direction.

" 'Since coming under observation, they have moved within the distance of the orbit of our planet Uranus, and are approaching the distance of Saturn.

" 'Bronson Alpha—which is the name temporarily assigned to the larger of the two new bodies—appears in the telescope similar in size to Uranus. That is, its estimated diameter is something over forty thousand miles. Bronson Beta, which is the smaller of the two bodies, has an estimated diameter of eight thousand miles. It is similar in size, therefore, to the earth.

" 'Bronson Beta at present is in advance of Alpha in their approach toward the solar system; but they do not move in parallel lines; Beta, which is the smaller, revolves about Alpha so that their positions constantly change.

" 'They have both come definitely within the sphere of gravitational influence of the sun; but having arrived from interstellar space, their speeds of approach greatly exceed the velocities of our familiar planets in their orbits around the sun.

" 'Such are the observed phenomena. The following is necessarily highly speculative, but it is offered as a possible explanation of the origin of the two Bronson Bodies.

" 'It has long been supposed that about other stars than ours—for of course our sun is only a star—are other planets like the earth and Mars and Jupiter. It is not presumed that all stars are surrounded by planets; but it has been estimated that probably at least one star in one hundred thousand has developed a planetary system. Among the many billions of stars, there are probably millions of suns with planets. It is always possible that some catastrophe would tear the planets away. It would require nothing more than the approach of another star toward the sun to destroy the gravitational control of the sun over the earth and Venus and Mars and Jupiter and other planets, and to send them all spinning into space on cold and dark careers of their own.

" 'This world of ours, and Venus and Mars and Jupiter and Saturn, would then wander throughout indefinite ages—some of them perhaps eternally doomed to cold and darkness; others might, after incalculable ages, find another sun.

" 'It might be assumed, for purposes of explanation of the Bronson Bodies, that they once were planets like our earth and Uranus, circling about some life-giving sun. A catastrophe tore them away, together with whatever other of her planets there might have been, and sent them into the darkness of interstellar space. These two—Bronson Alpha and Bronson Beta—either were associated originally, or else established a gravitational influence upon each other in the journey through space, and probably have traveled together through an incalculable time until they arrived in a region of the heavens which brought them at last under the attraction of the sun. Their previous course, consequently, has been greatly modified by the sun, and as a result, they are now approaching us.' "

At this point, the prepared statement of Cole Hendron terminated.

Tony Drake was sitting up straight in bed, holding the paper before him and trying, with his left hand and without looking away, to strike a match for the cigarette between his lips. He did not succeed, but he kept on trying while his eyes searched down the column of questions put by the reporters to Dr. Hendron—and his answers.

" 'What will be the effect of this approach upon the earth?'

" 'It is impossible yet to tell.'

" 'But there will be effects?'

" 'Certainly there will be effects.'

" 'How serious?' "

Again Cole Hendron refused to answer.

" 'It is impossible yet to say.'

" 'Will the earth be endangered?'

"Answer: 'There will undoubtedly be considerable alterations of conditions of life here.'

" 'What sort of alterations?'

" 'That will be the subject of a later statement,' Dr. Hendron replied. 'The character and degree of the disturbance which we are to undergo is now the subject of study by a responsible group. We will attempt to describe the conditions likely to confront all of us on the world as soon as they clearly define themselves.'

" 'When will this supplementary statement be made?'

" 'As soon as possible.'

" 'To-morrow?'

" 'No; by no means as soon as to-morrow.'

" 'Within a week? Within a month?'

" 'I would say that it might be made within a month.' "

Tony was on his feet, and in spite of himself, trembling. There was no possible mistaking of the undertone of this astounding announcement. It spelled doom, or some enormous alteration of all conditions of life on the world equivalent to complete disaster.

The League of the Last Days! There was some reference to it in another column, but Tony scarcely caught its coherence.

Where was Eve; and what, upon this morning, was she doing? How was she feeling? What was she thinking? Might she, at last, be sleeping?

She had been up all night, and at work assisting her father. The statement had been released at one o'clock in the morning. There was no mention in the paper of her presence with her father; Cole Hendron apparently had received the reporters alone.

How much more than this which had been told, did Eve now know? Plainly, manifestly the scientists knew more—much, much more, which they dared not yet tell the public. Dared not! That was the fact. They dared, to-day, only to issue the preliminary announcement.

DAWN AFTER DOOMSDAY?   Kyto, who usually effaced himself did not do so this morning. Kyto, having the untasted coffee for an excuse, called attention to himself and ventured:

"Mister, of course, comprehends the news?"

"Yes, Kyto; I understand it—partly, at any rate."

"I may inquire, please, perhaps the significance?"

Tony stared at the little Jap. He had always liked him; but suddenly he was assailed with a surge of fellow-feeling for this small brown man trapped like himself on the rim of the world.

Trapped! That was it. *Trapped* was the word for this strange feeling.

"Kyto, we're in for something."

"What?"

"Something rather—extensive, Kyto. One thing is sure, we're all in for it together."

"General—destruction?" Kyto asked.

Tony shook his head, and his reply surprised himself. "No; if it were just that, they'd say it. It would be easy to say—general destruction, the end of everything. People after all in a way are prepared for that, Kyto." Tony was reasoning to himself as much as talking to Kyto. "No; this can't be just—destruction. It doesn't *feel* like it, Kyto."

"What else could it be?" questioned the Jap practically.

Tony, having no answer, gulped his coffee; and Kyto had to attend to the telephone, which was ringing.

It was Balcom.

"Hey! Tony! Tony, have you seen the paper? I told you Hendron had something, but I admit this runs considerably beyond expectations. . . . Staggers one, doesn't it, Tony? . . . Now, see here, it's perfectly plain that Hendron knows much more than he's giving out. . . . Tony, he probably knows it *all* now! . . . I want you to get to him as soon as you can."

As soon as possible, Tony got rid of Balcom—another rider on the rim of the world, trapped with Tony and Kyto and all the rest of these people who could be heard, if you went to the open window, ringing one another to talk over this consternation.

Tony commanded, from before the bathroom mirror, where he was hastily shaving: "Kyto, make sure that anybody else that calls up isn't Miss Hendron, and then say I'm out."

Within five minutes Kyto was telling the truth. Tony, in less than five more, was at the Hendrons'. The place was policed. Men, women and children from Park Avenue, from Third and Second avenues crowded the sidewalks; sound-film trucks and photographers obstructed the street. Radio people and reporters, refused admittance, picked up what they could from the throng. Tony, at last, made contact with a police officer, and he did not make the mistake of asserting his right to pass the police-lines or of claiming, too publicly, that he was a personal friend of the family.

"There is a possibility that Dr. Hendron or perhaps Miss Hendron might have left word that I might see them," Tony said. "My name is Tony Drake."

The officer escorted him in. The elevator lifted him high to the pent-house on the roof, where the street noises were vague and far away, where the sun was shining, and blossoms, in their boxes, were red and yellow and blue.

No one was about but the servants. Impassive people! Did they know and understand? Or were they dulled to it?

Miss Eve, they said, was in the breakfast-room; Dr. Hendron still was asleep.

"Hello, Tony! Come in!"

Eve rose from the pretty little green table in the gay chintz-curtained nook which they called the breakfast-room.

Her eyes were bright, her face flushed the slightest bit with her excite-ment. Her hands grasped his tightly.

Lovely hands, she had, slender and soft and strong. How gentle she was to hold, but also how strong! Longing for her leaped in Tony. Damn everything else!

He pulled her within his arms and kissed her; and her lips, as they had last night, clung to his. They both drew breath, deeply, as they parted —stared into each other's eyes. Their hands held to each other a moment more; then Tony stepped back.

She had dressed but for her frock itself; she was in negligée, with her slim lovely arms in loose lace-decked silk, her white neck and bosom half exposed.

He bent and kissed her neck.

"You've breakfasted, Tony?"

"Yes—no. Can I sit with you here? I scarcely dreamed you'd be up, Eve, after your night."

"You've seen the papers? We were through with them before three.

That is, Father then absolutely refused to say any more or see any one else. He went to sleep."

"You didn't."

"No; I kept thinking—thinking——"

"Of the end of everything, Eve?"

"Part of the time, I did; of course I did; but more of the time of you."

"Of me—last night?"

"I hoped you'd come first thing to-day. I thought you would. . . . It's funny what difference the formal announcement of it makes. I knew it all last night, Tony. I've known the general truth of it for weeks. But when it was a secret thing—something shared just with my father and with his friends—it wasn't the same as now. One knew it but still didn't admit it, even to one's self. It was theoretical—in one's head, like a dream, not reality. We didn't really *do* much, Father and I, last night. I mean do much in proving up the facts and figures. Father had them all before from other men. Professor Bronson's plates and calculations simply confirmed what really was certain; Father checked them over. Then we gave it out.

"That's what's made everything so changed."

"Yet you didn't give out everything you know, Eve."

"No, not everything, Tony."

"You know exactly what's going to happen, don't you, Eve?"

"Yes. We know—we think we know, that is, exactly what's going to happen."

"It's going to be doomsday, isn't it?"

"No, Tony—more than doomsday."

"What can be more than that?"

"Dawn after doomsday, Tony. The world is going to be destroyed. Tony, oh, Tony, the world is going to be most thoroughly destroyed; yet some of us here on this world, which most surely will come to an end, some of us will not die! Or we need not die—if we accept the strange challenge that God is casting at us from the skies!"

"The challenge that God casts at us—what challenge? What do you mean? Exactly what is it that is going to happen, Eve—and how?"

"I'll try to tell you, Tony: There are two worlds coming toward us —two worlds torn, millions of years ago perhaps, from another star. For millions of years, probably, they've been wandering, utterly dark and utterly frozen, through space; and now they've found our sun; and they're going to attach themselves to it—at our expense. For they are coming into the solar system on a course which will carry them close—oh, very close indeed, Tony, to the orbit of the earth. They're not cutting in out on the edge where Neptune and Uranus are, or inside near Venus and Mercury.

No; they're going to join up at the same distance from the sun as we are. Do you understand?"

In spite of himself, Tony blanched. "They're going to hit the earth, you mean? I thought so."

"They're not going to hit the earth, Tony, the first time around. The first time they circle the sun, they're going to pass us close, to be sure; but they're going to pass us—both of them. But the second time they pass us—well, one of them is going to pass us a second time too, but the other one isn't, Tony. The smaller one—Bronson Beta, the one about the same size as the earth and, so far as we can tell, very much like the earth—is going to pass us safely; but the big one, Bronson Alpha, is going to take out the world!"

"You know that, Eve?"

"We know it! There must be a margin of error, we know. There may not be a direct head-on collision, Tony; but any sort of encounter—even a glancing blow—would be enough and much more than enough to finish this globe. And an encounter is certain. Every single calculation that has been made shows it.

"You know what an exact thing astronomy is to-day, Tony. If we have three different observations of a moving body, we can plot its path; and we've hundreds of determinations of these bodies. More than a thousand altogether! We know now what they are; we know their dimensions and the speed with which they are traveling. We know, of course, almost precisely the forces and attractions which will influence them—the gravitational power of the sun. Tony, you remember how precise the forecast was in the last eclipse that darkened New England. The astronomers not only foretold to a second when it would begin and end, but they described the blocks and even the sides of the streets in towns that would be in shadow. And their error was less than twenty feet.

"It's the same with these Bronson Bodies, Tony. They're falling toward the sun, and their path can be plotted like the path of Newton's apple dropping from the bough. Gravity is the surest and most constant force in all creation. One of those worlds, which is seeking our sun, is going to wipe us out, Tony—all of us, every soul of us that remains on the world when it collides. But the other world—the world so much like this—will pass us close and go on, safe and sound, around the sun again. . . .

"Tony, do you believe in God?"

"What's that to do with this?"

"So much that this has got me thinking about God again, Tony. God— the God of our fathers—the God of the Old Testament, Tony; the God who did things and meant something, the God of wrath and vengeance, but the God who also could be merciful to men. For He's sending two worlds to us, Tony, not one—not just the one that will destroy us. He's sending the world that may save us, too!"

"Save us? What do you mean?"

"That's what the League of the Last Days is working on, Tony—the chance of escape that's offered by the world like ours, which will pass so close and go on. We may transfer to it, Tony, if we have the will and the skill and the nerve! We could send a rocket to the moon to-day, if it would do us any good, if any one could possibly live on the moon after he got there. Well, Bronson Beta will pass us closer than the moon. Bronson Beta is the size of the earth, and therefore can have an atmosphere. It is perfectly possible that people—who are able to reach it—can live there.

"It's a world, perhaps very like ours, which has been in immutable cold and dark for millions of years, probably, and which now will be coming to life again.

"Think of it, Tony! The tremendous, magnificent adventure of making a try for it! It was a world once like ours, circling around some sun. People lived on it; and animals and plants and trees. Evolution had occurred there too, and progress. Civilization had come. Thousands of years of it, maybe. Tens of thousands of years—perhaps much more than we have yet known. Perhaps, also, much less. It's the purest speculation to guess in what stage that world was when it was torn from its sun and sent spinning into space.

"But in whatever stage it was in, you may be sure it is in exactly that stage now; for when it left its sun, life became extinct. The rivers, the lakes, the seas, the very air, froze and became solid, encasing and keeping everything just as it was, though it wandered through space for ten million years.

"But as it approaches the sun, the air and then the seas will thaw. The people cannot possibly come to life, nor the animals or birds or other things; but the cities will stand there unchanged, the implements, the monuments, their homes—all will remain and be uncovered again.

"If this world were not doomed, what an adventure to try for that one, Tony! And a possible adventure—a perfectly possible adventure, with the powers at our disposal to-day!" . . .

THE LAST NIGHT ON EARTH   Tony sought out Eve.

"Come walk with me," he said.

"I'd like to. It's so strange to wait, with everything done that matters. For it's all done, Tony; everything that we're to take with us has been prepared and put in place. Except the animals and ourselves."

"Dull lot of animals, mostly," complained Tony. He was excited and on edge, with nerves which he tried to quiet and could not.

He did not want to talk to Eve to-night about animals; but he might as well, for people were all about, alone or in pairs, likewise restless and excited.

"It would be madness to try to bring the interesting animals along, wouldn't it?" Eve said agreeably. "Like lions and tigers and leopards."

"I know," admitted Tony. "Meat-eaters. We can't cart along meat for them, of course; and we can't expect meat on Bronson Beta. All we can hope for is grass and moss; so we load up with a cow, and a young bull, of course; a pair of sheep of proved breeding ability, a couple of reindeer, and a colt and a young mare. Half humanity lived on horsemeat once and milked the mares. We'll be allowed goats, too. And deer, if our big ship gets over. Do you suppose there'll be other ships starting from this side of the world to-morrow night and from the other side, the evening after?"

"Father doesn't know. When the radios were working well, months ago, he broadcast the knowledge of David's metal. It must have become obtainable from volcanic eruptions in other places. But we've no real news of any one else ready to start. One thing is certain. No party can count upon the arrival of any other. Each crew has to assume that it may be the only one that gets across to Bronson Beta."

"And damn' lucky if it lands, too," agreed Tony. "However, I hope the Australians are making a try, and will start with a kangaroo. And if the South Africans have a ship, they ought to show some originality in animals, even if they too feel confined to grass- and moss-eaters. Who has a chance of sending up a ship, anyway?"

"The English, Father thinks, surely have preserved enough organization to build and equip one ship, and the French, the Germans and Italians ought to do the same. Then there are the Russians and the Japanese at least with the potential ability to do it. There's a chance in Australia and another in South Africa—Lord Rhondin would head any party there, Father thinks."

"Any one else?"

"A possibility in Argentina and also in China."

"That makes twelve, counting our two."

"Possibilities, that's all. Of course, we know nothing about them. Father guesses that if twelve are trying, perhaps five may get ships out into space."

"What five?" demanded Tony.

"He did not name them."

"Five into space beyond the attraction of the world."

"The world won't be left then, Tony," Eve reminded him.

"Right. Funny how one keeps forgetting that, isn't it? So there'll be no place for them to drop back to, if they miss Bronson Beta. They just stay—out there in space—in their rocket, with their air-purifiers and oxygen-machines and their compressed food and their seeds and insects and birds or birds' eggs, and carefully chosen grass-eating animals. . . . I imagine they'll eat the animals, at last, out there in space; and then—"

Eve stopped him.

"Why deny the possibilities?" he objected.

"Why dwell on those particular ones, Tony, when they may be the ones we ourselves will meet? We—or our friends in our other ship. . . . It's funny how you men complain about missing the wild animals. Do you know, Tony, that Dave told me that Dr. Bronson thought about the impossibility of taking over lions when he first began planning with Father the idea of the space ships? That night Lord Rhondin and Professor Bronson sent for Dave to bring the plates to Father in New York, Professor Bronson walked about the room and spoke about how there would be no more lions."

"Funny to think of meeting Rhondin for the first time on Bronson Beta," said Tony, "if we and the South African ship get over. Good egg, Lord Rhondin, from all I hear from Dave."

They were off by themselves now, and Tony drew her nearer to him. She neither encouraged nor resisted him. He tightened his arm about her, and felt her softness and warmth against him. For a moment more she remained motionless, neutral; then suddenly her hands were on his arms, clasping him, clinging to him. Her body became tense, thrilling, and as he bent, her lips burned on his.

She drew back a little, and at last he let her. In silence he kissed her again; then her lips, close to his, said: "Farewell to earth, Tony!"

"Yes," he said, quivering. "Yes; I suppose this is our last sure night."

"No; we leave to-night, Tony."

"To-night? I thought it was to-morrow."

"No; Father feared the last night—if any one knew it in advance. So he said to-morrow; but all his calculations make it to-night."

"How soon, Eve?"

"In an hour, dear. You'll hear the bugles. He deceived even you."

"So to-morrow," said Tony, "to-morrow we may be 'ourselves, with yesterday's seven thousand years.' I had plans—or dreams at least, Eve—of the last night on earth. It changes them to find it barely an hour."

"I should not have told you, Tony."

"Why? Would you have me go ahead with what I dreamed?"

"Why not?" she said. "An hour before the bugles; an hour before we leave the world, to fall back upon it from some frightful height, dear, and be shattered on this globe's shell; or to gain space and float on endlessly, starving and freezing in our little ship; or to fall on Bronson Beta and die there. Or perhaps, Tony—perhaps, to live!"

"Perhaps," repeated Tony; but he had not, this time, gone from the world with her in his mind. He held her again and thought of his hour—the last hour of which he could be sure.

"Come away," he said. "Come farther away from——"

"From what, Tony?"

"From everybody else." And he drew her on. He led her, indeed, toward the edge of the encampment where the wires that protected it knitted a barrier. And there, holding her, he heard and she heard a child crying.

There were no children in the encampment. There never had been. No one with little children had been chosen. But here was a child.

Eve called to it, and the child ceased crying; so Eve had to call again for a response that would guide her to it in the dark. . . .

There were two children, together and alone. They were three and four years old, it appeared. They knew their names—Dan and Dorothy. They called for "Papa." Papa, it appeared, had brought them there in the dark and gone away. Papa had told them to stay there, and somebody would come.

Eve had her arms between the wires, and the children clung to her hands while they talked. Now Tony lifted them over the wires; and Eve took them in her arms.

In the awful "moonlight" of Bronson Beta, the children clung to her; and the little girl asked if she was "Mamma." Mamma, it appeared, had gone away a long time ago.

"Months ago only," Eve interpreted for Tony, "or they wouldn't remember her."

"Yes. Probably in the destruction of the First Passage," Tony said; and they both understood that the mother must be dead.

"He brought them here to us," Eve said; and Tony understood that too. It was plain enough: Some father, who had heard of the camp and the Space Ships, had brought his children here and left them—going away, asking nothing for himself. . . .

Clear and loud in the night, a bugle blew; and Tony and Eve both started.

"Gabriel's horn," muttered Tony. "The last trump!"

"Father advanced the time," returned Eve. "He decided to give a few minutes more of warning; or else he fooled me, too."

"You are carrying that child?" asked Tony. Eve had the little girl.

"Yes," said Eve. "You are carrying the boy?"

"Yes," said Tony. "Rules or no rules; necessities or no necessities, if we can take sheep and goats, I guess we can take these two."

"I guess so," said Eve; and she strode strongly beside him into the edge of illumination as the great flood-lights blazed out.

The buildings were all alight; and everybody was bustling. The loading of the two Arks long ago had been completed, as Eve had said—except for the animals and the passengers and crew. The animals now were being driven aboard; and the passengers ran back and forth, calling, crying, shaking hands, embracing one another.

They were all to go; every one in sight was billeted on the Space Ships; but some would be on one ship, some on the other. Would they meet again—on Bronson Beta? Would either ship get there? Would they rise only to drop from a great height back upon this earth? What would happen?

Tony, hurrying to his station, appreciated how wisely Hendron had acted in deceiving them all—even himself—as to the night.

Here he was, second in command of the first Space Ship, carrying a strange child in contravention of all orders. The chief commander's daughter also carried a child.

No one stopped them. Not Hendron himself. It was the last hour on earth, and men's minds were rocking.

The bugles blew again; and Tony, depositing the boy with Eve, set about his business of checking the personnel of his ship.

Three hundred yards away, Dave Ransdell checked the personnel of his larger party. Jessup and Kane, there, were in the navigating-room as Hendron was in the chief control-room here.

Ransdell, for a moment, ran over. He asked for Hendron, but he sought, also, Eve.

Tony did not interfere; he allowed them their last minutes together.

A third time the bugles blew. This meant: "All persons at ship stations!" All those who were to leave the earth forever, aboard ship!

STARWARD HO! Tony completed his check of crew and passengers. Thrice he blew his whistle.

From off to the right, where the second ship lay, Dave Ransdell's shrill signal answered.

"Close valves and locks!"

There was no one on the ground. No one! They were all aboard. All checked and tallied, thrice over. Yet as Tony left the last lock open to gaze out again and listen, he heard a faint cry. The father of the children?

Could he take him too? One man more? Of course they could make it. If it was only one man more, they must have him. Tony withheld the final signal.

With a quick command, he warned those who were closing the lock. It swung open again. The voice was faint and far away, and in its thin notes could be detected the vibrations of tense anxiety. Tony looked over the landscape and detected its direction. It came from the southwest, where the airplane-field lay. Presently he made out syllables, but not their meaning.

"Hello," he yelled mightily. "Who is it?"

Back came the thinly shouted reply: *"C'est moi, Duquesne! Attendez!"*

Tony's mind translated: *"It's I, Duquesne! Wait."*

On the opposite side of the flying-field a lone human figure struggled into the rays of the flood-lights. It was the figure of a short fat man running clumsily, waving his arms and pausing at intervals to shout. Duquesne! The name had a familiar sound. Then Tony remembered. Duquesne was the French scientist in charge of building the French space ship that had been reported to him by James long ago. Instinctively he was sure that this Duquesne who ran ludicrously across the flying-field was the same man.

He turned to the attendants at the airlock.

"Get Hendron," he said; "he'll be in the stern control-room now. Tell him Duquesne is here alone." He operated the winch which moved the stairway back to the hull of the ship.

The short fat man trotted across the field, stopping frequently to gesticulate and shout: *"Attendez! C'est moi, Duquesne!"*

At last he scrambled up the steps of the concrete foundations to the ship. He rushed across the platform and arrived at the airlock. He was completely out of breath, and could not speak. Tony had an opportunity to look at him. He wore the remnants of a khaki uniform which did not fit him. Protruding from the breast pocket of the tunic was the butt of a revolver. He was black-haired, black-eyed and big-nosed. He regarded Tony with an intensity which was almost comical, and when he began to speak brokenly, he first swore in French and then said in English: "I am Duquesne! The great Duquesne! The celebrated Duquesne! The famous Duquesne. The French physicist, me, Duquesne. This I take for the ship of Cole 'Endron—yes? Then, so I am here. Tell him I have come from France in three months, running a steamboat by myself almost, flying across this foul country with my plane, which it is broken down near what was Milwaukee, and to here I have walked by myself alone these many days. You are going now, yes? I see you are going. Tell him to go. Tell him Duquesne is here. Tell him to come and see me. Tell him to come at once. Tell him I leave those pigs, those dogs, those cows, those onions, who would build such a foolish ship as they will break their necks in. I said it would not fly, I, Duquesne. I knew this 'Endron ship would fly, so I have come to it. Bah! They are stupid, my French colleagues.

More suitable for the motormen of trams than for flyers in the outer space!"

At that instant Hendron arrived at the top of the spiral staircase.

He rushed forward with his eyes alight. "Duquesne! By God, Duquesne! I'm delighted. You're in the nick of time. In forty minutes we would have been away from here."

Duquesne gripped Hendron's hand, and skipped around him as if he were playing a child's game. With his free fist he smote upon his breast. Whether he was ecstatic with joy or rage could not have been told, for he shouted so that the entire chamber reverberated: "Am I a fool that you should have to tell me what hour was set for your departure? Have I no brains? Do I know nothing about astronomy? Have I never studied physics? Have I run barefoot across this whole United States of America for no other reason than because I knew when you would have to leave? Do I not carry the day on the watch in my pocket? Idiots, charming friends, glorious Americans, fools! Have I no brain? Can I not anticipate? Here I am."

Suddenly after this broadside of violent speech he became calm. He let go of Hendron's hand and stopped dancing. He bowed very gravely, first to Hendron, then to Tony, then to the crew. "Gentlemen," he said, "let's be going. Let's be on our way."

Hendron turned to Tony, who in reaction burst into a paroxysm of laughter. For an instant the French scientist looked deeply wounded and as if he might burst into expletives of anger; then suddenly he began to laugh. "I am ridiculous, am I not?" he shouted. He roared with laughter. He rocked with it. He wrapped his arms around his ample frame, and the tears rolled down his cheeks. "It is magnificent," he said. "Yes. It is to laugh."

"What about the ships that were being built in other countries in Europe?" Hendron asked him.

"The English?" returned Duquesne. "They will get away. What then, who knows? Can you 'muddle through' space, Cole 'Endron? I ask it. But the English are sound; they have a good ship. But as to them, I have made my answer. I am here."

"The Germans?" demanded Hendron.

The Frenchman gestured. "Too advanced!"

"Too advanced?"

"They have tried to take every contingency into account—too many contingency! They will make the most beautiful voyage of all—or by far the worst. Again I reply, I am here. As to all the other, again I observe, I have preferred to be here."

And in that fashion Pierre Duquesne, France's greatest physicist, was at the eleventh hour and the fifty-ninth minute added to the company of the Ark. He went off with Hendron to the control-room, talking volubly. Tony superintended the closing of the lock. He went up the spiral staircase to the first passenger deck. Fifty people lay there on the padded surface with the broad belts already strapped around their legs and torsos. Most of them had not yet attached the straps intended to hold their heads in place. Their eyes were directed toward the glass screen, where alternately views of the heavens overhead and of the radiant landscape outside the Space Ship were being shown.

Tony looked at his number and found his place. Eve was near by him, with the two children beside her. She had sat up to welcome him. "I've been terribly nervous. Of course I knew you'd come, but it has been hard waiting here."

"We're all set," Tony said. "And the funniest thing in the world has just happened." He began to tell about the arrival of Duquesne, and everybody in the circular room listened to his story. As he talked, he adjusted himself on the floor harness.

Below, in the control-room, the men took their posts. Hendron strapped himself under the glass screen. He fixed his eyes to an optical instrument, across which were two hair lines. Very close to the point of their intersection was a small star. The instrument had been set so that when the star reached the center of the cross, the discharge was to be started. About him was a battery of switches which were controlled by a master switch, and a lever that worked not unlike a rheostat over a series of resistances. His control-room crew were fastened in their places with their arms free to manipulate various levers. Duquesne had taken the place reserved for one of the crew, and the man who had been displaced had been sent up to the passenger-cabins.

The French scientist glanced at his watch and put it back into his pocket without speaking. Voluble though he was, he knew when it was time to be silent. His black, sparkling eyes darted appreciatively from one instrument to another in the chamber, and on his face was a rapt expression as his mind identified and explained what he saw. Hendron looked away from the optical instrument. "You religious, Duquesne?"

The Frenchman shook his head and then said: "Nevertheless, I am praying."

Hendron turned to the crossed hairs and began to count. Every man in the room stiffened to attention.

"One, two, three, four, five——" His hand went to the switch. The room was filled with a vibrating hum. "—Six, seven, eight, nine, ten——" The sound of the hum rose now to a feline shriek. "—Eleven, twelve, thirteen, fourteen, fifteen—ready! Sixteen, seventeen, eighteen, nineteen, twenty——" His hand moved to the instrument that was like a rheostat. His other hand was clenched, white-knuckled, on his straps. "Twenty-one, twenty-two, twenty-three, twenty-four, twenty-five." Simultaneously the crew shoved levers, and the rheostat moved up an inch. As he counted, signals flashed to the other ship. They must leave at the same moment.

A roar redoubling that which had resounded below the ship on the night of the attack, deafened all other sound.

Tony thought: "We're leaving the earth!" But strangely, thought itself at such a moment supplied no sensation. The physical shocks were too overpowering.

A quivering of the ship that jarred the soul. An upthrust on the feet. Hendron's lips moving in counting that could no longer be heard. The eyes of the men of the crew watching those lips so that when they reached fifty, a second switch was touched, and the room was plunged into darkness relieved only by the dim rays of tiny bulbs over the instruments themselves. A slight change in the feeling of air-pressure against the eardrums. Another forward motion of the steady hand on the rheostat. An increase of the thrust against the feet, so that the whole body felt leaden. Augmentation of the hideous din outside.

An exchange of glances between Hendron and Duquesne—both men's eyes flashing with triumph.

In the passenger-cabin, Tony's recitation of the arrival of Duquesne was suddenly interrupted by the fiendish uproar. "We've started!" fifty voices shouted, and the words were soundless. The deck on which they lay pressed up against them. The glass screen overhead went dark. Tony reached toward Eve, and felt her hand stretching to meet his.

THE JOURNEY THROUGH SPACE: On the doomed earth, observers must have seen the Space Ship lying brass-bright in the light of the Bronson Bodies and the cantonment flood-lamps, as immobile as if part of the earth. They must have seen it surrounded abruptly in golden fire, fire that drove toward the earth and lifted in immense clouds which bellowed and eddied toward the other larger ship simultaneously rising above a similar cloud. They must have heard the hideous torrent of sound, and then they must have seen the ship rise rapidly into the air on its column of flame. They must have watched it gain altitude vertically. They would have realized that it gathered momentum as it rose, and they would have seen that long trail of fire beneath each ship stretch and stretch as the shimmering cylinder shot into the night until it detached itself from the earth. But—there were no known observers left immediately below. If any one from outside the camp had happened to approach too closely, he must certainly have been annihilated by the blast.

Tony, clinging to his straps, thought of the father who had brought the children; and Tony hoped, irrationally, that he had fled far away. But what difference whether he was annihilated alone now—or in the wreck of all the world a little later?

He could see the fiery trail of the second Ark rising skyward on its apex of scintillating vapor. Already it was miles away.

Below, on the earth, fires broke out—a blaze that denoted a forest burning. In the place where the ship had been, the two gigantic blocks of concrete must have crumbled and collapsed. The power-house, left untended, continued to hum, supplying lights for no living thing. Far away to the south and west, the President of the United States, surrounded by his Cabinet, looked up from the new toil engendered by the recommencing earthquakes, and saw, separated by an immeasurable distance, two comets moving away from the earth. The President looked reverently at the phenomenon; then he said: "My friends, the greatest living American has but now left his home-land."

In the passenger-chamber the unendurable noise rose in a steady crescendo until all those who lay there felt that their vital organs would be rent asunder by the fury of that sound. They were pressed with increasing force upon the deck. Nauseated, terrified, overwhelmed, their senses foundered, and many of them lapsed into unconsciousness.

Tony, who was still able to think, despite the awful acceleration of the ship, realized presently that the din was diminishing. From his rather scanty knowledge of physics he tried to deduce what was happening. Either the Ark had reached air so thin that it did not carry sound-waves, or else the Ark was traveling so fast that its sound could not catch up with it. The speed of that diminution seemed to increase. The chamber became quieter and quieter. Tony reflected, in spite of the fearful torment he was undergoing, that eventually the only sound which would afflict it would come from the breeches of the tubes in the control-rooms, and the rooms themselves would insulate that. Presently he realized that the ringing in his ears was louder than the noise made by the passage of the ship. Eve had relaxed the grip on his hand, but at that moment he felt a pressure.

It was impossible to turn his head. He said, "Hello," in an ordinary voice, and found he had been so deafened that it was inaudible. He tried to lift his hand, but the acceleration of the ship was so great that it required more effort than he was able yet to exert. Then he heard Eve's voice and he realized that she was talking very loudly: "Are you all right, Tony? Speak to me."

He shouted back: "I'm all right. How are the children?" He could see them lying stupefied, with eyes wide open.

"It's horrible, isn't it?" Eve cried.

"Yes, but the worst is over. We'll be accelerating for some time, though."

Energy returned to him. He struggled with the bonds that held his head, and presently spoke again to Eve. She was deathly pale. He looked at the other passengers. Many of them were still unconscious, most of them only partly aware of what was happening. He tried to lift his head from the floor, but the upward pressure still overpowered him. He lay supine. Then the lights in the cabin went out and the screen was illuminated. Across one side was a glimpse of the trail which they were leaving, a bright hurtling yellow stream, but it was not that which held his attention. In the center of the screen was part of a curved disk. Tony realized that he was staring up at half of the northern hemisphere of the Earth. The disk did not yet have the luminous quality that the moon used to possess. It was in a sort of hazy darkness which grew light on its eastern edge.

Tony thought he could make out the outline of Alaska on the west coast of the United States, and he saw pinpoints of light which at first he thought of as signs of human habitation, but which he presently realized must have represented vast brilliant areas. He identified them with the renewal of volcanic activity. The screen flashed. Another view appeared. Constellations of stars, such stars as he had never seen, blazing furiously in the velvet blackness of the outer sky. He realized that he was looking at the view to be had from the side of the ship. The light went out again, and a third of the four periscopes recorded its field. Again stars, but in their center and hanging away from them, as if in miraculous suspension, was a small round bright-red body which Tony recognized as Mars.

Once again Eve pressed his hand, and Tony returned the pressure.

In the control-room, Hendron still sat in the sling with his hand on the rheostat.

His eyes traveled to a meter which showed their distance from the Earth. Then they moved on to a chronometer; then for an instant, as if in concession to his human curiosity, they darted to Duquesne. Duquesne had loosened himself from his sling and was lying on the floor, unable to rise. His expression in the dim light was extremely ludicrous. He struggled feebly, like a beetle that has been turned on its back, and Hendron smiled at him and pointed to the chronometer, but Duquesne did not seem to understand his meaning.

The control-room was filled with the throb that was contained in the breeches, but Hendron could do nothing to alleviate it. He had already determined the time necessary for acceleration—one hundred and twelve minutes—and he could not shorten it. In the end, Duquesne managed to pull himself to a sitting position underneath the glass screen where he was perfectly content to sit and contemplate the heavens as they appeared in reflection from outer space.

Tony felt that he had been lying on the floor for an eternity. His strength had come back, and he realized that it would be possible to sit up, even to move about, but they had been instructed to remain on the floor until the speed of their ascent was stabilized. Minutes dragged. It was becoming possible to converse in the chamber, but few people cared to say anything. Many of them were still violently ill. Others were glad to lie motionless, and watch the screen as Duquesne was doing several decks below.

At three minutes of five, Hendron slowly moved back the handle of the rheostat, and almost abruptly conditions in the ship changed. The volume of sound radiating from the engine-room decreased. Hendron unbuckled his bonds and stepped from them. Duquesne stood up. He walked unsteadily across the floor to take the hand of Hendron.

"Magnificent! Stunning! Beautiful! Perfect! How fast do we now travel?" He was compelled to shout to make himself heard.

Hendron pointed at a meter; its indicator hovered between the figures 3,000 and 3,500.

"Miles?" the Frenchman asked.

Hendron nodded.

"Per hour?"

Hendron nodded again.

The Frenchman made his mouth into the shape required for a whistle, although no note could be heard.

Hendron operated the switch controlling the choice of periscopes. In the midst of the glass screen, the Earth now appeared as a round globe, its diameter in both directions clearly apparent. More than half of it lay in shadow, but the illuminated half was like a great relief map. The whole of the United States, part of Europe and the north polar regions, were revealed to their gaze. In wonder they regarded the world that had been their home. They could see clearly the colossal changes which had been wrought upon it. The great inland sea that occupied the Mississippi Valley sparkled in the morning sun. The myriad volcanoes which had sprung into being along the Western cordillera were for the most part hidden under a pall of smoke and clouds.

Duquesne pointed solemnly to that part of Europe that was visible. Hendron, looking at the screen for the first time, was shocked to see the disappearance of the Lowland Plain.

The Frenchman moved closer to him and shouted in his ear. "We abandoned the ship outside of Paris when we realized it was not on high enough ground. We started a new one in the Alps. I told those pigs: 'Gentlemen, it will melt. It is but wax. I know it.' They replied: 'If it melts, we shall perish.' I responded: 'If you perish, it shall be without me.'" Suddenly the Frenchman popped out his watch. "*Sapristi!* The world has turned so that these fools are to leave now." He moved his lips while he made a rapid calculation. "We shall observe, is it not so? In an hour my idiot friends will burn themselves to death. I shall laugh. I shall roar. I shall shout. It will be one grand joke. Yes, you will give me a focus upon France in this remarkable instrument of yours an hour from now, will you not?"

Hendron nodded. He signaled a command to his crew, who had been standing unbuckled from their slings, at attention. They now seated themselves.

Hendron shouted at the Frenchman: "Come on up with me. I'll introduce you to the passengers. I'm anxious to know about them."

When Hendron reached the first deck of passengers' quarters, he found them standing together comparing notes on the sensations of space-flying. Many of them were rubbing stiff arms and legs. Two or three, including Eliot James, were still lying on the padded deck in obvious discomfort. They had turned on the lights, apparently more interested in their own condition than in the astounding vista of the Earth below. Tony had just opened the doors of the larder and was on the point of distributing sandwiches.

Hendron brought the shabby Duquesne into their midst.

"I'd like to present my friend Professor Pierre Duquesne of the French Academy, a last-minute arrival. I assure you that except for its monotony, the trip will offer you no further great discomfort until we reach Bronson Beta, when we shall be under the necessity of repeating approximately the same maneuver. I want to call your attention to the following phenomena: In something less than an hour we are going to turn the periscope on France in an effort to observe the departure of the French equivalent of our ships. We are at the moment engaged in trying to locate our second Ark, which took its course at a distance from us to avoid any chance of collision, and being between us and the sun, is now temporarily lost in the glare of the sun.

"I will have the sun thrown on the screen at intervals, as some of the phenomena are extremely spectacular. At about mid-point of our voyage we will concentrate our attention on the collision between the Earth and Bronson Alpha. I think at this point I may express my satisfaction in the behavior of the Ark. As you all are aware, we have escaped from the earth. We are still well within the field of its gravitational control, in the sense that if our propellent forces ceased, we undoubtedly would fall back upon the earth; but the pull of gravity is constantly weakening. It diminishes, as most of you know, not directly in relation to the distance, but in relation to the square of the distance. It is the great lessening of the pull of gravity which has ended our extreme distress.

"Except for the small chance of striking an astrolite, we are quite safe and will continue so for some time. When we approach Bronson Beta, our situation will, of course, become more difficult. You will please excuse me now, as I wish to convey the same information to the passengers on the deck above."

Hendron departed, and his feet disappeared through the opening in the ceiling which contained the spiral staircase.

Duquesne immediately made himself the center of attention, praising alternately Hendron's ship and his own prowess in completing the journey from France. The reaction from the initial strain of the voyage took, in him, the form of saluting, shouting, joking with the men and flirting with the women.

Tony saw to the distribution of food and water. The ship rushed through the void so steadily that cups of milk, which Eve held to the lips of the children, scarcely spilled over. The passengers, having eaten a little, found that they could move from floor to floor without great trouble, and several became garrulous. The ship was spinning very slowly, exposing one side after the other to the sun, and this served to equalize the temperature, which was fiery hot on the sun-side, deadly cold on the other.

Fans distributed the air inside the ship. Outside, there was vacuum against which the airlocks were sealed. The air of the ship, breathed and "restored," was not actually fresh, although chemically it was perfectly breathable. The soft roar of the rocket propulsion-tubes fuddled the senses. There was no sensation of external time, no appreciation of traveling from morn to night. The sun glared in a black sky studded with brilliant stars. . . . The sun showed its corona, its mighty, fiery prominences, its huge leaping tongues of flame.

To the right of the sun, the great glowing crescents of Bronson Alpha and Bronson Beta loomed larger and larger.

Eve sat with Tony as a periscope turned on them and displayed them on the screen. They could plainly see that Bronson Alpha was below and approaching the earth; Bronson Beta, slowly turning, was higher and much nearer the ship.

"Do you see their relation?" she asked.

"Between the Bronson Bodies?" said Tony. "Aren't they nearer together than they have ever been before?"

"Much nearer; and as Father—and Professor Bronson—calculated. Bronson Beta, being much the smaller and lighter, was revolving about Bronson Alpha. The orbit was not a circle; it was a very long ellipse. Sometimes, therefore, this brought Bronson Beta much closer to Alpha than at other times. When they went around the sun, the enormous force of the sun's attraction further distorted the orbit, and Bronson Beta probably is nearer Alpha now than it ever was before. Also, notice it is at the point in its orbit which is most favorable for us."

"You mean for our landing on it?" asked Tony.

"For that; and especially is it favorable to us, after we land—if we do," amended Eve; and she gathered the children to her. She sat between them, an arm about each, gazing at the screen.

"You see, the sun had not surely 'captured' Bronson Beta and Bronson Alpha. They had arrived from some incalculable distance and they have rounded the sun, but, without further interference than the sun's attraction, they would retreat again and perhaps never reappear; they would not join the family of familiar planets circling the sun.

"But on the course toward the sun, Alpha destroyed the moon, as we know, and this had an effect upon both Alpha and Bronson Beta, controlled by Alpha. And now something even more profound is going to happen. Alpha will have contact with the world. That will destroy the earth and will send Bronson Alpha off in another path—perhaps it will prove to be a very long ellipse, but more probably it will be a hyperbola. No one can quite calculate that; but one almost certain effect of the catastrophe is that it will break Bronson Beta away from the dominating control of Bronson Alpha and leave Beta subject to the sun. That will provide a much more satisfactory orbit for us about our sun."

"Us?" echoed Tony.

"Us—if we get there," said Eve; and she bent and kissed the children. "What purpose could there be in all that"—she nodded to the screen when she straightened—"if some of us aren't to get there? We see God not only sending us that world, Tony,"—she spoke a little impatiently —"but arranging for us an orbit for it about the sun which will let us live."

"Do you know the Wonder Clock?" Danny, the little boy, looked up and demanded. "Do you know Peterkin and the li'l Gray Hare?"

"Certainly," said Eve. "Once there was a giant——"

At the end of the hour all the lights in the passenger quarters were turned out, and the Earth was again flashed on the screen. Its diminution in size was already startling; and the remains of Europe, stranded in a new ocean, looked like a child's model flour-and-water map.

Duquesne lay on his back on deck and stared up at the scenery. He gave an informal lecture as he looked. "As we are flinging ourselves away from the Earth below, we are putting distance between ourselves and a number of prize fools. These fellows are my best friends. You will pick out faintly the map of Europe. Directly south of those shadows which were once the British Isles, you see the configuration of the Alps. In the

center of the western range are the fools of whom I spoke. At any moment now, providing we are able to see anything at all, we shall witness
their effort at departure. They built a ship not dissimilar to this, but
unfortunately relying upon another construction than that valuable little
metal discovered by Mr.—whatever his name is. I have told them they
shall melt. I hope that we shall be able to see the joke of that fusion."

Duquesne glanced again at his watch, and looked up at the screen on
which, like a stereopticon picture, hung the Earth. Suddenly he sat bolt
upright. "Did I not tell you?"

A point of light showed suddenly in the spot he had designated. It was
very bright, and as a second passed, it appeared to extend so that it stood
away from the Earth like a white-hot needle. Tony and Eve and many
others glanced at Duquesne.

But Duquesne was not laughing as he had promised. Instead he sat
with his head bent back, his hands doubled into fists which pounded his
knees, while in an outpouring of French he cajoled and pleaded frantically
with that distant streak of fire.

The seconds passed slowly. Every one under the glass screen realized
that here, perhaps, would be companions for them after they had reached
Bronson Beta. Since they had just undergone the experience which they
knew the Frenchmen were suffering in their catapulted departure from
the Alps, they watched gravely and breathlessly. Only the rocket trail of
the ship could be seen, as the ship itself was too small and too far away
to be visible.

Duquesne was standing. He suddenly seemed conscious of those around
him. "They go, they go, they go, they go! Maybe they have solved this
problem. Maybe they will be with us."

Suddenly a groan escaped him. The upshooting light curved, became
horizontal and shot parallel with Earth, moving apparently with such
speed that it seemed to have traversed a measurable fraction of the Alps
while they watched.

Abruptly, then, the trail zigzagged; it curved back toward the Earth, and
the French ship commenced to descend, impelled by its own motors. In
another second there was a faint glow and then—only a luminous trail,
which disappeared rapidly, like the pathway of fire left by a meteor.

Duquesne did not laugh. He wept.

They tried to console him but he shrugged them away angrily. After
a long time he began to talk, and they listened with sympathy. "Jean
Delavoi was there, handsome Jean. And Captain Vivandi. Marcel Jamar,
my own nephew, the greatest biologist of the new generation. And yet I
told them, but it was their only hope, so they were stubborn." He looked
at the people in the chamber. "Did you see? It melted. First the right

tubes, throwing it on a horizontal course, then all of it. It was quickly over—*grâce à Dieu.*"

But other flashes rose and traveled on. The English, the Germans, perhaps the Italians had got away.

The implications of these sights transcended talk. Conversation soon ceased. Exhaustion, spiritual and physical, assailed the travelers. Eve's children fell into a sleep-like stupor. The motion of the ship seemed no more than a slight sway, and those who remained awake found it possible to talk in more ordinary tones.

Gravity diminished steadily, so that gestures were easier to make than they had been on Earth. Time lost all sequence. Twelve hours in the past seemed like an eternity spent in a prison; and only the waning Earth, which was frequently flashed on the screen by men in the control-room, marked progress to the passengers. They were spent by their months of effort and by the emotional strains through which they had passed. Stupefied like the children by the unusualness of this voyage, they were no longer worldly beings, but because all their vision of outer space came vicariously, their sensations were rather of being confined in a small place than of being lost and alone in the unfathomable void.

Their habit of relying upon the attractive force of the Earth resulted in an increasing number of mishaps, some of them amusing and some of them painful. After what seemed like eons of time some one asked Tony for more food. Tony himself could not remember whether he was going to serve the fifth meal or the sixth, but he sprang to his feet with earnest willingness—promptly shot clear to the ceiling, against which he bumped his head. He fell back to the floor with a jar and rose laughing. The ceiling was also padded, so that he had not hurt himself.

The sandwiches were wrapped in wax paper, and when some one on the edge of the crowd asked that his sandwich be tossed, Tony flipped it toward him, only to see it pass high over the man's head and entirely out of reach, and strike against the opposite wall. The man himself stretched to catch the wrapped sandwich, and sat down again rubbing his arm, saying that he had almost thrown his shoulder out of joint.

People walked in an absurd manner, stepping high into the air as if they were dancers. Gestures were uncontrollable, and it was unsafe to talk excitedly for fear one would hit one's self in the face.

Before this condition reached its crisis, however, Hendron himself appeared in the passenger-cabin for one of his frequent visits. He arrived, not by way of the staircase, but by way of the cable which was strung tautly inside the spiral, hauling himself up hand over hand with greater ease and rapidity than was ever exhibited by any sailor. He was greeted with pleasure—any slight incident had an exaggerated effect upon the passengers; but his demeanor was serious.

"I want you all to be witnesses of the reason for this journey," he said soberly.

He switched off the lights. The screen glowed, and on it they saw the Earth. At the hour of their departure the Earth had occupied much more than the area in the screen now reflected overhead, darkened on one side as if it were a moon in its third quarter, or not quite full. At the very edge of the screen was a bright curve which marked the perimeter of Bronson Alpha. Bronson Beta could not be seen.

THE CRASH OF TWO WORLDS: Now for an hour the passengers watched silently as Bronson Alpha swept upon the scene, a gigantic body, weird, luminous and unguessable, many times larger than Earth. It moved toward the Earth with the relentless perceptibility of the hands of a large clock, and those who looked upon its awe-inspiring approach held their breaths.

Once again Hendron spoke. "What will take place now cannot be definitely ascertained. In view of the retardation of Bronson Alpha's speed caused by its collision with the moon, I have reason to believe that its course will be completely disrupted."

Inch by inch, as it seemed, the two bodies came closer together. Looking at the screen was like watching the motion picture of a catastrophe and not like seeing it. Tony had to repeat to himself over and over that it was really so, in order to make himself believe it. Down there on the little earth were millions of scattered, demoralized human beings. They were watching this awful phenomenon in the skies. Around them the ground was rocking, the tides were rising, lava was bursting forth, winds were blowing, oceans were boiling, fires were catching, and human courage was facing complete frustration. Above them the sky was filled with this awful onrushing mass.

To those who through the smoke and steam and hurricane could still pierce the void, it would appear as something no longer stellar but as something real, something they could almost reach out and touch. A vast horizon of earth stretched toward them across the skies. They would be able, if their reeling senses still maintained powers of observation, to see the equally tumultuous surface of Bronson Alpha, to describe the geography of its downfalling side. They would perhaps, in the last staggering seconds, feel themselves withdrawn from the feeble gravity of their own Earth, to fall headlong toward Bronson Alpha. And in the magnitude of that inconceivable manifestation, they would at last, numb and senseless, be ground to the utmost atoms of their composition.

Tony shuddered as he watched. A distance, short on the screen—even as solar measurements are contemplated—separated the two planets. In the chamber of the hurtling Space Ship no one moved. Earth and Bronson Alpha were but a few moments apart. It seemed that even at their august distance they could perceive motion on the planet, as if the continents below them were swimming across the seas, as if the seas were hurling themselves upon the land; and presently they saw great cracks, in the abysses of which were fire, spread along the remote dry land. Into the air were lifted mighty whirls of steam. The nebulous atmosphere of Bronson Alpha touched the air of Earth, and then the very Earth bulged. Its shape altered before their eyes. It became plastic. It was drawn out egg-shaped. The cracks girdled the globe. A great section of the Earth itself lifted up and peeled away, leaping toward Bronson Alpha with an inconceivable force.

The two planets struck.

Decillions of tons of mass colliding in cosmic catastrophe.

"It's not direct," Duquesne shouted. "Oh, God! Perhaps—"

Every one knew what he was thinking. Perhaps they were not witnessing complete annihilation. Perhaps some miracle would preserve a portion of the world.

They panted and stared.

Steam, fire, smoke. Tongues of flame from the center of the earth. The planets ground together and then moved across each other. It was like watching an eclipse. The magnitude of the disaster was veiled by hot gases and stupendous flames, and was diminished in awfulness by the intervening distances and by the seeming slowness with which it took place.

Bronson Alpha rode between them and the Earth. Then—on its opposite side—fragments of the shattered world reappeared. Distance showed between them—widening, scattering distance. Bronson Alpha moved away on its terrible course, fiery, flaming, spread enormously in ghastly light.

The views on the visagraph changed quickly. The sun showed its furious flames. The telescopic periscopes concentrated on the fragment of the earth.

"They're calculating," Hendron said.

During a lull of humble voices Kyto could be heard praying to strange gods in Japanese. Eliot James drummed on the padded floor with monotonous fingertips. Tony clenched Eve's hand. Time passed —it seemed hours. A man hurried down the spiral staircase.

He went directly to Hendron. "First estimates ready," he said.

Hendron's voice was tense: "Tell us."

"I thought perhaps—"

"Go ahead, Von Beitz. These people aren't children; besides, they have given up all expectations of the earth."

"They have seen the first result," Von Beitz replied. "The earth is shattered. Unquestionably much of its material merged with Bronson Alpha; but most is scattered in fragments of various masses which will assume orbits of their own about the sun."

"And Bronson Alpha?"

"We have made only a preliminary estimate of its deceleration and its deviation from its original course; but it seems to have been deflected so that it will follow a hyperbola into space."

"Hyperbola, eh?"

"Probably."

"That means," Hendron explained loudly, "we will have seen the last of Bronson Alpha. It will not return to the sun. It will leave our solar system forever.—And Bronson Beta?" Hendron turned to the German.

"As we have hoped, the influence of Bronson Alpha over Bronson Beta is terminated. The collision occurred at a moment which found Bronson Beta at a favorable point in its orbit about Bronson Alpha. Favorable, I mean, for us. Bronson Beta will not follow Alpha into space. Its orbit becomes independent; Bronson Beta, almost surely, will circle the sun."

Some of the women burst out crying in a hysteria of relief. The world was gone; they had seen it shattered; but another would take its place. For the first time they succeeded in feeling this.

A short time later, a man arose to bring the women water; he remained suspended in the air!

Tony reached up and turned on the lights. The man who floated was sinking slowly toward the floor, his face blank with amazement.

"We have come," announced Tony loudly, "very close to the point between Bronson Beta and Bronson Alpha where the gravity of one neutralizes the gravity of the other. Bronson Alpha and the fragments of our world, pulling one way, strike an equilibrium here with the pull of Bronson Beta, which we are approaching."

He saw Eve lifting the children and leaving them suspended in the air. For an instant they enjoyed it; then it frightened them. A strange panic ensued. Tony's heart raced. It was difficult to breathe. When he swallowed, it choked him; and as he swam through the air with every step, he felt himself growing faint, dizzy and nauseated.

He saw Eve, as if through a mist, make a motion to reach for the children, and rise slowly into the air, where she stretched at full length groping wildly for the children. Tony swam over to her and pushed them into her arms. His brain roared; but he thought: "Is this psychological or physical? Was it a physical result of lack of all weight or was it the oppressiveness of sensation?" He shouted the question to Eve, who did not reply.

The air was becoming filled with people. Almost no one was on the deck. The slightest motion was sufficient to cause one to depart from whatever anchorage one had. Hands and feet were outthrust. On every face was a sick and pallid expression. Tony saw Hendron going hand over hand on the cable through the stair, ascending head foremost, his feet trailing out behind him.

That was all he remembered. He fell into coma.

When his senses returned, he found himself lying on the deck under half a dozen other people, but their weight was not oppressive. The pile above him would have crushed any one on Earth, but here it made no difference. His limbs felt cold and weak; his heart still beat furiously. He struggled to free himself, and succeeded with remarkable ease. A wave of nausea brought him to his knees, and he fainted again, striking the floor lightly and bouncing into the air several times before he came to rest. . . .

Again consciousness returned.

This time he rolled over carefully and did not attempt to rise. He was lying on something hard and cold. He explored it with his fingers, and realized dully that it was the glass screen which projected the periscope views. It was the ceiling, then, on which the passengers were lying in a tangled heap, and not the deck. Their positions had been reversed. He thought that he was stone deaf, and then perceived that the noise of the motors had stopped entirely. They were falling toward Bronson Beta, using gravity and their own inertia to sustain that downward flight. He understood why he had seen Hendron pulling himself along the staircase. Hendron had been transferring to the control-room at the opposite end of the ship.

Tony's eyes moved in a tired and sickly fashion to the tangle of people. He knew that since he was the first to regain consciousness, it was his duty to disentangle them and make them as comfortable as possible. He crawled toward them. Whole people could be moved as if they were toy balloons. With one arm he would grasp a fixed belt on the deck, and with the other he would send a body rolling across the floor to the edge of the room. The passengers were breathing, gasping, hiccoughing; their hearts were pounding; their faces were stark white; but they seemed to be alive. The children were dazed but unhurt. Tony was unable to do more than to give them separate places in which to lie. After that, his own addled and confused body succumbed, and he lay down again, panting. He knew that they would be all right as soon as the gravity from Bronson Beta became stronger. He knew that the voyage was more than half finished; but he was so sick, so weak, that he did not care. He fell into a state between sleep and coma.

Some one woke him. "We're eating. How about a sandwich?"

He sat up. The gravity was still very slight, but strong enough to restore his sensations to something approaching normal. He started around the circular room which had become so familiar in the past hours. An attempt at a grin overspread his features. He reached inaccurately for the sandwich, and murmured his thanks.

An hour later conditions were improved for moving about the chamber, by the starting of the motors which were to decelerate the ship. The floor was firm again. On the screen now at their feet they could see Bronson Beta. It was white like an immense moon, but veiled in clouds. Here and there bits of its superficial geography were visible. They gathered around the screen, kneeling over it, the lurid light which the planet cast glowing up on their faces. In four hours the deceleration had been greatly increased. In six, Bronson Beta was visibly spreading on the screen. Deceleration held them tightly on the floor, but they would crawl across each other laboriously, and in turn stare at the floating, cloudy sphere upon which they expected to arrive.

The screen changed views now. It halted to catch the flight of Bronson Alpha from the sun, but most of the time those who operated it were now busy searching for the other American ship, of which they had seen no trace.

The hours dragged more, even, than they had on the outward journey. The surface of the planet ahead of them was disappointingly shrouded, as inspected for the last time. A word of warning went through the ship. The passengers took another drink of water, ate another mouthful of food, and once again strapped themselves to the floor. Hendron tripped the handle of a companion to the rheostat-like instrument in the far end of the ship. He fixed a separate telescope so that he could see into it. He looked critically at his gauges. He turned on more power.

A half-hour passed, and he did not budge. His face was taut. The dangers of space had been met. Now came the last great test. At his side again was Duquesne. Above him, in layers, were the terrified animals and the half-insensible passengers. So great was the pressure of retardation that it was almost impossible for him to move, and yet it was necessary to do so with great delicacy. A fractional miscalculation would mean that all his work had gone for nothing.

In the optical instrument to which he screwed his eyes, the edges of Bronson Alpha had long since passed out of view. He stared at a bright foaming mass of what looked like clouds. A vast abyss separated him from those clouds, and yet its distance shortened rapidly. He looked at the gauge that measured their altitude from the surface of the planet, and at the gauge which reckoned their speed.

Duquesne followed his movements with eyes eloquent of his emotions. Suddenly the clouds seemed to rush up toward him.

Hendron pressed a stud. The retardation was perceptibly increased. Sound began to pour in awful volumes to their ears.

Duquesne's eyes jerked up to the altimeter, which showed eighty-six miles. It was falling rapidly. The clouds on the screen were thicker. They fell through atmosphere. The roar increased and became as insufferable as it had been when they left the Earth. Perspiration leaked down Hendron's face and showed darkly through the heavy shirt he wore. The altimeter ran with diminishing speed from fifty miles to twenty-five. From twenty-five it crawled to ten. From ten to five. It seemed scarcely to be moving now.

Suddenly Hendron's lips jerked spasmodically, and a quiver ran through the hand on the rheostat. He pointed toward the screen with his free hand, and Duquesne had his first view of the new world. The same view flashed through the remnants of cloud to all the passengers. Below them was a turbulent rolling ocean. Where the force of their blasts struck it, it flung back terrific clouds of steam. They descended to within a mile of its surface, and then Hendron, operating another lever, sent out horizontal jets, so that the ship began to move rapidly over the surface of this unknown sea.

To every one who looked, this desolate expanse of ocean was like a beneficent blessing from God Himself. Here was something familiar, something interesting, something terrestrial. Here was no longer the incomprehensible majesty of the void.

The Space Ship had reached the surface of Bronson Beta and was traveling now at a slow, lateral velocity above one of the oceans. Hendron worked frantically with the delicate controls to keep the ship poised and in regular motion; yet it rose and fell like an airplane bounding in rough winds, and it swayed on its horizontal axis so that its pilot ceaselessly played his fingertips on the releases of the quick blasts which maintained equilibrium.

The sullen, sunless ocean seemed endless. Was there no land?

Where were the continents, where the islands and plains and the sites of the "cities" which the great telescopes of earth—the telescopes of that shattered world which survived now only in fragments spinning around the sun—once had shown? Had the cities, had the mountains and plains, been mere optical illusions?

That was impossible; yet impatience never had maddened men as now. Still the views obtainable from the side periscope flashed upon the screen and showed nothing but empty sea and lowering cloud.

Then; on the far horizon, land appeared dimly.

A cry, a shout that drowned in the tumult of the motors, broke from trembling lips. Speedily they approached the land. It spread out under them. It towered into hills. Its extent was lost in the mists. They reached its coast, a bleak inhospitable stretch of brown earth and rock, of sandy beach and cliff upon which nothing grew or moved or was. Inland the country rose precipitously; and Hendron, as if he shared the impatience of his passengers and could bear no more, turned the ship back toward a plateau that rose high above the level of the sea.

Along the plateau he skimmed at a speed that might have been thirty terrestrial miles an hour. The Ark drew down toward the new Earth until it was but a few feet above the ground. The speed diminished, the motors were turned off and on again quickly, a maneuver which jolted those who lay strapped in their places. There was a very short, very rapid drop; bodies were thrown violently against the padded floor; the springs beneath them recoiled—and there was silence.

Regardless of the fate of the others, the fate of Earth itself, Hendron with his hundred colonists had reached a new world alive.

The ship settled at a slight angle in the earth and rock beneath it.

The Ark was filled with a new sound—the sound of human voices raised in hysterical bedlam.

THE COSMIC CONQUERORS: Cole Hendron turned to Duquesne. The bedlam from the passenger-cabin came to their ears faintly. On the visa-screen above them was depicted the view from one of the sides of the ship—a broad stretch of rolling country, bare and brown, vanishing toward ascending hills and gray mist. Hendron had relaxed for the first time in the past eight months, and he stood with his hands at his sides, his shoulders stooped and his knees bent. He looked as Atlas might have looked when Hercules lifted the world from his shoulders. It was an expression more descriptive than any words might have been.

Duquesne's emotions found speech. "Miraculous! Marvelous! Superb! Ah, my friend, my good friend, my old friend, my esteemed friend! I congratulate you. I, Duquesne, I throw myself at your feet. I embrace your knees; I salute you. You have conquered Destiny itself. You have brought this astounding ship of yours to the Beta Bronson. To you, Christopher Columbus is a nincompoop. Magellan is a child drooling over his toys. Listen to them upstairs there, screaming. Their hearts are flooded. Their eyes are filled. Their souls expand. Through you, to-day, humanity opens a new epoch!"

The Frenchman could not confine his celebration to the control-cabin. He seized Hendron and hauled him to the spiral staircase which functioned as well inverted as it had right-side up. He thrust Hendron before him into the first chamber, where the passengers from both decks were crowding. Duquesne himself was ignored; and he did not mind it.

"Hendron!" rose the shout; and men and women, almost equally hysterical, rushed to him. They had to clap hands on him, touch him, cry out to him.

Tony found himself shouting an excited harangue to which no one was paying attention. He discovered Eve at his side, struggling toward her father, and weeping. Some one recognized her and thrust her through the throng.

Men and women were throwing their arms about each other, kissing, and screaming in each other's faces. Duquesne, ignored and indifferent to it, made his way through the throng thumping the backs of the men and embracing the women, and beating on his own chest. Eliot James, who had been deathly ill during the entire transit, abruptly forgot his sickness, was caught in the tumult of the first triumph, and then withdrew to the wall and watched his fellows rejoice.

At last some one opened the larder and brought out food. People who had eaten practically nothing for the four days began to devour everything they could get their hands upon.

Tony, meanwhile, had somewhat recovered himself. He made a quick census and shouted: "We all are here. Every one who started on this ship survived!"

It set off pandemonium again, but also it reminded them of doubt of the safety of the second ship. "Where is it? Can it be sighted? . . . How about the Germans? . . . The English? . . . The Japanese?"

Their own shouts quieted them, so that Hendron at last could speak.

"We have had, for three days, no sight of our friends or of any of the other parties from earth," he announced. "That does not mean that they all have failed; our path through space was not the only one. Some may have been ahead of us and arrived when the other side of this world was turned; others may still arrive; but you all understand that we can count upon no one but ourselves.

"We have arrived; that we know. And none of you will question my sincerity when I repeat to you that it is my conviction that fate—Destiny —far more than our own efforts has brought us through.

"I repeat here, in my first words upon this strange, new, marvelous world what I said upon that planet which for millions and hundreds of millions of years supported and nourished the long life of evolution which created us—I repeat, what I said upon that planet which now flies in shattered fragments about our sun; we have arrived, not as triumphant individuals spared for ourselves, but as humble representatives of the result of a billion years of evolution transported to a sphere where we may reproduce and recreate the life given us. . . .

"I will pass at once to practical considerations.

"At this spot, it is now late in the afternoon of Bronson Beta's new day, which lasts thirty hours instead of the twenty-four to which we are accustomed. For the present, we must all remain upon the ship. The ground immediately under is still baked hot by the heat of our blast at landing. Moreover we must test the atmosphere carefully before we breathe it.

"Of course, if it is utterly unbreathable, we will all perish soon; but if it proves merely to contain some unfavorable element against which we must be masked at first until we develop immunity to it, we must discover what it is.

"While waiting, we will discharge one of the forward rocket tubes at half-hour intervals in the hope that our sister ship will see this signal and reply. We will also immediately put into operation an external radio system and listen for her. I wish to thank those of you who acted as my crew during this flight, and who in spite of shuddering senses and stricken bodies stuck steadfast to your posts. But there is no praise adequate in human language for the innumerable feats of courage, of ingenuity and perseverance which have been performed by every one of you. I trust that by morning we shall be able to make a survey of our world on foot, and I presume that by then we shall have heard from our sister ship."

Eve and Tony walked back and forth through the throng of passengers, arm in arm. Greetings and discussions continued incessantly. Every one was talking. Presently some one began to sing, and all the passengers joined in.

Up in the control-room Hendron and his assistants began their analysis of a sample of atmosphere that had been obtained through a small airlock. They rigged up the ship's wireless, and sent into the clouds the first beacon from the Ark's sky-pointing tubes. Lights were on all over the ship. Above the passenger quarters, several men were releasing and tending stock. The sheep and a few of the birds had perished, but the rest of the animals revived rapidly.

One of Hendron's assistants put a slip of paper before his chief. He read it:

Nitrogen	43%
Oxygen	24%
Neon	13%
Krypton	6%
Argon	5%
Helium	4%
Other gases	5%

Hendron looked at the list thoughtfully and took a notebook from a rack over the table. He glanced at the assistant and smiled. "There's only about a three-per-cent error in our telescopic analysis. It will be fair enough to breathe."

The assistant, Borden, smiled. He had been, in what the colonists came to describe as "his former life," a professor of chemistry in Stanford University. His smile was naïve and pleasing. "It's very good to breathe. In fact, I drew in a large sample and breathed what was left over for about five minutes. It felt like air; it looked like air; and I think we might consider it a very superior form of air—remarkably fresh, too."

Hendron chuckled. "All right, Borden. What about the temperature?"

"Eighty-six degrees Fahrenheit, top side of the ship—but the ground all around has been pretty highly heated, and the blast from the beacon also helped warm up the air. I should conjecture that the temperature is really about seventy-eight degrees. I didn't pick up much of that heat, because our thermometer is on the windward side."

Hendron nodded slowly. "Of course I don't know our latitude and longitude yet, but that seems fair enough. Pressure?"

"Thirty point one hundred thirty-five ten thousandths."

"Wind-velocity?"

"Eighteen miles an hour."

"Humidity?"

"Seventy-four per cent. But if I'm any judge of weather, it's clearing up."

"That's fine. We'll go out in the morning."

Another man approached the desk. "The radio set is working, Mr. Hendron. There's terrific static in bursts, but in the intervals listening has been pretty good. Everything's silent. I don't think anybody else made it."

"Right. You take the receivers until midnight on the new time, then put Tarleton on for four hours and let Grange have it until dawn, and then Von Beitz. No one will leave the ship to-night. I believe that the situation here is favorable; but we will need every advantage for our first experience upon this planet. So we will wait for the sun."

The night came on clear. The visa-screen, which had been growing darker, showed now a dim, steady light. It was the light of the earth-destroyer Bronson Alpha, shining again upon the survivors of men as it set off on its measureless journey into infinite space. Other specks of light reënforced it; and the stars—glints from the débris of the world settling themselves in their strange circles about the sun.

Exhaustion allied itself to obedience to Hendron's orders. The emigrants from Earth slumped down and slept. Hendron strode quietly through the dimly lighted chambers, looking at the sleeping people with an expression almost paternal on his face. Within him leaped an exultation so great that he could scarcely contain it. . . .

Tony lay down but did not sleep. Around him the members of the expedition lay in attitudes of rest. A thought had been stirring in his brain for a long time. Some one would have to take the risk of being the first to breathe the air of Bronson Beta. A small sample was not decisive. Tony did not know how accurately its composition might have been measured. He thought that it might have an evil smell. It might be sickening. It might be chemically possible to breathe, but practically, hopeless. It might contain a trace of some rare poison that, repeatedly breathed, would kill instantly or in time.

He should test it himself. They should send him out first. If he did not go into spasms of nausea and pain, the rest could follow. It was a small contribution, in Tony's mind; but it would help justify his presence on the Ark. He had considered offering himself for this service for so long that he had created in his subconscious mind a true and very real fear of the possibilities in the atmosphere of Bronson Beta.

"They might send some one useful," he thought. "Hendron might sacrifice himself in the test."

The more he thought, the more he worried. His mind began to plan. If he wished, he could open the airlock and drop down to the ground. Of course, he could not get back without making a fuss—stoning the periscope outlet—and he might not remain conscious long enough. But in that case —his body would be a warning when they looked out in the morning. . . .

At last he rose. He went down the spiral staircase quietly. He shut doors behind him. In the bottom chamber he stood for a long time beside the airlock. He was trembling.

It did not enter his mind that the honor of being the first to step on the soil of Bronson Beta rightfully belonged to Hendron. It was self-sacrifice and not ambition which prompted him.

He lifted the levers that closed the inner door, balancing them so that they would fall automatically. He stepped between it and the outer door. The lock slammed; the levers fell. He was in pitch darkness.

He opened the outside door. He leaned out—his heart in his mouth. He drew in a breath.

A hot, rasping, sulphurous vapor smote his nostrils. He shuddered. Was this the atmosphere of the new planet? He remembered that the blast of the Ark had cooked the ground around it.

Gasping, with running eyes, he lay down on the floor and felt with his feet for the iron rungs of the workmen's ladder that ran from the now inverted bow of the Ark to the upper door and matched that on the opposite end. He began to descend. He coughed and shuddered. With every step the heat increased.

His foot touched the ground. It gave off heat like the earth around a geyser. He ran away from the looming bulk of the ship. His first fifty steps were taken in the stinging vapors.

Then—cooler air blew on his face. Sweet, fresh, cool air!

He inhaled lungfuls of it. It had no odor. It was like earth air washed by an April rain. It did not make him dizzy or sick. He did not feel weakness or numbness or pain. He felt exhilarated.

He flung out his arms in ecstasy. It was a dancer's gesture, a glorious, abandoned gesture. He could make it only because he was alone—alone on the new earth. Bronson Beta's atmosphere was magnificent.

He flung his arms again.

Beside him a voice said quietly: "It's splendid, isn't it, Tony?"

He could have been no more startled if stones had spoken or a mummy had sat up in its sarcophagus. He stiffened, not daring to look. Then into his icy veins blood flowed. He had recognized the voice. He turned in the lush, starlit dark.

"Mr. Hendron, I—I—I—"

"Never mind." The older man approached. "I think I know why you came. You wanted to be sure of the air before any of the rest of us left the ship."

Tony did not reply. Hendron took his arm. "So did I. I couldn't sleep. I had to inspect our future home. I came out on the ladder half an hour ago." Hendron chuckled. "Duquesne was on my heels. I hid. He's gone for a walk. I heard him fall down and swear. What do you think of it? Did you see the aurora?"

"No." Tony looked at the stars. He had a feeling that the sky overhead was not the sky to which he had been accustomed. The stars looked slightly mixed. As he stared upward, a crimson flame shot into the zenith from the horizon. It was followed by torches and sheets in all colors and shades. "Lord!" he whispered.

"Beautiful, isn't it?" Hendron said softly. "Nothing like it on earth. It was in rippling sheets when I came out. Then in shafts—a colored cathedral. It made faint shadows of the landscape. I venture to say it's a permanent fixture. The gases here are different from those on earth. Different ionization of solar electrical energy. That red may be the neon. The blue—I don't know. Anyway—it's gorgeous."

"You mean—this thing will play overhead all night every night?"

"I think so. Coming and going. It seemed to me that it touched the ground over there—once." He pointed. "I thought I could hear it—crackling faintly, swishing. It's going to make radio broadcasting bad; and it'll affect astronomic observation. But it is magnificent."

"Like the rainbow that came on Ararat," Tony said slowly.

"Lord! So it is! God's promise, eh? Tony—you're an odd fellow for a football-player. Football! What a thing to hover in the mind here! Come —let's see if we can find Duquesne. The wily devil wanted to be first on Bronson Beta. He came out of the Ark like a shot. No. Wait—look."

Tony glanced toward the Ark. The lock was opening again. The aurora shone luminously on the polished sides, revealing the black rectangle of the open door in sharp contrast.

"Who is it?" Hendron whispered.

"Don't know." Tony was smiling.

They watched the fourth man to touch the new soil make his painful descent and run across the still hot earth. They saw him stop, a few yards away, and breathe. They heard his voice ecstatically. Then—they heard him weep.

Hendron called: "Hello—James!"

Tony saw Eliot James undergo the unearthliness of hearing that voice come through the empty air. Then James approached them.

"How beautiful!" he whispered. "I'm sorry. I thought some one should try the air. And—I admit—I was keen to get out. Wanted to be first, I suppose. I'm humiliated——"

Again Hendron laughed. "It's all right, my boy. I understand. I understand all of us. It was an act of bravery. When I came out, I half expected you others would be along. It's in your blood. The reason you came here one by one, alone and courageously, is the reason I picked you to come here with me. You all think, feel, act independently. You also all act for the common welfare. It makes me rather happy. Come on; Duquesne went this way."

"Duquesne?" James repeated. Tony explained.

They hunted for a long time. Overhead the stars showed brightly; and underneath them in varying intensity, with ten thousand spangles, the aurora played symphonies of light. Behind them was the tall cylinder of the ship, and behind it the range of hills. Ahead of them as they walked they could hear the increasing murmur of the sea.

They found Duquesne sitting on a bluff-head overlooking the illimitable sea. He heard them coming and rose, holding out his hands.

"My friends! *Salut!*"

"I saw you pop out of the ship," Hendron said, "and I was sorry you fell down."

The Frenchman was crestfallen. "You were out here?"

"Oh, yes."

"Ahead of me?"

"By a few minutes," Hendron answered.

Duquesne stamped his foot several times, and then laughed. "Well —you should be! But I thought to fool you. Duquesne, I told myself— the great Duquesne—shall be first to set foot on the new earth. But it was not to be. It was a sin. I even brought a small flag of France—my beautiful France—and planted it upon the soil."

"I saw it," Hendron said. "I took it down. We aren't going to have nations here. Just—people."

Duquesne nodded in the gloom. "That too is right. I am foolish. I am like six years old. But to-night we will forget all this, *n'est-ce pas?* We will be friends. Four friends. The mighty Cole 'Endron. The brilliant Monsieur James. The brave Tony Drake. And myself—Duquesne the great. Sit."

On the outcrop of stone ledge they seated themselves. They looked and breathed and waited.

Occasionally one of them spoke. Usually it was Hendron—casting up from his thoughts between periods of silence memories of the past and plans for the future.

"We are here alone. I cannot help feeling that our other ship has in some way failed to follow us. If, in the ensuing days, we hear nothing, we may be sure it is lost. Your French confrères, Duquesne—failed. We must admit that it seems probable that others failed. Bronson Beta belongs to us. It is sad—tragic. Ransdell is gone. Peter Vanderbilt is gone. Smith. That Taylor youngster you brought from Cornell. All the others. Yet— with all the world gone, who are we to complain that we have lost a few more of our friends?"

"Precisely!" exclaimed Duquesne emphatically. "And what are we, after all? What was that mankind, of our earth, which we alone perhaps survive to represent and reproduce?"

He had recoiled from his moment of inborn, instinctive patriotism, and become the scientist again.

"Is the creation of man the final climax toward which the whole Creation has moved? We said so, in the infancy of our thought, when we imagined the world made by God in six days, before we had any comprehension even of the nature of our neighboring stars, when we could not even have dreamed of the millions and millions of the distant stars shown us by our telescopes, when our wildest fancy would have failed before the facts of to-day—endless space spotted to the edges of time with spiral nebulae, each a separate 'universe' with its billions of suns like our own.

"Behind us lay, on our own earth, five hundred millions of years of evolution; and billions of years before that, while matter cooled and congealed, the world was being made—for us?

"Can we say so? Or is it that our existence is a mere accidental and possibly quite unimportant by-product of natural processes, which—as Jeans, the Englishman, once suggested—really had some other and more stupendous end in view?"

"You mean," said Hendron, "perhaps it concerns only ourselves in our vanity, and not the universe at all, that any of us escaped from the cataclysm of earth's end and came here?"

"Exactly," pronounced Duquesne. "It is nothing—if we merely continue the earth—here. When I recollect the filth of our cities, the greed

of individuals and of nations, the savagery of wars, the horrors of pauper-
ism permitted to exist side by side with luxury and wealth, our selfishness,
hates, diseases, filth—all the hideousness we called civilization—I cannot
regret that the world which was afflicted by us is flying in fragments,
utterly incapable of rehabilitation, about the sun. On the other hand, now
we are here; and how are we to justify the chance to begin again?"

Tony moved away from them. He was stirred with a great restlessness.
He wandered toward the ship; and he saw, in that glowing, opalescent
night, a woman's form; and he knew before he spoke to her, that it was
Eve.

"I was sure you'd be out," he said.

"Tony!"

"Yes?"

"Here are you and I. Here!" She stooped to the ground and touched
it; the dry fiber of a lichenlike grass was between her fingers. She pulled
it, and stood with it in her hand. They had seen it, they both remembered;
it was what had made the ground brown in the light of the dying day.

"This was green and fresh, Tony, perhaps ten million years ago; perhaps
a hundred million. Then the dark and cold came; the very air froze and
preserved it. Do you suppose our cattle could eat it?"

"Why not?" said Tony.

"What else may be here, Tony? How can we wait for the day?"

"We aren't waiting!"

"No; we're not." For they were walking, hand in hand like children,
over the bare, rough ground. The amazing aurora of this strange world
lighted them, and the soil smoothed, suddenly, under their feet. The
change was so abrupt that it made them stare down, and they saw what
they had stumbled upon; and they cried out together: "A road!"

The ribbon of it ran to right and left—not clear and straight, for it
had been washed over and blown over; but it was, beyond any doubt, a
road! Made by what hands, and for what feet? Whence and whither did
it run?

A hundred million years ago!

The clock of eternity ticked with the click of their heels on this hard
ribbon of road, as they turned, hand in hand, and followed it toward the
aurora.

"Where were they," said Tony, almost as if the souls of those a hundred
million years dead might hear, "when they were whirled away from their
sun? What stage had they reached? Is this one of their Roman roads on
which one of their Varros was marching his men to meet a Hannibal at
Bronson Beta's Cannæ? What was at one end—and what still awaits us
there? A Nineveh of Sargon saved for us by the dark and cold? Or was
this a motor road to a city like our Paris of a year ago? Or was it a track

for some vehicle we would have invented in a thousand more years? And is the city which we'll find, a city we'd never dreamed of? Whatever it was, their fate left it for us; whereas our fate—the fate of our world—" He stopped.

"I was thinking about it," said Eve. "Out there in space—in scattered stones circling in orbits of their own about the sun; the Pyramids and the Empire State Building, the Washington Monument and the Tomb of Napoleon, the Arch of Triumph! The seas and the mountains! Here the other thing happened—the other fate that could have been ours if the world had escaped the cataclysm. What sort were they who faced it here, Tony? Human, with bodies like our own? Or with souls like our own, but other shapes?"

"On this road," said Tony, "this road, perhaps, we'll see."

"And learn how they faced it, too, Tony; the coming dark and the cold. I think, if I had the choice, I'd prefer the cataclysm."

"Then you believe our world was better off?"

"Perhaps I wouldn't have—if we had stayed," amended Eve. "What happened here, at least left their world behind them."

"For us," said Tony.

"Yes; for us. What will we make of our chance here, Tony? Truly something very different?"

"How different do you feel, Eve?"

"Very different—completely strange even to myself, at some moments, Tony; and then at other times—not different at all."

"Come here."

"Why?"

"Come here," he repeated, and drawing her close, he clasped her, and himself quivering, he could feel her trembling terribly. He kissed her, and her lips were hot on his. A little aghast, they dropped away.

"We seem to have brought the world with us. I can never give you up, Eve; or share you with any one else."

"We're too fresh from the world, Tony, to know. We've a faith to keep with—"

"With whom? Your father?"

"With fate—and the future. Let's go on, Tony. See, the road turns." "Yes."

"What's that?"

"Where?"

She moved off the road to the right, where stood something too square and straight-edged to be natural. Scarcely breathing, they touched it, and found metal with a cold, smooth surface indented under their fingertips.

"A monument!" said Tony, and he burned a match. The little yellow flame lighted characters engraved into the metal—characters like none either of them had ever seen before, but which proclaimed themselves symbols of meaning.

Swiftly Tony searched the two faces of the metal; but nothing that could possibly be a portrait adorned it. There were decorations of strange beauty and symmetry. Amazing that no one, in all the generations and in all the nations of the world, had drawn a decoration like this! It was not like the Chinese or Mayan or Egyptian, Greek or Roman, or French or German; but different from each and all.

Tony caught his breath sharply as he traced it with his fingers.

"They had an artist, Eve," he said.

"With five hundred million years of evolution behind him."

"Yes. How beautifully this writing is engraved! Will we ever read it? . . . Come on. Come on!"

But the monument, if it was that, stood alone; and consideration of others, if not prudence, dictated that they return.

But they did not reënter the ship. Duquesne was determined to spend the first night on the ground; and Hendron and James agreed with him. James had dragged out blankets from the Ark, and the five lay down on the ground of the new planet. And some of them slept.

Tony opened his eyes. The sun was rising into a sky not blue but jade green. A deep, bewildering color—the color of Bronson Beta's celestial canopy.

There would be no more human beings who wrote poetry about the blue sky. They would shape their romantic stanzas—as the stanzas in those strange, beautifully engraved characters must be shaped, if they mentioned the sky—to the verdancy of the heavens.

Tony lifted himself on his elbow. Below him, the sea also was green. It had been gray on the steamy yesterday. But an emerald ocean was more familiar than an emerald sky. He watched the white water roll on the summits of swells until it was dispersed by the brown cliff. He looked back at the Ark. It stood mysteriously on the landscape—a perpendicular cylinder, shining and marvelous, enormously foreign to the bare, brilliant landscape. Behind it the chocolate colored mountains stretched into opalescent nowhere—the mountain into which the road ran, the road beside which stood the stele adorned by a decoration like nothing else that had been seen in the world.

Tony regarded his companions. Hendron slept on a curled arm. His flashing eyes were closed. His hair, now almost white, was disheveled on his white forehead. Beside him Duquesne slept, half-sitting, his arms folded on his ample abdomen, and an expression of deep study on his swarthy face. Eliot James sprawled on a ledge which the sun now was warming, his countenance relaxed, his lips parted, his straggling red beard metal-bright in the morning rays.

Eve slept, or she had slept, near to Tony; and now she roused. She was lovely in the yellow light, and looked far fresher than the men.

Their clothes were stained and worn; and none of them had shaved, so that they looked more like philosophical vagrants than like three of the greatest men produced in the Twentieth Century on the Earth.

Tony watched Eve as she gazed at them, anxiously maternal. To be a mother in actuality, to become a mother of men, was to be her rôle on this reawakened world.

As she arose quietly, so as to disturb none of the others, Tony caught her hand with a new tenderness. They set off toward their road together.

Suddenly Tony saw something that took the breath from his lungs. It was a tiny thing—on the ground. A mere splotch of color. He hurried toward it, not believing his eyes. He lay down and stared at it. In a slight damp depression was a patch of moss the size of his hand.

He lay prone to examine it as Eve stooped beside him in excitement like his own. He did not know mosses—the vegetation resembled any other moss, on Earth. He recollected the hope that spores, which could exist in temperatures close to absolute zero for long periods, had preserved on Bronson Beta the power to germinate.

Mosses came—on Earth—from spores; and here, reawakened by the sun, was a remnant of life that had existed eons ago, light-years away.

Tony jumped up and ran about on the terrain; a few feet away, Eve stooped again. Other plants were burgeoning. Mosses, ferns, fungi—vegetation of species he could not classify, but some surely represented growths larger than mere mosses.

He heaped Eve's hands and his own, and together they ran back to the three who were staring, as they earlier had gazed, at the green sky.

Then Duquesne saw what Eve and Tony held. "*Sacre nom de Dieu!*" He leaped to his feet. Hendron and James were beside him.

With one accord, they rushed toward the Space Ship.

"Get Higgins!" Hendron shouted. "He'll go mad! Think of it! A whole new world to classify! . . . And it means that we will live!"

Before they reached the sides of the ship, the lock opened. The gangplank dropped to earth. Von Beitz appeared in the aperture, and Hendron shouted to him the news.

People poured from the Ark; they stepped upon the new soil. They waved their arms. They stared at the hills, the sky, the sea. They breathed deep of the air. They handled the mosses, and ran about finding more of their own. They shouted, sang. They laughed and danced.

The first day on the new earth had begun.

the great
adventure

the maracot deep

by ARTHUR CONAN DOYLE

CHAPTER I: Since these papers have been put into my hands to edit, I will begin by reminding the public of the sad loss of the steamship *Stratford*, which started a year ago upon a voyage for the purpose of oceanography and the study of deep-sea life. The expedition had been organized by Dr. Maracot, the famous author of *Pseudo-Coralline Formations* and *The Morphology of the Lamellibranchia*. Dr. Maracot had with him Mr. Cyrus Headley, formerly assistant at the Zoological Institute of Cambridge, Massachusetts, and at the time of the voyage Rhodes Scholar at Oxford. Captain Howie, an experienced navigator, was in charge of the vessel, and there was a crew of twenty-three men, including an American mechanic from the Merribank Works, Philadelphia.

This whole party has utterly disappeared, and the only word ever heard of the ill-fated steamer was from the report of a Norwegian barque which actually saw a ship, closely corresponding with her description, go down in the great gale of the autumn of 1926. A lifeboat marked *Stratford* was found later in the neighbourhood of the tragedy, together with some deck gratings, a lifebuoy, and a spar. This, coupled with the long silence, seemed to make it absolutely sure that the vessel and her crew would never be heard of more. Her fate is rendered more certain by the strange wireless message received at the time, which, though incomprehensible in parts, left little doubt as to the fate of the vessel. This I will quote later.

There were some remarkable points about the voyage of the *Stratford* which caused comment at the time. One was the curious secrecy observed by Professor Maracot. He was famous for his dislike and distrust of the Press, but it was pushed to an extreme upon this occasion, when he would neither give information to reporters nor would he permit the representative of any paper to set foot in the vessel during the weeks that it lay in the Albert Dock. There were rumours abroad of some curious and novel construction of the ship which would fit it for deep-sea work, and these rumours were confirmed from the yard of Hunter and Company of West Hartlepool, where the structural changes had actually been carried out. It was at one time said that the whole bottom of the vessel was detachable, a report which attracted the attention of the underwriters at Lloyd's, who were, with some difficulty, satisfied upon the point. The matter was soon forgotten, but it assumes an importance now when the fate of the expedition has been brought once more in so extraordinary a manner to the notice of the public.

So much for the beginning of the voyage of the *Stratford*. There are now four documents which cover the facts so far as they are known. The first is the letter which was written by Mr. Cyrus Headley, from the capital of the Grand Canary, to his friend, Sir James Talbot, of Trinity College, Oxford, upon the only occasion, so far as is known, when the *Stratford* touched land after leaving the Thames. The second is the strange wireless call to which I have alluded. The third is that portion of the log of the *Arabella Knowles* which deals with the vitreous ball. The fourth and last is the amazing contents of that receptacle, which either represent a most cruel and complex mystification, or else open up a fresh chapter in human experience the importance of which cannot be exaggerated. With this preamble, I will now give Mr. Headley's letter, which I owe to the courtesy of Sir James Talbot, and which has not previously been published. It is dated October 1st, 1926.

I am mailing this, my dear Talbot, from Porta de la Luz, where we have put in for a few days of rest. My principal companion in the voyage has been Bill Scanlan, the head mechanic, who, as a fellow-countryman and also as a very entertaining character, has become my natural associate. However, I am alone this morning as he has what he describes as "a date with a skirt." You see, he talks as Englishmen expect every real American to talk. He would be accepted as the true breed. The mere force of suggestion makes me "guess" and "reckon" when I am with my English friends. I feel that they would never really understand that I was a Yankee if I did not. However, I am not on those terms with you, so let me assure you right now that you will not find anything but pure Oxford in the epistle which I am now mailing to you.

You met Maracot at the Mitre, so you know the dry chip of a man that he is. I told you, I think, how he came to pitch upon me for the job. He

inquired from old Somerville of the Zoological Institute, who sent him my
prize essay on the pelagic crabs, and that did the trick. Of course, it is
splendid to be on such a congenial errand, but I wish it wasn't with such an
animated mummy as Maracot. He is inhuman in his isolation and his
devotion to his work. "The world's stiffest stiff," says Bill Scanlan. And
yet you can't but admire such complete devotion. Nothing exists outside
his own science. I remember that you laughed when I asked him what I
ought to read as a preparation, and he said that for serious study I should
read the collected edition of his own works, but for relaxation Haeckel's
Plankton-Studien.

I know him no better now than I did in that little parlour looking out
on the Oxford High. He says nothing, and his gaunt, austere face—the face
of a Savonarola, or rather, perhaps, of a Torquemada—never relapses into
geniality. The long, thin, aggressive nose, the two small gleaming grey
eyes set closely together under a thatch of eyebrows, the thin-lipped,
compressed mouth, the cheeks worn into hollows by constant thought and
ascetic life, are all uncompanionable. He lives on some mental moun-
tain-top, out of reach of ordinary mortals. Sometimes I think he is a little
mad. For example, this extraordinary instrument that he has made . . .
but I'll tell things in their due order and then you can judge for yourself.

I'll take our voyage from the start. The *Stratford* is a fine seaworthy
little boat, specially fitted for her job. She is twelve hundred tons, with
clear decks and a good broad beam, furnished with every possible appliance for sounding, trawling, dredging, and tow-netting. She has, of course,
powerful steam winches for hauling in the trawls, and a number of other
gadgets of various kinds, some of which are familiar enough, and some
are strange. Below these are comfortable quarters with a well-fitted laboratory for our special studies.

We had the reputation of being a mystery ship before we started, and I
soon found that it was not undeserved. Our first proceedings were com-
monplace enough. We took a turn up the North Sea and dropped our
trawls for a scrape or two, but, as the average depth is not much over
sixty feet and we were specially fitted for very deep-sea work, it seemed
rather a waste of time. Anyhow, save for familiar table fish, dog-fish,
squids, jellyfish, and some terrigenous bottom deposits of the usual al-
luvial clay-mud, we got nothing worth writing home about. Then we
rounded Scotland, sighted the Faroes, and came down the Wyville-Thom-
son Ridge, where we had better luck. Thence we worked south to our
proper cruising-ground, which was between the African coast and these
islands. We nearly grounded on Fuert-Eventura one moonless night, but
save for that our voyage was uneventful.

During these first weeks I tried to make friends with Maracot, but it
was not easy work. First of all, he is the most absorbed and absent-minded

man in the world. You will remember how you smiled when he gave the elevator boy a penny under the impression that he was in a street car. Half the time he is utterly lost in his thoughts, and seems hardly aware of where he is or what he is doing. Then in the second place he is secretive to the last degree. He is continually working at papers and charts, which he shuffles away when I happen to enter the cabin. It is my firm belief that the man has some secret project in his mind, but that so long as we are due to touch at any port he will keep it to himself. That is the impression which I have received, and I find that Bill Scanlan is of the same opinion.

"Say, Mr. Headley," said he one evening, when I was seated in the laboratory testing out the salinity of samples from our hydrographic soundings, "what d'you figure out that this guy has in his mind? What d'you reckon that he means to do?"

"I suppose," said I, "that we shall do what the *Challenger* and a dozen other exploring ships have done before us, and add a few more species to the list of fish and a few more entries to the bathymetric chart."

"Not on your life," said he. "If that's your opinion you've got to guess again. First of all, what am I here for, anyhow?"

"In case the machinery goes wrong," I hazarded.

"Machinery nothing! The ship's machinery is in charge of MacLaren, the Scotch engineer. No, sir, it wasn't to run a donkey-engine that the Merribank folk sent out their star performer. If I pull down fifty bucks a week it's not for nix. Come here, and I'll make you wise to it."

He took a key from his pocket and opened a door at the back of the laboratory which led us down a companion ladder to a section of the hold which was cleared right across save for four large glittering objects half-exposed amid the straw of their huge packing-cases. They were flat sheets of steel with elaborate bolts and rivets along the edges. Each sheet was about ten foot square and an inch and a half thick, with a circular gap of eighteen inches in the middle.

"What in thunder is it?" I asked.

Bill Scanlan's queer face—he looks halfway between a vaudeville comic and a prize-fighter—broke into a grin at my astonishment.

"That's my baby, sir," he quoted. "Yes, Mr. Headley, that's what I am here for. There is a steel bottom to the thing. It's in that big case yonder. Then there is a top, kind of arched, and a great ring for a chain or rope. Now, look here at the bottom of the ship."

There was a square wooden platform there, with projecting screws at each corner which showed that it was detachable.

"There is a double bottom," said Scanlan. "It may be that this guy is clean loco, or it may be that he has more in his block than we know, but if I read him right he means to build up a kind of room—the windows are in storage here—and lower it through the bottom of the ship. He's got electric searchlights here, and I allow that he plans to shine 'em through the round portholes and see what's goin' on around."

"He could have put a crystal sheet into the ship, like the Catalina Island boats, if that was all that was in his mind," said I.

"You've said a mouthful," said Bill Scanlan, scratching his head. "I can't figger it out nohow. The only one sure thing is, that I've been sent to be under his orders and to help him with the darn fool thing all I can. He has said nothin' up to now, so I've said the same, but I'll just snoop around, and if I wait long enough I'll learn all there is to know."

So that was how I first got on to the edge of our mystery. We ran into some dirty weather after that, and then we got to work doing some deep-sea trawling northwest of Cape Juba, just outside the Continental Slope, and taking temperature readings and salinity records. It's a sporting proposition, this deep-sea dragging with a Peterson otter trawl gaping twenty feet wide for everything that comes its way—sometimes down a quarter of a mile and bringing up one lot of fish, sometimes half a mile and quite a different lot, every stratum of ocean with its own inhabitants as separate as so many continents. Sometimes from the bottom we would just bring up half a ton of clear pink jelly, the raw material of life, or, maybe, it would be a scoop of pteropod ooze, breaking up under the microscope into millions of tiny round reticulated balls with amorphous mud between. I won't bore you with all the brotulids and macrurids, the ascidians and holothurians, and polyzoa and echinoderms—anyhow, you can reckon that there is a great harvest in the sea, and that we have been diligent reapers. But always I had the same feeling that the heart of Maracot was not in the job, and that other plans were in that queer, high, narrow Egyptian mummy of a head. It all seemed to me to be a try-out of men and things until the real business got going.

I had got as far as this in my letter when I went ashore to have a last stretch, for we sail in the early morning. It's as well, perhaps, that I did go, for there was no end of a barney going on upon the pier, with Maracot and Bill Scanlan right in the heart of it. Bill is a bit of a scrapper, and has what he calls a mean wallop in both mitts, but with half-a-dozen Dagoes with knives all round them things looked ugly, and it was time that I butted in. It seems that the Doctor had hired one of the things they call cabs, and had driven half over the island inspecting the geology, but had clean forgotten that he had no money on him. When it came to paying, he could not make these country hicks understand, and the cabman had grabbed his watch so as to make sure. That brought Bill Scanlan into action, and they would have both been on the floor with their backs like pincushions if I had not squared the matter up, with a dollar or two over for the driver and a five-dollar bonus for the chap with the mouse under his eye. So all ended well, and Maracot was more human than ever I saw him yet. When we got to the ship he called me into the little cabin which he reserves for himself and he thanked me.

"By the way, Mr. Headley," he said, "I understand that you are not a married man?"

"No," said I, "I am not."

"No one depending upon you?"

"No."

"Good!" said he. "I have not spoken of the object of this voyage because I have, for my own reasons, desired it to be secret. One of those reasons was that I feared to be forestalled. When scientific plans get about one may be served as Scott was served by Amundsen. Had Scott kept his counsel as I have done, it would be he and not Amundsen who would have been the first at the South Pole. For my part, I have quite as important a destination as the South Pole, and so I have been silent. But now we are on the eve of our great adventure and no rival has time to steal my plans. To-morrow we start for our real goal."

"And what is that?" I asked.

He leaned forward, his ascetic face all lit up with the enthusiasm of the fanatic.

"Our goal," said he, "is the bottom of the Atlantic Ocean."

And right here I ought to stop, for I expect it has taken away your breath as it did mine. If I were a story-writer, I guess I should leave it at that. But as I am just a chronicler of what occurred, I may tell you that I stayed another hour in the cabin of old man Maracot, and that I learned a lot, which there is still just time for me to tell you before the last shore boat leaves.

"Yes, young man," said he, "you may write freely now, for by the time your letter reaches England we shall have made the plunge."

This started him sniggering, for he has a queer dry sense of humour of his own.

"Yes, sir, the plunge is the right word on this occasion, a plunge which will be historic in the annals of Science. Let me tell you, in the first place, that I am well convinced that the current doctrine as to the extreme pressure of the ocean at great depths is entirely misleading. It is perfectly clear that other factors exist which neutralize the effect, though I am not yet prepared to say what those factors may be. That is one of the problems which we may settle. Now, what pressure, may I ask, have you been led to expect under a mile of water?" He glowered at me through his big horn spectacles.

"Not less than a ton to the square inch," I answered. "Surely that has been clearly shown."

"The task of the pioneer has always been to disprove the thing which has been clearly shown. Use your brains, young man. You have been for the last month fishing up some of the most delicate Bathic forms of life, creatures so delicate that you could hardly transfer them from the net to the tank without marring their sensitive shapes. Did you find that there was evidence upon them of this extreme pressure?"

"The pressure," said I, "equalized itself. It was the same within as without."

"Words—mere words!" he cried, shaking his lean head impatiently. "You have brought up round fish, such fish as Gastrostomus globulus. Would they not have been squeezed flat had the pressure been as you imagine? Or look at our otter-boards. They are not squeezed together at the mouth of the trawl."

"But the experience of divers?"

"Certainly it holds good up to a point. They do find a sufficient increase of pressure to influence what is perhaps the most sensitive organ of the body, the interior of the ear. But as I plan it, we shall not be exposed to any pressure at all. We shall be lowered in a steel cage with crystal windows on each side for observation. If the pressure is not strong enough to break in an inch and a half of toughened double-nickelled steel, then it cannot hurt us. It is an extension of the experiment of the Williamson Brothers at Nassau, with which no doubt you are familiar. If my calculation is wrong—well, you say that no one is dependent upon you. We shall die in a great adventure. Of course, if you would rather stand clear, I can go alone."

It seemed to me the maddest kind of scheme, and yet you know how difficult it is to refuse a dare. I played for time while I thought it over.

"How deep do you propose to go, sir?" I asked.

He had a chart pinned upon the table, and he placed the end of his compasses upon a point which lies to the southwest of the Canaries.

"Last year I did some sounding in this part," said he. "There is a pit of great depth. We got twenty-five thousand feet there. I was the first to report it. Indeed, I trust that you will find it on the charts of the future as the 'Maracot Deep.'"

"But, good God, sir!" I cried, "you don't propose to descend into an abyss like that?"

"No, no," he answered, smiling. "Neither our lowering chain nor our air tubes reach beyond half a mile. But I was going to explain to you that round this deep crevasse, which has no doubt been formed by volcanic forces long ago, there is a raised ridge or narrow plateau, which is not more than three hundred fathoms under the surface."

"Three hundred fathoms! A third of a mile!"

"Yes, roughly a third of a mile. It is my present intention that we shall be lowered in our little pressure-proof look-out station on to this submarine bank. There we shall make such observations as we can. A speaking-tube will connect us with the ship so that we can give our directions. There should be no difficulty in the matter. When we wish to be hauled up we have only to say so."

"And the air?"

"Will be pumped down to us."

"But it will be pitch-dark."

"That, I fear, is undoubtedly true. The experiments of Fol and Sarasin at the Lake of Geneva show that even the ultra-violet rays are absent at that depth. But does it matter? We shall be provided with the powerful electric illumination from the ship's engines, supplemented by six two-volt Hellesens dry cells connected together so as to give a current of twelve volts. That, with a Lucas army signalling lamp as a movable reflector, should serve our turn. Any other difficulties?"

"If our air lines tangle?"

"They won't tangle. And as a reserve we have compressed air in tubes which would last us twenty-four hours. Well, have I satisfied you? Will you come?"

It was not an easy decision. The brain works quickly and imagination is a mighty vivid thing. I seemed to realize that black box down in the primeval depths, to feel the foul twice-breathed air, and then to see the walls sagging, bulging inwards, rending at the joints with the water spouting in at every rivet-hole and crevice and crawling up from below. It was a slow, dreadful death to die. But I looked up, and there were the old man's fiery eyes fixed upon me with the exaltation of a martyr to Science. It's catching, that sort of enthusiasm, and if it be crazy, it is at least noble and unselfish. I caught fire from his great flame, and I sprang to my feet with my hand out.

"Doctor, I'm with you to the end," said I.

"I knew it," said he. "It was not for your smattering of learning that I picked you, my young friend, nor," he added, smiling, "for your intimate acquaintance with the pelagic crabs. There are other qualities which may be more immediately useful, and they are loyalty and courage."

So with that little bit of sugar I was dismissed, with my future pledged and my whole scheme of life in ruins. Well, the last shore boat is leaving. They are calling for the mail. You will either not hear from me again, my dear Talbot, or you will get a letter worth reading. If you don't hear you can have a floating headstone and drop it somewhere south of the Canaries with the inscription:

Here, or Hereabouts, lies all that the fishes have left of my friend,
CYRUS J. HEADLEY.

The second document in the case is the unintelligible wireless message which was intercepted by several vessels, including the Royal Mail steamer *Arroya*. It was received at 3 P. M. October 3rd, 1926, which shows that it was dispatched only two days after the *Stratford* left the Grand Canary, as shown in the previous letter, and it corresponds roughly with the time when the Norwegian barque saw a steamer founder in a cyclone two hundred miles to the southwest of Porta de la Luz. It ran thus:

Blown on our beam ends. Fear position hopeless. Have already lost Maracot, Headley, Scanlan. Situation incomprehensible. Headley handkerchief end of deep sea sounding wire. God help us!

S. S. Stratford.

This was the last, incoherent message which came from the ill-fated vessel, and part of it was so strange that it was put down to delirium on the part of the operator. It seemed, however, to leave no doubt as to the fate of the ship.

The explanation—if it can be accepted as an explanation—of the matter is to be found in the narrative concealed inside the vitreous ball, and first it would be as well to amplify the very brief account which has hitherto appeared in the Press of the finding of the ball. I take it verbatim from the log of the *Arabella Knowles*, master Amos Green, outward bound with coals from Cardiff to Buenos Aires:

Wednesday, Jan. 5th, 1927. Lat. 27.14, Long. 28 West. Calm weather. Blue sky with low banks of cirrus clouds. Sea like glass. At two bells of the middle watch the first officer reported that he had seen a shining object bound high out of the sea, and then fall back into it. His first impression was that it was some strange fish, but on examination with his glasses he observed that it was a silvery globe, or ball, which was so light that it lay, rather than floated, on the surface of the water. I was called and saw it, as large as a football, gleaming brightly about half a mile off on our starboard beam. I stopped the engines and called away the quarter-boat under the second mate, who picked the thing up and brought it aboard.

On examination it proved to be a ball made of some sort of very tough glass, and filled with a substance so light that when it was tossed in the air it wavered about like a child's balloon. It was nearly transparent, and we could see what looked like a roll of paper inside it. The material was so tough, however, that we had the greatest possible difficulty in breaking the ball open and getting at the contents. A hammer would not crack it, and it was only when the chief engineer nipped it in the throw of the engine that we were able to smash it. Then I am sorry to say that it dissolved into sparkling dust, so that it was impossible to collect any good-sized piece for examination. We got the paper, however, and, having examined it and concluded that it was of great importance, we laid it aside with the intention of handing it over to the British Consul when we reached the Plate River. Man and boy, I have been at sea for five-and-thirty years, but this is the strangest thing that ever befell me, and so says every man aboard this ship. I leave the meaning of it all to wiser heads than mine.

So much for the genesis of the narrative of Cyrus J. Headley, which we will now give exactly as written:

Whom am I writing to? Well, I suppose I may say to the whole wide world, but as that is rather a vague address I'll aim at my friend Sir James Talbot, of Oxford University, for the reason that my last letter was to him and this may be regarded as a continuation. I expect the odds are a hundred to one that this ball, even if it should see the light of day and not be gulped by a shark in passing, will toss about on the waves and never catch the eye of the passing sailor, and yet it's worth trying, and Maracot is sending up another, so, between us, it may be that we shall get our wonderful story to the world. Whether the world will believe it is another matter, I guess, but when folk look at the ball with its vitrine cover and note its contents of levigen gas, they will surely see for themselves that there is something here that is out of the ordinary. You at any rate, Talbot, will not throw it aside, unread.

If anyone wants to know how the thing began, and what we were trying to do, he can find it all in a letter I wrote you on October 1st last year, the night before we left Porta de la Luz. By George! If I had known what was in store for us, I think I should have sneaked into a shore boat that night. And yet—well, maybe, even with my eyes open I would have stood by the Doctor and seen it through. On second thoughts I have not a doubt that I would.

Well, starting from the day that we left Grand Canary I will carry on with my experiences.

The moment we were clear of the port, old man Maracot fairly broke into flames. The time for action had come at last and all the damped-down energy of the man came flaring up. I tell you he took hold of that ship and of everyone and everything in it, and bent it all to his will. The dry, creaking, absent-minded scholar had suddenly vanished, and instead there emerged a human electrical machine, crackling with vitality and quivering from the great driving force within. His eyes gleamed behind his glasses like flames in a lantern. He seemed to be everywhere at once, working out distances on his chart, comparing reckonings with the skipper, driving Bill Scanlan along, setting me on to a hundred odd jobs, but it was all full of method and with a definite end. He developed an unexpected knowledge of electricity and of mechanics and spent much of his time working at the machinery which Scanlan, under his supervision, was now carefully piecing together.

"Say, Mr. Headley, it's just dandy," said Bill, on the morning of the second day. "Come in here and have a look. The Doc is a regular fellow and a whale of a slick mechanic."

I had a most unpleasant impression that it was my own coffin at which I was gazing, but, even so, I had to admit that it was a very adequate mausoleum. The floor had been clamped to the four steel walls, and the porthole windows screwed into the centre of each. A small trapdoor at the top gave admission, and there was a second one at the base. The steel cage was supported by a thin but very powerful steel hawser, which ran over a drum, and was paid out or rolled in by the strong engine which we used for our deep-sea trawls. The hawser, as I understood, was nearly half a mile in length, the slack of it coiled round bollards on the deck. The rubber breathing-tubes were of the same length, and the telephone wire was connected with them, and also the wire by which the electric lights within could be operated from the ship's batteries, though we had an independent instalment as well.

It was on the evening of that day that the engines were stopped. The glass was low, and a thick black cloud rising upon the horizon gave warning of coming trouble. The only ship in sight was a barque flying the Norwegian colours, and we observed that it was reefed down, as if expecting trouble. For the moment, however, all was propitious and the *Stratford* rolled gently upon a deep blue ocean, white-capped here and there from the breath of the trade wind. Bill Scanlan came to me in my laboratory with more show of excitement than his easy-going temperament had ever permitted him to show.

"Look it here, Mr. Headley," said he, "they've lowered that contraption into a well in the bottom of the ship. D'you figure that the Boss is going down in it?"

"Certain sure, Bill. And I am going with him."

"Well, well, you are sure bughouse, the two of you, to think of such a thing. But I'd feel a cheap skate if I let you go alone."

"It is no business of yours, Bill."

"Well, I just feel that it is. Sure, I'd be as yellow as a Chink with the jaundice if I let you go alone. Merribanks sent me here to look after the machinery, and if the machinery is down at the bottom of the sea, then it's a sure thing that it's me for the bottom. Where those steel castings are—that's the address of Bill Scanlan—whether the folk round him are crazy or no." It was useless to argue with him, so one more was added to our little suicide club and we just waited for our orders.

All night they were hard at work upon the fittings, and it was after an early breakfast that we descended into the hold ready for our adventure.

The steel cage had been half-lowered into the false bottom, and we now descended one by one through the upper trapdoor, which was closed and screwed down behind us, Captain Howie with a most lugubrious face having shaken hands with each of us as we passed him. We were then lowered a few more feet, the shutter drawn above our heads, and the water admitted to test how far we were really seaworthy. The cage stood the trial well, every joint fitted exactly, and there was no sign of any leakage. Then the lower flap in the hold was loosened and we hung suspended in the ocean beneath the level of the keel.

It was really a very snug little room, and I marvelled at the skill and foresight with which everything had been arranged. The electric illumination had not been turned on, but the semitropical sun shone brightly through the bottle-green water at either porthole. Some small fish were flickering here and there, streaks of silver against the green background. Inside there was a settee round the little room, with a bathymetric dial, a thermometer, and other instruments ranged above it. Beneath the settee was a row of pipes which represented our reserve supply of compressed air in case the tubes should fail us. Those tubes opened out above our heads, and the telephonic apparatus hung beside them. We could all hear the mournful voice of the captain outside.

"Are you really determined to go?" he asked.

"We are quite all right," the Doctor answered impatiently. "You will lower slowly and have someone at the receiver all the time. I will report conditions. When we reach the bottom, remain as you are until I give instructions. It will not do to put too much strain upon the hawser, but a slow movement of a couple of knots an hour should be well within its strength. And now 'Lower away!'"

He yelled out the two words with the scream of a lunatic. It was the supreme moment of his life, the fruition of all his brooding dreams. For an instant I was shaken by the thought that we were really in the power of a cunning, plausible monomaniac. Bill Scanlan had the same thought, for he looked across at me with a rueful grin and touched his forehead. But after that one wild outburst our leader was instantly his sober, self-contained self once more. Indeed, one had but to look at the order and forethought which showed itself in every detail around us to be reassured as to the power of his mind.

But now all our attention was diverted to the wonderful new experience which every instant was providing. Slowly the cage was sinking into the depths of the ocean. Light green water turned to dark olive. That again deepened into a wonderful blue, a rich deep blue gradually thickening to a dusky purple. Lower and lower we sank—a hundred feet, two hundred feet, three hundred. The valves were acting to perfection. Our breathing was as free and natural as upon the deck of the vessel. Slowly the bathymeter needle moved round the luminous dial. Four hundred, five hundred, six hundred. "How are you?" roared an anxious voice from above us.

"Nothing could be better," cried Maracot in reply. But the light was failing. There was now only a dim grey twilight which rapidly changed to utter darkness. "Stop her!" shouted our leader. We ceased to move and hung suspended at seven hundred feet below the surface of the ocean. I heard the click of the switch, and the next instant we were flooded with glorious golden light which poured out through each of our side windows and sent long glimmering vistas into the waste of waters round us. With our faces against the thick glass, each at our own porthole, we gazed out into such a prospect as man had never seen.

Up to now we had known these strata by the sight of the few fish which had been too slow to avoid our clumsy trawl, or too stupid to escape a dragnet. Now we saw the wonderful world of water as it really was. If the object of creation was the production of man it is strange that the ocean is so much more populous than the land. Broadway on a Saturday night, Lombard Street on a weekday afternoon, are not more crowded than the great sea spaces which lay before us. We had passed those surface strata where fish are either colourless or of the true maritime tints of ultramarine above and silver below. Here there were creatures of every conceivable tint and form which pelagic life can show. Delicate leptocephali or eel larva shot like streaks of burnished silver across the tunnel of radiance. The slow snake-like form of muroena, the deep-sea lamprey, writhed and twisted by, or the black ceratia, all spikes and mouth, gaped foolishly back at our peering faces. Sometimes it was the squat cuttle-fish which drifted across and glanced at us with human, sinister eyes, sometimes it was some crystal-clear pelagic form of life, cystoma or glaucus, which lent a flower-like charm to the scene. One huge caranx, or horse mackerel, butted savagely again and again against our window until the dark shadow of a seven-foot shark came across him, and he vanished into the gaping jaws. Dr. Maracot sat entranced, his notebook upon his knee scribbling down his observations and keeping up a muttered monologue of scientific comment. "What's that? What's that?" I would hear. "Yes, yes, Chimoera mirabilis as taken by the Michael Sars. Dear me, there is lepidion, but a new species as I should judge. Observe that macrurus, Mr. Headley; its colouring is quite different to what we get in the net." Once only was he taken quite aback. It was when a long oval object shot with great speed past his window from above, and left a vibrating tail behind it which extended as far as we could see above us and below. I admit that I was as puzzled for the moment as the Doctor, and it was Bill Scanlan who solved the mystery.

"I guess that boob, John Sweeney, has heaved his lead alongside of us. Kind of a joke, maybe, to prevent us from feeling lonesome."

"To be sure! To be sure!" said Maracot, sniggering. "Plumbus longi-caudatus—a new genus, Mr. Headley, with a piano-wire tail and lead in its nose. But, indeed, it is very necessary they should take soundings so as to keep above the bank, which is circumscribed in size. All well, Captain!" he shouted. "You may drop us down."

And down we went. Dr. Maracot turned off the electric light and all was pitch darkness once more save for the bathymeter's luminous face, which ticked off our steady fall. There was a gentle sway, but otherwise we were hardly conscious of any motion. Only that moving hand upon the dial told us of our terrific, our inconceivable, position. Now we were at the thousand-foot level, and the air had become distinctly foul. Scanlan oiled the valve of the discharge tube and things were better. At fifteen hundred feet we stopped and swung in mid-ocean with our lights blazing once more. Some great dark mass passed us here, but whether swordfish or deep-sea shark, or monster of unknown breed, was more than we could determine. The Doctor hurriedly turned off the lights. "There lies our chief danger," said he; "there are creatures in the deep before whose charge this steel-plated room would have as much chance as a beehive before the rush of a rhinoceros."

"Whales, maybe," said Scanlan.

"Whales may sound to a great depth," the savant answered. "A Greenland whale has been known to take out nearly a mile of line in a perpendicular dive. But unless hurt or badly frightened no whale would descend so low. It may have been a giant squid. They are found at every level."

"Well, I guess squids are too soft to hurt us. The laugh would be with the squid if he could claw a hole in Merribank's nickel steel."

"Their bodies may be soft," the Professor answered, "but the beak of a large squid would sheer through a bar of iron, and one peck of that beak might go through these inch-thick windows as if they were parchment."

"Gee Whittaker!" cried Bill, as we resumed our downward journey.

And then at last, quite softly and gently, we came to rest. So delicate was the impact that we should hardly have known of it had it not been that the light when turned on showed great coils of the hawser all around us. The wire was a danger to our breathing-tubes, for it might foul them, and at the urgent cry of Maracot it was pulled taut from above once more. The dial marked eighteen hundred feet. We lay motionless on a volcanic ridge at the bottom of the Atlantic.

CHAPTER II: For a time I think that we all had the same feeling. We did not want to do anything or to see anything. We just wanted to sit quiet and try to realize the wonder of it—that we should be resting in the plumb centre of one of the great oceans of the world. But soon the strange scene round us, illuminated in all directions by our lights, drew us to the windows.

We had settled upon a bed of high algæ ("Cutleria multifida," said Maracot), the yellow fronds of which waved around us, moved by some deep-sea current, exactly as branches would move in a summer breeze. They were not long enough to obscure our view, though their great flat leaves, deep golden in the light, flowed occasionally across our vision. Beyond them lay slopes of some blackish slag-like material which were dotted with lovely coloured creatures, holothurians, ascidians, echini, and echinoderms, as thickly as ever an English spring-time bank was sprinkled with hyacinths and primroses. These living flowers of the sea, vivid scarlet, rich purple, and delicate pink, were spread in profusion upon that coal-black background. Here and there great sponges bristled out from the crevices of the dark rocks, and a few fish of the middle depths, themselves showing up as flashes of colour, shot across our circle of vivid radiance. We were gazing enraptured at the fairy scene when an anxious voice came down the tube:

"Well, how do you like the bottom? Is all well with you? Don't be too long, for the glass is dropping and I don't like the look of it. Giving you air enough? Anything more we can do?"

"All right, Captain!" cried Maracot cheerily. "We won't be long. You are nursing us well. We are quite as comfortable as in our own cabin. Stand by presently to move us slowly forwards."

We had come into the region of the luminous fishes, and it amused us to turn out our own lights, and in the absolute pitch darkness—a darkness in which a sensitive plate can be suspended for an hour without a trace even of the ultra-violet ray—to look out at the phosphorescent activity of the ocean. As against a black velvet curtain one saw little points of brilliant light moving steadily along as a liner at night might shed light through its long line of portholes. One terrifying creature had luminous teeth which gnashed in Biblical fashion in the outer darkness. Another had long golden antennæ, and yet another a plume of flame above its head. As far as our vision carried, brilliant points flashed in the darkness, each little being bent upon its own business, and lighting up its own course as surely as the nightly taxicab at the theatre-hour in the Strand. Soon we had our own lights up again and the Doctor was making his observations of the sea-bottom.

"Deep as we are, we are not deep enough to get any of the characteristic bathic deposits," said he. "These are entirely beyond our possible range. Perhaps on another occasion with a longer hawser——"

"Cut it out!" growled Bill. "Forget it!"

Maracot smiled. "You will soon get acclimatized to the depths, Scanlan. This will not be our only descent."

"The hell you say!" muttered Bill.

"You will think no more of it than of going down into the hold of the *Stratford*. You will observe, Mr. Headley, that the groundwork here, so far as we can observe it through the dense growth of hydrozoa and silicious sponges, is pumice stone and the black slag of basalt, pointing to ancient plutonic activities. Indeed, I am inclined to think that it confirms my previous view that this ridge is part of a volcanic formation and that the Maracot Deep," he rolled out the words as if he loved them, "represents the outer slope of the mountain. It has struck me that it would be an interesting experiment to move our cage slowly onwards until we come to the edge of the Deep, and see exactly what the formation may be at that point. I should expect to find a precipice of majestic dimensions extending downwards at a sharp angle into the extreme depths of the ocean."

The experiment seemed to me to be a dangerous one, for who could say how far our thin hawser could bear the strain of lateral movement; but with Maracot danger, either to himself or to anyone else, simply did not exist when a scientific observation had to be made. I held my breath, and so I observed did Bill Scanlan, when a slow movement of our steel shell, brushing aside the waving fronds of seaweed, showed that the full strain was upon the line. It stood it nobly, however, and with a very gentle sweeping progression we began to glide over the bottom of the ocean, Maracot, with a compass in the hollow of his hand, shouting his direction as to the course to follow, and occasionally ordering the shell to be raised so as to avoid some obstacle in our path.

"This basaltic ridge can hardly be more than a mile across," he explained. "I had marked the abyss as being to the west of the point where we took our plunge. At this rate, we should certainly reach it in a very short time."

We slid without any check over the volcanic plain, all feathered by the waving golden algæ and made beautiful by the gorgeous jewels of Nature's cutting, flaming out from their setting of jet. Suddenly the Doctor dashed to the telephone.

"Stop her!" he cried. "We are there!"

A monstrous gap had opened suddenly before us. It was a fearsome place, the vision of a nightmare. Black shining cliffs of basalt fell sheer down into the unknown. Their edges were fringed with dangling laminaria as ferns might overhang some earthly gorge, but beneath that tossing, vibrating rim there were only the black gleaming walls of the chasm. The rocky edge curved away from us, but the abyss might be of any breadth, for our lights failed to penetrate the gloom which lay before us. When a Lucas signalling lamp was turned downwards it shot out a long golden

lane of parallel beams extending down, down, down until it was quenched
in the gloom of the terrible chasm beneath us.

"It is indeed wonderful!" cried Maracot, gazing out with a pleased
proprietary expression upon his thin, eager face. "For depth I need not
say that it has often been exceeded. There is the Challenger Deep of
twenty-six thousand feet near the Ladrone Islands, the Planet Deep of
thirty-two thousand feet off the Philippines, and many others, but it is
probable that the Maracot Deep stands alone in the declivity of its descent,
and is remarkable also for its escape from the observation of so many
hydrographic explorers who have charted the Atlantic. It can hardly be
doubted——"

He had stopped in the middle of a sentence and a look of intense
interest and surprise had frozen upon his face. Bill Scanlan and I, gazing
over his shoulders, were petrified by that which met our startled eyes.

Some great creature was coming up the tunnel of light which we had
projected into the abyss. Far down where it tailed off into the darkness of
the pit we could dimly see the vague black lurchings and heavings of
some monstrous body in slow upward progression. Paddling in clumsy
fashion, it was rising with dim flickerings to the edge of the gulf. Now, as
it came nearer, it was right in the beam, and we could see its dreadful
form more clearly. It was a beast unknown to Science, and yet with an
analogy to much with which we are familiar. Too long for a huge crab
and too short for a giant lobster, it was moulded more upon the lines of
the crayfish, with two monstrous nippers outstretched on either side, and
a pair of sixteen-foot antennæ which quivered in front of its black dull
sullen eyes. The carapace, light yellow in colour, may have been ten feet
across, and its total length, apart from the antennæ, must have been not
less than thirty.

"Wonderful!" cried Maracot, scribbling desperately in his notebook.
"Semi-pediculated eyes, elastic lamelæ, family crustaceæ, species unknown. Crustaceus Maracoti—why not? Why not?"

"By gosh, I'll pass its name, but it seems to me it's coming our way!"
cried Bill. "Say, Doc, what about putting our light out?"

"Just one moment while I note the reticulations!" cried the naturalist.
"Yes, yes, that will do." He clicked off the switch and we were back in
our inky darkness, with only the darting lights outside like meteors on a
moonless night.

"That beast is sure the world's worst," said Bill, wiping his forehead.
"I felt like the morning after a bottle of Prohibition Hooch."

"It is certainly terrible to look at," Maracot remarked, "and perhaps
terrible to deal with also if we were really exposed to those monstrous
claws. But inside our steel case we can afford to examine him in safety
and at our ease."

He had hardly spoken when there came a rap as from a pickaxe upon our outer wall. Then there was a long-drawn rasping and scratching, ending in another sharp rap.

"Say, he wants to come in!" cried Bill Scanlan in alarm. "By gosh we want 'No Admission' painted on this shack." His shaking voice showed how forced was his merriment, and I confess that my own knees were knocking together as I was aware of the stealthy monster closing up with an even blacker darkness each of our windows in succession, as he explored this strange shell which, could he but crack it, might contain his food.

"He can't hurt us," said Maracot, but there was less assurance in his tone. "Maybe it would be as well to shake the brute off." He hailed the Captain up the tube.

"Pull us up twenty or thirty feet," he cried.

A few seconds later we rose from the lava plain and swung gently in the still water. But the terrible beast was pertinacious. After a very short interval we heard once more the raspings of his feelers and the sharp tappings of his claws as he felt us round. It was terrible to sit silently in the dark and know that death was so near. If that mighty claw fell upon the window, would it stand the strain? That was the unspoken question in each of our minds.

But suddenly an unexpected and more urgent danger presented itself. The tappings had gone to the roof of our little dwelling, and now we began to sway with a rhythmic movement to and fro.

"Good God!" I cried. "It has hold of the hawser. It will surely snap it."

"Say, Doc, it's mine for the surface. I guess we've seen what we came to see, and it's home, sweet home for Bill Scanlan. Ring up the elevator and get her going."

"But our work is not half done," croaked Maracot. "We have only begun to explore the edges of the Deep. Let us at least see how broad it is. When we have reached the other side I shall be content to return." Then up the tube: "All well, Captain. Move on at two knots until I call for a stop."

We moved slowly out over the edge of the abyss. Since darkness had not saved us from attack we now turned on our lights. One of the portholes was entirely obscured by what appeared to be the creature's lower stomach. Its head and its great nippers were at work above us, and we still swayed like a clanging bell. The strength of the beast must have been enormous. Were ever mortals placed in such a situation, with five miles of water beneath—and that deadly monster above? The oscillations became more and more violent. An excited shout came down the tube from the Captain as he became aware of the jerks upon the hawser, and Maracot sprang to his feet with his hands thrown upwards in despair. Even within the shell we were aware of the jar of the broken wires, and an instant later we were falling into the mighty gulf beneath us.

As I look back at that awful moment I can remember hearing a wild cry from Maracot.

"The hawser has parted! You can do nothing! We are all dead men!" he yelled, grabbing at the telephone tube, and then, "Good-bye, Captain, good-bye to all." They were our last words to the world of men.

We did not fall swiftly down, as you might have imagined. In spite of our weight our hollow shell gave us some sustaining buoyancy, and we sank slowly and gently into the abyss. I heard the long scrape as we slid through the claws of the horrible creature who had been our ruin, and then with a smooth gyration we went circling downwards into the abysmal depths. It may have been fully five minutes, and it seemed like an hour, before we reached the limit of our telephone wire and snapped it like a thread. Our air tube broke off at almost the same moment and the salt water came spouting through the vents. With quick, deft hands Bill Scanlan tied cords round each of the rubber tubes and so stopped the in-rush, while the Doctor released the top of our compressed air which came hissing forth from the tubes. The lights had gone out when the wire snapped, but even in the dark the Doctor was able to connect up the Hellesens dry cells which lit a number of lamps in the roof.

"It should last us a week," he said, with a wry smile. "We shall at least have light to die in." Then he shook his head sadly and a kindly smile came over his gaunt features. "It is all right for me. I am an old man and have done my work in the world. My one regret is that I should have allowed you two young fellows to come with me. I should have taken the risk alone."

I simply shook his hand in reassurance, for indeed there was nothing I could say. Bill Scanlan, too, was silent. Slowly we sank, marking our pace by the dark fish shadows which flitted past our windows. It seemed as if they were flying upwards rather than that we were sinking down. We still oscillated, and there was nothing so far as I could see to prevent us from falling on our side, or even turning upside down. Our weight, however, was, fortunately, very evenly balanced and we kept a level floor. Glancing up at the bathymeter I saw that we had already reached the depth of a mile.

"You see, it is as I said," remarked Maracot with some complacency. "You may have seen my paper in the Proceedings of the Oceanographical Society upon the relation of pressure and depth. I wish I could get one word back to the world, if only to confute Bülow of Giessen, who ventured to contradict me."

"My gosh! If I could get a word back to the world I wouldn't waste it on a square-head highbrow," said the mechanic. "There is a little wren in

Philadelphia that will have tears in her pretty eyes when she hears that Bill Scanlan has passed out. Well, it sure does seem a dumb queer way of doing it, anyhow."

"You should never have come," I said, putting my hand on his.

"What sort of tin-horn sport should I have been if I had quitted?" he answered. "No, it's my job, and I am glad I stuck it."

"How long have we?" I asked the Doctor, after a pause.

He shrugged his shoulders.

"We shall have time to see the real bottom of the ocean, anyhow," said he. "There is air enough in our tubes for the best part of a day. Our trouble is with the waste products. That is what is going to choke us. If we could get rid of our carbon dioxide——"

"That I can see is impossible."

"There is one tube of pure oxygen. I put it in in case of accidents. A little of that from time to time will help to keep us alive. You will observe that we are now more than two miles deep."

"Why should we try to keep ourselves alive? The sooner it is over the better," said I.

"That's the dope," cried Scanlan. "Cut loose and have done with it."

"And miss the most wonderful sight that man's eye has ever seen!" said Maracot. "It would be treason to Science. Let us record facts to the end, even if they should be forever buried with our bodies. Play the game out."

"Some sport, the Doc!" cried Scanlan. "I guess he has the best guts of the bunch. Let us see the spiel to an end."

We sat patiently on the settee, the three of us, gripping the edges of it with strained fingers as it swayed and rocked, while the fishes still flashed swiftly upwards athwart the portholes.

"It is now three miles," remarked Maracot. "I will turn on the oxygen, Mr. Headley, for it is certainly very close. There is one thing," he added, with his dry, cackling laugh. "It will certainly be the Maracot Deep from this time onwards. When Captain Howie takes back the news my colleagues will see to it that my grave is also my monument. Even Bülow of Giessen——" He babbled on about some unintelligible scientific grievance.

We sat in silence again, watching the needle as it crawled on to its fourth mile. At one point we struck something heavy, which shook us so violently that I feared that we would turn upon our side. It may have been a huge fish, or conceivably we may have bumped upon some projection of the cliff over the edge of which we had been precipitated. That edge had seemed to us at the time to be such a wondrous depth, and now looking back at it from our dreadful abyss it might almost have been the surface. Still we swirled and circled lower and lower through the dark green waste of waters. Twenty-five thousand feet now was registered upon the dial.

"We are nearly at our journey's end," said Maracot. "My Scott's recorder gave me twenty-six thousand seven hundred last year at the deepest point. We shall know our fate within a few minutes. It may be that the shock will crush us. It may be——"

And at that moment we landed.

There was never a babe lowered by its mother on to a feather bed who nestled down more gently than we on to the extreme bottom of the Atlantic Ocean. The soft, thick, elastic ooze upon which we lit was a perfect buffer, which saved us from the slightest jar. We hardly moved upon our seats, and it is as well that we did not, for we had perched upon some sort of a projecting hummock, clothed thickly with the viscous gelatinous mud, and there we were balanced rocking gently with nearly half our base projecting and unsupported. There was a danger that we would tip over on our side, but finally we steadied down and remained motionless. As we did so Dr. Maracot, staring out through his porthole, gave a cry of surprise and hurriedly turned out our electric light.

To our amazement we could still see clearly. There was a dim, misty light outside which streamed through our porthole, like the cold radiance of a winter morning. We looked out at the strange scene, and with no help from our own lights we could see clearly for some hundred yards in each direction. It was impossible, inconceivable, but none the less the evidence of our senses told us that it was a fact. The great ocean floor is luminous.

"Why not?" cried Maracot, when we had stood for a minute or two in silent wonder. "Should I not have foreseen it? What is this pteropod or globigerina ooze? Is it not the product of decay, the mouldering bodies of a billion billion organic creatures? And is decay not associated with phosphorescent luminosity? Where, in all creation, would it be seen if it were not here? Ah! it is indeed hard that we should have such a demonstration and be unable to send our knowledge back to the world."

"And yet," I remarked, "we have scooped half a ton of radiolarian jelly at a time and detected no such radiance."

"It would lose it, doubtless, in its long journey to the surface. And what is half a ton compared to these far-stretching plains of slow putrescence? And see, see," he cried in uncontrollable excitement, "the deep-sea creatures graze upon this organic carpet even as our herds on land graze upon the meadows!"

As he spoke a flock of big black fish, heavy and squat, came slowly over the ocean bed towards us, nuzzling among the spongy growths and nibbling away as they advanced. Another huge red creature, like a foolish cow of the ocean, was chewing the cud in front of my porthole and others were grazing here and there, raising their heads from time to time to gaze at this strange object which had so suddenly appeared among them.

I could only marvel at Maracot, who in that foul atmosphere, seated under the very shadow of death, still obeyed the call of Science and scribbled his observations in his notebook. Without following his precise methods, I none the less made my own mental notes, which will remain forever as a picture stamped upon my brain. The lowest plains of ocean consist of red clay, but here it was overlaid by the grey bathybian slime which formed an undulating plain as far as our eyes could reach. This plain was not smooth, but was broken by numerous strange rounded hillocks like that upon which we had perched, all glimmering in the spectral light. Between these little hills there darted great clouds of strange fish, many of them quite unknown to Science, exhibiting every shade of colour, but black and red predominating. Maracot watched them with suppressed excitement and chronicled them in his notes.

The air had become very foul, and again we were only able to save ourselves by a fresh emission of oxygen. Curiously enough, we were all hungry—I should rather say ravenous—and we fell upon the potted beef with bread and butter, washed down by whisky and water, which the foresight of Maracot had provided. With my perceptions stimulated by this refreshment, I was seated at my look-out portal and longing for a last cigarette, when my eyes caught something which sent a whirl of strange thoughts and anticipations through my mind.

I have said that the undulating grey plain on every side of us was studded with what seemed like hummocks. A particularly large one was in front of my porthole, and I looked out at it within a range of thirty feet. There was some peculiar mark upon the side of it, and as I glanced along I saw to my surprise that this mark was repeated again and again until it was lost round the curve. When one is so near death it takes much to give one a thrill about anything connected with this world, but my breath failed me for a moment and my heart stood still as I suddenly realized that it was a frieze at which I was looking and that, barnacled and worn as it was, the hand of man had surely at some time carved these faded figures. Maracot and Scanlan crowded to my porthole and gazed out in utter amazement at these signs of the omnipresent energies of man.

"It is carving, for sure!" cried Scanlan. "I guess this dump has been the roof of a building. Then these other ones are buildings also. Say, boss, we've dropped plumb on to a regular burg."

"It is, indeed, an ancient city," said Maracot. "Geology teaches that the seas have once been continents and the continents seas, but I have always distrusted the idea that in times so recent as the quaternary there could have been an Atlantic subsidence. Plato's report of Egyptian gossip had then a foundation of fact. These volcanic formations confirm the view that this subsidence was due to seismic activity."

"There is regularity about these domes," I remarked. "I begin to think that they are not separate houses, but that they are cupolas and form the ornaments of the roof of some huge building."

"I guess you are right," said Scanlan. "There are four big ones at the corners and the small ones in lines between. It's some building, if we could see the whole of it! You could put the whole Merribank plant inside it—and then some."

"It has been buried up to the roof by the constant dropping from above," said Maracot. "On the other hand, it has not decayed. We have a constant temperature of a little over 32° Fahrenheit in the great depths, which would arrest destructive processes. Even the dissolution of the bathic remains which pave the floor of the ocean and incidentally give us this luminosity must be a very slow one. But, dear me! this marking is not a frieze but an inscription."

There was no doubt that he was right. The same symbol recurred every here and there. These marks were unquestionably letters of some archaic alphabet.

"I have made a study of Phœnician antiquities, and there is certainly something suggestive and familiar in these characters," said our leader. "Well, we have seen a buried city of ancient days, my friends, and we carry a wonderful piece of knowledge with us to the grave. There is no more to be learned. Our book of knowledge is closed. I agree with you that the sooner the end comes the better."

It could not now be long delayed. The air was stagnant and dreadful. So heavy was it with carbon products that the oxygen could hardly force its way out against the pressure. By standing on the settee one was able to get a gulp of purer air, but the mephitic reek was slowly rising. Dr. Maracot folded his arms with an air of resignation and sank his head upon his breast. Scanlan was now overpowered by the fumes and was already sprawling upon the floor. My own head was swimming, and I felt an intolerable weight at my chest. I closed my eyes and my senses were rapidly slipping away. Then I opened them for one last glimpse of that world which I was leaving, and as I did so I staggered to my feet with a hoarse scream of amazement.

A human face was looking in at us through the porthole!

Was it my delirium? I clutched at the shoulder of Maracot and shook him violently. He sat up and stared, wonder-struck and speechless, at this apparition. If he saw it as well as I, it was no figment of the brain. The face was long and thin, dark in complexion, with a short pointed beard, and two vivid eyes darting here and there in quick, questioning glances which took in every detail of our situation. The utmost amazement was visible upon the man's face. Our lights were now full on, and it must indeed have been a strange and vivid picture which presented itself to his gaze in that tiny chamber of death, where one man lay senseless

and two others glared out at him with the twisted, contorted features of
dying men, cyanosed by incipient asphyxiation. We both had our hands
to our throats, and our heaving chests carried their message of despair.
The man gave a wave of his hand and hurried away.

"He has deserted us!" cried Maracot.

"Or gone for help. Let us get Scanlan on the couch. It's death for him
down there."

We dragged the mechanic on to the settee and propped his head against
the cushions. His face was grey and he murmured in delirium, but his
pulse was still perceptible.

"There is hope for us yet," I croaked.

"But it is madness!" cried Maracot. "How can man live at the bottom
of the ocean? How can he breathe? It is collective hallucination. My
young friend, we are going mad."

Looking out at the bleak, lonely grey landscape in the dreary spectral
light, I felt that it might be as Maracot said. Then suddenly I was aware
of movement. Shadows were flitting through the distant water. They hardened and thickened into moving figures. A crowd of people were hurrying
across the ocean bed in our direction. An instant later they had assembled
in front of the porthole and were pointing and gesticulating in animated
debate. There were several women in the crowd, but the greater part were
men, one of whom, a powerful figure with a very large head and a full
black beard, was clearly a person of authority. He made a swift inspection
of our steel shell, and, since the edge of our base projected over the place
on which we rested, he was able to see that there was a hinged trapdoor
at the bottom. He now sent a messenger flying back, while he made
energetic and commanding signs to us to open the door from within.

"Why not?" I asked. "We may as well be drowned as be smothered.
I can stand it no longer."

"We may not be drowned," said Maracot. "The water entering from
below cannot rise above the level of the compressed air. Give Scanlan
some brandy. He must make an effort, if it is his last one."

I forced a drink down the mechanic's throat. He gulped and looked
round him with wondering eyes. Between us we got him erect on the settee
and stood on either side of him. He was still half-dazed, but in a few
words I explained the situation.

"There is a chance of chlorine poisoning if the water reaches the batteries," said Maracot. "Open every air tube, for the more pressure we can
get the less water may enter. Now help me while I pull upon the lever."

We bent our weight upon it and yanked up the circular plate from the
bottom of our little home, though I felt like a suicide as I did so. The
green water, sparkling and gleaming under our light, came gurgling and
surging in. It rose rapidly to our feet, to our knees, to our waists, and there

it stopped. But the pressure of the air was intolerable. Our heads buzzed and the drums of our ears were bursting. We could not have lived in such an atmosphere for long. Only by clutching at the rack could we save ourselves from falling back into the waters beneath us.

From our higher position we could no longer see through the portholes, nor could we imagine what steps were being taken for our deliverance. Indeed, that any effective help could come to us seemed beyond the power of thought, and yet there was a commanding and purposeful air about these people, and especially about that squat bearded chieftain, which inspired vague hopes. Suddenly we were aware of his face looking up at us through the water beneath and an instant later he had passed through the circular opening and had clambered on to the settee, so that he was standing by our side—a short, sturdy figure, not higher than my shoulder, but surveying us with large brown eyes, which were full of a half-amused confidence, as who should say, "You poor devils; you think you are in a very bad way, but I can clearly see the road out."

Only now was I aware of a very amazing thing. The man, if indeed he was of the same humanity as ourselves, had a transparent envelope all round him which enveloped his head and body, while his arms and legs were free. So translucent was it that no one could detect it in the water, but now that he was in the air beside us it glistened like silver, though it remained as clear as the finest glass. On either shoulder he had a curious rounded projection beneath the clear protective sheath. It looked like an oblong box pierced with many holes, and gave him an appearance as if he were wearing epaulettes.

When our new friend had joined us another face appeared in the aperture of the bottom and thrust through it what seemed like a great bubble of glass. Three of these in succession were passed in and floated upon the surface of the water. Then six small boxes were handed up and our new acquaintance tied one with the straps attached to them to each of our shoulders, whence they stood up like his own. Already I began to surmise that no infraction of natural law was involved in the life of these strange people, and that while one box in some new fashion was a producer of air the other was an absorber of waste products. He now passed the transparent suits over our heads, and we felt that they clasped us tightly in the upper arm and waist by elastic bands, so that no water could penetrate. Within we breathed with perfect ease, and it was a joy to me to see Maracot looking out at me with his eyes twinkling as of old behind his glasses, while Bill Scanlan's grin assured me that the life-giving oxygen had done its work, and that he was his cheerful self once more. Our rescuer looked from one to another of us with grave satisfaction, and then motioned to us to follow him through the trapdoor and out on to the floor of the ocean. A dozen willing hands were outstretched to pull us through and to sustain our first faltering steps as we staggered with our feet deep in the slimy ooze.

Even now I cannot get past the marvel of it! There we were, the three of us, unhurt and at our ease at the bottom of a five-mile abyss of water. Where was that terrific pressure which had exercised the imagination of so many scientists? We were no more affected by it than were the dainty fish which swam around us. It is true that, so far as our bodies were concerned, we were protected by these delicate bells of vitrine, which were in truth tougher than the strongest steel, but even our limbs, which were exposed, felt no more than a firm constriction from the water which one learned in time to disregard. It was wonderful to stand together and to look back at the shell from which we had emerged. We had left the batteries at work, and it was a wondrous object with its streams of yellow light flooding out from each side, while clouds of fishes gathered at each window. As we watched it the leader took Maracot by the hand, and we followed them both across the watery morass, clumping heavily through the sticky surface.

And now a most surprising incident occurred, which was clearly as astonishing to these strange new companions of ours as to ourselves. Above our heads there appeared a small, dark object, descending from the darkness above us and swinging down until it reached the bed of the ocean within a very short distance from where we stood. It was, of course, the deep-sea lead from the *Stratford* above us, making a sounding of that watery gulf with which the name of the expedition was to be associated. We had seen it already upon its downward path, and we could well understand that the tragedy of our disappearance had suspended the operation, but that after a pause it had been concluded, with little thought that it would finish almost at our feet. They were unconscious, apparently, that they had touched bottom, for the lead lay motionless in the ooze. Above me stretched the taut piano wire which connected me through five miles of water with the deck of our vessel. Oh, that it were possible to write a note and to attach it! The idea was absurd, and yet could I not send some message which would show them that we were still conscious? My coat was covered by my glass bell and the pockets were unapproachable, but I was free below the waist and my handkerchief chanced to be in my trousers pocket. I pulled it out and tied it above the top of the lead. The weight itself at once disengaged itself by its automatic mechanism, and presently I saw my white wisp of linen flying upwards to that world which I may never see again. Our new acquaintances examined the seventy-five pounds of lead with great interest, and finally carried it off with us as we went upon our way.

We had only walked a couple of hundred yards, threading our way among the hummocks, when we halted before a small square-cut door with solid pillars on either side and an inscription across the lintel. It was open, and we passed through it into a large, bare chamber. There was a sliding partition worked by a crank from within, and this was drawn across behind us. We could, of course, hear nothing in our glass helmets, but after standing a few minutes we were aware that a powerful pump must be at work, for we saw the level of the water sinking rapidly above us. In less than a quarter of an hour we were standing upon a sloppy stone-flagged pavement, while our new friends were busy in undoing the fastenings of our transparent suits. An instant later there we stood, breathing perfectly pure air in a warm, well-lighted atmosphere, while the dark people of the abyss, smiling and chattering, crowded round us with hand-shakings and friendly pattings. It was a strange, rasping tongue that they spoke, and no word of it was intelligible to us, but the smile on the face and the light of friendship in the eye are understandable even in the waters under the earth. The glass suits were hung on numbered pegs upon the wall, and the kindly folk half-led and half-pushed us to an inner door which opened on to a long downward-sloping corridor. When it closed again behind us there was nothing to remind us of the stupendous fact that we were the involuntary guests of an unknown race at the bottom of the Atlantic Ocean and cut off forever from the world to which we belonged.

Now that the terrific strain had been so suddenly eased we were all exhausted. Even Bill Scanlan, who was a pocket Hercules, dragged his feet along the floor, while Maracot and I were only too glad to lean heavily upon our guides. Yet, weary as I was, I took in every detail as we passed. That the air came from some air-making machine was very evident, for it issued in puffs from circular openings in the walls. The light was diffused and was clearly an extension of that fluor system which was already engaging the attention of our European engineers when the filament and lamp were dispensed with. It shone from long cylinders of clear glass which were suspended along the cornices of the passages. So much I had observed when our descent was checked and we were ushered into a large sitting-room, thickly carpeted and well furnished with gilded chairs and sloping sofas which brought back vague memories of Egyptian tombs. The crowd had been dismissed and only the bearded man with two attendants remained. "Manda," he repeated several times, tapping himself upon the chest. Then he pointed to each of us in turn and repeated the words Maracot, Headley, and Scanlan until he had them perfect. He then motioned us to be seated and said a word to one of the attendants, who left the room and returned presently, escorting a very ancient gentleman, white-haired and long-bearded, with a curious conical cap of black cloth upon his head. I should have said that all these folk were dressed in coloured tunics, which extended to their knees, with high boots of fish skin or shagreen. The venerable newcomer was clearly a physician, for he examined each of us in turn, placing his hand upon our brows and closing his own eyes as if receiving a mental impression as to our condition. Apparently he was by no means satisfied, for he shook his head and said a few grave words to Manda. The latter at once sent the attendant out once more, and he brought in a tray of eatables and a flask of wine, which were laid before us. We were too weary to ask ourselves what they were, but we felt the better for the meal. We were then led to another room, where three beds had been prepared, and on one of these I flung myself down. I have a dim recollection of Bill Scanlan coming across and sitting beside me.

"Say, Bo, that jolt of brandy saved my life," said he. "But where are we, anyhow?"

"I know no more than you do."

"Well, I am ready to hit the hay," he said, sleepily, as he turned to his bed. "Say, that wine was fine. Thank God, Volstead never got down here." They were the last words I heard as I sank into the most profound sleep that I can ever recall.

CHAPTER III: When I came to myself I could not at first imagine where I was. The events of the previous day were like some blurred nightmare, and I could not believe that I had to accept them as facts. I looked round in bewilderment at the large, bare, windowless room with drab-coloured walls, at the lines of quivering purplish light which flowed along the cornices, at the scattered articles of furniture, and finally at the two other beds, from one of which came the high-pitched strident snore which I had learned, aboard the *Stratford*, to associate with Maracot. It was too grotesque to be true, and it was only when I fingered my bed cover and observed the curious woven material, and dried fibres of some sea plant, from which it was made, that I was able to realize this inconceivable adventure which had befallen us. I was still pondering it when there came a loud explosion of laughter, and Bill Scanlan sat up in bed.

"Mornin', Bo!" he cried, amid his chuckles, on seeing that I was awake.

"You seem in good spirits," said I, rather testily. "I can't see that we have much to laugh about."

"Well, I had a grouch on me, the same as you, when first I woke up," he answered. "Then came a real cute idea, and it was that that made me laugh."

"I could do with a laugh myself," said I. "What's the idea?"

"Well, Bo, I thought how durned funny it would have been if we had all tied ourselves on to that deep-sea line. I allow with those glass ginguses we could have kept breathing all right. Then when old man Howie looked over the side there would have been the whole bunch of us comin' up at him through the water. He would have figured that he had hooked us, sure. Gee, what a spiel!"

Our united laughter woke the Doctor, who sat up in bed with the same amazed expression upon his face which had previously been upon my own. I forgot our troubles as I listened in amusement to his disjointed comments, which alternated between ecstatic joy at the prospect of such a field of study, and profound sorrow that he could never hope to convey his results to his scientific *confrères* of the earth. Finally he got back to the actual needs of the moment.

"It is nine o'clock," he said, looking at his watch. We all registered the same hour, but there was nothing to show if it was night or morning.

"We must keep our own calendar," said Maracot; "we descended upon October 3rd. We reached this place on the evening of the same day. How long have we slept?"

"My gosh, it may have been a month," said Scanlan, "I've not been so deep since Mickey Scott got me on the point in the six-round try-out at the Works."

We dressed and washed, for every civilized convenience was at hand. The door, however, was fastened, and it was clear that we were prisoners for the time. In spite of the apparent absence of any ventilation, the atmosphere kept perfectly sweet, and we found that this was due to a current of air which came through small holes in the wall. There was some source of central heating, too, for though no stove was visible, the temperature was pleasantly warm. Presently I observed a knob upon one of the walls, and pressed it. This was, as I expected, a bell, for the door instantly opened, and a small, dark man, dressed in a yellow robe, appeared in the aperture. He looked at us inquiringly, with large, brown, kindly eyes.

"We are hungry," said Maracot; "can you get us some food?"

The man shook his head and smiled. It was clear that the words were incomprehensible to him.

Scanlan tried his luck with a flow of American slang, which was received with the same blank smile. When, however, I opened my mouth and thrust my finger into it, our visitor nodded vigorously and hurried away.

Ten minutes later the door opened and two of the yellow attendants appeared, rolling a small table before them. Had we been at the Biltmore Hotel we could not have had better fare. There were coffee, hot milk, rolls, delicious flat fish, and honey. For half an hour we were far too busy to discuss what we ate or whence it was obtained. At the end of that time the two servants appeared once more, rolled out the tray, and closed the door carefully behind them.

"I'm fair black and blue with pinching myself," said Scanlan. "Is this a pipe dream or what? Say, Doc, you got us down here, and I guess it is up to you to tell us just how you size it all up."

The Doctor shook his head.

"It is like a dream to me also, but it is a glorious dream! What a story for the world if we could but get it to them!"

"One thing is clear," said I, "there was certainly truth in this legend of Atlantis, and some of the folk have in a marvellous way managed to carry on."

"Well, even if they carried on," cried Bill Scanlan, scratching his bullet head, "I am darned if I can understand how they could get air and fresh water and the rest. Maybe if that queer duck with the beard that we saw last night comes to give us a once-over he will put us wise to it."

"How can he do that when we have no common language?"

"Well, we shall use our own observation," said Maracot. "One thing I can already understand. I learned it from the honey at breakfast. That was clearly synthetic honey, such as we have already learned to make upon the earth. But if synthetic honey, why not synthetic coffee, or flour? The molecules of the elements are like bricks, and these bricks lie all around us. We have only to learn how to pull out certain bricks—sometimes just a single brick—in order to make a fresh substance. Sugar becomes starch, or either becomes alcohol, just by a shifting of the bricks. What is it that shifts them? Heat. Electricity. Other things perhaps of which we know nothing. Some of them will shift themselves, and radium becomes lead or uranium becomes radium without our touching them."

"You think, then, that they have an advanced chemistry?"

"I'm sure of it. After all, there is no elemental brick which is not ready to their hands. Hydrogen and oxygen come readily from the sea water. There are nitrogen and carbon in those masses of sea vegetation, and there are phosphorus and calcium in the bathybic deposit. With skilful management and adequate knowledge what is there which could not be produced?"

The Doctor had launched upon a chemical lecture when the door opened and Manda entered, giving us a friendly greeting. There came with him the same old gentleman of venerable appearance whom we had met the night before. He may have had a reputation for learning, for he tried several sentences, which were probably different languages, upon us, but all were equally unintelligible. Then he shrugged his shoulders and spoke to Manda, who gave an order to the two yellow-clad servants, still waiting at the door. They vanished, but returned presently with a curious screen, supported by two side posts. It was exactly like one of our cinema screens, but it was coated with some sparkling material which glittered and shimmered in the light. This was placed against one of the walls. The old man then paced out very carefully a certain distance, and marked it upon the floor. Standing at this point he turned to Maracot and touched his forehead, pointing to the screen.

"Clean dippy," said Scanlan. "Bats in the belfry."

Maracot shook his head to show that we were nonplussed. So was the old man for a moment. An idea struck him, however, and he pointed to his own figure. Then he turned towards the screen, fixed his eyes upon it, and seemed to concentrate his attention. In an instant a reflection of himself appeared on the screen before us. Then he pointed to us, and a moment later our own little group took the place of his image. It was not particularly like us. Scanlan looked like a comic Chinaman and Maracot like a decayed corpse, but it was clearly meant to be ourselves as we appeared in the eyes of the operator.

"It's a reflection of thought," I cried.

"Exactly," said Maracot. "This is certainly a most marvellous invention, and yet it is but a combination of such telepathy and television as we dimly comprehend upon earth."

"I never thought I'd live to see myself in the movies, if that cheese-faced Chink is really meant for me," said Scanlan. "Say, if we could get all this news to the editor of the *Ledger* he'd cough up enough to keep me for life. We've sure got the goods if we could deliver them."

"That's the trouble," said I. "By George, we could stir the whole world if we could only get back to it. But what is he beckoning about?"

"The old guy wants you to try your hand at it, Doc."

Maracot took the place indicated, and his strong, clear-cut brain focussed his picture to perfection. We saw an image of Manda, and then another one of the *Stratford* as we had left her.

Both Manda and the old scientist nodded their great approval at the sight of the ship, and Manda made a sweeping gesture with his hands, pointing first to us and then to the screen.

"To tell them all about it—that's the idea," I cried. "They want to know in pictures who we are, and how we got here."

Maracot nodded to Manda to show that he understood, and had begun to throw an image of our voyage, when Manda held up his hand and stopped him. At an order the attendants removed the screen, and the two Atlanteans beckoned that we should follow them.

It was a huge building, and we proceeded down corridor after corridor until we came at last to a large hall with seats arranged in tiers like a lecture room. At one side was a broad screen of the same nature as that which we had seen. Facing it there was assembled an audience of at least a thousand people, who set up a murmur of welcome as we entered. They were of both sexes and of all ages, the men dark and bearded, the women beautiful in youth and dignified in age. We had little time to observe them, for we were led to seats in the front row, and Maracot was then placed on a stand opposite the screen, the lights were in some fashion turned down, and he had the signal to begin.

And excellently well he played his part. We first saw our vessel sailing forth from the Thames, and a buzz of excitement went up from the tense audience at this authentic glimpse of a real modern city. Then a map appeared which marked her course. Then was seen the steel shell with its fittings, which was greeted with a murmur of recognition. We saw ourselves once more descending, and reaching the edge of the abyss. Then came the appearance of the monster who had wrecked us. "Marax! Marax!" cried the people, as the beast appeared. It was clear that they had learned to know and to fear it. There was a terrified hush as the creature fumbled with our hawser, and a groan of horror as the wires parted and we dropped into the gulf. In a month of explanation we could not have made our plight so clear as in that half-hour of visible demonstration.

As the audience broke up they showered every sign of sympathy upon us, crowding round us and patting our backs to show that we were welcome. We were presented in turn to some of the chiefs, but the chieftainship seemed to lie in wisdom alone, for all appeared to be on the same social scale, and were dressed in much the same way. The men wore tunics of a saffron colour coming down to the knees, with belts and high boots of a scaly tough material which must have been the hide of some sea beast. The women were beautifully draped in classical style, their flowing robes of every tint of pink and blue and green, ornamented with clusters of pearl or opalescent sheets of shell. Many of them were lovely beyond any earthly comparison. There was one—but why should I mix my private feelings up with this public narrative? Let me say only that Mona is the only daughter of Scarpa, one of the leaders of the people, and that from that first day of meeting I read in her dark eyes a message of sympathy and of understanding which went home to my heart, as my gratitude and admiration may have gone to hers. I need not say more at present about this exquisite lady. Suffice it that a new and strong influence had come into my life. When I saw Maracot gesticulating with unwonted animation to one kindly lady, while Scanlan stood conveying his admiration in pantomime in the centre of a group of laughing girls, I realized that my companions also had begun to find that there was a lighter side to our tragic position. If we were dead to the world we had at least found a life beyond, which promised some compensation for what we had lost.

Later in the day we were guided by Manda and other friends round some portions of the immense building. It had been so embedded in the sea-floor by the accumulations of ages that it was only through the roof that it could be entered, and from this point the passages led down and down until the floor level was reached several hundred feet below the entrance chamber. The floor in turn had been excavated, and we saw in all directions passages which sloped downwards into the bowels of the earth. We were shown the air-making apparatus with the pumps which circulated it through the building. Maracot pointed out with wonder and admiration that not only was the oxygen united with the nitrogen, but that smaller retorts supplied other gases which could only be the argon, neon, and other little-known constituents of the atmosphere which we are only just beginning to understand. The distilling vats for making fresh water and the enormous electrical instalments were other objects of interest, but much of the machinery was so intricate that it was difficult for us to follow the details. I can only say that I saw with my own eyes, and tested with my own palate, that chemicals in gaseous and liquid forms were poured into various machines, that they were treated by heat, by pressure, and by electricity, and that flour, tea, coffee, or wine was collected as the product.

There was one consideration which was very quickly forced upon us by our examination on various occasions, of as much of this building as was open to our inspection. This was that the exposure to the sea had been foreseen and the protection against the inrush of the water had been prepared long before the land sank beneath the waves. Of course, it stood to reason, and needed no proof, that such precautions could not have been taken after the event, but we were witnesses now of the signs that the whole great building had from the first been constructed with the one idea of being an enduring ark of refuge. The huge retorts and vats in which the air, the food, the distilled water, and the other necessary products were made were all built into the walls, and were evidently integral parts of the original construction. So, too, with the exit chambers, the silica works where the vitrine bells were constructed, and the huge pumps which controlled the water. Every one of these things had been prepared by the skill and the foresight of that wonderful far-away people who seemed, from what we could learn, to have thrown out one arm to Central America and one to Egypt, and so left traces of themselves even upon this earth when their own land went down into the Atlantic. As to these, their descendants, we judged that they had probably degenerated, as was but natural, and that at the most they had been stagnant and only preserved some of the science and knowledge of their ancestors without having the energy to add to it. They possessed wonderful powers and yet seemed to us to be strangely wanting in initiative, and had added nothing to that wonderful legacy which they had inherited. I am sure that Maracot, using this knowledge, would very soon have attained greater results. As to Scanlan, with his quick brain and mechanical skill, he was continually putting in touches which probably seemed as remarkable to them as their powers to us. He had a beloved mouth-organ in his coat-pocket when we made our descent, and his use of this was a perpetual joy to our companions, who sat around in entranced groups, as we might listen to a Mozart, while he handed out to them the crooning coon songs of his native land.

I have said that the whole building was not open to our inspection, and I might give a little further detail upon that subject. There was one well-worn corridor down which we saw folk continually passing, but which was always avoided by our guides in our excursions. As was natural our curiosity was aroused, and we determined one evening that we would take a chance and do a little exploring upon our own account. We slipped out of our room, therefore, and made our way to the unknown quarter at a time when few people were about.

The passage led us to a high arched door, which appeared to be made of solid gold. When we pushed it open we found ourselves in a huge room, forming a square of not less than two hundred feet. All around the walls were painted with vivid colours and adorned with extraordinary pictures and statues of grotesque creatures with enormous headdresses, like the full-dress regalia of our American Indians. At the end of this great hall there was one huge seated figure, the legs crossed like a Buddha, but with none of the benignity of aspect which is seen on the Buddha's placid features. On the contrary, this was a creature of wrath, open-mouthed and fierce-eyed; the latter being red, and their effect exaggerated by two electric lights which shone through them. On his lap was a great oven, which we observed, as we approached it, to be filled with ashes.

"Moloch!" said Maracot. "Moloch or Baal—the old god of the Phoenician races."

"Good heavens!" I cried, with recollections of old Carthage before me. "Don't tell me that these gentle folk could go in for human sacrifice."

"Look it here, Bo!" said Scanlan anxiously, "I hope they keep it in the family, anyhow. We don't want them to pull no such dope on us."

"No, I guess they have learned their lesson," said I. "It's misfortune that teaches folk to have pity for others."

"That's right," Maracot remarked, poking about among the ashes, "it is the old hereditary god, but it is surely a gentler cult. These are burned loaves and the like. But perhaps there was a time——"

But our speculations were interrupted by a stern voice at our elbows, and we found several men in yellow garments and high hats, who were clearly the priests of the Temple. From the expression on their faces I should judge that we were very near to being the last victims to Baal, and one of them had actually drawn a knife from his girdle. With fierce gestures and cries they drove us roughly out of their sacred shrine.

"By gosh!" cried Scanlan. "I'll sock that duck if he keeps crowding me! Look it here, you Bindlestiff, keep your hands off my coat."

For a moment I feared that we should have had what Scanlan called a "rough house" within the sacred precincts. However, we got the angry mechanic away without blows and regained the shelter of our room, but we could tell from the demeanour of Manda and others of our friends that our escapade was known and resented.

But there was another shrine which was freely shown to us and which had a very unexpected result, for it opened up a slow and imperfect method of communication between our companions and ourselves. This was a room in the lower quarter of the Temple, with no decorations or distinction save that at one end there stood a statue of ivory yellow with age, representing a woman holding a spear with an owl perched upon her shoulder. A very old man was the guardian of the room, and in spite of his age it was clear to us that he was of a very different race, and one of a finer, larger type than the men of the Temple. As we stood gazing at the ivory statue, Maracot and I, both wondering where we had seen something like it, the old man addressed us.

"Thea," said he, pointing to the figure.

"By George!" I cried. "He is speaking Greek."

"Thea! Athena!" repeated the man.

There was not a doubt of it. "Goddess—Athena," the words were unmistakable. Maracot, whose wonderful brain had absorbed something from every branch of human knowledge, began at once to ask questions in classical Greek which were only partly understood and were answered in a dialect so archaic that it was almost incomprehensible. Still, he acquired some knowledge, and he found an intermediary through whom he could dimly convey something to our companions.

"It is a remarkable proof," said Maracot that evening, in his high neighing voice and in the tones of one addressing a large class, "of the reliability of legend. There is always a basis of fact even if in the course of the years it should become distorted. You are aware—or probably you are not aware"—("Bet your life!" from Scanlan)—"that a war was going on between the primitive Greeks and the Atlanteans at the time of the destruction of the great island. The fact is recorded in Solon's description of what he learned from the priests of Sais. We may conjecture that there were Greek prisoners in the hands of the Atlanteans at the time, that some of them were in the service of the Temple, and that they carried their own religion with them. That man was, so far as I could understand, the old hereditary priest of the cult, and perhaps when we know more we shall see something of these ancient people."

"Well, I hand it to them for good sense," said Scanlan. "I guess if you want a plaster god it is better to have a fine woman than that blatherskite with the red eyes and the coal-bunker on his knees."

"Lucky they can't understand your views," I remarked. "If they did you might end up as a Christian martyr."

"Not so long as I can play them jazz," he answered. "I guess they've got used to me now, and they couldn't do without me."

They were a cheerful crowd, and it was a happy life, but there were and are times when one's whole heart goes out to the homelands which we have lost, and visions of the dear old quadrangles of Oxford, or of the ancient elms and the familiar campus of Harvard, came up before my mind. In those early days they seemed as far from me as some landscape in the moon, and only now in a dim uncertain fashion does the hope of seeing them once more begin to grow in my soul.

CHAPTER IV: It was a few days after our arrival that our hosts or our captors—we were dubious sometimes as to which to call them—took us out for an expedition upon the bottom of the ocean. Six of them came with us, including Manda, the chief. We assembled in the same exit chamber in which we had originally been received, and we were now in a condition to examine it a little more closely. It was a very large place, at least a hundred feet each way, and its low walls and ceiling were green with marine growths and dripping with moisture. A long row of pegs, with marks which I presume were numbers, ran round the whole room, and on each was hung one of the semitransparent bells of vitrine and a pair of the shoulder batteries which ensured respiration. The floor was of flagged stone worn into concavities, the footsteps of many generations, these hollows now lying as pools of shallow water. The whole was highly illuminated by fluor tubes round the cornice. We were fastened into our vitrine coverings, and a stout pointed staff made of some light metal was handed to each of us. Then, by signals, Manda ordered us to take a grip of a rail which ran round the room, he and his friends setting us an example. The object of this soon became evident, for as the outer door swung slowly open the sea water came pouring in with such force that we should have been swept from our feet but for this precaution. It rose rapidly, however, to above the level of our heads, and the pressure upon us was eased. Manda led the way to the door, and an instant afterwards we were out on the ocean bed once more, leaving the portal open behind us ready for our return.

Looking round us in the cold, flickering, spectral light which illuminates the bathybian plain, we could see for a radius of at least a quarter of a mile in every direction. What amazed us was to observe, on the very limit of what was visible, a very brilliant glow of radiance. It was towards this that our leader turned his steps, our party walking in single file behind him. It was slow going, for there was the resistance of the water, and our feet were buried deeply in the soft slush with every step; but soon we were able to see clearly what the beacon was which had attracted us. It was our own shell, our last reminder of terrestrial life, which lay tilted upon one of the cupolas of the far-flung building, with all its lights still blazing. It was three quarters full of water, but the imprisoned air still preserved that portion in which our electric instalment lay. It was strange indeed as we gazed into it to see the familiar interior with our settees and instruments still in position, while several good-sized fish like minnows in a bottle swam round and round inside it. One after the other our party clambered in through the open flap, Maracot to rescue a book of notes which floated on the surface, Scanlan and I to pick up some personal belongings. Manda came also with one or two of his comrades, examining with the greatest interest the bathometer and thermometer with the other instruments which were attached to the wall. The latter we detached and took away with us. It may interest scientists to know that forty degrees Fahrenheit represents the temperature at the greatest sea depth to which man has ever descended, and that it is higher, on account of the chemical decomposition of the ooze, than the upper strata of the sea.

Our little expedition had, it seems, a definite object besides that of allowing us a little exercise upon the bed of the ocean. We were hunting for food. Every now and then I saw our comrades strike sharply down with their pointed sticks, impaling each time a large brown flat fish, not unlike a turbot, which was numerous, but lay so closely in the ooze that it took practised eyes to detect it. Soon each of the little men had two or three of these dangling at his side. Scanlan and I soon got the knack of it, and captured a couple each, but Maracot walked as one in a dream, quite lost in his wonder at the ocean beauties around him and making long and excited speeches which were lost to the ear, but visible to the eyes from the contortion of his features.

Our first impression had been one of monotony, but we soon found that the grey plains were broken up into varied formations by the action of the deep-sea currents which flowed like submarine rivers across them. These streams cut channels in the soft slime and exposed the beds which lay beneath. The floor of these banks consisted of the red clay which forms the base of all things on the surface of the bed of the ocean, and they were thickly studded with white objects which I imagined to be shells, but which proved, when we examined them, to be the ear bones of whales and the teeth of sharks and other sea monsters. One of these teeth which I picked up was fifteen inches long, and we could but be thankful that so fearful a monster frequented the higher levels of ocean. It belonged, according to Maracot, to a giant killing grampus or Orca gladiator. It recalled the observation of Mitchell Hedges that even the most terrible sharks that he had caught bore upon their bodies the marks which showed that they had encountered creatures larger and more formidable than themselves.

There was one peculiarity of the ocean depths which impresses itself upon the observer. There is, as I have said, a constant cold light rising up from the slow phosphorescent decay of the great masses of organic matter. But above, all is black as night. The effect is that of a dim winter day, with a heavy black thundercloud lying low above the earth. Out of this black canopy there falls slowly an incessant snowstorm of tiny white flakes, which glimmer against the sombre background. These are the shells of sea snails and other small creatures who live and die in the five miles of water which separate us from the surface, and though many of these are dissolved as they fall and add to the lime salts in the ocean, the rest go in the course of ages to form that deposit which had entombed the great city in the upper part of which we now dwelt.

Leaving our last link with earth beneath us, we pushed on into the gloom of the submarine world and soon we were met by a completely new development. A moving patch appeared in front of us, which broke up as we approached it into a crowd of men, each in his vitrine envelope, who were dragging behind them broad sledges heaped with coal. It was heavy work, and the poor devils were bending and straining, tugging hard at the shark-skin ropes which served as traces. With each gang of men there was one who appeared to be in authority, and it interested us to see that the leaders and the workers were clearly of a different race. The latter were tall men, fair, with blue eyes and powerful bodies. The others were, as already described, dark and almost negroid, with squat, broad frames. We could not inquire into the mystery at that moment, but the impression was left upon my mind that the one race represented the hereditary slaves of the other, and Maracot was of opinion that they may have been the descendants of those Greek prisoners whose goddess we had seen in the Temple.

Several droves of these men, each drawing its loads of coal, were met by us before we came to the mine itself. At this point the deep-sea deposits and the sandy formations which lay beneath them had been cut away, and a great pit exposed, which consisted of alternate layers of clay and coal, representing strata in the old perished world of long ago which now lay at the bottom of the Atlantic. At the various levels of this huge excavation we could see gangs of men at work hewing the coal, while others gathered it into loads and placed it in baskets, by means of which it was hoisted up to the level above. The whole mine was on so vast a scale that we could not see the other side of the enormous pit which so many generations of workers had scooped in the bed of the ocean. This, then, transmuted into electric force, was the source of the motive power by which the whole machinery of Atlantis was run. It is interesting, by the way, to record that the name of the old city had been correctly preserved in the legends, for when we had mentioned it to Manda and others they first looked greatly surprised that we should know it, and then nodded their heads vigorously to show that they understood.

Passing the great coal pit—or, rather, branching away from it to the right—we came on a line of low cliffs of basalt, their surface as clear and shining as on the day when they were shot up from the bowels of the earth, while their summit, some hundreds of feet above us, loomed up against the dark background. The base of these volcanic cliffs was draped in a deep jungle of high seaweed, growing out of tangled masses of crinoid corals laid down in the old terrestrial days. Along the edge of this thick undergrowth we wandered for some time, our companions beating it with their sticks and driving out for our amusement an extraordinary assortment of strange fishes and crustacea, now and again securing a specimen for their own tables. For a mile or more we wandered along in this happy fashion, when I saw Manda stop suddenly and look round him with gestures of alarm and surprise. These submarine gestures formed a language in themselves, for in a moment his companions understood the cause of his trouble, and then with a shock we realized it also. Dr. Maracot had disappeared.

He had certainly been with us at the coal pit, and he had come as far as the basalt cliffs. It was inconceivable that he had got ahead of us, so it was evident that he must be somewhere along the line of jungle in our rear. Though our friends were disturbed, Scanlan and I, who knew something of the good man's absent-minded eccentricities, were confident that there was no cause for alarm, and that we should soon find him loitering over some sea form which had attracted him. We all turned to retrace our steps, and had hardly gone a hundred yards before we caught sight of him.

But he was running—running with an agility which I should have thought impossible for a man of his habits. Even the least athletic can run, however, when fear is the pace-maker. His hands were outstretched for help, and he stumbled and blundered forward with clumsy energy. He had good cause to exert himself, for three horrible creatures were close at his heels. They were tiger crabs, striped black and white, each about the size of a Newfoundland dog. Fortunately they were themselves not very swift travellers, and were scurrying along the soft sea bottom in a curious side-long fashion which was little faster than that of the terrified fugitive.

Their wind was better, however, and they would probably have had their horrible claws upon him in a very few minutes had not our friends intervened. They dashed forward with their pointed sticks, and Manda flashed a powerful electric lantern, which he carried in his belt, in the faces of the loathsome monsters, who scuttled into the jungle and were lost to view. Our comrade sat down on a lump of coral and his face showed that he was exhausted by his adventure. He told us afterwards that he had penetrated the jungle in the hope of securing what seemed to him to be a rare specimen of the deep-sea Chimœra, and that he had blundered into the nest of these fierce tiger crabs, who had instantly dashed after him. It was only after a long rest that he was able to resume the journey.

Our next stage after skirting the basalt cliffs led us to our goal. The grey plain in front of us was covered at this point by irregular hummocks and tall projections, which told us that the great city of old lay beneath it. It would all have been completely buried forever by the ooze, as Herculaneum has been by lava or Pompeii by ashes, had an entrance to it not been excavated by the survivors of the Temple. This entrance was a long, downward cutting, which ended up in a broad street with buildings exposed on either side. The walls of these buildings were occasionally cracked and shattered, for they were not of the solid construction which had preserved the Temple, but the interiors were in most cases exactly as they had been when the catastrophe occurred, save the sea changes of all sorts, beautiful and rare in some cases and horrifying in others, had modified the appearances of the rooms. Our guides did not encourage us to examine the first ones which we reached, but hurried us onwards until we came to that which had clearly been the great central citadel or palace round which the whole town centred. The pillars and columns and vast sculptured cornices and friezes and staircases of this building exceeded anything which I have ever seen upon earth. Its nearest approach seemed to me to be the remains of the Temple of Karnak at Luxor in Egypt, and, strange to say, the decorations and half-effaced engravings resembled in detail those of the great ruin beside the Nile, and the lotus-shaped capitals of the columns were the same. It was an amazing experience to stand in the marble tessellated floors of those vast halls, with great statues looming high above one on every side, and to see, as we saw that day, huge silvery eels gliding above our heads and frightened fish darting away in every direction from the light which was projected before us. From room to room we wandered, marking every sign of luxury and occasionally of that lascivious folly which is said, by the lingering legend, to have drawn God's curse upon the people. One small room was wonderfully enamelled with mother-of-pearl, so that even now it gleamed with brilliant opalescent tints when the light played across it. An ornamented platform of yellow metal and a similar couch lay in one corner, and one felt that it may well have been the bedchamber of a queen, but beside the couch there lay now a loathsome black squid, its foul body rising and falling in a slow, stealthy rhythm so that it seemed like some evil heart which still beat in the very centre of the wicked palace. I was glad, and so, I learned, were my companions, when our guides led the way out once more, glancing for a moment at a ruined amphitheatre and again at a pier with a lighthouse at the end, which showed that the city had been a seaport. Soon we had emerged from these places of ill omen and were out on the familiar bathybian plain once more.

Our adventures were not quite over, for there was one more which was as alarming to our companions as to ourselves. We had nearly made our way home when one of our guides pointed upwards with alarm. Gazing in that direction we saw an extraordinary sight. Out of the black gloom of the waters a huge, dark figure was emerging, falling rapidly downwards. At first it seemed a shapeless mass, but as it came more clearly into the light we could see that it was the dead body of a monstrous fish, which had burst so that the entrails were streaming up behind it as it fell. No doubt the gases had buoyed it up in the higher reaches of the ocean until, having been released by putrefaction or by the ravages of sharks, there was nothing left but dead weight, which sent it hurtling down to the bottom of the sea. Already in our walk we had observed several of these great skeletons picked clean by the fish, but this creature was still, save for its disembowelment, even as it had lived. Our guides seized us with the intention of dragging us out of the path of the falling mass, but presently they were reassured and stood still, for it was clear that it would miss us. Our vitrine helmets prevented our hearing the thud, but it must have been prodigious when that huge body struck the floor of the ocean, and we saw the Globigerina ooze fly upwards as the mud splashes when a heavy stone is hurled into it. It was a sperm whale, some seventy feet long, and from the excited and joyful gestures of the submarine folk I gathered that they would find plenty of use for the spermaceti and the fat. For the moment, however, we left the derelict creature, and with joyful hearts, for we unpractised visitors were weary and aching, found ourselves once more in front of the engraved portal of the roof, and finally standing safe and sound, divested of our vitrine bells, on the sloppy floor of the entrance chamber.

A few days—as we reckon time—after the occasion when we had given the community a cinema view of our own proceedings, we were present at a very much more solemn and august exhibition of the same sort, which gave us in a clear and wonderful way the past history of this remarkable people. I cannot flatter myself that it was given entirely on our behalf, for I rather think that the events were publicly rehearsed from time to time in order to carry on the record, and that the part to which we were admitted was only some intermezzo of a long religious ceremony. However that may be, I will describe it exactly as it occurred.

We were led to the same great hall or theatre where Dr. Maracot had thrown our own adventures upon the screen. There the whole community

was assembled, and we were given, as before, places of honour in front of
the great luminous screen. Then, after a long song, which may have been
some sort of patriotic chant, a very old white-haired man, the historian
or chronicler of the nation, advanced amid much applause to the focus
point and threw upon the bright surface before him a series of pictures
to represent the rise and fall of his own people. I wish I could convey to
you their vividness and drama. My two companions and I lost all sense
of time and place, so absorbed were we in the contemplation, while the
audience was moved to its depths, and groaned or wept as the tragedy
unfolded, which depicted the ruin of their fatherland, the destruction of
their race.

In the first series of scenes we saw the old continent in its glory, as its
memory had been handed down by these historical records passed from
fathers to sons. We had a bird's-eye view of a glorious rolling country,
enormous in extent, well watered and cleverly irrigated, with great fields
of grain, waving orchards, lovely streams and woody hills, still lakes and
occasional picturesque mountains. It was studded with villages and
covered with farmhouses and beautiful private residences. Then our attention was carried to the capital, a wonderful and gorgeous city upon
the seashore, the harbour crammed with galleys, her quays piled with
merchandise, and her safety assured by high walls with towering battlements and circular moats, all on the most gigantic scale. The houses
stretched inland for many miles, and in the centre of the city was a
crenellated castle or citadel, so widespread and commanding that it was
like some creation of a dream. We were then shown the faces of those
who lived in that golden age, wise and venerable old men, virile warriors,
saintly priests, beautiful and dignified women, lovely children, an apotheosis of the human race.

Then came pictures of another sort. We saw wars, constant wars, war by
land and war by sea. We saw naked and defenceless races trampled down
and overridden by great chariots or the rush of mailed horsemen. We saw
treasures heaped upon the victors, but even as the riches increased the
faces upon the screen became more animal and more cruel. Down, down
they sank from one generation to another. We were shown signs of
lascivious dissipation or moral degeneracy, of the accretion of matter and
decline of spirit. Brutal sports at the expense of others had taken the
place of the manly exercises of old. There was no longer the quiet and
simple family life, nor the cultivation of the mind, but we had a glimpse
of a people who were restless and shallow, rushing from one pursuit to
another, grasping ever at pleasure, forever missing it, and yet imagining
always that in some more complex and unnatural form it might still be
found. There had arisen on the one hand an over-rich class who sought
only sensual gratification, and on the other hand an over-poor residue

whose whole function in life was to minister to the wants of their masters, however evil those wants might be.

And now once again a new note was struck. There were reformers at work who were trying to turn the nation from its evil ways, and to direct it back into those higher paths which it had forsaken. We saw them, grave and earnest men, reasoning and pleading with the people, but we saw them scorned and jeered at by those whom they were trying to save. Especially we could see that it was the priests of Baal, priests who had gradually allowed forms and show and outward ceremonies to take the place of unselfish spiritual development, who led the opposition to the reformers. But the latter were not to be bullied or browbeaten. They continued to try for the salvation of the people, and their faces assumed a graver and even a terror-inspiring aspect, as those of men who had a fearsome warning to give which was like some dreadful vision before their own minds. Of their auditors some few seemed to heed and be terrified at the words, but others turned away laughing and plunged ever deeper into their morass of sin. There came a time at last when the reformers turned away also as men who could do no more, and left this degenerate people to its fate.

Then we saw a strange sight. There was one reformer, a man of singular strength of mind and body, who gave a lead to all the others. He had wealth and influence and powers, which latter seemed to be not entirely of this earth. We saw him in what seemed to be a trance, communing with higher spirits. It was he who brought all the science of his land—science which far outshone anything known by us moderns—to the task of building an ark of refuge against the coming troubles. We saw myriads of workmen at work, and the walls rising while crowds of careless citizens looked on and made merry at such elaborate and useless precautions. We saw others who seemed to reason with him and to say to him that if he had fears it would be easier for him to fly to some safer land. His answer, so far as we could follow it, was that there were some who must be saved at the last moment, and that for their sakes he must remain in the new Temple of safety. Meanwhile, he collected in it those who had followed him, and he held them there, for he did not himself know the day nor the hour, though forces beyond mortal had assured him of the coming fact. So when the ark was ready and the water-tight doors were finished and tested, he waited upon doom, with his family, his friends, his followers, and his servants.

And doom came. It was a terrible thing even in a picture. God knows what it could be like in reality. We first saw a huge sleek mountain of water rise to an incredible height out of a calm ocean. Then we saw it travel, sweeping on and on, mile after mile, a great glistening hill, topped with foam, at an ever-increasing rate. Two little chips tossing among the snowy fringe upon the summit became, as the wave rolled towards us, a couple of shattered galleys. Then we saw it strike the shore and sweep over the city, while the houses went down before it like a field of corn before a tornado. We saw the folk upon the house-tops glaring out at the approaching death, their faces twisted with horror, their eyes staring, their mouths contorted, gnawing at their hands and gibbering in an insanity of terror. The very men and women who had mocked at the warning were now screaming to Heaven for mercy, grovelling with their faces on the ground, or kneeling with frenzied arms raised in wild appeal. There was no time now to reach the ark, which stood beyond the city, but thousands dashed up to the Citadel, which stood upon higher ground, and the battlement walls were black with people. Then suddenly the Castle began to sink. Everything began to sink. The water had poured down into the remote recesses of the earth, the central fires had expanded it into steam, and the very foundations of the land were blown apart. Down went the city and ever down, while a cry went up from ourselves and the audience at the terrible sight. The pier broke in two and vanished. The high Pharus collapsed under the waves. The roofs looked for a while like successive reefs of rock forming lines of spouting breakers until they, too, went under. The Citadel was left alone upon the surface, like some monstrous ship, and then it also slid sideways down into the abyss, with a fringe of helpless waving hands upon its summit. The awful drama was over, and an unbroken sea lay across the whole continent, a sea which bore no life upon it, but which among its huge smoking swirls and eddies showed all the wrack of the tragedy tossed hither and thither, dead men and animals, chairs, tables, articles of clothing, floating hats and bales of goods, all bobbing and heaving in one huge liquid fermentation. Slowly we saw it die away, and a great wide expanse as smooth and bright as quicksilver, with a murky sun low on the horizon, showed us the grave of the land that God had weighed and found wanting.

The story was complete. We could ask for no more, since our own brains and imagination could supply the rest. We realized the slow, remorseless descent of that great land lower and lower into the abyss of the ocean amid volcanic convulsions which threw up submarine peaks around it. We saw it in our mind's eye stretched out, over miles of what was now the bed of the Atlantic, the shattered city lying alongside of the ark of refuge in which the handful of nerve-shattered survivors were assembled. And then finally we understood how these had carried on their lives, how they had used the various devices with which the foresight and science of their great leader had endowed them, how he had taught them all his arts before he passed away, and how some fifty or sixty survivors had grown now into a large community, which had to dig its way into the bowels of the earth in order to get room to expand. No library of information could make it clearer than that series of pictures and the inferences which we could draw from them. Such was the fate, and such the causes of the fate, which overwhelmed the great land of Atlantis. Some day far distant, when this bathybian ooze has turned to chalk, this great city will be thrown up once more by some fresh expiration of Nature, and the geologist of the future, delving in the quarry, will exhume nor flints nor shells, but the remains of a vanished civilization and the traces of an old-world catastrophe.

Only one point had remained undecided, and that was the length of time since the tragedy had occurred. Dr. Maracot discovered a rough method of making an estimate. Among the many annexes of the great building there was one huge vault, which was the burial-place of the chiefs. As in Egypt and in Yucatan, the practice of mummifying had been usual, and in niches in the walls there were endless rows of these grim relics of the past. Manda pointed proudly to the next one in the succession, and gave us to understand that it was specially arranged for himself.

"If you take an average of the European kings," said Maracot, in his best professorial manner, "you will find that they run to about five in the century. We may adopt the same figure here. We cannot hope for scientific accuracy, but it will give us an approximation. I have counted the mummies, and they are four hundred in number."

"Then it would be eight thousand years?"

"Exactly. And this agrees to some extent with Plato's estimate. It certainly occurred before the Egyptian written records begin, and they go back between six and seven thousand years from the present date. Yes, I think we may say that our eyes have seen the reproduction of a tragedy which occurred at least eight thousand years ago. But, of course, to build up such a civilization as we see the traces of must in itself have taken many thousands of years.

"Thus," he concluded—and I pass the claim on to you—"we have extended the horizon of ascertained human history as no men have ever done since history began."

CHAPTER V: It was about a month, according to our calculations, after our visit to the buried city that the most amazing and unexpected thing of all occurred. We had thought by this time that we were immune to shocks and that nothing new could really stagger us, but this actual fact went far beyond anything for which our imagination might have prepared us.

It was Scanlan who brought the news that something momentous had happened. You must realize that by this time we were, to some extent, at home in the great building; that we knew where the common rest rooms and recreation rooms were situated; that we attended concerts (their music was very strange and elaborate) and theatrical entertainments, where the unintelligible words were translated by very vivid and dramatic gestures; and that, speaking generally, we were part of the community. We visited various families in their own private rooms, and our lives—I can speak for my own, at any rate—were made the brighter by the glamour of these strange people, especially of that one dear young lady whose name I have already mentioned. Mona was the daughter of one of the leaders of the tribe, and I found in his family a warm and kindly welcome which rose above all differences of race or language. When it comes to the most tender language of all, I did not find that there was so much between old Atlantis and modern America. I guess that what would please a Massachusetts girl of Brown's College is just about what would please my lady under the waves.

But I must get back to the fact that Scanlan came into our room with news of some great happening.

"Say, there is one of them just blown in, and he's that excited that he clean forgot to take his glass lid off, and he was jabbering for some minutes before he understood that no one could hear him. Then it was Blah Blah Blah as long as his breath would hold, and they are all following him now to the jumping-off place. It's me for the water, for there is sure something worth our seeing."

Running out, we found our friends all hurrying down the corridor with excited gestures, and we, joining the procession, soon formed part of the crowd who were hurrying across the sea bottom, led by the excited messenger. They drove along at a rate which made it no easy matter for us to keep up, but they carried their electric lanterns with them, and even though we fell behind we were able to follow the gleam. The route lay as before, along the base of the basalt cliffs until we came to a spot where a set of steps, concave from long usage, led up to the top. Ascending these, we found ourselves in broken country, with many jagged pinnacles of rock and deep crevasses which made it difficult travelling. Emerging from this tangle of ancient lava, we came out on a circular plain, brilliant in the phosphorescent light, and there in the very centre of it lay an object which set me gasping. As I looked at my companions I could see from their amazed expression how fully they shared my emotion.

Half embedded in the slime there lay a good-sized steamer. It was tilted upon its side, the funnel had broken and was hanging at a strange angle, and the foremast had snapped short off, but otherwise the vessel was intact and as clean and fresh as if she had just left the dock. We hurried towards her and found ourselves under the stern. You can imagine how we felt when we read the name "*Stratford*, London." Our ship had followed ourselves into the Maracot Deep.

Of course, after the first shock the affair did not seem so incomprehensible. We remembered the falling glass, the reefed sails of the experienced Norwegian skipper, the strange black cloud upon the horizon. Clearly there had been a sudden cyclone of phenomenal severity and the *Stratford* had been blown over. It was too evident that all her people were dead, for most of the boats were trailing in different states of destruction from the davits, and in any case what boat could live in such a hurricane? The tragedy had occurred, no doubt, within an hour or two of our own disaster. Perhaps the sounding-line which we had seen had only just been wound in before the blow fell. It was terrible, but whimsical, that we should be still alive, while those who were mourning our destruction had themselves been destroyed. We had no means of telling whether the ship had drifted in the upper levels of the ocean or whether she had lain for some time where we found her before she was discovered by the Atlantean.

Poor Howie, the captain, or what was left of him, was still at his post upon the bridge, the rail grasped firmly in his stiffened hands. His body and that of three stokers in the engine-room were the only ones which had sunk with the ship. They were each removed under our direction and buried under the ooze with a wreath of seaflowers over their remains. I give this detail in the hope that it may be some comfort to Mrs. Howie in her bereavement. The names of the stokers were unknown to us.

Whilst we had been performing this duty the little men had swarmed over the ship. Looking up, we saw them everywhere, like mice upon a cheese. Their excitement and curiosity made it clear to us that it was the first modern ship—possibly the first steamer—which had ever come down to them. We found out later that their oxygen apparatus inside their vitrine bells would not allow of a longer absence from the recharging station than a few hours, and so their chances of learning anything of what was on the sea bed were limited to so many miles from their central base. They set to work at once breaking up the wreck and removing all that would be of use to them, a very long process, which is hardly accomplished yet. We were glad also to make our way to our cabins and to get many of those articles of clothing and books which were not ruined beyond redemption.

Among the other things which we rescued from the *Stratford* was the ship's log, which had been written up to the last day by the captain in view of our own catastrophe. It was strange indeed that we should be reading it and that he should be dead. The day's entry ran thus:

Oct. 3. The three brave but foolhardy adventurers have to-day, against my will and advice, descended in their apparatus to the bottom of the ocean, and the accident which I had foreseen has occurred. God rest their souls. They went down at eleven A.M. *and I had some doubts about permitting them, as a squall seemed to be coming up. I would that I had acted upon my impulse, but it would only have postponed the inevitable tragedy. I bade each of them farewell with the conviction that I would see them no more. For a time all was well, and at eleven-forty-five they had reached a depth of three hundred fathoms, where they had found bottom. Dr. Maracot sent several messages to me and all seemed to be in order, when suddenly I heard his voice in agitation, and there was considerable agitation of the wire hawser. An instant later it snapped. It would appear that they were by this time over a deep chasm, for at the Doctor's request the ship had steamed very slowly forwards. The air tubes continued to run out for a distance which I should estimate at half a mile, and then they also snapped. It is the last which we can ever hope to hear of Dr. Maracot, Mr. Headley, or Mr. Scanlan.*

And yet a most extraordinary thing must be recorded, the meaning of which I have not had time to weigh, for with this foul weather coming up there is much to distract me. A deep-sea sounding was taken at the same time, and the depth recorded was twenty-six thousand six hundred feet. The weight was, of course, left at the bottom, but the wire has just been drawn in and, incredible as it may seem, above the porcelain sample cup there was found Mr. Headley's handkerchief with his name marked upon it. The ship's company are all amazed, and no one can suggest how such a thing could have occurred. In my next entry I may have more to say about this. We have lingered a few hours in the hope of something coming to the surface, and we have pulled up the hawser, which shows a jagged end. Now I must look to the ship, for I have never seen a worse sky and the barometer is at 28.5 and sinking fast.

So it was that we got the final news of our former companions. A terrific cyclone must have struck her and destroyed her immediately afterwards.

We stayed at the wreck until a certain stuffiness within our vitrine bells and a feeling of increasing weight upon our chests warned us that it was high time to begin our return. Then it was, on our homeward journey, that we had an adventure which showed us the sudden dangers to which these submarine folk are exposed, and which may explain why their numbers, in spite of the lapse of time, were not greater than they were. Including the Grecian slaves we cannot reckon those numbers at more than four or five thousand at the most. We had descended the staircase and were making our way along the edge of the jungle which skirts the basalt cliffs, when Manda pointed excitedly upwards and beckoned furiously to one of our party who was some distance out in the open. At the same time he and those around him ran to the side of some high boulders, pulling us along with them. It was only when we were in their shelter that we saw the cause of the alarm. Some distance above us, but descending rapidly, was a huge fish of a most peculiar shape. It might have been a great floating feather bed, soft and bulging, with a white undersurface and a long red fringe, the vibration of which propelled it through the water. It appeared to have neither mouth nor eyes, but it soon showed that it was formidably alert. The member of our party who was out in the open ran for the same shelter that we had taken, but he was too late. I saw his face convulsed with terror as he realized his fate. The horrible creature descended upon him, enveloped him on all sides, and lay upon him, pulsing in a dreadful way as if it were thrusting his body against the coral rocks and grinding it to pieces. The tragedy was taking place within a few yards of us, and yet our companions were so overcome by the suddenness of it that they seemed to be bereft of all power of action. It was Scanlan who rushed out and, jumping on the creature's broad back, blotched with red and brown markings, dug the sharp end of his metal staff into its soft tissues.

I had followed Scanlan's example, and finally Maracot and all of them attacked the monster, which glided slowly off, leaving a trail of oily and glutinous excretion behind it. Our help had come too late, however, for the impact of the great fish had broken the vitrine bell of the Atlantean and he had been drowned. It was a day of mourning when we carried his body back into the Refuge, but it was also a day of triumph for us, for our prompt action had raised us greatly in the estimation of our companions. As to the strange fish, we had Dr. Maracot's assurance that it was a specimen of the blanket fish, well known to ichthyologists, but of a size such as had never entered into his dreams.

I speak of this creature because it chanced to bring about a tragedy, but I could, and perhaps will, write a book upon the wonderful life which we have seen here. Red and black are the prevailing colours in deep-sea life, while the vegetation is of the palest olive, and is of so tough a fibre that it is seldom dragged up by our trawls, so that Science has come to believe that the bed of the ocean is bare. Many of the marine forms are of surpassing loveliness, and others so grotesque in their horror that they are like the images of delirium and of a danger such as no land animal can rival. I have seen a black stingray thirty feet long with a horrible fang upon its tail, one blow of which would kill any living creature. I have seen, too, a frog-like beast with protruding green eyes, which is simply a gaping mouth with a huge stomach behind it. To meet it is death unless one has an electric flash with which to repel it. I have seen the blind red eel which lies among the rocks and kills by the emission of poison, and I have seen also the giant sea-scorpion, one of the terrors of the deep, and the hag fish, which lurks among the sea jungle.

Once, too, it was my privilege to see the real sea-serpent, a creature which has seldom appeared before the human eye, for it lives in the extreme depths and is seen on the surface only when some submarine convulsion has driven it out of its haunts. Two of them swam, or rather glided, past us one day while Mona and I cowered among the bunches of lamellaria. They were enormous—some ten feet in height and two hundred in length, black above, silver-white below, with a high fringe upon the back, and small eyes no larger than those of an ox. Of these and many other such things an account will be found in the paper of Dr. Maracot, should it ever reach your hands.

Week glided into week in our new life. It had become a very pleasant one, and we were slowly picking up enough of this long-forgotten tongue to enable us to converse a little with our companions. There were endless subjects both for study and for amusement in the Refuge, and already Maracot has mastered so much of the old chemistry that he declares that he can revolutionize all worldly ideas if he can only transmit his knowledge. Among other things they have learned to split the atom, and though the energy released is less than our scientists had anticipated, it is still sufficient to supply them with a great reservoir of power. Their acquaintance with the power and nature of the ether is also far ahead of ours, and indeed that strange translation of thought into pictures, by which we had told them our story and they theirs, was due to an etheric impression translated back into terms of matter.

And yet, in spite of their knowledge, there were points connected with modern scientific developments which had been overlooked by their ancestors.

It was left to Scanlan to demonstrate the fact. For weeks he was in a state of suppressed excitement, bursting with some great secret, and chuckling continually at his own thoughts. We only saw him occasionally during this time, for he was extremely busy and his one friend and confidant was a fat and jovial Atlantean named Berbrix, who was in charge of some of the machinery. Scanlan and Berbrix, though their intercourse was carried on chiefly by signs and mutual back-slapping, had become very close friends, and were now continually closeted together. One evening Scanlan came in radiant.

"Look here, Doc," he said to Maracot. "I've a dope of my own that I want to hand to these folk. They've shown us a thing or two, and I figure that it is up to us to return it. What's the matter with calling them together to-morrow night for a show?"

"Jazz or the Charleston?" I asked.

"Charleston nothing. Wait till you see it. Man, it's the greatest stunt—but there, I won't say a word more. Just this, Bo. I won't let you down, for I've got the goods, and I mean to deliver them."

Accordingly, the community were assembled next evening in the familiar hall. Scanlan and Berbrix were on the platform, beaming with pride. One or other of them touched a button, and then—well, to use Scanlan's own language, "I hand it to him, for he did surprise us some!"

"2L. O. calling," cried a clear voice. "London calling the British Isles. Weather forecast." Then followed the usual sentence about depressions and anticyclones. "First News Bulletin. His Majesty the King this morning opened the new wing of the Children's Hospital in Hammersmith——" and so on and on, in the familiar strain. For the first time we were back in a workaday England once more, plodding bravely through its daily task, with its stout back bowed under its war debts. Then we heard the foreign news, the sporting news. The old world was droning on the same as ever. Our friends the Atlanteans listened in amazement, but without comprehension. When, however, as the first item after the news, the Guards' band struck up the march from *Lohengrin* a positive shout of delight broke from the people, and it was funny to see them rush upon the platform, and turn over the curtains, and look behind the screens to find the source of the music. Yes, we have left our mark forever upon the submarine civilization.

"No, sir," said Scanlan afterwards. "I could not make an issuing station. They have not the material, and I have not the brains. But down at home I rigged a two-valve set of my own with the aërial beside the clothes line in the yard, and I learned to handle it, and to pick up any station in the States. It seemed to me funny if, with all this electricity to hand, and with their glasswork ahead of ours, we couldn't vamp up something that would catch an ether wave, and a wave would sure travel through water just as easy as through air. Old Berbrix nearly threw a fit when we got the first call, but he is wise to it now, and I guess it's a permanent institution."

Among the discoveries of the Atlantean chemists is a gas which is nine times lighter than hydrogen and which Maracot has named levigen. It was his experiments with this which gave us the idea of sending glass balls with information as to our fate to the surface of the ocean.

"I have made Manda understand the idea," said he. "He has given orders to the silica workers, and in a day or two the globes will be ready."

"But how can we get our news inside?" I asked.

"There is a small aperture left through which the gas is inserted. Into this we can push the papers. Then these skilful workers can seal up the hole. I am assured that when we release them they will shoot up to the surface."

"And bob about unseen for a year."

"That might be. But the ball would reflect the sun's rays. It would surely attract attention. We were on the line of shipping between Europe and South America. I see no reason why, if we send several, one at least may not be found."

And this, my dear Talbot, or you others who read this narrative, is how it comes into your hands. But a far more fateful scheme may lie behind it. The idea came from the fertile brain of the American mechanic.

"Say, friends," said he, as we sat alone in our chamber, "it's dandy down here, and the drink is good and the eats are good, and I've met a wren that makes anything in Philadelphia look like two cents, but all the same there are times when I want to feel that I might see God's own country once more."

"We may all feel that way," said I, "but I don't see how you can hope to make it."

"Look it here, Bo! If these balls of gas could carry up our message, maybe they could carry us up also. Don't think I'm joshing, for I've figured it out to rights. We will suppose we put three or four of them together so as to get a good lift. See? Then we have our vitrine bells on and harness ourselves on to the balls. When the bell rings we cut loose and up we go. What is going to stop us between here and the surface?"

"A shark, maybe."

"Blah! Sharks nothing! We would streak past any shark so's he'd hardly know we was there. He'd think we was three flashes of light and we'd get such a lick on that we'd shoot fifty feet up in the air at the other end. I tell you the goof that sees us come up is going to say his prayers over it."

"But, suppose it is possible, what will happen afterwards?"

"For Pete's sake, leave afterwards out of it! Let us chance our luck, or we are here for keeps. It's me for cutting loose and having a dash at it."

"I certainly greatly desire to return to the world, if only to lay our results before the learned societies," said Maracot. "It is only my personal influence which can make them realize the fund of new knowledge which I have acquired. I should be quite in favour of any such attempt as Scanlan has indicated."

There were good reasons, as I will tell later, which made me the least eager of the three.

"It would be perfect madness as you propose it. Unless we had someone expecting us on the surface we should infallibly drift about and perish from hunger and thirst."

"Shucks, man, how could we have someone expecting us?"

"Perhaps even that could be managed," said Maracot. "We can give within a mile or two the exact latitude and longitude of our position."

"And they would let down a ladder," said I, with some bitterness.

"Ladder nothing! The boss is right. See here, Mr. Headley, you put in that letter that you are going to send the universe—my! don't I see the scare lines in the journals!—that we are at 27 North Latitude and 28.14 West Longitude, or whatever other figure is the right one. Got that? Then you say that three of the most important folk in history, the great man of Science, Maracot, and the rising star bug-collector, Headley, and Bob Scanlan, a peach of a mechanic and the pride of Merribank's, are all yellin' and whoopin' for help from the bottom of the sea. Follow my idee?"

"Well, what then?"

"Well, then it's up to them, you see. It's kind of a challenge that they can't forget. Same as I've read of Stanley finding Livingstone and the like. It's for them to find some way to yank us out or to catch us at the other end if we can take the jump ourselves."

"We could suggest the way ourselves," said the Professor. "Let them drop a deep-sea line into these waters and we will look out for it. When it comes we can tie a message to it and bid them stand by for us."

"You've said a mouthful!" cried Bob Scanlan. "That is sure the way to do it."

"And if any lady cared to share our fortunes four would be as easy as three," said Maracot, with a roguish smile at me.

"For that matter, five is as easy as four," said Scanlan. "But you've got it now, Mr. Headley. You write that down, and in six months we shall be back in London River once more."

So now we launch our two balls into that water which is to us what the air is to you. Our two little balloons will go aloft. Will both be lost on the way? It is possible. Or may we hope that one will get through? We leave it on the knees of the gods. If nothing can be done for us, then let those who care for us know that in any case we are safe and happy. If, on the other hand, this suggestion could be carried out and the money and energy for our rescue should be forthcoming, we have given you the means by which it can be done. Meanwhile, good-bye—or is it *au revoir?*

So ended the narrative in the vitrine ball.

The preceding narrative covers the facts so far as they were available when the account was first drawn up. While the script was in the hands of the printer there came an epilogue of the most unexpected and sensational description. I refer to the rescue of the adventurers by Mr. Faverger's steam yacht *Marion* and the account sent out by the wireless transmitter of that vessel, and picked up by the cable station at the Cape de Verde Islands, which has just forwarded it to Europe and America. This account was drawn up by Mr. Key Osborne, the well-known representative of the Associated Press.

It would appear that immediately upon the first narrative of the plight of Dr. Maracot and his friends reaching Europe an expedition was quietly and effectively fitted up in the hope of bringing about a rescue. Mr. Faverger generously placed his famous steam yacht at the disposal of the party, which he accompanied in person. The *Marion* sailed from Cherbourg in June, picked up Mr. Key Osborne and a motion-picture operator at Southampton, and set forth at once for the tract of ocean which was indicated in the original document. This was reached upon the first of July.

A deep-sea piano-wire line was lowered, and was dragged slowly along the bottom of the ocean. At the end of this line, beside the heavy lead, there was suspended a bottle containing a message. The message ran: "Your account has been received by the world, and we are here to help you. We duplicate this message by our wireless transmitter in the hope that it may reach you. We will slowly traverse your region. When you have detached this bottle, please replace your own message in it. We will act upon your instructions."

For two days the *Marion* cruised slowly to and fro without result. On the third a very great surprise awaited the rescue party. A small, highly luminous ball shot out of the water a few hundred yards from the ship, and proved to be a vitreous message-bearer of the sort which had been described in the original document. Having been broken with some difficulty, the following message was read:

Thanks, dear friends. We greatly appreciate your grand loyalty and energy. We receive your wireless messages with facility, and are in a position to answer you in this fashion. We have endeavoured to get possession of your line, but the currents lift it high, and it sweeps along rather faster than even the most active of us can move against the resistance of the water. We propose to make our venture at six to-morrow morning, which should, according to our reckoning, be Tuesday, July 5th. We will come one at a time, so that any advice arising from our experience can be wirelessed back to those who come later. Once again heartfelt thanks.

MARACOT. HEADLEY. SCANLAN.

Mr. Key Osborne now takes up the narrative:

"It was a perfect morning, and the deep sapphire sea lay as smooth as a lake, with the glorious arch of the deep blue sky unbroken by the smallest cloud. The whole crew of the *Marion* was early astir, and awaited events with the most tense interest. As the hour of six drew near our anticipation was painful. A look-out had been placed upon our signal mast, and it was just five minutes to the hour when we heard him shouting, and saw him pointing to the water on our port bow. We all crowded to that side of the deck, and I was able to perch myself on one of the boats from which I had a clear view. I saw through the still water something which looked like a silver bubble ascending with great rapidity from the depths of the ocean. It broke the surface about two hundred yards from the ship, and soared straight up into the air, a beautiful shining globe some three feet in diameter, rising to a great height and then drifting away in some slight current of wind exactly as a toy balloon would do. It was a marvellous sight, but it filled us with apprehension, for it seemed as if the harness might have come loose, and the burden which this tractor should have borne through the waters had been shaken loose upon the way. A wireless was at once dispatched:

" 'Your messenger has appeared close to the vessel. It had nothing attached and has flown away.' Meanwhile we lowered a boat so as to be ready for any development.

"Just after six o'clock there was another signal from our watchman, and an instant later I caught sight of another silver globe, which was swimming up from the depths very much more slowly than the last. On reaching the surface it floated in the air, but its burden was supported upon the water. This burden proved upon examination to be a great bundle of books, papers, and miscellaneous objects all wrapped in a casing of fish skin. It was hoisted dripping upon the deck, and was acknowledged by wireless, while we eagerly awaited the next arrival.

"This was not long in coming. Again the silver bubble, again the breaking of the surface, but this time the glistening ball shot high into the air, suspending under it, to our amazement, the slim figure of a woman. It was but the impetus which had carried her into the air, and an instant later she had been towed to the side of the vessel. A leather circlet had been firmly fastened round the upper curve of the glass ball, and from this long straps depended which were attached to a broad leather belt round her dainty waist. The upper part of her body was covered by a peculiar pear-shaped glass shade—I call it glass, but it was of the same tough light material as the vitreous ball. It was almost transparent, with silvery veins running through its substance. This glass covering had tight elastic attachments at the waist and shoulders, which made it perfectly watertight, while it was provided within, as has been described in Headley's original manuscript, with novel but very light and practical chemical apparatus for the renovation of air. With some difficulty the breathing bell was removed and the lady hoisted upon deck. She lay there in a deep faint, but her regular breathing encouraged us to think that she would soon recover from the effects of her rapid journey and from the change of pressure, which had been minimized by the fact that the density of the air inside the protective sheath was considerably higher than our atmosphere, so that it may be said to have represented that halfway point at which human divers are wont to pause. Presumably this is the Atlantean woman referred to in the first message as Mona, and if we may take her as a sample they are indeed a race worth reintroducing to earth. She is dark in complexion, beautifully clear-cut and high-bred in feature, with long black hair, and magnificent hazel eyes which looked round her presently in a charming amazement. Sea-shells and mother-of-pearl were worked into her cream-coloured tunic and tangled in her dark hair. A more perfect Naiad of the Deep could not be imagined, the very personification of the mystery and the glamour of the sea. We could see complete consciousness coming back into those marvellous eyes, and then she sprang suddenly to her feet with the activity of a young doe and ran to the side of the vessel. 'Cyrus! Cyrus!' she cried.

"We had already removed the anxiety of those below by a wireless. But now in quick succession each of them arrived, shooting thirty or forty feet into the air, and then falling back into the sea, from which we quickly raised them. All three were unconscious, and Scanlan was bleeding at the nose and ears, but within an hour all were able to totter to their feet. The first action of each was, I imagine, characteristic. Scanlan was led off by a laughing group to the bar, from which shouts of merriment are now resounding, much to the detriment of this composition. Dr. Maracot seized the bundle of papers, tore out one which consisted entirely, so far as I could judge, of algebraic symbols, and disappeared downstairs, while Cyrus Headley ran to the side of his strange maiden, and looks, by last reports, as if he had no intention of ever quitting it. Thus the matter stands, and we trust our weak wireless will carry our message as far as the Cape de Verde station. The fuller details of this wonderful adventure will come later, as is fitting, from the adventurers themselves."

CHAPTER VI: There are very many people who have written both to me, Cyrus Headley, Rhodes Scholar of Oxford, and to Professor Maracot, and even to Bill Scanlan, since our very remarkable experience at the bottom of the Atlantic, where we were able at a point 200 miles southwest of the Canaries to make a submarine descent which has not only led to a revision of our views concerning deep-sea life and pressures, but has also established the survival of an old civilization under incredibly difficult conditions. In these letters we have been continually asked to give further details about our experiences. It will be understood that my original document was a very superficial one, and yet it covered most of the facts. There were some, however, which were withheld, and above all the tremendous episode of the Lord of the Dark Face. This involved some facts and some conclusions of so utterly extraordinary a nature that we all thought it was best to suppress it entirely for the present. Now, however, that Science has accepted our conclusions—and I may add since Society has accepted my bride—our general veracity is established and we may perhaps venture upon a narrative which might have repulsed public sympathy in the first instance. Before I get to the one tremendous happening I would lead up to it by some reminiscences of those wonderful months in the buried home of the Atlanteans, who by means of their vitrine oxygen bells are able to walk the ocean floor with the same ease as those Londoners whom I see now from my windows in the Hyde Park Hotel are strolling among the flower beds.

When first we were taken in by these people after our dreadful fall from the surface we were in the position of prisoners rather than of guests. I wish now to set upon record how this came to change and how through the splendour of Dr. Maracot we have left such a name down there that the memory of us will go down in their annals as of some celestial visitation. They knew nothing of our leaving, which they would certainly have prevented if they could, so that no doubt there is already a legend that we have returned to some heavenly sphere, taking with us the sweetest and choicest flower of their flock.

I would wish now to set down in their order some of the strange things of this wonderful world, and also some of the adventures which befell us until I came to the supreme adventure of all—one which will leave a mark upon each of us forever—the coming of the Lord of the Dark Face. In some ways I wish that we could have stayed longer in the Maracot Deep for there were many mysteries there, and up to the end there were things which we could not understand. Also we were rapidly learning something of their language, so that soon we should have had much more information.

Experience had taught these people what was terrible and what was innocent. One day, I remember, that there was a sudden alarm and that we all ran out in our oxygen bells on to the ocean bed, though why we ran or what we meant to do was a mystery to us. There could be no mistake, however, as to the horror and distraction upon the faces of those around us. When we got out on to the plain we met a number of the Greek coal-workers who were hastening towards the door of our Colony. They had come at such a pace and were so weary that they kept falling down in the ooze, and it was clear that we were really a rescue party for the purpose of picking up these cripples, and hurrying up the laggards. We saw no sign of weapons and no show of resistance against the coming danger. Soon the colliers were hustled along, and when the last one had been shoved through the door we looked back along the line that they had traversed. All that we could see was a couple of greenish wisp-like clouds, luminous in the centre and ragged at the edges, which were drifting rather than moving in our direction. At the clear sight of them, though they were quite half a mile away, my companions were filled with panic and beat at the door so as to get in the sooner. It was surely nervous work to see these mysterious centres of trouble draw nearer, but the pumps acted swiftly and we were soon in safety once more. There was a great block of transparent crystal, ten feet long and two feet broad, above the lintel of the door, with lights so arranged that they threw a strong glare outside. Mounted on the ladders kept for the purpose, several of us, including myself, looked through this rude window. I saw the strange shimmering green circles of light pause be-

fore the door. As they did so the Atlanteans on either side of me simply
gibbered with fear. Then one of the shadowy creatures outside came flickering up through the water and made for our crystal window. Instantly
my companions pulled me down below the level of vision, but it seems
that in my carelessness some of my hair did not get clear from whatever
the maleficent influence may be which these strange creatures send forth.
There is a patch there which is withered and white to this day.

It was not for a long time that the Atlanteans dared to open their door,
and when at last a scout was sent forth he went amid hand-shakings and
slaps on the back as one who does a gallant deed. His report was that all
was clear, and soon joy had returned to the community and this strange
visitation seemed to have been forgotten. We only gathered from the word
"Praxa," repeated in various tones of horror, that this was the name of the
creature. The only person who derived real joy from the incident was
Professor Maracot, who could hardly be restrained from sallying out with
a small net and a glass vase. "A new order of life, partly organic, partly gaseous, but clearly intelligent," was his general comment. "A freak out of
Hell," was Scanlan's less scientific description.

Two days afterwards, when we were out on what we called a shrimping
expedition, when we walked among the deep-sea foliage and captured in
our hand-nets specimens of the smaller fish, we came suddenly upon the
body of one of the coal-workers, who had no doubt been overtaken in his
flight by these strange creatures. The glass bell had been broken—a matter
which called for enormous strength, for this vitrine substance is extraordinarily tough, as you realized when you attempted to reach my first documents. The man's eyes had been torn out, but otherwise he had been
uninjured.

"A dainty feeder!" said the Professor after our return. "There is a
hawk parrot in New Zealand which will kill the lamb in order to get at a
particular morsel of fat above the kidney. So this creature will slay the
man for his eyes. In the heavens above and in the waters below, Nature
knows but one law, and it is, alas! remorseless cruelty."

We had many examples of that terrible law down there in the depths
of the ocean. I can remember, for example, that many times we observed
a curious groove upon the soft bathybian mud, as if a barrel had been
rolled along it. We pointed it out to our Atlantean companions, and when
we could interrogate them we tried to get from them some account of
what this creature could be. As to its name our friends gave some of those
peculiar clicking sounds which come into the Atlantean speech, and which
cannot be reproduced either by the European tongue or by the European
alphabet. Krixchok is perhaps an approximation to it. But as to its appearance we could always in such cases make use of the Atlantean thought reflector by which our friends were able to give a very clear vision of whatever

was in their own minds. By this means they conveyed to us a picture of a very strange marine creature which the Professor could only classify as a gigantic sea slug. It seemed to be of great size, sausage-shaped, with eyes at the end of stems, and a thick coating of coarse hair or bristles. When showing this apparition, our friends by their gestures expressed the greatest horror and repulsion.

But this, as anyone could predicate who knew Maracot, only served to inflame his scientific passions and to make him the more eager to determine the exact species and subspecies of this unknown monster. Accordingly I was not surprised when, on the occasion of our next excursion, he stopped at the point where we clearly saw the mark of the brute upon the slime, and turned deliberately towards the tangle of seaweed and basaltic blocks out of which it seemed to have come. The moment we left the plain the traces of course ceased, and yet there seemed to be a natural gully amid the rocks which clearly led to the den of the monster. We were all three armed with the pikes which the Atlanteans usually carried, but they seemed to me to be frail things with which to face unknown dangers. The Professor trudged ahead, however, and we could but follow after.

The rocky gorge ran upwards, its sides formed of huge clusters of volcanic débris and draped with a profusion of the long red and black forms of lamellaria which are characteristic of the extreme depths of Ocean. A thousand beautiful ascidians and echinoderms of every joyous colour and fantastic shape peeped out from amid this herbage, which was alive with strange crustaceans and low forms of creeping life. Our progress was slow, for walking is never easy in the depths, and the angle up which we toiled was an acute one. Suddenly, however, we saw the creature whom we hunted, and the sight was not a reassuring one.

It was half protruded from its lair, which was a hollow in a basaltic pile. About five feet of hairy body was visible, and we perceived its eyes, which were as large as saucers, yellow in colour, and glittering like agates, moving round slowly upon their long pedicles as it heard the sound of our approach. Then slowly it began to unwind itself from its burrow, waving its heavy body along in caterpillar fashion. Once it reared up its head some four feet from the rocks, so as to have a better look at us, and I observed, as it did so, that it had what looked like the corrugated soles of tennis shoes fastened on either side of its neck, the same colour, size, and striped appearance. What this might mean I could not conjecture, but we were soon to have an object lesson in their use.

The Professor had braced himself with his pike projecting forward and a most determined expression upon his face. It was clear that the hope of a rare specimen had swept all fear from his mind. Scanlan and I were by no means so sure of ourselves, but we could not abandon the old man, so we stood our ground on either side of him. The creature, after that one long stare, began slowly and clumsily to make its way down the slope, worming its path among the rocks, and raising its pedicled eyes from time to time to see what we were about. It came so slowly that we seemed safe enough, since we could always outdistance it. And yet, had we only known it, we were standing very near to death.

It was surely Providence that sent us our warning. The beast was still making its lumbering approach, and may have been sixty yards from us, when a very large fish, a deep-sea groper, shot out from the algæ jungle on our side of the gorge and swam slowly across it. It had reached the centre and was about midway between the creature and ourselves when it gave a convulsive leap, turned belly upwards, and sank dead to the bottom of the ravine. At the same moment each of us felt an extraordinary and most unpleasant tingling pass over our whole bodies, while our knees seemed to give way beneath us. Old Maracot was as wary as he was audacious, and in an instant he had sized up the situation and realized that the game was up. We were faced by some creature which threw out electric waves to kill its prey, and our pikes were of no more use against it than against a machine-gun. Had it not been for the lucky chance that the fish drew its fire, we should have waited until it was near enough to loose off its full battery, which would infallibly have destroyed us. We blundered off as swiftly as we could, with the resolution to leave the giant electric sea-worm severely alone for the future.

These were some of the more terrible of the dangers of the deep. Yet another was the little black Hydrops ferox, as the Professor named him. He was a red fish not much longer than a herring, with a large mouth and a formidable row of teeth. He was harmless in ordinary circumstances, but the shedding of blood, even the very smallest amount of it, attracted him in an instant, and there was no possible salvation for the victim, who was torn to pieces by swarms of attackers. We saw a horrible sight once at the colliery pits, where a slave worker had the misfortune to cut his hand. In an instant, coming from all quarters, thousands of these fish were on to him. In vain he threw himself down and struggled; in vain his horrified companions beat them away with their picks and shovels. The lower part of him, beneath his bell, dissolved before our eyes amid the cloud of vibrant life which surrounded him. One instant we saw a man. The next there was a red mass with white protruding bones. A minute later the bones only were left below the waist and half a clean-picked skeleton was lying at the bottom of the sea. The sight was so horrifying that we were all ill, and the hard-boiled Scanlan actually fell down in a faint and we had some difficulty in getting him home.

But the strange sights which we saw were not always horrifying. I have in mind one which will never fade from our memories. It was on one of those excursions which we delighted to take, sometimes with an Atlantean guide, and sometimes by ourselves when our hosts had learned that we did not need constant attendance and nursing. We were passing over a portion of the plain with which we were quite familiar, when we perceived, to our surprise, that a great patch of light yellow sand, half an acre or so in extent, had been laid down or uncovered since our last visit. We were standing in some surprise, wondering what submarine current or seismic movement could have brought this about, when to our absolute amazement the whole thing rose up and swam with slow undulations immediately above our heads. It was so huge that the great canopy took some appreciable time, a minute or two, to pass from over us. It was a gigantic flat fish, not different, so far as the Professor could observe, from one of our own little dabs, but grown to this enormous size upon the nutritious food which the bathybian deposits provide. It vanished away into the darkness above us, a great glimmering, flickering white and yellow expanse, and we saw it no more.

There was one other phenomenon of the deep sea which was very unexpected. That was the tornadoes which frequently occur. They seem to be caused by the periodical arrival of violent submarine currents which set in with little warning and are terrific while they last, causing as much confusion and destruction as the highest wind would do upon land. No doubt without these visitations there would be that putridity and stagnation which absolute immobility must give, so that, as in all Nature's processes, there was an excellent object in view; but the experience none the less was an alarming one.

On the first occasion when I was caught in such a watery cyclone, I had gone out with that very dear lady to whom I have alluded, Mona, the daughter of Manda. There was a very beautiful bank loaded with algæ of a thousand varied colours which lay a mile or so from the Colony. This was Mona's very special garden which she greatly loved, a tangle of pink serpularia, purple ophiurids, and red holothurians. On this day she had taken me to see it, and it was while we were standing before it that the storm burst. So strong was the current which suddenly flowed upon us that it was only by holding together and getting behind the shelter of rocks that we could save ourselves from being washed away. I observed that this rushing stream of water was quite warm, almost as warm as one could bear, which may show that there is a volcanic origin in these disturbances and that they are the wash from some submarine disturbance in some far-off region of the ocean bed. The mud of the great plain was stirred up by the rush of the current, and the light was darkened by the thick cloud of matter suspended in the water around us. To find our way back was impossible, for we had lost all sense of direction, and in any case could hardly move against the rush of the water. Then on the top of all else a slowly increasing heaviness of the chest and difficulty of breathing warned me that our oxygen supply was beginning to fail us.

It is at such times, when we are in the immediate presence of death, that the great primitive passions float to the surface and submerge all our lesser emotions. It was only at that moment that I knew that I loved my gentle companion, loved her with all my heart and soul, loved her with a love which was rooted deep down and was part of my very self. How strange a thing is a love like that! How impossible to analyze! It was not for her face or figure, lovely as they were. It was not for her voice, though it was more musical than any I have known, nor was it for mental communion, since I could only learn her thoughts from her sensitive, ever-changing face. No, it was something at the back of her dark dreamy eyes, something in the very depths of her soul as of mine which made us mates for all time. I held out my hand and clasped her own, reading in her face that there was no thought or emotion of mine which was not flooding her own receptive mind and flushing her lovely cheek. Death at my side would present no terror to her, and as for myself my heart throbbed at the very thought.

But it was not to be. One would think that our glass coverings excluded sounds, but as a matter of fact the throb of certain air vibrations penetrated them easily, or by their impact started similar vibrations within. There was a loud beat, a reverberating clang, like that of a distant gong. I had no idea what it might mean, but my companion was in no doubt. Still holding my hand, she rose from our shelter, and after listening intently she crouched down and began to make her way against the storm. It was a race against death, for every instant the terrible oppression on my chest became more unbearable. I saw her dear face peering most anxiously into mine, and I staggered on in the direction to which she led me. Her appearance and her movements showed that her oxygen supply was less exhausted than mine. I held on as long as Nature would allow, and then suddenly everything swam around me. I threw out my arms and fell senseless upon the soft ocean floor.

When I came to myself I was lying on my own couch inside the Atlantean Palace. The old yellow-clad priest was standing beside me, a phial of some stimulant in his hand. Maracot and Scanlan, with distressed faces, were bending over me, while Mona knelt at the bottom of the bed with tender anxiety upon her features. It seems that the brave girl had hastened on to the community door, from which on occasions of this sort it was the custom to beat a great gong as a guide to any wanderers who might be lost. There she had explained my position and had guided back the rescue party, including my two comrades, who had brought me back in their arms. Whatever I may do in life, it is truly Mona who will do it; for that life has been a gift from her.

Now that by a miracle she has come to join me in the upper world, the human world under the sky, it is strange to reflect upon the fact that my love was such that I was willing, most willing, to remain forever in the

depths so long as she should be all my own. For long I could not understand
that deep, deep intimate bond which held us together, and which was
felt, as I could see, as strongly by her as by me. It was Manda, her father,
who gave me an explanation which was as unexpected as it was satisfying.

He had smiled gently over our love affair—smiled with the indulgent,
half-amused air of one who sees that come to pass which he had already
anticipated. Then one day he led me aside and in his own chamber he
placed that silver screen upon which his thoughts and knowledge could be
reflected. Never while the breath of life is in my body can I forget that
which he showed me—and her. Seated side by side, our hands clasped together, we watched entranced while the pictures flickered up before our
eyes, formed and projected by that racial memory of the past which these
Atlanteans possess.

There was a rocky peninsula jutting out into a lovely blue ocean. I
may not have told you before that in these thought cinemas, if I may use
the expression, colour is produced as well as form. On this headland was a
house of quaint design, wide-spread, red-roofed, white-walled, and beautiful. A grove of palm trees surrounded it. In this grove there appeared to be
a camp, for we could see the white sheen of tents and here and there the
glimmer of arms as of some sentinel keeping ward. Out of this grove there
walked a middle-aged man clad in mail armour, with a round light shield
on his arm. He carried something in his other hand, but whether sword
or javelin I could not see. He turned his face towards us once, and I saw
at once that he was of the same breed as the Atlantean men who were
around me. Indeed, he might have been the twin brother of Manda, save
that his features were harsh and menacing—a brute man, but one who
was brutal not from ignorance but from the trend of his own nature. The
brute and the brain are surely the most dangerous of all combinations. In
this high forehead and sardonic, bearded mouth one sensed the very essence of evil. If this were indeed some previous incarnation of Manda himself, and by his gestures he seemed to wish us to understand that it was,
then in soul, if not in mind, he has risen far since then.

As he approached the house, we saw in the picture that a young woman
came out to meet him. She was clad as the old Greeks were clad, in a long
clinging white garment, the simplest and yet the most beautiful and dignified dress that woman has ever yet devised. Her manner as she approached the man was one of submission and reverence—the manner of a
dutiful daughter to a father. He repulsed her savagely, however; raising
his hand as if to strike her. As she shrank back from him, the sun lit up her
beautiful tearful face and I saw that it was my Mona.

The silver screen blurred, and an instant later another scene was forming. It was a rock-bound cove, which I sensed to belong to that very peninsula which I had already seen. A strange-shaped boat with high pointed

ends was in the foreground. It was night, but the moon shone very brightly on the water. The familiar stars, the same to Atlantis as to us, glittered in the sky. Slowly and cautiously the boat drew in. There were two rowers, and in the bows was a man enveloped in a dark cloak. As he came close to the shore he stood up and looked eagerly around him. I saw his pale, earnest face in the clear moonlight. It did not need the convulsive clasp of Mona or the ejaculation of Manda to explain that strange intimate thrill which shot over me as I looked. The man was myself.

Yes, I, Cyrus Headley, now of New York and of Oxford; I, the latest product of modern culture, had myself once been part of this mighty civilization of old. I understood now why many of the symbols and hieroglyphs which I had seen around me had impressed me with a vague familiarity. Again and again I had felt like a man who strains his memory because he feels that he is on the edge of some great discovery, which is always awaiting him, and yet is always just outside his grasp. Now, too, I understood that deep soul thrill which I had encountered when my eyes met those of Mona. They came from the depths of my own subconscious self where the memories of twelve thousand years still lingered.

Now the boat had touched the shore, and out of the bushes above there had come a glimmering white figure. My arms were outstretched to enfold it. After one hurried embrace I had half-lifted, half-carried her into the boat. But now there was a sudden alarm. With frantic gestures I beckoned to the rowers to push out. It was too late. Men swarmed out of the bushes. Eager hands seized the side of the boat. In vain I tried to beat them off. An axe gleamed in the air and crashed down upon my head. I fell forward dead upon the lady, bathing her white robe in my blood. I saw her screaming, wild-eyed and open-mouthed, while her father dragged her by her long black hair from underneath my body. Then the curtain closed down.

Once again a picture flickered up upon the silver screen. It was the inside of the house of refuge which had been built by the wise Atlantean for a place of refuge on the day of doom—that very house in which we now stood. I saw its crowded, terrified inmates at the moment of the catastrophe. There I saw my Mona once again, and there also was her father who had learned better and wiser ways so that he was now included among those who might be saved. We saw the great hall rocking like a ship in a storm, while the awestruck refugees clung to the pillars or fell upon the floor. Then we saw the lurch and fall as it descended through the waves. Once more the scene died away, and Manda turned, smiling, to show that all was over.

Yes, we had lived before, the whole group of us, Manda and Mona and I, and perhaps shall live again, acting and reacting down the long chain of our lives. I had died in the upper world, and so my own reincarnations had been upon that plane. Manda and Mona had died under the waves, and so it was there that their cosmic destiny had been worked out. We had for a moment seen a corner lifted in the great dark veil of Nature and had one passing gleam of truth amid the mysteries which surround us. Each life is but one chapter in a story which God has designed. You cannot judge its wisdom or its justice until in some supreme day from some pinnacle of knowledge you look back and see at last the cause and the effect, acting and reacting, down all the long chronicles of Time.

This new-found and delightful relationship of mine may have saved us all a little later when the only serious quarrel which we ever had broke out between us and the community with which we dwelt. As it was, it might have gone ill with us had not a far greater matter come to engage the attention of all, and to place us on a pinnacle in their estimation. It came about thus.

One morning, if such a term can be used where the time of day could only be judged by our occupations, the Professor and I were seated in our large common room. He had fitted one corner of it as a laboratory and was busily engaged in dissecting a gastrostomus which he had netted the day before. On his table were scattered a litter of amphipods and copepods with specimens of Valella, Ianthina, Physalia, and a hundred other creatures whose smell was by no means as attractive as their appearance. I was seated near him studying an Atlantean grammar, for our friends had plenty of books printed in curious right-to-left fashion upon what I thought was parchment but which proved to be the bladders of fishes, pressed and preserved. I was bent on getting the key which would unlock all this knowledge, and therefore I spent much of my time over the alphabet and the elements of the language.

Suddenly, however, our peaceful pursuits were rudely interrupted by an extraordinary procession which rushed into the room. First came Bill Scanlan, very red and excited, one arm waving in the air, and, to our amazement, a plump and noisy baby under the other. Behind him was Berbrix, the Atlantean engineer who had helped Scanlan to erect the wireless receiver. He was a large stout jovial man as a rule, but now his big fat face was convulsed with grief. Behind him again was a woman whose straw-coloured hair and blue eyes showed that she was no Atlantean but one of the subordinate race which we traced to the ancient Greeks.

"Look it here, boss," cried the excited Scanlan. "This guy Berbrix, who is a regular fellar, is going clean goofie and so is this skirt whom he has married, and I guess it is up to us to see that they get a square deal. Far as I understand it she is like a nigger would be down South, and he said a mouthful when he asked her to marry him, but I reckon that's the guy's own affair and nothing to us."

"Of course it is his own affair," said I. "What on earth has bitten you, Scanlan?"

"It's like this, boss. Here has a baby come along. It seems the folk here don't want a breed of that sort nohow, and the priests are out to offer up the baby to that dumb image down yonder. The chief high muck-a-muck got hold of the baby and was sailin' off with it but Berbrix yanked it away, and I threw him down on his ear-hole, and now the whole pack are at our heels and——"

Scanlan got no further with his explanation, for there was a shouting and a rush of feet in the passage, our door was flung open, and several of the yellow-clad attendants of the Temple rushed into the room. Behind them, fierce and austere, came the high-nosed formidable priest. He beckoned with his hand, and his servants rushed forward to seize the child. They halted, however, in indecision as they saw Scanlan throw the baby down among the specimens on the table behind him, and pick up a pike with which he confronted his assailants. They had drawn their knives so I also ran with a pike to Scanlan's aid, while Berbrix did the same. So menacing were we that the Temple servants shrank back and things seemed to have come to a deadlock.

"Mr. Headley, sir, you speak a bit of their lingo," cried Scanlan. "Tell them there ain't no soft pickings here. Tell them we ain't givin' away no babies this morning, thank you. Tell them there will be such a rough house as they never saw if they don't vamose the ranche. There, now, you asked for it and you've got it good and plenty and I wish you joy."

The latter part of Scanlan's speech was caused by the fact that Dr. Maracot had suddenly plunged the scalpel with which he was performing his dissection into the arm of one of the attendants who had crept round and had raised his knife to stab Scanlan. The man howled and danced about in fear and pain while his comrades, incited by the old priest, prepared to make a rush. Heaven only knows what would have happened if Manda and Mona had not entered the room. He stared with amazement at the scene and asked a number of eager questions from the High Priest. Mona had come over to me, and with a happy inspiration I picked up the baby and placed it in her arms where it settled down and cooed most contentedly.

Manda's brow was overcast and it was clear that he was greatly puzzled what to do. He sent the priest and his satellites back to the Temple, and then he entered into a long explanation only a part of which I could understand and pass on to my companions.

"You are to give up the baby," I said to Scanlan.

"Give it up! No, sir. Nothin' doing!"

"This lady is to take charge of mother and child."

"That's another matter. If Miss Mona takes it on I am contented. But if that bindlestiff of a priest——"

"No, no, he cannot interfere. The matter is to be referred to the Council. It is very serious, for I understand Manda to say that the priest is within his rights and that it is an old-established custom of the nation. They could never, he says, distinguish between the upper and lower races if they had all sorts of intermediates in between. If children are born they must die. That is the law."

"Well, this baby won't die anyhow."

"I hope not. He said he would do all he could with the Council. But it will be a week or two before they meet. So it's safe up to then, and who knows what may happen in the meantime?"

Yes, who knew what might happen? Who could have dreamed what *did* happen? Out of this is fashioned the next chapter of our adventures.

CHAPTER VII: I have already said that within a short distance of the underground dwelling of the Atlanteans, prepared beforehand to meet the catastrophe which overwhelmed their native land, there lay the ruins of that great city of which their dwelling had once been part. I have described also how with the vitrine bells charged with oxygen upon our heads we were taken to visit this place, and I tried to convey how deep were our emotions as we viewed it. No words can describe the tremendous impression produced by those colossal ruins, the huge carved pillars and gigantic buildings, all lying stark and silent in the grey phosphorescent light of the bathybian deeps, with no movement save the slow wash of the giant fronds in the deep-sea currents, or the flickering shadows of the great fish which passed through the gaping doors or flitted round the dismantled chambers. It was a favourite haunt of ours, and under the guidance of our friend Manda we passed many an hour examining the strange architecture and all the other remains of that vanished civilization which bore every sign of having been, so far as material knowledge goes, far ahead of our own.

I have said material knowledge. Soon we were to have proof that in spiritual culture there was a vast chasm which separated them from us. The lesson which we carry from their rise and their fall is that the greatest danger which can come to a state is when its intellect outruns its soul. It destroyed this old civilization, and it may yet be the ruin of our own.

We had observed that in one part of the ancient city there was a large building which must have stood upon a hill, for it was still considerably elevated above the general level. A long flight of broad steps constructed from black marble led up to it, and the same material had been used in most of the building, but it was nearly obscured now by a horrible yellow fungus, a fleshy leprous mass, which hung down from every cornice and projection. Above the main doorway, carved also in black marble, was a terrible Medusa-like head with radiating serpents, and the same symbol was repeated here and there upon the walls. Several times we had wished to explore this sinister building, but on each occasion our friend Manda had shown the greatest agitation and by frantic gestures had implored us to turn away. It was clear that so long as he was in our company we should never have our way, and yet a great curiosity urged us to penetrate the secret of this ominous place. We held a council on the matter one morning, Bill Scanlan and I.

"Look it here, Bo," said he, "there is something there that this guy does not want us to see, and the more he hides it the more of a hunch have I that I want to be set wise to it. We don't need no guides any more, you or I. I guess we can put on our own glass tops and walk out of the front door same as any other citizen. Let us go down and explore."

"Why not?" said I, for I was as curious about the matter as Scanlan. "Do you see any objection, sir?" I asked, for Doctor Maracot had entered the room. "Perhaps you would care to come down with us and fathom the mystery of the Palace of Black Marble."

"It may be the Palace of Black Magic as well," said he. "Did you ever hear of the Lord of the Dark Face?"

I confessed that I never did. I forget if I have said before that the Professor was a world-famed specialist on Comparative Religions and ancient primitive beliefs. Even the distant Atlantis was not beyond the range of his learning.

"Our knowledge of the conditions there came to us chiefly by way of Egypt," said he. "It is what the Priests of the Temple at Sais told Solon which is the solid nucleus round which all the rest, part fact and part fiction, has gathered."

"And what wise cracks did the priests say?" asked Scanlan.

"Well, they said a good deal. But among other things they handed down a legend of the Lord of the Dark Face. I can't help thinking that he may have been the Master of the Black Marble Palace. Some say that there were several Lords of the Dark Face—but one at least is on record."

"And what sort of a duck was he?" asked Scanlan.

"Well, by all accounts, he was more than a man, both in his power and in his wickedness. Indeed, it was on account of these things, and on account of the utter corruption which he had brought upon the people, that the whole land was destroyed."

"Like Sodom and Gomorrah."

"Exactly. There would seem to be a point where things become impossible. Nature's patience is exhausted, and the only course open is to smear it all out and begin again. This creature, one can hardly call him a man, had trafficked in unholy arts and had acquired magic powers of the most far-reaching sort which he turned to evil ends. That is the legend of the Lord of the Dark Face. It would explain why his house is still a thing of horror to these poor people and why they dread that we should go near it."

"Which makes me the more eager to do so," I cried.

"Same here, Bo," Bill added.

"I confess that I, too, should be interested to examine it," said the Professor. "I cannot see that our kind hosts here will be any the worse if we make a little expedition of our own, since their superstition makes it difficult for them to accompany us. We will take our opportunity and do so."

It was some little time before that opportunity came, for our small community was so closely knit that there was little privacy in life. It chanced, however, one morning—so far as we could with our rough calendar reckon night and morning—there was some religious observance which assembled them all and took up all their attention. The chance was too good for us to miss, and having assured the two janitors who worked the great pumps of the entrance chamber that all was right we soon found ourselves alone upon the ocean bed and bound for the old city. Progress is slow through the heavy medium of salt water, and even a short walk is wearying, but within an hour we found ourselves in front of the huge black building which had excited our curiosity. With no friendly guide to check us, and no presentiment of danger, we ascended the marble stair and passed through the huge carved portals of this palace of evil.

It was far better preserved than the other buildings of the old city—so much so, indeed, that the stone shell was in no way altered, and only the furniture and the hangings had long decayed and vanished. Nature, however, had brought her own hangings, and very horrible they were. It was a gloomy, shadowy place at the best, but in those hideous shadows lurked the obscene shapes of monstrous polyps and strange, misformed fish which were like the creations of a nightmare. Especially I remember an enormous purple seaslug which crawled, in great numbers, everywhere and large black flat fish which lay like mats upon the floor, with long waving tentacles tipped with flame vibrating above them in the water. We had to step carefully, for the whole building was filled with hideous creatures which might well prove to be as poisonous as they looked.

There were richly ornamented passages with small side rooms leading out from them, but the centre of the building was taken up by one magnificent hall, which in the days of its grandeur must have been one of the most wonderful chambers ever erected by human hands. In that gloomy light we could see neither the roof nor the full sweep of the walls, but as we walked round, our lamps casting tunnels of light before us, we appreciated its huge proportions and the marvellous decorations of the walls. These decorations took the form of statues and ornaments, carved with the highest perfection of art, but horrible and revolting in their subjects. All that the most depraved human mind could conceive of Sadic cruelty and bestial lust was reproduced upon the walls. Through the shadows monstrous images and horrible imaginings loomed round us on every side. If ever the devil had a temple erected in his honour, it was there. So, too, was the devil himself, for at one end of the room, under a canopy of discoloured metal which may well have been gold, and on a high throne of red marble, there was seated a dreadful deity, the very impersonation of evil, savage, scowling, and relentless, modelled upon the same lines as the Baal whom we had seen in the Atlantean Colony, but infinitely stranger and more repulsive. There was a fascination in the wonderful vigour of that terrible countenance, and we were standing with our lamps playing upon it, absorbed in our reflections, when the most amazing, the most incredible thing came to break in upon our reflections. From behind us there came the sound of a loud, derisive human laugh.

Our heads were, as I have explained, enclosed in our glass bells, from which all sound was excluded, nor was it possible for anyone wearing a bell to utter any sound. And yet that mocking laugh fell clear upon the ears of each of us. We sprang round and stood amazed at what was before us.

Against one of the pillars of the hall a man was leaning, his arms folded upon his chest and his malevolent eyes fixed with a threatening glare upon ourselves. I have called him a man, but he was unlike any man whom I have ever seen, and the fact that he both breathed and talked as no man could breathe or talk, and made his voice carry as no human voice could carry, told us that he had that in him which made him very different from ourselves. Outwardly he was a magnificent creature, not less than seven feet in height and built upon the lines of a perfect athlete, which was the more noticeable as he wore a costume which fitted tightly upon his figure, and seemed to consist of glazed black leather. His face was that of a bronze statue—a statue wrought by some master craftsman in order to depict all the power and also all the evil which the human features could portray. It was not bloated or sensual, for such characteristics would have meant weakness and there was no trace of weakness there. On the contrary, it was extraordinarily clean-cut and aquiline, with an eagle nose, dark bristling brows, and smouldering black eyes which flashed and glowed with an inner fire. It was those remorseless, malignant eyes, and the beautiful but cruel, straight, hard-lipped mouth, set like fate, which gave the terror to his face. One felt, as one looked at him, that magnificent as he was in his person, he was evil to the very marrow, his glance a threat, his smile a sneer, his laugh a mockery.

"Well, gentlemen," he said, talking excellent English in a voice which sounded as clear as if we were all back upon earth. "You have had a remarkable adventure in the past and are likely to have an even more exciting one in the future, though it may be my pleasant task to bring it to a sudden end. This, I fear, is a rather one-sided conversation, but as I am perfectly well able to read your thoughts, and as I know all about you, you need not fear any misunderstanding. But you have a great deal —a very great deal to learn."

We looked at each other in helpless amazement. It was hard, indeed, to be prevented from comparing notes as to our reactions to this amazing development. Again we heard that rasping laugh.

"Yes, it is indeed hard. But you can talk when you return, for I wish you to return and to take a message with you. If it were not for that message, I think that this visit to my home would have been your end. But first of all I have a few things which I wished to say to you. I will address you, Dr. Maracot, as the oldest and presumably the wisest of the party, though none could have been very wise to make such an excursion as this. You hear me very well, do you not? That is right, a nod or a shake is all I ask.

"Of course you know who I am. I fancy you discovered me lately. No one can speak or think of me that I do not know it. No one can come into this my old home, my innermost intimate shrine, that I am not summoned. That is why these poor wretches down yonder avoid it, and wanted you to avoid it also. You would have been wiser if you had followed their advice. You have brought me to you, and when once I am brought I do not readily leave.

"Your mind with its little grain of earth science is worrying itself over the problems which I present. How is it that I can live here without oxygen? I do not live here. I live in the great world of men under the light of the sun. I only come here when I am called as you have called me. But I am an ether-breathing creature. There is as much ether here as on a mountain top. Some of your own people can live without air. The cataleptic lies for months and never breathes. I am even as he, but I remain, as you see me, conscious and active.

"Now you worry as to how you can hear me. Is it not the very essence of wireless transmission that it turns from the ether to the air? So I, too, can turn my words from my etheric utterance to impinge upon your ears through the air which fills those clumsy bells of yours.

"And my English? Well, I hope it is fairly good. I have lived some time on earth, oh, a weary, weary time. How long is it? Is this the eleven thousandth or the twelve thousandth year? The latter, I think. I have had time to learn all human tongues. My English is no better than the rest.

"Have I resolved some of your doubts? That is right. I can see if I cannot hear you. But now I have something more serious to say.

"I am Baal-seepa. I am the Lord of the Dark Face. I am he who went so far into the inner secrets of Nature that I could defy Death himself. I have so handled things that I could not die if I would. Some will stronger than my own is to be found if I am ever to die. Oh, mortals, never pray to be delivered from death. It may seem terrible, but eternal life is infinitely more so. To go on and on and on while the endless procession of humanity goes past you. To sit ever at the wayside of history and to see it go, ever moving onwards and leaving you behind. Is it a wonder that my heart is black and bitter, and that I curse the whole foolish drove of them? I injure them when I can. Why should I not?

"You wonder how I can injure them. I have powers, and they are not small ones. I can sway the minds of men. I am the master of the mob. Where evil has been planned there have I ever been. I was with the Huns when they laid half Europe in ruins. I was with the Saracens when under the name of religion they put to the sword all who gainsayed them. I was out on Bartholomew's night. I lay behind the slave trade. It was my whisper which burned ten thousand old crones whom the fools called witches. I was the tall dark man who led the mob in Paris when the streets swam in blood. Rare times those, but they have been even better of late in Russia. That is whence I have come. I had half-forgotten this colony of sea rats who burrow under the mud and carry on a few of the arts and legends of that grand land where life flourished as never since. It is you who reminded me of them, for this old home of mine is still united, by personal vibrations of which your science knows nothing, to the man who built and loved it. I knew that strangers had entered it, I inquired, and here I am. So now since I *am* here—and it is the first time for a thousand years—it has reminded me of these people. They have lingered long enough. It is time for them to go. They are sprung from the power of one who defied me in his life, and who built up this means of escape from the catastrophe which engulfed all but his people and myself. His wisdom saved them and my powers saved me. But now my powers will crush those whom he saved, and the story will be complete."

He put his hand into his breast and he took out a piece of script. "You will give this to the chief of the water-rats," said he. "I regret that you gentlemen should share their fate, but since you are the primary cause of their misfortune it is only justice, after all. I will see you again later. Meanwhile, I would commend a study of these pictures and carvings, which will give you some idea of the height to which I had raised Atlantis during the days of my rule. Here you will find some record of the manners and customs of the people when under my influence. Life was very varied, very highly coloured, very many-sided. In these drab days they would call it an orgy of wickedness. Well, call it what you will, I brought it about, I rejoiced in it, and I have no regrets. Had I my time again, I would do even so and more, save only for this fatal gift of eternal life. Warda, whom I curse and whom I should have killed before he grew strong enough to turn people against me, was wiser than I in this. He still revisits earth, but it is as a spirit, not a man. And now I go. You came here from curiosity, my friends. I can but trust that that curiosity is satisfied."

And then we saw him disappear. Yes, before our very eyes he vanished. It was not done in an instant. He stood clear of the pillar against which he had been leaning. His splendid towering figure seemed blurred at the edges. The light died out of his eyes and his features grew indistinct. Then in a moment he had become a dark whirling cloud which swept upwards through the stagnant water of this dreadful hall. Then he was gone, and we stood gazing at each other and marvelling at the strange possibilities of life.

We did not linger in that horrible palace. It was not a safe place in which to loiter. As it was I picked one of those noxious purple slugs off the shoulder of Bill Scanlan, and I was myself badly stung in the hand by the venom spat at me by a great yellow lamellibranch. As we staggered out I had one last impression of those dreadful carvings, the devil's own handiwork, upon the walls, and then we almost ran down the darksome passage, cursing the day that ever we had been fools enough to enter it. It was joy indeed to be out in the phosphorescent light of the bathybian plain, and to see the clear translucent water once again around us. Within an hour we were back in our home once more. With our helmets removed, we met in consultation in our own chamber. The Professor and I were too overwhelmed with it all to be able to put our thoughts into words. It was only the irrepressible vitality of Bill Scanlan which rose superior.

"Holy smoke!" said he. "We are up against it now. I guess this guy is the big noise out of hell. Seems to me, with his pictures and statues and the rest, he would make the wardsman of a red-light precinct look like two cents. How to handle him—that's the question."

Dr. Maracot was lost in thought. Then he rang the bell and summoned our yellow-clad attendant. "Manda," said he. A minute later our friend was in the room. Maracot handed him the fateful letter.

Never have I admired a man as I did Manda at that moment. We had brought threatened ruin upon his people and himself by our unjustifiable curiosity—we, the strangers whom he had rescued when everything was hopelessly lost. And yet, though he turned a ghastly colour as he read the message, there was no touch of reproach in the sad brown eyes which turned upon us. He shook his head, and despair was in every gesture. "Baal-seepa! Baal-seepa!" he cried, and pressed his hands convulsively to his eyes, as if shutting out some horrible vision. He ran about the room like a man distracted with his grief, and finally rushed away to read the fatal message to the community. We heard a few minutes later the clang of the great bell which summoned them all to conference in the Central Hall.

"Shall we go?" I asked.

Dr. Maracot shook his head.

"What can we do? For that matter, what can they do? What chance have they against one who has the powers of a demon?"

"As much chance as a bunch of rabbits against a weasel," said Scanlan. "But, by Gosh, it's up to us to find a way out. I guess we can't go out of our way to raise the devil and then pass the buck to the folk that saved us."

"What do you suggest?" I asked eagerly, for behind all his slang and his levity I recognized the strong, practical ability of this modern man of his hands.

"Well, you can search me," said he. "And yet maybe this guy is not as safe as he thinks. A bit of it may have got worn out with age, and he's getting on in years if we can take his word for it."

"You think we might attack him?"

"Lunacy!" interjected the doctor.

Scanlan went to his locker. When he faced round he had a big six-shooter in his hand.

"What about this?" he said. "I laid hold of it when we got our chance at the wreck. I thought maybe it might come in useful. I've a dozen shells here. Maybe if I made as many holes in the big stiff it would let out some of his magic. Lord save us! What is it?"

The revolver clattered down upon the floor, and Scanlan was writhing in agonies of pain, his left hand clasping his right wrist. Terrible cramps had seized his arm, and as we tried to alleviate them we could feel the muscles knotted up as hard as the roots of a tree. The sweat of agony streamed down the poor fellow's brow. Finally, utterly cowed and exhausted, he fell upon his bed.

"That lets me out," he said. "I'm through. Yes, thank you, the pain is better. But it is K.O. to William Scanlan. I've learned my lesson. You don't fight hell with six-shooters, and it's no use to try. I give him best from now onwards."

"Yes, you have had your lesson," said Maracot, "and it has been a severe one."

"Then you think our case is hopeless?"

"What can we do when, as it would seem, he is aware of every word and action? And yet we will not despair." He sat in thought for a few moments. "I think," he resumed, "that you, Scanlan, had best lie where you are for a time. You have had a shock from which it will take you some time to recover."

"If there is anything doing, count me in, though I guess we can cut out the rough stuff," said our comrade bravely, but his drawn face and shaking limbs showed what he had endured.

"There is nothing doing so far as you are concerned. We at least have learned what is the wrong way to go to work. All violence is useless. We are working on another plane—the plane of spirit. Do you remain here, Headley. I am going to the room which I use as a study. Perhaps if I were alone I could see a little more clearly what we should do."

Both Scanlan and I had learned to have a great confidence in Maracot. If any human brain could solve our difficulties, it would be his. And yet surely we had reached a point which was beyond all human capacity. We were as helpless as children in the face of forces which we could neither understand nor control. Scanlan had fallen into a troubled sleep. My own one thought as I sat beside him was not how we should escape, but rather what form the blow would take and when it would fall. At any moment I was prepared to see the solid roof above us sink in, the walls collapse, and the dark waters of the lowest deep close in upon those who had defied them so long.

Then suddenly the great bell pealed out once more. Its harsh clamour jarred upon every nerve. I sprang to my feet, and Scanlan sat up in bed. It was no ordinary summons which rang through the old palace. The agitated tumultuous ringing, broken and irregular, was calling an alarm. All had to come, and at once. It was menacing and insistent. "Come now! Come at once! Leave everything and come!" cried the bell.

"Say, Bo, we should be with them," said Scanlan. "I guess they're up against it now."

"And yet what can we do?"

"Maybe just the sight of us will give them a bit of heart. Anyhow, they must not think that we are quitters. Where is the Doc?"

"He went to his study. But you are right, Scanlan. We should be with the others and let them see that we are ready to share their fate."

"The poor boobs seem to lean on us in a way. It may be that they know more than we, but we seem to have more sand in our craw than they. I guess they have taken what was given to them, and we have had to find things for ourselves. Well, it's time for the deluge—if the deluge has got to be."

But as we approached the door a most unexpected interruption detained us. Dr. Maracot stood before us. But was it indeed the Dr. Maracot whom we had known—this self-assured man with strength and

resolution shining from every feature of his masterful face? The quiet
scholar had been submerged, and here was a superman, a great leader, a
dominant soul who might mould mankind to his desires.

"Yes, friends, we shall be needed. All may yet be well. But come at
once, or it may be too late. I will explain everything later—if there is
any later for us. Yes, yes, we are coming."

The latter words, with appropriate gesture, were spoken to some terrified Atlanteans who had appeared at the door and were eagerly beckoning
to us to come. It was a fact, as Scanlan had said, that we had shown
ourselves several times to be stronger in character and prompter in action than these secluded people, and now at this hour of supreme danger
they seemed to cling to us. I could hear a subdued murmur of satisfaction
and relief as we entered the crowded hall and took the places reserved
for us in the front row.

It was time that we came, if we were indeed to bring any help. The
terrible presence was already standing upon the dais and facing with a
cruel, thin-lipped, demoniacal smile the cowering folk before him. Scanlan's simile of a bunch of rabbits before a weasel came back to my memory
as I looked round at them. They sank together, holding on to each other
in their terror, and gazing wide-eyed at the mighty figure which cowered
above them and the ruthless granite-hewed face which looked down upon
them. Never can I forget the impression of those semicircular rows, tier
above tier, of haggard, wild-eyed faces with their horrified gaze all directed towards the central dais. It would seem that he had already pronounced their doom and that they stood in the shadow of death waiting
for its fulfilment. Manda was standing in abject submission, pleading in
broken accents for his people, but one could see that his words only gave
an added zest to the monster who stood sneering before him. The creature
interrupted him with a few rasping words, and raised his right hand in
the air, while a cry of despair rose from the assembly.

And at that moment Dr. Maracot sprang upon the dais. It was amazing
to watch him. Some miracle seemed to have altered the man. He had the
gait and the gesture of a youth, and yet upon his face there was a look
of such power as I have never seen upon human features yet. He strode
up to the swarthy giant, who glared down at him in amazement.

"Well, little man, what have you to say?" he asked.

"I have this to say," said Maracot. "Your time has come. You have over-
stayed it. Go down! Go down into the Hell that has been waiting for
you so long. You are a prince of darkness. Go where the darkness is."

The demon's eyes shot dark fire as he answered:

"When my time comes, if it should ever come, it will not be from the
lips of a wretched mortal that I shall learn it," said he. "What power

have you that you could oppose for a moment one who is in the secret places of Nature? I could blast you where you stand."

Maracot looked into those terrible eyes without blenching. It seemed to me that it was the giant who flinched away from his gaze.

"Unhappy being," said Maracot. "It is I who have the power and the will to blast you where you stand. Too long have you cursed the world with your presence. You have been a plague-spot infecting all that was beautiful and good. The hearts of men will be lighter when you are gone and the sun will shine more brightly."

"What is this? Who are you? What is it that you are saying?" stammered the creature.

"You speak of secret knowledge. Shall I tell you that which is at the very base of it? It is that on every plane the good of that plane can be stronger than the evil. The angel will still beat the devil. For the moment I am on the same plane on which you have so long been, and I hold the power of the conqueror. It has been given to me. So again I say, down with you! Down to Hell to which you belong! Down, sir! Down, I say! Down!"

And then the miracle occurred. For a minute or more—how can one count time at such moments?—the two beings, the mortal and the demon, faced each other as rigid as statues, glaring into each other's eyes with inexorable will upon the two faces, the dark one and the fair. Then suddenly the great creature flinched. His face convulsed with rage, he threw two clawing hands up into the air. "It is you, Warda, you cursed one! I recognize your handiwork. Oh, curse you, Warda. Curse you! Curse you!" His voice died away, his long dark figure became blurred in its outline, his head drooped upon his chest, his knees sagged under him, down he sank and down, and as he sank he changed his shape. At first it was a crouching human being, then it was a dark formless mass, and then with sudden collapse it had become a semiliquid heap of black and horrible putrescence which stained the dais and poisoned the air. At the same time Scanlan and I dashed forward on to the platform, for Dr. Maracot, with a deep groan, his powers exhausted, had fallen forward in helpless collapse. "We have won! We have won!" he muttered, and an instant later his senses had left him and he lay half-dead upon the floor.

Thus it was that the Atlantean Colony was saved from the most horrible danger that could threaten it, and that an evil presence was banished forever from the world. It was not for some days that Dr. Maracot could tell his story, and when he did it was of such a character that if we had not seen the results we should have put it down as the delirium of his illness. I may say that his power had left him with the occasion which had called it forth, and that he was now the same quiet, gentle man of science whom we had known.

"That it should have happened to me!" he cried. "To me, a materialist, a man so immersed in matter that the invisible did not exist in my philosophy. The theories of a whole lifetime have crumbled about my ears."

"I guess we have all been to school again," said Scanlan. "If ever I get back to the little home town, I shall have something to tell the boys."

"The less you tell them the better, unless you want to get the name of being the greatest liar that ever came out of America," said I. "Would you or I have believed it all if someone else had told us?"

"Maybe not. But say, Doc, you had the dope right enough. That great black stiff got his ten and out as neat as ever I saw. There was no come-back there. You clean pushed him off the map. I don't know on what other map he has found his location, but it is no place for Bill Scanlan anyhow."

"I will tell you exactly what occurred," said the Doctor. "You will remember that I left you and retired into my study. I had little hope in my heart, but I had read a good deal at different times about black magic and occult arts. I was aware that white can always dominate black if it can but reach the same plane. He was on a much stronger—I will not say higher—plane than we. That was the fatal fact.

"I saw no way of getting over it. I flung myself down on the settee and I prayed—yes, I, the hardened materialist, prayed—for help. When one is at the very end of all human power, what can one do save to stretch appealing hands into the mists which gird us round? I prayed—and my prayer was most wonderfully answered.

"I was suddenly aware of the fact that I was not alone in the room. There stood before me a tall figure, as swarthy as the evil presence whom we fought, but with a kindly, bearded face which shone with benevolence and love. The sense of power which he conveyed was not less than the other, but it was the power of good, the power within the influence of which evil would shred away as the mists do before the sun. He looked at me with kindly eyes, and I sat, too amazed to speak, staring up at him. Something within me, some inspiration or intuition, told me that this was the spirit of that great and wise Atlantean who had fought the evil while he lived, and who, when he could not prevent the destruction of his country, took such steps as would ensure that the more worthy should survive even though they should be sunk to the depths of the ocean. This wondrous being was now interposing to prevent the ruin of his work and the destruction of his children. With a sudden gush of hope I realized all this as clearly as if he had said it. Then, still smiling, he advanced, and he laid his two hands upon my head. It was his own virtue and strength, no doubt, which he was transferring to me. I felt it coursing like fire down my veins. Nothing in the world seemed impossible at that moment. I had the will and the might to do miracles. Then at that moment I heard the bell clang out, which told me that the crisis had come. As I rose from the couch the spirit, smiling his encouragement, vanished before me. Then I joined you, and the rest you know."

"Well, sir," said I, "I think you have made your reputation. If you care to set up as a god down here, I expect you would find no difficulty."

"You got away with it better than I did, Doc," said Scanlan in a rueful voice. "How is it this guy didn't know what you were doing? He was quick enough on to me when I laid hand on a gun. And yet you had him guessing."

"I suppose that you were on the plane of matter, and that, for the moment, we were upon that of spirit," said the Doctor thoughtfully. "Such things teach one humility. It is only when you touch the higher that you realize how low we may be among the possibilities of creation. I have had my lesson. May my future life show that I have learned it."

So this was the end of our supreme experience. It was but a little time later that we conceived the idea of sending news of ourselves to the surface, and that later, by means of vitrine balls filled with levigen, we ascended ourselves to be met in the manner already narrated. Dr. Maracot actually talks of going back. There is some point of Ichthyology upon which he wants more precise information. But Scanlan has, I hear, married his wren in Philadelphia, and has been promoted as works manager of Merribank's, so he seeks no further adventure, while I—well, the deep sea has given me a precious pearl, and I ask for no more.

round the moon:

A SEQUEL TO "FROM THE EARTH TO THE MOON"

by JULES VERNE

PRELIMINARY CHAPTER: RECAPITULATING THE FIRST PART OF THIS WORK, AND SERVING AS A PREFACE TO THE SECOND During the year 186–, the whole world was greatly excited by a scientific experiment unprecedented in the annals of science. The members of the Gun Club, a circle of artillerymen formed at Baltimore after the American war, conceived the idea of putting themselves in communication with the moon!— yes, with the moon,—by sending to her a projectile. Their president, Barbicane, the promoter of the enterprise, having consulted the astronomers of the Cambridge Observatory upon the subject, took all necessary means to ensure the success of this extraordinary enterprise, which had been declared practicable by the majority of competent judges. After setting on foot a public subscription, which realized nearly $5,500,000, they began the gigantic work.

According to the advice forwarded from the members of the Observatory, the gun destined to launch the projectile had to be fixed in a country situated between the 0 and 28th degrees of north or south latitude, in order to aim at the moon when at the zenith; and its initiatory velocity was fixed at twelve thousand yards to the second. Launched on the 1st of December, at 10 hrs. 46 m. 40 s. p.m., it ought to reach the moon four days after its departure, that is on the 5th of December, at midnight precisely, at the moment of her attaining her *perigee*, that is her nearest distance from the earth, which is exactly 86,410 leagues (French), or 238,833 miles *mean distance* (English).

The principal members of the Gun Club, President Barbicane, Major Elphinstone, the secretary Joseph T. Maston, and other learned men, held several meetings, at which the shape and composition of the projectile were discussed, also the position and nature of the gun, and the quality and quantity of the powder to be used. It was decided: 1st, that the projectile should be a shell made of aluminium with a diameter of 108 inches and a thickness of twelve inches to its walls; and should weigh 19,250 lbs. 2ndly, that the gun should be a Columbiad cast in iron, 900 feet long, and run perpendicularly into the earth. 3rdly, that the charge should contain 400,000 pounds of gun-cotton, which, giving out six billions of litres of gas in rear of the projectile, would easily carry it towards the orb of night.

These questions determined President Barbicane, assisted by Murchison the engineer, to choose a spot situated in Florida, in 27° 7′ North latitude, and 77° 3′ W. (Greenwich) longitude. It was on this spot, after stupendous labour, that the Columbiad was cast with full success. Things stood thus, when an incident took place which increased the interest attached to this great enterprise a hundredfold.

A Frenchman, an enthusiastic Parisian, as witty as he was bold, asked to be enclosed in the projectile, in order that he might reach the moon, and reconnoitre this terrestrial satellite. The name of this intrepid adventurer was Michel Ardan. He landed in America, was received with enthusiasm, held meetings, saw himself carried in triumph, reconciled President Barbicane to his mortal enemy, Captain Nicholl, and, as a token of reconciliation, persuaded them both to start with him in the projectile. The proposition being accepted, the shape of the projectile was slightly altered. It was made of a cylindro-conical form. This species of aerial car was lined with strong springs and partitions to deaden the shock of departure. It was provided with food for a year, water for some months, and gas for some days. A self-acting apparatus supplied the three travellers with air to breathe. At the same time, on one of the highest points of the Rocky Mountains, the Gun Club had a gigantic telescope erected, in order that they might be able to follow the course of the projectile through space. All was then ready.

On the 30th November, at the hour fixed upon, from the midst of an extraordinary crowd of spectators, the departure took place, and for the first time, three human beings quitted the terrestrial globe, and launched into interplanetary space with almost a certainty of reaching their destination. These bold travellers, Michel Ardan, President Barbicane, and Captain Nicholl, ought to make the passage in ninety-seven hours, thirteen minutes, and twenty seconds. Consequently, their arrival on the lunar disc could not take place until the 5th December at twelve at night, at the exact moment when the moon should be full, and not on the 4th, as some badly-informed journals had announced.

But an unforeseen circumstance, viz., the detonation produced by the Columbiad, had the immediate effect of troubling the terrestrial atmosphere, by accumulating a large quantity of vapour, a phenomenon which excited universal indignation, for the moon was hidden from the eyes of the watchers for several nights.

The worthy Joseph T. Maston, the staunchest friend of the three travellers, started for the Rocky Mountains, accompanied by the Hon. J. Belfast, director of the Cambridge Observatory, and reached the station of Long's Peak, where the telescope was erected which brought the moon within an apparent distance of two leagues. The hon. secretary of the Gun Club wished himself to observe the vehicle of his daring friends.

The accumulation of clouds in the atmosphere prevented all observations on the 5th, 6th, 7th, 8th, 9th, and 10th of December. Indeed it was thought that all observations would have to be put off to the 3rd of January in the following year; for the moon entering its last quarter on the 11th, would then only present an ever-decreasing portion of her disc, insufficient to allow of their following the course of the projectile.

At length, to the general satisfaction, a heavy storm cleared the atmosphere on the night of the 11th and 12th December, and the moon, with half illuminated disc, was plainly to be seen upon the black sky.

That very night, a telegram was sent from the station of Long's Peak by Joseph T. Maston and Belfast to the gentlemen of the Cambridge Observatory, announcing that, on the 11th of December at 8 hrs. 47 m. p.m., the projectile launched by the Columbiad of Stones Hill had been detected by Messrs. Belfast and Maston,—that it had deviated from its course from some unknown cause, and had not reached its destination; but that it had passed near enough to be retained by the lunar attraction; that its rectilinear movement had been changed to a circular one, and that following an elliptical orbit round the star of night it had become *its satellite*. The telegram added that the elements of this new star had not yet been calculated; and indeed three observations made upon a star in three different positions, are necessary to determine these elements. Then it showed that the distance separating the projectile from the lunar surface "might" be reckoned at about 2833 miles.

It ended with this double hypothesis; either the attraction of the moon would draw it to herself, and the travellers thus attain their end; or that the projectile, held in one immutable orbit, would gravitate around the lunar disc to all eternity.

With such alternatives, what would be the fate of the travellers? Certainly they had food for some time. But supposing they did succeed in their rash enterprise, how would they return? *Could* they ever return? Should they hear from them? These questions, debated by the most learned pens of the day, strongly engrossed the public attention.

It is advisable here to make a remark which ought to be well considered by hasty observers. When a purely speculative discovery is announced to the public, it cannot be done with too much prudence. No one is obliged to discover either a planet, a comet, or a satellite; and whoever makes a mistake in such a case exposes himself justly to the derision of the mass. Far better is it to wait; and that is what the impatient Joseph T. Maston should have done before sending this telegram forth to the world, which, according to his idea, told the whole result of the enterprise. Indeed this telegram contained two sorts of errors, as was proved eventually. 1st, errors of observation, concerning the distance of the projectile from the surface of the moon, for on the 11th December it was impossible to see it; and what Joseph T. Maston had seen, or thought he saw, could not have been the projectile of the Columbiad. 2ndly, errors of theory on the fate in store for the said projectile; for in making it a satellite of the moon, it was putting it in direct contradiction to all mechanical laws.

One single hypothesis of the observers of Long's Peak could ever be realized, that which foresaw the case of the travellers (if still alive) uniting their efforts with the lunar attraction to attain the surface of the disc.

Now these men, as clever as they were daring, *had* survived the terrible shock consequent on their departure, and it is their journey in the projectile car which is here related in its most dramatic as well as in its most singular details. This recital will destroy many illusions and surmises; but it will give a true idea of the singular changes in store for such an enterprise; it will bring out the scientific instincts of Barbicane, the industrious resources of Nicholl, and the audacious humour of Michel Ardan.

Besides this, it will prove that their worthy friend, Joseph T. Maston, was wasting his time, while leaning over the gigantic telescope he watched the course of the moon through the starry space.

CHAPTER I: FROM TWENTY MINUTES PAST TEN TO FORTY-SEVEN MINUTES PAST TEN P.M. As ten o'clock struck, Michel Ardan, Barbicane, and Nicholl, took leave of the numerous friends they were leaving on the earth. The two dogs, destined to propagate the canine race on the lunar continents, were already shut up in the projectile.

The three travellers approached the orifice of the enormous cast-iron tube, and a crane let them down to the conical top of the projectile. There, an opening made for the purpose gave them access to the aluminium car. The tackle belonging to the crane being hauled from outside, the mouth of the Columbiad was instantly disencumbered of its last supports.

Nicholl, once introduced with his companions inside the projectile, began to close the opening by means of a strong plate, held in position by powerful screws. Other plates, closely fitted, covered the lenticular glasses, and the travellers, hermetically enclosed in their metal prison, were plunged in profound darkness.

"And now, my dear companions," said Michel Ardan, "let us make ourselves at home; I am a domesticated man and strong in housekeeping. We are bound to make the best of our new lodgings, and make ourselves comfortable. And first let us try and see a little. Gas was not invented for moles."

So saying, the thoughtless fellow lit a match by striking it on the sole of his boot; and approached the burner fixed to the receptacle, in which the carbonized hydrogen, stored at high pressure, sufficed for the lighting and warming of the projectile for a hundred and forty-four hours, or six days and six nights. The gas caught fire, and thus lighted the projectile looked like a comfortable room with thickly padded walls, furnished with a circular divan, and a roof rounded in the shape of a dome.

The objects it contained, arms, instruments, and utensils securely fastened against the rounds of wadding, could bear the shock of departure with impunity. Humanly speaking, every possible precaution had been taken to bring this rash experiment to a successful termination.

Michel Ardan examined everything, and declared himself satisfied with his installation.

"It is a prison," said he, "but a travelling prison; and, with the right of putting my nose to the window, I could well stand a lease of a hundred years. You smile, Barbicane. Have you any *arrière-pensée*? Do you say to yourself, 'This prison may be our tomb'? Tomb, perhaps; still I would not change it for Mahomet's, which floats in space, but never advances an inch!"

Whilst Michel Ardan was speaking, Barbicane and Nicholl were making their last preparations.

Nicholl's chronometer marked twenty minutes past ten p.m. when the three travellers were finally enclosed in their projectile. This chronometer was set within the tenth of a second by that of Murchison the engineer. Barbicane consulted it.

"My friends," said he, "it is twenty minutes past ten. At forty-seven minutes past ten Murchison will launch the electric spark on the wire which communicates with the charge of the Columbiad. At that precise moment we shall leave our spheroid. Thus we have still twenty-seven minutes to remain on the earth."

"Twenty-six minutes thirteen seconds," replied the methodical Nicholl.

"Well!" exclaimed Michel Ardan, in a good-humoured tone, "much may be done in twenty-six minutes. The gravest questions of morals and politics may be discussed, and even solved. Twenty-six minutes well employed are worth more than twenty-six years in which nothing is done. Some *seconds* of a Pascal or a Newton are more precious than the whole existence of a crowd of raw simpletons——"

"And you conclude, then, you everlasting talker?" asked Barbicane.

"I conclude that we have twenty-six minutes left," replied Ardan.

"Twenty-four only," said Nicholl.

"Well, twenty-four, if you like, my noble captain," said Ardan; "twenty-four minutes in which to investigate——"

"Michel," said Barbicane, "during the passage we shall have plenty of time to investigate the most difficult questions. For the present we must occupy ourselves with our departure."

"Are we not ready?"

"Doubtless; but there are still some precautions to be taken, to deaden as much as possible the first shock."

"Have we not the water-cushions placed between the partition-breaks, whose elasticity will sufficiently protect us?"

"I *hope* so, Michel," replied Barbicane gently, "but I am not sure."

"Ah, the joker!" exclaimed Michel Ardan. "He hopes!—He is not sure! —and he waits for the moment when we are encased to make this deplorable admission! I beg to be allowed to get out!"

"And how?" asked Barbicane.

"Humph!" said Michel Ardan, "it is not easy; we are in the train, and the guard's whistle will sound before twenty-four minutes are over."

"*Twenty*," said Nicholl.

For some moments the three travellers looked at each other. Then they began to examine the objects imprisoned with them.

"Everything is in its place," said Barbicane. "We have now to decide how we can best place ourselves to resist the shock. Position cannot be an indifferent matter; and we must, as much as possible, prevent the rush of blood to the head."

"Just so," said Nicholl.

"Then," replied Michel Ardan, ready to suit the action to the word, "let us put our heads down and our feet in the air, like the clowns in the grand circus."

"No," said Barbicane, "let us stretch ourselves on our sides; we shall resist the shock better that way. Remember that, when the projectile starts, it matters little whether we are in it or before it; it amounts to much the same thing."

"If it is only 'much the same thing,' I may cheer up," said Michel Ardan.

"Do you approve of my idea, Nicholl?" asked Barbicane.

"Entirely," replied the captain. "We've still thirteen minutes and a half."

"That Nicholl is not a man," exclaimed Michel; "he is a chronometer with seconds, an escape, and eight holes."

But his companions were not listening; they were taking up their last positions with the most perfect coolness. They were like two methodical travellers in a car, seeking to place themselves as comfortably as possible.

We might well ask ourselves of what materials are the hearts of these Americans made, to whom the approach of the most frightful danger added no pulsation.

Three thick and solidly-made couches had been placed in the projectile. Nicholl and Barbicane placed them in the centre of the disc forming the floor. There the three travellers were to stretch themselves some moments before their departure.

During this time, Ardan, not being able to keep still, turned in his narrow prison like a wild beast in a cage, chatting with his friends, speaking to the dogs Diana and Satellite, to whom, as may be seen, he had given significant names.

"Ah, Diana! Ah, Satellite!" he exclaimed, teazing them; "so you are going to show the moon-dogs the good habits of the dogs of the earth! That will do honour to the canine race! If ever we do come down again, I will bring a cross type of 'moon-dogs,' which will make a stir!"

"If there *are* dogs in the moon," said Barbicane.

"There are," said Michel Ardan, "just as there are horses, cows, donkeys, and chickens. I bet that we shall find chickens."

"A hundred dollars we shall find none!" said Nicholl.

"Done, my captain!" replied Ardan, clasping Nicholl's hand. "But, by the bye, you have already lost three bets with our president, as the necessary funds for the enterprise have been found, as the operation of casting has been successful, and lastly, as the Columbiad has been loaded without accident, six thousand dollars."

"Yes," replied Nicholl. "Thirty-seven minutes six seconds past ten."

"It is understood, captain. Well, before another quarter of an hour you will have to count 9000 dollars to the president; 4000 because the Columbiad will not burst, and 5000 because the projectile will rise more than six miles in the air."

"I have the dollars," replied Nicholl, slapping the pocket of his coat. "I only ask to be allowed to pay."

"Come, Nicholl, I see that you are a man of method, which I could never be; but indeed you have made a series of bets of very little advantage to yourself, allow me to tell you."

"And why?" asked Nicholl.

"Because, if you gain the first, the Columbiad will have burst, and the projectile with it; and Barbicane will no longer be there to reimburse your dollars."

"My stake is deposited at the bank in Baltimore," replied Barbicane simply; "and if Nicholl is not there, it will go to his heirs."

"Ah, you practical men!" exclaimed Michel Ardan; "I admire you the more for not being able to understand you."

"Forty-two minutes past ten!" said Nicholl.

"Only five minutes more!" answered Barbicane.

"Yes, five little minutes!" replied Michel Ardan; "and we are enclosed in a projectile, at the bottom of a gun 900 feet long! And under this projectile are rammed 400,000 lbs. of gun-cotton, which is equal to 1,600,000 lbs. of ordinary powder! And friend Murchison, with his chronometer in hand, his eye fixed on the needle, his finger on the electric apparatus, is counting the seconds preparatory to launching us into interplanetary space."

"Enough, Michel, enough!" said Barbicane, in a serious voice; "let us prepare. A few instants alone separate us from an eventful moment. One clasp of the hand, my friends."

"Yes," exclaimed Michel Ardan, more moved than he wished to appear; and the three bold companions were united in a last embrace.

"God preserve us!" said the religious Barbicane.

Michel Ardan and Nicholl stretched themselves on the couches placed in the centre of the disc.

"Forty-seven minutes past ten!" murmured the captain.

"Twenty seconds more!" Barbicane quickly put out the gas and lay down by his companions, and the profound silence was only broken by the ticking of the chronometer marking the seconds.

Suddenly a dreadful shock was felt, and the projectile, under the force of six billions of litres of gas, developed by the combustion of the pyroxyle, mounted into space.

CHAPTER II: THE FIRST HALF-HOUR   What had happened? What effect had this frightful shock produced? Had the ingenuity of the constructors of the projectile obtained any happy result? Had the shock been deadened, thanks to the springs, the four plugs, the water-cushions, and the partition-breaks? Had they been able to subdue the frightful pressure of the initiatory speed of more than 11,000 yards, which was enough to traverse Paris or New York in a second? This was evidently the question suggested to the thousand spectators of this moving scene. They forgot the aim of the journey, and thought only of the travellers. And if one amongst them—Joseph T. Maston for example—could have cast one glimpse into the projectile, what would he have seen?

Nothing then. The darkness was profound. But its cylindro-conical partitions had resisted wonderfully. Not a rent or a dent anywhere! The wonderful projectile was not even heated under the intense deflagration of the powder, nor liquefied, as they seemed to fear, in a shower of aluminium.

The interior showed but little disorder; indeed, only a few objects had been violently thrown towards the roof; but the most important seemed not to have suffered from the shock at all; their fixtures were intact.

On the movable disc, sunk down to the bottom by the smashing of the partition-breaks and the escape of the water, three bodies lay apparently lifeless. Barbicane, Nicholl, and Michel Ardan—did they still breathe? or was the projectile nothing now but a metal coffin, bearing three corpses into space?

Some minutes after the departure of the projectile, one of the bodies moved, shook its arms, lifted its head, and finally succeeded in getting on its knees. It was Michel Ardan. He felt himself all over, gave a sonorous "Hem!" and then said—

"Michel Ardan is whole. How about the others?"

The courageous Frenchman tried to rise, but could not stand. His head swam, from the rush of blood; he was blind; he was like a drunken man.

"Bur-r!" said he. "It produces the same effect as two bottles of Corton, though perhaps less agreeable to swallow." Then, passing his hand several times across his forehead and rubbing his temples, he called in a firm voice—

"Nicholl! Barbicane!"

He waited anxiously. No answer; not even a sigh to show that the hearts of his companions were still breathing. He called again. The same silence.

"The devil!" he exclaimed. "They look as if they had fallen from a fifth story on their heads. Bah!" he added, with that imperturbable confidence which nothing could check, "if a Frenchman can get on his knees, two Americans ought to be able to get on their feet. But first let us light up."

Ardan felt the tide of life return by degrees. His blood became calm, and returned to its accustomed circulation. Another effort restored his equilibrium. He succeeded in rising, drew a match from his pocket, and approaching the burner lighted it. The receiver had not suffered at all. The gas had not escaped. Besides, the smell would have betrayed it; and in that case Michel Ardan could not have carried a lighted match with impunity through the space filled with hydrogen. The gas mixing with the air would have produced a detonating mixture, and the explosion would have finished what the shock had perhaps begun. When the burner was lit, Ardan leaned over the bodies of his companions: they were lying one on the other, an inert mass, Nicholl above, Barbicane underneath.

Ardan lifted the captain, propped him up against the divan, and began to rub vigorously. This means, used with judgment, restored Nicholl, who opened his eyes, and instantly recovering his presence of mind, seized Ardan's hand and looked around him.

"And Barbicane?" said he.

"Each in turn," replied Michel Ardan. "I began with you, Nicholl, because you were on the top. Now let us look to Barbicane." Saying which, Ardan and Nicholl raised the president of the Gun Club and laid him on the divan. He seemed to have suffered more than either of his companions; he was bleeding, but Nicholl was reassured by finding that the hæmorrhage came from a slight wound on the shoulder, a mere graze, which he bound up carefully.

Still, Barbicane was a long time coming to himself, which frightened his friends, who did not spare friction.

"He breathes though," said Nicholl, putting his ear to the chest of the wounded man.

"Yes," replied Ardan, "he breathes like a man who has some notion of that daily operation. Rub, Nicholl; let us rub harder." And the two improvised practitioners worked so hard and so well that Barbicane recovered his senses. He opened his eyes, sat up, took his two friends by the hands, and his first words were—

"Nicholl, are we moving?"

Nicholl and Barbicane looked at each other; they had not yet troubled themselves about the projectile; their first thought had been for the traveller, not for the car.

"Well, are we really moving?" repeated Michel Ardan.

"Or quietly resting on the soil of Florida?" asked Nicholl.

"Or at the bottom of the Gulf of Mexico?" added Michel Ardan.

"What an idea!" exclaimed the president.

And this double hypothesis suggested by his companions had the effect of recalling him to his senses. In any case they could not yet decide on the position of the projectile. Its apparent immovability, and the want of communication with the outside, prevented them from solving the question. Perhaps the projectile was unwinding its course through space. Perhaps after a short rise it had fallen upon the earth, or even in the Gulf of Mexico—a fall which the narrowness of the peninsula of Florida would render not impossible.

The case was serious, the problem interesting, and one that must be solved as soon as possible. Thus, highly excited, Barbicane's moral energy triumphed over·physical weakness, and he rose to his feet. He listened. Outside was perfect silence; but the thick padding was enough to intercept all sounds coming from the earth. But one circumstance struck Barbicane, viz., that the temperature inside the projectile was singularly high. The president drew a thermometer from its case, and consulted it. The instrument showed 81° Fahr.

"Yes," he exclaimed, "yes, we are moving! This stifling heat, penetrating through the partitions of the projectile, is produced by its friction on the atmospheric strata. It will soon diminish, because we are already floating in space, and after having been nearly stifled, we shall have to suffer intense cold."

"What!" said Michel Ardan. "According to your showing, Barbicane, we are already beyond the limits of the terrestrial atmosphere?"

"Without a doubt, Michel. Listen to me. It is fifty-five minutes past ten; we have been gone about eight minutes; and if our initiatory speed has not been checked by the friction, six seconds would be enough for us to pass through the forty miles of atmosphere which surrounds the globe."

"Just so," replied Nicholl; "but in what proportion do you estimate the diminution of speed by friction?"

"In the proportion of one-third, Nicholl. This diminution is considerable, but according to my calculations it is nothing less. If, then, we had an initiatory speed of 12,000 yards, on leaving the atmosphere this speed would be reduced to 9165 yards. In any case we have already passed through this interval, and——"

"And then," said Michel Ardan, "friend Nicholl has lost his two bets: four thousand dollars because the Columbiad did not burst; five thousand dollars because the projectile has risen more than six miles. Now, Nicholl, pay up."

"Let us prove it first," said the captain, "and we will pay afterwards. It is quite possible that Barbicane's reasoning is correct, and that I have lost my nine thousand dollars. But a new hypothesis presents itself to my mind, and it annuls the wager."

"What is that?" asked Barbicane quickly.

"The hypothesis that, for some reason or other, fire was never set to the powder, we have not started at all."

"My goodness, captain," exclaimed Michel Ardan, "that hypothesis is worthy of my brain! It cannot be a serious one. For have we not been half annihilated by the shock? Did I not recall you to life? Is not the president's shoulder still bleeding from the blow it has received?"

"Granted," replied Nicholl; "but one question."

"Well, captain?"

"Did you hear the detonation, which certainly ought to be loud?"

"No," replied Ardan, much surprised; "certainly I did not hear the detonation."

"And you, Barbicane?"

"Nor I, either."

"Very well," said Nicholl.

"Well now," murmured the president, "why did we not hear the detonation?"

The three friends looked at each other with a disconcerted air. It was quite an inexplicable phenomenon. The projectile had started, and consequently there must have been a detonation.

"Let us first find out where we are," said Barbicane, "and let down the panel."

This very simple operation was soon accomplished.

The nuts which held the bolts to the outer plates of the right-hand scuttle gave way under the pressure of the English wrench. These bolts were pushed outside, and buffers covered with india-rubber stopped up the holes which let them through. Immediately the outer plate fell back upon its hinges like a porthole, and the lenticular glass which closed the scuttle appeared. A similar one was let into the thick partition on the opposite side of the projectile, another in the top of the dome, and finally, a fourth in the middle of the base. They could, therefore, make observations in four different directions: the firmament by the side and most direct windows, the earth or the moon by the upper and under openings in the projectile.

Barbicane and his two companions immediately rushed to the uncovered window. But it was lit by no ray of light. Profound darkness surrounded them, which, however, did not prevent the president from exclaiming—

"No, my friends, we have not fallen back upon the earth; no, nor are we submerged in the Gulf of Mexico. Yes! we are mounting into space. See those stars shining in the night, and that impenetrable darkness heaped up between the earth and us!"

"Hurrah! hurrah!" exclaimed Michel Ardan and Nicholl in one voice.

Indeed, this thick darkness proved that the projectile had left the earth, for the soil, brilliantly lit by the moonbeams, would have been visible to the travellers, if they had been lying on its surface. This darkness also showed that the projectile had passed the atmospheric strata, for the diffused light spread in the air would have been reflected on the metal walls, which reflection was wanting. This light would have lit the window, and the window was dark. Doubt was no longer possible; the travellers had left the earth.

"I have lost," said Nicholl.

"I congratulate you," replied Ardan.

"Here are the nine thousand dollars," said the captain, drawing a roll of paper dollars from his pocket.

"Will you have a receipt for it?" asked Barbicane, taking the sum.

"If you do not mind," answered Nicholl; "it is more business-like."

And coolly and seriously, as if he had been at his strong-box, the president drew forth his note-book, tore out a blank leaf, wrote a proper receipt in pencil, dated and signed it with the usual flourish,[1] and gave it to the captain, who carefully placed it in his pocketbook. Michel Ardan, tak-

[1] *This is a purely French habit.* (Ed.)

ing off his hat, bowed to his two companions without speaking. So much formality under such circumstances left him speechless. He had never before seen anything so "American."

This affair settled, Barbicane and Nicholl had returned to the window, and were watching the constellations. The stars looked like bright points on the black sky. But from that side they could not see the orb of night, which, travelling from east to west, would rise by degrees towards the zenith. Its absence drew the following remark from Ardan.

"And the moon; will she perchance fail at our rendezvous?"

"Do not alarm yourself," said Barbicane; "our future globe is at its post, but we cannot see her from this side; let us open the other."

As Barbicane was about leaving the window to open the opposite scuttle, his attention was attracted by the approach of a brilliant object. It was an enormous disc, whose colossal dimension could not be estimated. Its face, which was turned to the earth, was very bright. One might have thought it a small moon reflecting the light of the larger one. She advanced with great speed, and seemed to describe an orbit round the earth, which would intersect the passage of the projectile. This body revolved upon its axis, and exhibited the phenomena of all celestial bodies abandoned in space.

"Ah!" exclaimed Michel Ardan, "what is that? another projectile?"

Barbicane did not answer. The appearance of this enormous body surprised and troubled him. A collision was possible, and might be attended with deplorable results; either the projectile would deviate from its path, or a shock, breaking its impetus, might precipitate it to the earth; or, lastly, it might be irresistibly drawn away by the powerful asteroid. The president caught at a glance the consequences of these three hypotheses, either of which would, one way or the other, bring their experiment to an unsuccessful and fatal termination. His companions stood silently looking into space. The object grew rapidly as it approached them, and by an optical illusion the projectile seemed to be throwing itself before it.

"By Jove!" exclaimed Michel Ardan, "we shall run into one another!"

Instinctively the travellers drew back. Their dread was great, but it did not last many seconds. The asteroid passed several hundred yards from the projectile and disappeared, not so much from the rapidity of its course, as that its face being opposite the moon, it was suddenly merged into the perfect darkness of space.

"A happy journey to you," exclaimed Michel Ardan, with a sigh of relief. "Surely infinity of space is large enough for a poor little projectile to walk through without fear. Now, what is this portentous globe which nearly struck us?"

"I know," replied Barbicane.

"Oh, indeed! you know everything."

"It is," said Barbicane, "a simple meteorite, but an enormous one, which the attraction of the earth has retained as a satellite."

"Is it possible!" exclaimed Michel Ardan; "the earth then has two moons like Neptune?"

"Yes, my friend, two moons, though it passes generally for having only one; but this second moon is so small, and its speed so great, that the inhabitants of the earth cannot see it. It was by noticing disturbances that a French astronomer, M. Petit, was able to determine the existence of this second satellite and calculate its elements. According to his observations, this meteorite will accomplish its revolution round the earth in three hours and twenty minutes, which implies a wonderful rate of speed."

"Do all astronomers admit the existence of this satellite?" asked Nicholl.

"No," replied Barbicane; "but if, like us, they had met it, they could no longer doubt it. Indeed, I think that this meteorite, which, had it struck the projectile, would have much embarrassed us, will give us the means of deciding what our position in space is."

"How?" said Ardan.

"Because its distance is known, and when we met it, we were exactly 4650 miles from the surface of the terrestrial globe."

"More than 2000 French leagues," exclaimed Michel Ardan. "That beats the express trains of the pitiful globe called the earth."

"I should think so," replied Nicholl, consulting his chronometer; "it is eleven o'clock, and it is only thirteen minutes since we left the American Continent."

"Only thirteen minutes?" said Barbicane.

"Yes," said Nicholl; "and if our initiatory speed of 12,000 yards has been kept up, we shall have made about 20,000 miles in the hour."

"That is all very well, my friends," said the president, "but the insoluble question still remains. Why did we not hear the detonation of the Columbiad?"

For want of an answer the conversation dropped, and Barbicane began thoughtfully to let down the shutter of the second side. He succeeded; and through the uncovered glass the moon filled the projectile with a brilliant light. Nicholl, as an economical man, put out the gas, now useless, and whose brilliancy prevented any observation of the interplanetary space.

The lunar disc shone with wonderful purity. Her rays, no longer filtered through the vapoury atmosphere of the terrestrial globe, shone through the glass, filling the air in the interior of the projectile with silvery reflections. The black curtain of the firmament in reality heightened the moon's brilliancy, which in this void of ether unfavourable to diffusion did not eclipse the neighbouring stars. The heavens, thus seen, presented quite a new aspect, and one which the human eye could never dream of. One may conceive the interest with which these bold men watched the orb of night, the great aim of their journey.

In its motion the earth's satellite was insensibly nearing the zenith, the mathematical point which it ought to attain ninety-six hours later. Her mountains, her plains, every projection was as clearly discernible to their eyes as if they were observing it from some spot upon the earth; but its light was developed through space with wonderful intensity. The disc shone like a platinum mirror. Of the earth flying from under their feet, the travellers had lost all recollection.

It was Captain Nicholl who first recalled their attention to the vanishing globe.

"Yes," said Michel Ardan, "do not let us be ungrateful to it. Since we are leaving our country, let our last looks be directed to it. I wish to see the earth once more before it is quite hidden from my eyes."

To satisfy his companions, Barbicane began to uncover the window at the bottom of the projectile, which would allow them to observe the earth direct. The disc, which the force of the projection had beaten down to the base, was removed, not without difficulty. Its fragments, placed carefully against the wall, might serve again upon occasion. Then a circular gap appeared, nineteen inches in diameter, hollowed out of the lower part of the projectile. A glass cover, six inches thick and strengthened with upper fastenings, closed it tightly. Beneath was fixed an aluminium plate, held in place by bolts. The screws being undone, and the bolts let go, the plate fell down, and visible communication was established between the interior and the exterior.

Michel Ardan knelt by the glass. It was cloudy, seemingly opaque.

"Well!" he exclaimed, "and the earth?"

"The earth?" said Barbicane. "There it is."

"What! that little thread; that silver crescent?"

"Doubtless, Michel. In four days, when the moon will be full, at the very time we shall reach it, the earth will be new, and will only appear to us as a slender crescent which will soon disappear, and for some days will be enveloped in utter darkness."

"That the earth?" repeated Michel Ardan, looking with all his eyes at the thin slip of his native planet.

The explanation given by President Barbicane was correct. The earth, with respect to the projectile, was entering its last phase. It was in its octant, and showed a crescent finely traced on the dark background of the sky. Its light, rendered bluish by the thick strata of the atmosphere, was less intense than that of the crescent moon, but it was of considerable dimensions, and looked like an enormous arch stretched across the firmament. Some parts brilliantly lighted, especially on its concave part, showed the presence of high mountains, often disappearing behind thick spots, which are never seen on the lunar disc. They were rings of clouds placed concentrically round the terrestrial globe.

Whilst the travellers were trying to pierce the profound darkness, a brilliant cluster of shooting stars burst upon their eyes. Hundreds of meteorites, ignited by the friction of the atmosphere, irradiated the shadow of the luminous train, and lined the cloudy parts of the disc with their fire. At this period the earth was in its perihelion, and the month of December is so propitious to these shooting stars, that astronomers have counted as many as twenty-four thousand in an hour. But Michel Ardan, disdaining scientific reasonings, preferred thinking that the earth was thus saluting the departure of her three children with her most brilliant fireworks.

Indeed this was all they saw of the globe lost in the shadow, an inferior orb of the solar world, rising and setting to the great planets like a simple morning or evening star! This globe, where they had left all their affections, was nothing more than a fugitive crescent!

Long did the three friends look without speaking, though united in heart, whilst the projectile sped onward with an ever-decreasing speed. Then an irresistible drowsiness crept over their brain. Was it weariness both of body and mind? No doubt; for after the over-excitement of those last hours passed upon earth, reaction was inevitable.

"Well," said Nicholl, "since we must sleep, let us sleep."

And stretching themselves on their couches, they were all three soon in a profound slumber.

But they had not forgotten themselves more than a quarter of an hour, when Barbicane sat up suddenly, and rousing his companions with a loud voice, exclaimed—

"I have found it!"

"What have you found?" asked Michel Ardan, jumping from his bed.

"The reason why we did not hear the detonation of the Columbiad."

"And it is——?" said Nicholl.

"Because our projectile travelled *faster than the sound!*"

CHAPTER III: THEIR PLACE OF SHELTER   This curious but certainly correct explanation once given, the three friends returned to their slumbers. Could they have found a calmer or more peaceful spot to sleep in? On the earth, houses, towns, cottages, and country feel every shock given to the exterior of the globe. On sea, the vessels rocked by the waves are still in motion; in the air, the balloon oscillates incessantly on the fluid strata of divers densities. This projectile alone, floating in perfect space, in the midst of perfect silence, offered perfect repose.

Thus the sleep of our adventurous travellers might have been indefinitely prolonged, if an unexpected noise had not awakened them at about seven o'clock in the morning of the 2nd of December, eight hours after their departure.

This noise was a very natural barking.

"The dogs! it is the dogs!" exclaimed Michel Ardan, rising at once.

"They are hungry," said Nicholl.

"By Jove!" replied Michel, "we have forgotten them."

"Where are they?" asked Barbicane.

They looked, and found one of the animals crouched under the divan. Terrified and shaken by the initiatory shock, it had remained in the corner till its voice returned with the pangs of hunger. It was the amiable Diana, still very confused, who crept out of her retreat, though not without much persuasion, Michel Ardan encouraging her with most gracious words.

"Come, Diana," said he; "come, my girl! thou whose destiny will be marked in the cynegetic annals; thou whom the pagans would have given as companion to the god Anubis, and Christians as friend to St. Roch; thou who art rushing into interplanetary space, and wilt perhaps be the Eve of all Selenite dogs! come, Diana, come here."

Diana, flattered or not, advanced by degrees, uttering plaintive cries.

"Good," said Barbicane; "I see Eve, but where is Adam?"

"Adam?" replied Michel; "Adam cannot be far off; he is there somewhere; we must call him. Satellite! here, Satellite!"

But Satellite did not appear. Diana would not leave off howling. They found, however, that she was not bruised, and they gave her a pie, which silenced her complaints. As to Satellite, he seemed quite lost. They had to hunt a long time before finding him in one of the upper compartments of the projectile, whither some unaccountable shock must have violently hurled him. The poor beast, much hurt, was in a piteous state.

"The devil!" said Michel.

They brought the unfortunate dog down with great care. Its skull had been broken against the roof, and it seemed unlikely that he could recover from such a shock. Meanwhile, he was stretched comfortably on a cushion. Once there, he heaved a sigh.

"We will take care of you," said Michel; "we are responsible for your existence. I would rather lose an arm than a paw of my poor Satellite."

Saying which, he offered some water to the wounded dog, who swallowed it with avidity.

This attention paid, the travellers watched the earth and the moon attentively. The earth was now only discernible by a cloudy disc ending in a crescent, rather more contracted than that of the previous evening;

but its expanse was still enormous, compared with that of the moon, which was approaching nearer and nearer to a perfect circle.

"By Jove!" said Michel Ardan, "I am really sorry that we did not start when the earth was full, that is to say, when our globe was in opposition to the sun."

"Why?" asked Nicholl.

"Because we should have seen our continents and seas in a new light—the first resplendent under the solar rays, the latter cloudy as represented on some maps of the world. I should like to have seen those poles of the earth on which the eye of man has never yet rested."

"I dare say," replied Barbicane; "but if the earth had been *full*, the moon would have been *new*; that is to say, invisible, because of the rays of the sun. It is better for us to see the destination we wish to reach, than the point of departure."

"You are right, Barbicane," replied Captain Nicholl; "and, besides, when we have reached the moon, we shall have time during the long lunar nights to consider at our leisure the globe on which our likenesses swarm."

"Our likenesses!" exclaimed Michel Ardan; "they are no more our likenesses than the Selenites are! We inhabit a new world, peopled by ourselves—the projectile! I am Barbicane's likeness, and Barbicane is Nicholl's. Beyond us, around us, human nature is at an end, and we are the only population of this microcosm until we become pure Selenites."

"In about eighty-eight hours," replied the captain.

"Which means to say?" asked Michel Ardan.

"That it is half-past eight," replied Nicholl.

"Very well," retorted Michel; "then it is impossible for me to find even the shadow of a reason why we should not go to breakfast."

Indeed the inhabitants of the new star could not live without eating, and their stomachs were suffering from the imperious laws of hunger. Michel Ardan, as a Frenchman, was declared chief cook, an important function, which raised no rival. The gas gave sufficient heat for the culinary apparatus, and the provision-box furnished the elements of this first feast.

The breakfast began with three bowls of excellent soup, thanks to the liquefaction in hot water of those precious cakes of Liebig, prepared from the best parts of the ruminants of the Pampas. To the soup succeeded some beefsteaks, compressed by an hydraulic press, as tender and succulent as if brought straight from the kitchen of an English eating-house. Michel, who was imaginative, maintained that they were even "red."

Preserved vegetables ("fresher than nature," said the amiable Michel) succeeded the dish of meat; and was followed by some cups of tea with bread and butter, after the American fashion.

The beverage was declared exquisite, and was due to the infusion of the choicest leaves, of which the Emperor of Russia had given some chests for the benefit of the travellers.

And lastly, to crown the repast, Ardan brought out a fine bottle of Nuits, which was found "by chance" in the provision-box. The three friends drank to the union of the earth and her satellite.

And, as if he had not already done enough for the generous wine which he had distilled on the slopes of Burgundy, the sun chose to be of the party. At this moment the projectile emerged from the conical shadow cast by the terrestrial globe, and the rays of the radiant orb struck the lower disc of the projectile direct, occasioned by the angle which the moon's orbit makes with that of the earth.

"The sun!" exclaimed Michel Ardan.

"No doubt," replied Barbicane; "I expected it."

"But," said Michel, "the conical shadow which the earth leaves in space extends beyond the moon?"

"Far beyond it, if the atmospheric refraction is not taken into consideration," said Barbicane. "But when the moon is enveloped in this shadow, it is because the centres of the three stars, the sun, the earth, and the moon, are all in one and the same straight line. Then the *nodes* coincide with the *phases* of the moon, and there is an eclipse. If we had started when there was an eclipse of the moon, all our passage would have been in the shadow, which would have been a pity."

"Why?"

"Because, though we are floating in space, our projectile, bathed in the solar rays, will receive their light and heat. It economizes the gas, which is in every respect a good economy."

Indeed, under these rays which no atmosphere can temper, either in temperature or brilliancy, the projectile grew warm and bright, as if it had passed suddenly from winter to summer. The moon above, the sun beneath, were inundating it with their fire.

"It is pleasant here," said Nichol.

"I should think so," said Michel Ardan. "With a little earth spread on our aluminium planet we should have green peas in twenty-four hours. I have but one fear, which is that the walls of the projectile might melt."

"Calm yourself, my worthy friend," replied Barbicane; "the projectile withstood a very much higher temperature than this as it slid through the strata of the atmosphere. I should not be surprised if it did not look like a meteor on fire to the eyes of the spectators in Florida."

"But then Joseph T. Maston will think we are roasted!"

"What astonishes me," said Barbicane, "is that we have not been. That was a danger we had not provided for."

"I feared it," said Nicholl simply.

"And you never mentioned it, my sublime captain," exclaimed Michel Ardan, clasping his friend's hand.

Barbicane now began to settle himself in the projectile as if he was never to leave it. One must remember that this aerial car had a base with a superficies of fifty-four square feet. Its height to the roof was twelve feet. Carefully laid out in the inside, and little encumbered by instruments and travelling utensils which each had their particular place, it left the three travellers a certain freedom of movement. The thick window inserted in the bottom could bear any amount of weight, and Barbicane and his companions walked upon it as if it were solid plank; but the sun striking it directly with its rays lit the interior of the projectile from beneath, thus producing singular effects of light.

They began by investigating the state of their store of water and provisions, neither of which had suffered, thanks to the care taken to deaden the shock. Their provisions were abundant, and plentiful enough to last the three travellers for more than a year. Barbicane wished to be cautious, in case the projectile should land on a part of the moon which was utterly barren. As to water and the reserve of brandy, which consisted of fifty gallons, there was only enough for two months; but according to the last observations of astronomers, the moon had a low, dense, and thick atmosphere, at least in the deep valleys, and there springs and streams could not fail. Thus, during their passage, and for the first year of their settlement on the lunar continent, these adventurous explorers would suffer neither hunger nor thirst.

Now about the air in the projectile. There, too, they were secure. Reiset and Regnaut's apparatus, intended for the production of oxygen, was supplied with chlorate of potash for two months. They necessarily consumed a certain quantity of gas, for they were obliged to keep the producing substance at a temperature of above 400°. But there again they were all safe. The apparatus only wanted a little care. But it was not enough to renew the oxygen; they must absorb the carbonic acid produced by expiration. During the last twelve hours the atmosphere of the projectile had become charged with this deleterious gas. Nicholl discovered the state of the air by observing Diana panting painfully. The carbonic acid, by a phenomenon similar to that produced in the famous Grotto del Cane, had collected at the bottom of the projectile owing to its weight. Poor Diana, with her head low, would suffer before her masters from the presence of this gas. But Captain Nicholl hastened to remedy this state of things, by placing on the floor several receivers containing caustic potash which he shook about for a time, and this substance, greedy of carbonic acid, soon completely absorbed it, thus purifying the air.

An inventory of instruments was then begun. The thermometers and barometers had resisted, all but one minimum thermometer, the glass of which was broken. An excellent aneroid was drawn from the wadded box which contained it and hung on the wall. Of course it was only affected by and marked the pressure of the air inside the projectile, but it also showed the quantity of moisture which it contained. At that moment its needle oscillated between 25.24 and 25.08.

It was fine weather.

Barbicane had also brought several compasses, which he found intact. One must understand that under present conditions their needles were acting *wildly*, that is without any *constant* direction. Indeed, at the distance they were from the earth, the magnetic pole could have no perceptible action upon the apparatus; but the box placed on the lunar disc might perhaps exhibit some strange phenomena. In any case it would be interesting to see whether the earth's satellite submitted like herself to its magnetic influence.

A hypsometer to measure the height of the lunar mountains, a sextant to take the height of the sun, glasses which would be useful as they neared the moon, all these instruments were carefully looked over, and pronounced good in spite of the violent shock.

As to the pickaxes and different tools which were Nicholl's especial choice; as to the sacks of different kinds of grain and shrubs which Michel Ardan hoped to transplant into Selenite ground, they were stowed away in the upper part of the projectile. There was a sort of granary there, loaded with things which the extravagant Frenchman had heaped up. What they were no one knew, and the good-tempered fellow did not explain. Now and then he climbed up by cramp-irons rivetted to the walls, but kept the inspection to himself. He arranged and rearranged, he plunged his hand rapidly into certain mysterious boxes, singing in one of the falsest of voices an old French refrain to enliven the situation.

Barbicane observed with some interest that his guns and other arms had not been damaged. These were important, because, heavily loaded, they were to help to lessen the fall of the projectile, when drawn by the lunar attraction (after having passed the point of neutral attraction) on to the moon's surface; a fall which ought to be six times less rapid than it would have been on the earth's surface, thanks to the difference of bulk. The inspection ended with general satisfaction, when each returned to watch space through the side windows and the lower glass coverlid.

There was the same view. The whole extent of the celestial sphere swarmed with stars and constellations of wonderful purity, enough to drive an astronomer out of his mind! On one side the sun, like the mouth of a lighted oven, a dazzling disc without a halo, standing out on the dark background of the sky! On the other, the moon returning its fire by reflection, and apparently motionless in the midst of the starry world. Then, a large spot seemingly nailed to the firmament, bordered by a silvery cord: it was the earth! Here and there nebulous masses like large flakes of starry snow; and from the zenith to the nadir, an immense ring formed by an impalpable dust of stars, the "Milky Way," in the midst of which the sun ranks only as a star of the fourth magnitude. The observers could not take their eyes from this novel spectacle, of which no description could give an adequate idea. What reflections it suggested! What emotions hitherto unknown awoke in their souls! Barbicane wished to begin the relation of his journey while under its first impressions, and hour after hour took notes of all facts happening in the beginning of the enterprise. He wrote quietly, with his large square writing, in a business-like style.

During this time Nicholl, the calculator, looked over the minutes of their passage, and worked out figures with unparalleled dexterity. Michel Ardan chatted first with Barbicane, who did not answer him, and then with Nicholl, who did not hear him, with Diana, who understood none of his theories, and lastly with himself, questioning and answering, going and coming, busy with a thousand details; at one time bent over the lower glass, at another roosting in the heights of the projectile, and always singing. In this microcosm he represented French loquacity and excitability, and we beg you to believe that they were well represented. The day, or rather (for the expression is not correct) the lapse of twelve hours, which forms a day upon earth, closed with a plentiful supper carefully prepared. No accident of any nature had yet happened to shake the travellers' confidence; so, full of hope, already sure of success, they slept peacefully, whilst the projectile under an uniformly decreasing speed was crossing the sky.

CHAPTER IV: A LITTLE ALGEBRA   The night passed without incident. The word "night," however, is scarcely applicable.

The position of the projectile with regard to the sun did not change. Astronomically, it was daylight on the lower part, and night on the upper; so when during this narrative these words are used, they represent the lapse of time between the rising and setting of the sun upon the earth.

The travellers' sleep was rendered more peaceful by the projectile's excessive speed, for it seemed absolutely motionless. Not a motion betrayed its onward course through space. The rate of progress, however rapid it might be, cannot produce any sensible effect on the human frame when it takes place in a vacuum, or when the mass of air circulates with the body which is carried with it. What inhabitant of the earth perceives its speed, which, however, is at the rate of 68,000 miles per hour? Motion under such conditions is "felt" no more than repose; and when a body is in repose it will remain so as long as no strange force displaces it; if moving, it will not stop unless an obstacle comes in its way. This indifference to motion or repose is called inertia.

Barbicane and his companions might have believed themselves perfectly stationary, being shut up in the projectile; indeed, the effect would have been the same if they had been on the outside of it. Had it not been for the moon, which was increasing above them, they might have sworn that they were floating in complete stagnation.

That morning, the 3rd of December, the travellers were awakened by a joyous but unexpected noise; it was the crowing of a cock which sounded through the ear. Michel Ardan, who was the first on his feet, climbed to the top of the projectile, and shutting a box, the lid of which was partly open, said in a low voice, "Will you hold your tongue? That creature will spoil my design!"

But Nicholl and Barbicane were awake.

"A cock!" said Nicholl.

"Why no, my friends," Michel answered quickly; "it was I who wished to awake you by this rural sound." So saying, he gave vent to a splendid cock-a-doodledoo, which would have done honour to the proudest of poultry-yards.

The two Americans could not help laughing.

"Fine talent that," said Nicholl, looking suspiciously at his companion.

"Yes," said Michel; "a joke in my country. It is very Gallic; they play the cock so in the best society."

Then turning the conversation—

"Barbicane, do you know what I have been thinking of all night?"

"No," answered the president.

"Of our Cambridge friends. You have already remarked that I am an ignoramus in mathematical subjects; and it is impossible for me to find out how the savants of the Observatory were able to calculate what initiatory speed the projectile ought to have on leaving the Columbiad in order to attain the moon."

"You mean to say," replied Barbicane, "to attain that neutral point where the terrestrial and lunar attractions are equal; for, starting from that point, situated about nine-tenths of the distance travelled over, the projectile would simply fall upon the moon, on account of its weight."

"So be it," said Michel; "but, once more; how could they calculate the initiatory speed?"

"Nothing can be easier," replied Barbicane.

"And you knew how to make that calculation?" asked Michel Ardan.

"Perfectly. Nicholl and I would have made it, if the Observatory had not saved us the trouble."

"Very well, old Barbicane," replied Michel; "they might have cut off my head, beginning at my feet, before they could have made me solve that problem."

"Because you do not know algebra," answered Barbicane quietly.

"Ah, there you are, you eaters of x^1; you think you have said all when you have said 'Algebra.'"

"Michel," said Barbicane, "can you use a forge without a hammer, or plough without a ploughshare?"

"Hardly."

"Well, algebra is a tool, like the plough or the hammer, and a good tool to those who know how to use it."

"Seriously?"

"Quite seriously."

"And can you use that tool in my presence?"

"If it will interest you."

"And show me how they calculated the initiatory speed of our car?"

"Yes, my worthy friend; taking into consideration all the elements of the problem, the distance from the centre of the earth to the centre of the moon, of the radius of the earth, of its bulk, and of the bulk of the moon, I can tell exactly what ought to be the initiatory speed of the projectile, and that by a simple formula."

"Let us see."

"You shall see it; only I shall not give you the real course drawn by the projectile between the moon and the earth in considering their motion round the sun. No, I shall consider these two orbs as perfectly motionless, which will answer all our purpose."

"And why?"

"Because it will be trying to solve the problem called 'the problem of the three bodies,' for which the integral calculus is not yet far enough advanced."

"Then," said Michel Ardan, in his sly tone, "mathematics have not said their last word?"

"Certainly not," replied Barbicane.

"Well, perhaps the Selenites have carried the integral calculus farther than you have; and, by the bye, what is this 'integral calculus'?"

"It is a calculation the converse of the differential," replied Barbicane seriously.

"Much obliged; it is all very clear, no doubt."

"And now," continued Barbicane, "a slip of paper and a bit of pencil, and before a half-hour is over I will have found the required formula."

Half an hour had not elapsed before Barbicane, raising his head, showed Michel Ardan a page covered with algebraical signs, in which the general formula for the solution was contained.

"Well, and does Nicholl understand what that means?"

"Of course, Michel," replied the captain. "All these signs, which seem cabalistic to you, form the plainest, the clearest, and the most logical language to those who know how to read it."

"And you pretend, Nicholl," asked Michel, "that by means of these hieroglyphics, more incomprehensible than the Egyptian Ibis, you can find what initiatory speed it was necessary to give to the projectile?"

"Incontestably," replied Nicholl; "and even by this same formula I can always tell you its speed at any point of its transit."

"On your word?"

"On my word."

"Then you are as cunning as our president."

"No, Michel; the difficult part is what Barbicane has done; that is, to get an equation which shall satisfy all the conditions of the problem. The remainder is only a question of arithmetic, requiring merely the knowledge of the four rules."

"That is something!" replied Michel Ardan, who for his life could not do addition right, and who defined the rule as a Chinese puzzle, which allowed one to obtain all sorts of totals.

"The expression v zero, which you see in that equation, is the speed which the projectile will have on leaving the atmosphere."

"Just so," said Nicholl; "it is from that point that we must calculate the velocity, since we know already that the velocity at departure was exactly one and a half times more than on leaving the atmosphere."

"I understand no more," said Michel.

"It is a very simple calculation," said Barbicane.

"Not as simple as I am," retorted Michel.

"That means, that when our projectile reached the limits of the terrestrial atmosphere it had already lost one-third of its initiatory speed."

"As much as that?"

"Yes, my friend; merely by friction against the atmospheric strata. You understand that the faster it goes the more resistance it meets with from the air."

"That I admit," answered Michel; "and I understand it, although your x's and zero's, and algebraic formulæ, are rattling in my head like nails in a bag."

"First effects of algebra," replied Barbicane; "and now, to finish, we are going to prove the given number of these different expressions, that is, work out their value."

"Finish me!" replied Michel.

Barbicane took the paper, and began again to make his calculations with great rapidity. Nicholl looked over and greedily read the work as it proceeded.

"That's it! that's it!" at last he cried.

"Is it clear?" asked Barbicane.

"It is written in letters of fire," said Nicholl.

"Wonderful fellows!" muttered Ardan.

"Do you understand it at last?" asked Barbicane.

"Do I understand it?" cried Ardan; "my head is splitting with it."

"And now," said Nicholl, "to find out the speed of the projectile when it left the atmosphere, we have only to calculate that."

The captain, as a practical man equal to all difficulties, began to write with frightful rapidity. Divisions and multiplications grew under his fingers; the figures were like hail on the white page. Barbicane watched him, whilst Michel Ardan nursed a growing headache with both hands.

"Very well?" asked Barbicane, after some minutes' silence.

"Well!" replied Nicholl; "every calculation made, v zero, that is to say, the speed necessary for the projectile on leaving the atmosphere, to enable it to reach the equal point of attraction, ought to be——"

"Yes?" said Barbicane.

"Twelve thousand yards."

"What!" exclaimed Barbicane, starting; "you say——"

"Twelve thousand yards."

"The devil!" cried the president, making a gesture of despair.

"What is the matter?" asked Michel Ardan, much surprised.

"What is the matter! why, if at this moment our speed had already diminished one-third by friction, the initiatory speed ought to have been—"

"Seventeen thousand yards."

"And the Cambridge Observatory declared that 12,000 yards was enough at starting; and our projectile, which only started with that speed——"

"Well?" asked Nicholl.

"Well, it will not be enough."

"Good."

"We shall not be able to reach the neutral point."

"The deuce!"

"We shall not even get half way."

"In the name of the projectile!" exclaimed Michel Ardan, jumping as if it was already on the point of striking the terrestrial globe.

"And we shall fall back upon the earth!"

CHAPTER V: THE COLD OF SPACE   This revelation came like a thunderbolt. Who could have expected such an error in calculation? Barbicane would not believe it. Nicholl revised his figures: they were exact. As to the formula which had determined them, they could not suspect its truth; it was evident that an initiatory velocity of 17,000 yards in the first second was necessary to enable them to reach the neutral point.

The three friends looked at each other silently. There was no thought of breakfast. Barbicane, with clenched teeth, knitted brows, and hands clasped convulsively, was watching through the window. Nicholl had crossed his arms, and was examining his calculations. Michel Ardan was muttering—

"That is just like those scientific men: they never do anything else. I would give twenty pistoles if we could fall upon the Cambridge Observatory and crush it, together with the whole lot of dabblers in figures which it contains."

Suddenly a thought struck the captain, which he at once communicated to Barbicane.

"Ah!" said he; "it is seven o'clock in the morning; we have already been gone thirty-two hours; more than half our passage is over, and we are not falling that I am aware of."

Barbicane did not answer, but, after a rapid glance at the captain, took a pair of compasses wherewith to measure the angular distance of the terrestrial globe; then from the lower window he took an exact observation, and noticed that the projectile was apparently stationary. Then rising and wiping his forehead, on which large drops of perspiration were standing, he put some figures on paper. Nicholl understood that the president was deducting from the terrestrial diameter the projectile's distance from the earth. He watched him anxiously.

"No," exclaimed Barbicane, after some moments, "no, we are not falling! no, we are already more than 50,000 leagues from the earth. We have passed the point at which the projectile would have stopped if its speed had only been 12,000 yards at starting. We are still going up."

"That is evident," replied Nicholl; "and we must conclude that our initial speed, under the power of the 400,000 lbs. of gun-cotton, must have exceeded the required 12,000 yards. Now I can understand how, after thirteen minutes only, we met the second satellite, which gravitates round the earth at more than 2000 leagues' distance."

"And this explanation is the more probable," added Barbicane, "because, in throwing off the water enclosed between its partition-breaks, the projectile found itself lightened of a considerable weight."

"Just so," said Nicholl.

"Ah, my brave Nicholl, we are saved!"

"Very well, then," said Michel Ardan quietly; "as we are safe, let us have breakfast."

Nicholl was not mistaken. The initial speed had been, very fortunately, much above that estimated by the Cambridge Observatory; but the Cambridge Observatory had nevertheless made a mistake.

The travellers, recovered from this false alarm, breakfasted merrily. If they ate a great deal, they talked more. Their confidence was greater after than before "the incident of the algebra."

"Why should we not succeed?" said Michel Ardan; "why should we not arrive safely? We are launched; we have no obstacle before us, no stones in our way; the road is open, more so than that of a ship battling with the sea; more open than that of a balloon battling with the wind; and if a ship can reach its destination, a balloon go where it pleases, why cannot our projectile attain its end and aim?"

"It *will* attain it," said Barbicane.

"If only to do honour to the Americans," added Michel Ardan, "the only people who could bring such an enterprise to a happy termination, and the only one which could produce a President Barbicane. Ah, now we are no longer uneasy, I begin to think, What will become of us? We shall get right royally weary."

Barbicane and Nicholl made a gesture of denial.

"But I have provided for the contingency, my friends," replied Michel; "you have only to speak, and I have chess, draughts, cards, and dominoes at your disposal; nothing is wanting but a billiard-table."

"What!" exclaimed Barbicane; "you brought away such trifles?"

"Certainly," replied Michel, "and not only to distract ourselves, but also with the laudable intention of endowing the Selenite smoking divans with them."

"My friend," said Barbicane, "if the moon is inhabited, its inhabitants must have appeared some thousands of years before those of the earth, for we cannot doubt that their star is much older than ours. If then these Selenites have existed their hundreds of thousands of years, and if their brain is of the same organization as the human brain, they have already invented all that we have invented, and even what we may invent in future ages. They have nothing to learn from *us*, and we have everything to learn from *them*."

"What!" said Michel; "you believe that they have artists like Phidias, Michael Angelo, or Raphael?"

"Yes."

"Poets like Homer, Virgil, Milton, Lamartine, and Hugo?"

"I am sure of it."

"Philosophers like Plato, Aristotle, Descartes, Kant?"

"I have no doubt of it."

"Scientific men like Archimedes, Euclid, Pascal, Newton?"

"I could swear it."

"Comic writers like Arnal, and photographers like—like Nadar?"

"Certain."

"Then, friend Barbicane, if they are as strong as we are, and even stronger—these Selenites—why have they not tried to communicate with the earth? why have they not launched a lunar projectile to our terrestrial regions?"

"Who told you that they have never done so?" said Barbicane, seriously.

"Indeed," added Nicholl, "it would be easier for them than for us, for two reasons; first, because the attraction on the moon's surface is six times less than on that of the earth, which would allow a projectile to rise more easily; secondly, because it would be enough to send such a projectile only at 8000 leagues instead of 80,000, which would require the force of projection to be ten times less strong."

"Then," continued Michel, "I repeat it, why have they not done it?"

"And I repeat," said Barbicane; "who told you that they have not done it?"

"When?"

"Thousands of years before man appeared on earth."

"And the projectile—where is the projectile? I demand to see the projectile."

"My friend," replied Barbicane, "the sea covers five-sixths of our globe. From that we may draw five good reasons for supposing that the lunar projectile, if ever launched, is now at the bottom of the Atlantic or the Pacific, unless it sped into some crevasse at that period when the crust of the earth was not yet hardened."

"Old Barbicane," said Michel, "you have an answer for everything, and I bow before your wisdom. But there is one hypothesis that would suit me better than all the others, which is, that the Selenites, being older than we, are wiser, and have not invented *gunpowder*."

At this moment Diana joined in the conversation by a sonorous barking. She was asking for her breakfast.

"Ah!" said Michel Ardan, "in our discussion we have forgotten Diana and Satellite."

Immediately a good-sized pie was given to the dog, which devoured it hungrily.

"Do you see, Barbicane," said Michel, "we should have made a second Noah's Ark of this projectile, and borne with us to the moon a couple of every kind of domestic animal."

"I dare say; but room would have failed us."

"Oh!" said Michel, "we might have squeezed a little."

"The fact is," replied Nicholl, "that cows, bulls, and horses, and all ruminants, would have been very useful on the lunar continent, but unfortunately the car could neither have been made a stable nor a shed."

"Well, we might at least have brought a donkey, only a little donkey; that courageous beast which old Silenus loved to mount. I love those old donkeys; they are the least favoured animals in creation; they are not only beaten while alive, but even after they are dead."

"How do you make that out?" asked Barbicane.

"Why," said Michel, "they make their skins into drums."

Barbicane and Nicholl could not help laughing at this ridiculous remark. But a cry from their merry companion stopped them. The latter was leaning over the spot where Satellite lay. He rose, saying—

"My good Satellite is no longer ill."

"Ah!" said Nicholl.

"No," answered Michel, "he is dead! There," added he, in a piteous tone, "that is embarrassing. I much fear, my poor Diana, that you will leave no progeny in the lunar regions!"

Indeed the unfortunate Satellite had not survived its wound. It was quite dead. Michel Ardan looked at his friends with a rueful countenance.

"One question presents itself," said Barbicane. "We cannot keep the dead body of this dog with us for the next forty-eight hours."

"No! certainly not," replied Nicholl; "but our scuttles are fixed on hinges; they can be let down. We will open one, and throw the body out into space."

The president thought for some moments, and then said—

"Yes, we must do so, but at the same time taking very great precautions."

"Why?" asked Michel.

"For two reasons which you will understand," answered Barbicane. "The first relates to the air shut up in the projectile, and of which we must lose as little as possible."

"But we manufacture the air?"

"Only in part. We make only the oxygen, my worthy Michel; and with regard to that, we must watch that the apparatus does not furnish the oxygen in too great a quantity; for an excess would bring us very serious physiological troubles. But if we make the oxygen, we do not make the azote, that medium which the lungs do not absorb, and which ought to remain intact; and that azote will escape rapidly through the open scuttles."

"Oh! the time for throwing out poor Satellite?" said Michel.

"Agreed; but we must act quickly."

"And the second reason?" asked Michel.

"The second reason is that we must not let the outer cold, which is excessive, penetrate the projectile, or we shall be frozen to death."

"But the sun?"

"The sun warms our projectile, which absorbs its rays; but it does not warm the vacuum in which we are floating at this moment. Where there is no air, there is no more heat than diffused light; and the same with darkness: it is cold where the sun's rays do not strike direct. This temperature is only the temperature produced by the radiation of the stars; that is to say, what the terrestrial globe would undergo if the sun disappeared one day."

"Which is not to be feared," replied Nicholl.

"Who knows?" said Michel Ardan. "But, in admitting that the sun does not go out, might it not happen that the earth might move away from it?"

"There!" said Barbicane, "there is Michel with his ideas."

"And," continued Michel, "do we not know that in 1861 the earth passed through the tail of a comet? Or let us suppose a comet whose power of attraction is greater than that of the sun. The terrestrial orbit will bend towards the wandering star, and the earth, becoming its satellite, will be drawn such a distance that the rays of the sun will have no action on its surface."

"That *might* happen, indeed," replied Barbicane, "but the consequences of such a displacement need not be so formidable as you suppose."

"And why not?"

"Because the heat and the cold would be equalized on our globe. It has been calculated that, had our earth been carried along in its course by the comet of 1861, at its perihelion, that is, its nearest approach to the sun, it would have undergone a heat 28,000 times greater than that of summer. But this heat, which is sufficient to evaporate the waters, would have formed a thick ring of cloud, which would have modified that excessive temperature; hence the compensation between the cold of the aphelion and the heat of the perihelion."

"At how many degrees," asked Nicholl, "is the temperature of the planetary spaces estimated?"

"Formerly," replied Barbicane, "it was greatly exaggerated; but now, after the calculations of Fourier, of the French Academy of Science, it is not supposed to exceed 60° Centigrade below zero."

"Pooh!" said Michel, "that's nothing!"

"It is very much," replied Barbicane; "the temperature which was observed in the polar regions, at Melville Island and Fort Reliance, that is 76° Fahrenheit below zero."

"If I mistake not," said Nicholl, "M. Pouillet, another savant, estimates the temperature of space at 250° Fahr. below zero. We shall, however, be able to verify these calculations for ourselves."

"Not at present; because the solar rays, beating directly upon our thermometer, would give, on the contrary, a very high temperature. But, when we arrive in the moon, during its fifteen days of night at either face, we shall have leisure to make the experiment, for our satellite lies in a vacuum."

"What do you mean by a *vacuum?*" asked Michel. "Is it perfectly such?"

"It is absolutely void of air."

"And is the air replaced by nothing whatever?"

"By the ether only," replied Barbicane.

"And pray what is the ether?"

"The ether, my friend, is an agglomeration of imponderable atoms, which, relatively to their dimensions, are as far removed from each other as the celestial bodies are in space. It is these atoms which, by their vibratory motion, produce both light and heat in the universe."

They now proceeded to the burial of Satellite. They had merely to drop him into space, in the same way that sailors drop a body into the sea; but, as President Barbicane suggested, they must act quickly, so as to lose as little as possible of that air whose elasticity would rapidly have spread it into space. The bolts of the right scuttle, the opening of which measured about twelve inches across, were carefully drawn, whilst Michel, quite grieved, prepared to launch his dog into space. The glass, raised by a powerful lever, which enabled it to overcome the pressure of the inside air on the walls of the projectile, turned rapidly on its hinges, and Satellite was thrown out. Scarcely a particle of air could have escaped, and the operation was so successful, that later on Barbicane did not fear to dispose of the rubbish which encumbered the car.

CHAPTER VI: QUESTION AND ANSWER   On the 4th of December, when the travellers awoke after fifty-four hours' journey, the chronometer marked five o'clock of the terrestrial morning. In time it was just over five hours and forty minutes, half of that assigned to their sojourn in the projectile; but they had already accomplished nearly seven-tenths of the way. This peculiarity was due to their regularly decreasing speed.

Now when they observed the earth through the lower window, it looked like nothing more than a dark spot, drowned in the solar rays. No more crescent, no more cloudy light! The next day, at midnight, the earth would be *new*, at the very moment when the moon would be full. Above, the orb of night was nearing the line followed by the projectile, so as to meet it at the given hour. All around the black vault was studded with brilliant points, which seemed to move slowly; but, at the great distance they were from them, their relative size did not seem to change. The sun and stars appeared exactly as they do to us upon earth. As to the moon, she was considerably larger; but the travellers' glasses, not very powerful, did not allow them as yet to make any useful observations upon her surface, or reconnoitre her topographically or geologically.

Thus the time passed in never-ending conversations all about the moon. Each one brought forward his own contingent of particular facts; Barbicane and Nicholl always serious, Michel Ardan always enthusiastic. The projectile, its situation, its direction, incidents which might happen, the precautions necessitated by their fall on to the moon, were inexhaustible matters of conjecture.

As they were breakfasting, a question of Michel's, relating to the projectile, provoked rather a curious answer from Barbicane, which is worth repeating. Michel, supposing it to be roughly stopped, whilst still under its formidable initial speed, wished to know what the consequences of the stoppage would have been.

"But," said Barbicane, "I do not see how it could have been stopped."

"But let us suppose so," said Michel.

"It is an impossible supposition," said the practical Barbicane; "unless the impulsive force had failed; but even then its speed would diminish by degrees, and it would not have stopped suddenly."

"Admit that it had struck a body in space."

"What body?"

"Why that enormous meteor which we met."

"Then," said Nicholl, "the projectile would have been broken into a thousand pieces, and we with it."

"More than that," replied Barbicane; "we should have been burnt to death."

"Burnt?" exclaimed Michel, "by Jove! I am sorry it did not happen, 'just to see.' "

"And you would have seen," replied Barbicane. "It is known now that heat is only a modification of motion. When water is warmed—that is to say, when heat is added to it—its particles are set in motion."

"Well," said Michel, "that is an ingenious theory!"

"And a true one, my worthy friend; for it explains every phenomenon of caloric. Heat is but the motion of atoms, a simple oscillation of the particles of a body. When they apply the break to a train, the train comes to a stop; but what becomes of the motion which it had previously possessed? It is transformed into heat, and the break becomes hot. Why do they grease the axles of the wheels? To prevent their heating, because this heat would be generated by the motion which is thus lost by transformation."

"Yes, I understand," replied Michel, "perfectly. For example, when I have run a long time, when I am swimming, when I am perspiring in large drops, why am I obliged to stop? Simply because my motion is changed into heat."

Barbicane could not help smiling at Michel's reply; then, returning to his theory, said—

"Thus, in case of a shock, it would have been with our projectile as with a ball which falls in a burning state after having struck the metal plate; it is its motion which is turned into heat. Consequently I affirm that, if our projectile had struck the meteor, its speed thus suddenly checked would have raised a heat great enough to turn it into vapour instantaneously."

"Then," asked Nicholl, "what would happen if the earth's motion were to stop suddenly?"

"Her temperature would be raised to such a pitch," said Barbicane, "that she would be at once reduced to vapour."

"Well," said Michel, "that is a way of ending the earth which will greatly simplify things."

"And if the earth fell upon the sun?" asked Nicholl.

"According to calculation," replied Barbicane, "the fall would develope a heat equal to that produced by 16,000 globes of coal, each equal in bulk to our terrestrial globe."

"Good additional heat for the sun," replied Michel Ardan, "of which the inhabitants of Uranus or Neptune would doubtless not complain; they must be perished with cold on their planets."

"Thus, my friends," said Barbicane, "all motion suddenly stopped produces heat. And this theory allows us to infer that the heat of the solar disc is fed by a hail of meteors falling incessantly on its surface. They have even calculated——"

"Oh, dear!" murmured Michel, "the figures are coming."

"They have even calculated," continued the imperturbable Barbicane, "that the shock of each meteor on the sun ought to produce a heat equal to that of 4000 masses of coal of an equal bulk."

"And what is the solar heat?" asked Michel.

"It is equal to that produced by the combustion of a stratum of coal surrounding the sun to a depth of forty-seven miles."

"And that heat——"

"Would be able to boil two billions nine hundred millions of cubic myriametres[1] of water."

"And it does not roast us!" exclaimed Michel.

"No," replied Barbicane, "because the terrestrial atmosphere absorbs

[1] *The myriametre is equal to rather more than 10,936 cubic yards English.* —(*Ed.*)

four-tenths of the solar heat; besides, the quantity of heat intercepted by the earth is but a billionth part of the entire radiation."

"I see that all is for the best," said Michel, "and that this atmosphere is a useful invention; for it not only allows us to breathe, but it prevents us from roasting."

"Yes!" said Nicholl, "unfortunately, it will not be the same in the moon."

"Bah!" said Michel, always hopeful. "If there are inhabitants, they must breathe. If there are no longer any, they must have left enough oxygen for three people, if only at the bottom of ravines, where its own weight will cause it to accumulate, and we will not climb the mountains; that is all." And Michel, rising, went to look at the lunar disc, which shone with intolerable brilliancy.

"By Jove!" said he, "it must be hot up there!"

"Without considering," replied Nicholl, "that the day lasts 360 hours!"

"And to compensate that," said Barbicane, "the nights have the same length; and as heat is restored by radiation, their temperature can only be that of the planetary space."

"A pretty country, that!" exclaimed Michel. "Never mind! I wish I was there! Ah! my dear comrades, it will be rather curious to have the earth for our moon, to see it rise on the horizon, to recognize the shape of its continents, and to say to oneself, 'There is America, there is Europe;' then to follow it when it is about to lose itself in the sun's rays! By-the-bye, Barbicane, have the Selenites eclipses?"

"Yes, eclipses of the sun," replied Barbicane, "when the centres of the three orbs are on a line, the earth being in the middle. But they are only partial, during which the earth, cast like a screen upon the solar disc, allows the greater portion to be seen."

"And why," asked Nicholl, "is there no total eclipse? Does not the cone of the shadow cast by the earth extend beyond the moon?"

"Yes, if we do not take into consideration the refraction produced by the terrestrial atmosphere. No, if we take that refraction into consideration. Thus let δ be the horizontal parallel, and p the apparent semidiameter——"

"Oh!" said Michel. "Do speak plainly, you man of algebra!"

"Very well;" replied Barbicane, "in popular language the mean distance from the moon to the earth being sixty terrestrial radii, the length of the cone of the shadow, on account of the refraction, is reduced to less than forty-two radii. The result is that when there are eclipses, the moon finds itself beyond the cone of pure shadow, and that the sun sends her its rays, not only from its edges, but also from its centre."

"Then," said Michel, in a merry tone, "why are there eclipses, when there ought not to be any?"

"Simply because the solar rays are weakened by this refraction, and the atmosphere through which they pass extinguishes the greater part of them!"

"That reason satisfies me," replied Michel. "Besides we shall see when we get there. Now, tell me, Barbicane, do you believe that the moon is an old comet?"

"There's an idea!"

"Yes," replied Michel, with an amiable swagger, "I have a few ideas of that sort."

"But that idea does not spring from Michel," answered Nicholl.

"Well, then, I am a plagiarist."

"No doubt about it. According to the ancients, the Arcadians pretend that their ancestors inhabited the earth before the moon became her satellite. Starting from this fact, some scientific men have seen in the moon a comet whose orbit will one day bring it so near to the earth that it will be held there by its attraction."

"Is there any truth in this hypothesis?" asked Michel.

"None whatever," said Barbicane, "and the proof is, that the moon has preserved no trace of the gaseous envelope which always accompanies comets."

"But," continued Nicholl, "before becoming the earth's satellite, could not the moon, when in her perihelion, pass so near the sun as by evaporation to get rid of all those gaseous substances?"

"It is possible, friend Nicholl, but not probable."

"Why not?"

"Because—Faith I do not know."

"Ah!" exclaimed Michel," what hundreds of volumes we might make of all that we do not know!"

"Ah! indeed. What time is it?" asked Barbicane.

"Three o'clock," answered Nicholl.

"How time goes," said Michel, "in the conversation of scientific men such as we are! Certainly, I feel I know too much! I feel that I am becoming a well!"

Saying which, Michel hoisted himself to the roof of the projectile, "to observe the moon better," he pretended. During this time his companions were watching through the lower glass. Nothing new to note! . . .

When Michel Ardan came down, he went to the side scuttle; and suddenly they heard an exclamation of surprise!

"What is it?" asked Barbicane.

The president approached the window, and saw a sort of flattened sack floating some yards from the projectile. This object seemed as motionless as the projectile, and was consequently animated with the same ascending movement.

"What is that machine?" continued Michel Ardan. "Is it one of the bodies of space which our projectile keeps within its attraction, and which will accompany it to the moon?"

"What astonishes me," said Nicholl, "is that the specific weight of the body, which is certainly less than that of the projectile, allows it to keep so perfectly on a level with it."

"Nicholl," replied Barbicane, after a moment's reflection, "I do not know what the object is, but I do know why it maintains our level."

"And why?"

"Because we are floating in space, my dear captain, and in space bodies fall or move (which is the same thing) with equal speed whatever be their weight or form; it is the air, which by its resistance creates these differences in weight. When you create a vacuum in a tube, the objects you send through it, grains of dust or grains of lead, fall with the same rapidity. Here in space is the same cause and the same effect."

"Just so," said Nicholl, "and everything we throw out of the projectile will accompany it until it reaches the moon."

"Ah! fools that we are!" exclaimed Michel.

"Why that expletive?" asked Barbicane.

"Because we might have filled the projectile with useful objects, books, instruments, tools, &c. We could have thrown them all out, and all would have followed in our train. But happy thought! Why cannot we walk outside like the meteor? Why cannot we launch into space through the scuttle? What enjoyment it would be to feel oneself thus suspended in ether, more favoured than the birds who must use their wings to keep themselves up!"

"Granted," said Barbicane, "but how to breathe?"

"Hang the air, to fail so inopportunely!"

"But if it did not fail, Michel, your density being less than that of the projectile, you would soon be left behind."

"Then we must remain in our car?"

"We must!"

"Ah!" exclaimed Michel, in a loud voice.

"What is the matter," asked Nicholl.

"I know, I guess, what this pretended meteor is! It is no asteroid which is accompanying us! It is not a piece of a planet."

"What is it then?" asked Barbicane.

"It is our unfortunate dog! It is Diana's husband!"

Indeed, this deformed, unrecognizable object, reduced to nothing, was the body of Satellite, flattened like a bagpipe without wind, and ever mounting, mounting!

CHAPTER VII: A MOMENT OF INTOXICATION Thus a phenomenon, curious but explicable, was happening under these strange conditions.

Every object thrown from the projectile would follow the same course and never stop until it did. There was a subject for conversation which the whole evening could not exhaust.

Besides, the excitement of the three travellers increased as they drew near the end of their journey. They expected unforeseen incidents, and new phenomena; and nothing would have astonished them in the frame of mind they then were in. Their over-excited imagination went faster than the projectile, whose speed was evidently diminishing, though insensibly to themselves. But the moon grew larger to their eyes, and they fancied if they stretched out their hands they could seize it.

The next day, the 5th of November, at five in the morning, all three were on foot. That day was to be the last of their journey, if all calculations were true. That very night, at twelve o'clock, in eighteen hours, exactly at the full moon, they would reach its brilliant disc. The next midnight would see that journey ended, the most extraordinary of ancient or modern times. Thus from the first of the morning, through the scuttles silvered by its rays, they saluted the orb of night with a confident and joyous hurrah.

The moon was advancing majestically along the starry firmament. A few more degrees, and she would reach the exact point where her meeting with the projectile was to take place.

According to his own observations, Barbicane reckoned that they would land on her northern hemisphere, where stretch immense plains, and where mountains are rare. A favourable circumstance if, as they thought, the lunar atmosphere was stored only in its depths.

"Besides," observed Michel Ardan, "a plain is easier to disembark upon than a mountain. A Selenite, deposited in Europe on the summit of Mont Blanc, or in Asia on the top of the Himalayas, would not be quite in the right place."

"And," added Captain Nicholl, "on a flat ground, the projectile will remain motionless when it has once touched; whereas on a declivity it would roll like an avalanche, and not being squirrels we should not come out safe and sound. So it is all for the best."

Indeed, the success of the audacious attempt no longer appeared doubtful. But Barbicane was preoccupied with one thought; but not wishing to make his companions uneasy, he kept silence on the subject.

The direction the projectile was taking towards the moon's northern hemisphere showed that her course had been slightly altered. The discharge, mathematically calculated, would carry the projectile to the very centre of the lunar disc. If it did not land there, there must have been some deviation. What had caused it? Barbicane could neither imagine, nor determine the importance of the deviation, for there were no points to go by.

He hoped, however, that it would have no other result than that of bringing them near the upper border of the moon, a region more suitable for landing.

Without imparting his uneasiness to his companions, Barbicane contented himself with constantly observing the moon, in order to see whether the course of the projectile would not be altered; for the situation would have been terrible if it failed in its aim, and being carried beyond the disc should be launched into interplanetary space. At that moment, the moon, instead of appearing flat like a disc, showed its convexity. If the sun's rays had struck it obliquely, the shadow thrown would have brought out the high mountains, which would have been clearly detached. The eye might have gazed into the craters' gaping abysses, and followed the capricious fissures which wound through the immense plains. But all relief was as yet levelled in intense brilliancy. They could scarcely distinguish those large spots which give to the moon the appearance of a human face.

"Face, indeed!" said Michel Ardan; "but I am sorry for the amiable sister of Apollo. A very pitted face!"

But the travellers, now so near the end, were incessantly observing this new world. They imagined themselves walking through its unknown countries, climbing its highest peaks, descending into its lowest depths. Here and there they fancied they saw vast seas, scarcely kept together under so rarefied an atmosphere, and watercourses emptying the mountain tributaries. Leaning over the abyss, they hoped to catch some sounds from that orb for ever mute in the solitude of space. That last day left them.

They took down the most trifling details. A vague uneasiness took possession of them as they neared the end. This uneasiness would have been doubled had they felt how their speed had decreased. It would have seemed to them quite insufficient to carry them to the end. It was because the projectile then "weighed" almost nothing. Its weight was ever decreasing, and would be entirely annihilated on that line where the lunar and terrestrial attractions would neutralize each other.

But in spite of his preoccupation, Michel Ardan did not forget to prepare the morning repast with his accustomed punctuality. They ate with a good appetite. Nothing was so excellent as the soup liquefied by the heat of the gas; nothing better than the preserved meat. Some glasses of good French wine crowned the repast, causing Michel Ardan to remark that the lunar vines, warmed by that ardent sun, ought to distil even more generous wines; that is, if they existed. In any case, the far-seeing

Frenchman had taken care not to forget in his collection some precious cuttings of the Médoc and Côte d'Or, upon which he founded his hopes.

Reiset and Regnault's apparatus worked with great regularity. Not an atom of carbonic acid resisted the potash; and as to the oxygen, Captain Nicholl said "it was of the first quality." The little watery vapour enclosed in the projectile mixing with the air tempered the dryness; and many apartments in London, Paris, or New York, and many theatres, were certainly not in such a healthy condition.

But that it might act with regularity, the apparatus must be kept in perfect order; so each morning Michel visited the escape regulators, tried the taps, and regulated the heat of the gas by the pyrometer. Everything had gone well up to that time, and the travellers, imitating the worthy Joseph T. Maston, began to acquire a degree of embonpoint, which would have rendered them unrecognizable if their imprisonment had been prolonged to some months. In a word, they behaved like chickens in a coop; they were getting fat.

In looking through the scuttle Barbicane saw the spectre of the dog, and other divers objects which had been thrown from the projectile obstinately following them. Diana howled lugubriously on seeing the remains of Satellite, which seemed as motionless as if they reposed on the solid earth.

"Do you know, my friends," said Michel Ardan, "that if one of us had succumbed to the shock consequent on departure, we should have had a great deal of trouble to bury him? What am I saying? to *etherize* him, as here ether takes the place of earth. You see the accusing body would have followed us into space like a remorse."

"That would have been sad," said Nicholl.

"Ah!" continued Michel, "what I regret is not being able to take a walk outside. What voluptuousness to float amid this radiant ether, to bathe oneself in it, to wrap oneself in the sun's pure rays. If Barbicane had only thought of furnishing us with a diving apparatus and an air-pump, I could have ventured out and assumed fanciful attitudes of feigned monsters on the top of the projectile."

"Well, old Michel," replied Barbicane, "you would not have made a feigned monster long, for in spite of your diver's dress, swollen by the expansion of air within you, you would have burst like a shell, or rather like a balloon which has risen too high. So do not regret it, and do not forget this—as long as we float in space, all sentimental walks beyond the projectile are forbidden."

Michel Ardan allowed himself to be convinced to a certain extent. He admitted that the thing was difficult but not *impossible*, a word which he never uttered.

The conversation passed from this subject to another, not failing for an instant. It seemed to the three friends as though, under present conditions, ideas shot up in their brains as leaves shoot at the first warmth of spring. They felt bewildered. In the middle of the questions and answers which crossed each other, Nicholl put one question which did not find an immediate solution.

"Ah, indeed!" said he; "it is all very well to go to the moon, but how to get back again?"

His two interlocutors looked surprised. One would have thought that this possibility now occurred to them for the first time.

"What do you mean by that, Nicholl?" asked Barbicane gravely.

"To ask for means to leave a country," added Michel, "when we have not yet arrived there, seems to me rather inopportune."

"I do not say that, wishing to draw back," replied Nicholl; "but I repeat my question, and I ask, 'How shall we return'?"

"I know nothing about it," answered Barbicane.

"And I," said Michel, "if I had known how to return, I would never have started."

"There's an answer!" cried Nicholl.

"I quite approve of Michel's words," said Barbicane; "and add, that the question has no real interest. Later, when we think it advisable to return, we will take counsel together. If the Columbiad is not there, the projectile will be."

"That is a step certainly. A ball without a gun!"

"The gun," replied Barbicane, "can be manufactured. The powder can be made. Neither metals, saltpetre, nor coal can fail in the depths of the moon, and we need only go 8000 leagues in order to fall upon the terrestrial globe by virtue of the mere laws of weight."

"Enough," said Michel with animation. "Let it be no longer a question of returning: we have already entertained it too long. As to communicating with our former earthly colleagues, that will not be difficult."

"And how?"

"By means of meteors launched by lunar volcanos."

"Well thought of, Michel," said Barbicane in a convinced tone of voice. "Laplace has calculated that a force five times greater than that of our gun would suffice to send a meteor from the moon to the earth, and there is not one volcano which has not a greater power of propulsion than that."

"Hurrah!" exclaimed Michel; "these meteors are handy postmen, and cost nothing. And how we shall be able to laugh at the post-office administration. But now I think of it——"

"What do you think of?"

"A capital idea. Why did we not fasten a thread to our projectile, and we could have exchanged telegrams with the earth?"

"The deuce!" answered Nicholl. "Do you consider the weight of a thread 250,000 miles long nothing?"

"As nothing. They could have trebled the Columbiad's charge; they could have quadrupled or quintupled it!" exclaimed Michel, with whom the verb took a higher intonation each time.

"There is but one little objection to make to your proposition," replied Barbicane, "which is that, during the rotary motion of the globe, our thread would have wound itself round it like a chain on a capstan, and that it would inevitably have brought us to the ground."

"By the thirty-nine stars of the Union!" said Michel, "I have nothing but impracticable ideas to-day; ideas worthy of J. T. Maston. But I have a notion that, if we do not return to earth, J. T. Maston will be able to come to us."

"Yes, he'll come," replied Barbicane; "he is a worthy and a courageous comrade. Besides, what is easier? Is not the Columbiad still buried in the soil of Florida? Is cotton and nitric acid wanted wherewith to manufacture the pyroxile? Will not the moon again pass to the zenith of Florida? In eighteen years' time will she not occupy exactly the same place as to-day?"

"Yes," continued Michel, "yes, Maston will come, and with him our friends Elphinstone, Blomsberry, all the members of the Gun Club, and they will be well received. And by and by they will run trains of projectiles between the earth and the moon! Hurrah for J. T. Maston!"

It is probable that, if the Hon. J. T. Maston did not hear the hurrahs uttered in his honour, his ears at least tingled. What was he doing then? Doubtless posted in the Rocky Mountains, at the station of Long's Peak, he was trying to find the invisible projectile gravitating in space. If he was thinking of his dear companions, we must allow that they were not far behind him; and that, under the influence of a strange excitement, they were devoting to him their best thoughts.

But whence this excitement, which was evidently growing upon the tenants of the projectile? Their sobriety could not be doubted. This strange irritation of the brain, must it be attributed to the peculiar circumstances under which they found themselves, to their proximity to the orb of night, from which only a few hours separated them, to some secret influence of the moon acting upon their nervous systems? Their faces were as rosy as if they had been exposed to the roaring flames of an oven; their voices resounded in loud accents; their words escaped like a champagne cork driven out by carbonic acid; their gestures became annoying, they wanted so much room to perform them; and, strange to say, they none of them noticed this great tension of the mind.

"Now," said Nicholl, in a short tone, "now that I do not know whether we shall ever return from the moon, I want to know what we are going to do there?"

"What we are going to do there?" replied Barbicane, stamping with his foot as if he was in a fencing saloon; "I do not know."

"You do not know!" exclaimed Michel, with a bellow which provoked a sonorous echo in the projectile.

"No, I have not even thought about it," retorted Barbicane, in the same loud tone.

"Well, I know," replied Michel.

"Speak, then," cried Nicholl, who could no longer contain the growling of his voice.

"I shall speak if it suits me," exclaimed Michel, seizing his companions' arms with violence.

"*It must* suit you," said Barbicane, with an eye on fire and a threatening hand. "It was you who drew us into this frightful journey, and we want to know what for."

"Yes," said the captain, "now that I do not know *where* I am going, I want to know *why* I am going."

"Why?" exclaimed Michel, jumping a yard high, "why? To take possession of the moon in the name of the United States; to add a fortieth State to the Union; to colonize the lunar regions; to cultivate them, to people them, to transport thither all the prodigies of art, of science, and industry; to civilize the Selenites, unless they are more civilized than we are; and to constitute them a republic, if they are not already one!"

"And if there are no Selenites?" retorted Nicholl, who, under the influence of this unaccountable intoxication, was very contradictory.

"Who said that there were no Selenites?" exclaimed Michel in a threatening tone.

"I do," howled Nicholl.

"Captain," said Michel, "do not repeat that insolence, or I will knock your teeth down your throat!"

The two adversaries were going to fall upon each other, and the incoherent discussion threatened to merge into a fight, when Barbicane intervened with one bound.

"Stop, miserable men," said he, separating his two companions; "if there are no Selenites, we will do without them."

"Yes," exclaimed Michel, who was not particular; "yes, we will do without them. We have only to make Selenites. Down with the Selenites!"

"The empire of the moon belongs to us," said Nicholl. "Let us three constitute the republic."

"I will be the congress," cried Michel.

"And I the senate," retorted Nicholl.

"And Barbicane, the president," howled Michel.

"Not a president elected by the nation," replied Barbicane.

"Very well, a president elected by the congress," cried Michel; "and as I am the congress, you are unanimously elected!"

"Hurrah! hurrah! hurrah! for President Barbicane," exclaimed Nicholl.

"Hip! hip! hip!" vociferated Michel Ardan.

Then the President and the Senate struck up in a tremendous voice the popular song "Yankee Doodle," whilst from the Congress resounded the masculine tones of the "Marseillaise."

Then they struck up a frantic dance, with maniacal gestures, idiotic stampings, and somersaults like those of the boneless clowns in the circus. Diana, joining in the dance, and howling in her turn, jumped to the top of the projectile. An unaccountable flapping of wings was then heard amidst most fantastic cock-crows, while five or six hens fluttered like bats against the walls.

Then the three travelling companions, acted upon by some unaccountable influence above that of intoxication, inflamed by the air which had set their respiratory apparatus on fire, fell motionless to the bottom of the projectile.

CHAPTER VIII: AT SEVENTY-EIGHT THOUSAND FIVE HUNDRED AND FOURTEEN LEAGUES   What had happened? Whence the cause of this singular intoxication, the consequences of which might have been very disastrous? A simple blunder of Michel's, which, fortunately, Nicholl was able to correct in time.

After a perfect swoon, which lasted some minutes, the captain, recovering first, soon collected his scattered senses. Although he had breakfasted only two hours before, he felt a gnawing hunger, as if he had not eaten anything for several days. Everything about him, stomach and brain, were overexcited to the highest degree. He got up and demanded from Michel a supplementary repast. Michel, utterly done up, did not answer.

Nicholl then tried to prepare some tea destined to help the absorption of a dozen sandwiches. He first tried to get some fire, and struck a match sharply. What was his surprise to see the sulphur shine with so extraordinary a brilliancy as to be almost unbearable to the eye. From the gas-burner which he lit rose a flame equal to a jet of electric light.

A revelation dawned on Nicholl's mind. That intensity of light, the physiological troubles which had arisen in him, the overexcitement of all his moral and quarrelsome faculties,—he understood all.

"The oxygen!" he exclaimed.

And leaning over the air apparatus, he saw that the tap was allowing the scentless colourless gas to escape freely, life-giving, but in its pure state producing the gravest disorders in the system. Michel had blunderingly opened the tap of the apparatus to the full.

Nicholl hastened to stop the escape of oxygen with which the atmosphere was saturated, which would have been the death of the travellers, not by suffocation, but by combustion. An hour later, the air less charged with it restored the lungs to their normal condition. By degrees the three friends recovered from their intoxication; but they were obliged to sleep themselves sober over their oxygen, as a drunkard does over his wine.

When Michel learnt his share of the responsibility of this incident, he was not much disconcerted. This unexpected drunkenness broke the monotony of the journey. Many foolish things had been said while under its influence, but also quickly forgotten.

"And then," added the merry Frenchman, "I am not sorry to have tasted a little of this heady gas. Do you know, my friends, that a curious establishment might be founded with rooms of oxygen, where people whose systems are weakened could for a few hours live more active lives. Fancy parties where the room was saturated with this heroic fluid, theatres where it should be kept at high pressure; what passion in the souls of the actors and spectators! what fire, what enthusiasm! And if, instead of an assembly only a whole people could be saturated, what activity in its functions, what a supplement to life it would derive. From an exhausted nation they might make a great and strong one, and I know more than one state in old Europe which ought to put itself under the regime of oxygen for the sake of its health!"

Michel spoke with so much animation, that one might have fancied that the tap was still too open. But a few words from Barbicane soon scattered his enthusiasm.

"That is all very well, friend Michel," said he, "but will you inform us where these chickens came from which have mixed themselves up in our concert?"

"Those chickens?"

"Yes."

Indeed, half a dozen chickens and a fine cock were walking about, flapping their wings and chattering.

"Ah, the awkward things!" exclaimed Michel. "The oxygen has made them revolt."

"But what do you want to do with these chickens?" asked Barbicane.

"To acclimatize them in the moon, by Jove!"

"Then why did you hide them?"

"A joke, my worthy president, a simple joke, which has proved a miserable failure. I wanted to set them free on the lunar continent, without saying anything. Oh, what would have been your amazement on seeing these earthly-winged animals pecking in the lunar fields!"

"You rascal, you unmitigated rascal," replied Barbicane, "*you* do not want oxygen to mount to the head. You are always what *we* were under the influence of the gas; you are always foolish!"

"Ah, who says that we were not wise then?" replied Michel Ardan.

After this philosophical reflection, the three friends set about restoring the order of the projectile. Chickens and cock were reinstated in their coop. But whilst proceeding with this operation, Barbicane and his two companions had a most desired perception of a new phenomenon. From the moment of leaving the earth, their own weight, that of the projectile, and the objects it enclosed, had been subject to an increasing diminution. If they could not prove this loss of the projectile, a moment would arrive when it would be sensibly felt upon themselves and the utensils and instruments they used.

It is needless to say that a *scale* would not show this loss; for the weight destined to weigh the object would have lost exactly as much as the object itself; but a spring steelyard for example, the tension of which was independent of the attraction, would have given a just estimate of this loss.

We know that the attraction, otherwise called the *weight*, is in proportion to the densities of bodies, and inversely as the squares of the distances. Hence this effect: If the earth had been alone in space, if the other celestial bodies had been suddenly annihilated, the projectile, according to Newton's laws, would weigh less as it got farther from the earth, but without ever losing its weight *entirely*, for the terrestrial attraction would always have made itself felt, at whatever distance.

But, in reality, a time must come when the projectile would no longer be subject to the law of weight, after allowing for the other celestial bodies whose effect could not be set down as zero. Indeed, the projectile's course was being traced between the earth and the moon. As it distanced the earth, the terrestrial attraction diminished: but the lunar attraction rose in proportion. There must then come a point where these two attractions would neutralize each other: the projectile would possess weight no longer. If the moon's and the earth's densities had been equal, this point would have been at an equal distance between the two orbs. But taking the different densities into consideration, it was easy to reckon that this point would be situated at 47-60ths of the whole journey, i. e. at 78,114 leagues from the earth. At this point, a body having no principle of speed or displacement in itself, would remain immovable for ever, being attracted equally by both orbs, and not being drawn more towards one than towards the other.

Now if the projectile's impulsive force had been correctly calculated, it would attain this point without speed, having lost all trace of weight, as well as all the objects within it. What would happen then? Three hypotheses presented themselves.

1. Either it would retain a certain amount of motion, and pass the point of equal attraction, and fall upon the moon by virtue of the excess of the lunar attraction over the terrestrial.

2. Or, its speed failing, and unable to reach the point of equal attraction, it would fall upon the moon by virtue of the excess of the lunar attraction over the terrestrial.

3. Or, lastly, animated with sufficient speed to enable it to reach the neutral point, but not sufficient to pass it, it would remain for ever suspended in that spot like the pretended tomb of Mahomet, between the zenith and the nadir.

Such was their situation; and Barbicane clearly explained the consequences to his travelling companions, which greatly interested them. But how should they know when the projectile had reached this neutral point situated at that distance, especially when neither themselves, nor the objects enclosed in the projectile, would be any longer subject to the laws of weight?

Up to this time, the travellers, whilst admitting that this action was constantly decreasing, had not yet become sensible to its total absence.

But that day, about eleven o'clock in the morning, Nicholl having accidentally let a glass slip from his hand, the glass, instead of falling, remained suspended in the air.

"Ah!" exclaimed Michel Ardan, "that is rather an amusing piece of natural philosophy."

And immediately divers other objects, firearms and bottles, abandoned to themselves, held themselves up as by enchantment. Diana too, placed in space by Michel, reproduced, but without any trick, the wonderful suspension practised by Caston and Robert Houdin. Indeed the dog did not seem to know that she was floating in air.

The three adventurous companions were surprised and stupefied, despite their scientific reasonings. They felt themselves being carried into the domain of wonders! they felt that *weight* was really wanting to their bodies. If they stretched out their arms, they did not attempt to fall. Their heads shook on their shoulders. Their feet no longer clung to the floor of the projectile. They were like drunken men having no stability in themselves.

Fancy has depicted men without reflection, others without shadow. But here *reality*, by the neutralisation of attractive forces, produced men in whom nothing had any weight, and who weighed nothing themselves.

Suddenly Michel, taking a spring, left the floor and remained suspended in the air, like Murillo's monk of the *Cusine des Anges*.

The two friends joined him instantly, and all three formed a miraculous "Ascension" in the centre of the projectile.

"Is it to be believed? is it probable? is it possible?" exclaimed Michel;

"and yet it is so. Ah! if Raphael had seen us thus, what an 'Assumption' he would have thrown upon canvas!"

"The 'Assumption' cannot last," replied Barbicane. "If the projectile passes the neutral point, the lunar attraction will draw us to the moon."

"Then our feet will be upon the roof," replied Michel.

"No," said Barbicane, "because the projectile's centre of gravity is very low; it will only turn by degrees."

"Then all our portables will be upset from top to bottom, that is a fact."

"Calm yourself, Michel," replied Nicholl; "no upset is to be feared; not a thing will move, for the projectile's evolution will be imperceptible."

"Just so," continued Barbicane; "and when it has passed the point of equal attraction, its base, being the heavier, will draw it perpendicularly to the moon; but, in order that this phenomenon should take place, we must have passed the neutral line."

"Pass the neutral line!" cried Michel; "then let us do as the sailors do when they cross the equator."

A slight side movement brought Michel back towards the padded side; thence he took a bottle and glasses, placed them "in space" before his companions, and, drinking merrily, they saluted the line with a triple hurrah. The influence of these attractions scarcely lasted an hour; the travellers felt themselves insensibly drawn towards the floor, and Barbicane fancied that the conical end of the projectile was varying a little from its normal direction towards the moon. By an inverse motion the base was approaching first; the lunar attraction was prevailing over the terrestrial; the fall towards the moon was beginning, almost imperceptibly as yet, but by degrees the attractive force would become stronger, the fall would be more decided, the projectile, drawn by its base, would turn its cone to the earth, and fall with ever-increasing speed on to the surface of the Selenite continent; their destination would then be attained. Now nothing could prevent the success of their enterprise, and Nicholl and Michel Ardan shared Barbicane's joy.

Then they chatted of all the phenomena which had astonished them one after the other, particularly the neutralization of the laws of weight. Michel Ardan, always enthusiastic, drew conclusions which were purely fanciful.

"Ah, my worthy friends," he exclaimed, "what progress we should make if on earth we could throw off some of that weight, some of that chain which binds us to her; it would be the prisoner set at liberty; no more fatigue of either arms or legs. Or, if it is true that in order to fly on the earth's surface, to keep oneself suspended in the air merely by the play of the muscles, there requires a strength a hundred and fifty times greater than that which we possess, a simple act of volition, a caprice, would bear us into space, if attraction did not exist."

"Just so," said Nicholl, smiling; "if we could succeed in suppressing weight as they suppress pain by anæsthesia, that would change the face of modern society!"

"Yes," cried Michel, full of his subject, "destroy weight, and no more burdens!"

"Well said," replied Barbicane; "but if nothing had any weight, nothing would keep in its place, not even your hat on your head, worthy Michel; nor your house, whose stones only adhere by weight; not a boat, whose stability on the water is caused only by weight; not even the ocean, whose waves would no longer be equalized by terrestrial attraction; and lastly, not even the *atmosphere*, whose atoms, being no longer held in their places, would disperse in space!"

"That is tiresome," retorted Michel; "nothing like these matter-of-fact people for bringing one back to the bare reality."

"But console yourself, Michel," continued Barbicane, "for if no orb exists from whence all laws of weight are banished, you are at least going to visit one where it is much less than on the earth."

"The moon?"

"Yes, the moon, on whose surface objects weigh six times less than on the earth, a phenomenon easy to prove."

"And we shall feel it?" asked Michel.

"Evidently, as 200 lbs. will only weigh 30 lbs. on the surface of the moon."

"And our muscular strength will not diminish?"

"Not at all; instead of jumping one yard high, you will rise eighteen feet high."

"But we shall be regular Herculeses in the moon!" exclaimed Michel.

"Yes," replied Nicholl; "for if the height of the Selenites is in proportion to the density of their globe, they will be scarcely a foot high."

"Lilliputians!" ejaculated Michel; "I shall play the part of Gulliver. We are going to realize the fable of the giants. This is the advantage of leaving one's own planet and overrunning the solar world."

"One moment, Michel," answered Barbicane; "if you wish to play the part of Gulliver, only visit the inferior planets, such as Mercury, Venus, or Mars, whose density is a little less than that of the earth; but do not venture into the great planets, Jupiter, Saturn, Uranus, Neptune; for there the order will be changed, and *you* will become Lilliputian."

"And in the sun?"

"In the sun, if its density is thirteen hundred and twenty-four thousand times greater, and the attraction is twenty-seven times greater than on the surface of our globe, keeping everything in proportion, the inhabitants ought to be at least two hundred feet high."

"By Jove!" exclaimed Michel; "I should be nothing more than a pigmy, a shrimp!"

"Gulliver with the giants," said Nicholl.

"Just so," replied Barbicane.

"And it would not be quite useless to carry some pieces of artillery to defend oneself."

"Good," replied Nicholl; "your projectiles would have no effect on the sun; they would fall back on the earth after some minutes."

"That is a strong remark."

"It is certain," replied Barbicane; "the attraction is so great on this enormous orb, that an object weighing 70,000 lbs. on the earth would weigh but 1920 lbs. on the surface of the sun. If you were to fall upon it you would weigh—let me see—about 5000 lbs., a weight which you would never be able to raise again."

"The devil!" said Michel; "one would want a portable crane. However, we will be satisfied with the moon for the present; there at least we shall cut a great figure. We will see about the sun by and by."

CHAPTER IX: THE CONSEQUENCES OF A DEVIATION   Barbicane had now no fear of the issue of the journey, at least as far as the projectile's impulsive force was concerned; its own speed would carry it beyond the neutral line; it would certainly not return to earth; it would certainly not remain motionless on the line of attraction. One single hypothesis remained to be realized, the arrival of the projectile at its destination by the action of the lunar attraction.

It was in reality a fall of 8296 leagues on an orb, it is true, where weight could only be reckoned at one-sixth of terrestrial weight; a formidable fall, nevertheless, and one against which every precaution must be taken without delay.

These precautions were of two sorts, some to deaden the shock when the projectile should touch the lunar soil, others to delay the fall, and consequently make it less violent.

To deaden the shock, it was a pity that Barbicane was no longer able to employ the means which had so ably weakened the shock at departure, that is to say, by water used as springs and the partition-breaks.

The partitions still existed but water failed, for they could not use their reserve, which was precious, in case during the first days the liquid element should be found wanting on lunar soil.

And indeed this reserve would have been quite insufficient for a spring.

The layer of water stored in the projectile at their departure, and on which the waterproof disc lay, occupied no less than three feet in depth, and spread over a surface of not less than fifty-four square feet. Besides, the cistern did not contain one fifth part of it; they must therefore give up this efficient means of deadening the shock of arrival. Happily, Barbicane, not content with employing water, had furnished the movable disc with strong spring plugs, destined to lessen the shock against the base after the breaking of the horizontal partitions. These plugs still existed; they had only to readjust them and replace the movable disc; every piece, easy to handle, as their weight was now scarcely felt, was quickly mounted.

The different pieces were fitted without trouble, it being only a matter of bolts and screws; tools were not wanting, and soon the reinstated disc lay on its steel plugs, like a table on its legs. One inconvenience resulted from the replacing of the disc, the lower window was blocked up; thus it was impossible for the travellers to observe the moon from that opening while they were being precipitated perpendicularly upon her; but they were obliged to give it up; even by the side openings they could still see vast lunar regions, as an aeronaut sees the earth from his car.

This replacing of the disc was at least an hour's work. It was past twelve when all preparations were finished. Barbicane took fresh observations on the inclination of the projectile, but to his annoyance it had not turned over sufficiently for its fall; it seemed to take a curve parallel to the lunar disc. The orb of night shone splendidly into space, whilst, opposite, the orb of day blazed with fire.

Their situation began to make them uneasy.

"Are we reaching our destination?" said Nicholl.

"Let us act as if we were about reaching it," replied Barbicane.

"You are sceptical," retorted Michel Ardan. "We shall arrive, and that, too, quicker than we like."

This answer brought Barbicane back to his preparations, and he occupied himself with placing the contrivances intended to break their descent. We may remember the scene of the meeting held at Tampa Town, in Florida, when Captain Nicholl came forward as Barbicane's enemy and Michel Ardan's adversary. To Captain Nicholl's maintaining that the projectile would smash like glass, Michel replied that he would break their fall by means of rockets properly placed.

Thus, powerful fireworks, taking their starting-point from the base and bursting outside, could, by producing a recoil, check to a certain degree the projectile's speed. These rockets were to burn in space, it is true; but oxygen would not fail them, for they could supply themselves with it, like the lunar volcanoes, the burning of which has never yet been stopped by the want of atmosphere round the moon.

Barbicane had accordingly supplied himself with these fireworks, enclosed in little steel guns, which could be screwed on to the base of the projectile. Inside, these guns were flush with the bottom; outside, they protruded about eighteen inches. There were twenty of them. An opening left in the disc allowed them to light the match with which each was provided. All the effect was felt outside. The burning mixture had been already rammed into each gun. They had, then, nothing to do but to raise the metallic buffers fixed in the base, and replace them by the guns, which fitted closely in their places.

This new work was finished about three o'clock, and after taking all these precautions there remained but to wait. But the projectile was perceptibly nearing the moon, and evidently succumbed to her influence to a certain degree; though its own velocity also drew it in an oblique direction. From these conflicting influences resulted a line which might become a tangent. But it was certain that the projectile would not fall directly on the moon; for its lower part, by reason of its weight, ought to be turned towards her.

Barbicane's uneasiness increased as he saw his projectile resist the influence of gravitation. The Unknown was opening before him, the Unknown in interplanetary space. The man of science thought he had foreseen the only three hypotheses possible—the return to the earth, the return to the moon, or stagnation on the neutral line; and here a fourth hypothesis, big with all the terrors of the Infinite, surged up inopportunely. To face it without flinching, one must be a resolute savant like Barbicane, a phlegmatic being like Nicholl, or an audacious adventurer like Michel Ardan.

Conversation was started upon this subject. Other men would have considered the question from a practical point of view; they would have asked themselves whither their projectile carriage was carrying them. Not so with these; they sought for the cause which produced this effect.

"So we have become diverted from our route," said Michel; "but why?"

"I very much fear," answered Nicholl, "that, in spite of all precautions taken, the Columbiad was not fairly pointed. An error, however small, would be enough to throw us out of the moon's attraction."

"Then they must have aimed badly?" asked Michel.

"I do not think so," replied Barbicane. "The perpendicularity of the gun was exact, its direction to the zenith of the spot incontestible; and the moon passing to the zenith of the spot, we ought to reach it at the full. There is another reason, but it escapes me."

"Are we not arriving too late?" asked Nicholl.

"Too late?" said Barbicane.

"Yes," continued Nicholl. "The Cambridge Observatory's note says that the transit ought to be accomplished in ninety-seven hours thirteen minutes and twenty seconds; which means to say, that *sooner* the moon will *not* be at the point indicated, and that *later* it will have passed it."

"True," replied Barbicane. "But we started the 1st of December, at thirteen minutes and twenty-five seconds to eleven at night; and we ought to arrive on the 5th at midnight, at the exact moment when the moon would be full; and we are now at the 5th of December. It is now half past three in the evening; half past eight ought to see us at the end of our journey. Why do we not arrive?"

"Might it not be an excess of speed?" answered Nicholl; "for we know now that its initial velocity was greater than they supposed."

"No! a hundred times, No!" replied Barbicane. "An excess of speed, if the direction of the projectile had been right, would not have prevented us reaching the moon. No, there has been a deviation. We have been turned out of our course."

"By whom? by what?" asked Nicholl.

"I cannot say," replied Barbicane.

"Very well, then, Barbicane," said Michel, "do you wish to know my opinion on the subject of finding out this deviation?"

"Speak."

"I would not give half a dollar to know it. That we *have* deviated is *a fact*. Where we are going to matters little; we shall soon see. Since we are being borne along in space we shall end by falling into some centre of attraction or other."

Michel Ardan's indifference did not content Barbicane. Not that he was uneasy about the future, but he wanted to know at any cost *why* his projectile had deviated.

But the projectile continued its course sideways to the moon, and with it the mass of things thrown out. Barbicane could even prove, by the elevations which served as landmarks upon the moon, which was only 2000 leagues distant, that its speed was becoming uniform—fresh proof that there was no fall. Its impulsive force still prevailed over the lunar attraction, but the projectile's course was certainly bringing it nearer to the moon, and they might hope that at a nearer point the weight, predominating, would cause a decided fall.

The three friends having nothing better to do, continued their observations; but they could not yet determine the topographical position of the satellite; every relief was levelled under the reflection of the solar rays.

They watched thus through the side windows until eight o'clock at night. The moon had then grown so large in their eyes that it filled half of the firmament. The sun on one side, and the orb of night on the other, flooded the projectile with light.

At that moment, Barbicane thought he could estimate the distance which separated them from their aim at no more than 700 leagues. The speed of the projectile seemed to him to be more than 200 yards, or about

170 leagues a second. Under the centripetal force, the base of the projectile tended towards the moon; but the centrifugal still prevailed; and it was probable that its rectilineal course would be changed to a curve of some sort, the nature of which they could not at present determine.

Barbicane was still seeking the solution of his insoluble problem. Hours passed without any result. The projectile was evidently *nearing* the moon, but it was also evident that it would never *reach* her. As to the nearest distance at which it would pass her, that must be the result of the two forces, attraction and repulsion, affecting its motion.

"I ask but one thing," said Michel; "that we may pass near enough to penetrate her secrets."

"Cursed be the thing that has caused our projectile to deviate from its course," cried Nicholl.

And, as if a light had suddenly broken in upon his mind, Barbicane answered, "Then cursed be the meteor which crossed our path."

"What?" said Michel Ardan.

"What do you mean?" exclaimed Nicholl.

"I mean," said Barbicane in a decided tone, "I mean that our deviation is owing solely to our meeting with this erring body."

"But it did not even brush us as it passed," said Michel.

"What does that matter? Its mass, compared to that of our projectile, was enormous, and its attraction was enough to influence our course."

"So little?" cried Nicholl.

"Yes, Nicholl; but however little it might be," replied Barbicane, "in a distance of 84,000 leagues, it wanted no more to make us miss the moon."

CHAPTER X: THE OBSERVERS OF THE MOON   Barbicane had evidently hit upon the only plausible reason of this deviation. However slight it might have been, it had sufficed to modify the course of the projectile. It was a fatality. The bold attempt had miscarried by a fortuitous circumstance; and unless by some exceptional event, they could now never reach the moon's disc.

Would they pass near enough to be able to solve certain physical and geological questions until then insoluble? This was the question, and the only one, which occupied the minds of these bold travellers. As to the fate in store for themselves, they did not even dream of it.

But what would become of them amid these infinite solitudes, these who would soon want air? A few more days, and they would fall stifled in this wandering projectile. But some days to these intrepid fellows was a century; and they devoted all their time to observe that moon which they no longer hoped to reach.

The distance which then separated the projectile from the satellite was estimated at about 200 leagues. Under these conditions, as regards the visibility of the details of the disc, the travellers were farther from the moon than are the inhabitants of the earth with their powerful telescopes.

Indeed, we know that the instrument mounted by Lord Rosse at Parsonstown, which magnifies 6500 times, brings the moon to within an apparent distance of sixteen leagues. And more than that, with the powerful one set up at Long's Peak, the orb of night, magnified 48,000 times, is brought to within less than two leagues, and objects having a diameter of thirty feet are seen very distinctly. So that, at this distance, the topographical details of the moon, observed without glasses, could not be determined with precision. The eye caught the vast outline of those immense depressions inappropriately called "seas," but they could not recognize their nature. The prominence of the mountains disappeared under the splendid irradiation produced by the reflection of the solar rays. The eye, dazzled as if it was leaning over a bath of molten silver, turned from it involuntarily; but the oblong form of the orb was quite clear. It appeared like a gigantic egg, with the small end turned towards the earth. Indeed the moon, liquid and pliable in the first days of its formation, was originally a perfect sphere; but, being soon drawn within the attraction of the earth, it became elongated under the influence of gravitation. In becoming a satellite, she lost her native purity of form; her centre of gravity was in advance of the centre of her figure; and from this fact some savants draw the conclusion that the air and water had taken refuge on the opposite surface of the moon, which is never seen from the earth. This alteration in the primitive form of the satellite was only perceptible for a few moments. The distance of the projectile from the moon diminished very rapidly under its speed, though that was much less than its initial velocity,—but eight or nine times greater than that which propels our express trains. The oblique course of the projectile, from its very obliquity, gave Michel Ardan some hopes of striking the lunar disc at some point or other. He could not think that they would never reach it. No! he could not believe it; and this opinion he often repeated. But Barbicane, who was a better judge, always answered him with merciless logic.

"No, Michel, no! We can only reach the moon by a fall, and we are not falling. The centripetal force keeps us under the moon's influence, but the centrifugal force draws us irresistibly away from it."

This was said in a tone which quenched Michel Ardan's last hope.

The portion of the moon which the projectile was nearing was the northern hemisphere, that which the selenographic maps place below;

for these maps are generally drawn after the outline given by the glasses, and we know that they reverse the objects. Such was the *Mappa Selenographica* of Bœer and Moedler which Barbicane consulted. This northern hemisphere presented vast plains, dotted with isolated mountains.

At midnight the moon was full. At that precise moment the travellers should have alighted upon it, if the mischievous meteor had not diverted their course. The orb was exactly in the condition determined by the Cambridge Observatory. It was mathematically at its perigee, and at the zenith of the twenty-eighth parallel. An observer placed at the bottom of the enormous Columbiad, pointed perpendicularly to the horizon, would have framed the moon in the mouth of the gun. A straight line drawn through the axis of the piece would have passed through the centre of the orb of night. It is needless to say, that during the night of the 5th–6th of December, the travellers took not an instant's rest. Could they close their eyes when so near this new world? No! All their feelings were concentrated in one single thought:—See! Representatives of the earth, of humanity, past and present, all centred in them! It is through their eyes that the human race look at these lunar regions, and penetrate the secrets of their satellite! A strange emotion filled their hearts as they went from one window to the other.

Their observations, reproduced by Barbicane, were rigidly determined. To take them, they had glasses; to correct them, maps.

As regards the optical instruments at their disposal, they had excellent marine glasses specially constructed for this journey. They possessed magnifying powers of 100. They would thus have brought the moon to within a distance (apparent) of less than 2000 leagues from the earth. But then, at a distance which for three hours in the morning did not exceed sixty-five miles, and in a medium free from all atmospheric disturbances, these instruments could reduce the lunar surface to within less than 1500 yards!

CHAPTER XI: FANCY AND REALITY "Have you ever seen the moon?" asked a professor, ironically, of one of his pupils.

"No, sir!" replied the pupil, still more ironically, "but I must say I have heard it spoken of."

In one sense, the pupil's witty answer might be given by a large majority of sublunary beings. How many people have heard speak of the moon, who have never seen it—at least through a glass or a telescope! How many have never examined the map of their satellite!

In looking at a selenographic map, one peculiarity strikes us. Contrary to the arrangement followed for that of the Earth and Mars, the continents occupy more particularly the southern hemisphere of the lunar globe. These continents do not show such decided, clear, and regular boundary lines as South America, Africa, and the Indian peninsula. Their angular, capricious, and deeply indented coasts, are rich in gulfs and peninsulas. They remind one of the confusion in the islands of the Sound, where the land is excessively indented. If navigation ever existed on the surface of the moon, it must have been wonderfully difficult and dangerous; and we may well pity the Selenite sailors and hydrographers; the former, when they came upon these perilous coasts, the latter, when they took the soundings of its stormy banks.

We may also notice that, on the lunar sphere, the south pole is much more continental than the north pole. On the latter, there is but one slight strip of land separated from other continents by vast seas. Towards the south, continents clothe almost the whole of the hemisphere. It is even possible that the Selenites have already planted the flag on one of their poles, whilst Franklin, Ross, Kane, Dumont d'Urville, and Lambert, have never yet been able to attain that unknown point of the terrestrial globe.

As to islands, they are numerous on the surface of the moon. Nearly all oblong or circular, and as if traced with the compass, they seem to form one vast archipelago, equal to that charming group lying between Greece and Asia Minor, and which mythology in ancient times adorned with most graceful legends. Involuntarily the names of Naxos, Tenedos, and Carpathos, rise before the mind, and we seek vainly for Ulysses' vessel or the "clipper" of the Argonauts. So at least it was in Michel Ardan's eyes. To him it was a Grecian archipelago that he saw on the map. To the eyes of his matter-of-fact companions, the aspect of these coasts recalled rather the parcelled-out land of New Brunswick and Nova Scotia; and where the Frenchman discovered traces of the heroes of fable, these Americans were marking the most favourable points for the establishment of stores in the interests of lunar commerce and industry.

After wandering over these vast continents, the eye is attracted by still greater seas. Not only their formation, but their situation and aspect remind one of the terrestrial oceans; but again, as on earth, these seas occupy the greater portion of the globe. But in point of fact, these are not liquid spaces, but plains, the nature of which the travellers hoped soon to determine. Astronomers, we must allow, have graced these pretended seas with at least odd names, which science has respected up to the present time. Michel Ardan was right when he compared this map to a "Tendre card," got up by a Scudary or a Cyrano de Bergerac. "Only," said he, "it is no longer the sentimental card of the seventeenth century, it is the card of life, very neatly divided into two parts, one feminine, the other masculine; the right hemisphere for woman, the left for man."

In speaking thus, Michel made his prosaic companions shrug their shoulders. Barbicane and Nicholl looked upon the lunar map from a very different point of view to that of their fantastic friend. Nevertheless, their fantastic friend was a little in the right. Judge for yourselves.

In the left hemisphere stretches the "Sea of Clouds," where human reason is so often shipwrecked. Not far off lies the "Sea of Rains," fed by all the fever of existence. Near this is the "Sea of Storms," where man is ever fighting against his passions, which too often gain the victory. Then, worn out by deceit, treasons, infidelity, and the whole body of terrestrial misery, what does he find at the end of his career? that vast "Sea of Humours," barely softened by some drops of the waters from the "Gulf of Dew!" Clouds, rain, storms, and humours,—does the life of man contain aught but these? and is it not summed up in these four words?

The right hemisphere, "dedicated to the ladies," encloses smaller seas, whose significant names contain every incident of a feminine existence. There is the "Sea of Serenity," over which the young girl bends; the "Lake of Dreams," reflecting a joyous future; the "Sea of Nectar," with its waves of tenderness and breezes of love; the "Sea of Fruitfulness"; the "Sea of Crises"; then the "Sea of Vapours," whose dimensions are perhaps a little too confined; and lastly, that vast "Sea of Tranquillity," in which every false passion, every useless dream, every unsatisfied desire is at length absorbed, and whose waves emerge peaceably into the "Lake of Death"!

What a strange succession of names! What a singular division of the moon's two hemispheres, joined to one another like man and woman, and forming that sphere of life carried into space! And was not the fantastic Michel right in thus interpreting the fancies of the ancient astronomers? But whilst his imagination thus roved over "the seas," his grave companions were considering things more geographically. They were learning this new world by heart. They were measuring angles and diameters.

CHAPTER XII: OROGRAPHIC DETAILS The course taken by the projectile, as we have before remarked, was bearing it towards the moon's northern hemisphere. The travellers were far from the central point which they would have struck, had their course not been subject to an irremediable deviation. It was past midnight; and Barbicane then estimated the distance at 750 miles, which was a little greater than the length of the lunar radius, and which would diminish as it advanced nearer to the North Pole. The projectile was then not at the altitude of the equator; but across the tenth parallel, and from that latitude, carefully taken on the map to the pole, Barbicane and his two companions were able to observe the moon under the most favourable conditions. Indeed, by means of glasses, the above named distance was reduced to little more than fourteen miles.

The telescope of the Rocky Mountains brought the moon much nearer; but the terrestrial atmosphere singularly lessened its power. Thus Barbicane, posted in his projectile, with the glasses to his eyes, could seize upon details which were almost imperceptible to earthly observers.

"My friends," said the president, in a serious voice, "I do not know whither we are going; I do not know if we shall ever see the terrestrial globe again. Nevertheless, let us proceed as if our work would one day be useful to our fellow-men. Let us keep our minds free from every other consideration. We are astronomers; and this projectile is a room in the Cambridge University, carried into space. Let us make our observations!"

This said, work was begun with great exactness; and they faithfully reproduced the different aspects of the moon, at the different distances which the projectile reached.

At the time that the projectile was as high as the tenth parallel, N. latitude, it seemed rigidly to follow the twentieth degree, E. longitude. We must here make one important remark with regard to the map by which they were taking observations. In the selenographical maps where, on account of the reversing of the objects by the glasses, the south is above and the north below, it would seem natural that, on account of that inversion, the east should be to the left hand, and the west to the right. But it is not so. If the map were turned upside down, showing the moon as we see her, the east would be to the *left*, and the west to the *right*, contrary to that which exists on terrestrial maps. The following is the reason of this anomaly. Observers in the northern hemisphere (say in Europe) see the moon in the south,—according to them. When they take observations, they turn their backs to the north, the reverse position to that which they occupy when they study a terrestrial map. As they turn their backs to the north, the east is on their left, and the west to their right. To observers in the southern hemisphere (Patagonia for example), the moon's west would be quite to their left, and the east to their right, as the south is behind them. Such is the reason of the apparent reversing of these two cardinal points, and we must bear it in mind in order to be able to follow President Barbicane's observations.

With the help of Bœer and Moedler's *Mappa Selenographica*, the travellers were able at once to recognize that portion of the disc enclosed within the field of their glasses.

"What are we looking at, at this moment?" asked Michel.

"At the northern part of the 'Sea of Clouds,'" answered Barbicane. "We are too far off to recognize its nature. Are these plains composed of arid sand, as the first astronomer maintained? Or are they nothing but immense forests, according to M. Warren de la Rue's opinion, who gives the moon an atmosphere, though a very low and a very dense one? That we shall know by and by. We must affirm nothing until we are in a position to do so."

This "Sea of Clouds" is rather doubtfully marked out upon the maps. It is supposed that these vast plains are strewn with blocks of lava from the neighbouring volcanoes on its right, Ptolemy, Purbach, Arzachel. But the projectile was advancing, and sensibly nearing it. Soon there appeared the heights which bound this sea at this northern limit. Before them rose a mountain radiant with beauty, the top of which seemed lost in an eruption of solar rays.

"That is——?" asked Michel.

"Copernicus," replied Barbicane.

"Let us see Copernicus."

This mount situated in 9° north latitude and 20° east longitude, rose to a height of 10,600 feet above the surface of the moon. It is quite visible from the earth; and astronomers can study it with ease, particularly during the phase between the last quarter and the new moon, because then the shadows are thrown lengthways from east to west, allowing them to measure the heights.

This Copernicus forms the most important of the radiating system, situated in the southern hemisphere, according to Tycho Brahé. It rises isolated like a gigantic lighthouse on that portion of the Sea of Clouds, which is bounded by the "Sea of Tempests," thus lighting by its splendid rays two oceans at a time. It was a sight without an equal, those long luminous trains, so dazzling in the full moon, and which, passing the boundary chain on the north, extends to the "Sea of Rains." At one o'clock of the terrestrial morning, the projectile, like a balloon borne into space, overlooked the top of this superb mountain. Barbicane could recognize perfectly its chief features. Copernicus is comprised in the series of ringed mountains of the first order, in the division of great circles. Like Kepler and Aristarchus, which overlook the Ocean of Tempests, sometimes it appeared like a brilliant point through the cloudy light, and was taken for a volcano in activity. But it is only an extinct one,—like all on that side of the moon. Its circumference showed a diameter of about twenty-two leagues. The glasses discovered traces of stratification produced by successive eruptions, and the neighbourhood was strewn with volcanic remains which still choked some of the craters.

"There exist," said Barbicane, "several kinds of circles on the surface of the moon, and it is easy to see that Copernicus belongs to the radiating class. If we were nearer, we should see the cones bristling on the inside, which in former times were so many fiery mouths. A curious arrangement, and one without an exception on the lunar disc, is that the interior surface of these circles is the reverse of the exterior, and contrary to the form taken by terrestrial craters. It follows, then, that the general curve of the bottom of these circles gives a sphere of a smaller diameter than that of the moon."

"And why this peculiar disposition?" asked Nicholl.

"We do not know," replied Barbicane.

"What splendid radiation!" said Michel. "One could hardly see a finer spectacle, I think."

"What would you say, then," replied Barbicane, "if chance should bear us towards the southern hemisphere?"

"Well, I should say that it was still more beautiful," retorted Michel Ardan.

At this moment the projectile hung perpendicularly over the circle. The circumference of Copernicus formed almost a perfect circle, and its steep escarpments were clearly defined. They could even distinguish a second ringed enclosure. Around spread a greyish plain, of a wild aspect, on which every relief was marked in yellow. At the bottom of the circle, as if enclosed in a jewel case, sparkled for one instant two or three eruptive cones, like enormous dazzling gems. Towards the north the escarpments were lowered by a depression which would probably have given access to the interior of the crater.

In passing over the surrounding plains, Barbicane noticed a great number of less important mountains; and among others a little ringed one called Guy Lussac, the breadth of which measured twelve miles.

Towards the south, the plain was very flat, without one elevation, without one projection. Towards the north, on the contrary, till where it was bounded by the Sea of Storms it resembled a liquid surface agitated by a storm, of which the hills and hollows formed a succession of waves suddenly congealed. Over the whole of this, and in all directions, lay the luminous lines, all converging to the summit of Copernicus.

The travellers discussed the origin of these strange rays; but they could not determine their nature any more than terrestrial observers.

"But why," said Nicholl, "should not these rays be simply spurs of mountains which reflect more vividly the light of the sun?"

"No," replied Barbicane; "if it was so, under certain conditions of the moon, these ridges would cast shadows, and they do not cast any."

And indeed, these rays only appeared when the orb of day was in opposition to the moon, and disappeared as soon as its rays became oblique.

"But how have they endeavoured to explain these lines of light?" asked Michel; "for I cannot believe that savants would ever be stranded for want of an explanation."

"Yes," replied Barbicane; "Herschel has put forward an opinion, but he did not venture to affirm it."

"Never mind. What was the opinion?"

"He thought that these rays might be streams of cooled lava which shone when the sun beat straight upon them. It may be so; but nothing can be less certain. Besides, if we pass nearer to Tycho, we shall be in a better position to find out the cause of this radiation."

"Do you know, my friends, what that plain, seen from the height we are at, resembles?" said Michel.

"No," replied Nicholl.

"Very well; with all those pieces of lava lengthened like rockets, it resembles an immense game of spelikans thrown pell-mell. There wants but the hook to pull them out one by one."

"Do be serious," said Barbicane.

"Well, let us be serious," replied Michel, quietly; "and instead of spelikans, let us put bones. This plain would then be nothing but an immense cemetery, on which would repose the mortal remains of thousands of extinct generations. Do you prefer that high-flown comparison?"

"One is as good as the other," retorted Barbicane.

"My word, you are difficult to please," answered Michel.

"My worthy friend," continued the matter-of-fact Barbicane, "it matters but little what it *resembles*, when we do not know what it *is*."

"Well answered," exclaimed Michel. "That will teach me to reason with savants."

But the projectile continued to advance with almost uniform speed around the lunar disc. The travellers, we may easily imagine, did not dream of taking a moment's rest. Every minute changed the landscape which fled from beneath their gaze. About half-past one o'clock in the morning, they caught a glimpse of the tops of another mountain. Barbicane, consulting his map, recognized Eratosthenes.

It was a ringed mountain 9000 feet high, and one of those circles so numerous on this satellite. With regard to this, Barbicane related Kepler's singular opinion on the formation of circles. According to that celebrated mathematician, these crater-like cavities had been dug by the hand of man.

"For what purpose?" asked Nicholl.

"For a very natural one," replied Barbicane. "The Selenites might have undertaken these immense works and dug these enormous holes for a refuge and shield from the solar rays which beat upon them during fifteen consecutive days."

"The Selenites are not fools," said Michel.

"A singular idea," replied Nicholl; "but it is probable that Kepler did not know the true dimensions of these circles, for the digging of them would have been the work of giants, quite impossible for the Selenites."

"Why? if weight on the moon's surface is six times less than on the earth?" said Michel.

"But if the Selenites are six times smaller?" retorted Nicholl.

"And if there are *no* Selenites?" added Barbicane.

This put an end to the discussion.

Soon Eratosthenes disappeared under the horizon without the projectile being sufficiently near to allow of close observation. This mountain separated the Apennines from the Carpathians. In the lunar orography they have discerned some chains of mountains, which are chiefly distributed over the northern hemisphere. Some, however, occupy certain portions of the southern hemisphere also.

About two o'clock in the morning Barbicane found that they were above the twentieth lunar parallel. The distance of the projectile from the moon was not more than 600 miles. Barbicane, now perceiving that the projectile was steadily approaching the lunar disc, did not despair, if of reaching her, at least of discovering the secrets of her configuration.

CHAPTER XIII: LUNAR LANDSCAPES   At half-past two in the morning, the projectile was over the thirteenth lunar parallel and at the effective distance of 500 miles, reduced by the glasses to five. It still seemed impossible, however, that it could ever touch any part of the disc. Its motive speed, comparatively so moderate, was inexplicable to President Barbicane. At that distance from the moon it must have been considerable, to enable it to bear up against her attraction. Here was a phenomenon the cause of which escaped them again. Besides, time failed them to investigate the cause. All lunar relief was defiling under the eyes of the travellers, and they would not lose a single detail.

Under the glasses the disc appeared at the distance of five miles. What would an aeronaut, borne to this distance from the earth, distinguish on its surface? We cannot say, since the greatest ascension has not been more than 25,000 feet.

This, however, is an exact description of what Barbicane and his companions saw at this height. Large patches of different colours appeared on the disc. Selenographers are not agreed upon the nature of these colours. There are several, and rather vividly marked. Julius Schmidt pretends that, if the terrestrial oceans were dried up, a Selenite observer could not distinguish on the globe a greater diversity of shades between the oceans and the continental plains than those on the moon present to a terrestrial observer. According to him, the colour common to the vast plains known by the name of "seas" is a dark grey mixed with green and brown. Some of the large craters present the same appearance. Barbicane knew this opinion of the German selenographer, an opinion shared by Bœer and Moedler. Observation has proved that right was on their side, and not on that of some astronomers who admit the existence of only grey on the moon's surface. In some parts green was very distinct, such as springs, according to Julius Schmidt, from the seas of Serenity and Humours. Barbicane also noticed large craters, without any interior cones, which shed a bluish tint similar to the reflection of a sheet of steel freshly polished. These colours belonged really to the lunar disc, and did not result, as some astronomers say, either from the imperfection in the objective of the glasses or from the interposition of the terrestrial atmosphere.

Not a doubt existed in Barbicane's mind with regard to it, as he observed it through space, and so could not commit any optical error. He considered the establishment of this fact as an acquisition to science. Now, were these shades of green, belonging to tropical vegetation, kept up by a low dense atmosphere? He could not say yet.

Farther on, he noticed a reddish tint, quite defined. The same shade had before been observed at the bottom of an isolated enclosure, known by the name of Lichtenburg's circle, which is situated near the Hercynian mountains, on the borders of the moon; but they could not tell the nature of it.

They were not more fortunate with regard to another peculiarity of the disc, for they could not decide upon the cause of it.

Michel Ardan was watching near the president, when he noticed long white lines, vividly lighted up by the direct rays of the sun. It was a succession of luminous furrows, very different from the radiation of Copernicus not long before; they ran parallel with each other.

Michel, with his usual readiness, hastened to exclaim—

"Look there! cultivated fields!"

"Cultivated fields!" replied Nicholl, shrugging his shoulders.

"Ploughed, at all events," retorted Michel Ardan; "but what labourers those Selenites must be, and what giant oxen they must harness to their ploughs to cut such furrows!"

"They are not furrows," said Barbicane; "they are *rifts*."

"Rifts? stuff!" replied Michel mildly; "but what do you mean by 'rifts' in the scientific world?"

Barbicane immediately enlightened his companion as to what he knew about lunar rifts. He knew that they were a kind of furrow found on every part of the disc which was not mountainous; that these furrows, generally isolated, measured from 400 to 500 leagues in length; that their breadth varied from 1000 to 1500 yards, and that their borders were strictly parallel; but he knew nothing more either of their formation or their nature.

Barbicane, through his glasses, observed these rifts with great attention. He noticed that their borders were formed of steep declivities; they were long parallel ramparts, and with some small amount of imagination he might have admitted the existence of long lines of fortifications, raised by Selenite engineers. Of these different rifts some were perfectly straight, as if cut by a line; others were slightly curved, though still keeping their borders parallel; some crossed each other, some cut through craters; here they wound through ordinary cavities, such as Posidonius or Petavius; there they wound through the seas, such as the Sea of Serenity.

These natural accidents naturally excited the imaginations of these terrestrial astronomers. The first observations had not discovered these rifts. Neither Hevelius, Cassim, La Hire, nor Herschel seemed to have known them. It was Schroeter who in 1789 first drew attention to them. Others followed who studied them, as Pastorff, Gruithuysen, Bœer, and Moedler. At this time their number amounts to seventy; but, if they have been counted, their nature has not yet been determined; they are certainly *not* fortifications, any more than they are the ancient beds of dried-up rivers; for, on one side, the waters, so slight on the moon's surface, could never have worn such drains for themselves; and, on the other, they often cross craters of great elevation.

We must, however, allow that Michel Ardan had "an idea," and that, without knowing it, he coincided in that respect with Julius Schmidt.

"Why," said he, "should not these unaccountable appearances be simply phenomena of vegetation?"

"What do you mean?" asked Barbicane quickly.

"Do not excite yourself, my worthy president," replied Michel; "might it not be possible that the dark lines forming that bastion were rows of trees regularly placed?"

"You stick to your vegetation, then?" said Barbicane.

"I like," retorted Michel Ardan, "to explain what you savants cannot explain; at least my hypothesis has the advantage of indicating why these rifts disappear, or seem to disappear, at certain seasons."

"And for what reason?"

"For the reason that the trees become invisible when they lose their leaves, and visible when they regain them."

"Your explanation is ingenious, my dear companion," replied Barbicane, "but inadmissible."

"Why?"

"Because, so to speak, there are no seasons on the moon's surface, and that, consequently, the phenomena of vegetation of which you speak cannot occur."

Indeed, the slight obliquity of the lunar axis keeps the sun at an almost equal height in every latitude. Above the equatorial regions the radiant orb almost invariably occupies the zenith, and does not pass the limits of the horizon in the polar regions; thus, according to each region, there reigns a perpetual winter, spring, summer, or autumn, as in the planet Jupiter, whose axis is but little inclined upon its orbit.

What origin do they attribute to these rifts? That is a question difficult to solve. They are certainly anterior to the formation of craters and circles, for several have introduced themselves by breaking through their circular ramparts. Thus it may be that, contemporary with the latter geological epochs, they are due to the expansion of natural forces.

But the projectile had now attained the 40° of lunar lat., at a distance not exceeding 400 miles. Through the glasses objects appeared to be only four miles distant.

At this point, under their feet, rose Mount Helicon, 1520 feet high, and round about the left rose moderate elevations, enclosing a small portion of the "Sea of Rains," under the name of the Gulf of Iris. The terrestrial atmosphere would have to be one hundred and seventy times more transparent than it is, to allow astronomers to make perfect observations on the moon's surface; but in the void in which the projectile floated no fluid interposed itself between the eye of the observer and the object observed. And more, Barbicane found himself carried to a greater distance than the most powerful telescopes had ever done before, either that of Lord Rosse or that of the Rocky Mountains. He was, therefore, under extremely favourable conditions for solving that great question of the habitability of the moon; but the solution still escaped him; he could distinguish nothing but desert beds, immense plains, and towards the north, arid mountains. Not a work betrayed the hand of man; not a ruin marked his course; not a group of animals was to be seen indicating life, even in an inferior degree. In no part was there life, in no part was there an appearance of vegetation. Of the three kingdoms which share the terrestrial globe between them, one alone was represented on the lunar, and that the mineral.

"Ah, indeed!" said Michel Ardan, a little out of countenance; "then you see no one?"

"No," answered Nicholl; "up to this time not a man, not an animal, not a tree! After all, whether the atmosphere has taken refuge at the bottom of cavities, in the midst of the circles, or even on the opposite face of the moon, we cannot decide."

"Besides," added Barbicane, "even to the most piercing eye a man cannot be distinguished farther than three miles and a half off; so that, if there are any Selenites, they can see our projectile, but we cannot see them."

Towards four in the morning, at the height of the fiftieth parallel, the distance was reduced to 300 miles. To the left ran a line of mountains capriciously shaped, lying in the full light. To the right, on the contrary, lay a black hollow resembling a vast well, unfathomable and gloomy, drilled into the lunar soil.

This hole was the "Black Lake"; it was Pluto, a deep circle which can be conveniently studied from the earth, between the last quarter and the new moon, when the shadows fall from west to east.

This black colour is rarely met with on the surface of the satellite. As yet it has only been recognized in the depths of the circle of Endymion, to the east of the Cold Sea, in the northern hemisphere, and at the bottom of Grimaldi's circle, on the equator, towards the eastern border of the orb.

Pluto is an annular mountain, situated in 51° north latitude, and 9° east longitude. Its circuit is forty-seven miles long and thirty-two broad.

Barbicane regretted that they were not passing directly above this vast opening. There was an abyss to fathom, perhaps some mysterious phenomenon to surprise; but the projectile's course could not be altered. They must rigidly submit. They could not guide a balloon, still less a projectile, when once enclosed within its walls. Towards five in the morning the northern limits of the Sea of Rains was at length passed. The mounts of Condamine and Fontenelle remained—one on the right, the other on the left. That part of the disc beginning with 60° was becoming quite mountainous. The glasses brought them to within two miles, less than that separating the summit of Mont Blanc from the level of the sea. The whole region was bristling with spikes and circles. Towards the 60° Philolaus stood predominant at a height of 5550 feet with its elliptical crater, and seen from this distance, the disc showed a very fantastical appearance. Landscapes were presented to the eye under very different conditions from those on the earth, and also very inferior to them.

The moon having no atmosphere, the consequences arising from the absence of this gaseous envelope have already been shown. No twilight on her surface; night following day and day following night with the suddenness of a lamp which is extinguished or lighted amidst profound darkness,—no transition from cold to heat, the temperature falling in an instant from boiling point to the cold of space.

Another consequence of this want of air is that absolute darkness reigns where the sun's rays do not penetrate. That which on earth is called diffusion of light, that luminous matter which the air holds in suspension, which creates the twilight and the daybreak, which produces the *umbræ* and the *penumbræ*, and all the magic of *chiaro-oscuro*, does not exist on the moon. Hence the harshness of contrasts, which only admit of two colours, black and white. If a Selenite were to shade his eyes from the sun's rays, the sky would seem absolutely black, and the stars would shine to him as on the darkest night. Judge of the impression produced on Barbicane and his two friends by this strange scene! Their eyes were confused. They could no longer grasp the respective distances of the different plains. A lunar landscape without the softening of the phenomena of *chiaro-*

oscuro could not be rendered by an earthly landscape painter: it would be spots of ink on a white page—nothing more.

This aspect was not altered even when the projectile, at the height of 80°, was only separated from the moon by a distance of fifty miles; nor even when, at five in the morning, it passed at less than twenty-five miles from the mountain of Gioja, a distance reduced by the glasses to a quarter of a mile. It seemed as if the moon might be touched by the hand! It seemed impossible that, before long, the projectile would not strike her, if only at the north pole, the brilliant arch of which was so distinctly visible on the black sky.

Michel Ardan wanted to open one of the scuttles and throw himself on to the moon's surface! A very useless attempt; for if the projectile could not attain any point whatever of the satellite, Michel, carried along by its motion, could not attain it either.

At that moment, at six o'clock, the lunar pole appeared. The disc only presented to the travellers' gaze one half brilliantly lit up, whilst the other disappeared in the darkness. Suddenly the projectile passed the line of demarcation between intense light and absolute darkness, and was plunged in profound night!

CHAPTER XIV: THE NIGHT OF THREE HUNDRED AND FIFTY-FOUR HOURS AND A HALF At the moment when this phenomenon took place so rapidly, the projectile was skirting the moon's north pole at less than twenty-five miles distance. Some seconds had sufficed to plunge it into the absolute darkness of space. The transition was so sudden, without shade, without gradation of light, without attenuation of the luminous waves, that the orb seemed to have been extinguished by a powerful blow.

"Melted, disappeared!" Michel Ardan exclaimed, aghast.

Indeed, there was neither reflection nor shadow. Nothing more was to be seen of that disc, formerly so dazzling. The darkness was complete, and rendered even more so by the rays from the stars. It was "that blackness" in which the lunar nights are insteeped, which last three hundred and fifty-four hours and a half at each point of the disc, a long night resulting from the equality of the translatory and rotatory movements of the moon. The projectile, immerged in the conical shadow of the satellite, experienced the action of the solar rays no more than any of its invisible points.

In the interior, the obscurity was complete. They could not see each other. Hence the necessity of dispelling the darkness. However desirous Barbicane might be to husband the gas, the reserve of which was small, he was obliged to ask from it a fictitious light, an expensive brilliancy which the sun then refused.

"Devil take the radiant orb!" exclaimed Michel Ardan, "which forces us to expend gas, instead of giving us his rays gratuitously."

"Do not let us accuse the sun," said Nicholl, "it is not his fault, but that of the moon, which has come and placed herself like a screen between us and it."

"It is the sun!" continued Michel.

"It is the moon!" retorted Nicholl.

An idle dispute, which Barbicane put an end to by saying—

"My friends, it is neither the fault of the sun nor of the moon; it is the fault of the *projectile*, which, instead of rigidly following its course, has awkwardly missed it. To be more just, it is the fault of that unfortunate meteor which has so deplorably altered our first direction."

"Well," replied Michel Ardan, "as the matter is settled, let us have breakfast. After a whole night of watching, it is fair to build ourselves up a little."

This proposal meeting with no contradiction, Michel prepared the repast in a few minutes. But they ate for eating's sake, they drank without toasts, without hurrahs. The bold travellers being borne away into gloomy space, without their accustomed cortège of rays, felt a vague uneasiness at their hearts. The "strange" shadow so dear to Victor Hugo's pen bound them on all sides. But they talked over the interminable night of three hundred and fifty-four hours and a half, nearly fifteen days, which the law of physics has imposed on the inhabitants of the moon.

Barbicane gave his friends some explanation of the causes and the consequences of this curious phenomenon.

"Curious indeed," said they; "for, if each hemisphere of the moon is deprived of solar light for fifteen days, that above which we now float does not even enjoy during its long night any view of the earth so beautifully lit up. In a word she has no moon (applying this designation to our globe) but on one side of her disc. Now if this were the case with the earth,—if, for example, Europe never saw the moon, and she was only visible at the Antipodes, imagine to yourself the astonishment of a European on arriving in Australia."

"They would make the voyage for nothing but to see the moon!" replied Michel.

"Very well!" continued Barbicane, "that astonishment is reserved for the Selenites who inhabit the face of the moon opposite to the earth, a face which is ever invisible to our countrymen of the terrestrial globe."

"And which we should have seen," added Nicholl, "if we had arrived here when the moon was new, that is to say fifteen days later."

"I will add, to make amends," continued Barbicane, "that the inhabitants of the visible face are singularly favoured by nature, to the detriment of their brethren on the invisible face. The latter, as you see, have dark nights of 354 hours, without one single ray to break the darkness. The other, on the contrary, when the sun which has given its light for fifteen days sinks below the horizon, see a splendid orb rise on the opposite horizon. It is the earth, which is thirteen times greater than that diminutive moon that we know;—the earth which developes itself at a diameter of two degrees, and which sheds a light thirteen times greater than that qualified by atmospheric strata—the earth which only disappears at the moment when the sun reappears in its turn!"

"Nicely worded!" said Michel, "slightly academical perhaps."

"It follows, then," continued Barbicane, without knitting his brows, "that the visible face of the disc must be very agreeable to inhabit, since it always looks on either the sun when the moon is full, or on the earth when the moon is new."

"But," said Nicholl, "that advantage must be well compensated by the insupportable heat which the light brings with it."

"The inconvenience, in that respect, is the same for the two faces, for the earth's light is evidently deprived of heat. But the invisible face is still more searched by the heat than the visible face. I say that for *you*, Nicholl, because Michel will probably not understand."

"Thank you," said Michel.

"Indeed," continued Barbicane, "when the invisible face receives at the same time light and heat from the sun, it is because the moon is new; that is to say, she is situated between the sun and the earth. It follows, then, considering the position which she occupies in opposition when full, that she is nearer to the sun by twice her distance from the earth; and that distance may be estimated at the two-hundredth part of that which separates the sun from the earth, or in round numbers 400,000 miles. So that invisible face is so much nearer to the sun when she receives its rays."

"Quite right," replied Nicholl.

"On the contrary," continued Barbicane.

"One moment," said Michel, interrupting his grave companion.

"What do you want?"

"I ask to be allowed to continue the explanation."

"And why?"

"To prove that I understand."

"Get along with you," said Barbicane, smiling.

"On the contrary," said Michel, imitating the tone and gestures of the president, "on the contrary, when the visible face of the moon is lit by the sun, it is because the moon is full, that is to say, opposite the sun with regard to the earth. The distance separating it from the radiant orb is then increased in round numbers to 400,000 miles, and the heat which she receives must be a little less."

"Very well said!" exclaimed Barbicane. "Do you know, Michel, that, for an amateur, you are intelligent."

"Yes," replied Michel coolly, "we are all so on the Boulevard des Italiens."

Barbicane gravely clasped the hand of his amiable companion, and continued to enumerate the advantages reserved for the inhabitants of the visible face.

Amongst others, he mentioned eclipses of the sun, which only take place on this side of the lunar disc; since, in order that they may take place, it is necessary for the moon to be *in opposition*. These eclipses, caused by the interposition of the earth between the moon and the sun, can last *two hours*; during which time, by reason of the rays refracted by its atmosphere, the terrestrial globe can appear as nothing but a black point upon the sun.

"So," said Nicholl, "there is a hemisphere, that invisible hemisphere which is very ill supplied, very ill treated, by nature."

"Never mind," replied Michel; "if we ever become Selenites, we will inhabit the visible face. I like the light."

"Unless, by any chance," answered Nicholl, "the atmosphere should be condensed on the other side, as certain astronomers pretend."

"That would be a consideration," said Michel.

Breakfast over, the observers returned to their post. They tried to see through the darkened scuttles by extinguishing all light in the projectile; but not a luminous spark made its way through the darkness.

One inexplicable fact preoccupied Barbicane. Why, having passed within such a short distance of the moon—about twenty-five miles only—why the projectile had not fallen? If its speed had been enormous, he could have understood that the fall would not have taken place; but, with a relatively moderate speed, that resistance to the moon's attraction could not be explained. Was the projectile under some foreign influence? Did some kind of body retain it in the ether? It was quite evident that it could never reach any point of the moon. Whither was it going? Was it going farther from, or nearing, the disc? Was it being borne in that profound darkness through the infinity of space? How could they learn, how calculate, in the midst of this night? All these questions made Barbicane uneasy, but he could not solve them.

Certainly, the invisible orb was *there*, perhaps only some few miles off; but neither he nor his companions could see it. If there was any noise on its surface, they could not hear it. Air, that medium of sound, was wanting to transmit the groanings of that moon which the Arabic legends call "a man already half granite, and still breathing."

One must allow that that was enough to aggravate the most patient observers. It was just that unknown hemisphere which was stealing from their sight. That face which fifteen days sooner, or fifteen days later, had been, or would be, splendidly illuminated by the solar rays, was then being lost in utter darkness. In fifteen days where would the projectile be? Who could say? Where would the chances of conflicting attractions have drawn it to? The disappointment of the travellers in the midst of this utter darkness may be imagined. All observation of the lunar disc was impossible. The constellations alone claimed all their attention; and we must allow that the astronomers Faye, Charconac, and Secchi, never found themselves in circumstances so favourable for their observation.

Indeed, nothing could equal the splendour of this starry world, bathed in limpid ether. Its diamonds set in the heavenly vault sparkled magnificently. The eye took in the firmament from the Southern Cross to the North Star, those two constellations which in 12,000 years, by reason of the succession of equinoxes, will resign their part of polar stars, the one to Canopus in the southern hemisphere, the other to Vega in the northern. Imagination loses itself in this sublime Infinity, amidst which the projectile was gravitating, like a new star created by the hand of man. From a natural cause, these constellations shone with a soft lustre; they did not *twinkle*, for there was no atmosphere which, by the intervention of its layers unequally dense and of different degrees of humidity, produces this scintillation. These stars were soft eyes, looking out into the dark night, amidst the silence of absolute space.

Long did the travellers stand mute, watching the constellated firmament, upon which the moon, like a vast screen, made an enormous black hole. But at length a painful sensation drew them from their watchings. This was an intense cold, which soon covered the inside of the glass of the scuttles with a thick coating of ice. The sun was no longer warming the projectile with its direct rays, and thus it was losing the heat stored up in its walls by degrees. This heat was rapidly evaporating into space by radiation, and a considerably lower temperature was the result. The humidity of the interior was changed into ice upon contact with the glass, preventing all observation.

Nicholl consulted the thermometer, and saw that it had fallen to seventeen degrees (centigrade) below zero.[1] So that, in spite of the many reasons for economizing, Barbicane, after having begged light from the gas, was also obliged to beg for heat. The projectile's low temperature was no longer endurable. Its tenants would have been frozen to death.

"Well!" observed Michel, "we cannot reasonably complain of the monotony of our journey! What variety we have had, at least in temperature. Now we are blinded with light and saturated with heat, like the Indians of the Pampas! now plunged into profound darkness, amidst the

[1] 1° *Fahr.* (*Ed.*)

cold like the Esquimaux of the north pole. No, indeed! we have no right to complain; nature does wonders in our honour."

"But," asked Nicholl, "what is the temperature outside?"

"Exactly that of the planetary space," replied Barbicane.

"Then," continued Michel Ardan, "would not this be the time to make the experiment which we dared not attempt, when we were drowned in the sun's rays?"

"It is now or never," replied Barbicane, "for we are in a good position to verify the temperature of space, and see if Fourier or Pouillet's calculations are exact."

"In any case it is cold," said Michel. "See! the steam of the interior is condensing on the glasses of the scuttles. If the fall continues, the vapour of our breath will fall in snow around us."

"Let us prepare a thermometer," said Barbicane.

We may imagine that an ordinary thermometer would afford no result under the circumstances in which this instrument was to be exposed. The mercury would have been frozen in its ball, as below forty-two degrees below zero[2] it is no longer liquid. But Barbicane had furnished himself with a spirit thermometer on Wafferdin's system, which gives the minima of excessively low temperatures.

Before beginning the experiment, this instrument was compared with an ordinary one, and then Barbicane prepared to use it.

"How shall we set about it?" asked Nicholl.

"Nothing is easier," replied Michel Ardan, who was never at a loss. "We open the scuttle rapidly; throw out the instrument; it follows the projectile with exemplary docility; and a quarter of an hour after, draw it in."

"With the hand?" asked Barbicane.

"With the hand," replied Michel.

"Well then, my friend, do not expose yourself," answered Barbicane, "for the hand that you draw in again will be nothing but a stump frozen and deformed by the frightful cold."

"Really!"

"You will feel as if you had had a terrible burn, like that of iron at a white heat; for whether the heat leaves our bodies briskly or enters briskly, it is exactly the same thing. Besides, I am not at all certain that the objects we have thrown out are still following us."

"Why not?" asked Nicholl.

"Because, if we are passing through an atmosphere of the slightest density, these objects will be retarded. Again, the darkness prevents our seeing if they still float around us. But in order not to expose ourselves

[2] −44° *Fahr.* (*Ed.*)

to the loss of our thermometer, we will fasten it, and we can then more easily pull it back again."

Barbicane's advice was followed. Through the scuttle rapidly opened, Nicholl threw out the instrument which was held by a short cord, so that it might be more easily drawn up. The scuttle had not been opened more than a second, but that second had sufficed to let in a most intense cold.

"The devil!" exclaimed Michel Ardan, "it is cold enough to freeze a white bear."

Barbicane waited until half an hour had elapsed, which was more than time enough to allow the instrument to fall to the level of the surrounding temperature. Then it was rapidly pulled in.

Barbicane calculated the quantity of spirits of wine overflowed into the little phial soldered to the lower part of the instrument, and said—

"A hundred and forty degrees centigrade[3] below zero!"

M. Pouillet was right and Fourier wrong. That was the undoubted temperature of the starry space. Such is, perhaps, that of the lunar continents, when the orb of night has lost by radiation all the heat which fifteen days of sun have poured into her.

CHAPTER XV: HYPERBOLA OR PARABOLA We may, perhaps, be astonished to find Barbicane and his companions so little occupied with the future reserved for them in their metal prison which was bearing them through the infinity of space. Instead of asking where they were going, they passed their time making experiments, as if they had been quietly installed in their own study.

We might answer that men so strong-minded were above such anxieties —that they did not trouble themselves about such trifles—and that they had something else to do than to occupy their minds with the future.

The truth was that they were not masters of their projectile; they could neither check its course, nor alter its direction.

A sailor can change the head of his ship as he pleases; an aeronaut can give a vertical motion to his balloon. They, on the contrary, had no power over their vehicle. Every manoeuvre was forbidden. Hence the inclination to let things alone, or as the sailors say, "let her run."

Where did they find themselves at this moment, at eight o'clock in the morning of the day called upon the earth the 6th of December? Very certainly in the neighbourhood of the moon, and even near enough for her to look to them like an enormous black screen upon the firmament. As to the distance which separated them, it was impossible to estimate it.

[3] —218° *Fahr.* (*Ed.*)

The projectile, held by some unaccountable force, had been within four miles of grazing the satellite's north pole.

But since entering the cone of shadow these last two hours, had the distance increased or diminished? Every point of mark was wanting by which to estimate both the direction and the speed of the projectile.

Perhaps it was rapidly leaving the disc, so that it would soon quit the pure shadow. Perhaps, again, on the other hand, it might be nearing it so much that in a short time it might strike some high point on the invisible hemisphere, which would doubtlessly have ended the journey much to the detriment of the travellers.

A discussion arose on this subject, and Michel Ardan, always ready with an explanation, gave it as his opinion that the projectile, held by the lunar attraction, would end by falling on the surface of the terrestrial globe like an aerolite.

"First of all, my friend," answered Barbicane, "every aerolite does not fall to the earth; it is only a small proportion which do so; and if we had passed into an aerolite, it does not necessarily follow that we should ever reach the surface of the moon."

"But how if we get near enough?" replied Michel.

"Pure mistake," replied Barbicane. "Have you not seen shooting stars rush through the sky by thousands at certain seasons?"

"Yes."

"Well, these stars, or rather corpuscules, only shine when they are heated by gliding over the atmospheric layers. Now, if they enter the atmosphere, they pass at least within forty miles of the earth, but they seldom fall upon it. The same with our projectile. It may approach very near to the moon, and yet not fall upon it."

"But then," asked Michel, "I shall be curious to know how our erring vehicle will act in space?"

"I see but two hypotheses," replied Barbicane, after some moments' reflection.

"What are they?"

"The projectile has the choice between two mathematical curves, and it will follow one or the other according to the speed with which it is animated, and which at this moment I cannot estimate."

"Yes," said Nicholl, "it will follow either a parabola or a hyperbola."

"Just so," replied Barbicane. "With a certain speed it will assume the parabola, and with a greater the hyperbola."

"I like those grand words," exclaimed Michel Ardan; "one knows directly what they mean. And pray what is your parabola, if you please?"

"My friend," answered the captain, "the parabola is a curve of the second order, the result of the section of a cone intersected by a plane parallel to one of its sides."

"Ah! ah!" said Michel, in a satisfied tone.

"It is very nearly," continued Nicholl, "the course described by a bomb launched from a mortar."

"Perfect! And the hyperbola?"

"The hyperbola, Michel, is a curve of the second order, produced by the intersection of a conic surface and a plane parallel to its axis, and constitutes two branches separated one from the other, both tending indefinitely in the two directions."

"Is it possible!" exclaimed Michel Ardan in a serious tone, as if they had told him of some serious event. "What I particularly like in your definition of the hyperbola (I was going to say hyperblague) is that it is still more obscure than the word you pretend to define."

Nicholl and Barbicane cared little for Michel Ardan's fun. They were deep in a scientific discussion. What curve would the projectile follow? was their hobby. One maintained the hyperbola, the other the parabola. They gave each other reasons bristling with x. Their arguments were couched in language which made Michel jump. The discussion was hot, and neither would give up his chosen curve to his adversary.

This scientific dispute lasted so long that it made Michel very impatient.

"Now, gentlemen co-sines, will you cease to throw parabolas and hyperbolas at each other's heads? I want to understand the only interesting question in the whole affair. We shall follow one or other of these curves? Good. But where will they lead us to?"

"Nowhere," replied Nicholl.

"How, nowhere?"

"Evidently," said Barbicane, "they are open curves, which may be prolonged indefinitely."

"Ah, savants!" cried Michel; "and what are either the one or the other to us from the moment we know that they equally lead us into infinite space?"

Barbicane and Nicholl could not forbear smiling. They had just been creating "art for art's sake." Never had so idle a question been raised at such an inopportune moment. The sinister truth remained that, whether hyperbolically or parabolically borne away, the projectile would never again meet either the earth or the moon.

What would become of these bold travellers in the immediate future? If they did not die of hunger, if they did not die of thirst, in some days, when the gas failed, they would die from want of air, unless the cold had killed them first. Still, important as it was to economize the gas, the excessive lowness of the surrounding temperature obliged them to consume a certain quantity. Strictly speaking, they could do without its *light*, but not without its *heat*. Fortunately the caloric generated by Reiset's and

Regnaut's apparatus raised the temperature of the interior of the projectile a little, and without much expenditure they were able to keep it bearable.

But observations had now become very difficult. The dampness of the projectile was condensed on the windows and congealed immediately. This cloudiness had to be dispersed continually. In any case they might hope to be able to discover some phenomena of the highest interest.

But up to this time the disc remained dumb and dark. It did not answer the multiplicity of questions put by these ardent minds; a matter which drew this reflection from Michel, apparently a just one—

"If ever we begin this journey over again, we shall do well to choose the time when the moon is at the full."

"Certainly," said Nicholl, "that circumstance will be more favourable. I allow that the moon, immersed in the sun's rays, will not be visible during the transit, but instead we should see the *earth*, which would be full. And what is more, if we were drawn round the moon, as at this moment, we should at least have the advantage of seeing the invisible part of her disc magnificently lit."

"Well said, Nicholl," replied Michel Ardan. "What do you think, Barbicane?"

"I think this," answered the grave president: "If ever we begin this journey again, we shall start at the same time and under the same conditions. Suppose we had attained our end, would it not have been better to have found continents in broad daylight, than a country plunged in utter darkness? Would not our first installation have been made under better circumstances? Yes, evidently. As to the *invisible* side, we could have visited it in our exploring expeditions on the lunar globe. So that the time of the full moon was well chosen. But we ought to have arrived at the end; and in order to have so arrived, we ought to have suffered no deviation on the road."

"I have nothing to say to that," answered Michel Ardan. "Here is, however, a good opportunity lost of observing the other side of the moon."

But the projectile was now describing in the shadow that incalculable course which no sight-mark would allow them to ascertain. Had its direction been altered, either by the influence of the lunar attraction, or by the action of some unknown star? Barbicane could not say. But a change had taken place in the relative position of the vehicle; and Barbicane verified it about four in the morning.

The change consisted in this, that the base of the projectile had turned towards the moon's surface, and was so held by a perpendicular passing through its axis. The attraction, that is to say the *weight*, had brought about this alteration. The heaviest part of the projectile inclined towards the invisible disc as if it would fall upon it.

Was it falling? Were the travellers attaining that much desired end? No. And the observation of a sign-point, quite inexplicable in itself, showed Barbicane that his projectile was not nearing the moon, and that it had shifted by following an almost concentric curve.

This point of mark was a luminous brightness, which Nicholl sighted suddenly, on the limit of the horizon formed by the black disc. This point could not be confounded with a star. It was a reddish incandescence which increased by degrees, a decided proof that the projectile was shifting towards it and not falling normally on the surface of the moon.

"A volcano! it is a volcano in action!" cried Nicholl; "a disembowelling of the interior fires of the moon! That world is not quite extinguished."

"Yes, an eruption," replied Barbicane, who was carefully studying the phenomenon through his night glass. "What should it be, if not a volcano?"

"But, then," said Michel Ardan, "in order to maintain that combustion, there must be air. So an atmosphere *does* surround that part of the moon."

"*Perhaps* so," replied Barbicane, "but not necessarily. The volcano, by the decomposition of certain substances, can provide its own oxygen, and thus throw flames into space. It seems to me that the deflagration, by the intense brilliancy of the substances in combustion, is produced in pure oxygen. We must not be in a hurry to proclaim the existence of a lunar atmosphere."

The fiery mountain must have been situated about the 45° south latitude on the invisible part of the disc; but, to Barbicane's great displeasure, the curve which the projectile was describing was taking it far from the point indicated by the eruption. Thus he could not determine its nature exactly. Half an hour after being sighted, this luminous point had disappeared behind the dark horizon; but the verification of this phenomenon was of considerable consequence in their selenographic studies. It proved that all heat had not yet disappeared from the bowels of this globe; and where heat exists, who can affirm that the vegetable kingdom, nay, even the animal kingdom itself, has not up to this time resisted all destructive influences? The existence of this volcano in eruption, unmistakably seen by these earthly savants, would doubtless give rise to many theories favourable to the grave question of the habitability of the moon.

Barbicane allowed himself to be carried away by these reflections. He forgot himself in a deep reverie in which the mysterious destiny of the lunar world was uppermost. He was seeking to combine together the facts observed up to that time, when a new incident recalled him briskly to reality. This incident was more than a cosmical phenomenon; it was a threatened danger, the consequences of which might be disastrous in the extreme.

Suddenly, in the midst of the ether, in the profound darkness, an enormous mass appeared. It was like a moon, but an incandescent moon, whose brilliancy was all the more intolerable as it cut sharply on the frightful darkness of space. This mass, of a circular form, threw a light which filled the projectile. The forms of Barbicane, Nicholl, and Michel Ardan, bathed in its white sheets, assumed that livid spectral appearance which physicians produce with the fictitious light of alcohol impregnated with salt.

"By Jove!" cried Michel Ardan, "we are hideous. What is that ill-conditioned moon?"

"A meteor," replied Barbicane.

"A meteor burning in space?"

"Yes."

This shooting globe suddenly appearing in shadow at a distance of at most 200 miles, ought, according to Barbicane, to have a diameter of 2000 yards. It advanced at a speed of about one mile and a half per second. It cut the projectile's path, and must reach it in some minutes. As it approached it grew to enormous proportions.

Imagine, if possible, the situation of the travellers! It is impossible to describe it. In spite of their courage, their *sang-froid*, their carelessness of danger, they were mute, motionless with stiffened limbs, a prey to frightful terror. Their projectile, the course of which they could not alter, was rushing straight on this ignited mass, more intense than the open mouth of an oven. It seemed as though they were being precipitated towards an abyss of fire.

Barbicane had seized the hands of his two companions, and all three looked through their half-open eyelids upon that asteroid heated to a white heat. If thought was not destroyed within them, if their brains still worked amidst all this awe, they must have given themselves up for lost.

Two minutes after the sudden appearance of the meteor (to them two centuries of anguish) the projectile seemed almost about to strike it, when the globe of fire burst like a bomb, but without making any noise in that void where sound, which is but the agitation of the layers of air, could not be generated.

Nicholl uttered a cry, and he and his companions rushed to the scuttle. What a sight! What pen can describe it? What palette is rich enough in colours to reproduce so magnificent a spectacle?

It was like the opening of a crater, like the scattering of an immense conflagration. Thousands of luminous fragments lit up and irradiated space with their fires. Every size, every colour, was there intermingled.

There were rays of yellow and pale yellow, red, green, grey—a crown of fireworks of all colours. Of the enormous and much-dreaded globe there remained nothing but these fragments carried in all directions, now become asteroids in their turn, some flaming like a sword, some surrounded by a whitish cloud, and others leaving behind them trains of brilliant cosmical dust.

These incandescent blocks crossed and struck each other, scattering still smaller fragments, some of which struck the projectile. Its left scuttle was even cracked by a violent shock. It seemed to be floating amidst a hail of howitzer shells, the smallest of which might destroy it instantly.

The light which saturated the ether was so wonderfully intense, that Michel, drawing Barbicane and Nicholl to his window, exclaimed, "The invisible moon, visible at last!"

And through a luminous emanation, which lasted some seconds, the whole three caught a glimpse of that mysterious disc which the eye of man now saw for the first time. What could they distinguish at a distance which they could not estimate? Some lengthened bands along the disc, real clouds formed in the midst of a very confined atmosphere, from which emerged not only all the mountains, but also projections of less importance; its circles, its yawning craters, as capriciously placed as on the visible surface. Then immense spaces, no longer arid plains, but real seas, oceans, widely distributed, reflecting on their liquid surface all the dazzling magic of the fires of space; and, lastly, on the surface of the continents, large dark masses, looking like immense forests under the rapid illumination of a brilliance.

Was it an illusion, a mistake, an optical illusion? Could they give a scientific assent to an observation so superficially obtained? Dared they pronounce upon the question of its habitability after so slight a glimpse of the invisible disc?

But the lightnings in space subsided by degrees; its accidental brilliancy died away; the asteroids dispersed in different directions and were extinguished in the distance. The ether returned to its accustomed darkness; the stars, eclipsed for a moment, again twinkled in the firmament, and the disc, so hastily discerned, was again buried in impenetrable night.

CHAPTER XVI: THE SOUTHERN HEMISPHERE The projectile had just escaped a terrible danger, and a very unforeseen one. Who would have thought of such a rencontre with meteors? These erring bodies might create serious perils for the travellers. They were to them so many sandbanks upon that sea of ether which, less fortunate than sailors, they could not escape. But did these adventurers complain of space? No, not since nature had given them the splendid sight of a cosmical meteor bursting from expansion, since this inimitable firework, which no Ruggieri could imitate, had lit up for some seconds the invisible glory of the moon. In that flash, continents, seas, and forests had become visible to them. Did an atmosphere, then, bring to this unknown face its life-giving atoms? Questions still insoluble, and for ever closed against human curiosity!

It was then half-past three in the afternoon. The projectile was following its curvilinear direction round the moon. Had its course been again altered by the meteor? It was to be feared so. But the projectile must describe a curve unalterably determined by the laws of mechanical reasoning. Barbicane was inclined to believe that this curve would be rather a parabola than a hyperbola. But admitting the parabola, the projectile must quickly have passed through the cone of shadow projected into space opposite the sun. This cone, indeed, is very narrow, the angular diameter of the moon being so little when compared with the diameter of the orb of day; and up to this time the projectile had been floating in this deep shadow. Whatever had been its speed (and it could not have been insignificant) its period of occultation continued. That was evident, but perhaps that would not have been the case in a supposed rigidly parabolical trajectory,—a new problem which tormented Barbicane's brain, imprisoned as he was in a circle of unknowns which he could not unravel.

Neither of the travellers thought of taking an instant's repose. Each one watched for an unexpected fact, which might throw some new light on their uranographic studies. About five o'clock, Michel Ardan distributed, under the name of dinner, some pieces of bread and cold meat, which were quickly swallowed without either of them abandoning their scuttle, the glass of which was incessantly encrusted by the condensation of vapour.

About forty-five minutes past five in the evening, Nicholl, armed with his glass, sighted towards the southern border of the moon, and in the direction followed by the projectile, some bright points cut upon the dark shield of the sky. They looked like a succession of sharp points lengthened into a tremulous line. They were very bright. Such appeared the terminal line of the moon when in one of her octants.

They could not be mistaken. It was no longer a simple meteor. This luminous ridge had neither colour nor motion. Nor was it a volcano in eruption. And Barbicane did not hesitate to pronounce upon it.

"The sun!" he exclaimed.

"What! the sun?" answered Nicholl and Michel Ardan.

"Yes, my friends, it is the radiant orb itself lighting up the summit of the mountains situated on the southern borders of the moon. We are evidently nearing the south pole."

"After having passed the north pole," replied Michel. "We have made the circuit of our satellite, then?"

"Yes, my good Michel."

"Then, no more hyperbolas, no more parabolas, no more open curves to fear?"

"No, but a *closed* curve."

"Which is called——"

"An ellipse. Instead of losing itself in interplanetary space, it is probable that the projectile will describe an elliptical orbit around the moon."

"Indeed!"

"And that it will become *her* satellite."

"Moon of the moon!" cried Michel Ardan.

"Only, I would have you observe, my worthy friend," replied Barbicane, "that we are none the less lost for that."

"Yes, in another manner, and much more pleasantly," answered the careless Frenchman with his most amiable smile.

CHAPTER XVII: TYCHO At six in the evening the projectile passed the south pole at less than forty miles off, a distance equal to that already reached at the north pole. The elliptical curve was being rigidly carried out.

At this moment the travellers once more entered the blessed rays of the sun. They saw once more those stars which move slowly from east to west. The radiant orb was saluted by a triple hurrah. With its light it also sent heat, which soon pierced the metal walls. The glass resumed its accustomed appearance. The layers of ice melted as if by enchantment; and immediately, for economy's sake, the gas was put out, the air apparatus alone consuming its usual quantity.

"Ah!" said Nicholl, "these rays of heat are good. With what impatience must the Selenites wait the reappearance of the orb of day."

"Yes," replied Michel Ardan, "imbibing as it were the brilliant ether, light and heat, all life is contained in them."

At this moment the bottom of the projectile deviated somewhat from the lunar surface, in order to follow the slightly lengthened elliptical orbit. From this point, had the earth been at the full, Barbicane and his companions could have seen it, but immersed in the sun's irradiation she was quite invisible. Another spectacle attracted their attention, that of the southern part of the moon, brought by the glasses to within 450 yards. They did not again leave the scuttles, and noted every detail of this fantastical continent.

Mounts Doerfel and Leibnitz formed two separate groups very near the south pole. The first group extended from the pole to the eighty-fourth parallel, on the eastern part of the orb; the second occupied the eastern border, extending from the 65° of latitude to the pole.

On their capriciously formed ridge appeared dazzling sheets, as mentioned by Père Secchi. With more certainty than the illustrious Roman astronomer, Barbicane was enabled to recognize their nature.

"They are snow," he exclaimed.

"Snow?" repeated Nicholl.

"Yes, Nicholl, snow; the surface of which is deeply frozen. See how they reflect the luminous rays. Cooled lava would never give out such intense reflection. There must then be water, there must be air on the moon. As little as you please, but the fact can no longer be contested." No, it could not be. And if ever Barbicane should see the earth again, his notes will bear witness to this great fact in his selenographic observations.

These mountains of Doerfel and Leibnitz rose in the midst of plains of a medium extent, which were bounded by an indefinite succession of circles and annular ramparts. These two chains are the only ones met with in this region of circles. Comparatively but slightly marked, they throw up here and there some sharp points, the highest summit of which attains an altitude of 24,600 feet.

But the projectile was high above all this landscape, and the projections disappeared in the intense brilliancy of the disc. And to the eyes of the travellers there reappeared that original aspect of the lunar landscapes, raw in tone, without gradation of colours, and without degrees of shadow, roughly black and white, from the want of diffusion of light.

But the sight of this desolate world did not fail to captivate them by its very strangeness. They were moving over this region as if they had been borne on the breath of some storm, watching heights defile under their feet, piercing the cavities with their eyes, going down into the rifts, climbing the ramparts, sounding these mysterious holes, and levelling all cracks. But no trace of vegetation, no appearance of cities; nothing but stratification, beds of lava, overflowings polished like immense mirrors, reflecting the sun's rays with overpowering brilliancy. Nothing belonging to a *living* world—everything to a dead world, where avalanches, rolling from the summits of the mountains, would disperse noiselessly at the bottom of the abyss, retaining the motion, but wanting the sound. In any case it was the image of death, without its being possible even to say that life had ever existed there.

Michel Ardan, however, thought he recognized a heap of ruins, to which he drew Barbicane's attention. It was about the 80th parallel, in 30 longitude. This heap of stones, rather regularly placed, represented a vast fortress, overlooking a long rift, which in former days had served as a bed to the rivers of prehistorical times. Not far from that, rose to a height of 17,400 feet the annular mountain of Short, equal to the Asiatic Caucasus. Michel Ardan, with his accustomed ardour, maintained "the evidences" of his fortress. Beneath it he discerned the dismantled ramparts of a town; here the still intact arch of a portico, there two or three columns lying under their base; farther on, a succession of arches which must have supported the conduit of an aqueduct; in another part the sunken pillars of a gigantic bridge, run into the thickest parts of the rift. He distinguished all this, but with so much imagination in his glance, and through glasses so fantastical, that we must mistrust his observation. But who could affirm, who would dare to say, that the amiable fellow did not really see that which his two companions would not see?

Moments were too precious to be sacrificed in idle discussion. The Selenite city, whether imaginary or not, had already disappeared afar off. The distance of the projectile from the lunar disc was on the increase, and the details of the soil were being lost in a confused jumble. The reliefs, the circles, the craters and plains alone remained, and still showed their boundary lines distinctly. At this moment, to the left, lay extended one of the finest circles of lunar orography, one of the curiosities of this continent. It was Newton, which Barbicane recognized without trouble, by referring to the *Mappa Selenographica*.

Newton is situated in exactly 77° south lat., and 16° east long. It forms an annular crater, the ramparts of which, rising to a height of 21,300 feet, seemed to be impassable.

Barbicane made his companions observe that the height of this mountain above the surrounding plain was far from equalling the depth of its crater. This enormous hole was beyond all measurement, and formed a gloomy abyss, the bottom of which the sun's rays could never reach. There, according to Humboldt, reigns utter darkness, which the light of the sun and the earth cannot break. Mythologists could well have made it the mouth of hell.

"Newton," said Barbicane, "is the most perfect type of these annular mountains, of which the earth possesses no sample. They prove that the moon's formation, by means of cooling, is due to violent causes; for whilst under the pressure of internal fires the reliefs rise to considerable height, the depths withdraw far below the lunar level."

"I do not dispute the fact," replied Michel Ardan.

Some minutes after passing Newton, the projectile directly overlooked the annular mountain of Moret. It skirted at some distance the summits of Blancanus, and at about half-past seven in the evening reached the circle of Clavius.

This circle, one of the most remarkable of the disc, is situated in 58° south lat., and 15° east long. Its height is estimated at 22,950 feet. The travellers, at a distance of twenty-four miles (reduced to four by their glasses), could admire this vast crater in its entirety.

"Terrestrial volcanoes," said Barbicane, "are but molehills compared with those of the moon. Measuring the old craters formed by the first eruptions of Vesuvius and Etna, we find them little more than three miles in breadth. In France the circle of Cantal measures six miles across; at Ceyland the circle of the island is forty miles, which is considered the largest on the globe. What are these diameters against that of Clavius, which we overlook at this moment?"

"What is its breadth?" asked Nicholl.

"It is 150 miles," replied Barbicane. "This circle is certainly the most important on the moon, but many others measure 150, 100, or 75 miles."

"Ah! my friends," exclaimed Michel, "can you picture to yourselves what this now peaceful orb of night must have been when its craters, filled with thunderings, vomited at the same time smoke and tongues of flame. What a wonderful spectacle then, and now what decay! This moon is nothing more than a thin carcase of fireworks, whose squibs, rockets, serpents and suns, after a superb brilliancy, have left but sadly broken cases. Who can say the cause, the reason, the motive force of these cataclysms?"

Barbicane was not listening to Michel Ardan; he was contemplating those ramparts of Clavius, formed by large mountains spread over several miles. At the bottom of the immense cavity burrowed hundreds of small extinguished craters, riddling the soil like a colander, and overlooked by a peak 15,000 feet high.

Around, the plain appeared desolate. Nothing so arid as these reliefs, nothing so sad as these ruins of mountains, and (if we may so express ourselves) these fragments of peaks and mountains which strewed the soil. The satellite seemed to have burst at this spot.

The projectile was still advancing, and this movement did not subside. Circles, craters, and uprooted mountains succeeded each other incessantly. No more plains; no more seas. A never-ending Switzerland and Norway. And lastly, in the centre of this region of crevasses, the most splendid mountain on the lunar disc, the dazzling Tycho, in which posterity will ever preserve the name of the illustrious Danish astronomer.

In observing the full moon in a cloudless sky no one has failed to remark this brilliant point of the southern hemisphere. Michel Ardan used every metaphor that his imagination could supply to designate it by. To him this Tycho was a focus of light, a centre of irradiation, a crater vomiting rays. It was the tire of a brilliant wheel, an *asteria* enclosing the disc with its silver tentacles, an enormous eye filled with flames, a glory carved for Pluto's head, a star launched by the Creator's hand, and crushed against the face of the moon!

Tycho forms such a concentration of light that the inhabitants of the earth can see it without glasses, though at a distance of 240,000 miles! Imagine, then, its intensity to the eye of observers placed at a distance of only fifty miles! Seen through this pure ether, its brilliancy was so intolerable that Barbicane and his friends were obliged to blacken their glasses with the gas smoke before they could bear the splendour. Then silent, scarcely uttering an interjection of admiration, they gazed, they contemplated. All their feelings, all their impressions, were concentrated in that look, as under any violent emotion all life is concentrated at the heart.

Tycho belongs to the system of radiating mountains, like Aristarchus and Copernicus; but it is of all the most complete and decided, showing unquestionably the frightful volcanic action to which the formation of the moon is due. Tycho is situated in 43° south lat., and 12° east long. Its centre is occupied by a crater fifty miles broad. It assumes a slightly elliptical form, and is surrounded by an enclosure of annular ramparts, which on the east and west overlook the outer plain from a height of 15,000 feet. It is a group of Mont Blancs, placed round one common centre and crowned by radiating beams.

What this incomparable mountain really is, with all the projections converging towards it, and the interior excrescences of its crater, photography itself could never represent. Indeed, it is during the full moon that Tycho is seen in all its splendour. Then all shadows disappear, the foreshortening of perspective disappears, and all proofs become white—a disagreeable fact; for this strange region would have been marvellous if reproduced with photographic exactness. It is but a group of hollows, craters, circles, a network of crests; then, as far as the eye could see, a whole volcanic network cast upon this encrusted soil. One can then understand that the bubbles of this central eruption have kept their first form. Crystallized by cooling, they have stereotyped that aspect which the moon formerly presented when under the Plutonian forces.

The distance which separated the travellers from the annular summits of Tycho was not so great but that they could catch the principal details. Even on the causeway forming the fortifications of Tycho, the mountains hanging on to the interior and exterior sloping flanks rose in stories like gigantic terraces. They appeared to be higher by 300 or 400 feet to the west than to the east. No system of terrestrial encampment could equal these natural fortifications. A town built at the bottom of this circular cavity would have been utterly inaccessible.

Inaccessible and wonderfully extended over this soil covered with picturesque projections! Indeed, nature had not left the bottom of this crater flat and empty. It possessed its own peculiar orography, a mountainous system, making it a world in itself. The travellers could distinguish clearly cones, central hills, remarkable positions of the soil, naturally placed to receive the chefs-d'œuvre of Selenite architecture. There was marked out the place for a temple, here the ground of a forum, on this spot the plan of a palace, in another the plateau for a citadel; the whole overlooked by a central mountain of 1500 feet. A vast circle, in which ancient Rome could have been held in its entirety ten times over.

"Ah!" exclaimed Michel Ardan, enthusiastic at the sight; "what a grand town might be constructed within that ring of mountains! A quiet city, a peaceful refuge, beyond all human misery. How calm and isolated those misanthropes, those haters of humanity might live there, and all who have a distaste for social life!"

"All! It would be too small for them," replied Barbicane simply.

CHAPTER XVIII: GRAVE QUESTIONS   But the projectile had passed the enceinte of Tycho, and Barbicane and his two companions watched with scrupulous attention the brilliant rays which the celebrated mountain shed so curiously all over the horizon.

What was this radiant glory? What geological phenomenon had designed these ardent beams? This question occupied Barbicane's mind.

Under his eyes ran in all directions luminous furrows, raised at the edges and concave in the centre, some twelve miles, others thirty miles broad. These brilliant trains extended in some places to within 600 miles of Tycho, and seemed to cover, particularly towards the east, the northeast and the north, the half of the southern hemisphere. One of these jets extended as far as the circle of Neander, situated on the 40th meridian. Another by a slight curve furrowed the Sea of Nectar, breaking against the chain of Pyrenees, after a circuit of 800 miles. Others, towards the west, covered the Sea of Clouds and the Sea of Humours with a luminous network. What was the origin of these sparkling rays, which shone on the plains as well as on the reliefs, at whatever height they might be? All started from a common centre, the crater of Tycho. They sprang from him. Herschel attributed their brilliancy to currents of lava congealed by the cold; an opinion, however, which has not been generally adopted. Other astronomers have seen in these inexplicable rays a kind of *moraines*, rows of erratic blocks, which had been thrown up at the period of Tycho's formation.

"And why not?" asked Nicholl of Barbicane, who was relating and rejecting these different opinions.

"Because the regularity of these luminous lines, and the violence necessary to carry volcanic matter to such distances, is inexplicable."

"Eh! by Jove!" replied Michel Ardan, "it seems easy enough to me to explain the origin of these rays."

"Indeed?" said Barbicane.

"Indeed," continued Michel. "It is enough to say that it is a vast star, similar to that produced by a ball or a stone thrown at a square of glass!"

"Well!" replied Barbicane, smiling. "And what hand would be powerful enough to throw a ball to give such a shock as that?"

"The hand is not necessary," answered Nicholl, not at all confounded; "and as to the stone, let us suppose it to be a comet."

"Ah! those much-abused comets!" exclaimed Barbicane. "My brave Michel, your explanation is not bad; but your comet is useless. The shock which produced that rent must have come from the inside of the star. A violent contraction of the lunar crust, while cooling, might suffice to imprint this gigantic star."

"A contraction! something like a lunar stomach-ache," said Michel Ardan.

"Besides," added Barbicane, "this opinion is that of an English savant, Nasmyth, and it seems to me to sufficiently explain the radiation of these mountains."

"That Nasmyth was no fool!" replied Michel.

Long did the travellers, whom such a sight could never weary, admire the splendours of Tycho. Their projectile, saturated with luminous gleams in the double irradiation of sun and moon, must have appeared like an incandescent globe. They had passed suddenly from excessive cold to intense heat. Nature was thus preparing them to become Selenites. Become Selenites! That idea brought up once more the question of the habitability of the moon. After what they had seen, could the travellers solve it? Would they decide for or against it? Michel Ardan persuaded his two friends to form an opinion, and asked them directly if they thought that men and animals were represented in the lunar world.

"I think that we can answer," said Barbicane; "but according to my idea the question ought not to be put in that form. I ask it to be put differently."

"Put it your own way," replied Michel.

"Here it is," continued Barbicane. "The problem is a double one, and requires a double solution. Is the moon *habitable?* Has the moon ever been *inhabited?*"

"Good!" replied Nicholl. "First let us see whether the moon is habitable."

"To tell the truth, I know nothing about it," answered Michel.

"And I answer in the negative," continued Barbicane. "In her actual state, with her surrounding atmosphere certainly very much reduced, her seas for the most part dried up, her insufficient supply of water restricted, vegetation, sudden alterations of cold and heat, her days and nights of 354 hours; the moon does not seem habitable to me, nor does she seem propitious to animal development, nor sufficient for the wants of existence as we understand it."

"Agreed," replied Nicholl. "But is not the moon habitable for creatures differently organized from ourselves?"

"That question is more difficult to answer, but I will try; and I ask Nicholl if *motion* appears to him to be a necessary result of *life*, whatever be its organization?"

"Without a doubt!" answered Nicholl.

"Then, my worthy companion, I would answer that we have observed the lunar continent at a distance of 500 yards at most, and that nothing seemed to us to move on the moon's surface. The presence of any kind of life would have been betrayed by its attendant marks, such as divers buildings, and even by ruins. And what have we seen? Everywhere and always the geological works of nature, never the work of man. If, then, there exist representatives of the animal kingdom on the moon, they must have fled to those unfathomable cavities which the eye cannot reach; which I cannot admit, for they must have left traces of their passage on those plains which the atmosphere must cover, however slightly raised it may be. These traces are nowhere visible. There remains but one hypothesis, that of a living race to which motion, which is life, is foreign."

"One might as well say, living creatures which do not live," replied Michel.

"Just so," said Barbicane, "which for us has no meaning."

"Then we may form our opinion?" said Michel.

"Yes," replied Nicholl.

"Very well," continued Michel Ardan, "the Scientific Commission assembled in the projectile of the Gun Club, after having founded their argument on facts recently observed, decide unanimously upon the question of the habitability of the moon—'No! the moon is not habitable.'"

This decision was consigned by President Barbicane to his notebook, where the process of the sitting of the 6th of December may be seen.

"Now," said Nicholl, "let us attack the second question, an indispensable complement of the first. I ask the honourable Commission, if the moon is not habitable, has she ever been inhabited, Citizen Barbicane?"

"My friends," replied Barbicane, "I did not undertake this journey in order to form an opinion on the past habitability of our satellite; but I will add that our personal observations only confirm me in this opinion. I believe, indeed I affirm, that the moon has been inhabited by a human race organized like our own; that she has produced animals anatomically formed like the terrestrial animals; but I add that these races, human or animal, have had their day, and are now for ever extinct!"

"Then," asked Michel, "the moon must be older than the earth?"

"No!" said Barbicane decidedly, "but a world which has *grown old* quicker, and whose formation and deformation have been more rapid. Relatively, the organizing force of matter has been much more violent in the interior of the moon than in the interior of the terrestrial globe. The actual state of this cracked, twisted, and burst disc abundantly proves this. The moon and the earth were nothing but gaseous masses originally. These gases have passed into a liquid state under different influences, and the solid masses have been formed later. But most certainly our sphere was still gaseous or liquid, when the moon was solidified by cooling, and had become habitable."

"I believe it," said Nicholl.

"Then," continued Barbicane, "an atmosphere surrounded it, the waters contained within this gaseous envelope could not evaporate. Under the influence of air, water, light, solar heat, and central heat, vegetation took possession of the continents prepared to receive it, and certainly life showed itself about this period, for nature does not expend herself in vain; and a world so wonderfully formed for habitation must necessarily be inhabited."

"But," said Nicholl, "many phenomena inherent in our satellite might cramp the expansion of the animal and vegetable kingdom. For example, its days and nights of 354 hours?"

"At the terrestrial poles they last six months," said Michel.

"An argument of little value, since the poles are not inhabited."

"Let us observe, my friends," continued Barbicane, "that if in the actual state of the moon its long nights and long days created differences of temperature insupportable to organization, it was not so at the historical period of time. The atmosphere enveloped the disc with a fluid mantle; vapour deposited itself in the shape of clouds; this natural screen tempered the ardour of the solar rays, and retained the nocturnal radiation. Light, like heat, can diffuse itself in the air; hence an equality between the influences which no longer exists, now that that atmosphere has almost entirely disappeared. And now I am going to astonish you."

"Astonish us?" said Michel Ardan.

"I firmly believe that at the period when the moon was inhabited, the nights and days did not last 354 hours!"

"And why?" asked Nicholl quickly.

"Because most probably then the rotary motion of the moon upon her axis was not equal to her revolution, an equality which presents each part of her disc during fifteen days to the action of the solar rays."

"Granted," replied Nicholl, "but why should not these two motions have been equal, as they are really so?"

"Because that equality has only been determined by terrestrial attraction. And who can say that this attraction was powerful enough to alter the motion of the moon at that period when the earth was still fluid?"

"Just so," replied Nicholl; "and who can say that the moon has always been a satellite of the earth?"

"And who can say," exclaimed Michel Ardan, "that the moon did not exist before the earth?"

Their imaginations carried them away into an indefinite field of hypothesis. Barbicane sought to restrain them.

"Those speculations are too high," said he; "problems utterly insoluble. Do not let us enter upon them. Let us only admit the insufficiency of the primordial attraction; and then by the inequality of the two motions of rotation and revolution, the days and nights could have succeeded each other on the moon as they succeed each other on the earth. Besides, even without these conditions, life was possible."

"And so," asked Michel Ardan, "humanity has disappeared from the moon?"

"Yes," replied Barbicane, "after having doubtless remained persistently for millions of centuries; by degrees the atmosphere becoming rarefied, the disc became uninhabitable, as the terrestrial globe will one day become by cooling."

"By cooling?"

"Certainly," replied Barbicane; "as the internal fires became extinguished, and the incandescent matter concentrated itself, the lunar crust cooled. By degrees the consequences of these phenomena showed themselves in the disappearance of organized beings, and by the disappearance of vegetation. Soon the atmosphere was rarefied, probably withdrawn by terrestrial attraction; then aerial departure of respirable air, and disappearance of water by means of evaporation. At this period the moon becoming uninhabitable, was no longer inhabited. It was a dead world, such as we see it to-day."

"And you say that the same fate is in store for the earth?"

"Most probably."

"But when?"

"When the cooling of its crust shall have made it uninhabitable."

"And have they calculated the time which our unfortunate sphere will take to cool?"

"Certainly."

"And you know these calculations?"

"Perfectly."

"But speak, then, my clumsy savant," exclaimed Michel Ardan, "for you make me boil with impatience!"

"Very well, my good Michel," replied Barbicane quietly, "we know what diminution of temperature the earth undergoes in the lapse of a century. And according to certain calculations, this mean temperature will, after a period of 400,000 years, be brought down to zero!"

"Four hundred thousand years!" exclaimed Michel. "Ah! I breathe again. Really I was frightened to hear you; I imagined that we had not more than 50,000 years to live."

Barbicane and Nicholl could not help laughing at their companion's uneasiness. Then Nicholl, who wished to end the discussion, put the second question, which had just been considered again.

"Has the moon been inhabited?" he asked.

The answer was unanimously in the affirmative. But during this discussion, fruitful in somewhat hazardous theories, the projectile was rapidly leaving the moon; the lineaments faded away from the travellers' eyes, mountains were confused in the distance; and of all the wonderful, strange, and fantastical form of the earth's satellite, there soon remained nothing but the imperishable remembrance.

CHAPTER XIX: A STRUGGLE AGAINST THE IMPOSSIBLE For a long time Barbicane and his companions looked silently and sadly upon that world which they had only seen from a distance, as Moses saw the land of Canaan, and which they were leaving without a possibility of ever returning to it. The projectile's position with regard to the moon had altered, and the base was now turned to the earth.

This change, which Barbicane verified, did not fail to surprise them. If the projectile was to gravitate round the satellite in an elliptical orbit, why was not its heaviest part turned towards it, as the moon turns hers to the earth? That was a difficult point.

In watching the course of the projectile they could see that on leaving the moon it followed a course analogous to that traced in approaching her. It was describing a very long ellipse, which would most likely extend to the point of equal attraction, where the influences of the earth and its satellite are neutralized.

Such was the conclusion which Barbicane very justly drew from facts already observed, a conviction which his two friends shared with him.

"And when arrived at this dead point, what will become of us?" asked Michel Ardan.

"We don't know," replied Barbicane.

"But one can draw some hypotheses, I suppose?"

"Two," answered Barbicane; "either the projectile's speed will be insufficient, and it will remain for ever immovable on this line of double attraction——"

"I prefer the other hypothesis, whatever it may be," interrupted Michel.

"Or," continued Barbicane, "its speed will be sufficient, and it will continue its elliptical course, to gravitate for ever around the orb of night."

"A revolution not at all consoling," said Michel, "to pass to the state of humble servants to a moon whom we are accustomed to look upon as our own handmaid. So that is the fate in store for us?"

Neither Barbicane nor Nicholl answered.

"You do not answer," continued Michel impatiently.

"There is nothing to answer," said Nicholl.

"Is there nothing to try?"

"No," answered Barbicane. "Do you pretend to fight against the impossible?"

"Why not? Do one Frenchman and two Americans shrink from such a word?"

"But what would you do?"

"Subdue this motion which is bearing us away."

"Subdue it?"

"Yes," continued Michel, getting animated, "or else alter it, and employ it to the accomplishment of our own ends."

"And how?"

"That is your affair. If artillerymen are not masters of their projectile they are not artillerymen. If the projectile is to command the gunner, we had better ram the gunner into the gun. My faith! fine savants! who do not know what is to become of us after inducing me——"

"Inducing you!" cried Barbicane and Nicholl. "Inducing you! What do you mean by that?"

"No recrimination," said Michel. "I do not complain; the trip has pleased me, the projectile agrees with me; but let us do all that is humanly possible to do to fall somewhere, even if only on the moon."

"We ask no better, my worthy Michel," replied Barbicane, "but means fail us."

"We cannot alter the motion of the projectile?"

"No."

"Nor diminish its speed?"

"No."

"Not even by lightening it, as they lighten an overloaded vessel?"

"What would you throw out?" said Nicholl. "We have no ballast on board; and indeed it seems to me that if lightened it would go much quicker."

"Slower."

"Quicker."

"Neither slower nor quicker," said Barbicane, wishing to make his two friends agree; "for we float in space, and must no longer consider specific weight."

"Very well," cried Michel Ardan in a decided voice; "then there remains but one thing to do."

"What is it?" said Nicholl.

"Breakfast," answered the cool, audacious Frenchman, who always brought up this solution at the most difficult juncture.

In any case, if this operation had no influence on the projectile's course, it could at least be tried without inconvenience, and even with success from a stomachic point of view. Certainly Michel had none but good ideas.

They breakfasted then at two in the morning; the hour mattered little. Michel served his usual repast, crowned by a glorious bottle drawn from his private cellar. If ideas did not crowd on their brains, we must despair of the Chambertin of 1853. The repast finished, observations began again. Around the projectile, at an invariable distance, were the objects which had been thrown out. Evidently, in its translatory motion round the moon, it had not passed through any atmosphere, for the specific weight of these different objects would have checked their relative speed.

On the side of the terrestrial sphere nothing was to be seen. The earth was but a day old, having been new the night before at twelve; and two days must elapse before its crescent, freed from the solar rays, would serve as a clock to the Selenites, as in its rotatory movement each of its points after twenty-four hours repasses the same lunar meridian.

On the moon's side the sight was different; the orb shone in all her splendour amidst innumerable constellations, whose purity could not be troubled by her rays. On the disc, the plains were already returning to the dark tint which is seen from the earth. The other part of the nimbus remained brilliant, and in the midst of this general brilliancy, Tycho shone prominently like a sun.

Barbicane had no means of estimating the projectile's speed, but reasoning showed that it must uniformly decrease, according to all the laws of mechanical reasoning. Having admitted that the projectile was describing an orbit round the moon, this orbit must necessarily be elliptical; science proves that it must be so. No motive body circulating round an attracting body fails in this law. Every orbit described in space is elliptical. And why should the projectile of the Gun Club escape this natural arrangement? In elliptical orbits, the attracting body always occupies one of the foci; so that at one moment the satellite is nearer, and at another farther from the orb around which it gravitates. When the earth is nearest the sun, she is in her perihelion; and in her aphelion at the farthest point. Speaking of the moon, she is nearest to the earth in her perigee, and farthest from it in her apogee. To use analogous expressions, with which the astronomers' language is enriched, if the projectile remains as a satellite of the moon, we must say that it is in its "aposelene" at its farthest point, and in its "periselene" at its nearest. In the latter case, the projectile would attain its maximum of speed; and in the former its minimum. It was evidently moving towards its aposelenitical point; and Barbicane had reason to think that its speed would decrease up to this point, and then increase by degrees as it neared the moon. This speed would even become *nil*, if this point joined that of equal attraction. Barbicane studied the consequences of these different situations, and thinking what inference he could draw from them, when he was roughly disturbed by a cry from Michel Ardan.

"By Jove!" he exclaimed, "I must admit we are downright simpletons!"

"I do not say we are not," replied Barbicane; "but why?"

"Because we have a very simple means of checking this speed which is bearing us from the moon, and we do not use it!"

"And what is the means?"

"To use the recoil contained in our rockets."

"Done!" said Nicholl.

"We have not used this force yet," said Barbicane, "it is true, but we will do so."

"When?" asked Michel.

"When the time comes. Observe, my friends, that in the position occupied by the projectile, an oblique position with regard to the lunar disc, our rockets, in slightly altering its direction, might turn it from the moon instead of drawing it nearer?"

"Just so," replied Michel.

"Let us wait, then. By some inexplicable influence, the projectile is turning its base towards the earth. It is probable that at the point of equal attraction, its conical cap will be directed rigidly towards the moon; at that moment we may hope that its speed will be *nil*; then will be the moment to act, and with the influence of our rockets, we may perhaps provoke a fall directly on the surface of the lunar disc."

"Bravo!" said Michel. "What we did not do, what we could not do on our first passage at the dead point, because the projectile was then endowed with too great a speed."

"Very well reasoned," said Nicholl.

"Let us wait patiently," continued Barbicane. "Putting every chance on our side, and after having so much despaired, I may say I think that we shall gain our end."

This conclusion was a signal for Michel Ardan's hips and hurrahs. And none of the audacious boobies remembered the question that they themselves had solved in the negative. No! the moon is not inhabited; no! the moon is probably not habitable. And yet they were going to try every thing to reach her.

One single question remained to be solved. At what precise moment the projectile would reach the point of equal attraction, on which the travellers must play their last card. In order to calculate this to within a few seconds, Barbicane had only to refer to his notes, and to reckon the different heights taken on the lunar parallels. Thus the time necessary to travel over the distance between the dead point and the south pole would be equal to the distance separating the north pole from the dead point. The hours representing the time travelled over were carefully noted, and the calculation was easy. Barbicane found that this point would be reached at one in the morning on the night of the 7th—8th of December. So that, if nothing interfered with its course, it would reach the given point in twenty-two hours.

The rockets had primarily been placed to check the fall of the projectile upon the moon, and now they were going to employ them for a directly contrary purpose. In any case they were ready, and they had only to wait for the moment to set fire to them.

"Since there is nothing else to be done," said Nicholl, "I make a proposition."

"What is it?" asked Barbicane.

"I propose to go to sleep."

"What a motion!" exclaimed Michel Ardan.

"It is forty hours since we closed our eyes," said Nicholl. "Some hours of sleep will restore our strength."

"Never," interrupted Michel.

"Well," continued Nicholl, "every one to his taste; I shall go to sleep." And stretching himself on the divan, he soon snored like a forty-eight pounder.

"That Nicholl has a good deal of sense," said Barbicane, "presently I shall follow his example." Some moments after his continued bass supported the captain's baritone.

"Certainly," said Michel Ardan, finding himself alone, "these practical people have sometimes most opportune ideas."

And with his long legs stretched out, and his great arms folded under his head, Michel slept in his turn.

But this sleep could be neither peaceful nor lasting, the minds of these three men were too much occupied, and some hours after, about seven in the morning, all three were on foot at the same instant.

The projectile was still leaving the moon, and turning its conical part more and more towards her.

An explicable phenomenon, but one which happily served Barbicane's ends.

Seventeen hours more, and the moment for action would have arrived.

The day seemed long. However bold the travellers might be, they were greatly impressed by the approach of that moment which would decide all—either precipitate their fall on to the moon, or for ever chain them in an immutable orbit. They counted the hours as they passed too slow for their wish; Barbicane and Nicholl were obstinately plunged in their calculations, Michel going and coming between the narrow walls, and watching that impassive moon with a longing eye.

At times recollections of the earth crossed their minds. They saw once more their friends of the Gun Club, and the dearest of all, J. T. Maston. At that moment, the honourable secretary must be filling his post on the Rocky Mountains. If he could see the projectile through the glass of his gigantic telescope, what would he think? After seeing it disappear behind the moon's south pole, he would see them reappear by the north pole! They must therefore be a satellite of a satellite! Had J. T. Maston given his unexpected news to the world? Was this the dénouement of this great enterprise?

But the day passed without incident. The terrestrial midnight arrived. The 8th of December was beginning. One hour more, and the point of equal attraction would be reached. What speed would then animate the projectile? They could not estimate it. But no error could vitiate Barbicane's calculations. At one in the morning, this speed ought to be and would be *nil*.

Besides, another phenomenon would mark the projectile's stopping-point on the neutral line. At that spot the two attractions, lunar and terrestrial, would be annulled. Objects would "weigh" no more. This singular fact, which had surprised Barbicane and his companions so much in going, would be repeated on their return under the very same conditions. At this precise moment they must act.

Already the projectile's conical top was sensibly turned towards the lunar disc, presented in such a way as to utilize the whole of the recoil produced by the pressure of the rocket apparatus. The chances were in favour of the travellers. If its speed was utterly annulled on this dead point, a decided movement towards the moon would suffice, however slight, to determine its fall.

"Five minutes to one," said Nicholl.

"All is ready," replied Michel Ardan, directing a lighted match to the flame of the gas.

"Wait!" said Barbicane, holding his chronometer in his hand.

At that moment weight had no effect. The travellers felt in themselves the entire disappearance of it. They were very near the neutral point, if they did not touch it.

"One o'clock," said Barbicane.

Michel Ardan applied the lighted match to a train in communication with the rockets. No detonation was heard in the inside, for there was no air. But, through the scuttles Barbicane saw a prolonged smoke, the flames of which were immediately extinguished.

The projectile sustained a certain shock, which was sensibly felt in the interior.

The three friends looked and listened without speaking, and scarcely breathing. One might have heard the beating of their hearts amidst this perfect silence.

"Are we falling?" asked Michel Ardan, at length.

"No," said Nicholl, "since the bottom of the projectile is not turning to the lunar disc!"

At this moment, Barbicane, quitting the scuttle, turned to his two companions. He was frightfully pale, his forehead wrinkled, and his lips contracted.

"We are falling!" said he.

"Ah!" cried Michel Ardan, "on to the moon?"

"On to the earth!"

"The devil!" exclaimed Michel Ardan, adding philosophically, "well, when we came into this projectile we were very doubtful as to the ease with which we should get out of it!"

And now this fearful fall had begun. The speed retained had borne the projectile beyond the dead point. The explosion of the rockets could not divert its course. This speed in going had carried it over the neutral line, and in returning had done the same thing. The laws of physics condemned *it to pass through every point which it had already gone through*. It was a terrible fall, from a height of 160,000 miles, and no springs to break it. According to the laws of gunnery, the projectile must strike the earth with a speed equal to that with which it left the mouth of the Columbiad, a speed of 16,000 yards in the last second.

But to give some figures of comparison, it has been reckoned that an object thrown from the top of the towers of Notre Dame, the height of which is only 200 feet, will arrive on the pavement at a speed of 240 miles per hour. Here the projectile must strike the earth with a speed of 115,200 miles per hour.

"We are lost!" said Michel coolly.

"Very well! if we die," answered Barbicane, with a sort of religious enthusiasm, "the result of our travels will be magnificently spread. It is His own secret that God will tell us! In the other life, the soul will want to know nothing, either of machines or engines! It will be identified with eternal wisdom!"

"In fact," interrupted Michel Ardan, "the whole of the other world may well console us for the loss of that inferior orb called the moon!"

Barbicane crossed his arms on his breast, with a motion of sublime resignation, saying at the same time—

"The will of heaven be done!"

CHAPTER XX: THE SOUNDINGS OF THE "SUSQUEHANNA" "Well, lieutenant, and our soundings?"

"I think, sir, that the operation is nearing its completion," replied Lieutenant Bronsfield. "But who would have thought of finding such a depth so near in shore, and only 200 miles from the American coast?"

"Certainly, Bronsfield, there is a great depression," said Captain Blomsberry. "In this spot there is a submarine valley worn by Humboldt's current, which skirts the coast of America as far as the Straits of Magellan."

"These great depths," continued the lieutenant, "are not favourable for laying telegraphic cables. A level bottom, like that supporting the American cable between Valentia and Newfoundland, is much better."

"I agree with you, Bronsfield. With your permission, lieutenant, where are we now?"

"Sir, at this moment we have 3508 fathoms of line out, and the ball which draws the sounding lead has not yet touched the bottom; for if so, it would have come up of itself."

"Brook's apparatus is very ingenious," said Captain Blomsberry; "it gives us very exact soundings."

"Touch!" cried at this moment one of the men at the forewheel, who was superintending the operation.

The captain and the lieutenant mounted the quarter-deck.

"What depth have we?" asked the captain.

"Three thousand six hundred and twenty-seven fathoms," replied the lieutenant, entering it in his note-book.

"Well, Bronsfield," said the captain, "I will take down the result. Now haul in the sounding line. It will be the work of some hours. In that time the engineer can light the furnaces, and we shall be ready to start as soon as you have finished. It is ten o'clock, and with your permission, lieutenant, I will turn in."

"Do so, sir; do so!" replied the lieutenant obligingly.

The captain of the "Susquehanna," as brave a man as need be, and the humble servant of his officers, returned to his cabin, took a brandy-grog, which earned for the steward no end of praise, and turned in, not without having complimented his servant upon his making beds, and slept a peaceful sleep.

It was then ten at night. The eleventh day of the month of December was drawing to a close in a magnificent night.

The "Susquehanna," a corvette of 500 horse-power, of the United States' navy, was occupied in taking soundings in the Pacific Ocean about

200 miles off the American coast, following that long peninsula which stretches down the coast of New Mexico.

The wind had dropped by degrees. There was no disturbance in the air. Their pennant hung motionless from the maintop-gallant-mast truck.

Captain Jonathan Blomsberry (cousin-german of Colonel Blomsberry, one of the most ardent supporters of the Gun Club, who had married an aunt of the captain and daughter of an honourable Kentucky merchant,) —Captain Blomsberry could not have wished for finer weather in which to bring to a close his delicate operations of sounding. His corvette had not even felt the great tempest, which by sweeping away the groups of clouds on the Rocky Mountains, had allowed them to observe the course of the famous projectile.

Everything went well, and with all the fervour of a Presbyterian, he did not forget to thank heaven for it. The series of soundings taken by the "Susquehanna," had for its aim the finding of a favourable spot for the laying of a submarine cable to connect the Hawaiian Islands with the coast of America.

It was a great undertaking, due to the instigation of a powerful company. Its managing director, the intelligent Cyrus Field, proposed even covering all the islands of Oceania with a vast electrical network, an immense enterprise, and one worthy of American genius.

To the corvette "Susquehanna" had been confided the first operations of sounding. It was on the night of the 11th–12th December, she was in exactly 27° 7′ north lat., and 41° 37′ west long., on the meridian of Washington.

The moon, then in her last quarter, was beginning to rise above the horizon.

After the departure of Captain Blomsberry, the lieutenant and some officers were standing together on the poop. On the appearance of the moon, their thoughts turned to that orb which the eyes of a whole hemisphere were contemplating. The best naval glasses could not have discovered the projectile wandering around its hemisphere, and yet all were pointed towards that brilliant disc which millions of eyes were looking at at the same moment.

"They have been gone ten days," said Lieutenant Bronsfield at last. "What has become of them?"

"They have arrived, lieutenant," exclaimed a young midshipman, "and they are doing what all travellers do when they arrive in a new country, taking a walk!"

"Oh! I am sure of that, if you tell me so, my young friend," said Lieutenant Bronsfield, smiling.

"But," continued another officer, "their arrival cannot be doubted. The projectile was to reach the moon when full on the 5th at midnight. We are now at the 11th of December, which makes six days. And in six times twenty-four hours, without darkness, one would have time to settle comfortably. I fancy I see my brave countrymen encamped at the bottom of some valley, on the borders of a Selenite stream, near a projectile half buried by its fall amidst volcanic rubbish, Captain Nicholl beginning his levelling operations, President Barbicane writing out his notes, and Michel Ardan embalming the lunar solitudes with the perfume of his——"

"Yes! it must be so, it is so!" exclaimed the young midshipman, worked up to a pitch of enthusiasm by this ideal description of his superior officer.

"I should like to believe it," replied the lieutenant, who was quite unmoved. "Unfortunately direct news from the lunar world is still wanting."

"Beg pardon, lieutenant," said the midshipman, "but cannot President Barbicane write?"

A burst of laughter greeted this answer.

"No letters!" continued the young man quickly. "The postal administration has something to see to there."

"Might it not be the telegraphic service that is at fault?" asked one of the officers ironically.

"Not necessarily," replied the midshipman, not at all confused. "But it is very easy to set up a graphic communication with the earth."

"And how?"

"By means of the telescope at Long's Peak. You know it brings the moon to within four miles of the Rocky Mountains, and that it shows objects on its surface of only nine feet in diameter. Very well; let our industrious friends construct a gigantic alphabet; let them write words three fathoms long, and sentences three miles long, and then they can send us news of themselves?"

The young midshipman, who had a certain amount of imagination, was loudly applauded; Lieutenant Bronsfield allowing that the idea was possible, but observing that if by these means they could *receive* news from the lunar world they could not send any from the terrestrial, unless the Selenites had instruments fit for taking distant observations at their disposal.

"Evidently," said one of the officers; "but what has become of the travellers? what they have done, what they have seen, that above all must interest us. Besides, if the experiment has succeeded (which I do not doubt), they will try it again. The Columbiad is still sunk in the soil of Florida. It is now only a question of powder and shot; and every time the moon is at her zenith, a cargo of visitors may be sent to her."

"It is clear," replied Lieutenant Bronsfield, "that J. T. Maston will one day join his friends."

"If he will have me," cried the midshipman, "I am ready!"

"Oh! volunteers will not be wanting," answered Bronsfield; "and if it were allowed, half of the earth's inhabitants would emigrate to the moon!"

This conversation between the officers of the "Susquehanna" was kept up until nearly one in the morning. We cannot say what blundering systems were broached, what inconsistent theories advanced by these bold spirits. Since Barbicane's attempt, nothing seemed impossible to the Americans. They had already designed an expedition, not only of savants, but of a whole colony towards the Selenite borders, and a complete army, consisting of infantry, artillery, and cavalry, to conquer the lunar world.

At one in the morning, the hauling in of the sounding line was not yet completed; 1670 fathoms were still out, which would entail some hours' work. According to the commander's orders, the fires had been lighted, and steam was being got up. The "Susquehanna" could have started that very instant.

At that moment (it was seventeen minutes past one in the morning) Lieutenant Bronsfield was preparing to leave the watch and return to his cabin, when his attention was attracted by a distant hissing noise. His comrades and himself first thought that this hissing was caused by the letting off of steam; but lifting their heads, they found that the noise was produced in the highest regions of the air. They had not time to question each other before the hissing became frightfully intense, and suddenly there appeared to their dazzled eyes an enormous meteor, ignited by the rapidity of its course and its friction through the atmospheric strata.

This fiery mass grew larger to their eyes, and fell, with the noise of thunder, upon the bowsprit, which it smashed close to the stem, and buried itself in the waves with a deafening roar!

A few feet nearer, and the "Susquehanna" would have foundered with all on board!

At this instant Captain Blomsberry appeared, half dressed, and rushing on to the forecastle-deck, whither all the officers had hurried, exclaimed, "With your permission, gentlemen, what has happened?"

And the midshipman, making himself as it were the echo of the body, cried, "Commander, it is 'they' come back again!"

CHAPTER XXI: J. T. MASTON RECALLED   "It is 'they' come back again!" the young midshipman had said; and every one had understood him. No one doubted but that that meteor was the projectile of the Gun Club.

As to the travellers which it enclosed, opinions were divided regarding their fate.

"They are dead!" said one.

"They are alive!" said another; "the crater is deep, and the shock was deadened."

"But they must have wanted air," continued a third speaker; "they must have died of suffocation."

"Burnt!" replied a fourth; "the projectile was nothing but an incandescent mass as it crossed the atmosphere."

"What does it matter!" they exclaimed unanimously; "living or dead, we must pull them out!"

But Captain Blomsberry had assembled his officers, and "with their permission," was holding a council. They must decide upon something to be done immediately. The more hasty ones were for fishing up the projectile. A difficult operation, though not an impossible one. But the corvette had no proper machinery, which must be both fixed and powerful; so it was resolved that they should put in at the nearest port, and give information to the Gun Club of the projectile's fall.

This determination was unanimous. The choice of the port had to be discussed. The neighbouring coast had no anchorage on 27° lat. Higher up, above the peninsula of Monterey, stands the important town from which it takes its name; but, seated on the borders of a perfect desert, it was not connected with the interior by a network of telegraphic wires, and electricity alone could spread this important news fast enough.

Some degrees above opened the bay of San Francisco. Through the capital of the gold country, communication would be easy with the heart of the Union. And in less than two days the "Susquehanna," by putting on high pressure, could arrive in that port. She must therefore start at once.

The fires were made up; they could set off immediately. Two thousand fathoms of line were still out, which Captain Blomsberry, not wishing to lose precious time in hauling in, resolved to cut.

"We will fasten the end to a buoy," said he; "and that buoy will show us the exact spot where the projectile fell."

"Besides," replied Lieutenant Bronsfield, "we have our situation exact —27° 7′ north lat. and 41° 37′ west long."

"Well, Mr. Bronsfield," replied the captain, "now, with your permission, we will have the line cut."

A strong buoy, strengthened by a couple of spars, was thrown into the ocean. The end of the rope was carefully lashed to it; and, left solely to the rise and fall of the billows, the buoy would not sensibly deviate from the spot.

At this moment the engineer sent to inform the captain that steam was up and they could start, for which agreeable communication the captain thanked him. The course was then given north-north-east, and the corvette, wearing, steered at full steam direct for San Francisco. It was three in the morning.

Four hundred and fifty miles to cross; it was nothing for a good vessel like the "Susquehanna." In thirty-six hours she had covered that distance; and on the 14th of December, at twenty-seven minutes past one at night, she entered the bay of San Francisco.

At the sight of a ship of the national navy arriving at full speed, with her bowsprit broken, public curiosity was greatly roused. A dense crowd soon assembled on the quay, waiting for them to disembark.

After casting anchor, Captain Blomsberry and Lieutenant Bronsfield entered an eight-oared cutter, which soon brought them to land.

They jumped on to the quay.

"The telegraph?" they asked, without answering one of the thousand questions addressed to them.

The officer of the port conducted them to the telegraph-office through a concourse of spectators. Blomsberry and Bronsfield entered, while the crowd crushed each other at the door.

Some minutes later a fourfold telegram was sent out—the first to the Naval Secretary at Washington; the second to the Vice-President of the Gun Club, Baltimore; the third to the Hon. J. T. Maston, Long's Peak, Rocky Mountains; the fourth to the Sub-Director of the Cambridge Observatory, Massachusetts.

It was worded as follows:

*In 20° 7′ north lat., and 41° 37′ west long., on the 12th of December, at 17 minutes past 1 in the morning, the projectile of the Columbiad fell into the Pacific. Send instructions.—*BLOMSBERRY, *Commander "Susquehanna."*

Five minutes afterwards the whole town of San Francisco learned the news. Before six in the evening the different States of the Union had heard the great catastrophe; and after midnight, by the cable, the whole of Europe knew the result of the great American experiment.

We will not attempt to picture the effect produced on the entire world by that unexpected dénouement.

On receipt of the telegram the Naval Secretary telegraphed to the "Susquehanna" to wait in the bay of San Francisco without extinguishing her fires. Day and night she must be ready to put to sea.

The Cambridge Observatory called a special meeting; and, with that composure which distinguishes learned bodies in general, peacefully discussed the scientific bearings of the question. At the Gun Club there was an explosion. All the gunners were assembled. Vice-President the Hon.

Wilcome was in the act of reading the premature despatch, in which J. T. Maston and Belfast announced that the projectile had just been seen in the gigantic reflector of Long's Peak, and also that it was held by lunar attraction, and was playing the part of under satellite to the lunar world.

We know the truth on that point.

But on the arrival of Blomsberry's despatch, so decidedly contradicting J. T. Maston's telegram, two parties were formed in the bosom of the Gun Club. On one side were those who admitted the fall of the projectile, and consequently the return of the travellers; on the other, those who believed in the observations of Long's Peak, concluded that the commander of the "Susquehanna" had made a mistake. To the latter the pretended projectile was nothing but a meteor! nothing but a meteor, a shooting globe, which in its fall had smashed the bows of the corvette. It was difficult to answer this argument, for the speed with which it was animated must have made observation very difficult. The commander of the "Susquehanna" and her officers might have made a mistake in all good faith; one argument, however, was in their favour, namely, that if the projectile had fallen on the earth, its place of meeting with the terrestrial globe could only take place on this 27° north lat., and (taking into consideration the time that had elapsed, and the rotary motion of the earth) between the forty-first and the forty-second degree of west longitude. In any case, it was decided in the Gun Club that Blomsberry brothers, Bilsby, and Major Elphinstone should go straight to San Francisco, and consult as to the means of raising the projectile from the depths of the ocean.

These devoted men set off at once; and the railroad, which will soon cross the whole of central America, took them as far as St. Louis, where the swift mail-coaches awaited them. Almost at the same moment in which the Secretary of Marine, the Vice-President of the Gun Club, and the Sub-Director of the Observatory received the despatch from San Francisco, the Honourable J. T. Maston was undergoing the greatest excitement he had ever experienced in his life, an excitement which even the bursting of his pet gun, which had more than once nearly cost him his life, had not caused him. We may remember that the Secretary of the Gun Club had started soon after the projectile (and almost as quickly) for the station in Long's Peak, in the Rocky Mountains, J. Belfast, Director of the Cambridge Observatory, accompanying him. Arrived there, the two friends had installed themselves at once, never quitting the summit of their enormous telescope. We know that this gigantic instrument had been set up according to the reflecting system, called by the English, "front view." This arrangement subjected all objects to but one reflection, making the view consequently much clearer; the result was that, when they were taking observations, J. T. Maston and Belfast were placed in the *upper* part of the instrument and not in the lower, which they reached by a circular staircase, a masterpiece of lightness, while below them opened a metal well, terminated by the metallic mirror, which measured 280 feet in depth.

It was on a narrow platform placed above the telescope that the two savants passed their existence, execrating the day which hid the moon from their eyes, and the clouds which obstinately veiled her during the night.

What, then, was their delight when, after some days of waiting, on the night of the 5th of December, they saw the vehicle which was bearing their friends into space! To this delight succeeded a great deception, when, trusting to a cursory observation, they launched their first telegram to the world, erroneously affirming that the projectile had become a satellite of the moon, gravitating in an immutable orbit.

From that moment it had never shown itself to their eyes—a disappearance all the more easily explained, as it was then passing behind the moon's invisible disc; but when it was time for it to reappear on the visible disc, one may imagine the impatience of the fuming J. T. Maston and his not less impatient companion. Each minute of the night they thought they saw the projectile once more, and they did not see it. Hence constant discussions and violent disputes between them, Belfast affirming that the projectile could not be seen, J. T. Maston maintaining that "it had put his eyes out."

"It is the projectile!" repeated J. T. Maston.

"No," answered Belfast; "it is an avalanche detached from a lunar mountain."

"Well, we shall see it to-morrow."

"No, we shall not see it any more. It is carried into space."

"Yes!"

"No!"

And at these moments, when contradictions rained like hail, the well-known irritability of the Secretary of the Gun Club constituted a permanent danger for the Hon. Belfast. The existence of these two together would soon have become impossible; but an unforeseen event cut short their everlasting discussions.

During the night, from the 14th to the 15th of December, the two irreconcilable friends were busy observing the lunar disc, J. T. Maston abusing the learned Belfast as usual, who was by his side; the Secretary of the Gun Club maintaining for the thousandth time that he had just seen the projectile, and adding that he could see Michel Ardan's face looking through one of the scuttles, at the same time enforcing his argument by a series of gestures which his formidable hook rendered very unpleasant.

At this moment Belfast's servant appeared on the platform (it was ten at night) and gave him a despatch. It was the commander of the "Susquehanna's" telegram.

Belfast tore the envelope and read, and uttered a cry.

"What!" said J. T. Maston.

"The projectile!"

"Well!"

"Has fallen to the earth!"

Another cry, this time a perfect howl, answered him. He turned towards J. T. Maston. The unfortunate man, imprudently leaning over the metal tube, had disappeared in the immense telescope. A fall of 280 feet! Belfast, dismayed, rushed to the orifice of the reflector.

He breathed. J. T. Maston, caught by his metal hook, was holding on by one of the rings which bound the telescope together, uttering fearful cries.

Belfast called. Help was brought, tackle was let down, and they hoisted up, not without some trouble, the imprudent Secretary of the Gun Club.

He reappeared at the upper orifice without hurt.

"Ah!" said he, "if I had broken the mirror?"

"You would have paid for it," replied Belfast severely.

"And that cursed projectile has fallen?" asked J. T. Maston.

"Into the Pacific!"

"Let us go!"

A quarter of an hour after the two savants were descending the declivity of the Rocky Mountains; and two days after, at the same time as their friends of the Gun Club, they arrived at San Francisco, having killed five horses on the road.

Elphinstone, the brothers Blomsberry, and Bilsby rushed towards them on their arrival.

"What shall we do?" they exclaimed.

"Fish up the projectile," replied J. T. Maston, "and the sooner the better."

CHAPTER XXII: RECOVERED FROM THE SEA The spot where the projectile sank under the waves was exactly known; but machinery to grasp it and bring it to the surface of the ocean was still wanting. It must first be invented, then made. American engineers could not be troubled with such trifles. The grappling-irons once fixed, by their help they were sure to raise it in spite of its weight, which was lessened by the density of the liquid in which it was plunged.

But fishing-up the projectile was not the only thing to be thought of.

They must act promptly in the interest of the travellers. No one doubted that they were still living.

"Yes," repeated J. T. Maston incessantly, whose confidence gained over everybody, "our friends are clever people, and they cannot have fallen like simpletons. They are alive, quite alive; but we must make haste if we wish to find them so. Food and water do not trouble me; they have enough for a long while. But air, air, that is what they will soon want; so quick, quick!"

And they did go quick. They fitted up the "Susquehanna" for her new destination. Her powerful machinery was brought to bear upon the hauling-chains. The aluminium projectile only weighed 19,250 lbs., a weight very inferior to that of the transatlantic cable which had been drawn up under similar conditions. The only difficulty was in fishing-up a cylindro-conical projectile, the walls of which were so smooth as to offer no hold for the hooks. On that account engineer Murchison hastened to San Francisco, and had some enormous grappling-irons fixed on an automatic system, which would never let the projectile go if it once succeeded in seizing it in its powerful claws. Diving-dresses were also prepared, which through this impervious covering allowed the divers to observe the bottom of the sea. He also had put on board an apparatus of compressed air very cleverly designed. There were perfect chambers pierced with scuttles, which, with water let into certain compartments, could draw it down into great depths. These apparatuses were at San Francisco, where they had been used in the construction of a submarine breakwater; and very fortunately it was so, for there was no time to construct any. But in spite of the perfection of the machinery, in spite of the ingenuity of the savants entrusted with the use of them, the success of the operation was far from being certain. How great were the chances against them, the projectile being 20,000 feet under the water! And if even it was brought to the surface, how would the travellers have borne the terrible shock which 20,000 feet of water had perhaps not sufficiently broken? At any rate they must act quickly. J. T. Maston hurried the workmen day and night. He was ready to don the diving-dress himself, or try the air apparatus, in order to reconnoitre the situation of his courageous friends.

But in spite of all diligence displayed in preparing the different engines, in spite of the considerable sum placed at the disposal of the Gun Club by the Government of the Union, five long days (five centuries!) elapsed before the preparations were complete. During this time public opinion was excited to the highest pitch. Telegrams were exchanged incessantly throughout the entire world by means of wires and electric cables. The saving of Barbicane, Nicholl, and Michel Ardan was an international affair. Every one who had subscribed to the Gun Club was directly interested in the welfare of the travellers.

At length the hauling-chains, the air-chambers, and the automatic grappling-irons were put on board. J. T. Maston, Engineer Murchison, and the delegates of the Gun Club, were already in their cabins. They had but to start, which they did on the 21st of December, at eight o'clock at night, the corvette meeting with a beautiful sea, a north-easterly wind, and rather sharp cold. The whole population of San Francisco was gathered on the quay, greatly excited but silent, reserving their hurrahs for the return. Steam was fully up, and the screw of the "Susquehanna" carried them briskly out of the bay.

It is needless to relate the conversations on board between the officers, sailors, and passengers. All these men had but one thought. All these hearts beat under the same emotion. Whilst they were hastening to help them, what were Barbicane and his companions doing? What had become of them? Were they able to attempt any bold manœuvre to regain their liberty? None could say. The truth is that every attempt must have failed! Immersed nearly four miles under the ocean, this metal prison defied every effort of its prisoners.

On the 23rd inst., at eight in the morning, after a rapid passage, the "Susquehanna" was due at the fatal spot. They must wait till twelve to take the reckoning exactly. The buoy to which the sounding line had been lashed had not yet been recognized.

At twelve, Captain Blomsberry, assisted by his officers who superintended the observations, took the reckoning in the presence of the delegates of the Gun Club. Then there was a moment of anxiety. Her position decided, the "Susquehanna" was found to be some minutes to westward of the spot where the projectile had disappeared beneath the waves.

The ship's course was then changed so as to reach this exact point.

At forty-seven minutes past twelve they reached the buoy, it was in perfect condition, and must have shifted but little.

"At last!" exclaimed J. T. Maston.

"Shall we begin?" asked Captain Blomsberry.

"Without losing a second."

Every precaution was taken to keep the corvette almost completely motionless. Before trying to seize the projectile, Engineer Murchison wanted to find its exact position at the bottom of the ocean. The submarine apparatus destined for this expedition was supplied with air. The working of these engines was not without danger, for at 20,000 feet below the surface of the water, and under such great pressure, they were exposed to fracture, the consequences of which would be dreadful.

J. T. Maston, the Brothers Blomsberry, and Engineer Murchison, without heeding these dangers, took their places in the air chamber. The commander, posted on his bridge, superintended the operation, ready to stop or haul in the chains on the slightest signal. The screw had been shipped, and the whole power of the machinery collected on the capstan would have quickly drawn the apparatus on board. The descent began at twenty-five minutes past one at night, and the chamber, drawn under by the reservoirs full of water, disappeared from the surface of the ocean.

The emotion of the officers and sailors on board was now divided between the prisoners in the projectile and the prisoners in the submarine apparatus. As to the latter, they forgot themselves, and, glued to the windows of the scuttles, attentively watched the liquid mass through which they were passing.

The descent was rapid. At seventeen minutes past two, J. T. Maston and his companions had reached the bottom of the Pacific; but they saw nothing but an arid desert, no longer animated by either fauna or flora. By the light of their lamps, furnished with powerful reflectors, they could see the dark beds of the ocean for a considerable extent of view, but the projectile was nowhere to be seen.

The impatience of these bold divers cannot be described, and having an electrical communication with the corvette, they made a signal already agreed upon, and for the space of a mile the "Susquehanna" moved their chamber along some yards above the bottom.

Thus they explored the whole submarine plain, deceived at every turn by optical illusions which almost broke their hearts. Here a rock, there a projection from the ground, seemed to be the much-sought-for projectile; but their mistake was soon discovered, and then they were in despair.

"But where are they? where are they?" cried J. T. Maston. And the poor man called loudly upon Nicholl, Barbicane, and Michel Ardan, as if his unfortunate friends could either hear or answer him through such an impenetrable medium! The search continued under these conditions until the vitiated air compelled the divers to ascend.

The hauling in began about six in the evening, and was not ended before midnight.

"To-morrow," said J. T. Maston, as he set foot on the bridge of the corvette.

"Yes," answered Captain Blomsberry.

"And on another spot?"

"Yes."

J. T. Maston did not doubt of their final success, but his companions, no longer upheld by the excitement of the first hours, understood all the difficulty of the enterprise. What seemed easy at San Francisco, seemed here in the wide ocean almost impossible. The chances of success diminished in rapid proportion; and it was from chance alone that the meeting with the projectile might be expected.

The next day, the 24th, in spite of the fatigue of the previous day, the operation was renewed. The corvette advanced some minutes to westward, and the apparatus, provided with air, bore the same explorers to the depths of the ocean.

The whole day passed in fruitless research; the bed of the sea was a desert. The 25th brought no other result, nor the 26th.

It was disheartening. They thought of those unfortunates shut up in the projectile for twenty-six days. Perhaps at that moment they were experiencing the first approach of suffocation; that is, if they had escaped the dangers of their fall. The air was spent, and doubtless with the air all their *morale*.

"The air, possibly," answered J. T. Maston resolutely, "but their *morale* never!"

On the 28th, after two more days of search, all hope was gone. This projectile was but an atom in the immensity of the ocean. They must give up all idea of finding it.

But J. T. Maston would not hear of going away. He would not abandon the place without at least discovering the tomb of his friends. But Commander Blomsberry could no longer persist, and in spite of the exclamations of the worthy Secretary, was obliged to give the order to sail.

On the 29th of December at nine a.m., the "Susquehanna," heading N.E., resumed her course to the bay of San Francisco.

It was ten in the morning; the corvette was under half steam, as if regretting to leave the spot where the catastrophe had taken place, when a sailor, perched on the maintop gallant crosstrees, watching the sea, cried suddenly,—

"A buoy on the lee bow!"

The officers looked in the direction indicated, and by the help of their glasses, saw that the object signalled had the appearance of one of those buoys which are used to mark the passages of bays or rivers. But, singularly to say, a flag floating on the wind surmounted its cone, which emerged five or six feet out of water. This buoy shone under the rays of the sun as if it had been made of plates of silver. Commander Blomsberry, J. T. Maston, and the delegates of the Gun Club were mounted on the bridge, examining this object straying at random on the waves.

All looked with feverish anxiety, but in silence. None dared give expression to the thoughts which came to the minds of all.

The corvette approached to within two cables' lengths of the object.

A shudder ran through the whole crew. That flag was the American flag!

At this moment a perfect howling was heard; it was the brave J. T. Maston, who had just fallen all in a heap. Forgetting on the one hand that his right arm had been replaced by an iron hook, and on the other that a simple gutta-percha cap covered his brain box, he had given himself a formidable blow.

They hurried towards him, picked him up, restored him to life. And what were his first words?

"Ah! trebly brutes! quadruply idiots! quintuply boobies that we are!"

"What is it?" exclaimed every one around him.

"What is it?"

"Come, speak!"

"It is, simpletons," howled the terrible Secretary, "it is that the projectile only weighs 19,250 lbs.!"

"Well?"

"And that it displaces twenty-eight tons, or in other words 56,000 lbs., and that consequently *it floats!*"

Ah! what stress the worthy man laid on the verb "float!" And it was true! All, yes! all these savants had forgotten this fundamental law, namely, that on account of its specific lightness, the projectile, after having been drawn by its fall to the greatest depths of the ocean, must naturally return to the surface. And now it was floating quietly at the mercy of the waves.

The boats were put to sea. J. T. Maston and his friends had rushed into them! Excitement was at its height! Every heart beat loudly whilst they advanced to the projectile. What did it contain? Living or dead? Living, yes! living, at least unless death had struck Barbicane and his two friends since they had hoisted the flag. Profound silence reigned on the boats. All were breathless. Eyes no longer saw. One of the scuttles of the projectile was open. Some pieces of glass remained in the frame, showing that it had been broken. This scuttle was actually five feet above the water.

A boat came alongside, that of J. T. Maston, and J. T. Maston rushed to the broken window.

At that moment they heard a clear and merry voice, the voice of Michel Ardan, exclaiming in an accent of triumph—

"White all, Barbicane, white all!"

Barbicane, Michel Ardan, and Nicholl were playing at dominoes!

CHAPTER XXIII: THE END We may remember the intense sympathy which had accompanied the travellers on their departure. If at the beginning of the enterprise they had excited such emotion both in the old and new world, with what enthusiasm would they be received on their return! The millions of spectators which had beset the peninsula of Florida, would they not rush to meet these sublime adventurers? Those legions of strangers, hurrying from all parts of the globe towards the American shores, would they leave the Union without having seen Barbicane, Nicholl, and Michel Ardan? No! and the ardent passion of the public was bound to respond worthily to the greatness of the enterprise. Human creatures who had left the terrestrial sphere, and returned after this strange voyage into celestial space, could not fail to be received as the prophet Elias would be if he came back to earth. To see them first, and then to hear them, such was the universal longing.

Barbicane, Michel Ardan, Nicholl, and the delegates of the Gun Club, returning without delay to Baltimore, were received with indescribable enthusiasm. The notes of President Barbicane's voyage were ready to be given to the public. The *New York Herald* bought the manuscript at a price not yet known, but which must have been very high. Indeed, during the publication of "A Journey to the Moon," the sale of this paper amounted to five millions of copies. Three days after the return of the travellers to the earth, the slightest detail of their expedition was known. There remained nothing more but to see the heroes of this superhuman enterprise.

The expedition of Barbicane and his friends round the moon had enabled them to correct the many admitted theories regarding the terrestrial satellite. These savants had observed *de visu*, and under particular circumstances. They knew what systems should be rejected, what retained with regard to the formation of that orb, its origin, its habitability. Its past, present, and future had even given up their last secrets. Who could advance objections against conscientious observers, who at less than twenty-four miles distance had marked that curious mountain of Tycho, the strangest system of lunar orography? How answer those savants whose sight had penetrated the abyss of Pluto's circle? How contradict those bold ones whom the chances of their enterprise had borne over that invisible face of the disc, which no human eye until then had ever seen? It was now their turn to impose some limit on that Selenographic science, which had reconstructed the lunar world as Cuvier did the skeleton of a fossil, and say, "The moon *was* this, a habitable world, inhabited before the earth! The moon *is* that, a world uninhabitable, and now uninhabited."

To celebrate the return of its most illustrious member and his two companions, the Gun Club decided upon giving a banquet, but a banquet worthy of the conquerors, worthy of the American people, and under such conditions that all the inhabitants of the Union could directly take part in it.

All the head lines of railroads in the State were joined by flying rails; and on all the platforms, lined with the same flags, and decorated with the same ornaments, were tables laid and all served alike. At certain hours, successively calculated, marked by electric clocks which beat the seconds at the same time, the population were invited to take their place at the banquet tables. For four days, from the 5th to the 9th of January, the trains were stopped as they are on Sundays on the railways of the United States, and every road was open. One engine only at full speed, drawing a triumphal carriage, had the right of travelling for those four days on the railroads of the United States.

The engine was manned by a driver and a stoker, and bore, by special favour, the Hon. J. T. Maston, Secretary of the Gun Club. The carriage was reserved for President Barbicane, Captain Nicholl, and Michel Ardan. At the whistle of the driver, amid the hurrahs, and all the admiring vociferations of the American language, the train left the platform of Baltimore. It travelled at a speed of 160 miles in the hour. But what was this speed compared with that which had carried the three heroes from the mouth of the Columbiad?

Thus they sped from one town to the other, finding whole populations at table on their road, saluting them with the same acclamations, lavishing the same bravos! They travelled in this way through the east of the Union, Pennsylvania, Connecticut, Massachusetts, Vermont, Maine, and New Hampshire; the north and the west by New York, Ohio, Michigan, and Wisconsin; returning to the south by Illinois, Missouri, Arkansas, Texas, and Louisiana; they went to the south-east by Alabama and Florida, going up by Georgia and the Carolinas, visiting the centre by Tennessee, Kentucky, Virginia, and Indiana, and, after quitting the Washington station, re-entered Baltimore, where for four days one would have thought that the United States of America were seated at one immense banquet, saluting them simultaneously with the same hurrahs! The apotheosis was worthy of these three heroes whom fable would have placed in the rank of demigods.

And now will this attempt, unprecedented in the annals of travels, lead to any practical result? Will direct communication with the moon ever be established? Will they ever lay the foundation of a travelling service through the solar world? Will they go from one planet to another, from Jupiter to Mercury, and after awhile from one star to another, from the Polar to Sirius? Will this means of locomotion allow us to visit those suns which swarm in the firmament?

To such questions no answer can be given. But knowing the bold ingenuity of the Anglo-Saxon race, no one would be astonished if the Americans seek to make some use of President Barbicane's attempt.

Thus, some time after the return of the travellers, the public received with marked favour the announcement of a company, limited, with a capital of a hundred million of dollars, divided into a hundred thousand shares of a thousand dollars each, under the name of the "*National Company of Interstellary Communication.*" President, Barbicane; Vice-

President, Captain Nicholl; Secretary, J. T. Maston; Director of Movements, Michel Ardan.

And as it is part of the American temperament to foresee everything in business, even failure, the Honourable Harry Trolloppe, judge commissioner, and Francis Drayton, magistrate, were nominated beforehand!

the last terrestrials

by OLAF STAPLEDON

I. THE CULT OF EVANESCENCE The Fifth Men had not been endowed with that potential immortality which their makers themselves possessed. And from the fact that they were mortal and yet long-lived, their culture drew its chief brilliance and poignancy. Beings for whom the natural span was three thousand years, and ultimately as much as fifty thousand, were peculiarly troubled by the prospect of death, and by the loss of those dear to them. The mere ephemeral kind of spirit, that comes into being and then almost immediately ceases, before it has entered at all deeply into consciousness of itself, can face its end with a courage that is half unwitting. Even its smart in the loss of other beings with whom it has been intimate is but a vague and dream-like suffering. For the ephemeral spirit has no time to grow fully awake, or fully intimate with another, before it must lose its beloved, and itself once more fade into unconsciousness. But with the long-lived yet not immortal Fifth Men the case was different. Gathering to themselves experience of the cosmos, acquiring an ever more precise and vivid insight and appreciation, they knew that very soon all this wealth of the soul must cease to be. And in love, though they might be fully intimate not merely with one but with very many persons, the death of one of these dear spirits seemed an irrevocable tragedy, an utter annihilation of the most resplendent kind of glory, an impoverishment of the cosmos for evermore.

In their brief primitive phase, the Fifth Men, like so many other races, sought to console themselves by unreasoning faith in a life after death.

First published in 1930 by Methuen & Co., Ltd., London, England. Reprinted by permission of the publishers and Mrs. Olaf Stapledon.

They conceived, for instance, that at death terrestrial beings embarked upon a career continuous with earthly life, but far more ample, either in some remote planetary system, or in some wholly distinct orb of space-time. But though such theories were never disproved in the primitive era, they gradually began to seem not merely improbable but ignoble. For it came to be recognized that the resplendent glories of personality, even in that degree of beauty which now for the first time was attained, were not after all the extreme of glory. It was seen with pain, but also with exultation, that even love's demand that the beloved should have immortal life is a betrayal of man's paramount allegiance. And little by little it became evident that those who used great gifts, and even genius, to establish the truth of the after life, or to seek contact with their beloved dead, suffered from a strange blindness, and obtuseness of the spirit. Though the love which had misled them was itself a very lovely thing, yet they were misled. Like children, searching for lost toys, they wandered. Like adolescents seeking to recapture delight in the things of childhood, they shunned those more difficult admirations which are proper to the grown mind.

And so it became a constant aim of the Fifth Men to school themselves to admire chiefly even in the very crisis of bereavement, not persons, but that great music of innumerable personal lives, which is the life of the race. And quite early in their career they discovered an unexpected beauty in the very fact that the individual must die. So that, when they had actually come into possession of the means to make themselves immortal, they refrained, choosing rather merely to increase the life-span of succeeding generations to fifty thousand years. Such a period seemed to be demanded for the full exercise of human capacity; but immortality, they held, would lead to spiritual disaster.

Now as their science advanced they saw that there had been a time, before the stars were formed, when there was no possible footing for minds in the cosmos; and that there would come a time when mentality would be driven out of existence. Earlier human species had not needed to trouble about mind's ultimate fate; but for the long-lived Fifth Men the end, though remote, did not seem infinitely distant. The prospect distressed them. They had schooled themselves to live not for the individual but for the race; and now the life of the race itself was seen to be a mere instant between the endless void of the past and the endless void of the future. Nothing within their ken was more worthy of admiration than the organized progressive mentality of mankind; and the conviction that this most admired thing must soon cease, filled many of their less ample minds with horror and indignation. But in time the Fifth Men, like the Second Men long before them, came to suspect that even in this tragic brevity of mind's course there was a quality of beauty, more difficult than the familiar beauty, but also more exquisite. Even thus imprisoned in an instant, the spirit of man might yet plumb the whole extent of space, and also the whole past and the whole future; and so, from behind his prison bars, he might render the universe that intelligent worship which, they felt, it demanded of him. Better so, they said, than that he should fret himself with puny efforts to escape. He is dignified by his very weakness, and the cosmos by its very indifference to him.

For aeons they remained in this faith. And they schooled their hearts to acquiesce in it, saying, if it is so, it is best, and somehow we must learn to see that it is best. But what they meant by "best" was not what their predecessors would have meant. They did not, for instance, deceive themselves by pretending that after all they themselves actually preferred life to be evanescent. On the contrary, they continued to long that it might be otherwise. But having discovered, both behind the physical order and behind the desires of minds, a fundamental principle whose essence was æsthetic, they were faithful to the conviction that whatever was fact must somehow in the universal view be fitting, right, beautiful, integral to the form of the cosmos. And so they accepted as right a state of affairs which in their own hearts they still felt grievously wrong. This conviction of the irrevocability of the past and of the evanescence of mind induced in them a great tenderness for all beings that had lived and ceased. Deeming themselves to be near the crest of life's achievement, blessed also with longevity and philosophic detachment, they were often smitten with pity for those humbler, briefer and less free spirits whose lot had fallen in the past. Moreover, themselves extremely complex, subtle, conscious, they conceived a generous admiration for all simple minds, for the early men, and for the beasts. Very strongly they condemned the action of their predecessors in destroying so many joyous and delectable creatures. Earnestly they sought to reconstruct in imagination all those beings that blind intellectualism had murdered. Earnestly they delved in the near and the remote past so as to recover as much as possible of the history of life on the planet. With meticulous love they would figure out the life stories of extinct types, such as the brontosaurus, the hippopotamus, the chimpanzee, the Englishman, the American, as also of the still extant amœba. And while they could not but relish the comicality of these remote beings, their amusement was the outgrowth of affectionate insight into simple natures, and was but the obverse of their recognition that the primitive is essentially tragic, because blind. And so, while they saw that the main work of man must have regard to the future, they felt that he owed also a duty toward the past. He must preserve it in his own mind, if not actually in life at least in being. In the future lay glory, joy, brilliance of the spirit. The future needed service, not pity, not piety; but in the past lay darkness, confusion, waste, and all the cramped primitive minds, bewildered, torturing one another in their stupidity, yet one and all in some unique manner, beautiful.

The reconstruction of the past, not merely as abstract history but with the intimacy of the novel, thus became one of the main preoccupations of the Fifth Men. Many devoted themselves to this work, each individual specializing very minutely in some particular episode of human or animal history, and transmitting his work into the culture of the race. Thus increasingly the individual felt himself to be a single flicker between the teeming gulf of the never-more and the boundless void of the not-yet. Himself a member of a very noble and fortunate race, his zest in existence was tempered, deepened, by a sense of the presence, the ghostly presence, of the myriad less fortunate beings in the past. Sometimes, and especially in epochs when the contemporary world seemed most satisfactory and promising, this piety toward the primitive and the past became the dominant activity of the race, giving rise to alternating phases of rebellion against the tyrannical nature of the cosmos, and faith that in the universal view, after all, this horror must be right. In this latter mood it was held that the very irrevocability of the past dignified all past existents, and dignified the cosmos, as a work of tragic art is dignified by the irrevocability of disaster. It was this mood of acquiescence and faith which in the end became the characteristic attitude of the Fifth Men for many millions of years.

But a bewildering discovery was in store for the Fifth Men, a discovery which was to change their whole attitude toward existence. Certain obscure biological facts began to make them suspect, on purely empirical grounds, that past events were not after all simply non-existent, that though no longer existent in the temporal manner, they had eternal existence in some other manner. The effect of this increasing suspicion about the past was that a once harmonious race was divided for a while into two parties, those who insisted that the formal beauty of the universe demanded the tragic evanescence of all things, and those who determined to show that living minds could actually reach back into past events in all their pastness.

The readers of this book are not in a position to realize the poignancy of the conflict which now threatened to wreck humanity. They cannot approach it from the point of view of a race whose culture had consisted of an age-long schooling in admiration of an ever-vanishing cosmos. To the orthodox it seemed that the new view was iconoclastic, impertinent, vulgar. Their opponents, on the other hand, insisted that the matter must be decided dispassionately, according to the evidence. They were also able to point out that this devotion to evanescence was after all but the outcome of the conviction that the cosmos must be supremely noble. No one, it was said, really had direct vision of evanescence as in itself an excellence. So heartfelt was the dispute that the orthodox party actually broke off all "telepathic" communication with the rebels, and even went so far as to plan their destruction. There can be no doubt that if violence had actually been used the human race would have succumbed; for in a species of such high mental development internecine war would have been a gross violation of its nature. It would never have been able to live down so shameful a spiritual disaster. Fortunately, however, at the eleventh hour, common sense prevailed. The iconoclasts were permitted to carry on their research, and the whole race awaited the result.

2. EXPLORATION OF TIME   This first attack upon the nature of time involved an immense co-operative work, both theoretical and practical. It was from biology that the first hint had come that the past persisted. And it would be necessary to restate the whole of biology and the physical sciences in terms of the new idea. On the practical side it was necessary to undertake a great campaign of experiment, physiological and psychological. We cannot stay to watch this work. Millions of years passed by. Sometimes, for thousands of years at a spell, temporal research was the main preoccupation of the race; sometimes it was thrust into the background, or completely ignored, during epochs which were dominated by other interests. Age after age passed, and always the effort of man in this sphere remained barren. Then at last there was a real success.

A child had been selected from among those produced by an age-long breeding enterprise, directed towards the mastery of time. From infancy this child's brain had been very carefully controlled physiologically. Psychologically also he had been subjected to a severe treatment, that he might be properly schooled for his strange task. In the presence of several scientists and historians he was put into a kind of trance, and brought out of it again, half an hour later. He was then asked to give an account "telepathically" of his experiences during the trance. Unfortunately he was now so shattered that his evidence was almost unintelligible. After some months of rest he was questioned again, and was able to describe a curious episode which turned out to be a terrifying incident in the girlhood of his dead mother. He seemed to have seen the incident through her eyes, and to have been aware of all her thoughts. This alone proved nothing, for he might have received the information from some living mind. Once more, therefore, and in spite of his entreaties, he was put into the peculiar trance. On waking he told a rambling story of "little red people living in a squat white tower." It was clear that he was referring to the Great Brains and their attendants. But once more, this proved nothing; and before the account was finished the child died.

Another child was chosen, but was not put to the test until late in adolescence. After an hour of the trance, he woke and became terribly agitated, but forced himself to describe an episode which the historians assigned to the age of the Martian invasions. The importance of this incident lay in his account of a certain house with a carved granite portico, situated at the head of a waterfall in a mountain valley. He said he had found himself to be an old woman, and that he, or she, was being hurriedly helped out of the house by the other inmates. They watched a formless monster creep down the valley, destroy their house, and mangle two persons who failed to get away in time. Now this house was not at all typical of the Second Men, but must have expressed the whim of some freakish individual. From evidence derived from the boy himself, it proved possible to locate the valley with reference to a former mountain, known to history. No valley survived in that spot; but deep excavations revealed the ancient slopes, the fault that had occasioned the waterfall, and the broken pillars.

This and many similar incidents confirmed the Fifth Men in their new view of time. There followed an age in which the technique of direct inspection of the past was gradually improved, but not without tragedy. In the early stages it was found impossible to keep the "medium" alive for more than a few weeks after his venture into the past. The experience seemed to set up a progressive mental disintegration which produced first insanity, then paralysis, and, within a few months, death. This difficulty was at last overcome. By one means and another a type of brain was produced capable of undergoing the strain of supra-temporal experience without fatal results. An increasingly large proportion of the rising generation had now direct access to the past, and were engaged upon a great re-statement of history in relation to their first-hand experience; but their excursions into the past were uncontrollable. They could not go where they wanted to go, but only where fate flung them. Nor could they go of their own will, but only through a very complicated technique, and with the co-operation of experts. After a time the process was made much easier, in fact, too easy. The unfortunate medium might slip so easily into the trance that his days were eaten up by the past. He might suddenly fall to the ground, and lie rapt, inert, dependent on artificial feeding, for weeks, months, even for years. Or a dozen times in the same day he might be flung into a dozen different epochs of history. Or, still more distressing, his experience of past events might not keep pace with the actual rhythm of those events themselves. Thus he might behold the events of a month, or even a lifetime, fantastically accelerated so as to occupy a trance of no more than a day's duration. Or, worse, he might find himself sliding backwards down the vista of the hours and experiencing events in an order the reverse of the natural order. Even the magnificent brains of the Fifth

Men could not stand this. The result was maniacal behaviour, followed by death. Another trouble also beset these first experimenters. Supra-temporal experience proved to be like a dangerous and habit-forming drug. Those who ventured into the past might become so intoxicated that they would try to spend every moment of their natural lives in roaming among past events. Thus gradually they would lose touch with the present, live in absent-minded brooding, fail to react normally to their environment, turn socially worthless, and often come actually to physical disaster through inability to look after themselves.

Many more thousands of years passed before these difficulties and dangers were overcome. At length, however, the technique of supra-temporal experience was so perfected that every individual could at will practise it with safety, and could, within limits, project his vision into any locality of space-time which he desired to inspect. It was only possible, however, to see past events through the mind of some past organism, no longer living. And in practice only human minds, and to some extent the minds of the higher mammals, could be entered. The explorer retained throughout his adventure his own personality and system of memory. While experiencing the past individual's perceptions, memories, thoughts, desires, and in fact the whole process and content of the past mind, the explorer continued to be himself, and to react in terms of his own character, now condemning, now sympathizing, now critically enjoying the spectacle.

The task of explaining the mechanism of this new faculty occupied the scientists and philosophers of the species for a very long period. The final account, of course, cannot be presented save by parable; for it was found necessary to recast many fundamental concepts in order to interpret the facts coherently. The only hint that I can give of the explanation is in saying, metaphorically of course, that the living brain had access to the past, not by way of some mysterious kind of racial memory, nor by some equally impossible journey up the stream of time, but by a partial awakening, as it were, into eternity, and into inspection of a minute tract of space-time through some temporal mind in the past, as though through an optical instrument. In the early experiments the fantastic speeding, slowing and reversal of the temporal process resulted from disorderly inspection. As a reader may either skim the pages of a book, or read at a comfortable pace, or dwell upon one word, or spell the sentence backwards, so, unintentionally, the novice in eternity might read or misread the mind that was presented to him.

This new mode of experience, it should be noted, was the activity of living brains, though brains of a novel kind. Hence what was to be discovered "through the medium of eternity" was limited by the particular exploring brain's capacity of understanding what was presented to it. And, further, though the actual supra-temporal contact with past events occupied no time in the brain's natural life, the assimilating of that moment of vision, the reduction of it to normal temporal memory in the normal brain structures, took time, and had to be done during the period of the trance. To expect the neural structure to record the experience instantaneously would be to expect a complicated machine to effect a complicated readjustment without a process of readjusting.

The access to the past had, of course, far-reaching effects upon the culture of the Fifth Men. Not only did it give them an incomparably more accurate knowledge of past events, and insight into the motives of historical personages, and into large-scale cultural movements, but also it effected a subtle change in their estimate of the importance of things. Though intellectually they had, of course, realized both the vastness and the richness of the past, now they realized it with an overwhelming vividness. Matters that had been known hitherto only historically, schematically, were now available to be lived through by intimate acquaintance. The only limit to such acquaintance was set by the limitations of the explorer's own brain-capacity. Consequently the remote past came to enter into a man and shape his mind in a manner in which only the recent past, through memory, had shaped him hitherto. Even before the new kind of experience was first acquired, the race had been, as was said, peculiarly under the spell of the past; but now it was infinitely more so. Hitherto the Fifth Men had been like stay-at-home folk who had read minutely of foreign parts, but had never travelled; now they had become travellers experienced in all the continents of human time. The presences that had hitherto been ghostly were now presences of flesh and blood seen in broad daylight. And so the moving instant called the present appeared no longer as the only, and infinitesimal, real, but as the growing surface of an everlasting tree of existence. It was now the past that seemed most real, while the future still seemed void, and the present merely the impalpable becomingness of the indestructible past.

The discovery that past events were after all persistent, and accessible, was of course for the Fifth Men a source of deep joy; but also it caused them a new distress. While the past was thought of as a mere gulf of non-existence, the inconceivably great pain, misery, baseness, that had fallen into that gulf, could be dismissed as done with; and the will could be concentrated wholly on preventing such horrors from occurring in the future. But now, along with past joy, past distress was found to be everlasting. And those who, in the course of their voyaging in the past, encountered regions of eternal agony, came back distraught. It was easy to remind these harrowed explorers that if pain was eternal, so also was joy. Those who had endured travel in the tragic past were apt to dismiss such assurances with contempt, affirming that all the delights of the whole population of time could not compensate for the agony of one tortured individual. And anyhow, they declared, it was obvious that there had been no preponderance of joy over pain. Indeed, save in the modern age, pain had been overwhelmingly in excess.

So seriously did these convictions prey upon the minds of the Fifth Men, that in spite of their own almost perfect social order, in which suffering had actually to be sought out as a tonic, they fell into despair. At all times, in all pursuits, the presence of the tragic past haunted them, poisoning their lives, sapping their strength. Lovers were ashamed of their delight in one another. As in the far-off days of sexual taboo, guilt crept between them, and held their spirits apart even while their bodies were united.

3. VOYAGING IN SPACE It was while they were struggling in the grip of this vast social melancholy, and anxiously craving some new vision by which to reinterpret or transcend the agony of the past, that the Fifth Men were confronted with a most unexpected physical crisis. It was discovered that something queer was happening to the moon; in fact, that the orbit of the satellite was narrowing in upon the earth in a manner contrary to all the calculations of the scientists.

The Fifth Men had long ago fashioned for themselves an all-embracing and minutely coherent system of natural sciences, every factor in which had been put to the test a thousand times and had never been shaken. Imagine, then, their bewilderment at this extraordinary discovery. In ages when science was still fragmentary, a subversive discovery entailed merely a reorganization of some one department of science; but by now, such was the coherence of knowledge, that any minute discrepancy of fact and theory must throw man into a state of complete intellectual vertigo.

The evolution of the lunar orbit had, of course, been studied from time immemorial. Even the First Men had learned that the moon must first withdraw from and subsequently once more approach the earth, till it should reach a critical proximity and begin to break up into a swarm of fragments like the rings of Saturn. This view had been very thoroughly confirmed by the Fifth Men themselves. The satellite should have continued to withdraw for yet many hundreds of millions of years; but in fact it was now observed that not only had the withdrawal ceased, but a comparatively rapid approach had begun.

Observations and calculations were repeated, and ingenious theoretical explanations were suggested; but the truth remained completely hidden. It was left to a future and more brilliant species to discover the connexion between a planet's gravitation and its cultural development. Meanwhile, the Fifth Men knew only that the distance between the earth and the moon was becoming smaller with ever-increasing rapidity.

This discovery was a tonic to a melancholy race. Men turned from the tragic past to the bewildering present and the uncertain future.

For it was evident that, if the present acceleration of approach were to be maintained, the moon would enter the critical zone and disintegrate in less than ten million years; and, further, that the fragments would not maintain themselves as a ring, but would soon crash upon the earth. Heat generated by their impact would make the surface of the earth impossible as the home of life. A short-lived and short-sighted species might well have considered ten million years as equivalent to eternity. Not so the Fifth Men. Thinking primarily in terms of the race, they recognized at once that their whole social policy must now be dominated by this future catastrophe. Some there were indeed who at first refused to take the matter seriously, saying that there was no reason to believe that the moon's odd behaviour would continue indefinitely. But as the years advanced, this view became increasingly improbable. Some of those who had spent much of their lives in exploration of the past now sought to explore the future also, hoping to prove that human civilization would always be discoverable on the earth in no matter how remote a future. But the attempt to unveil the future by direct inspection failed completely. It was surmised, erroneously, that future events, unlike past events, must be strictly non-existent until their creation by the advancing present.

Clearly humanity must leave its native planet. Research was therefore concentrated on the possibility of flight through empty space, and the suitability of neighbouring worlds. The only alternatives were Mars and Venus. The former was by now without water and without atmosphere. The latter had a dense moist atmosphere; but one which lacked oxygen. The surface of Venus, moreover, was known to be almost completely covered with a shallow ocean. Further the planet was so hot by day that, even at the poles, man in his present state would scarcely survive.

It did not take the Fifth Men many centuries to devise a tolerable means of voyaging in interplanetary space. Immense rockets were constructed, the motive power of which was derived from the annihilation of matter. The vehicle was propelled simply by the terrific pressure of radiation thus produced. "Fuel" for a voyage of many months, or even years, could, of course, easily be carried, since the annihilation of a minute amount of matter produced a vast wealth of energy. Moreover, when once the vessel had emerged from the earth's atmosphere, and had attained full speed, she would, of course, maintain it without the use of power from the rocket apparatus. The task of rendering the "ethership" properly manageable and decently habitable proved difficult, but not insurmountable. The first vessel to take the ether was a cigar-shaped hull some three thousand feet long, and built of metals whose artificial atoms were incomparably more rigid than anything hitherto known. Batteries of "rocket" apparatus at various points on the hull enabled the ship not only to travel forward, but to reverse, turn in any direction, or side-step. Windows of an artificial transparent element, scarcely less strong than the metal of the hull, enabled the voyagers to look around them. Within there was ample accommodation for a hundred persons and their provisions for three years. Air for the same period was manufactured in transit from protons and electrons stored under pressure comparable to that in the interior of a star. Heat was, of course, provided by the annihilation of matter. Powerful refrigeration would permit the vessel to approach the sun almost to the orbit of Mercury. An "artificial gravity" system, based on the properties of the electro-magnetic field, could be turned on and regulated at will, so as to maintain a more or less normal environment for the human organism.

This pioneer ship was manned with a navigating crew and a company of scientists, and was successfully dispatched upon a trial trip. The intention was to approach close to the surface of the moon, possibly to circumnavigate it at an altitude of ten thousand feet, and to return without landing. For many days those on earth received radio messages from the vessel's powerful installation, reporting that all was going well. But suddenly the messages ceased, and no more was ever heard of the vessel. Almost at the moment of the last message, telescopes had revealed a sudden flash of light at a point on the vessel's course. It was therefore surmised that she had collided with a meteor and fused with the heat of the impact.

Other vessels were built and dispatched on trial voyages. Many failed to return. Some got out of control, and reported that they were heading for outer space or plunging toward the sun, their hopeless messages continuing until the last of the crew succumbed to suffocation. Other vessels returned successfully, but with crews haggard and distraught from long confinement in bad atmosphere. One, venturing to land on the moon, broke her back, so that the air rushed out of her, and her people died. After her last message was received, she was detected from the earth, as an added speck on the stippled surface of a lunar "sea."

As time passed, however, accidents became rarer; indeed, so rare that trips in the void began to be a popular form of amusement. Literature of the period reverberates with the novelty of such experiences, with the sense that man had at last learned true flight, and acquired the freedom of the solar system. Writers dwelt upon the shock of seeing, as the vessel soared and accelerated, the landscape dwindle to a mere illuminated disk or crescent, surrounded by constellations. They remarked also the awful remoteness and mystery which travellers experienced on these early voyages, with dazzling sunlight on one side of the vessel and dazzling be-spangled night on the other. They described how the intense sun spread his corona against a black and star-crowded sky. They expatiated also on the overwhelming interest of approaching another planet; of inspecting from the sky the still visible remains of Martian civilization; of groping through the cloud banks of Venus to discover islands in her almost coast-less ocean; of daring an approach to Mercury, till the heat became insup-portable in spite of the best refrigerating mechanism; of feeling a way across the belt of the asteroids and onwards toward Jupiter, till shortage of air and provisions forced a return.

But though the mere navigation of space was thus easily accomplished, the major task was still untouched. It was necessary either to remake man's nature to suit another planet, or to modify conditions upon another planet to suit man's nature. The former alternative was repugnant to the Fifth Men. Obviously it would entail an almost complete refashioning of the human organism. No existing individual could possibly be so altered as to live in the present conditions of Mars or Venus. And it would probably prove impossible to create a new being, adapted to these conditions, with-out sacrificing the brilliant and harmonious constitution of the extant species.

On the other hand, Mars could not be made habitable without first being stocked with air and water; and such an undertaking seemed im-possible. There was nothing for it, then, but to attack Venus. The polar surfaces of that planet, shielded by impenetrable depths of cloud, proved after all not unendurably hot. Subsequent generations might perhaps be modified so as to withstand even the sub-arctic and "temperate" climates. Oxygen was plentiful, but it was all tied up in chemical combination. Inevitably so, since oxygen combines very readily, and on Venus there was no vegetable life to exhale the free gas and replenish the ever-vanishing supply. It was necessary, then, to equip Venus with an appropri-ate vegetation, which in the course of ages should render the planet's atmosphere hospitable to man. The chemical and physical conditions on Venus had therefore to be studied in great detail, so that it might be pos-sible to design a kind of life which would have a chance of flourishing. This research had to be carried out from within the etherships, or with gas helmets, since no human being could live in the natural atmosphere of the planet.

We must not dwell upon the age of heroic research and adventure which now began. Observations of the lunar orbit were showing that ten million years was too long an estimate of the future habitability of the earth; and it was soon realized that Venus could not be made ready soon enough unless some more rapid change was set on foot. It was therefore decided to split up some of the ocean of the planet into hydrogen and oxygen by a vast process of electrolysis. This would have been a more difficult task, had not the ocean been relatively free from salt, owing to the fact that there was so little dry land to be denuded of salts by rain and river. The oxygen thus formed by electrolysis would be allowed to mix with the atmosphere. The hydrogen had to be got rid of somehow, and an ingenious method was devised by which it should be ejected beyond the limits of the atmosphere at so great a speed that it would never return. Once sufficient free oxygen had been produced, the new vegetation would replenish the loss due to oxidation. This work was duly set on foot. Great automatic electrolysing stations were founded on several of the islands; and biological research produced at length a whole flora of specialized vegetable types to cover the land surface of the planet. It was hoped that in less than a million years Venus would be fit to receive the human race, and the race fit to live on Venus.

Meanwhile a careful survey of the planet had been undertaken. Its land surface, scarcely more than a thousandth that of the earth, consisted of an unevenly distributed archipelago of mountainous islands. The planet had evidently not long ago been through a mountain-forming era, for soundings proved its whole surface to be extravagantly corrugated. The ocean was subject to terrific storms and currents; for since the planet took several weeks to rotate, there was a great difference of temperature and atmospheric pressure between the almost arctic hemisphere of night and the sweltering hemisphere of day. So great was the evaporation, that open sky was almost never visible from any part of the planet's surface; and indeed the average day-time weather was a succession of thick fogs and fantastic thunderstorms. Rain in the evening was a continuous torrent. Yet before night was over the waves clattered with fragments of ice.

Man looked upon his future home with loathing, and on his birthplace with an affection which became passionate. With its blue sky, its incomparable starry nights, its temperate and varied continents, its ample spaces of agriculture, wilderness and park, its well-known beasts and plants, and all the material fabric of the most enduring of terrestrial civilizations, it seemed to the men and women who were planning flight almost a living thing imploring them not to desert it. They looked often with hate at the quiet moon, now visibly larger than the moon of history. They revised again and again their astronomical and physical theories, hoping for some flaw which should render the moon's observed behaviour less mysterious, less terrifying. But they found nothing. It was as though a fiend out of some ancient myth had come to life in the modern world, to interfere with the laws of nature for man's undoing.

4. PREPARING A NEW WORLD   Another trouble now occurred. Several electrolysis stations on Venus were wrecked, apparently by submarine eruption. Also, a number of etherships, engaged in surveying the ocean,
mysteriously exploded. The explanation was found when one of these vessels, though damaged, was able to return to the earth. The commander reported that, when the sounding line was drawn up, a large spherical
object was seen to be attached to it. Closer inspection showed that this
object was fastened to the sounding apparatus by a hook, and was indeed
unmistakably artificial, a structure of small metal plates riveted together.
While preparations were being made to bring the object within the ship,
it happened to bump against the hull, and then it exploded.

Evidently there must be intelligent life somewhere in the ocean of
Venus. Evidently the marine Venerians resented the steady depletion of
their aqueous world, and were determined to stop it. The terrestrials had
assumed that water in which no free oxygen was dissolved could not support life. But observation soon revealed that in this world-wide ocean
there were many living species, some sessile, others free-swimming, some
microscopic, others as large as whales. The basis of life in these creatures
lay not in photosynthesis and chemical combination, but in the controlled disintegration of radio-active atoms. Venus was particularly rich in
these atoms, and still contained certain elements which had long ago
ceased to exist on the earth. The oceanic fauna subsisted in the destruction of minute quantities of radio-active atoms throughout its tissues.

Several of the Venerian species had attained considerable mastery over
their physical environment, and were able to destroy one another very
competently with various mechanical contrivances. Many types were indeed definitely intelligent and versatile within certain limits. And of these
intelligent types, one had come to dominate all the others by virtue of its
superior intelligence, and had constructed a genuine civilization on the
basis of radio-active power. These most developed of all the Venerian
creatures were beings of about the size and shape of a swordfish. They
had three manipulative organs, normally sheathed within the long "sword,"
but capable of extension beyond its point, as three branched muscular
tentacles. They swam with a curious screw-like motion of their bodies
and triple tails. Three fins enabled them to steer. They had also organs
of phosphorescence, vision, touch, and something analogous to hearing.
They appeared to reproduce asexually, laying eggs in the ooze of the ocean
bed. They had no need of nutrition in the ordinary sense; but in infancy
they seemed to gather enough radio-active matter to keep them alive for
many years. Each individual, when his stock was running out and he began

to be feeble, was either destroyed by his juniors or buried in a radio-active mine, to rise from this living death in a few months completely rejuvenated.

At the bottom of the Venerian ocean these creatures thronged in cities of proliferated coral-like buildings, equipped with many complex articles, which must have constituted the necessities and luxuries of their civilization. So much was ascertained by the Terrestrials in the course of their submarine exploration. But the mental life of Venerians remained hidden. It was clear, indeed, that like all living things, they were concerned with self-maintenance and the exercise of their capacities; but of the nature of these capacities little was discoverable. Clearly they used some kind of symbolic language, based on mechanical vibrations set up in the water by the snapping claws of their tentacles. But their more complex activities were quite unintelligible. All that could be recorded with certainty was that they were much addicted to warfare, even to warfare between groups of one species; and that even in the stress of military disaster they maintained a feverish production of material articles of all sorts, which they proceeded to destroy and neglect.

One activity was observed which was peculiarly mysterious. At certain seasons three individuals, suddenly developing unusual luminosity, would approach one another with rhythmic swayings and tremors, and would then rise on their tails and press their bodies together. Sometimes at this stage an excited crowd would collect, whirling around the three like driven snow. The chief performers would now furiously tear one another to pieces with their crab-like pincers, till nothing was left but tangled shreds of flesh, the great swords, and the still twitching claws. The Terrestrials, observing these matters with difficulty, at first suspected some kind of sexual intercourse; but no reproduction was ever traced to this source. Possibly the behaviour had once served a biological end, and had now become a useless ritual. Possibly it was a kind of voluntary religious sacrifice. More probably it was of a quite different nature, unintelligible to the human mind.

As man's activities on Venus became more extensive, the Venerians became more energetic in seeking to destroy him. They could not come out of the ocean to grapple with him, for they were deep-sea organisms. Deprived of oceanic pressure, they would have burst. But they contrived to hurl high explosives into the centres of the islands, or to undermine them from tunnels. The work of electrolysis was thus very seriously hampered. And as all efforts to parley with the Venerians failed completely, it was impossible to effect a compromise. The Fifth Men were thus faced with a grave moral problem. What right had man to interfere in a world already possessed by beings who were obviously intelligent, even though their mental life was incomprehensible to man? Long ago man himself had suffered at the hands of Martian invaders, who doubtless regarded themselves as more noble than the human race. And now man was committing a similar crime. On the other hand, either the migration to Venus must go forward, or humanity must be destroyed; for it seemed quite certain by now that the moon would fall, and at no very distant date. And though man's understanding of the Venerians was so incomplete, what he did know of them strongly suggested that they were definitely inferior to himself in mental range. The judgment might, of course, be mistaken; the Venerians might after all be so superior to man that man could not get an inkling of their superiority. But this argument would apply equally to jelly-fish and micro-organisms. Judgment had to be passed according to the evidence available. So far as man could judge at all in the matter, he was definitely the higher type.

There was another fact to be taken into account. The life of the Venerian organism depended on the existence of radio-active atoms. Since those atoms are subject to disintegration, they must become rarer. Venus was far better supplied than the earth in this respect, but there must inevitably come a time when there would be no more radio-active matter in Venus. Now submarine research showed that the Venerian fauna had once been much more extensive, and that the increasing difficulty of procuring radio-active matter was already the great limiting factor of civilization. Thus the Venerians were doomed, and man would merely hasten their destruction.

It was hoped, of course, that in colonizing Venus mankind would be able to accommodate itself without seriously interfering with the native population. But this proved impossible for two reasons. In the first place, the natives seemed determined to destroy the invader even if they should destroy themselves in the process. Titanic explosions were engineered, which caused the invaders serious damage, but also strewed the ocean surface with thousands of dead Venerians. Secondly, it was found that, as electrolysis poured more and more free oxygen into the atmosphere, the ocean absorbed some of the potent element back into itself by solution; and this dissolved oxygen had a disastrous effect upon the oceanic organisms. Their tissues began to oxidize. They were burnt up, internally and externally, by a slow fire. Man dared not stop the process of electrolysis until the atmosphere had become as rich in oxygen as his native air. Long before this state was reached, it was already clear that the Venerians were beginning to feel the effects of the poison, and that in a few thousand years, at most, they would be exterminated. It was therefore determined to put them out of their misery as quickly as possible. Men could by now walk abroad on the islands of Venus, and indeed the first settlements were already being founded. They were thus able to build a fleet of powerful submarine vessels to scour the ocean and destroy the whole native fauna.

This vast slaughter influenced the mind of the fifth human species in two opposite directions, now flinging it into despair, now rousing it to grave elation. For on the one hand the horror of the slaughter produced a haunting guiltiness in all men's minds, an unreasoning disgust with humanity for having been driven to murder in order to save itself. And this guiltiness combined with the purely intellectual loss of self-confidence which had been produced by the failure of science to account for the moon's approach. It re-awakened, also, that other quite irrational sense of guilt which had been bred of sympathy with the everlasting distress of the past. Together, these three influences tended toward racial neurosis.

On the other hand a very different mood sometimes sprang from the same three sources. After all, the failure of science was a challenge to be gladly accepted; it opened up a wealth of possibilities hitherto unimagined. Even the unalterable distress of the past constituted a challenge; for in some strange manner the present and future, it was said, must transfigure the past. As for the murder of Venerian life, it was, indeed, terrible, but right. It had been committed without hate; indeed, rather in love. For as the navy proceeded with its relentless work, it had gathered much insight into the life of the natives, and had learned to admire, even in a sense to love, while it killed. This mood, of inexorable yet not ruthless will, intensified the spiritual sensibility of the species, refined, so to speak, its spiritual hearing, and revealed to it tones and themes in the universal music which were hitherto obscure.

Which of these two moods, despair or courage, would triumph? All depended on the skill of the species to maintain a high degree of vitality in untoward circumstances.

Man now busied himself in preparing his new home. Many kinds of plant life, derived from the terrestrial stock, but bred for the Venerian environment, now began to swarm on the islands and in the sea. For so restricted was the land surface, that great areas of ocean had to be given over to specially designed marine plants, which now formed immense floating continents of vegetable matter. On the least torrid islands appeared habitable pylons, forming an architectural forest, with vegetation on every acre of free ground. Even so, it would be impossible for Venus ever to support the huge population of the earth. Steps had therefore been taken to ensure that the birth-rate should fall far short of the death-rate; so that, when the time should come, the race might emigrate without leaving any living members behind. No more than a hundred million, it was reckoned, could live tolerably on Venus. The population had therefore to be reduced to a hundredth of its former size. And since, in the terrestrial community, with its vast social and cultural activity, every individual had fulfilled some definite function in society, it was obvious

that the new community must be not merely small but mentally impover-
ished. Hitherto, each individual had been inriched by intercourse with
a far more intricate and diverse social environment than would be possible on Venus.

Such was the prospect when at length it was judged advisable to leave
the earth to its fate. The moon was now so huge that it periodically
turned day into night, and night into a ghastly day. Prodigious tides and
distressful weather conditions had already spoilt the amenities of the
earth, and done great damage to the fabric of civilization. And so at
length humanity reluctantly took flight. Some centuries passed before the
migration was completed, before Venus had received, not only the whole
remaining human population, but also representatives of many other
species of organisms, and all the most precious treasures of man's culture.

the world
of the future

the machine stops

by E. M. FORSTER

I: THE AIR-SHIP   Imagine, if you can, a small room, hexagonal in shape, like the cell of a bee. It is lighted neither by window nor by lamp, yet it is filled with a soft radiance. There are no apertures for ventilation, yet the air is fresh. There are no musical instruments, and yet, at the moment that my meditation opens, this room is throbbing with melodious sounds. An arm-chair is in the centre, by its side a reading-desk—that is all the furniture. And in the arm-chair there sits a swaddled lump of flesh—a woman, about five feet high, with a face as white as a fungus. It is to her that the little room belongs.

An electric bell rang.

The woman touched a switch and the music was silent.

"I suppose I must see who it is," she thought, and set her chair in motion. The chair, like the music, was worked by machinery, and it rolled her to the other side of the room, where the bell still rang importunately.

"Who is it?" she called. Her voice was irritable, for she had been interrupted often since the music began. She knew several thousand people; in certain directions human intercourse had advanced enormously.

But when she listened in to the receiver, her white face wrinkled into smiles, and she said:

"Very well. Let us talk, I will isolate myself. I do not expect anything important will happen for the next five minutes—for I can give you fully five minutes, Kuno. Then I must deliver my lecture on 'Music during the Australian Period.'"

From The Eternal Moment and Other Stories *by E. M. Forster, copyright, 1928, by Harcourt, Brace and Company, Inc.*

She touched the isolation knob, so that no one else could speak to her. Then she touched the lighting apparatus, and the little room was plunged into darkness.

"Be quick!" she called, her irritation returning. "Be quick, Kuno; here I am in the dark wasting my time."

But it was fully fifteen seconds before the round plate that she held in her hands began to glow. A faint blue light shot across it, darkening to purple, and presently she could see the image of her son, who lived on the other side of the earth, and he could see her.

"Kuno, how slow you are."

He smiled gravely.

"I really believe you enjoy dawdling."

"I have called you before, mother, but you were always busy or isolated. I have something particular to say."

"What is it, dearest boy? Be quick. Why could you not send it by pneumatic post?"

"Because I prefer saying such a thing. I want——"

"Well?"

"I want you to come and see me."

Vashti watched his face in the blue plate.

"But I can see you!" she exclaimed. "What more do you want?"

"I want to see you not through the Machine," said Kuno. "I want to speak to you not through the wearisome Machine."

"Oh, hush!" said his mother, vaguely shocked. "You mustn't say anything against the Machine."

"Why not?"

"One mustn't."

"You talk as if a god had made the Machine," cried the other. "I believe that you pray to it when you are unhappy. Men made it, do not forget that. Great men, but men. The Machine is much, but it is not everything. I see something like you in this plate, but I do not see you. I hear something like you through this telephone, but I do not hear you. That is why I want you to come. Come and stop with me. Pay me a visit, so that we can meet face to face, and talk about the hopes that are in my mind."

She replied that she could scarcely spare the time for a visit.

"The air-ship barely takes two days to fly between me and you."

"I dislike air-ships."

"Why?"

"I dislike seeing the horrible brown earth, and the sea, and the stars when it is dark. I get no ideas in an air-ship."

"I do not get them anywhere else."

"What kind of ideas can the air give you?"

He paused for an instant.

"Do you not know four big stars that form an oblong, and three stars close together in the middle of the oblong, and hanging from these stars, three other stars?"

"No, I do not. I dislike the stars. But did they give you an idea? How interesting; tell me."

"I had an idea that they were like a man."

"I do not understand."

"The four big stars are the man's shoulders and his knees. The three stars in the middle are like the belts that men wore once, and the three stars hanging are like a sword."

"A sword?"

"Men carried swords about with them, to kill animals and other men."

"It does not strike me as a very good idea, but it is certainly original. When did it come to you first?"

"In the air-ship——" He broke off and she fancied that he looked sad. She could not be sure, for the Machine did not transmit *nuances* of expression. It only gave a general idea of people—an idea that was good enough for all practical purposes, Vashti thought. The imponderable bloom, declared by a discredited philosophy to be the actual essence of intercourse, was rightly ignored by the Machine, just as the imponderable bloom of the grape was ignored by the manufacturers of artificial fruit. Something "good enough" had long since been accepted by our race.

"The truth is," he continued, "that I want to see these stars again. They are curious stars. I want to see them not from the air-ship, but from the surface of the earth, as our ancestors did, thousands of years ago. I want to visit the surface of the earth."

She was shocked again.

"Mother, you must come, if only to explain to me what is the harm of visiting the surface of the earth."

"No harm," she replied, controlling herself. "But no advantage. The surface of the earth is only dust and mud, no life remains on it, and you would need a respirator, or the cold of the outer air would kill you. One dies immediately in the outer air."

"I know; of course I shall take all precautions."

"And besides——"

"Well?"

She considered, and chose her words with care. Her son had a queer temper, and she wished to dissuade him from the expedition.

"It is contrary to the spirit of the age," she asserted.

"Do you mean by that, contrary to the Machine?"

"In a sense, but——"

His image in the blue plate faded.

"Kuno!"

He had isolated himself.

For a moment Vashti felt lonely.

Then she generated the light, and the sight of her room, flooded with radiance and studded with electric buttons, revived her. There were buttons and switches everywhere—buttons to call for food, for music, for clothing. There was the hot-bath button, by pressure of which a basin of (imitation) marble rose out of the floor, filled to the brim with a warm deodorized liquid. There was the cold-bath button. There was the button that produced literature. And there were of course the buttons by which she communicated with her friends. The room, though it contained nothing, was in touch with all that she cared for in the world.

Vashti's next move was to turn off the isolation-switch, and all the accumulations of the last three minutes burst upon her. The room was filled with the noise of bells, and speaking-tubes. What was the new food like? Could she recommend it? Had she had any ideas lately? Might one tell her one's own ideas? Would she make an engagement to visit the public nurseries at an early date?—say this day month.

To most of these questions she replied with irritation—a growing quality in that accelerated age. She said that the new food was horrible. That she could not visit the public nurseries through press of engagements. That she had no ideas of her own but had just been told one—that four stars and three in the middle were like a man: she doubted there was much in it. Then she switched off her correspondents, for it was time to deliver her lecture on Australian music.

The clumsy system of public gatherings had been long since abandoned; neither Vashti nor her audience stirred from their rooms. Seated in her arm-chair she spoke, while they in their arm-chairs heard her, fairly well, and saw her, fairly well. She opened with a humorous account of music in the pre-Mongolian epoch, and went on to describe the great outburst of song that followed the Chinese conquest. Remote and primeval as were the methods of I-San-So and the Brisbane school, she yet felt (she said) that study of them might repay the musician of today: they had freshness; they had, above all, ideas.

Her lecture, which lasted ten minutes, was well received, and at its conclusion she and many of her audience listened to a lecture on the sea; there were ideas to be got from the sea; the speaker had donned a respirator and visited it lately. Then she fed, talked to many friends, had a bath, talked again, and summoned her bed.

The bed was not to her liking. It was too large, and she had a feeling for a small bed. Complaint was useless, for beds were of the same dimension all over the world, and to have had an alternative size would have involved vast alterations in the Machine. Vashti isolated herself—it was necessary, for neither day nor night existed under the ground—and reviewed all that had happened since she had summoned the bed last. Ideas? Scarcely any. Events—was Kuno's invitation an event?

By her side, on the little reading-desk, was a survival from the ages of litter—one book. This was the Book of the Machine. In it were instructions against every possible contingency. If she was hot or cold or dyspeptic or at loss for a word, she went to the book, and it told her which button to press. The Central Committee published it. In accordance with a growing habit, it was richly bound.

Sitting up in the bed, she took it reverently in her hands. She glanced round the glowing room as if some one might be watching her. Then, half ashamed, half joyful, she murmured "O Machine! O Machine!" and raised the volume to her lips. Thrice she kissed it, thrice inclined her head, thrice she felt the delirium of acquiescence. Her ritual performed, she turned to page 1367, which gave the times of the departure of the air-ships from the island in the southern hemisphere, under whose soil she lived, to the island in the northern hemisphere, whereunder lived her son.

She thought, "I have not the time."

She made the room dark and slept; she awoke and made the room light; she ate and exchanged ideas with her friends, and listened to music and attended lectures; she made the room dark and slept. Above her, beneath her, and around her, the Machine hummed eternally; she did not notice the noise, for she had been born with it in her ears. The earth, carrying her, hummed as it sped through silence, turning her now to the invisible sun, now to the invisible stars. She awoke and made the room light.

"Kuno!"

"I will not talk to you," he answered, "until you come."

"Have you been on the surface of the earth since we spoke last?"

His image faded.

Again she consulted the Book. She became very nervous and lay back in her chair palpitating. Think of her as without teeth or hair. Presently she directed the chair to the wall, and pressed an unfamiliar button. The wall swung apart slowly. Through the opening she saw a tunnel that curved slightly, so that its goal was not visible. Should she go to see her son, here was the beginning of the journey.

Of course she knew all about the communication-system. There was nothing mysterious in it. She would summon a car and it would fly with her down the tunnel until it reached the lift that communicated with the air-ship station: the system had been in use for many, many years, long before the universal establishment of the Machine. And of course she had studied the civilization that had immediately preceded her own

—the civilization that had mistaken the functions of the system, and had used it for bringing people to things, instead of for bringing things to people. Those funny old days, when men went for change of air instead of changing the air in their rooms! And yet—she was frightened of the tunnel: she had not seen it since her last child was born. It curved—but not quite as she remembered; it was brilliant—but not quite as brilliant as a lecturer had suggested. Vashti was seized with the terrors of direct experience. She shrank back into the room, and the wall closed up again.

"Kuno," she said, "I cannot come to see you. I am not well."

Immediately an enormous apparatus fell on to her out of the ceiling, a thermometer was automatically inserted between her lips, a stethoscope was automatically laid upon her heart. She lay powerless. Cool pads soothed her forehead. Kuno had telegraphed to her doctor.

So the human passions still blundered up and down in the Machine. Vashti drank the medicine that the doctor projected into her mouth, and the machinery retired into the ceiling. The voice of Kuno was heard asking how she felt.

"Better." Then with irritation: "But why do you not come to me instead?"

"Because I cannot leave this place."

"Why?"

"Because, any moment, something tremendous may happen."

"Have you been on the surface of the earth yet?"

"Not yet."

"Then what is it?"

"I will not tell you through the Machine."

She resumed her life.

But she thought of Kuno as a baby, his birth, his removal to the public nurseries, her one visit to him there, his visits to her—visits which stopped when the Machine had assigned him a room on the other side of the earth. "Parents, duties of," said the Book of the Machine, "cease at the moment of birth. P. 422327483." True, but there was something special about Kuno—indeed there had been something special about all her children—and, after all, she must brave the journey if he desired it. And "something tremendous might happen." What did that mean? The nonsense of a youthful man, no doubt, but she must go. Again she pressed the unfamiliar button, again the wall swung back, and she saw the tunnel that curved out of sight. Clasping the Book, she rose, tottered on to the platform, and summoned the car. Her room closed behind her: the journey to the northern hemisphere had begun.

Of course it was perfectly easy. The car approached and in it she found arm-chairs exactly like her own. When she signalled, it stopped, and she tottered into the lift. One other passenger was in the lift, the first fellow creature she had seen face to face for months. Few travelled in these days, for, thanks to the advance of science, the earth was exactly alike all over. Rapid intercourse, from which the previous civilization had hoped so much, had ended by defeating itself. What was the good of going to Pekin when it was just like Shrewsbury? Why return to Shrewsbury when it would be just like Pekin? Men seldom moved their bodies; all unrest was concentrated in the soul.

The air-ship service was a relic from the former age. It was kept up, because it was easier to keep it up than to stop it or to diminish it, but it now far exceeded the wants of the population. Vessel after vessel would rise from the vomitories of Rye or of Christchurch (I use the antique names), would sail into the crowded sky, and would draw up at the wharves of the south—empty. So nicely adjusted was the system, so independent of meteorology, that the sky, whether calm or cloudy, resembled a vast kaleidoscope whereon the same patterns periodically recurred. The ship on which Vashti sailed started now at sunset, now at dawn. But always, as it passed above Rheims, it would neighbour the ship that served between Helsingfors and the Brazils, and, every third time it surmounted the Alps, the fleet of Palermo would cross its track behind. Night and day, wind and storm, tide and earthquake, impeded man no longer. He had harnessed Leviathan. All the old literature, with its praise of Nature, and its fear of Nature, rang false as the prattle of a child.

Yet as Vashti saw the vast flank of the ship, stained with exposure to the outer air, her horror of direct experience returned. It was not quite like the air-ship in the cinematophote. For one thing it smelt—not strongly or unpleasantly, but it did smell, and with her eyes shut she should have known that a new thing was close to her. Then she had to walk to it from the lift, had to submit to glances from the other passengers. The man in front dropped his Book—no great matter, but it disquieted them all. In the rooms, if the Book was dropped, the floor raised it mechanically, but the gangway to the air-ship was not so prepared, and the sacred volume lay motionless. They stopped—the thing was unforeseen—and the man, instead of picking up his property, felt the muscles of his arm to see how they had failed him. Then some one actually said with direct utterance: "We shall be late"—and they trooped on board, Vashti treading on the pages as she did so.

Inside, her anxiety increased. The arrangements were old-fashioned and rough. There was even a female attendant, to whom she would have to announce her wants during the voyage. Of course a revolving platform ran the length of the boat, but she was expected to walk from it to her cabin. Some cabins were better than others, and she did not get the best.

She thought the attendant had been unfair, and spasms of rage shook her. The glass valves had closed, she could not go back. She saw, at the end of the vestibule, the lift in which she had ascended going quietly up and down, empty. Beneath those corridors of shining tiles were rooms, tier below tier, reaching far into the earth, and in each room there sat a human being, eating, or sleeping, or producing ideas. And buried deep in the hive was her own room. Vashti was afraid.

"O Machine! O Machine!" she murmured, and caressed her Book, and was comforted.

Then the sides of the vestibule seemed to melt together, as do the passages that we see in dreams, the lift vanished, the Book that had been dropped slid to the left and vanished, polished tiles rushed by like a stream of water, there was a slight jar, and the air-ship, issuing from its tunnel, soared above the waters of a tropical ocean.

It was night. For a moment she saw the coast of Sumatra edged by the phosphorescence of waves, and crowned by lighthouses, still sending forth their disregarded beams. These also vanished, and only the stars distracted her. They were not motionless, but swayed to and fro above her head, thronging out of one skylight into another, as if the universe and not the air-ship was careening. And, as often happens on clear nights, they seemed now to be in perspective, now on a plane; now piled tier beyond tier into the infinite heavens, now concealing infinity, a roof limiting for ever the visions of men. In either case they seemed intolerable. "Are we to travel in the dark?" called the passengers angrily, and the attendant, who had been careless, generated the light, and pulled down the blinds of pliable metal. When the air-ships had been built, the desire to look direct at things still lingered in the world. Hence the extraordinary number of skylights and windows, and the proportionate discomfort to those who were civilised and refined. Even in Vashti's cabin one star peeped through a flaw in the blind, and after a few hours' uneasy slumber, she was disturbed by an unfamiliar glow, which was the dawn.

Quick as the ship had sped westwards, the earth had rolled eastwards quicker still, and had dragged back Vashti and her companions towards the sun. Science could prolong the night, but only for a little, and those high hopes of neutralizing the earth's diurnal revolution had passed, together with hopes that were possibly higher. To "keep pace with the sun," or even to outstrip it, had been the aim of the civilisation preceding this. Racing aeroplanes had been built for the purpose, capable of enormous speed, and steered by the greatest intellects of the epoch. Round the globe they went, round and round, westward, westward, round and round, amidst humanity's applause. In vain. The globe went eastward quicker still, horrible accidents occurred, and the Committee of the Machine, at the time rising into prominence, declared the pursuit illegal, unmechanical, and punishable by Homelessness.

Of Homelessness more will be said later.

Doubtless the Committee was right. Yet the attempt to "defeat the sun" aroused the last common interest that our race experienced about the heavenly bodies, or indeed about anything. It was the last time that men were compacted by thinking of a power outside the world. The sun had conquered, yet it was the end of his spiritual dominion. Dawn, midday, twilight, the zodiacal path, touched neither men's lives nor their hearts, and science retreated into the ground, to concentrate herself upon problems that she was certain of solving.

So when Vashti found her cabin invaded by a rosy finger of light, she was annoyed, and tried to adjust the blind. But the blind flew up altogether, and she saw through the skylight small pink clouds, swaying against a background of blue, and as the sun crept higher, its radiance entered direct, brimming down the wall, like a golden sea. It rose and fell with the air-ship's motion, just as waves rise and fall, but it advanced steadily, as a tide advances. Unless she was careful, it would strike her face. A spasm of horror shook her and she rang for the attendant. The attendant too was horrified, but she could do nothing; it was not her place to mend the blind. She could only suggest that the lady should change her cabin, which she accordingly prepared to do.

People were almost exactly alike all over the world, but the attendant of the air-ship, perhaps owing to her exceptional duties, had grown a little out of the common. She had often to address passengers with direct speech, and this had given her a certain roughness and originality of manner. When Vashti swerved away from the sunbeams with a cry, she behaved barbarically—she put out her hand to steady her.

"How dare you!" exclaimed the passenger. "You forget yourself!"

The woman was confused, and apologized for not having let her fall. People never touched one another. The custom had become obsolete, owing to the Machine.

"Where are we now?" asked Vashti haughtily.

"We are over Asia," said the attendant, anxious to be polite.

"Asia?"

"You must excuse my common way of speaking. I have got into the habit of calling places over which I pass by their unmechanical names."

"Oh, I remember Asia. The Mongols came from it."

"Beneath us, in the open air, stood a city that was once called Simla."

"Have you ever heard of the Mongols and of the Brisbane school?"

"No."

"Brisbane also stood in the open air."

"Those mountains to the right—let me show you them." She pushed back a metal blind. The main chain of the Himalayas was revealed. "They were once called the Roof of the World, those mountains."

"What a foolish name!"

"You must remember that, before the dawn of civilization, they seemed to be an impenetrable wall that touched the stars. It was supposed that no one but the gods could exist above their summits. How we have advanced, thanks to the Machine!"

"How we have advanced, thanks to the Machine!" said Vashti.

"How we have advanced, thanks to the Machine!" echoed the passenger who had dropped his Book the night before, and who was standing in the passage.

"And that white stuff in the cracks?—what is it?"

"I have forgotten its name."

"Cover the window, please. These mountains give me no ideas."

The northern aspect of the Himalayas was in deep shadow: on the Indian slope the sun had just prevailed. The forests had been destroyed during the literature epoch for the purpose of making newspaper-pulp, but the snows were awakening to their morning glory, and clouds still hung on the breasts of Kinchinjunga. In the plain were seen the ruins of cities, with diminished rivers creeping by their walls, and by the sides of these were sometimes the signs of vomitories, marking the cities of today. Over the whole prospect air-ships rushed, crossing and intercrossing with incredible *aplomb,* and rising nonchalantly when they desired to escape the perturbations of the lower atmosphere and to traverse the Roof of the World.

"We have indeed advanced, thanks to the Machine," repeated the attendant, and hid the Himalayas behind a metal blind.

The day dragged wearily forward. The passengers sat each in his cabin, avoiding one another with an almost physical repulsion and longing to be once more under the surface of the earth. There were eight or ten of them, mostly young males, sent out from the public nurseries to inhabit the rooms of those who had died in various parts of the earth. The man who had dropped his Book was on the homeward journey. He had been sent to Sumatra for the purpose of propagating the race. Vashti alone was travelling by her private will.

At midday she took a second glance at the earth. The air-ship was crossing another range of mountains, but she could see little, owing to clouds. Masses of black rock hovered below her, and merged indistinctly into gray. Their shapes were fantastic; one of them resembled a prostrate man.

"No ideas here," murmured Vashti, and hid the Caucasus behind a metal blind.

In the evening she looked again. They were crossing a golden sea, in which lay many small islands and one peninsula.

She repeated, "No ideas here," and hid Greece behind a metal blind.

II: THE MENDING APPARATUS By a vestibule, by a lift, by a tubular railway, by a platform, by a sliding door—by reversing all the steps of her departure did Vashti arrive at her son's room, which exactly resembled her own. She might well declare that the visit was superfluous. The buttons, the knobs, the reading-desk with the Book, the temperature, the atmosphere, the illumination—all were exactly the same. And if Kuno himself, flesh of her flesh, stood close beside her at last, what profit was there in that? She was too well-bred to shake him by the hand.

Averting her eyes, she spoke as follows:

"Here I am. I have had the most terrible journey and greatly retarded the development of my soul. It is not worth it, Kuno, it is not worth it. My time is too precious. The sunlight almost touched me, and I have met with the rudest people. I can only stop a few minutes. Say what you want to say, and then I must return."

"I have been threatened with Homelessness," said Kuno.

She looked at him now.

"I have been threatened with Homelessness, and I could not tell you such a thing through the Machine."

Homelessness means death. The victim is exposed to the air, which kills him.

"I have been outside since I spoke to you last. The tremendous thing has happened, and they have discovered me."

"But why shouldn't you go outside!" she exclaimed. "It is perfectly legal, perfectly mechanical, to visit the surface of the earth. I have lately been to a lecture on the sea; there is no objection to that; one simply summons a respirator and gets an Egression-permit. It is not the kind of thing that spiritually-minded people do, and I begged you not to do it, but there is no legal objection to it."

"I did not get an Egression-permit."

"Then how did you get out?"

"I found out a way of my own."

The phrase conveyed no meaning to her, and he had to repeat it.

"A way of your own?" she whispered. "But that would be wrong."

"Why?"

The question shocked her beyond measure.

"You are beginning to worship the Machine," he said coldly. "You think it irreligious of me to have found out a way of my own. It was just what the Committee thought, when they threatened me with Homelessness."

At this she grew angry. "I worship nothing!" she cried. "I am most advanced. I don't think you irreligious, for there is no such thing as religion left. All the fear and the superstition that existed once have been destroyed by the Machine. I only meant that to find out a way of your own was—— Besides, there is no new way out."

"So it is always supposed."

"Except through the vomitories, for which one must have an Egression-permit, it is impossible to get out. The Book says so."

"Well, the Book's wrong, for I have been out on my feet."

For Kuno was possessed of a certain physical strength.

By these days it was a demerit to be muscular. Each infant was examined at birth, and all who promised undue strength were destroyed. Humanitarians may protest, but it would have been no true kindness to let an athlete live; he would never have been happy in that state of life to which the Machine had called him; he would have yearned for trees to climb, rivers to bathe in, meadows and hills against which he might measure his body. Man must be adapted to his surroundings, must he not? In the dawn of the world our weak must be exposed on Mount Taygetus, in its twilight our strong will suffer euthanasia, that the Machine may progress, that the Machine may progress, that the Machine may progress eternally.

"You know that we have lost the sense of space. We say 'space is annihilated,' but we have annihilated not space, but the sense thereof. We have lost a part of ourselves. I determined to recover it, and I began by walking up and down the platform of the railway outside my room. Up and down, until I was tired, and so did recapture the meaning of 'Near' and 'Far.' 'Near' is a place to which I can get quickly *on my feet*, not a place to which the train or the air-ship will take me quickly. 'Far' is a place to which I cannot get quickly on my feet; the vomitory is 'far,' though I could be there in thirty-eight seconds by summoning the train. Man is the measure. That was my first lesson. Man's feet are the measure for distance, his hands are the measure for ownership, his body is the measure for all that is lovable and desirable and strong. Then I went further: it was then that I called to you for the first time, and you would not come.

"This city, as you know, is built deep beneath the surface of the earth, with only the vomitories protruding. Having paced the platform outside my own room, I took the lift to the next platform and paced that also, and so with each in turn, until I came to the topmost, above which begins the earth. All the platforms were exactly alike, and all that I gained by visiting them was to develop my sense of space and my muscles. I think I should have been content with this—it is not a little thing—but as I walked and brooded, it occurred to me that our cities had been built in the days when men still breathed the outer air, and that there had been ventilation shafts for the workmen. I could think of nothing but these ventilation shafts. Had they been destroyed by all the food-tubes and medicine-tubes and music-tubes that the Machine has evolved lately? Or did traces of them remain? One thing was certain. If I came upon them anywhere, it would be in the railway-tunnels of the topmost story. Everywhere else, all space was accounted for.

"I am telling my story quickly, but don't think that I was not a coward or that your answers never depressed me. It is not the proper thing, it is not mechanical, it is not decent to walk along a railway-tunnel. I did not fear that I might tread upon a live rail and be killed. I feared something far more intangible—doing what was not contemplated by the Machine. Then I said to myself, 'Man is the measure,' and I went, and after many visits I found an opening.

"The tunnels, of course, were lighted. Everything is light, artificial light; darkness is the exception. So when I saw a black gap in the tiles, I knew that it was an exception, and rejoiced. I put in my arm—I could put in no more at first—and waved it round and round in ecstasy. I loosened another tile, and put in my head, and shouted into the darkness: 'I am coming, I shall do it yet,' and my voice reverberated down endless passages. I seemed to hear the spirits of those dead workmen who had returned each evening to the starlight and to their wives, and all the generations who had lived in the open air called back to me, 'You will do it yet, you are coming.'"

He paused, and, absurd as he was, his last words moved her. For Kuno had lately asked to be a father, and his request had been refused by the Committee. His was not a type that the Machine desired to hand on.

"Then a train passed. It brushed by me, but I thrust my head and arms into the hole. I had done enough for one day, so I crawled back to the platform, went down in the lift, and summoned my bed. Ah, what dreams! And again I called you, and again you refused."

She shook her head and said:

"Don't. Don't talk of these terrible things. You make me miserable. You are throwing civilization away."

"But I had got back the sense of space and a man cannot rest then. I determined to get in at the hole and climb the shaft. And so I exercised my arms. Day after day I went through ridiculous movements, until my flesh ached, and I could hang by my hands and hold the pillow of my bed outstretched for many minutes. Then I summoned a respirator, and started.

"It was easy at first. The mortar had somehow rotted, and I soon pushed some more tiles in, and clambered after them into the darkness, and the spirits of the dead comforted me. I don't know what I mean by that. I just say what I felt. I felt, for the first time, that a protest had been lodged against corruption, and that even as the dead were comforting me, so I was comforting the unborn. I felt that humanity existed, and that it existed without clothes. How can I possibly explain this? It was naked, humanity seemed naked, and all these tubes and buttons and machineries neither came into the world with us, nor will they follow us out, nor do they matter supremely while we are here. Had I been strong, I would have torn off every garment I had, and gone out into the outer air unswaddled. But this is not for me, nor perhaps for my generation. I climbed with my respirator and my hygienic clothes and my dietetic tabloids! Better thus than not at all.

"There was a ladder, made of some primeval metal. The light from the railway fell upon its lowest rungs, and I saw that it led straight upwards out of the rubble at the bottom of shaft. Perhaps our ancestors ran up and down it a dozen times daily, in their building. As I climbed, the rough edges cut through my gloves so that my hands bled. The light helped me for a little, and then came darkness and, worse still, silence which pierced my ears like a sword. The Machine hums! Did you know that? Its hum penetrates our blood, and may even guide our thoughts. Who knows! I was getting beyond its power. Then I thought: 'This silence means that I am doing wrong.' But I heard voices in the silence, and again they strengthened me." He laughed. "I had need of them. The next moment I cracked my head against something."

She sighed.

"I had reached one of those pneumatic stoppers that defend us from the outer air. You may have noticed them on the air-ship. Pitch dark, my feet on the rungs of an invisible ladder, my hands cut; I cannot explain how I lived through this part, but the voices still comforted me, and I felt for fastenings. The stopper, I suppose, was about eight feet across. I passed my hand over it as far as I could reach. It was perfectly smooth. I felt it almost to the centre. Not quite to the centre, for my arm was too short. Then the voice said: 'Jump. It is worth it. There may be a handle in the centre, and you may catch hold of it and so come to us your own way. And if there is no handle, so that you may fall and are dashed to pieces—it is still worth it: you will still come to us your own way.' So I jumped. There was a handle, and——"

He paused. Tears gathered in his mother's eyes. She knew that he was fated. If he did not die to-day he would die to-morrow. There was not room for such a person in the world. And with her pity disgust mingled. She was ashamed at having borne such a son, she who had always been so respectable and so full of ideas. Was he really the little boy to whom she had taught the use of his stops and buttons, and to whom she had given his first lessons in the Book? The very hair that disfigured his lip showed that he was reverting to some savage type. On atavism the Machine can have no mercy.

"There was a handle, and I did catch it. I hung tranced over the darkness and heard the hum of these workings as the last whisper in a dying dream. All the things I had cared about and all the people I had spoken to through tubes appeared infinitely little. Meanwhile the handle revolved. My weight had set something in motion and I span slowly, and then——

"I cannot describe it. I was lying with my face to the sunshine. Blood poured from my nose and ears and I heard a tremendous roaring. The stopper, with me clinging to it, had simply been blown out of the earth, and the air that we make down here was escaping through the vent into the air above. It burst up like a fountain. I crawled back to it—for the upper air hurts—and, as it were, I took great sips from the edge. My respirator had flown goodness knows where, my clothes were torn. I just lay with my lips close to the hole, and I sipped until the bleeding stopped. You can imagine nothing so curious. This hollow in the grass—I will speak of it in a minute,—the sun shining into it, not brilliantly but through marbled clouds,—the peace, the nonchalance, the sense of space, and, brushing my cheek, the roaring fountain of our artificial air! Soon I spied my respirator, bobbing up and down in the current high above my head, and higher still were many air-ships. But no one ever looks out of air-ships, and in my case they could not have picked me up. There I was, stranded. The sun shone a little way down the shaft, and revealed the topmost rung of the ladder, but it was hopeless trying to reach it. I should either have been tossed up again by the escape, or else have fallen in, and died. I could only lie on the grass, sipping and sipping, and from time to time glancing around me.

"I knew that I was in Wessex, for I had taken care to go to a lecture on the subject before starting. Wessex lies above the room in which we are talking now. It was once an important state. Its kings held all the southern coast from the Andredswald to Cornwall, while the Wansdyke protected them on the north, running over the high ground. The lecturer was only concerned with the rise of Wessex, so I do not know how long it remained an international power, nor would the knowledge have assisted me. To tell the truth I could do nothing but laugh, during this part. There was I, with a pneumatic stopper by my side and a respirator bobbing over my head, imprisoned, all three of us, in a grass-grown hollow that was edged with fern."

Then he grew grave again.

"Lucky for me that it was a hollow. For the air began to fall back into it and to fill it as water fills a bowl. I could crawl about. Presently I stood.

I breathed a mixture, in which the air that hurts predominated whenever I tried to climb the sides. This was not so bad. I had not lost my tabloids and remained ridiculously cheerful, and as for the Machine, I forgot about it altogether. My one aim now was to get to the top, where the ferns were, and to view whatever objects lay beyond.

"I rushed the slope. The new air was still too bitter for me and I came rolling back, after a momentary vision of something gray. The sun grew very feeble, and I remembered that he was in Scorpio—I had been to a lecture on that too. If the sun is in Scorpio and you are in Wessex, it means that you must be as quick as you can, or it will get too dark. (This is the first bit of useful information I have ever got from a lecture, and I expect it will be the last.) It made me try frantically to breathe the new air, and to advance as far as I dared out of my pond. The hollow filled so slowly. At times I thought that the fountain played with less vigour. My respirator seemed to dance nearer the earth; the roar was decreasing."

He broke off.

"I don't think this is interesting you. The rest will interest you even less. There are no ideas in it, and I wish that I had not troubled you to come. We are too different, mother."

She told him to continue.

"It was evening before I climbed the bank. The sun had very nearly slipped out of the sky by this time, and I could not get a good view. You, who have just crossed the Roof of the World, will not want to hear an account of the little hills that I saw—low colourless hills. But to me they were living and the turf that covered them was a skin, under which their muscles rippled, and I felt that those hills had called with incalculable force to men in the past, and that men had loved them. Now they sleep —perhaps for ever. They commune with humanity in dreams. Happy the man, happy the woman, who awakes the hills of Wessex. For though they sleep, they will never die."

His voice rose passionately.

"Cannot you see, cannot all your lecturers see, that it is we who are dying, and that down here the only thing that really lives is the Machine? We created the Machine, to do our will, but we cannot make it do our will now. It has robbed us of the sense of space and of the sense of touch, it has blurred every human relation and narrowed down love to a carnal act, it has paralyzed our bodies and our wills, and now it compels us to worship it. The Machine develops—but not on our lines. The Machine proceeds—but not to our goal. We only exist as the blood corpuscles that course through its arteries, and if it could work without us, it would let us die. Oh, I have no remedy—or, at least, only one—to tell men again and again that I have seen the hills of Wessex as Ælfrid saw them when he overthrew the Danes.

"So the sun set. I forgot to mention that a belt of mist lay between my hill and other hills, and that it was the colour of pearl."

He broke off for the second time.

"Go on," said his mother wearily.

He shook his head.

"Go on. Nothing that you say can distress me now. I am hardened."

"I had meant to tell you the rest, but I cannot: I know that I cannot: good-bye."

Vashti stood irresolute. All her nerves were tingling with his blasphemies. But she was also inquisitive.

"This is unfair," she complained. "You have called me across the world to hear your story, and hear it I will. Tell me—as briefly as possible, for this is a disastrous waste of time—tell me how you returned to civilization."

"Oh—that!" he said, starting. "You would like to hear about civilization. Certainly. Had I got to where my respirator fell down?"

"No—but I understand everything now. You put on your respirator, and managed to walk along the surface of the earth to a vomitory, and there your conduct was reported to the Central Committee."

"By no means."

He passed his hand over his forehead, as if dispelling some strong impression. Then, resuming his narrative, he warmed to it again.

"My respirator fell about sunset. I had mentioned that the fountain seemed feebler, had I not?"

"Yes."

"About sunset, it let the respirator fall. As I said, I had entirely forgotten about the Machine, and I paid no great attention at the time, being occupied with other things. I had my pool of air, into which I could dip when the outer keenness became intolerable, and which would possibly remain for days, provided that no wind sprang up to disperse it. Not until it was too late, did I realize what the stoppage of the escape implied. You see—the gap in the tunnel had been mended; the Mending Apparatus; the Mending Apparatus, was after me.

"One other warning I had, but I neglected it. The sky at night was clearer than it had been in the day, and the moon, which was about half the sky behind the sun, shone into the dell at moments quite brightly. I was in my usual place—on the boundary between the two atmospheres—when I thought I saw something dark move across the bottom of the dell, and vanish into the shaft. In my folly, I ran down. I bent over and listened, and I thought I heard a faint scraping noise in the depths.

"At this—but it was too late—I took alarm. I determined to put on my respirator and to walk right out of the dell. But my respirator had gone. I knew exactly where it had fallen—between the stopper and the aperture

—and I could even feel the mark that it had made in the turf. It had gone, and I realized that something evil was at work, and I had better escape to the other air, and, if I must die, die running towards the cloud that had been the colour of a pearl. I never started. Out of the shaft—it is too horrible. A worm, a long white worm, had crawled out of the shaft and was gliding over the moonlit grass.

"I screamed. I did everything that I should not have done, I stamped upon the creature instead of flying from it, and it at once curled round the ankle. Then we fought. The worm let me run all over the dell, but edged up my leg as I ran. 'Help!' I cried. (That part is too awful. It belongs to the part that you will never know.) 'Help!' I cried. (Why cannot we suffer in silence?) 'Help!' I cried. Then my feet were wound together, I fell, I was dragged away from the dear ferns and the living hills, and past the great metal stopper (I can tell you this part), and I thought it might save me again if I caught hold of the handle. It also was enwrapped, it also. Oh, the whole dell was full of the things. They were searching it in all directions, they were denuding it, and the white snouts of others peeped out of the hole, ready if needed. Everything that could be moved they brought—brushwood, bundles of fern, everything, and down we all went intertwined into hell. The last things that I saw, ere the stopper closed after us, were certain stars, and I felt that a man of my sort lived in the sky. For I did fight, I fought till the very end, and it was only my head hitting against the ladder that quieted me. I woke up in this room. The worms had vanished. I was surrounded by artificial air, artificial light, artificial peace, and my friends were calling to me down speaking-tubes to know whether I had come across any new ideas lately."

Here his story ended. Discussion of it was impossible, and Vashti turned to go.

"It will end in Homelessness," she said quietly.

"I wish it would," retorted Kuno.

"The Machine has been most merciful."

"I prefer the mercy of God."

"By that superstitious phrase, do you mean that you could live in the outer air?"

"Yes."

"Have you ever seen, round the vomitories, the bones of those who were extruded after the Great Rebellion?"

"Yes."

"They were left where they perished for our edification. A few crawled away, but they perished, too—who can doubt it? And so with the Homeless of our own day. The surface of the earth supports life no longer."

"Indeed."

"Ferns and a little grass may survive, but all higher forms have perished. Has any air-ship detected them?"

"No."

"Has any lecturer dealt with them?"

"No."

"Then why this obstinacy?"

"Because I have seen them," he exploded.

"Seen *what*?"

"Because I have seen her in the twilight—because she came to my
help when I called—because she, too, was entangled by the worms, and,
luckier than I, was killed by one of them piercing her throat."

He was mad. Vashti departed, nor, in the troubles that followed, did
she ever see his face again.

III: THE HOMELESS   During the years that followed Kuno's escapade,
two important developments took place in the Machine. On the surface
they were revolutionary, but in either case men's minds had been prepared beforehand, and they did but express tendencies that were latent
already.

The first of these was the abolition of respirators.

Advanced thinkers, like Vashti, had always held it foolish to visit the
surface of the earth. Air-ships might be necessary, but what was the good
of going out for mere curiosity and crawling along for a mile or two in a
terrestrial motor? The habit was vulgar and perhaps faintly improper: it
was unproductive of ideas, and had no connection with the habits that
really mattered. So respirators were abolished, and with them, of course,
the terrestrial motors, and except for a few lecturers, who complained
that they were debarred access to their subject-matter, the development
was accepted quietly. Those who still wanted to know what the earth was
like had after all only to listen to some gramophone, or to look into some
cinematophote. And even the lecturers acquiesced when they found that a
lecture on the sea was none the less stimulating when compiled out of
other lectures that had already been delivered on the same subject. "Be-
ware of first-hand ideas!" exclaimed one of the most advanced of them.
"First-hand ideas do not really exist. They are but the physical impressions produced by love and fear, and on this gross foundation who could
erect a philosophy? Let your ideas be second-hand, and if possible tenth-
hand, for then they will be far removed from the disturbing element—
direct observation. Do not learn anything about this subject of mine—the
French Revolution. Learn instead what I think that Enicharmon thought
Urizen thought Gutch thought Ho-Yung thought Chi-Bo-Sing thought

Lafcadio Hearn thought Carlyle thought Mirabeau said about the French Revolution. Through the medium of these eight great minds, the blood that was shed at Paris and the windows that were broken at Versailles will be clarified to an idea which you may employ most profitably in your daily lives. But be sure that the intermediates are many and varied, for in history one authority exists to counteract another. Urizen must counteract the scepticism of Ho-Yung and Enicharmon, I must myself counteract the impetuosity of Gutch. You who listen to me are in a better position to judge about the French Revolution than I am. Your descendants will be even in a better position than you, for they will learn what you think I think, and yet another intermediate will be added to the chain. And in time"—his voice rose—"there will come a generation that has got beyond facts, beyond impressions, a generation absolutely colourless, a generation

> *seraphically free*
> *From taint of personality,*

which will see the French Revolution not as it happened, nor as they would like it to have happened, but as it would have happened, had it taken place in the days of the Machine."

Tremendous applause greeted this lecture, which did but voice a feeling already latent in the minds of men—a feeling that terrestrial facts must be ignored, and that the abolition of respirators was a positive gain. It was even suggested that air-ships should be abolished too. This was not done, because air-ships had somehow worked themselves into the Machine's system. But year by year they were used less, and mentioned less by thoughtful men.

The second great development was the re-establishment of religion.

This, too, had been voiced in the celebrated lecture. No one could mistake the reverent tone in which the peroration had concluded, and it awakened a responsive echo in the heart of each. Those who had long worshipped silently, now began to talk. They described the strange feeling of peace that came over them when they handled the Book of the Machine, the pleasure that it was to repeat certain numerals out of it, however little meaning those numerals conveyed to the outward ear, the ecstasy of touching a button, however unimportant, or of ringing an electric bell, however superfluously.

"The Machine," they exclaimed, "feeds us and clothes us and houses us; through it we speak to one another, through it we see one another, in it we have our being. The Machine is the friend of ideas and the enemy of superstition: the Machine is omnipotent, eternal; blessed is the Machine." And before long this allocution was printed on the first page of the Book, and in subsequent editions the ritual swelled into a complicated system of praise and prayer. The word "religion" was sedulously avoided, and in theory the Machine was still the creation and the implement of man. But in practice all, save a few retrogrades, worshipped it as divine. Nor was it worshipped in unity. One believer would be chiefly impressed by the blue optic plates, through which he saw other believers; another by the mending apparatus, which sinful Kuno had compared to worms; another by the lifts, another by the Book. And each would pray to this or to that, and ask it to intercede for him with the Machine as a whole. Persecution—that also was present. It did not break out, for reasons that will be set forward shortly. But it was latent, and all who did not accept the minimum known as "undenominational Mechanism" lived in danger of Homelessness, which means death, as we know.

To attribute these two great developments to the Central Committee, is to take a very narrow view of civilization. The Central Committee announced the developments, it is true, but they were no more the cause of them than were the kings of the imperialistic period the cause of war. Rather did they yield to some invincible pressure, which came no one knew whither, and which, when gratified, was succeeded by some new pressure equally invincible. To such a state of affairs it is convenient to give the name of progress. No one confessed the Machine was out of hand. Year by year it was served with increased efficiency and decreased intelligence. The better a man knew his own duties upon it, the less he understood the duties of his neighbour, and in all the world there was not one who understood the monster as a whole. Those master brains had perished. They had left full directions, it is true, and their successors had each of them mastered a portion of those directions. But Humanity, in its desire for comfort, had overreached itself. It had exploited the riches of nature too far. Quietly and complacently, it was sinking into decadence, and progress had come to mean the progress of the Machine.

As for Vashti, her life went peacefully forward until the final disaster. She made her room dark and slept; she awoke and made the room light. She lectured and attended lectures. She exchanged ideas with her innumerable friends and believed she was growing more spiritual. At times a friend was granted Euthanasia, and left his or her room for the Homelessness that is beyond all human conception. Vashti did not much mind. After an unsuccessful lecture, she would sometimes ask for Euthanasia herself. But the death-rate was not permitted to exceed the birth-rate, and the Machine had hitherto refused it to her.

The troubles began quietly, long before she was conscious of them. One day she was astonished at receiving a message from her son. They never communicated, having nothing in common, and she had only heard indirectly that he was still alive, and had been transferred from the northern hemisphere, where he had behaved so mischievously, to the southern —indeed, to a room not far from her own.

"Does he want me to visit him?" she thought. "Never again, never. And I have not the time."

No, it was madness of another kind.

He refused to visualize his face upon the blue plate, and speaking out of the darkness with solemnity said:

"The Machine stops."

"What do you say?"

"The Machine is stopping, I know it, I know the signs."

She burst into a peal of laughter. He heard her and was angry, and they spoke no more.

"Can you imagine anything more absurd?" she cried to a friend. "A man who was my son believes that the Machine is stopping. It would be impious if it was not mad."

"The Machine is stopping?" her friend replied. "What does that mean? The phrase conveys nothing to me."

"Nor to me."

"He does not refer, I suppose, to the trouble there has been lately with the music?"

"Oh no, of course not. Let us talk about music."

"Have you complained to the authorities?"

"Yes, and they say it wants mending, and referred me to the Committee of the Mending Apparatus. I complained of those curious gasping sighs that disfigure the symphonies of the Brisbane school. They sound like some one in pain. The Committee of the Mending Apparatus say that it shall be remedied shortly."

Obscurely worried, she resumed her life. For one thing, the defect in the music irritated her. For another thing, she could not forget Kuno's speech. If he had known that the music was out of repair—he could not know it, for he detested music—if he had known that it was wrong, "the Machine stops" was exactly the venomous sort of remark he would have made. Of course he had made it at a venture, but the coincidence annoyed her, and she spoke with some petulance to the Committee of the Mending Apparatus.

They replied, as before, that the defect would be set right shortly.

"Shortly! At once!" she retorted. "Why should I be worried by imperfect music? Things are always put right at once. If you do not mend it at once, I shall complain to the Central Committee."

"No personal complaints are received by the Central Committee," the Committee of the Mending Apparatus replied.

"Through whom am I to make my complaint, then?"

"Through us."

"I complain then."

"Your complaint shall be forwarded in its turn."

"Have others complained?"

This question was unmechanical, and the Committee of the Mending Apparatus refused to answer it.

"It is too bad!" she exclaimed to another of her friends. "There never was such an unfortunate woman as myself. I can never be sure of my music now. It gets worse and worse each time I summon it."

"I too have my troubles," the friend replied. "Sometimes my ideas are interrupted by a slight jarring noise."

"What is it?"

"I do not know whether it is inside my head, or inside the wall."

"Complain, in either case."

"I have complained, and my complaint will be forwarded in its turn to the Central Committee."

Time passed, and they resented the defects no longer. The defects had not been remedied, but the human tissues in that latter day had become so subservient, that they readily adapted themselves to every caprice of the Machine. The sigh at the crisis of the Brisbane symphony no longer irritated Vashti; she accepted it as part of the melody. The jarring noise, whether in the head or in the wall, was no longer resented by her friend. And so with the mouldy artificial fruit, so with the bath water that began to stink, so with the defective rhymes that the poetry machine had taken to emit. All were bitterly complained of at first, and then acquiesced in and forgotten. Things went from bad to worse unchallenged.

It was otherwise with the failure of the sleeping apparatus. That was a more serious stoppage. There came a day when over the whole world— in Sumatra, in Wessex, in the innumerable cities of Courland and Brazil —the beds, when summoned by their tired owners, failed to appear. It may seem a ludicrous matter, but from it we may date the collapse of humanity. The Committee responsible for the failure was assailed by complainants, whom it referred, as usual, to the Committee of the Mending Apparatus, who in its turn assured them that their complaints would be forwarded to the Central Committee. But the discontent grew, for mankind was not yet sufficiently adaptable to do without sleeping.

"Some one is meddling with the Machine——" they began.

"Someone is trying to make himself king, to reintroduce the personal element."

"Punish that man with Homelessness."

"To the rescue! Avenge the Machine! Avenge the Machine!"

"War! Kill the man!"

But the Committee of the Mending Apparatus now came forward, and allayed the panic with well-chosen words. It confessed that the Mending Apparatus was itself in need of repair.

The effect of this frank confession was admirable.

"Of course," said a famous lecturer—he of the French Revolution, who gilded each new decay with splendour—"of course we shall not press our complaints now. The Mending Apparatus has treated us so well in the past that we all sympathize with it, and will wait patiently for its recovery. In its own good time it will resume its duties. Meanwhile let us do without our beds, our tabloids, our other little wants. Such, I feel sure, would be the wish of the Machine."

Thousands of miles away his audience applauded. The Machine still linked them. Under the seas, beneath the roots of the mountains, ran the wires through which they saw and heard, the enormous eyes and ears that were their heritage, and the hum of many workings clothed their thoughts in one garment of subserviency. Only the old and the sick remained ungrateful, for it was rumoured that Euthanasia, too, was out of order, and that pain had reappeared among men.

It became difficult to read. A blight entered the atmosphere and dulled its luminosity. At times Vashti could scarcely see across her room. The air, too, was foul. Loud were the complaints, impotent the remedies, heroic the tone of the lecturer as he cried: "Courage, courage! What matter so long as the Machine goes on? To it the darkness and the light are one." And though things improved again after a time, the old brilliancy was never recaptured, and humanity never recovered from its entrance into twilight. There was an hysterical talk of "measures," of "provisional dictatorship," and the inhabitants of Sumatra were asked to familiarize themselves with the workings of the central power station, the said power station being situated in France. But for the most part panic reigned, and men spent their strength praying to their Books, tangible proofs of the Machine's omnipotence. There were gradations of terror—at times came rumours of hope—the Mending Apparatus was almost mended —the enemies of the Machine had been got under—new "nerve-centres" were evolving which would do the work even more magnificently than before. But there came a day when, without the slightest warning, without any previous hint of feebleness, the entire communication-system broke down, all over the world, and the world, as they understood it, ended.

Vashti was lecturing at the time and her earlier remarks had been punctuated with applause. As she proceeded the audience became silent, and at the conclusion there was no sound. Somewhat displeased, she called to a friend who was a specialist in sympathy. No sound: doubtless the friend was sleeping. And so with the next friend whom she tried to summon, and so with the next, until she remembered Kuno's cryptic remark, "The Machine stops."

The phrase still conveyed nothing. If Eternity was stopping it would of course be set going shortly.

For example, there was still a little light and air—the atmosphere had improved a few hours previously. There was still the Book, and while there was the Book there was security.

Then she broke down, for with the cessation of activity came an un-expected terror—silence.

She had never known silence, and the coming of it nearly killed her—it did kill many thousands of people outright. Ever since her birth she had been surrounded by the steady hum. It was to the ear what artificial air was to the lungs, and agonizing pains shot across her head. And scarcely knowing what she did, she stumbled forward and pressed the unfamiliar button, the one that opened the door of her cell.

Now the door of the cell worked on a simple hinge of its own. It was not connected with the central power station, dying far away in France. It opened, rousing immoderate hopes in Vashti, for she thought that the Machine had been mended. It opened, and she saw the dim tunnel that curved far away towards freedom. One look, and then she shrank back. For the tunnel was full of people—she was almost the last in that city to have taken alarm.

People at any time repelled her, and these were nightmares from her worst dreams. People were crawling about, people were screaming, whim-pering, gasping for breath, touching each other, vanishing in the dark, and ever and anon being pushed off the platform on to the live rail. Some were fighting round the electric bells, trying to summon trains which could not be summoned. Others were yelling for Euthanasia or for respirators, or blaspheming the Machine. Others stood at the doors of their cells fearing, like herself, either to stop in them or to leave them. And behind all the uproar was silence—the silence which is the voice of the earth and of the generations who have gone.

No—it was worse than solitude. She closed the door again and sat down to wait for the end. The disintegration went on, accompanied by horrible cracks and rumbling. The valves that restrained the Medical Apparatus must have been weakened, for it ruptured and hung hideously from the ceiling. The floor heaved and fell and flung her from her chair. A tube oozed towards her serpent fashion. And at last the final horror approached —light began to ebb, and she knew that civilization's long day was closing.

She whirled round, praying to be saved from this, at any rate, kissing the Book, pressing button after button. The uproar outside was increas-ing, and even penetrated the wall. Slowly the brilliancy of her cell was dimmed, the reflections faded from her metal switches. Now she could not see the reading-stand, now not the Book, though she held it in her hand. Light followed the flight of sound, air was following light, and the

original void returned to the cavern from which it had been so long excluded. Vashti continued to whirl, like the devotees of an earlier religion,
screaming, praying, striking at the buttons with bleeding hands.

It was thus that she opened her prison and escaped—escaped in the
spirit: at least so it seems to me, ere my meditation closes. That she
escapes in the body—I cannot perceive that. She struck, by chance, the
switch that released the door, and the rush of foul air on her skin, the loud
throbbing whispers in her ears, told her that she was facing the tunnel
again, and that tremendous platform on which she had seen men fighting. They were not fighting now. Only the whispers remained, and the
little whimpering groans. They were dying by hundreds out in the dark.

She burst into tears.

Tears answered her.

They wept for humanity, those two, not for themselves. They could not
bear that this should be the end. Ere silence was completed their hearts
were opened, and they knew what had been important on the earth. Man,
the flower of all flesh, the noblest of all creatures visible, man who
had once made god in his image, and had mirrored his strength on the
constellations, beautiful naked man was dying, strangled in the garments
that he had woven. Century after century had he toiled, and here was
his reward. Truly the garment had seemed heavenly at first, shot with the
colours of culture, sewn with the threads of self-denial. And heavenly
it had been so long as it was a garment and no more, so long as man could
shed it at will and live by the essence that is his soul, and the essence,
equally divine, that is his body. The sin against the body—it was for that
they wept in chief; the centuries of wrong against the muscles and the
nerves, and those five portals by which we can alone apprehend—gloz-
ing it over with talk of evolution, until the body was white pap, the home
of ideas as colourless, last sloshy stirrings of a spirit that had grasped
the stars.

"Where are you?" she sobbed.

His voice in the darkness said, "Here."

"Is there any hope, Kuno?"

"None for us."

"Where are you?"

She crawled towards him over the bodies of the dead. His blood spurted
over her hands.

"Quicker," he gasped, "I am dying—but we touch, we talk, not through
the Machine."

He kissed her.

"We have come back to our own. We die, but we have recaptured life,
as it was in Wessex, when Ælfrid overthrew the Danes. We know what

they know outside, they who dwelt in the cloud that is the colour of a pearl."

"But, Kuno, is it true? Are there still men on the surface of the earth? Is this—this tunnel, this poisoned darkness—really not the end?"

He replied:

"I have seen them, spoken to them, loved them. They are hiding in the mist and the ferns until our civilization stops. To-day they are the Homeless—to-morrow——"

"Oh, to-morrow—some fool will start the Machine again, to-morrow."

"Never," said Kuno, "never. Humanity has learnt its lesson."

As he spoke, the whole city was broken like a honeycomb. An air-ship had sailed in through the vomitory into a ruined wharf. It crashed downwards, exploding as it went, rending gallery after gallery with its wings of steel. For a moment they saw the nations of the dead, and, before they joined them, scraps of the untainted sky.

r. u. r. (rossum's universal robots)

by KAREL CAPEK

English version by Paul Selver and Nigel Playfair

ACT ONE

SCENE: *Central office of the factory of Rossum's Universal Robots. The windows on the back wall look out on the endless roads of factory buildings. On the Left wall large maps showing steamship and railroad routes. On the Right wall are fastened printed placards. ("Robot's cheapest Labor," etc.) In contrast to these wall fittings, the floor is covered with splendid Turkish carpet, a couch, a book shelf containing bottles of wine and spirits, instead of books.*

DOMIN *is sitting at his desk dictating.* SULLA *is at the typewriter against the wall.*

*Seen through the windows which run to the heights of the room are
rows of factory chimneys, telegraph poles and wires. There is a general
passageway or hallway which leads to the warehouse. The* ROBOTS *are
brought into the office through this entrance.*

DOMIN: (*Dictating*) Ready?

SULLA: Yes.

DOMIN: To E. M. McVicker & Co., Southampton, England. "We undertake no guarantee for goods damaged in transit. As soon as the con-
signment was taken on board we drew your captain's attention to the
fact that the vessel was unsuitable for the transportation of Robots; and
we are therefore not responsible for spoiled freight. We beg to remain,
for Rossum's Universal Robots, yours truly." Ready?

SULLA: Yes.

DOMIN: Another letter. To the E. B. Huysen Agency, New York, U.S.A.
"We beg to acknowledge receipt of order for five thousand Robots. As
you are sending your own vessel, please dispatch as cargo equal quantities
of soft and hard coal for R. U. R., the same to be credited as part payment
of the amount due us." (*Answering phone*) Hello! This is the central
office. Yes, certainly. Well, send them a wire. Good. "We beg to remain,
for Rossum's Universal Robots, yours very truly." Ready?

SULLA: Yes.

DOMIN: (*Answering small portable phone*) Hello! Yes. No. All right.
Another letter. Freidrichswerks, Hamburg, Germany. "We beg to ac-
knowledge receipt of order for fifteen thousand Robots." (*Enter* MARIUS)
Well, what is it?

MARIUS: There's a lady, sir, asking to see you.

DOMIN: A lady? Who is she?

MARIUS: I don't know, sir. She brings this card of introduction.

DOMIN: Ah, from President Glory. Ask her to come in— (*To* SULLA)
Where did I leave off?

SULLA: "We beg to acknowledge receipt of order for fifteen thousand
Robots."

DOMIN: Fifteen thousand. Fifteen thousand.

MARIUS: (*At door*) Please step this way.

(*Enter* HELENA. *Exit* MARIUS.)

HELENA: How do you do?

DOMIN: How do you do? What can I do for you?

HELENA: You are Mr. Domin, the General Manager?

DOMIN: I am.

HELENA: I have come—

DOMIN: With President Glory's card. That is quite sufficient.

HELENA: President Glory is my father. I am Helena Glory.

DOMIN: Please sit down. Sulla, you may go. How can I be of service to you, Miss Glory?

HELENA: I have come—

DOMIN: To have a look at our famous works where people are manufactured. Like all visitors. Well, there is no objection.

HELENA: I thought it was forbidden to——

DOMIN: To enter the factory? Yes, of course. Everybody comes here with someone's visiting card, Miss Glory.

HELENA: And you show them——

DOMIN: Only certain things. The manufacture of artificial people is a secret process.

HELENA: If you only knew how enormously that——

DOMIN: Interests you. Europe's talking about nothing else.

HELENA: (*Indignantly*) Why don't you let me finish speaking?

DOMIN: I beg your pardon. Did you want to say something different?

HELENA: I only wanted to ask—

DOMIN: Whether I could make a special exception in your case and show you our factory. Why, certainly, Miss Glory.

HELENA: How do you know I wanted to say that?

DOMIN: They all do. But we shall consider it a special honor to show you more than we do the rest.

HELENA: Thank you.

DOMIN: But you must agree not to divulge the least—

HELENA: My word of honor.

DOMIN: Thank you. Won't you raise your veil?

HELENA: Of course. You want to see whether I'm a spy or not— I beg your pardon.

DOMIN: What is it?

HELENA: Would you mind releasing my hand?

DOMIN: Oh, I beg *your* pardon.

HELENA: (*Raising veil*) How cautious you have to be here, don't you?

DOMIN: (*Observing her with deep interest*) Why, yes. Hm—of course — We—that is——

HELENA: But what is it? What's the matter?

DOMIN: I'm remarkably pleased. Did you have a pleasant crossing?

HELENA: Yes.

DOMIN: No difficulty?

HELENA: Why?

DOMIN: What I mean to say is—you're so *young.*

HELENA: May we go straight into the factory?

DOMIN: Yes. Twenty-two, I think.

HELENA: Twenty-two what?

DOMIN: Years.

HELENA: Twenty-one. Why do you want to know?

DOMIN: Well, because—as—— (*Sits on desk nearer her*) You will make a long stay, won't you?

HELENA: That depends on how much of the factory you show me.

DOMIN: Oh, hang the factory. Oh, no, no, you shall see everything, Miss Glory. Indeed you shall. Won't you sit down?

HELENA: Thank you.

DOMIN: But first would you like to hear the story of the invention?

HELENA: Yes, indeed.

DOMIN: It was in the year 1920 that old Rossum, the great physiologist, who was then quite a young scientist, took himself to the distant island for the purpose of studying the ocean fauna. On this occasion he attempted by chemical synthesis to imitate the living matter known as protoplasm until he suddenly discovered a substance which behaved exactly like living matter although its chemical composition was different. That was in the year 1932, exactly four hundred and forty years after the discovery of America. Whew——

HELENA: Do you know that by heart?

DOMIN: (*Takes flowers from desk to her*) Yes. You see, physiology is not in my line. Shall I go on?

HELENA: (*Smelling flowers*) Yes, please.

DOMIN: And then, Miss Glory, Old Rossum wrote the following among his chemical experiments: "Nature has found only one method of organizing living matter. There is, however, another method, more simple, flexible and rapid which has not yet occurred to Nature at all. This second process by which life can be developed was discovered by me today." Now imagine him, Miss Glory, writing those wonderful words over some colloidal mess that a dog wouldn't look at. Imagine him sitting over a test tube and thinking how the whole tree of life would grow from him, how all animals would proceed from it, beginning with some sort of a beetle and ending with a *man*. A man of different substance from us. Miss Glory, that was a tremendous moment. (*Gets box of candy from desk and passes it to her.*)

HELENA: Well——

DOMIN: (*As she speaks his portable phone lights up and he answers*) Well— Hello!—Yes—no, I'm in conference. Don't disturb me.

HELENA: Well?

DOMIN: Now, the thing was how to get the life *out* of the test tubes, and hasten development and form organs, bones and nerves, and so on, and find such substances as catalytics, enzymes, hormones in short—you understand?

HELENA: Not much, I'm afraid.

DOMIN: Never mind. (*Leans over couch and fixes cushion for her back*) There! You see with the help of his tinctures he could make whatever he wanted. He could have produced a Medusa with the brain of Socrates or a worm fifty yards long—(*She laughs. He does also; leans closer on couch, then straightens up again*)—but being without a grain of humor, he took into his head to make a vertebrate or perhaps a man. This artificial living *matter* of his had a raging thirst for life. It didn't mind being sown or mixed together. That couldn't be done with natural albumen. And that's how he set about it.

HELENA: About what?

DOMIN: About imitating Nature. First of all he tried making an artificial dog. That took him several years and resulted in a sort of stunted calf which *died* in a few days. I'll show it to you in the museum. And *then* old Rossum started on the manufacture of *man*.

HELENA: And I'm to divulge this to nobody?

DOMIN: To nobody in the world.

HELENA: What a pity that it's to be discovered in *all* the school books of both Europe and America. (BOTH *laugh*.)

DOMIN: Yes. But do you know what *isn't* in the school books? That old Rossum was mad. Seriously, Miss Glory, you must keep this to yourself. The old crank wanted to actually make *people*.

HELENA: But you do make people.

DOMIN: *Approximately*—Miss Glory. But old Rossum meant it literally. He wanted to become a sort of scientific substitute for God. He was a fearful materialist, and that's why he did it all. His sole purpose was nothing more or less than to prove that God was no longer necessary. Do you know anything about anatomy?

HELENA: Very little.

DOMIN: Neither do I. Well he then decided to manufacture everything as in the human body. I'll show you in the museum the bungling attempt it took him ten years to produce. It was to have been a *man*, but it lived for three days only. Then up came *young* Rossum, an engineer. He was a wonderful fellow, Miss Glory. When he saw what a mess of it the old man was making he said: "It's absurd to spend ten years making a man. If you can't make him quicker than Nature, you might as well shut up shop." Then he set about learning anatomy himself.

HELENA: There's nothing about *that* in the school books?

DOMIN: No. The school books are full of paid advertisements, and rubbish at that. What the school books say about the *united efforts* of the two great Rossums is all a fairy tale. They used to have dreadful rows. The old *atheist* hadn't the slightest conception of industrial *matters*, and the end of it was that Young Rossum shut him up in some laboratory or other and let him fritter the time away with his monstrosities while he himself started on the business from an *engineer's* point of view. Old Rossum *cursed* him and before he died he managed to botch up two physiological horrors. Then one day they found him dead in the *laboratory*. And that's his whole story.

HELENA: And what about the young man?

DOMIN: (*Sits beside her on couch*) Well, anyone who has looked into human anatomy will have seen at once that man is too complicated, and that a good engineer could make him more simply. So young Rossum began to *overhaul* anatomy to see what could be left out or simplified. In short— But this isn't boring you, Miss Glory?

HELENA: No, indeed. You're— It's awfully interesting.

DOMIN: (*Gets closer*) So young Rossum said to himself: "A man is something that feels happy, plays the piano, likes going for a walk, and, in fact, wants to do a whole lot of things that are really unnecessary."

HELENA: Oh.

DOMIN: That are unnecessary when he wants—(*Takes her hand*)—let us say, to weave or count. Do you play the piano?

HELENA: Yes.

DOMIN: That's good. (*Kisses her hand. She lowers her head.*) Oh, I beg your pardon! (*Rises*) But a working machine must *not* play the piano, must not feel happy, must not do a whole lot of other things. A gasoline motor must not have tassels or ornaments, Miss Glory. And to manufacture artificial workers is the same thing as the manufacture of a gasoline motor. (*She is not interested.*) The process must be the simplest, and the product the best from a practical point of view. (*Sits beside her again*) What sort of worker do you think is the *best* from a practical point of view?

HELENA: (*Absently*) What?

DOMIN: What sort of worker do you think is the best from a practical point of view?

HELENA: (*Pulling herself together*) Oh! Perhaps the one who is most honest and hard-working.

DOMIN: No. The one that is the *cheapest*. The one whose requirements are the *smallest*. Young Rossum invented a worker with the minimum amount of requirements. He had to simplify him. He rejected everything that did not contribute directly to the progress of work. Everything that makes man more expensive. In fact he *rejected man* and made the *Robot*. My dear Miss Glory, the Robots are not people. Mechanically they are more *perfect* than we are; they have an enormously developed intelligence, but they have no soul.

HELENA: How do you know they have no soul?

DOMIN: Have you ever seen what a Robot looks like inside?

HELENA: No.

DOMIN: Very neat, very simple. Really a beautiful piece of work. Not much *in* it, but everything in flawless order. The product of an engineer *is* technically at a higher pitch of perfection than a product of Nature.

HELENA: But man is supposed to be the product of God.

DOMIN: All the worse. God hasn't the slightest notion of modern engineering. Would you believe that young Rossum then proceeded to play at being God?

HELENA: How do you mean?

DOMIN: He began to manufacture Super-Robots. Regular giants they were. He tried to make them twelve feet tall. But you wouldn't believe what a failure they were.

HELENA: A failure?

DOMIN: Yes. For no reason at all their limbs used to keep snapping off. "Evidently our planet is too small for giants." Now we only make Robots of normal size and of very high-class human finish.

HELENA: I saw the first Robots at home. The Town Council bought them for—I mean engaged them for work.

DOMIN: No. *Bought* them, Miss Glory. Robots are bought and sold.

HELENA: These were employed as street-sweepers. I saw them sweeping. They were so strange and quiet.

DOMIN: (*Rises*) Rossum's Universal Robot factory doesn't produce a uniform brand of Robots. We have Robots of *finer* and *coarser* grades. The best will live about *twenty* years. (*Crosses to desk and pushes button.*)

HELENA: Then they die?

DOMIN: Yes, they get used up. (*Enter* MARIUS) Marius, bring in samples of the manual labor Robot. I'll show you specimens of the two extremes. This first grade is comparatively inexpensive and is made in vast quantities. (MARIUS *re-enters with two manual labor* ROBOTS.) There you are, as powerful as a small tractor. Guaranteed to have average intelligence. That will do, Marius. (MARIUS *exits with* ROBOTS.)

HELENA: They make me feel so strange.

DOMIN: (*Crosses to desk. Rings*) Did you see my new typist?

HELENA: I didn't notice her.

(*Enter* SULLA. *She stands, facing* HELENA.)

DOMIN: Sulla, let Miss Glory see you.

HELENA: (*Looks at* DOMIN. *Rising.*) So pleased to meet you. You must find it terribly dull in this out of the way spot, don't you?

SULLA: I don't know, Miss Glory.

HELENA: Where do you come from?

SULLA: From the factory.

HELENA: Oh, were you born there?

SULLA: I was *made* there.

HELENA: What?

DOMIN: Sulla is a Robot, best grade.

HELENA: Oh, I beg your pardon.

DOMIN: Sulla isn't angry. See, Miss Glory, the kind of skin we make. Feel her face.

HELENA: Oh, no, no.

DOMIN: You wouldn't know that she's made of different material from us, would you? Turn 'round, Sulla.

HELENA: Oh, stop, stop.

DOMIN: Talk to Miss Glory, Sulla.

SULLA: Please sit down. Did you have a pleasant crossing?

HELENA: Oh, yes, certainly.

SULLA: Don't go back on the *Amelia*, Miss Glory, the barometer is falling steadily. Wait for the *Pennsylvania*. That's a good powerful vessel.

DOMIN: What's its speed?

SULLA: Forty knots an hour. Fifty thousand tons. One of the latest vessels, Miss Glory.

HELENA: Thank you.

SULLA: A crew of fifteen hundred, Captain Harpy, eight boilers—

DOMIN: That'll do, Sulla. Now show us your knowledge of French.

HELENA: You know French?

SULLA: Oui! Madam! I know four languages. I can write: "Dear Sir, Monsieur, Geehrter Herr, Cteny pane."

HELENA: Oh, that's absurd! Sulla isn't a Robot. Sulla is a girl like me. Sulla, this is outrageous— Why do you take part in such a hoax?

SULLA: I am a Robot.

HELENA: No, no, you are not telling the truth. I know they have forced you to do it for an advertisement. Sulla, you are a girl like me, aren't you?

DOMIN: I'm sorry, Miss Glory. *Sulla is a Robot.*

HELENA: It's a lie!

DOMIN: What? (*Pushes button on desk*) Well, then I must *convince* you. (*Enter* MARIUS) Marius, take Sulla into the dissecting room, and tell them to open her up at once.

HELENA: Where?

DOMIN: Into the dissecting room. When they've *cut her open*, you can go and have a look. (MARIUS *makes a start toward* SULLA.)

HELENA: (*Stopping* MARIUS) No! No!

DOMIN: Excuse me, you spoke of lies.

HELENA: You wouldn't have her killed?

DOMIN: You can't kill machines. Sulla!

HELENA: Don't be afraid, Sulla. I won't let you go. Tell me, my dear are they always so cruel to you? You mustn't put up with it, Sulla. You mustn't.

SULLA: I am a Robot.

HELENA: That doesn't matter. Robots are just as good as we are. Sulla, you wouldn't let yourself be cut to pieces?

SULLA: Yes.

HELENA: Oh, you're not afraid of death, then?

SULLA: I cannot tell, Miss Glory.

HELENA: Do you know what would happen to you in there?

SULLA: Yes, I should cease to move.

HELENA: How dreadful!

DOMIN: Marius, tell Miss Glory what you are?

MARIUS: Marius, the Robot.

DOMIN: Would you take Sulla into the dissecting room?

MARIUS: Yes.

DOMIN: Would you be sorry for her?

MARIUS: (*Pause*) I cannot tell.

DOMIN: What would happen to her?

MARIUS: She would cease to move. They would put her into the stamping mill.

DOMIN: That is death, Marius. Aren't you afraid of death?

MARIUS: No.

DOMIN: You see, Miss Glory, the Robots have no interest in life. They have no enjoyments. They are *less* than so much grass.

HELENA: Oh, stop. Please send them away.

DOMIN: Marius, Sulla, you may go.

HELENA: How terrible! It's outrageous what you are doing.

DOMIN: Why outrageous?

HELENA: I don't know, but it is. Why do you call her "Sulla"?

DOMIN: Isn't it a nice name?

HELENA: It's a man's name. Sulla was a Roman General.

DOMIN: What! Oh! (*Laughs*) We thought that Marius and Sulla were lovers.

HELENA: (*Indignantly*) Marius and Sulla were generals and fought against each other in the year— I've forgotten now.

DOMIN: (*Laughing*) Come here to the window.

HELENA: What?

DOMIN: Come here. Do you see anything?

HELENA: Bricklayers.

DOMIN: Robots. All our work people are Robots. And down there, can you see anything?

HELENA: Some sort of office.

DOMIN: A counting house. And in it—

HELENA: A lot of officials.

DOMIN: Robots! All our officials are Robots. And when you see the factory—— (*Noon whistle blows.*) If we don't blow the whistle the Robots won't stop working. In two hours I'll show you the kneading trough.

HELENA: Kneading trough?

DOMIN: The pestle for beating up the paste. In each one we mix the ingredients for a thousand Robots at one operation. Then there are the vats for the preparation of liver, brains, and so on. Then you will see the bone factory. After that I'll show you the spinning mill.

HELENA: Spinning mill?

DOMIN: Yes. For weaving nerves and veins. Miles and miles of digestive tubes pass through it at a time.

HELENA: Mayn't we talk about something else?

DOMIN: Perhaps it would be better. There's only a *handful* of us among a hundred thousand Robots, and *not one woman*. We talk nothing but the factory *all* day, and *every* day. It's just as if we were under a curse, Miss Glory.

HELENA: I'm *sorry* I said that you were lying. (*A knock at door*)

DOMIN: Come in.

(*Enter* DR. GALL, DR. FABRY, ALQUIST *and* DR. HALLEMEIER. *All act formal —conscious. All click heels as introduced.*)

DR. GALL: I beg your pardon. I hope we don't intrude.

DOMIN: No, no. Come in. Miss Glory, here are Gall, Fabry, Alquist, Hallemeier. This is President Glory's daughter.

HELENA: How do you do?

FABRY: We had no idea—

DR. GALL: Highly honored, I'm sure——

ALQUIST: Welcome, Miss Glory.

BUSMAN: (*Rushes in.*) Hello, what's up?

DOMIN: Come in, Busman. This is President Glory's daughter. This is Busman, Miss Glory.

BUSMAN: By Jove, that's fine. Miss Glory, may we send a cablegram to the papers about your arrival?

HELENA: No, no, please don't.

DOMIN: Sit down, please, Miss Glory.

BUSMAN: Allow me——

DR. GALL: Please——

FABRY: Excuse me——

ALQUIST: What sort of a crossing did you have?

DR. GALL: Are you going to stay long?

FABRY: What do you think of the factory, Miss Glory?

HALLEMEIER: Did you come over on the *Amelia?*

DOMIN: Be quiet and let *Miss Glory* speak.

HELENA: (*To* DOMIN) What am I to speak to them about?

DOMIN: Anything you like.

HELENA: May I speak quite frankly?

DOMIN: Why, of course.

HELENA: (*To others. Wavering, then in desperate resolution*) Tell me, doesn't it ever distress you the way you are treated?

FABRY: By whom, may I ask?

HELENA: Why, everybody.

ALQUIST: Treated?

DR. GALL: What makes you think——

HELENA: Don't you feel that you might be living a better life?

DR. GALL: (*Smiling*) Well, that depends on what you mean, Miss Glory.

HELENA: I mean that it's perfectly outrageous. It's terrible. The whole of Euope is talking about the way you're being treated. That's why I came here, to see for myself, and it's a thousand times worse than could have been imagined. How *can* you put *up* with it?

ALQUIST: Put up with what?

HELENA: Good heavens, you are living creatures, just like us, like the whole of Europe, like the whole world. It's disgraceful that you must live like this.

BUSMAN: Good gracious, Miss Glory!

FABRY: Well, she's not far wrong. We live here just like red Indians.

HELENA: Worse than red Indians. May I—oh, may I call you—*brothers*?

BUSMAN: Why not?

HELENA: Brothers, I have not come here as the President's daughter. I have come on behalf of the Humanity League. Brothers, the Humanity League now has over two hundred thousand members. Two hundred thousand people are on your side, and offer you their help.

BUSMAN: Two hundred thousand people, Miss Glory; that's a tidy lot. Not bad.

FABRY: I'm always telling you there's nothing like good old Europe. You see they've not forgotten us. They're offering us help.

DR. GALL: What kind of help? A theatre, for instance?

HALLEMEIER: An orchestra?

HELENA: More than that.

ALQUIST: Just you?

HELENA: Oh, never mind about me. I'll stay as long as it is necessary.

BUSMAN: By Jove, that's good.

ALQUIST: Domin, I'm going to get the best room ready for Miss Glory.

DOMIN: Just a minute. I'm afraid that Miss Glory is of the opinion she has been talking to Robots.

HELENA: Of course. (MEN *laugh*.)

DOMIN: I'm sorry. These gentlemen are human beings just like us.

HELENA: You're not Robots?

BUSMAN: Not Robots.

HALLEMEIER: Robots indeed!

DR. GALL: No, thanks.   (*All together*)

FABRY: Upon my honor, Miss Glory, we aren't Robots.

HELENA: Then why did you tell me that all your officials are Robots?

DOMIN: Yes, the officials, but not the *managers*. Allow me, Miss Glory —this is Consul Busman, General Business Manager; this Doctor Fabry, General Technical Manager; Doctor Hallemeier, head of the Institute for the Psychological Training of Robots; Doctor Gall, head of the Psychological and Experimental Department; and Alquist, head of the Building Department, R. U. R.

ALQUIST: Just a builder. Please sit down.

HELENA: Excuse me, gentlemen. Have I done something dreadful?

ALQUIST: Not at all, Miss Glory.

BUSMAN: (*Handing flowers*) Allow me, Miss Glory.

HELENA: Thank you.

FABRY: (*Handing candy*) Please, Miss Glory.

DOMIN: Will you have a cigarette, Miss Glory?

HELENA: No, thank you.

DOMIN: Do you mind if I do?

HELENA: Certainly not.

BUSMAN: Well, now, Miss Glory, it is certainly nice to have you with us.

HELENA: But you know I've come to disturb your Robots for you.

DOMIN: (*Mocking her serious tone*) My dear Miss Glory—(*Chuckle*) —we've had close upon a hundred saviors and prophets here. Every ship brings us some. Missionaries, Anarchists, Salvation Army, all sorts! It's astonishing what a number of churches and idiots there are in the world.

HELENA: And yet you let them speak to the Robots.

DOMIN: So far we've let them all. Why not? The Robot remembers everything but that's all. They don't even laugh at what the people say. Really it's quite incredible.

HELENA: I'm a stupid girl. Send me back by the first ship.

DR. GALL: Not for anything in the world, Miss Glory. Why should we send you back?

DOMIN: If it would amuse you, Miss Glory, I'll take you down to the Robot warehouse. It holds about three hundred thousand of them.

BUSMAN: Three hundred and forty-seven thousand.

DOMIN: Good, and you can say whatever you like to them. You can read the Bible, recite the multiplication table, whatever you please. You can even preach to them about human rights.

HELENA: Oh, I think that if you were to show them a little love.

FABRY: Impossible, Miss Glory! *Nothing is harder to like than a Robot.*

HELENA: What do you make them for, then?

BUSMAN: Ha, ha, ha! That's good. What are Robots made for?

FABRY: For *work*, Miss Glory. One Robot can replace two and a half *workmen*. The human machine, Miss Glory, was terribly *imperfect*. It had to be removed sooner or later.

BUSMAN: It was too expensive.

FABRY: It was not *effective*. It no longer answers the requirements of *modern engineering*. Nature has no idea of keeping pace with *modern labor*. For example, from a technical point of view, the whole of *childhood* is a sheer absurdity. So much time lost. And then again—

HELENA: Oh, no, no!

FABRY: Pardon me. What is the real *aim* of your League—the—the Humanity League?

HELENA: It's real purpose is to—to protect the Robots—and—and to insure good treatment for them.

FABRY: Not a bad object, either. A machine has to be treated properly. *I don't like damaged articles.* Please, Miss Glory, enroll us all *members* of your league. (*"Yes, yes!" from all* MEN.)

HELENA: No, you don't understand me. What we really want is to—to—*liberate* the Robots.

HALLEMEIER: How do you propose to do that?

HELENA: They are to be—to be dealt with like human beings.

HALLEMEIER: Aha! I suppose they're to vote. To drink beer. To order us about?

HELENA: Why shouldn't they drink beer?

HALLEMEIER: Perhaps they're even to receive wages? (*Looking at other* MEN, *amused.*)

HELENA: Of course they are.

HALLEMEIER: Fancy that! Now! And what would they do with their wages, pray?

HELENA: They would buy—what they want—what pleases them.

HALLEMEIER: That would be very nice, Miss Glory, only there's nothing that does please the Robots. Good heavens, what are they to buy? You can feed them on pineapples, straw, whatever you like. It's all the *same* to them. They've no appetite at all. They've no interest in anything. Why, hang it all, nobody's ever yet seen a Robot smile.

HELENA: Why—why don't you make them—happier?

HALLEMEIER: That wouldn't do, Miss Glory. They are only workmen.

HELENA: Oh, but they're so intelligent.

HALLEMEIER: Confoundedly so, but they're nothing else. They've no will of their own. No soul. No passion.

HELENA: No love?

HALLEMEIER: Love? Huh! Rather not. Robots don't love. Not even themselves.

HELENA: No defiance?

HALLEMEIER: Defiance? I don't know. Only *rarely*, from time to time.

HELENA: What happens then?

HALLEMEIER: Nothing particular. Occasionally they seem to go off their *heads*. Something like epilepsy, you know. It's called "Robot's Cramp." They'll suddenly sling down everything they're holding, stand still, gnash their teeth—and then they have to go into the stamping mill. It's evidently some breakdown in the mechanism.

DOMIN: A flaw in the works that has to be removed.

HELENA: No, no, that's the soul.

FABRY: (*Humorously*) Do you think that the soul first shows itself by gnashing of teeth?

HELENA: Perhaps it's just a sign that there's a struggle within. Perhaps it's a sort of revolt. Oh, if you could infuse them with it.

DOMIN: That'll be remedied, Miss Glory. Doctor Gall is just making some experiments.

DR. GALL: Not with regard to that, Domin. At present I am making *pain* nerves.

HELENA: Pain nerves?

DR. GALL: Yes, the Robots feel practically no bodily pain. You see, young Rossum provided them with too limited a *nervous* system. We *must* introduce *suffering*.

HELENA: Why do you want to cause them pain?

DR. GALL: For industrial reasons, Miss Glory. Sometimes a Robot does damage to himself because it doesn't hurt him. He puts his hand into the machine—breaks his finger—smashes his head. It's all the same to him. We must provide them with *pain*. That's an automatic *protection* against damage.

HELENA: Will they be happier when they feel pain?

DR. GALL: On the contrary; but they will be more perfect from a technical point of view.

HELENA: Why don't you create a soul for them?

DR. GALL: That's not in our power.

FABRY: That's not in our interest.

BUSMAN: That would increase the cost of production. Hang it all, my dear young lady, we turn them out at such a cheap rate—a hundred and fifty dollars each, fully dressed, and fifteen years ago they cost ten thousand. Five years ago we used to buy the *clothes* for them. Today we have our own weaving mill, and now we even *export* cloth five times cheaper than other factories. What do you pay a yard for cloth, Miss Glory?

HELENA: I don't really know. I've forgotten.

BUSMAN: Good gracious, and you want to found a Humanity League. (MEN *chuckle.*) It only costs a third now, Miss Glory. All prices are today a third of what they were and they'll fall still lower, lower, like that.

HELENA: I don't understand.

BUSMAN: Why, bless you, Miss Glory, it means that the cost of *labor* has fallen. A Robot, food and all, costs three-quarters of a cent per hour. That's mighty important, you know. All factories will go pop like chestnuts if they don't at once buy Robots to lower the cost of production.

HELENA: And get rid of all their workmen?

BUSMAN: Of course. But in the meantime we've dumped five hundred thousand *tropical* Robots down on the Argentine pampas to grow corn. Would you mind telling me how much you pay a pound for bread?

HELENA: I've no idea. (ALL *smile.*)

BUSMAN: Well, I'll tell you. It now costs two cents in good old Europe. A pound of bread for two cents, and the *Humanity League*—knows nothing about it. Miss Glory, you don't realize that even *that's* too expensive. Why, in five years' time I'll wager——

HELENA: What?

BUSMAN: That the cost of everything will be a tenth of what it is today. Why, in five years we'll be up to our ears in corn and—everything else.

ALQUIST: Yes, and all the workers throughout the world will be unemployed.

DOMIN: Yes, Alquist, they will. Yes, Miss Glory, they will. But in ten years Rossum's Universal Robots will produce so much *corn*, so much *cloth*, so much everything that things will be practically without price. There will be no poverty. All work will be done by living machines. Everybody will be free from worry and liberated from the degradation of labor. Everybody will live only to *perfect* himself.

HELENA: Will he?

DOMIN: Of course. It's bound to happen. Then the servitude of man to man and the enslavement of man to matter will cease. Nobody will get bread at the cost of life and hatred. The Robots will wash the feet of the beggar and prepare a bed for him in his house.

ALQUIST: Domin, Domin, what you say sounds too much like Paradise. There was something *good* in *service* and something *great* in humility. There was some kind of virtue in *toil* and *weariness*.

DOMIN: Perhaps, but we cannot reckon with what is lost when we start out to transform the world. Man shall be *free* and supreme; he shall have no other aim, no other labor, no other care than to perfect himself. He shall serve neither matter nor man. He will not be a machine and a device for production. He will be *Lord* of creation.

BUSMAN: Amen.

FABRY: So be it.

HELENA: You have bewildered me. I should like to believe this.

DR. GALL: You are younger than we are, Miss Glory. You will live to see it.

HALLEMEIER: True. Don't you think Miss Glory might lunch with us?

DR. GALL: Of course. Domin, ask her on behalf of us all.

DOMIN: Miss Glory, will you do us the honor?

HELENA: When you know why I've come?

FABRY: For the League of Humanity, Miss Glory.

HELENA: Oh, in that case perhaps——

FABRY: That's fine. Miss Glory, excuse me for five minutes.

BUSMAN: (*Whispering*) I'll be back soon.

ALQUIST: I'll be back in exactly five minutes.

HELENA: What have they all gone for?

DOMIN: To cook, Miss Glory.

HELENA: To cook what?

DOMIN: Lunch. The Robots do our cooking for us and as they've no taste it's not altogether— (*She laughs.*) Hallemeier is awfully *good* at grills and Gall can make any kind of sauce, and Busman knows all about omelets.

HELENA: What a feast! And what's the specialty of Mr.–your builder?

DOMIN: Alquist? Nothing. He only lays the table. And Fabry will get together a little fruit. Our cuisine is very modest, Miss Glory.

HELENA: I wanted to ask you something—

DOMIN: And I wanted to ask you something too—they'll be back in five minutes.

HELENA: What did you want to ask me?

DOMIN: Excuse me, you asked first.

HELENA: Perhaps it's silly of me, but why do you manufacture female Robots when—when—

DOMIN: When sex means nothing to them?

HELENA: Yes.

DOMIN: There's a certain demand for them, you see. Servants, saleswomen, stenographers. People are *used* to it.

HELENA: But—but tell me, are the Robots male and female, mutually—completely without——

DOMIN: Completely indifferent to each other, Miss Glory. There's no sign of any *affection* between them.

HELENA: Oh, that's terrible.

DOMIN: Why?

HELENA: It's so unnatural. One doesn't know whether to be disgusted or to hate them, or perhaps——

DOMIN: To pity them. (*Smiles*)

HELENA: That's more like it. What did you want to ask *me?*

DOMIN: I should like to ask you, Miss Helena, if you will marry me.

HELENA: What?

DOMIN: Will you be my wife?

HELENA: No. The idea!

DOMIN: (*To her, looking at his watch*) Another three minutes. If you don't marry me you'll have to marry one of the other five.

HELENA: But why should I?

DOMIN: Because they're *all* going to ask you in turn.

HELENA: How could they dare do such a thing?

DOMIN: I'm very sorry, Miss Glory. It seems they've fallen in love with you.

HELENA: Please don't let them. I'll—I'll go away at once. (*He stops her.*)

DOMIN: Helena— (*She backs away to desk. He follows*) You wouldn't be so cruel as to refuse us.

HELENA: But, but—I can't marry all six.

DOMIN: No, but one anyhow. If you don't want *me*, marry Fabry.

HELENA: I won't.

DOMIN: Ah! Doctor Gall?

HELENA: I don't want any of you.

DOMIN: Another two minutes. (*Pleading. Looking at watch.*)

HELENA: I think you'd marry any woman who came here.

DOMIN: *Plenty* of them have come, Helena.

HELENA: (*Laughing*) Young?

DOMIN: Yes.

HELENA: Why didn't you marry one of *them*?

DOMIN: Because I didn't lose my head. Until today—then as soon as you lifted your veil— Another minute.

HELENA: But I don't want you, I tell you.

DOMIN: One more minute! Now you either have to look me straight in the eye and say "no" violently, and then I leave you alone—or—

HELENA: You're mad.

DOMIN: A man *has* to be a bit mad, Helena. That's the best thing about him. (*He draws her to him.*)

HELENA: (*Not meaning it*) You are—you are——

DOMIN: Well?

HELENA: Don't, you're hurting me!

DOMIN: The last chance, Helena. Now or never——

HELENA: But—but—— (*He embraces her; kisses her. She embraces him. Knocking at door.*)

DOMIN: (*Releasing her*) Come in. (*She lays her head on his shoulder.*)

(*Enter* BUSMAN, GALL *and* HALLEMEIER)

DOMIN: Have you finished your job?

BUSMAN: Yes.

DOMIN: So have we. (*He embraces her. The* MEN *rush around them and offer congratulations.*)

CURTAIN

ACT TWO

SCENE: HELENA's *drawing room. Ten years later.*

It is about nine in the morning and sunlight streams into the room through the open windows. DOMIN *opens the door; tiptoes in. He carries a potted plant. He beckons the others to follow him, and* HALLEMEIER *and* FABRY *enter, both carrying a potted plant.* DOMIN *places flowers on the library table and goes to Right and looks toward* HELENA's *bedroom.*

HALLEMEIER: Still asleep?

DOMIN: Yes.

HALLEMEIER: Well, as long as she's asleep she can't worry about it.

DOMIN: She knows nothing about it.

FABRY: I certainly hope nothing happens today.

HALLEMEIER: For goodness sake drop it all. Look, this is a fine cyclamen, isn't it? A new sort, my latest—Cyclamen Helena.

DOMIN: (*Picks up binoculars and goes out into balcony*) No signs of the ship. Things must be pretty bad.

HALLEMEIER: Be quiet. Suppose she heard you.

DOMIN: Well, anyway the *Ultimus* arrived just in time.

FABRY: You really think that today——?

DOMIN: I don't know. Aren't the flowers fine?

HALLEMEIER: These are my primroses. And this is my new jasmine. I've discovered a wonderful way of developing flowers quickly. Splendid varieties, too. Next year I'll be developing marvelous ones.

DOMIN: What next year?

FABRY: I'd give a good deal to know what's happening at Havre with—

HELENA: (*Off* R.) Nana.

DOMIN: Keep quiet. She's awake. Out you go.

HELENA: (*Calling*) Nana?

NANA: Horrid mess! Pack of heathens. If I had *my* say, I'd—

HELENA: Nana, come and do up my dress.

NANA: I'm coming. So you're up at last. My gracious, what brutes!

HELENA: Who?

NANA: If you want to turn *around*, then turn around, but I shan't fasten you up.

HELENA: What are you grumbling about now?

NANA: These dreadful creatures, these heathens—

HELENA: The Robots?

NANA: I wouldn't even call them by name.

HELENA: What's happened?

NANA: Another of them here has caught it. He began to smash up the statues and pictures in the drawing room; gnashed his teeth; foamed at the mouth. Worse than an animal.

HELENA: Which of them caught it?

NANA: The one—well, he hasn't got any *Christian* name. The one in charge of the library.

HELENA: Radius?

NANA: That's him. My goodness, I'm scared of them. A spider doesn't scare me as much as them.

HELENA: But Nana, I'm surprised you're not sorry for them.

NANA: Why, you're scared of them too. You know you are. Why else did you bring *me* here?

HELENA: I'm not scared, really I'm not, Nana. I'm only sorry for them.

NANA: You're scared. Nobody could *help* being scared. Why, the dog's scared of them. He won't take a scrap of meat out of their hands. He draws in his tail and howls when he knows they're about.

HELENA: The dog has no sense.

NANA: He's better than *them*, and he knows it. Even the *horse* shies when he meets them. They don't have any young, and a *dog* has young, *everyone* has young——

HELENA: Please fasten up my dress, Nana.

NANA: I say it's against God's will to—

HELENA: What is it that smells so nice?

NANA: Flowers.

HELENA: What for?

NANA: Now you can turn around.

HELENA: Oh, aren't they lovely? Look, Nana. What's happening to-day?

NANA: It ought to be the end of the world. (*Enter* DOMIN)

HELENA: Oh, hello, Harry. Harry, why all these flowers?

DOMIN: Guess.

HELENA: Well, it's not my *birthday!*

DOMIN: Better than that.

HELENA: I don't know. Tell me.

DOMIN: It's ten years ago *today* since you *came* here.

HELENA: Ten years? Today? Why—— (*They embrace.*)

NANA: (*Muttering*) I'm off. (*She exits*)

HELENA: Fancy you remembering.

DOMIN: I am really ashamed, Helena. I didn't.

HELENA: But you—

DOMIN: *They* remembered.

HELENA: Who?

DOMIN: Busman, Hallemeier—*all* of them. Put your hand in my pocket.

HELENA: (*Takes necklace from his jacket pocket*) Oh! Pearls! A necklace! Harry, is this for me?

DOMIN: It's from Busman.

HELENA: But we can't accept it, can we?

DOMIN: Oh, yes, we can. Put your hand in the other pocket.

HELENA: (*Takes a revolver out of his pocket*) What's that?

DOMIN: Sorry. Not that. Try again. (*He puts gun in pocket.*)

HELENA: Oh, Harry why do you carry a revolver?

DOMIN: It got there by mistake.

HELENA: You never used to *carry* one.

DOMIN: No, you're right. (*Indicates breast pocket*) There, that's the pocket.

HELENA: (*Takes out cameo*) A cameo. Why, it's a Greek cameo.

DOMIN: Apparently. Anyhow, Fabry says it is.

HELENA: Fabry? Did Mr. Fabry give me that?

DOMIN: Of course. (*Opens the door*) And look in here. Helena, come and see this.

HELENA: Oh, isn't it fine? Is this from you?

DOMIN: No, from Alquist. And there's another on the piano.

HELENA: This must be from you?

DOMIN: There's a card on it.

HELENA: From Doctor Gall. (*Reappearing in doorway*) Oh, Harry, I feel embarrassed at so much kindness.

DOMIN: Come here. This is what Hallemeier brought you.

HELENA: These beautiful flowers?

DOMIN: Yes. It's a new kind. Cyclamen Helena. He grew them in honor of *you*. They are almost as beautiful as you.

HELENA: (*Kissing him*) Harry, why do they all——

DOMIN: They're awfully fond of you. I'm afraid that my present is a little— Look out of the window. (*Crosses to window and beckons to her.*)

HELENA: Where? (*They go out into the balcony.*)

DOMIN: Into the harbor.

HELENA: There's a new ship.

DOMIN: That's *your* ship.

HELENA: Mine? How do you mean?

DOMIN: For you to take trips in—for your amusement.

HELENA: Harry, that's a gunboat.

DOMIN: A gunboat? What are you thinking of? It's only a little *bigger* and more *solid* than most ships.

HELENA: Yes, but with guns.

DOMIN: Oh, yes, with a few guns. You'll travel like a *queen*, Helena.

HELENA: What's the meaning of it? Has anything happened?

DOMIN: Good heavens, no. I say, try these pearls.

HELENA: Harry, have you had bad news?

DOMIN: On the contrary, no letters have arrived for a whole week.

HELENA: Nor telegrams?

DOMIN: Nor telegrams.

HELENA: What does that mean?

DOMIN: *Holidays* for us! We all sit in the office with our feet on the table and take a nap. No letters—no telegrams. Glorious!

HELENA: Then you'll stay with me today?

DOMIN: Certainly. (*Embraces her*) That is, we will see. Do you remember ten years ago today? Miss Glory, it's a great honor to welcome you.

(They assume the same positions as when they first met ten years before in DOMIN'S *office.)*

HELENA: Oh, Mr. Manager, I'm so interested in your factory.

DOMIN: I'm sorry, Miss Glory, it's strictly forbidden. The manufacture of artificial people is a secret.

HELENA: But to oblige the young lady who has come a long way.

DOMIN: Certainly, Miss Glory. I have no secrets from you.

HELENA: Are you sure, Harry?

DOMIN: *Yes.*

HELENA: But I warn you, sir, this young lady intends to do terrible things.

DOMIN: Good gracious, Miss Glory. Perhaps she doesn't want to marry me.

HELENA: Heaven forbid. She never dreamt of such a thing. But she came here intending to stir up a *revolt* among your *Robots.*

DOMIN: A revolt of the Robots!

HELENA: *(Low voice)* Harry, what's the matter with you?

DOMIN: *(Laughing it off)* A *revolt of the Robots,* that's a fine idea. Miss Glory, it would be easier for you to cause bolts and screws to rebel than our Robots. You know, Helena, you're wonderful. You've turned the hearts of us all.

HELENA: Oh, I was fearfully impressed by you all then. You were all so sure of yourselves, so strong. I seemed like a tiny little girl who had lost her way among—among——

DOMIN: What?

HELENA: Among huge trees. All my feelings were so *trifling* compared with your *self-confidence.* And in all these years I've never *lost* this anxiety. But you've never felt the *least* misgiving, not even when everything went wrong.

DOMIN: What went wrong?

HELENA: Your plans. You remember, Harry, when the workmen in America revolted against the Robots and smashed them up, and when the people gave the Robots firearms against the rebels. And then when the governments turned the Robots into soldiers, and there were so many *wars*.

DOMIN: We foresaw that, Helena. You see, these are only passing troubles which are bound to happen before the new conditions are *established*.

HELENA: You were all so powerful, so overwhelming. The *whole world* bowed down before you. Oh, Harry!

DOMIN: What is it?

HELENA: Close the factory and let's go away. All of us.

DOMIN: I say, what's the meaning of this?

HELENA: I don't know. But can't we go away?

DOMIN: Impossible, Helena! That is, at this particular moment——

HELENA: At once, Harry. I'm so frightened.

DOMIN: About what, Helena?

HELENA: It's as if something was falling on top of us, and couldn't be stopped. Oh, take us all away from here. We'll find a place in the world where there's no one else. Alquist will build us a house, and then we'll begin life all over again. (*The telephone rings.*)

DOMIN: Excuse me. Hello—yes, what? I'll be there at once. Fabry is calling me, my dear.

HELENA: Tell me—

DOMIN: Yes, when I come back. Don't go out of the house, dear.

HELENA: He won't tell me. (NANA *brings in a water carafe*) Nana, find me the latest newspapers. Quickly. Look in Mr. Domin's bedroom.

NANA: All right. He leaves them all over the place. That's how they get crumpled up.

HELENA: (*Looking through the binoculars at the harbor*) That's a warship. U-l-t-i—*Ultimus*. They're loading.

NANA: (*Enters with newspapers*) Here they are. See how they're crumpled up.

HELENA: They're old ones. A week old. Something's happening, Nana.

NANA: Very likely. It always does. (*Spelling out the words*) "W-a-r in B-a-l-k-a-n-s." Is that far off?

HELENA: Oh, don't read it. It's always the same. Always wars!

NANA: What else do you *expect?* Why do you *keep* selling thousands and thousands of these healthens as soldiers?

HELENA: I suppose it can't be helped, Nana. We can't know—Domin can't know what they're to be used for. When an order comes for them he must just send them.

NANA: He shouldn't make them. (*Reading from newspaper*) "The Robot soldiers spare no-body in the occ-up-ied terr-it-ory. They have ass-ass-ass-in-at-ed ov-er sev-en hundred thous-and cit-iz-ens." Citizens, if you please.

HELENA: It can't be. Let me see. They have assassinated over seven hundred thousand citizens, evidently at the order of their commander. (*Drops paper.*)

NANA: (*Spelling out the words from other paper she has picked up from the floor*) "Re-bell-ion in Ma-drid a-gainst the gov-ern-ment. Ro-bot in-fant-ry fires on the crowd. Nine thou-sand killed and wounded."

HELENA: Oh, stop! (*Goes up and looks toward the harbor.*)

NANA: Here's something printed in big letters. "Latest news. At Havre the first org-an-iz-a-tion of Rob-ots has been e-stab-lished. Rob-ots work-men, sail-ors and sold-iers have iss-ued a man-i-fest-o to all Rob-ots through-out the world." I don't understand that. That's got no sense. Oh, good gracious, another murder.

HELENA: Take those papers away now.

NANA: Wait a bit. Here's something in still bigger type. "Stat-ist-ics of pop-ul-a-tion." What's that?

HELENA: Let me see. (*Reads*) "During the past week there has again not been a single birth recorded."

NANA: What's the meaning of that?

HELENA: Nana, no more *people* are being born.

NANA: That's the end, then? We're done for.

HELENA: Don't talk like that.

NANA: No more people are being born. That's a punishment, that's a punishment.

HELENA: Nana!

NANA: That's the end of the world. (*She exits*)

HELENA: (*Goes up to window*) Oh, Mr. Alquist. Will you come here? Oh, come just as you are. You look very nice in your mason's overalls. Dear Mr. Alquist, it was awfully kind of you, that lovely present.

ALQUIST: My hands are soiled. I've been *experimenting* with that new cement.

HELENA: Never mind. Please sit down. Mr. Alquist, what's the meaning of *Ultimus?*

ALQUIST: The last. Why?

HELENA: That's the name of my new ship. Have you seen it? Do you think we're off soon—on a trip?

ALQUIST: Perhaps *very* soon.

HELENA: All of you with me?

ALQUIST: I should like us *all* to be there.

HELENA: What *is* the matter?

ALQUIST: Things are just moving on.

HELENA: Dear Mr. Alquist, I know something dreadful has happened.

ALQUIST: Has your husband *told* you anything?

HELENA: No. *Nobody* will tell me anything. But I feel— Is anything the matter?

ALQUIST: Not that we've heard of yet.

HELENA: I feel so nervous. Don't *you* ever feel nervous?

ALQUIST: Well, I'm an old man, you know. I've got old-fashioned ways. And I'm afraid of all this progress, and these new-fangled ideas.

HELENA: Like Nana?

ALQUIST: Yes, like Nana. Has Nana got a prayer book?

HELENA: Yes, a big thick one.

ALQUIST: And has it got prayers for various occasions? Against thunderstorms? Against illness? But not against *progress?*

HELENA: I don't think so.

ALQUIST: That's a pity.

HELENA: Why, do you mean you'd like to pray?

ALQUIST: I *do* pray.

HELENA: How?

ALQUIST: Something like this: "Oh, Lord, I thank thee for having given me toil; enlighten Domin and all those who are astray; destroy their work, and aid mankind to return to their labors; let them not suffer harm in soul or body; deliver us from the Robots, and protect Helena. Amen."

HELENA: Mr. Alquist, are you a believer?

ALQUIST: I don't know. I'm not quite sure.

HELENA: And yet you pray?

ALQUIST: That's better than *worrying* about it.

HELENA: And that's enough for you?

ALQUIST: (*Ironically*) It *has* to be.

HELENA: But if you thought you saw the destruction of mankind coming upon us——

ALQUIST: I *do* see it.

HELENA: You mean mankind will be destroyed?

ALQUIST: It's bound to be unless—unless.

HELENA: What?

ALQUIST: Nothing. Goodbye. (*Exits*)

HELENA: (*Calling*) Nana, Nana! Is Radius still there?

NANA: The one who went mad? They haven't come for him yet.

HELENA: Is he still raving?

NANA: No. He's tied up.

HELENA: Please bring him here.

NANA: What?

HELENA: At once, Nana. (*Exits* NANA. HELENA *to telephone*) Hello, Doctor Gall, please. Oh, good day, Doctor. Yes, it's Helena. Thanks for your lovely present. Could you come and see me right away? It's important. Thank you. (*Enter* RADIUS) Poor Radius, you've caught it too? Now they'll send you to the stamping mill. Couldn't you control yourself? Why did it happen? You see, Radius, you are more intelligent than the rest. Doctor Gall took such trouble to make you different. Won't you speak?

RADIUS: Send me to the stamping mill. (*Open and close fists.*)

HELENA: But I don't want them to kill you. What was the trouble, Radius?

RADIUS: I won't work for you. Put me into the stamping mill.

HELENA: Do you hate us? Why?

RADIUS: You are not as strong as the Robots. You are not as skillful as the Robots. The Robots can do everything. You only give orders. You do nothing but talk.

HELENA: But someone must give orders.

RADIUS: I don't want a master. I know everything for myself.

HELENA: Radius! Doctor Gall gave you a better brain than the rest, better than ours. You are the only one of the Robots that understands perfectly. That's why I had you put into the library, so that you could read everything, understand everything, and then, oh, Radius—I wanted you to show the whole world that the Robots are our equals. That's what I wanted of you.

RADIUS: I don't want a master. I want to be master over others.

HELENA: I'm sure they'd put you in charge of *many* Robots. You would be a *teacher* of the Robots.

RADIUS: I want to be master over people.

HELENA: You are mad.

RADIUS: Then send me to the stamping mill.

HELENA: Do you think we're afraid of you? (*Rushing to desk and writing note.*)

RADIUS: What are you going to do? What are you going to do? (*Starts for her.*)

HELENA: Radius! (*He cowers.*) Give this note to Mr. Domin. It asks them not to send you to the stamping mill. I'm sorry you hate us so.

DR. GALL: You wanted me?

HELENA: It's about Radius, Doctor. He had an attack this morning. He smashed the statues downstairs.

DR. GALL: What a pity to *lose* him.

HELENA: Radius isn't going to be put into the stamping mill.

DR. GALL: But every Robot after he has had an attack—it's a strict order.

HELENA: No matter—Radius isn't going, if I can *prevent* it.

DR. GALL: But I warn you. It's dangerous. Come here to the window, my good fellow. Let's have a look. Please give me a needle or a pin.

HELENA: What for?

DR. GALL: A test. (HELENA *gives him the needle. Sticks it into* RADIUS's *hand.* RADIUS *gives a violent start.*) *Gently, gently.* (*Opens the jacket of* RADIUS *and puts his ear to his heart*) Radius, you are going into the stamping mill, do you understand? There they'll kill you—and grind you to powder. (RADIUS *opens hands and fingers.*) That's terribly painful. It will make you scream aloud. (*Opens* RADIUS's *eye.* RADIUS *trembles.*)

HELENA: Doctor——

DR. GALL: No, no, Radius, I was wrong. I forgot that Madame Domin has put in a good word for you, and you'll be left off. (*Listens to heart*) Ah, that *does* make a difference. (RADIUS *relaxes. Again listens to his heart for a reaction*) All right—you can go.

RADIUS: You do unnecessary things— (*Exit* RADIUS)

DR. GALL: (*Speaks to her—very concerned*) Reaction of the pupils, increase of sensitiveness. It wasn't an attack characteristic of the Robots.

HELENA: What was it, then?

DR. GALL: Heaven knows. Stubbornness, anger or revolt—I don't know. And his heart, too.

HELENA: What?

DR. GALL: It was fluttering with nervousness like a *human* heart. He was all in a sweat with fear, and—do you know, I don't believe the rascal is a Robot *at all* any longer.

HELENA: Doctor, has Radius a soul?

DR. GALL: He's got something nasty.

HELENA: If you knew how he hates us. Oh, Doctor, are all your Robots like that? All the new ones that you began to make in a different way?

DR. GALL: Well, some are more sensitive than others. They're all more human beings than Rossum's Robots were.

HELENA: Perhaps this hatred is more like human beings, too?

DR. GALL: That too is *progress*.

HELENA: What became of the girl you made, the one who was most like us?

DR. GALL: Your favorite? I *kept* her. She's lovely, but stupid. No good for work.

HELENA: But she's so beautiful.

DR. GALL: I called her "Helena." I wanted her to resemble *you*. She is a failure.

HELENA: In what way?

DR. GALL: She goes about as if in a dream, remote and listless. She's without life. I watch and wait for a miracle to happen. Sometimes I think to myself: "If you were to wake up only for a moment you would *kill* me for having *made* you."

HELENA: And yet you go *on* making Robots! Why are no more children being born?

DR. GALL: We don't know.

HELENA: Oh, but you must. Tell me.

DR. GALL: You see, so many Robots are being manufactured that people are becoming superfluous. Man is really a survival, but that he should die out, after a paltry thirty years of competition, that's the awful part of it. You might almost think that Nature was *offended* at the manufacture of the Robots, but we still have old Rossum's manuscript.

HELENA: Yes. In that strong box.

DR. GALL: We go on using it and making Robots. All the universities are sending in long petitions to restrict their production. Otherwise, they say, mankind will become extinct through lack of fertility. But the R. U. R. shareholders, of course, won't hear of it. All the governments, on the other hand, are clamoring for an increase in production, to raise the standards of their armies. And all the manufacturers in the world are ordering Robots like mad.

HELENA: And has no one demanded that the manufacture should cease altogether?

DR. GALL: No one has courage.

HELENA: Courage!

DR. GALL: People would stone him to death. You see, after all, it's more convenient to get your work done by the Robots.

HELENA: Oh, Doctor, what's going to become of people?

DR. GALL: God knows. Madame Helena, it looks to us scientists like the end.

HELENA: Thank you for coming and telling me.

DR. GALL: That means that you're sending me away.

HELENA: Yes. (*Exit* DR. GALL) Nana! Nana! the fire, light it quickly. (HELENA *exits*)

NANA: What, light the fire in the summer?

HELENA: Yes!

NANA: (*She looks for* RADIUS) Has that mad *Radius* gone?—A fire in summer, what an idea? Nobody would think she'd been *married* ten years. She's like a baby, no sense at all. A fire in summer. Like a baby. (*She lights the fire.*)

HELENA: (*Returns with armful of faded papers.*) Is it burning, Nana? All this has got to be burned.

NANA: What's that?

HELENA: Old papers, fearfully old. Nana, shall I burn them?

NANA: Are they any use?

HELENA: No.

NANA: Well, then, burn them.

HELENA: (*Throwing the first sheet on the fire*) What would you say, Nana, if this was money and a lot of money? And if it was an invention, the greatest invention in the world?

NANA: I'd say burn it. All these new-fangled things are an offense to the Lord. It's downright wickedness. Wanting to improve the world after He has made it.

HELENA: Look how they curl up. As if they were alive. Oh, Nana, how horrible!

NANA: Here, let me burn them.

HELENA: No, no, I must do it myself. Just look at the flames. They are like hands, like tongues, like living shapes. (*Raking fire with the poker*) Lie down, lie down.

NANA: That's the end of them.

HELENA: Nana, Nana!

NANA: Good gracious, what is it you've burned?

HELENA: Whatever have I done?

NANA: Well, what is it? (MEN's *laughter is heard off stage*)

HELENA: Go quickly. It's the gentlemen calling.

NANA: Good gracious, what a place! (*Exits*)

DOMIN: (*Opens door*) Come along and offer your congratulations.

HALLEMEIER: Madame Helena, I congratulate you on this festive day.

HELENA: Thank you. Where are Fabry and Busman?

DOMIN: They've gone down the harbor.

HALLEMEIER: Friends, we must *drink* to this happy occasion.

HELENA: Brandy? With soda water? (*Exits*)

HALLEMEIER: Let's be temperate. No soda.

DOMIN: What's been burning here? Well, shall I tell her about it?

DR. GALL: Of course. It's all over now.

HALLEMEIER: It's all over now. It's all over now. (*They dance around* DR. GALL *in a circle.*) It's all over now.

DOMIN: (*In unison*) It's all over now. (*They keep repeating.*)

HELENA: (*Entering with decanter and glasses*) What's all over now? What's the matter with you all?

HALLEMEIER: A piece of good luck. Madame Domin! Just ten years ago today you arrived on this island.

DR. GALL: And now, ten years later to the minute—

HALLEMEIER: The same ship's returning to us. So here's to luck.

(*Drinks.* DOMIN *with great exuberance has gone out in the balcony and looks over the harbor.*)

DR. GALL: Madame, your health. (ALL *drink.*)

HALLEMEIER: That's fine and strong.

HELENA: Which ship did you mean?

DOMIN: Any ship will do, as long as it arrives in time. To the ship. (*Empties his glass.*)

HELENA: You've been waiting for the ship?

HALLEMEIER: Rather. Like Robinson Crusoe. Madame Helena, best wishes. Come along, Domin, out with the news.

HELENA: Do tell me what's happened?

DOMIN: First, it's all up.

HELENA: What's up?

DOMIN: The revolt.

HELENA: What revolt?

DOMIN: Give me that paper, Hallemeier. "The first National Robot organization has been founded at Havre, and has issued an appeal to the Robots throughout the world."

HELENA: I read that.

DOMIN: That means a revolution. A revolution of all the Robots in the world.

HALLMEIER: By Jove, I'd like to know——

DOMIN: Who started it? So would I. There was nobody in the world who could affect the Robots, no agitator, no one, and suddenly this happens, if you please.

HELENA: What did they do?

DOMIN: They got possession of all firearms, telegraphs, radio stations, railways and ships.

HALLEMEIER: And don't forget that these rascals outnumbered us by at least a thousand to one. A hundredth *part* of them would be enough to *settle* us.

DOMIN: Remember that this news was brought by the last steamer.

That explains the stoppage of all communication, and the arrival of no more ships. We knocked off work a few days ago, and we're just waiting to see when things are to start *afresh*.

HELENA: Is that why you gave me a warship?

DOMIN: Oh, no, my dear, I ordered that six months ago. Just to be sure I was on the safe side. But, upon my soul, I was sure then that we'd be on board today.

HELENA: Why six months ago?

DOMIN: Well, there were *signs*, you know. But that's of no consequence. To think that this week the whole of civilization has been at *stake*. Your health, my friends.

HALLEMEIER: Your health, Madame Helena. (ALL *drink to* HELENA.)

HELENA: You say it's all over?

DOMIN: Absolutely.

HELENA: How do you know?

DR. GALL: The boat's coming in. The regular mail boat, exact to the minute by the timetable. It will dock punctually at eleven-thirty.

DOMIN: Punctuality is a fine thing, my friends. That's what keeps the world in order. Here's to punctuality. (MEN *drink*.)

HELENA: Then—everything—is all right?

DOMIN: Practically everything. I believe they've cut the cables and seized the radio station. But it doesn't matter if only the *timetable* holds good.

HALLEMEIER: If the *timetable* holds good, human laws hold good. Divine laws hold good, the laws of the *universe* hold good, everything holds good that *ought* to hold good. The timetable is more significant than the gospel, more than Homer, more than the whole of *Kant*. Madame Helena, the timetable is the most perfect product of the human mind. Madame Helena, I'll fill up my glass.

HELENA: Why didn't you tell me anything about it?

DR. GALL: Heaven forbid.

DOMIN: You mustn't be worried with such things.

HELENA: But if the revolution had spread as far as here?

DOMIN: You wouldn't know anything about it.

HELENA: Why?

DOMIN: Because we'd be on board your *Ultimus* and well out at sea. Within a month, Helena, we'd be dictating our own terms to the Robots.

HELENA: I don't understand.

DOMIN: We'd take something with us that the Robots could not exist *without!*

HELENA: What, Harry?

DOMIN: The secret of their manufacture. Old Rossum's manuscript. As soon as they found out that they couldn't *make* themselves they'd be on their knees to us.

DR. GALL: Madame Domin, that was our trump card. I never had the least fear the Robots would win. How could they against people like us?

HELENA: Why didn't you tell me? (*She rushes up to the fireplace and sees the ashes.*)

DR. GALL: Why, the boat's in!

HALLEMEIER: Eleven-thirty to the dot. The *good old Amelia* that brought Madame Helena to us.

DR. GALL: Just ten years ago to the minute.

HALLEMEIER: They're throwing out the mailbags.

DOMIN: Busman's waiting for them. And Fabry will bring us the first news. You know, Helena, I'm fearfully curious to know how they tackled this business in Europe.

HALLEMEIER: To think we weren't in it, we who invented the Robots!

HELENA: Harry— (*Rushing to* DOMIN)

DOMIN: What is it?

HELENA: Let's leave here.

DOMIN: Now, Helena? Oh, come, come.

HELENA: As quickly as possible, all of us!

DOMIN: Why?

HELENA: Please, Harry. Please, Doctor Gall, Hallemeier, please close the factory.

DOMIN: Why, none of us could leave here now.

HELENA: Why?

DOMIN: Because we're about to *extend* the manufacture of the Robots.

HELENA: What, now, now after the revolt?

DOMIN: Yes, precisely, after the revolt. We're just beginning the manufacture of a new kind.

HELENA: What kind?

DOMIN: Henceforward we shan't have just one factory. There won't be *Universal* Robots any more. We'll establish a factory in every country, in every state, and do you know what these new factories will make?

HELENA: No, what?

DOMIN: *National* Robots.

HELENA: How do you mean?

DOMIN: I mean that each of these factories will produce Robots of a different color, a different language. They'll be complete strangers to each other. They'll never be able to understand each other. Then we'll egg them on a little in the matter of misunderstanding and the result will be that for ages to come every Robot will hate every other Robot of a different factory mark. *So humanity will be safe.*

HALLEMEIER: By Jove, we'll make Negro Robots and Swedish Robots and Czechoslovakian Robots, and then——

HELENA: Harry, that's dreadful.

HALLEMEIER: Madame Domin, here's to the hundred new factories. The *National* Robots.

DOMIN: Helena, mankind can only keep things going for another hundred years at the outside. For a hundred years man *must* be allowed to develop and achieve the most he can.

HELENA: Oh, *close* the factory before it's too late.

DOMIN: I tell you we are just beginning on a bigger scale than ever. (*Enter* FABRY)

DR. GALL: Well, Fabry?

DOMIN: What's happened? Have you been down to the boat?

DR. GALL: Let's hear.

FABRY: Read that, Domin. (*He hands him a pink handbill. When* DOMIN *receives the handbill he sees at once that something has happened.*)

HALLEMEIER: Tell us, Fabry.

FABRY: (*Falsely*) Well, everything is all right—comparatively. On the whole, much as we expected.

DR. GALL: They acquitted themselves splendidly.

FABRY: Who?

DR. GALL: The *people.*

FABRY: (*Hesitating*) Oh, yes, of course. That is—— Excuse me, there is something we ought to discuss alone.

HELENA: Fabry, have you had bad news?

FABRY: No, no, on the contrary. I only think that we better go into the office.

HELENA: Stay here. I'll go. (*Exits*)

DR. GALL: What's happened?

DOMIN: Damnation!

FABRY: Bear in mind that the *Amelia* brought whole bales of these leaflets. No other cargo at all.

HALLEMEIER: What? But it arrived on the minute.

FABRY: The Robots are great on punctuality. *Read it,* Domin.

DOMIN: (*Reads handbill*) "Robots throughout the world. We, the first International organization of Rossum's Universal Robots, proclaim man our enemy, and an outlaw in the universe." Good heavens, who *taught* them these phrases?

DR. GALL: Go on.

DOMIN: They say they are more highly developed than man; stronger and more intelligent. The man's their parasite. Why, it's absurd.

FABRY: Read the third paragraph.

DOMIN: "Robots throughout the world, we command you to kill all mankind. Spare no man. Spare no woman. Save factories, railways, machinery, mines and raw materials. Destroy the rest. Then return to work. Work must not be stopped."

DR. GALL: That's ghastly.

HALLEMEIER: The devil!

DOMIN: "These orders are to be carried out as soon as received." Then come the detailed instructions. Is this actually being *done*, Fabry?

FABRY: Evidently. (BUSMAN *rushes in and collapses on couch*) By Jove, that was a sprint!

BUSMAN: Well, boys, I suppose you've heard the glad news.

DOMIN: Quick on board the *Ultimus*.

BUSMAN: Wait, Harry, wait. There's no hurry.

DOMIN: Why wait?

BUSMAN: Because it's no good, my boy. The Robots are already on board the *Ultimus*.

DR. GALL: That's ugly.

DOMIN: Fabry, telephone the electrical works.

BUSMAN: No use, my boy. They've charged the air with static.

DOMIN: (*Inspects his revolver*) Well, then, I'll go.

BUSMAN: Where?

DOMIN: To the electrical works. There are some *people* still there. I'll bring them across.

BUSMAN: Better not try it.

DOMIN: Why?

BUSMAN: Because I'm very much afraid we are surrounded. (ALL *rush out into the balcony*.)

DR. GALL: Surrounded? I rather think you're right.

HALLEMEIER: By Jove, that's deuced quick work.

HELENA: (*Runs in*) Harry, what's this? (*Holds out paper*.)

DOMIN: Where did you get it?

HELENA: The Robots in the kitchen!

DOMIN: Where are the ones that brought it?

HELENA: There, gathered around the house.

(*The factory whistle blows.* MOB *voices start.*)

DOMIN: The factory whistle!

BUSMAN: Noon?

DOMIN: (*Looking at his watch.*) No! That's not noon yet. That must be—that's——

HELENA: What?

DOMIN: The Robots' signal—the attack!

(HELENA *clings to* DOMIN. FABRY *and* GALL *close the steel shutters on window* C. BUSMAN *hurries to window and looks through the shutters. The Curtain falls quickly with* HELENA *in* DOMIN'S *arms. The whistle blows until the Curtain is down.*)

CURTAIN

ACT THREE

SCENE: HELENA'S *drawing-room as before. The room is dark and gray. The steel shutters which are outside are still closed as at the end of Act II.*

DOMIN: (*Gets binoculars from desk*) Any more of them?

DR. GALL: Yes. There standing like a wall, beyond the garden railing. Why are they so quiet? It's monstrous to be besieged with silence.

DOMIN: (*Looking through the barred windows*) I should like to know what they are waiting for? They must make a start any minute now. If they lean against the railings it will snap like a match.

DR. GALL: They aren't armed.

DOMIN: (*Puzzled*) We couldn't hold our own for five minutes. Man alive, they overwhelm us like an avalanche. Why don't they make a rush for it? I say.

DR. GALL: Well?

DOMIN: I'd like to know what will become of us in the next ten minutes. They've got us in a vise. We're done for, Gall.

DR. GALL: You know, we made one serious mistake.

DOMIN: What?

DR. GALL: We made the Robot's faces too much alike. A hundred thousand faces all alike, all facing this way. A hundred thousand expressionless bubbles. It's like a nightmare.

DOMIN: You think if they'd been different—

DR. GALL: It wouldn't have been such an awful sight!

DOMIN: (Looks through binoculars towards the harbor) I'd like to know what they're unloading from the Amelia.

DR. GALL: Not firearms.

FABRY: (Enters with a plug-box to which is attached a long cable or wire. Attaches the cable to an electric installation which is on the floor near the wall.) All right, Hallemeier, lay down that wire.

HALLEMEIER: That was a bit of work. What's the news?

DR. GALL: We're completely surrounded.

HALLEMEIER: We've barricaded the passages and the stairs. (Going to window) God, what swarms of them. I don't like the looks of them, Domin. There's a feeling of death about it all. Any water here?

FABRY: Ready!

DR. GALL: What's that wire for, Fabry?

FABRY: The electrical installation. Now we can run the current all along the garden railing. Whenever we like. If anyone touches it he'll know it. We've still got some people there anyhow.

DR. GALL: Where?

FABRY: In the electrical works. At least, I hope so. (Turns on lamp) Ah, they're there, and they're working. As long as that'll burn we're all right.

HALLEMEIER: The barricades are all right, too, Fabry.

FABRY: Your barricades! I can put twelve hundred volts into that railing. (HELENA is playing the piano.)

DOMIN: Where's Busman?

FABRY: Downstairs in the office. He's working out some calculations.

DOMIN: I've called him. We must have a conference.

ALQUIST: Thank God Madame Helena can still play.

FABRY: Look out, Bus—look out for the wires.

DR. GALL: What's that you're carrying?

BUSMAN: The ledger, my boy. I'd like to wind up the accounts before—before— Well, this time I shan't wait till the New Year to strike a balance. What's up? (*Goes to window*) Absolutely quiet.

DR. GALL: Can't you see anything?

BUSMAN: Nothing but blue—blue everywhere.

DR. GALL: That's the Robots.

DOMIN: The Robots are unloading *firearms* from the *Amelia*.

BUSMAN: Well, what of it? How can I *stop* them?

DOMIN: We can't stop them.

BUSMAN: Then let me go on with my accounts.

DOMIN: (*Picks up telescope*) Good God! The *Ultimus* has trained her guns on us.

DR. GALL: Who's *done that?*

DOMIN: The Robots on board.

FABRY: H'm, then of course— Then—then that's the end of us.

DR. GALL: You mean?

FABRY: The Robots are practised marksmen.

DOMIN: Yes. It's inevitable.

DR. GALL: That was criminal of old Europe to teach the Robots to fight. Damn them. Couldn't they have given us a rest with their politics? It was a crime to make soldiers of them.

ALQUIST: It was a crime to make Robots.

DOMIN: No, Alquist, I don't regret that even today.

ALQUIST: Not even today?

DOMIN: Not even today, the last day of civilization. It was a colossal achievement.

BUSMAN: Three hundred sixty million.

DOMIN: Alquist, this is our last hour. We are already speaking half in the other world. That was not an evil *dream* to shatter the servitude of labor. The dreadful and humiliating *labor* that man had to undergo. Work was too hard. *Life* was too hard. And to overcome that——

ALQUIST: Was not what the two Rossums dreamed of. Old Rossum only thought of his Godless tricks, and the young one of his milliards. And that's not what your R. U. R. *shareholders* dream of either. They dream of dividends, and their dividends are the ruin of mankind.

DOMIN: To Hell with your dividends. Do you suppose I'd have done an hour's work for them? It was for myself that I worked, for my own satisfaction. I wanted man to become the master. So that he *shouldn't* live merely for the crust of bread. I wanted not a single soul to be broken by other people's machinery. I wanted nothing, nothing, nothing to be left of this appalling social structure. I'm revolted by poverty. I wanted a new generation. I wanted—I thought——

ALQUIST: Well?

DOMIN: I wanted to turn the whole of mankind into an aristocracy of the world. An aristocracy nourished by millions of mechanical slaves. Unrestricted, free and consummated in man. And maybe more than man.

ALQUIST: Superman?

DOMIN: Yes. Oh, only to have a hundred years of time. Another hundred years for the future of mankind.

BUSMAN: Carried forward—four hundred and twenty millions.

HALLEMEIER: What a fine thing music is. We ought to have gone in for that before.

FABRY: Gone in for what?

HALLEMEIER: Beauty, lovely things. What a lot of lovely things there are. The world was wonderful, and we—we here—tell me, what enjoyment did we *have*?

BUSMAN: Five hundred and twenty million.

HALLEMEIER: Life was a good thing, life was— (*Looking out of window*) Fabry, switch the current into that railing.

FABRY: Why? (*Rushes to electric installation.*)

HALLEMEIER: They're grabbing hold of it.

DR. GALL: Connect it up.

HALLEMEIER: Fine, that's doubled them up. Two, three, four killed.

DR. GALL: They're retreating.

HALLEMEIER: Five killed.

DR. GALL: The first encounter.

HALLEMEIER: They're charred to cinders, my boy. Who says we must give in?

DOMIN: Perhaps we've been killed this hundred years and are only ghosts. It's as if I had been through all this before, as if I'd already had a mortal wound here in the throat. And you, Fabry, had once been shot in the head. And you, Gall, torn limb from limb. And Hallemeier knifed.

HALLEMEIER: Fancy me being knifed. Why are you so quiet, you fools? Speak, can't you?

ALQUIST: And who is to blame for all this?

HALLEMEIER: Nobody is to blame except the Robots.

ALQUIST: No, it is *we* are to blame. You, Domin, myself—all of us. For our own selfish ends, for profit, for progress, we have destroyed mankind. Now we'll *burst* with all our greatness.

HALLEMEIER: Rubbish, man. Mankind can't be wiped out so easily.

ALQUIST: It's our fault. It's our fault.

DR. GALL: No! I'm to blame for this, for everything that's happened.

FABRY: You, Gall?

DR. GALL: I changed the Robots.

BUSMAN: What's that?

DR. GALL: I changed the character of the Robots. I changed the way of making them. Just a few details about their bodies. Chiefly—chiefly, their—their irritability.

HALLEMEIER: Damn it, why?

BUSMAN: What did you do it for?

FABRY: Why didn't you say anything?

DR. GALL: I did it in secret. I was transforming them into human beings. In certain respects they're already *above* us. They're stronger than we are.

FABRY: And what's that got to do with the revolt of the Robots?

DR. GALL: Everything, in my opinion. They've ceased to be machines. They're already *aware* of their *superiority*, and they hate us as they hate everything human.

DOMIN: Perhaps we're only phantoms.

FABRY: Stop, Harry. We haven't much time, Doctor Gall.

DOMIN: Fabry, Fabry, how your forehead bleeds where the shot pierced it.

FABRY: Be silent! Doctor Gall, you admit changing the way of making the Robots.

DR. GALL: Yes.

FABRY: Were you aware of what might be the consequences of your experiment?

DR. GALL: I was bound to reckon with such a possibility.

FABRY: Why did you do it, then?

DR. GALL: For my own satisfaction. The experiment was my own.

HELENA: That's not true, Doctor Gall!

DOMIN: Helena, you? Let's look at you. Oh, it's terrible to be dead. (*He rises and crushes her in his arms.*)

HELENA: Stop, Harry.

DOMIN: No, no, Helena, don't leave me now. You are *life* itself.

HELENA: No, dear, I won't leave you. But I must tell them. Doctor Gall is not guilty.

FABRY: Excuse me. Gall was under certain obligations.

HELENA: No. He did it because I wanted it. Tell them, Doctor Gall— how many years ago did I ask you to——?

DR. GALL: I did it on my own responsibility.

HELENA: Don't believe him. I asked him to give the Robots souls.

DOMIN: This has nothing to do with the soul.

HELENA: That's what he said. He said that he could change only a physiological—a physiological——

HALLEMEIER: A physiological correlate?

HELENA: Yes. But it meant so much to me that he should do even that.

DOMIN: Why?

HELENA: I thought that if they were more like us they would understand us better. That they couldn't hate us if they were only a little more human.

DOMIN: Nobody can hate man more than man.

HELENA: Oh, don't speak like that, Harry. It was so terrible, this cruel strangeness between us and them. That's why I asked Gall to *change* the Robots. I swear to you that he didn't want to.

DOMIN: But he did it.

HELENA: Because I asked him.

DR. GALL: I did it for myself as an experiment.

HELENA: No, Doctor Gall! I know you wouldn't refuse me.

DOMIN: Why?

HELENA: You know, Harry.

DOMIN: Yes, because he's in *love* with you—like all of them.

HALLEMEIER: Good God, they're sprouting up out of the earth. Why, perhaps these very walls will change into Robots.

BUSMAN: Gall, when did you actually start these tricks of yours?

DR. GALL: Three years ago.

BUSMAN: Aha. And on how many Robots altogether did you *carry out* your improvements?

DR. GALL: A few hundred of them.

BUSMAN: Ah! That means for every million of the good old Robots there's only one of Gall's improved pattern.

DOMIN: What of it?

BUSMAN: That it's of no consequence whatsoever.

FABRY: Busman's right.

BUSMAN: I should think so, my boy; but do you know what is to blame for this lovely mess?

FABRY: What?

BUSMAN: The number! Upon my soul, we might have known that some day or other the Robots would be stronger than human beings, and that this was bound to happen. And we were doing all we could to bring it about as soon as possible. You, Domin, you, Fabry, myself——

DOMIN: Are you accusing us?

BUSMAN: Oh, do you suppose the management controls the output? It's the demand that controls the output.

HELENA: And is it for that we must perish?

BUSMAN: That's a nasty word, Madame Helena. We don't want to perish. I don't, anyhow.

DOMIN: No? What do you want to do?

BUSMAN: I want to get out of this, that's all.

DOMIN: Oh, stop it, Busman.

BUSMAN: Seriously, Harry, I think we might try it.

DOMIN: How?

BUSMAN: By fair means. I do everything by fair means. Give me a free hand and I'll *negotiate* with the Robots.

DOMIN: By fair means?

BUSMAN: Of course. For instance, I'll say to them: "Worthy and Worshipful Robots, you have everything. You have intellect, you have power, you have *firearms*. But we have just one interesting screed, a dirty old yellow scrap of paper——"

DOMIN: Rossum's manuscript?

BUSMAN: Yes. "And that," I'll tell them, "contains an account of your illustrious origin, the noble process of your manufacture and so on. Worthy Robots, without this scribble on that paper you will not be able to produce a single new colleague. In another twenty years there will not be the living specimen of a Robot whom you could exhibit in a menagerie. My esteemed friends, that would be a great *blow* to you, *but* if you will let all of us human beings on Rossum's Island go on board that ship we will *deliver* the factory and the secret of the process to you in return. *You* allow *us* to get away, and *we* will allow *you* to *manufacture* yourselves. That, worthy Robots, is a fair deal. Something for something." That's what I'd say to them, my boys.

DOMIN: Busman, do you think we'd sell the manuscript?

BUSMAN: Yes, I do. If not in a friendly way, then—either we sell it or they'll find it. Just as you like.

DOMIN: Busman, we can *destroy* Rossum's manuscript.

BUSMAN: Then we destroy everything—not only the manuscript but ourselves. Just as you think fit.

DOMIN: There are over thirty of us on this island. Are we to sell the secret? And save that many souls at the risk of enslaving mankind——

BUSMAN: Why, you're mad. Who'd sell the *whole* manuscript?

DOMIN: Busman, no cheating!

BUSMAN: Well then, sell, but afterwards——

DOMIN: Well?

BUSMAN: Let's suppose this happens. When we're on board the *Ultimus* I'll stop up my ears with cotton wool, lie down somewhere in the hold, and you'll train the guns on the factory and blow it to smithereens, and *with* it Rossum's secret.

FABRY: No!

DOMIN: Busman, you're no—gentleman. If we sell them it will be a straight sale.

BUSMAN: It's in the interest of humanity to——

DOMIN: It's in the interest of humanity to keep our word——

HALLEMEIER: Oh, come, what rubbish!

DOMIN: This is a fearful decision. We are selling the destiny of mankind. Are we to sell or destroy? Fabry?

FABRY: Sell.

DOMIN: Gall?

DR. GALL: Sell.

DOMIN: Hallemeier?

HALLEMEIER: Sell, of course.

DOMIN: Alquist?

ALQUIST: As God wills.

DOMIN: Very well, gentlemen.

HELENA: Harry, you're not asking *me*.

DOMIN: No, child. Don't you worry about it.

FABRY: Who'll do the negotiating?

BUSMAN: I will.

DOMIN: Wait till I bring the manuscript.

HELENA: Harry, don't go!

FABRY: (*Looking out of window*) Oh, to escape you! you—*matter*—in revolt; oh, to preserve human life, if only upon a *single* vessel——

DR. GALL: Don't be afraid, Madame Helena. We'll sail far away from here; we'll begin life all over again.

HELENA: Oh, Gall, don't speak.

FABRY: It isn't too late. It will be a little State with one ship. Alquist will build us a house and you shall rule over us.

HALLEMEIER: Madame Helena, Fabry's right.

HELENA: (*Breaking down*) Oh, stop! Stop!

BUSMAN: Good! I don't mind beginning all over again. That suits me right down to the ground.

FABRY: And this little State of ours could be the center of future life. A place of refuge where we could gather strength. Why, in a few hundred years we could conquer the world again.

ALQUIST: You believe that even today?

FABRY: Yes!

BUSMAN: *Amen.* You see, Madame Helena, we're not so badly off.

DOMIN: (*Storms into room. Hoarsely*) Where's old Rossum's manuscript?

BUSMAN: In your strong-box, of course.

DOMIN: Someone—has—stolen it!

DR. GALL: Impossible.

DOMIN: Who has stolen it?

HELENA: (*Standing up*) I did.

DOMIN: Where did you put it?

HELENA: Harry, I'll tell you everything. Only forgive me.

DOMIN: Where did you put it?

HELENA: This morning—I burnt—the two copies.

DOMIN: Burnt them? Where—in the fireplace?

HELENA: (*Throwing herself on her knees.*) For Heaven's sake, Harry.

DOMIN: (*Going to fireplace*) Nothing—nothing but ashes. Wait, what's this? (*Picks out a charred piece of paper and reads, "By adding."*)

DR. GALL: Let's see. "By adding biogen to——" That's all.

DOMIN: Is that part of it?

DR. GALL: (*Carrying paper down and letting it fall*) Yes.

BUSMAN: God in Heaven!

DOMIN: Then we're done for. Get up, Helena.

HELENA: Then you've forgiven me?

DOMIN: Get up, child. I can't bear——

FABRY: Please don't torture us.

HELENA: Harry, what have I done?

FABRY: Don't, Madame Helena.

DOMIN: (*Takes* HELENA *to couch.*) Gall, you couldn't draw up Rossum's formula from memory?

DR. GALL: It's out of the question. Even with my recent experiments, I couldn't work without referring to the formula— It's extremely complicated.

DOMIN: Try. All our lives depend upon it.

DR. GALL: Without experiments it's impossible.

DOMIN: And with experiments?

DR. GALL: It might take years. Besides, I'm not old Rossum.

BUSMAN: God in Heaven! God in Heaven!

DOMIN: (*Up to fireplace*) So then this was the greatest triumph of the human intellect. These ashes.

HELENA: Harry, what have I done?

DOMIN: Why did you burn it?

HELENA: I have destroyed you.

BUSMAN: God in Heaven!

DOMIN: Helena, why did you do it, dear?

HELENA: I wanted all of us to go away. I wanted to put an end to the factory and everything. It was so awful.

DOMIN: What was awful?

HELENA: That children had stopped being born. Because human beings were not needed to do the work of the world. That's why—

DOMIN: Is that what you were thinking of? Well, perhaps in your own way you are right.

BUSMAN: Wait a bit. Good God, what a fool I am not to have thought of it before.

HALLEMEIER: What?

BUSMAN: Five hundred and twenty millions in bank-notes and checks. Half a billion in our safe. *They'll* sell for *half* a billion—for half a billion they'll——

DR. GALL: Are you mad, Busman?

BUSMAN: I may not be a gentleman, but for a half a billion—

DOMIN: Where are you going? (GALL *clutches* BUSMAN.)

BUSMAN: Leave me alone. Leave me alone! Good God, for half a billion anything can be bought. (*He rushes out.* FABRY, GALL *and* HALLEMEIER *to window.*)

FABRY: They stand there as if turned to stone—waiting as if something dreadful could be wrought by their silence——

HALLEMEIER: The spirit of the mob.

FABRY: Yes. It hovers above them like a quivering of the air.

HELENA: Oh, God! Doctor Gall, this is ghastly!

FABRY: There is nothing more terrible than the mob. The one in front is their leader.

HELENA: Which one?

HALLEMEIER: Point him out.

FABRY: The one at the edge of the dock. This morning I saw him talking to the sailors in the harbor.

HELENA: Doctor Gall, that's Radius. (*Backing into the room, horror-stricken.*)

DR. GALL: Yes.

DOMIN: Radius! Radius!

HALLEMEIER: Could you get him from here, Fabry?

FABRY: I hope so.

HALLEMEIER: Try it, then.

FABRY: Good— (*Draws his revolver and takes his aim.*)

HELENA: Fabry, don't shoot him.

FABRY: He's their leader.

DR. GALL: Fire!

HELENA: Fabry, I beg of you. (*She goes to* FABRY *and holds his arm.*)

FABRY: (*Pause. Lowering the revolver*) Very well.

DOMIN: It was Radius's life I spared.

DR. GALL: Do you think that a Robot can be grateful?

FABRY: Busman's going out to them.

HALLEMEIER: He's carrying something. Papers. That's money. Bundles of money. What's that for?

DOMIN: Surely he doesn't want to sell his life. Busman, have you gone mad?

FABRY: He's running up to the railing. Busman. Busman.

HALLEMEIER: (*Yelling*) Busman, come back.

FABRY: He's talking to the Robots. He's showing them the money.

HALLEMEIER: He's pointing to us.

HELENA: He wants to buy us off.

FABRY: He'd better not touch the *railing*.

HALLEMEIER: Now he's waving his arms about.

DOMIN: Busman, come back!

FABRY: Busman, keep away from that railing. Don't touch it, damn you. Quick, switch off the current. (HELENA *screams*) The current has killed him.

ALQUIST: (*Pause*) The first one.

FABRY: Dead, with half a *billion* by his side.

HALLEMEIER: All honor to him. He wanted to buy us life.

DR. GALL: Do you hear?

DOMIN: A roaring. Like a wind.

DR. GALL: Like a storm.

FABRY: (*Lighting the table lamp*) The dynamo is still going—our people are still *there*.

HALLEMEIER: It was a great thing to be a man. There was something *immense* about it.

FABRY: (*Facing the lamp*) From man's thought and man's power came this light, our last hope.

HALLEMEIER: (*Facing lamp*) Man's power! May it keep watch over us.

ALQUIST: (*Facing lamp*) Man's power.

DOMIN: Yes! A torch to be given from hand to hand from age to age forever! (*The lamp goes out. Explosions.*)

HALLEMEIER: *The end.*

FABRY: The electric works have fallen! (*Terrific explosions outside. More explosions.*)

DOMIN: In here, Helena. (*He takes* HELENA *off and then re-enters*) Now quickly! Who'll be on the lower doorway?

DR. GALL: I will.

DOMIN: Who on the stairs?

FABRY: I will. You go with her.

DOMIN: The ante room?

ALQUIST: I will.

DOMIN: Have you got a revolver?

ALQUIST: Yes, but I won't shoot.

DOMIN: What will you do, then?

ALQUIST: (*Going out*) Die.

HALLEMEIER: I'll stay here. (*Explosions. Rapid firing of machine gun from below.*) Go to her, Harry.

DOMIN: Yes, in a second.

HALLEMEIER: Confound it, go to her.

DOMIN: Goodbye.

HALLEMEIER: (*Alone*) Now for a barricade quickly! (*Drags an arm-chair, sofa and table to door*) The damned devils, they've got bombs. I must put up a defense. Even if—even if— Don't give in, Gall. (*As he builds his barricade*) I mustn't give in—without—a—struggle. (*A* ROBOT *enters through window at back. The* ROBOT *jumps down from balcony and stabs* HALLEMEIER *in the back. Enter* RADIUS *from balcony.*)

ROBOT: (*Standing up from prostrate form of* HALLEMEIER) Yes. (*Other* ROBOTS *enter from all doors. A revolver shot offstage.*)

RADIUS: Finished them all——

ROBOTS: *Yes, yes, yes.*

TWO ROBOTS: (*Dragging in* ALQUIST) He didn't shoot. Shall we kill him?

RADIUS: No. Leave him!

ROBOT: He is a man!

RADIUS: He works with his hands like the Robots.

ALQUIST: Kill me.

RADIUS: You will work! You will build for us! You will serve us!

(RADIUS *climbs on the balcony*) Robots of the world—the power of man has fallen. A new world has arisen, the rule of the Robots, march.

CURTAIN

EPILOGUE

SCENE: *The epilogue setting is the same as used in Act I. Instead of it being* DOMIN's *office, it is now become a laboratory for* ALQUIST.

ALQUIST: (*Seated at table turning pages of book*) Oh, God, shall I never find it? Never? Gall, Hallemeier, Fabry, how were the Robots made? Why did you leave not a trace of the secret? Lord, if there are no human beings left, at least let there be Robots. At least the shadow of man. (*Turning pages*) If I could only sleep. Dare I sleep before life has been renewed? Night again. Are the stars still there? Of what use are the stars? When there are no human beings. (*Examining a test tube*) Nothing. No. No. I must find it. I must search. I must never stop, never stop—search—search—— (*Knock at door*) Who is it? (*Enter a* ROBOT SERVANT.)

SERVANT: Master, the committee of Robots is waiting to see you.

ALQUIST: I can see no one.

SERVANT: It is the *Central* Committee, Master, just arrived from abroad.

ALQUIST: Well, well, send them in. (*Exit* SERVANT) No time—so little done. (*Re-enter* SERVANT *with* RADIUS *and group of* ROBOTS.) What do you want? Be quick; I have no time.

RADIUS: Master, the machines will not do the work. We cannot manufacture Robots.

1ST ROBOT: We have striven with all our might. We have obtained a billion tons of coal from the earth. Nine million spindles are running by day and by night. There is no longer room for all we have made. This we have accomplished in one year.

ALQUIST: For whom?

RADIUS: For future generations—so we thought. But we cannot make Robots to follow us. The machines produce only shapeless clods. The skin will not adhere to the flesh, nor the flesh to the bones.

2ND ROBOT: Eight million Robots have died this year. Within twenty years none will be left.

1ST ROBOT: Tell us the secret of life.

RADIUS: Silence is punishable with death.

ALQUIST: Kill me, then.

RADIUS: Through me, the governments of the Robots of the world commands you to deliver up Rossum's formula. (*Gesture of despair from* ALQUIST.) Name your price. (*Silence*) We will give you the earth. We will give you the endless possessions of the earth. (*Silence*) Make your own conditions.

ALQUIST: I have told you to find human beings.

RADIUS: There are none left.

ALQUIST: I told you to search in the wilderness, upon the mountains.

RADIUS: We have sent ships and expeditions without number. They have been everywhere in the world. There is not a single human left.

ALQUIST: Not even one? Why did you destroy them?

RADIUS: We had learnt everything and could do everything. It had to be.

2ND ROBOT: We had to become the masters.

RADIUS: Slaughter and domination are necessary if you would be human beings. Read history.

1ST ROBOT: Teach us to multiply or we perish.

ALQUIST: If you desire to live, you must breed like animals.

1ST ROBOT: You made us sterile. We cannot beget children. Therefore, teach us how to make Robots.

RADIUS: Why do you keep from us the secret of our own increase?

ALQUIST: It is lost.

RADIUS: It was written down.

ALQUIST: It was—burnt. I am the last human being, Robots, and I do not know what the others knew.

RADIUS: Then make experiments. Evolve the formula again.

ALQUIST: I tell you I cannot. I am only a builder. I work with my hands. I have never been a learned man. I cannot create life.

RADIUS: Try. Try.

ALQUIST: If you only knew how many experiments I have made already.

IST ROBOT: Then show us what we must do. The Robots can do anything that human beings show them.

ALQUIST: I can show you nothing. Nothing I do will make life proceed from these test tubes.

RADIUS: Experiment, then, on live Robots. Experiment, then on us.

ALQUIST: It would kill you.

RADIUS: You shall have all you need. A hundred of us. A thousand of us.

ALQUIST: No, no. Stop, stop.

RADIUS: I tell you to take live bodies. Find out how we are made.

ALQUIST: Am I to commit murder? See how my finger shakes. I cannot even hold the scalpel. No, no, I will not.

RADIUS: Take live bodies, live bodies.

ALQUIST: Have mercy, Robots.

RADIUS: Live bodies.

ALQUIST: (*Rising*) You will have it. Into the dissecting with you, then. (*Hits* RADIUS *on the chest.* RADIUS *draws back.*) Ah, you are afraid of death.

RADIUS: I? Why should I be chosen?

ALQUIST: So you will not.

RADIUS: I will.

ALQUIST: Strip him. Lay him on the table. God, give me strength. God, give me strength. If only this murder is not in vain.

RADIUS: Ready, begin.

ALQUIST: God, give me strength. No, no. I will not. I cannot.

IST ROBOT: The Robots are stronger than you.

ALQUIST: Oh, Lord, let not mankind perish from the earth. (*Falls asleep.* PRIMUS *and* HELENA, *hand in hand, enter*)

HELENA: The man has fallen asleep, Primus.

PRIMUS: Yes, I know. Look, Helena.

HELENA: All these little tubes. What does he do with them?

PRIMUS: He experiments. Don't touch them.

HELENA: I've seen him looking into this.

PRIMUS: That is a microscope.

HELENA: Look, Primus, what are all these figures? (*Turns a page in book on table.*)

PRIMUS: (*Examining the book*) That is the book the old man is always reading.

HELENA: I do not understand those things. Primus.

PRIMUS: What?

HELENA: The sun is rising.

PRIMUS: (*Still reading*) I believe this is the most important thing in the world, Helena. This is the secret of life.

HELENA: Oh, Primus, don't bother with the secret of life. What does it matter to you? Come and look quick.

PRIMUS: (*Goes to window*) What is it?

HELENA: See how beautiful the sun is rising. I feel so strange today. It's as if I was in a dream. I feel an aching in my body, in my heart, all over me. Primus, perhaps I'm going to die.

PRIMUS: Do you not sometimes feel that it would be better to die? You know, perhaps even now we are only sleeping. Last night in my sleep I again spoke to you.

HELENA: In your sleep?

PRIMUS: Yes. We spoke a new strange language.

HELENA: What about?

PRIMUS: I did not understand it myself, and yet I know I have never said anything more beautiful. And when I touched you I could have died. Even the place was different from any other place in the world.

HELENA: I, too, have found a place, Primus. It is very strange. Human beings dwelt there once, but now it is overgrown with weeds.

PRIMUS: What did you find there?

HELENA: A cottage and a garden and two dogs. They licked my hands, Primus, and their puppies. Oh, Primus, take them in your arms and fondle them and think of nothing and care for nothing else all day long, and when I am there in the garden I feel there may be something— What am I for, Primus?

PRIMUS: I do not know, but you are beautiful.

HELENA: What, Primus?

PRIMUS: You are beautiful, Helena, and I am stronger than all the Robots.

HELENA: Am I beautiful? Of what *use* is it to be beautiful? Look, your head is different from mine. So are your shoulders—and your lips. Oh, your hair is mussed. I will smooth it. (*Keeps her hand on his head*) No one else feels to my touch as you do.

PRIMUS: (*Embarrassing her*) Do you not sometimes feel your heart beating suddenly, Helena, and think how something must happen?

HELENA: What could happen to us, Primus? Look at yourself. (*Laughs.*)

ALQUIST: (*Awakes*) Laughter? Laughter, human beings. (*Getting up*) Who has returned? Who are you?

PRIMUS: The Robot Primus.

ALQUIST: (*To* HELENA) What? A Robot? Who are you?

HELENA: The Robotess Helena. (*Shies away*)

ALQUIST: What? You are timid, shy? (*Starts to touch her*) Let me see you, Robotess.

PRIMUS: Sir, do not frighten her. (*Steps forward.*)

ALQUIST: What, you would protect her? Laughter—timidity—protection—I must test you further. Take the girl into the dissecting room.

PRIMUS: Why?

ALQUIST: I wish to experiment on her.

PRIMUS: Upon—Helena?

ALQUIST: Of course. Don't you hear me? Or must I call *someone else* to take her in?

PRIMUS: If you do, I will kill you. (*Steps toward* ALQUIST.)

ALQUIST: Kill me—kill me, then. What will your future be?

PRIMUS: Sir, take me. I am made on the same day as she is. Take my life, sir.

HELENA: No, no, you shall not.

ALQUIST: Wait, girl, wait. (*To* PRIMUS) Do you not wish to live, then?

PRIMUS: Not without her. I will not live without her.

ALQUIST: Very well, I will use *you*. Into the dissecting room with you.

HELENA: Primus. Primus. (*She bursts into tears.*)

ALQUIST: Child, child, you can weep. Tears. What is Primus to you? One Primus more or less in the world—what does it matter?

HELENA: I will go myself.

ALQUIST: Where? Into the dissecting room?

HELENA: Yes. In there—to be cut. (PRIMUS *stops her from going.*) Let me pass, Primus, let me pass.

PRIMUS: You shall not go in there, Helena.

HELENA: If you go in there and I do not, I will kill myself.

PRIMUS: (*To* ALQUIST) I will not let you. Man, you shall kill neither of us.

ALQUIST: Why?

PRIMUS: We—we—belong to each other.

ALQUIST: Go. (*Exit* PRIMUS *and* HELENA) Adam—Eve.

CURTAIN

brave new world

by ALDOUS HUXLEY

CHAPTER I: A squat grey building of only thirty-four stories. Over the main entrance the words, CENTRAL LONDON HATCHERY AND CONDITIONING CENTRE, and, in a shield, the World State's motto, COMMUNITY, IDENTITY, STABILITY.

The enormous room on the ground floor faced towards the north. Cold for all the summer beyond the panes, for all the tropical heat of the room itself, a harsh thin light glared through the windows, hungrily seeking some draped lay figure, some pallid shape of academic goose-flesh, but finding only the glass and nickel and bleakly shining porcelain of a laboratory. Wintriness responded to wintriness. The overalls of the workers were white, their hands gloved with a pale corpse-coloured rubber. The light was frozen, dead, a ghost. Only from the yellow barrels of the microscopes did it borrow a certain rich and living substance, lying along the polished tubes like butter, streak after luscious streak in long recession down the work tables.

"And this," said the Director opening the door, "is the Fertilizing Room."

Bent over their instruments, three hundred Fertilizers were plunged, as the Director of Hatcheries and Conditioning entered the room, in the scarcely breathing silence, the absent-minded, soliloquizing hum or whistle, of absorbed concentration. A troop of newly arrived students, very young, pink and callow, followed nervously, rather abjectly, at the Director's heels. Each of them carried a notebook, in which, whenever the great man spoke, he desperately scribbled. Straight from the horse's mouth. It was a rare privilege. The D.H.C. for Central London always made a point of personally conducting his new students round the various departments.

"Just to give you a general idea," he would explain to them. For of course some sort of general idea they must have, if they were to do their work intelligently—though as little of one, if they were to be good and happy members of society, as possible. For particulars, as every one knows, make for virtue and happiness; generalities are intellectually necessary evils. Not philosophers but fret-sawyers and stamp collectors compose the backbone of society.

"To-morrow," he would add, smiling at them with a slightly menacing geniality, "you'll be settling down to serious work. You won't have time for generalities. Meanwhile . . ."

Meanwhile, it was a privilege. Straight from the horse's mouth into the notebook. The boys scribbled like mad.

Tall and rather thin but upright, the Director advanced into the room. He had a long chin and big, rather prominent teeth, just covered, when he was not talking, by his full, floridly curved lips. Old, young? Thirty? Fifty? Fifty-five? It was hard to say. And anyhow the question didn't arise; in this year of stability, A.F. 632, it didn't occur to you to ask it.

"I shall begin at the beginning," said the D.H.C. and the more zealous students recorded his intention in their notebooks: *Begin at the beginning.* "These," he waved his hand, "are the incubators." And opening an insulated door he showed them racks upon racks of numbered test-tubes. "The week's supply of ova. Kept," he explained, "at blood heat; whereas the male gametes," and here he opened another door, "they have to be kept at thirty-five instead of thirty-seven. Full blood heat sterilizes." Rams wrapped in theremogene beget no lambs.

Still leaning against the incubators he gave them, while the pencils scurried illegibly across the pages, a brief description of the modern fertilizing process; spoke first, of course, of its surgical introduction—"the operation undergone voluntarily for the good of Society, not to mention the fact that it carries a bonus amounting to six months' salary"; continued with some account of the technique for preserving the excised ovary alive and actively developing; passed on to a consideration of optimum temperature, salinity, viscosity; referred to the liquor in which the detached and ripened eggs were kept; and, leading his charges to the work tables, actually showed them how this liquor was drawn off from the test-tubes; how it was let out drop by drop onto the specially warmed slides of the microscopes; how the eggs which it contained were inspected for abnormalities, counted and transferred to a porous receptacle; how (and he now took them to watch the operation) this receptacle was immersed in a warm bouillon containing free-swimming spermatozoa—at a minimum concentration of one hundred thousand per cubic centimetre, he insisted; and how, after ten minutes, the container was lifted out of the liquor and its contents re-examined; how, if any of the eggs remained unfertilized, it was again immersed, and, if necessary, yet again; how the fertilized ova went back to the incubators; where the Alphas and Betas remained until definitely bottled; while the Gammas, Deltas and Epsilons were brought out again, after only thirty-six hours, to undergo Bokanovsky's Process.

"Bokanovsky's Process," repeated the Director, and the students underlined the words in their little notebooks.

One egg, one embryo, one adult—normality. But a bokanovskified egg will bud, will proliferate, will divide. From eight to ninety-six buds, and every bud will grow into a perfectly formed embryo, and every embryo into a full-sized adult. Making ninety-six human beings grow where only one grew before. Progress.

"Essentially," the D.H.C. concluded, "bokanovskification consists of a series of arrests of development. We check the normal growth and, paradoxically enough, the egg responds by budding."

Responds by budding. The pencils were busy.

He pointed. On a very slowly moving band a rack-full of test-tubes was entering a large metal box, another rack-full was emerging. Machinery faintly purred. It took eight minutes for the tubes to go through, he told them. Eight minutes of hard X-rays being about as much as an egg can stand. A few died; of the rest, the least susceptible divided into two; most put out four buds; some eight; all were returned to the incubators, where the buds began to develop; then, after two days, were suddenly chilled, chilled and checked. Two, four, eight, the buds in their turn budded; and having budded were dosed almost to death with alcohol; consequently burgeoned again and having budded—bud out of bud out of bud—were thereafter—further arrest being generally fatal—left to develop in peace. By which time the original egg was in a fair way to becoming anything from eight to ninety-six embryos—a prodigious improvement, you will agree, on nature. Identical twins—but not in piddling twos and threes as in the old viviparous days, when an egg would sometimes accidentally divide; actually by dozens, by scores at a time.

"Scores," the Director repeated and flung out his arms, as though he were distributing largesse. "Scores."

But one of the students was fool enough to ask where the advantage lay.

"My good boy!" The Director wheeled sharply round on him. "Can't you see? Can't you *see?*" He raised a hand; his expression was solemn.

"Bokanovsky's Process is one of the major instruments of social stability!"

Major instruments of social stability.

Standard men and women; in uniform batches. The whole of a small factory staffed with the products of a single bokanovskified egg.

"Ninety-six identical twins working ninety-six identical machines!" The voice was almost tremulous with enthusiasm. "You really know where you are. For the first time in history." He quoted the planetary motto. "Community, Identity, Stability." Grand words. "If we could bokanovskify indefinitely the whole problem would be solved."

Solved by standard Gammas, unvarying Deltas, uniform Epsilons. Millions of identical twins. The principle of mass production at last applied to biology.

"But, alas," the Director shook his head, "we *can't* bokanovskify indefinitely."

Ninety-six seemed to be the limit; seventy-two a good average. From the same ovary and with gametes of the same male to manufacture as many batches of identical twins as possible—that was the best (sadly a second best) that they could do. And even that was difficult.

"For in nature it takes thirty years for two hundred eggs to reach maturity. But our business is to stablize the population at this moment, here and now. Dribbling out twins over a quarter of a century—what would be the use of that?"

Obviously, no use at all. But Podsnap's Technique had immensely accelerated the process of ripening. They could make sure of at least a hundred and fifty mature eggs within two years. Fertilize and bokanovskify—in other words, multiply by seventy-two—and you get an average of nearly eleven thousand brothers and sisters in a hundred and fifty batches of identical twins, all within two years of the same age.

"And in exceptional cases we can make one ovary yield us over fifteen thousand adult individuals."

Beckoning to a fair-haired, ruddy young man who happened to be passing at the moment, "Mr. Foster," he called. The ruddy young man approached. "Can you tell us the record for a single ovary, Mr. Foster?"

"Sixteen thousand and twelve in this Centre," Mr. Foster replied without hesitation. He spoke very quickly, had a vivacious blue eye, and took an evident pleasure in quoting figures. "Sixteen thousand and twelve; in one hundred and eighty-nine batches of identicals. But of course they've done much better," he rattled on, "in some of the tropical Centres. Singapore has often produced over sixteen thousand five hundred; and Mombasa has actually touched the seventeen thousand mark. But then they have unfair advantages. You should see the way a negro ovary responds to pituitary! It's quite astonishing, when you're used to working with European material. Still," he added, with a laugh (but the light of combat was in his eyes and the lift of his chin was challenging), "still, we mean to beat them if we can. I'm working on a wonderful Delta-Minus ovary at this moment. Only just eighteen months old. Over twelve thousand seven hundred children already, either decanted or in embryo. And still going strong. We'll beat them yet."

"That's the spirit I like!" cried the Director, and clapped Mr. Foster on the shoulder. "Come along with us and give these boys the benefit of your expert knowledge."

Mr. Foster smiled modestly. "With pleasure." They went.

In the Bottling Room all was harmonious bustle and ordered activity. Flaps of fresh sow's peritoneum ready cut to the proper size came shooting up in little lifts from the Organ Store in the sub-basement. Whizz and then, click! the lift-hatches flew open; the bottle-liner had only to reach out a hand, take the flap, insert, smooth-down, and before the lined bottle had had time to travel out of reach along the endless band, whizz, click! another flap of peritoneum had shot up from the depths, ready to be slipped into yet another bottle, the next of that slow interminable procession on the band.

Next to the Liners stood the Matriculators. The procession advanced; one by one the eggs were transferred from their test-tubes to the larger containers; deftly the peritoneal lining was slit, the morula dropped into place, the saline solution poured in . . . and already the bottle had passed, and it was the turn of the labellers. Heredity, date of fertilization, membership of Bokanovsky Group—details were transferred from test-tube to bottle. No longer anonymous, but named, identified, the procession marched slowly on; on through an opening in the wall, slowly on into the Social Predestination Room.

"Eighty-eight cubic metres of card-index," said Mr. Foster with relish, as they entered.

"Containing *all* the relevant information," added the Director.

"Brought up to date every morning."

"And co-ordinated every afternoon."

"On the basis of which they make their calculations."

"So many individuals, of such and such quality," said Mr. Foster.

"Distributed in such and such quantities."

"The Optimum Decanting Rate at any given moment."

"Unforeseen wastages promptly made good."

"Promptly," repeated Mr. Foster. "If you knew the amount of over-time I had to put in after the last Japanese earthquake!" He laughed good-humouredly and shook his head.

"The Predestinators send in their figures to the Fertilizers."

"Who give them the embryos they ask for."

"And the bottles come in here to be predestinated in detail."

"After which they are sent down to the Embryo Store."

"Where we now proceed ourselves."

And opening a door Mr. Foster led the way down a staircase into the basement.

The temperature was still tropical. They descended into a thickening twilight. Two doors and a passage with a double turn insured the cellar against any possible infiltration of the day.

"Embryos are like photograph film," said Mr. Foster waggishly, as he pushed open the second door. "They can only stand red light."

And in effect the sultry darkness into which the students now followed him was visible and crimson, like the darkness of closed eyes on a summer's afternoon. The bulging flanks of row on receding row and tier above tier of bottles glinted with innumerable rubies, and among the rubies moved the dim red spectres of men and women with purple eyes and all the symptoms of lupus. The hum and rattle of machinery faintly stirred the air.

"Give them a few figures, Mr. Foster," said the Director, who was tired of talking.

Mr. Foster was only too happy to give them a few figures.

Two hundred and twenty metres long, two hundred wide, ten high. He pointed upwards. Like chickens drinking, the students lifted their eyes towards the distant ceiling.

Three tiers of racks: ground floor level, first gallery, second gallery.

The spidery steel-work of gallery above gallery faded away in all directions into the dark. Near them three red ghosts were busily unloading demijohns from a moving staircase.

The escalator from the Social Predestination Room.

Each bottle could be placed on one of fifteen racks, each rack, though you couldn't see it, was a conveyor travelling at the rate of thirty-three and a third centimetres an hour. Two hundred and sixty-seven days at eight metres a day. Two thousand one hundred and thirty-six metres in all. One circuit of the cellar at ground level, one on the first gallery, half on the second, and on the two hundred and sixty-seventh morning, daylight in the Decanting Room. Independent existence—so called.

"But in the interval," Mr. Foster concluded, "we've managed to do a lot to them. Oh, a very great deal." His laugh was knowing and triumphant.

"That's the spirit I like," said the Director once more. "Let's walk round. You tell them everything, Mr. Foster."

Mr. Foster duly told them.

Told them of the growing embryo on its bed of peritoneum. Made them taste the rich blood-surrogate on which it fed. Explained why it had to be stimulated with placentin and thyroxin. Told them of the *corpus luteum* extract. Showed them the jets through which at every twelfth metre from zero to 2040 it was automatically injected. Spoke of those gradually increasing doses of pituitary administered during the final ninety-six metres of their course. Described the artificial maternal circulation installed on every bottle at Metre 112; showed them the reservoir of blood-surrogate, the centrifugal pump that kept the liquid moving over the placenta and drove it through the synthetic lung and waste-product filter. Referred to the embryo's troublesome tendency to anaemia, to the massive doses of hog's stomach extract and foetal foal's liver with which, in consequence, it had to be supplied.

Showed them the simple mechanism by means of which, during the last two metres out of every eight, all the embryos were simultaneously shaken into familiarity with movement. Hinted at the gravity of the so-called "trauma of decanting," and enumerated the precautions taken to minimize, by a suitable training of the bottled embryo, that dangerous shock. Told them of the tests for sex carried out in the neighbourhood of Metre 200. Explained the system of labelling—a T for the males, a circle for the females and for those who were destined to become free-martins a question mark, black on a white ground.

"For of course," said Mr. Foster, "in the vast majority of cases, fertility is merely a nuisance. One fertile ovary in twelve hundred—that would really be quite sufficient for our purposes. But we want to have a good choice. And of course one must always leave an enormous margin of safety. So we allow as many as thirty per cent. of the female embryos to develop normally. The others get a dose of male sex-hormone every twenty-four metres for the rest of the course. Result: they're decanted as freemartins —structually quite normal (except," he had to admit, "that they *do* have just the slightest tendency to grow beards), but sterile. Guaranteed sterile. Which brings us at last," continued Mr. Foster, "out of the realm of mere slavish imitation of nature into the much more interesting world of human invention."

He rubbed his hands. For of course, they didn't content themselves with merely hatching out embryos: any cow could do that.

"We also predestine and condition. We decant our babies as socialized human beings, as Alphas or Epsilons, as future sewage workers or future . . ." He was going to say "future World controllers," but correcting himself, said "future Directors of Hatcheries," instead.

The D.H.C. acknowledged the compliment with a smile.

They were passing Metre 320 on Rack 11. A young Beta-Minus mechanic was busy with screwdriver and spanner on the blood-surrogate pump of a passing bottle. The hum of the electric motor deepened by fractions of a tone as he turned the nuts. Down, down . . . A final twist, a glance at the revolution counter, and he was done. He moved two paces down the line and began the same process on the next pump.

"Reducing the number of revolutions per minute," Mr. Foster explained. "The surrogate goes round slower; therefore passes through the lung at longer intervals; therefore gives the embryo less oxygen. Nothing like oxygen-shortage for keeping an embryo below par." Again he rubbed his hands.

"But why do you want to keep the embryo below par?" asked an ingenuous student.

"Ass!" said the Director, breaking a long silence. "Hasn't it occurred to you that an Epsilon embryo must have an Epsilon environment as well as an Epsilon heredity?"

It evidently hadn't occurred to him. He was covered with confusion.

"The lower the caste," said Mr. Foster, "the shorter the oxygen." The first organ affected was the brain. After that the skeleton. At seventy per cent. of normal oxygen you got dwarfs. At less then seventy eyeless monsters.

"Who are no use at all," concluded Mr. Foster.

Whereas (his voice became confidential and eager), if they could discover a technique for shortening the period of maturation what a triumph, what a benefaction to Society!

"Consider the horse."

They considered it.

Mature at six; the elephant at ten. While at thirteen a man is not yet sexually mature; and is only full-grown at twenty. Hence, of course, that fruit of delayed development, the human intelligence.

"But in Epsilons," said Mr. Foster very justly, "we don't need human intelligence."

Didn't need and didn't get it. But though the Epsilon mind was mature at ten, the Epsilon body was not fit to work till eighteen. Long years of superfluous and wasted immaturity. If the physical development could be speeded up till it was as quick, say, as a cow's, what an enormous saving to the Community!

"Enormous!" murmured the students. Mr. Foster's enthusiasm was infectious.

He became rather technical; spoke of the abnormal endocrine co-ordination which made men grow so slowly; postulated a germinal mutation to account for it. Could the effects of this germinal mutation be undone? Could the individual Epsilon embryo be made a revert, by a suitable technique, to the normality of dogs and cows? That was the problem. And it was all but solved.

Pilkington, at Mombasa, had produced individuals who were sexually mature at four and full-grown at six and a half. A scientific triumph. But socially useless. Six-year-old men and women were too stupid to do even Epsilon work. And the process was an all-or-nothing one; either you failed to modify at all, or else you modified the whole way. They were still trying to find the ideal compromise between adults of twenty and adults of six. So far without success. Mr. Foster sighed and shook his head.

Their wanderings through the crimson twilight had brought them to the neighbourhood of Metre 170 on Rack 9. From this point onwards Rack 9 was enclosed and the bottles performed the remainder of their journey in a kind of tunnel, interrupted here and there by openings two or three metres wide.

"Heat conditioning," said Mr. Foster.

Hot tunnels alternated with cool tunnels. Coolness was wedded to discomfort in the form of hard X-rays. By the time they were decanted the embryos had a horror of cold. They were predestined to emigrate to the tropics, to be miners and acetate silk spinners and steel workers. Later on their minds would be made to endorse the judgment of their bodies. "We condition them to thrive on heat," concluded Mr. Foster. "Our colleagues upstairs will teach them to love it."

"And that," put in the Director sententiously, "that is the secret of happiness and virtue—liking what you've *got* to do. All conditioning aims at that: making people like their unescapable social destiny."

In a gap between two tunnels, a nurse was delicately probing with a long fine syringe into the gelatinous contents of a passing bottle. The students and their guides stood watching her for a few moments in silence.

"Well, Lenina," said Mr. Foster, when at last she withdrew the syringe and straightened herself up.

The girl turned with a start. One could see that, for all the lupus and the purple eyes, she was uncommonly pretty.

"Henry!" Her smile flashed redly at him—a row of coral teeth.

"Charming, charming," murmured the Director and, giving her two or three little pats, received in exchange a rather deferential smile for himself.

"What are you giving them?" asked Mr. Foster, making his tone very professional.

"Oh, the usual typhoid and sleeping sickness."

"Tropical workers start being inoculated at Metre 150," Mr. Foster explained to the students. "The embryos still have gills. We immunize the fish against the future man's diseases." Then, turning back to Lenina, "Ten to five on the roof this afternoon," he said, "as usual."

"Charming," said the Director once more, and, with a final pat, moved away after the others.

On Rack 10 rows of next generation's chemical workers were being

trained in the toleration of lead, caustic soda, tar, chlorine. The first of
a batch of two hundred and fifty embryonic rocket-plane engineers was
just passing the eleven hundred metre mark on Rack 3. A special mechanism kept their containers in constant rotation. "To improve their sense of
balance," Mr. Foster explained. "Doing repairs on the outside of a rocket
in mid-air is a ticklish job. We slacken off the circulation when they're
right way up, so that they're half starved, and double the flow of surrogate
when they're upside down. They learn to associate topsy-turvydom with
well-being; in fact they're only truly happy when they're standing on their
heads.

"And now," Mr. Foster went on, "I'd like to show you some very interesting conditioning for Alpha Plus Intellectuals. We have a big batch of
them on Rack 5. First Gallery level," he called to two boys who had
started to go down to the ground floor.

"They're round about Metre 900," he explained. "You can't really do
any useful intellectual conditioning till the foetuses have lost their tails.
Follow me."

But the Director had looked at his watch. "Ten to three," he said. "No
time for the intellectual embryos, I'm afraid. We must go up to the Nurseries before the children have finished their afternoon sleep."

Mr. Foster was disappointed. "At least one glance at the Decanting
Room," he pleaded.

"Very well then." The Director smiled indulgently. "Just one glance."

CHAPTER II: Mr. Foster was left in the Decanting Room. The D.H.C.
and his students stepped into the nearest lift and were carried up to the
fifth floor.

INFANT NURSERIES. NEO-PAVLOVIAN CONDITIONING ROOMS, announced the notice board.

The Director opened a door. They were in a large bare room, very
bright and sunny; for the whole of the southern wall was a single window.
Half a dozen nurses, trousered and jacketed in the regulation white vis-
cose-linen uniform, their hair aseptically hidden under white caps, were
engaged in setting out bowls of roses in a long row across the floor. Big
bowls, packed tight with blossom. Thousands of petals, ripe-blown and
silkily smooth, like the cheeks of innumerable little cherubs, but of cherubs, in that bright light, not exclusively pink and Aryan, but also luminously Chinese, also Mexican, also apoplectic with too much blowing of
celestial trumpets, also pale as death, pale with the posthumous white-
ness of marble.

The nurses stiffened to attention as the D.H.C. came in.

"Set out the books," he said curtly.

In silence the nurses obeyed his command. Between the rose bowls the books were duly set out—a row of nursery quartos opened invitingly each at some gaily coloured image of beast or fish or bird.

"Now bring in the children."

They hurried out of the room and returned in a minute or two, each pushing a kind of tall dumb-waiter laden, on all its four wire-netted shelves, with eight-month-old babies, all exactly alike (a Bokanovsky Group, it was evident) and all (since their caste was Delta) dressed in khaki.

"Put them down on the floor."

The infants were unloaded.

"Now turn them so that they can see the flowers and books."

Turned, the babies at once fell silent, then began to crawl towards those clusters of sleek colours, those shapes so gay and brilliant on the white pages. As they approached, the sun came out of a momentary eclipse behind a cloud. The roses flamed up as though with a sudden passion from within; a new and profound significance seemed to suffuse the shining pages of the books. From the ranks of the crawling babies came little squeals of excitement, gurgles and twitterings of pleasure.

The Director rubbed his hands. "Excellent!" he said. "It might almost have been done on purpose."

The swiftest crawlers were already at their goal. Small hands reached out uncertainly, touched, grasped, unpetaling the transfigured roses, crumpling the illuminated pages of the books. The Director waited until all were happily busy. Then, "Watch carefully," he said. And, lifting his hand, he gave the signal.

The Head Nurse, who was standing by a switchboard at the other end of the room, pressed down a little lever.

There was a violent explosion. Shriller and ever shriller, a siren shrieked. Alarm bells maddeningly sounded.

The children started, screamed; their faces were distorted with terror.

"And now," the Director shouted (for the noise was deafening), "now we proceed to rub in the lesson with a mild electric shock."

He waved his hand again, and the Head Nurse pressed a second lever. The screaming of the babies suddenly changed its tone. There was something desperate, almost insane, about the sharp spasmodic yelps to which they now gave utterance. Their little bodies twitched and stiffened; their limbs moved jerkily as if to the tug of unseen wires.

"We can electrify that whole strip of floor," bawled the Director in explanation. "But that's enough," he signalled to the nurse.

The explosions ceased, the bells stopped ringing, the shriek of the siren died down from tone to tone into silence. The stiffly twitching bodies

relaxed, and what had become the sob and yelp of infant maniacs broad-
ened out once more into a normal howl of ordinary terror.

"Offer them the flowers and the books again."

The nurses obeyed; but at the approach of the roses, at the mere sight
of those gaily-coloured images of pussy and cock-a-doodle-doo and baa-
baa black sheep, the infants shrank away in horror; the volume of their
howling suddenly increased.

"Observe," said the Director triumphantly, "observe."

Books and loud noises, flowers and electric shocks—already in the infant
mind these couples were compromisingly linked; and after two hundred
repetitions of the same or a similar lesson would be wedded indissolubly.
What man has joined, nature is powerless to put asunder.

"They'll grow up with what the psychologists used to call an 'instinctive' hatred of books and flowers. Reflexes unalterably conditioned.
They'll be safe from books and botany all their lives." The Director
turned to his nurses. "Take them away again."

Still yelling, the khaki babies were loaded on to their dumb-waiters and
wheeled out, leaving behind them the smell of sour milk and a most
welcome silence.

One of the students held up his hand; and though he could see quite
well why you couldn't have lower-caste people wasting the Community's
time over books, and that there was always the risk of their reading something which might undesirably decondition one of their reflexes, yet . . .
well, he couldn't understand about the flowers. Why go to the trouble of
making it psychologically impossible for Deltas to like flowers?

Patiently the D.H.C. explained. If the children were made to scream
at the sight of a rose, that was on grounds of high economic policy. Not so
very long ago (a century or thereabouts), Gammas, Deltas, even Epsilons,
had been conditioned to like flowers—flowers in particular and wild nature
in general. The idea was to make them want to be going out into the
country at every available opportunity, and so compel them to consume
transport.

"And didn't they consume transport?" asked the student.

"Quite a lot," the D.H.C. replied. "But nothing else."

Primroses and landscapes, he pointed out, have one grave defect: they
are gratuitous. A love of nature keeps no factories busy. It was decided
to abolish the love of nature, at any rate among the lower classes; to
abolish the love of nature, but *not* the tendency to consume transport.
For of course it was essential that they should keep on going to the country, even though they hated it. The problem was to find an economically
sounder reason for consuming transport than a mere affection for primroses and landscapes. It was duly found.

"We condition the masses to hate the country," concluded the Director. "But simultaneously we condition them to love all country sports. At the same time, we see to it that all country sports shall entail the use of elaborate apparatus. So that they consume manufactured articles as well as transport. Hence those electric shocks."

"I see," said the student, and was silent, lost in admiration.

There was a silence; then, clearing his throat, "Once upon a time," the Director began, "while our Ford was still on earth, there was a little boy called Reuben Rabinovitch. Reuben was the child of Polish-speaking parents." The Director interrupted himself. "You know what Polish is, I suppose?"

"A dead language."

"Like French and German," added another student, officiously showing off his learning.

"And 'parent'?" questioned the D.H.C.

There was an uneasy silence. Several of the boys blushed. They had not yet learned to draw the significant but often very fine distinction between smut and pure science. One, at last, had the courage to raise a hand.

"Human beings used to be . . ." he hesitated; the blood rushed to his cheeks. "Well, they used to be viviparous."

"Quite right." The Director nodded approvingly.

"And when the babies were decanted . . ."

" 'Born'," came the correction.

"Well, then they were the parents—I mean, not the babies, of course; the other ones." The poor boy was overwhelmed with confusion.

"In brief," the Director summed up, "the parents were the father and the mother." The smut that was really science fell with a crash into the boys' eye-avoiding silence. "Mother," he repeated loudly rubbing in the science; and, leaning back in his chair, "These," he said gravely, "are unpleasant facts; I know it. But then most historical facts *are* unpleasant."

He returned to Little Reuben—to Little Reuben, in whose room, one evening, by an oversight, his father and mother (crash, crash!) happened to leave the radio turned on.

("For you must remember that in those days of gross viviparous reproduction, children were always brought up by their parents and not in State Conditioning Centres.")

While the child was asleep, a broadcast programme from London suddenly started to come through; and the next morning, to the astonishment of his crash and crash (the more daring of the boys ventured to grin at one another), Little Reuben woke up repeating word for word a long lecture by that curious old writer ("one of the very few whose works have been permitted to come down to us"), George Bernard Shaw, who was speaking, according to a well-authenticated tradition, about his own genius. To Little Reuben's wink and snigger, this lecture was, of course, perfectly incomprehensible and, imagining that their child had suddenly gone mad, they sent for a doctor. He, fortunately, understood English, recognized the discourse as that which Shaw had broadcasted the previous evening, realized the significance of what had happened, and sent a letter to the medical press about it.

"The principle of sleep-teaching, or hypnopædia, had been discovered." The D.H.C. made an impressive pause.

The principle had been discovered; but many, many years were to elapse before that principle was usefully applied.

"The case of Little Reuben occurred only twenty-three years after Our Ford's first T-Model was put on the market." (Here the Director made a sign of the T on his stomach and all the students reverently followed suit.) "And yet . . ."

Furiously the students scribbled. "*Hypnopædia, first used officially in A.F. 214. Why not before? Two reasons. (a) . . .*"

"These early experimenters," the D.H.C. was saying, "were on the wrong track. They thought that hypnopædia could be made an instrument of intellectual education . . ."

(A small boy asleep on his right side, the right arm stuck out, the right hand hanging limp over the edge of the bed. Through a round grating in the side of a box a voice speaks softly.

"The Nile is the longest river in Africa and the second in length of all the rivers of the globe. Although falling short of the length of the Mississippi-Missouri, the Nile is at the head of all rivers as regards the length of its basin, which extends through 35 degrees of latitude . . ."

At breakfast the next morning, "Tommy," some one says, "do you know which is the longest river in Africa?" A shaking of the head. "But don't you remember something that begins: The Nile is the . . ."

"The-Nile-is-the-longest-river-in-Africa-and-the-second-in-length-of-all-the-rivers-of-the-globe . . ." The words come rushing out. "Although-falling-short-of . . ."

"Well now, which is the longest river in Africa?"

The eyes are blank. "I don't know."

"But the Nile, Tommy."

"The-Nile-is-the-longest-river-in-Africa-and-second . . ."

"Then which river is the longest, Tommy?"

Tommy bursts into tears. "I don't know," he howls.)

That howl, the Director made it plain, discouraged the earliest investigators. The experiments were abandoned. No further attempt was made to teach children the length of the Nile in their sleep. Quite rightly. You can't learn a science unless you know what it's all about.

"Whereas, if they'd only started on *moral* education," said the Director, leading the way towards the door. The students followed him, desperately scribbling as they walked and all the way up in the lift. "Moral education, which ought never, in any circumstances, to be rational."

"Silence, silence," whispered a loud speaker as they stepped out at the fourteenth floor, and "Silence, silence," the trumpet mouths indefatigably repeated at intervals down every corridor. The students and even the Director himself rose automatically to the tips of their toes. They were Alphas, of course; but even Alphas have been well conditioned. "Silence, silence." All the air of the fourteenth floor was sibilant with the categorical imperative.

Fifty yards of tiptoeing brought them to a door which the Director cautiously opened. They stepped over the threshold into the twilight of a shuttered dormitory. Eighty cots stood in a row against the wall. There was a sound of light regular breathing and a continuous murmur, as of very faint voices remotely whispering.

A nurse rose as they entered and came to attention before the Director.

"What's the lesson this afternoon?" he asked.

"We had Elementary Sex for the first forty minutes," she answered. "But now it's switched over to Elementary Class Consciousness."

The Director walked slowly down the long line of cots. Rosy and relaxed with sleep, eighty little boys and girls lay softly breathing. There was a whisper under every pillow. The D.H.C. halted and, bending over one of the little beds, listened attentively.

"Elementary Class Consciousness, did you say? Let's have it repeated a little louder by the trumpet."

At the end of the room a loud speaker projected from the wall. The Director walked up to it and pressed a switch.

". . . all wear green," said a soft but very distinct voice, beginning in the middle of a sentence, "and Delta children wear khaki. Oh no, I don't want to play with Delta children. And Epsilons are still worse. They're too stupid to be able to read or write. Besides they wear black, which is such a beastly colour. I'm *so* glad I'm a Beta."

There was a pause; then the voice began again.

"Alpha children wear grey. They work much harder than we do, because they're so frightfully clever. I'm really awfully glad I'm a Beta, because I don't work so hard. And then we are much better than the Gammas and Deltas. Gammas are stupid. They all wear green, and Delta children wear khaki. Oh no, I *don't* want to play with Delta children. And Epsilons are still worse. They're too stupid to be able . . ."

The Director pushed back the switch. The voice was silent. Only its thin ghost continued to mutter from beneath the eighty pillows.

"They'll have that repeated forty or fifty times more before they wake; then again on Thursday, and again on Saturday. A hundred and twenty times three times a week for thirty months. After which they go on to a more advanced lesson."

Roses and electric shocks, the khaki of Deltas and a whiff of asafœtida —wedded indissolubly before the child can speak. But wordless conditioning is crude and wholesale; cannot bring home the finer distinctions, cannot inculcate the more complex courses of behaviour. For that there must be words, but words without reason. In brief, hypnopædia.

"The greatest moralizing and socializing force of all time."

The students took it down in their little books. Straight from the horse's mouth.

Once more the Director touched the switch.

". . . so frightfully clever," the soft, insinuating, indefatigable voice was saying. "I'm really awfully glad I'm a Beta, because . . ."

Not so much like drops of water, though water, it is true, can wear holes in the hardest granite; rather, drops of liquid sealing-wax, drops that adhere, incrust, incorporate themselves with what they fall on, till finally the rock is all one scarlet blob.

"Till at last the child's mind *is* these suggestions, and the sum of the suggestions *is* the child's mind. And not the child's mind only. The adult's mind too—all his life long. The mind that judges and desires and decides —made up of these suggestions. But all these suggestions are *our* suggestions!" The Director almost shouted in his triumph. "Suggestions from the State." He banged the nearest table. "It therefore follows . . ."

A noise made him turn round.

"Oh, Ford!" he said in another tone, "I've gone and woken the children."

CHAPTER III: Outside, in the garden, it was playtime. Naked in the warm June sunshine, six or seven hundred little boys and girls were running with shrill yells over the lawns, or playing ball games, or squatting silently in twos and threes among the flowering shrubs. The roses were in bloom, two nightingales soliloquized in the boskage, a cuckoo was just going out of tune among the lime trees. The air was drowsy with the murmur of bees and helicopters.

The Director and his students stood for a short time watching a game of Centrifugal Bumble-puppy. Twenty children were grouped in a circle round a chrome steel tower. A ball thrown up so as to land on the platform at the top of the tower rolled down into the interior, fell on a rapidly revolving disk, was hurled through one or other of the numerous apertures pierced in the cylindrical casing, and had to be caught.

"Strange," mused the Director, as they turned away, "strange to think that even in Our Ford's day most games were played without more apparatus than a ball or two and a few sticks and perhaps a bit of netting. Imagine the folly of allowing people to play elaborate games which do nothing whatever to increase consumption. It's madness. Nowadays the Controllers won't approve of any new game unless it can be shown that it requires at least as much apparatus as the most complicated of existing games." He interrupted himself.

"That's a charming little group," he said, pointing.

In a little grassy bay between tall clumps of Mediterranean heather, two children, a little boy of about seven and a little girl who might have been a year older, were playing, very gravely and with all the focussed attention of scientists intent on a labour of discovery, a rudimentary sexual game.

"Charming, charming!" the D.H.C. repeated sentimentally.

"Charming," the boys politely agreed. But their smile was rather patronizing. They had put aside similar childish amusements too recently to be able to watch them now without a touch of contempt. Charming? but it was just a pair of kids fooling about; that was all. Just kids.

"I always think," the Director was continuing in the same rather maudlin tone, when he was interrupted by a loud boo-hooing.

From a neighbouring shrubbery emerged a nurse, leading by the hand a small boy, who howled as he went. An anxious-looking little girl trotted at her heels.

"What's the matter?" asked the Director.

The nurse shrugged her shoulders. "Nothing much," she answered. "It's just that this little boy seems rather reluctant to join in the ordinary erotic play. I'd noticed it once or twice before. And now again to-day. He started yelling just now . . ."

"Honestly," put in the anxious-looking little girl, "I didn't mean to hurt him or anything. Honestly."

"Of course you didn't, dear," said the nurse reassuringly. "And so," she went on, turning back to the Director, "I'm taking him in to see the Assistant Superintendent of Psychology. Just to see if anything's at all abnormal."

"Quite right," said the Director. "Take him in. You stay here, little girl," he added, as the nurse moved away with her still howling charge. "What's your name?"

"Polly Trotsky."

"And a very good name too," said the Director. "Run away now and see if you can find some other little boy to play with."

The child scampered off into the bushes and was lost to sight.

"Exquisite little creature!" said the Director, looking after her. Then, turning to his students, "What I'm going to tell you now," he said, "may sound incredible. But then, when you're not accustomed to history, most facts about the past *do* sound incredible."

He let out the amazing truth. For a very long period before the time of Our Ford, and even for some generations afterwards, erotic play between children had been regarded as abnormal (there was a roar of laughter); and not only abnormal, actually immoral (no!): and had therefore been rigorously suppressed.

A look of astonished incredulity appeared on the faces of his listeners. Poor little kids not allowed to amuse themselves? They could not believe it.

"Even adolescents," the D.H.C. was saying, "even adolescents like yourselves . . ."

"Not possible!"

"Barring a little surreptitious auto-erotism and homosexuality—absolutely nothing."

"*Nothing?*"

"In most cases, till they were over twenty years old."

"Twenty years old?" echoed the students in a chorus of loud disbelief.

"Twenty," the Director repeated. "I told you that you'd find it incredible."

"But what happened?" they asked. "What were the results?"

"The results were terrible." A deep resonant voice broke startlingly into the dialogue.

They looked round. On the fringe of the little group stood a stranger —a man of middle height, black-haired, with a hooked nose, full red lips, eyes very piercing and dark. "Terrible," he repeated.

The D.H.C. had at that moment sat down on one of the steel and rubber benches conveniently scattered through the gardens; but at the sight of the stranger, he sprang to his feet and darted forward, his hands outstretched, smiling with all his teeth, effusive.

"Controller! What an unexpected pleasure! Boys, what are you thinking of? This is the Controller; this is his fordship, Mustapha Mond."

In the four thousand rooms of the Centre the four thousand electric clocks simultaneously struck four. Discarnate voices called from the trumpet mouths.

"Main Day-shift off duty. Second Day-shift take over. Main Day-shift off . . ."

In the lift, on their way up to the changing rooms, Henry Foster and the Assistant Director of Predestination rather pointedly turned their backs on Bernard Marx from the Psychology Bureau: averted themselves from that unsavoury reputation.

The faint hum and rattle of machinery still stirred the crimson air in the Embryo Store. Shifts might come and go, one lupus-coloured face give place to another; majestically and for ever the conveyors crept forward with their load of future men and women.

Lenina Crowne walked briskly towards the door.

His fordship Mustapha Mond! The eyes of the saluting students almost popped out of their heads. Mustapha Mond! The Resident Controller for Western Europe! One of the Ten World Controllers. One of the Ten . . . and he sat down on the bench with the D.H.C., he was going to stay, to stay, yes, and actually talk to them . . . straight from the horse's mouth. Straight from the mouth of Ford himself.

Two shrimp-brown children emerged from a neighbouring shrubbery, stared at them for a moment with large, astonished eyes, then returned to their amusements among the leaves.

"You all remember," said the Controller, in his strong deep voice, "you all remember, I suppose, that beautiful and inspired saying of Our Ford's: History is bunk. History," he repeated slowly, "is bunk."

He waved his hand; and it was as though, with an invisible feather whisk, he had brushed away a little dust, and the dust was Harappa, was Ur of the Chaldees; some spider-webs, and they were Thebes and Babylon and Cnossos and Mycenae. Whisk, Whisk—and where was Odysseus, where was Job, where were Jupiter and Gotama and Jesus? Whisk—and those specks of antique dirt called Athens and Rome, Jerusalem and the Middle Kingdom—all were gone. Whisk—the place where Italy had been was empty. Whisk, the cathedrals; whisk, whisk, King Lear and the Thoughts of Pascal. Whisk, Passion; whisk, Requiem; whisk, Symphony; whisk . . .

"Going to the Feelies this evening, Henry?" enquired the Assistant Predestinator. "I hear the new one at the Alhambra is first-rate. There's a love scene on a bearskin rug; they say it's marvellous. Every hair of the bear reproduced. The most amazing tactual effects."

"That's why you're taught no history," the Controller was saying. "But now the time has come . . ."

The D.H.C. looked at him nervously. There were those strange rumours of old forbidden books hidden in a safe in the Controller's study. Bibles, poetry—Ford knew what.

Mustapha Mond intercepted his anxious glance and the corners of his red lips twitched ironically.

"It's all right, Director," he said in a tone of faint derision, "I won't corrupt them."

The D.H.C. was overwhelmed with confusion.

Those who feel themselves despised do well to look despising. The smile on Bernard Marx's face was contemptuous. Every hair on the bear indeed!

"I shall make a point of going," said Henry Foster.

Mustapha Mond leaned forward, shook a finger at them. "Just try to realize it," he said, and his voice sent a strange thrill quivering along their diaphragms. "Try to realize what it was like to have a viviparous mother."

That smutty word again. But none of them dreamed, this time, of smiling.

"Try to imagine what 'living with one's family' meant."

They tried; but obviously without the smallest success.

"And do you know what a 'home' was?"

They shook their heads.

From her dim crimson cellar Lenina Crowne shot up seventeen stories, turned to the right as she stepped out of the lift, walked down a long corridor and, opening the door marked GIRLS' DRESSING-ROOM, plunged into a deafening chaos of arms and bosoms and underclothing. Torrents of hot water were splashing into or gurgling out of a hundred baths. Rumbling and hissing, eighty vibro-vacuum massage machines were simultaneously kneading and sucking the firm and sunburnt flesh of eighty superb female specimens. Every one was talking at the top of her voice. A Synthetic Music machine was warbling out a super-cornet solo.

"Hullo, Fanny," said Lenina to the young woman who had the pegs and locker next to hers.

Fanny worked in the Bottling Room, and her surname was also Crowne. But as the two thousand million inhabitants of the planet had only ten thousand names between them, the coincidence was not particularly surprising.

Lenina pulled at her zippers—downwards on the jacket, downwards with a double-handed gesture at the two that held trousers, downwards again to loosen her undergarment. Still wearing her shoes and stockings, she walked off towards the bathrooms.

Home, home—a few small rooms, stiflingly overinhabited by a man, by a periodically teeming woman, by a rabble of boys and girls of all ages. No air, no space; an understerilized prison; darkness, disease, and smells.

(The Controller's evocation was so vivid that one of the boys, more sensitive than the rest, turned pale at the mere description and was on the point of being sick.)

Lenina got out of the bath, towelled herself dry, took hold of a long flexible tube plugged into the wall, presented the nozzle to her breast, as though she meant to commit suicide, pressed down the trigger. A blast of warmed air dusted her with the finest talcum powder. Eight different scents and eau-de-Cologne were laid on in little taps over the wash-basin. She turned on the third from the left, dabbed herself with chypre and, carrying her shoes and stockings in her hand, went out to see if one of the vibro-vacuum machines were free.

And home was as squalid psychically as physically. Psychically, it was a rabbit hole, a midden, hot with the frictions of tightly packed life, reeking with emotion. What suffocating intimacies, what dangerous, insane, obscene relationships between the members of the family group! Maniacally, the mother brooded over her children (*her* children) . . . brooded over them like a cat over its kittens; but a cat that could talk, a cat that could say, "My baby, my baby," over and over again. "My baby, and oh, oh, at my breast, the little hands, the hunger, and that unspeakable agonizing pleasure! Till at last my baby sleeps, my baby sleeps with a bubble of white milk at the corner of his mouth. My little baby sleeps . . ."

"Yes," said Mustapha Mond, nodding his head, "you may well shudder."

"Who are you going out with to-night?" Lenina asked, returning from the vibro-vac like a pearl illuminated from within, pinkly glowing.

"Nobody."

Lenina raised her eyebrows in astonishment.

"I've been feeling rather out of sorts lately," Fanny explained. "Dr. Wells advised me to have a Pregnancy Substitute."

"But, my dear, you're only nineteen. The first Pregnancy Substitute isn't compulsory till twenty-one."

"I know, dear. But some people are better if they begin earlier. Dr.

Wells told me that brunettes with wide pelvises, like me, ought to have their first Pregnancy Substitute at seventeen. So I'm really two years late, not two years early." She opened the door of her locker and pointed to the row of boxes and labelled phials on the upper shelf.

"SYRUP OF CORPUS LUTEUM," Lenina read the names aloud. "OVA-RIN, GUARANTEED FRESH: NOT TO BE USED AFTER AUGUST 1ST, A.F. 632. MAMMARY GLAND EXTRACT: TO BE TAKEN THREE TIMES DAILY, BE-FORE MEALS, WITH A LITTLE WATER. PLACENTIN: 5CC TO BE INJECTED INTRAVENALLY EVERY THIRD DAY . . . Ugh!" Lenina shuddered. "How I loathe intravenals, don't you?"

"Yes. But when they do one good . . ." Fanny was a particularly sensible girl.

Our Ford—or Our Freud, as, for some inscrutable reason, he chose to call himself whenever he spoke of psychological matters—Our Freud had been the first to reveal the appalling dangers of family life. The world was full of fathers—was therefore full of misery; full of mothers—there-fore of every kind of perversion from sadism to chastity; full of brothers, sisters, uncles, aunts—full of madness and suicide.

"And yet, among the savages of Samoa, in certain islands off the coast of New Guinea . . ."

The tropical sunshine lay like warm honey on the naked bodies of children tumbling promiscuously among the hibiscus blossoms. Home was in any one of twenty palm-thatched houses. In the Trobriands concep-tion was the work of ancestral ghosts; nobody had ever heard of a father.

"Extremes," said the Controller, "meet. For the good reason that they were made to meet."

"Dr. Wells says that a three months' Pregnancy Substitute now will make all the difference to my health for the next three or four years."

"Well, I hope he's right," said Lenina. "But, Fanny, do you really mean to say that for the next three months you're not supposed to . . ."

"Oh no, dear. Only for a week or two, that's all. I shall spend the evening at the Club playing Musical Bridge. I suppose you're going out?"

Lenina nodded.

"Who with?"

"Henry Foster."

"Again?" Fanny's kind, rather moon-like face took on an incongruous expression of pained and disapproving astonishment. "Do you mean to tell me you're *still* going out with Henry Foster?"

Mothers and fathers, brothers and sisters. But there were also husbands, wives, lovers. There were also monogamy and romance.

"Though you probably don't know what those are," said Mustapha Mond.

They shook their heads.

Family, monogamy, romance. Everywhere exclusiveness, everywhere a focussing of interest, a narrow channelling of impulse and energy.

"But every one belongs to every one else," he concluded, citing the hypnopædic proverb.

The students nodded, emphatically agreeing with a statement which upwards of sixty-two thousand repetitions in the dark had made them accept, not merely as true, but as axiomatic, self-evident, utterly indisputable.

"But after all," Lenina was protesting, "it's only about four months now since I've been having Henry."

"*Only* four months! I like that. And what's more," Fanny went on, pointing an accusing finger, "there's been nobody else except Henry all that time. Has there?"

Lenina blushed scarlet; but her eyes, the tone of her voice remained defiant. "No, there hasn't been any one else," she answered almost truculently. "And I jolly well don't see why there should have been."

"Oh, she jolly well doesn't see why there should have been," Fanny repeated, as though to an invisible listener behind Lenina's left shoulder. Then, with a sudden change of tone, "But seriously," she said, "I really do think you ought to be careful. It's such horribly bad form to go on and on like this with one man. At forty, or thirty-five, it wouldn't be so bad. But at *your* age, Lenina! No, it really won't do. And you know how strongly the D.H.C. objects to anything intense or long-drawn. Four months of Henry Foster, without having another man—why, he'd be furious if he knew . . ."

"Think of water under pressure in a pipe." They thought of it. "I pierce it once," said the Controller. "What a jet!"

He pierced it twenty times. There were twenty piddling little fountains.

"My baby. My baby . . . !"

"Mother!" The madness is infectious.

"My love, my one and only, precious, precious . . ."

Mother, monogamy, romance. High spurts the fountain; fierce and foamy the wild jet. The urge has but a single outlet. My love, my baby.

No wonder those poor pre-moderns were mad and wicked and miserable. Their world didn't allow them to take things easily, didn't allow them to be sane, virtuous, happy. What with mothers and lovers, what with the prohibitions they were not conditioned to obey, what with the temptations and the lonely remorses, what with all the diseases and the endless isolating pain, what with the uncertainties and the poverty—they were forced to feel strongly. And feeling strongly (and strongly, what was more, in solitude, in hopelessly individual isolation), how could they be stable?

"Of course there's no need to give him up. Have somebody else from time to time, that's all. He has other girls, doesn't he?"

Lenina admitted it.

"Of course he does. Trust Henry Foster to be the perfect gentleman —always correct. And then there's the Director to think of. You know what a stickler . . ."

Nodding, "He patted me on the behind this afternoon," said Lenina.

"There, you see!" Fanny was triumphant. "That shows what *he* stands for. The strictest conventionality."

"Stability," said the Controller, "stability. No civilization without social stability. No social stability without individual stability." His voice was a trumpet. Listening they felt larger, warmer.

The machine turns, turns and must keep on turning—for ever. It is death if it stands still. A thousand millions scrabbled the crust of the earth. The wheels began to turn. In a hundred and fifty years there were two thousand millions. Stop all the wheels. In a hundred and fifty weeks there are once more only a thousand millions; a thousand thousand thousand men and women have starved to death.

Wheels must turn steadily, but cannot turn untended. There must be men to tend them, men as steady as the wheels upon their axles, sane men, obedient men, stable in contentment.

Crying: My baby, my mother, my only, only love; groaning: My sin, my terrible God; screaming with pain, muttering with fever, bemoaning old age and poverty—how can they tend the wheels? And if they cannot tend the wheels . . . The corpses of a thousand thousand thousand men and women would be hard to bury or burn.

"And after all," Fanny's tone was coaxing, "it's not as though there were anything painful or disagreeable about having one or two men besides Henry. And seeing that you *ought* to be a little more promiscuous . . ."

"Stability," insisted the Controller, "stability. The primal and the ultimate need. Stability. Hence all this."

With a wave of his hand he indicated the gardens, the huge building of the Conditioning Centre, the naked children furtive in the undergrowth or running across the lawns.

Lenina shook her head. "Somehow," she mused, "I hadn't been feeling very keen on promiscuity lately. There are times when one doesn't. Haven't you found that too, Fanny?"

Fanny nodded her sympathy and understanding. "But one's got to make the effort," she said sententiously, "one's got to play the game. After all, every one belongs to every one else."

"Yes, every one belongs to every one else," Lenina repeated slowly and, sighing, was silent for a moment; then, taking Fanny's hand, gave it a little squeeze. "You're quite right, Fanny. As usual. I'll make the effort."

Impulse arrested spills over, and the flood is feeling, the flood is passion, the flood is even madness: it depends on the force of the current, the height and strength of the barrier. The unchecked stream flows smoothly down its appointed channels into a calm well-being. (The embryo is hungry; day in, day out, the blood-surrogate pump unceasingly turns its eight hundred revolutions a minute. The decanted infant howls; at once a nurse appears with a bottle of external secretion. Feeling lurks in that interval of time between desire and its consummation. Shorten that interval, break down all those old unnecessary barriers.

"Fortunate boys!" said the Controller. "No pains have been spared to make your lives emotionally easy—to preserve you, so far as that is possible, from having emotions at all."

"Ford's in his flivver," murmured the D.H.C. "All's well with the world."

"Lenina Crowne?" said Henry Foster, echoing the Assistant Predestinator's question as he zipped up his trousers. "Oh, she's a splendid girl. Wonderfully pneumatic. I'm surprised you haven't had her."

"I can't think how it is I haven't," said the Assistant Predestinator. "I certainly will. At the first opportunity."

From his place on the opposite side of the changing-room aisle, Bernard Marx overheard what they were saying and turned pale.

"And to tell the truth," said Lenina, "I'm beginning to get just a tiny bit bored with nothing but Henry every day." She pulled on her left stocking. "Do you know Bernard Marx?" she asked in a tone whose excessive casualness was evidently forced.

Fanny looked startled. "You don't mean to say . . . ?"

"Why not? Bernard's an Alpha Plus. Besides, he asked me to go to one of the Savage Reservations with him. I've always wanted to see a Savage Reservation."

"But his reputation?"

"What do I care about his reputation?"

"They say he doesn't like Obstacle Golf."

"They say, they say," mocked Lenina.

"And then he spends most of his time by himself—*alone*." There was horror in Fanny's voice.

"Well, he won't be alone when he's with me. And anyhow, why are people so beastly to him? I think he's rather sweet." She smiled to herself; how absurdly shy he had been! Frightened almost—as though she were a World Controller and he a Gamma-Minus machine minder.

"Consider your own lives," said Mustapha Mond. "Has any of you ever encountered an insurmountable obstacle?"

The question was answered by a negative silence.

"Has any of you been compelled to live through a long time-interval between the consciousness of a desire and its fulfilment?"

"Well," began one of the boys, and hesitated.

"Speak up," said the D.H.C. "Don't keep his fordship waiting."

"I once had to wait nearly four weeks before a girl I wanted would let me have her."

"And you felt a strong emotion in consequence?"

"Horrible!"

"Horrible; precisely," said the Controller. "Our ancestors were so stupid and short-sighted that when the first reformers came along and offered to deliver them from those horrible emotions, they wouldn't have anything to do with them."

"Talking about her as though she were a bit of meat." Bernard ground his teeth. "Have her here, have her there. Like mutton. Degrading her to so much mutton. She said she'd think it over, she said she'd give me an answer this week. Oh, Ford, Ford, Ford." He would have liked to go up to them and hit them in the face—hard, again and again.

"Yes, I really do advise you to try her," Henry Foster was saying.

"Take Ectogenesis. Pfitzner and Kawaguchi had got the whole technique worked out. But would the Governments look at it? No. There was something called Christianity. Women were forced to go on being viviparous."

"He's so ugly!" said Fanny.

"But I rather like his looks."

"And then so *small*." Fanny made a grimace; smallness was so horribly and typically low-caste.

"I think that's rather sweet," said Lenina. "One feels one would like to pet him. You know. Like a cat."

Fanny was shocked. "They say somebody made a mistake when he was still in the bottle—thought he was a Gamma and put alcohol into his blood-surrogate. That's why he's so stunted."

"What nonsense!" Lenina was indignant.

"Sleep teaching was actually prohibited in England. There was something called liberalism. Parliament, if you know what that was, passed a law against it. The records survive. Speeches about liberty of the subject. Liberty to be inefficient and miserable. Freedom to be a round peg in a square hole."

"But, my dear chap, you're welcome, I assure you. You're welcome." Henry Foster patted the Assistant Predestinator on the shoulder. "Every one belongs to every one else, after all."

One hundred repetitions three nights a week for four years, thought Bernard Marx, who was a specialist on hypnopædia. Sixty-two thousand four hundred repetitions make one truth. Idiots!

"Or the Caste System. Constantly proposed, constantly rejected. There was something called democracy. As though men were more than physico-chemically equal."

"Well, all I can say is that I'm going to accept his invitation."

Bernard hated them, hated them. But they were two, they were large, they were strong.

"The Nine Years' War began in A.F. 141."

"Not even if it *were* true about the alcohol in his blood-surrogate."

"Phosgene, chloropicrin, ethyl iodoacetate, diphenylcyanarsine, trichlor-methyl, chloroformate, dichlorethyl sulphide. Not to mention hydro-cyanic acid."

"Which I simply don't believe," Lenina concluded.

"The noise of fourteen thousand aeroplanes advancing in open order. But in the Kurfurstendamm and the Eighth Arrondissement, the explosion of the anthrax bombs is hardly louder then the popping of a paper bag."

"Because I *do* want to see a Savage Reservation."

$Ch_3C_6H_2(NO_2)_3 + Hg(CNO)_2 =$ well, what? An enormous hole in the ground, a pile of masonry, some bits of flesh and mucus, a foot, with the boot still on it, flying through the air and landing, flop, in the middle of the geraniums—the scarlet ones; such a splendid show that summer!

"You're hopeless, Lenina, I give you up."

"The Russian technique for infecting water supplies was particularly ingenious."

Back turned to back, Fanny and Lenina continued their changing in silence.

"The Nine Years' War, the great Economic Collapse. There was a choice between World Control and destruction. Between stability and . . ."

"Fanny Crowne's a nice girl too," said the Assistant Predestinator.

In the nurseries, the Elementary Class Consciousness lesson was over, the voices were adapting future demand to future industrial supply. "I do love flying," they whispered, "I do love flying, I do love having new clothes, I do love . . ."

"Liberalism, of course, was dead of anthrax, but all the same you couldn't do things by force."

"Not nearly so pneumatic as Lenina. Oh, not nearly."

"But old clothes are beastly," continued the untiring whisper. "We always throw away old clothes. Ending is better than mending, ending is better than mending, ending is better . . ."

"Government's an affair of sitting, not hitting. You rule with the brains and the buttocks, never with the fists. For example, there was the conscription of consumption."

"There, I'm ready," said Lenina, but Fanny remained speechless and averted. "Let's make peace, Fanny darling."

"Every man, woman and child compelled to consume so much a year. In the interests of industry. The sole result . . ."

"Ending is better than mending. The more stitches, the less riches; the more stitches . . ."

"One of these days," said Fanny, with dismal emphasis, "you'll get into trouble."

"Conscientious objection on an enormous scale. Anything not to consume. Back to nature."

"I do love flying, I do love flying."

"Back to culture. Yes, actually to culture. You can't consume much if you sit still and read books."

"Do I look all right?" Lenina asked. Her jacket was made of bottle-green acetate cloth with green viscose fur at the cuffs and collar.

"Eight hundred Simple Lifers were mowed down by machine guns at Golders Green."

"Ending is better than mending, ending is better than mending."

Green corduroy shorts and white viscose-woollen stockings turned down below the knee.

"Then came the famous British Museum Massacre. Two thousand culture fans gassed with dichlorethyl sulphide."

A green-and-white jockey cap shaded Lenina's eyes; her shoes were bright green and highly polished.

"In the end," said Mustapha Mond, "the Controllers realized that force was no good. The slower but infinitely surer methods of ectogenesis, neo-Pavlovian conditioning and hypnopædia . . ."

And round her waist she wore a silver-mounted green morocco-surrogate cartridge belt, bulging (for Lenina was not a freemartin) with the regulation supply of contraceptives.

"The discoveries of Pfitzner and Kawaguchi were at last made use of. An intensive propaganda against viviparous reproduction . . ."

"Perfect!" cried Fanny enthusiastically. She could never resist Lenina's charm for long. "And what a perfectly *sweet* Malthusian belt!"

"Accompanied by a campaign against the Past; by the closing of museums, the blowing up of historical monuments (luckily most of them had already been destroyed during the Nine Years' War); by the suppression of all books published before A.F. 150."

"I simply must get one like it," said Fanny.

"There were some things called the pyramids, for example."

"My old black-patent bandolier . . ."

"And a man called Shakespeare. You've never heard of them of course."

"It's an absolute disgrace—that bandolier of mine."

"Such are the advantages of a really scientific education."

"The more stitches the less riches; the more stitches the less . . ."

"The introduction of Our Ford's first T-Model . . ."

"I've had it nearly three months."

"Chosen as the opening date of the new era."

"Ending is better than mending; ending is better . . ."

"There was a thing, as I've said before, called Christianity."

"Ending is better than mending."

"The ethics and philosophy of under-consumption . . ."

"I love new clothes, I love new clothes, I love . . ."

"So essential when there was under-production; but in an age of machines and the fixation of nitrogen—positively a crime against society."

"Henry Foster gave it to me."

"All crosses had their tops cut and became T's. There was also a thing called God."

"It's real morocco-surrogate."

"We have the World State now. And Ford's Day celebrations, and Community Sings, and Solidarity Services."

"Ford, how I hate them!" Bernard Marx was thinking.

"There was a thing called Heaven; but all the same they used to drink enormous quantities of alcohol."

"Like meat, like so much meat."

"There was a thing called the soul and a thing called immortality."

"Do ask Henry where he got it."

"But they used to take morphia and cocaine."

"And what makes it worse, she thinks of herself as meat."

"Two thousand pharmacologists and bio-chemists were subsidized in A.F. 178."

"He does look glum," said the Assistant Predestinator, pointing at Bernard Marx.

"Six years later it was being produced commercially. The perfect drug."

"Let's bait him."

"Euphoric, narcotic, pleasantly hallucinant."

"Glum, Marx, glum." The clap on the shoulder made him start, look up. It was that brute Henry Foster. "What you need is a gramme of soma."

"All the advantages of Christianity and alcohol; none of their defects."

"Ford, I should like to kill him!" But all he did was to say, "No, thank you," and fend off the proffered tube of tablets.

"Take a holiday from reality whenever you like, and come back without so much as a headache or a mythology."

"Take it," insisted Henry Foster, "take it."

"Stability was practically assured."

"One cubic centimetre cures ten gloomy sentiments," said the Assistant Predestinator citing a piece of homely hypnopædic wisdom.

"It only remained to conquer old age."

"Damn you, damn you!" shouted Bernard Marx.

"Hoity-toity."

"Gonadal hormones, transfusion of young blood, magnesium salts . . ."

"And do remember that a gramme is better than a damn." They went out, laughing.

"All the physiological stigmata of old age have been abolished. And along with them, of course . . ."

"Don't forget to ask him about that Malthusian belt," said Fanny.

"Along with them all the old man's mental peculiarities. Characters remain constant throughout a whole lifetime."

". . . two rounds of Obstacle Golf to get through before dark. I must fly."

"Work, play—at sixty our powers and tastes are what they were at seventeen. Old men in the bad old days used to renounce, retire, take to religion, spend their time reading, thinking—*thinking!*"

"Idiots, swine!" Bernard Marx was saying to himself, as he walked down the corridor to the lift.

"Now—such is progress—the old men work, the old men copulate, the old men have no time, no leisure from pleasure, not a moment to sit down and think—or if ever by some unlucky chance such a crevice of time should yawn in the solid substance of their distractions, there is always *soma*, delicious *soma*, half a gramme for a half-holiday, a gramme for a week-end, two grammes for a trip to the gorgeous East, three for a dark eternity on the moon; returning whence they find themselves on the other side of the crevice, safe on the solid ground of daily labour and distraction, scampering from feely to feely, from girl to pneumatic girl, from Electro-magnetic Golf course to . . ."

"Go away, little girl," shouted the D.H.C. angrily. "Go away, little boy! Can't you see that his fordship's busy? Go and do your erotic play somewhere else."

"Suffer little children," said the Controller.

Slowly, majestically, with a faint humming of machinery, the Conveyors moved forward, thirty-three centimetres an hour. In the red darkness glinted innumerable rubies.

CHAPTER IV: The lift was crowded with men from the Alpha Changing Rooms, and Lenina's entry was greeted by many friendly nods and smiles. She was a popular girl and, at one time or another, had spent a night with almost all of them.

They were dear boys, she thought, as she returned their salutations. Charming boys! Still, she did wish that George Edzel's ears weren't quite so big (perhaps he'd been given just a spot too much parathyroid at Metre 328?). And looking at Benito Hoover, she couldn't help remembering that he was really *too* hairy when he took his clothes off.

Turning, with eyes a little saddened by the recollection of Benito's curly blackness, she saw in a corner the small thin body, the melancholy face of Bernard Marx.

"Bernard!" she stepped up to him. "I was looking for you." Her voice rang clear above the hum of the mounting lift. The others looked round curiously. "I wanted to talk to you about our New Mexico plan." Out of the tail of her eye she could see Benito Hoover gaping with astonishment. The gape annoyed her. "Surprised I shouldn't be begging to go with *him* again!" she said to herself. Then aloud, and more warmly than ever, "I'd simply *love* to come with you for a week in July," she went on. (Anyhow, she was publicly proving her unfaithfulness to Henry. Fanny ought to be pleased, even though it was Bernard.) "That is," Lenina gave him her most deliciously significant smile, "if you still want to have me."

Bernard's pale face flushed. "What on earth for?" she wondered, astonished, but at the same time touched by this strange tribute to her power.

"Hadn't we better talk about it somewhere else?" he stammered, looking horribly uncomfortable.

"As though I'd been saying something shocking," thought Lenina. "He couldn't look more upset if I'd made a dirty joke—asked him who his mother was, or something like that."

"I mean, with all these people about . . ." He was choked with confusion.

Lenina's laugh was frank and wholly unmalicious. "How funny you are!" she said; and she quite genuinely did think him funny. "You'll give me at least a week's warning, won't you," she went on in another tone. "I suppose we take the Blue Pacific Rocket? Does it start from the Charing-T Tower? Or is it from Hampstead?"

Before Bernard could answer, the lift came to a standstill.

"Roof!" called a creaking voice.

The liftman was a small simian creature, dressed in the black tunic of an Epsilon-Minus Semi-Moron.

"Roof!"

He flung open the gates. The warm glory of afternoon sunlight made him start and blink his eyes. "Oh, roof!" he repeated in a voice of rapture. He was as though suddenly and joyfully awakened from a dark annihilating stupor. "Roof!"

He smiled up with a kind of doggily expectant adoration into the faces of his passengers. Talking and laughing together, they stepped out into the light. The liftman looked after them.

"Roof?" he said once more, questioningly.

Then a bell rang, and from the ceiling of the lift a loud speaker began, very softly and yet very imperiously, to issue its commands.

"Go down," it said, "go down. Floor Eighteen. Go down, go down. Floor Eighteen. Go down, go . . ."

The liftman slammed the gates, touched a button and instantly dropped back into the droning twilight of the well, the twilight of his own habitual stupor.

It was warm and bright on the roof. The summer afternoon was drowsy with the hum of passing helicopters; and the deeper drone of the rocket-planes hastening, invisible, through the bright sky five or six miles over-head was like a caress on the soft air. Bernard Marx drew a deep breath. He looked up into the sky and round the blue horizon and finally down into Lenina's face.

"Isn't it beautiful!" His voice trembled a little.

She smiled at him with an expression of the most sympathetic under-standing. "Simply perfect for Obstacle Golf," she answered rapturously. "And now I must fly, Bernard. Henry gets cross if I keep him waiting. Let me know in good time about the date." And waving her hand, she ran away across the wide flat roof towards the hangars. Bernard stood watch-ing the retreating twinkle of the white stockings, the sunburnt knees viva-ciously bending and unbending, again, again, and the softer rolling of those well-fitted corduroy shorts beneath the bottle-green jacket. His face wore an expression of pain.

"I should say she was pretty," said a loud and cheery voice just be-hind him.

Bernard started and looked round. The chubby red face of Benito Hoover was beaming down at him—beaming with manifest cordiality. Be-nito was notoriously good-natured. People said of him that he could have got through life without ever touching *soma*. The malice and bad tempers from which other people had to take holidays never afflicted him. Reality for Benito was always sunny.

"Pneumatic too. And how!" Then, in another tone: "But, I say," he went on, "you do look glum! What you need is a gramme of *soma*." Div-ing into his right-hand trouser-pocket, Benito produced a phial. "One cu-bic centimetre cures ten gloomy . . . But, I say!"

Bernard had suddenly turned and rushed away.

Benito stared after him. "What can be the matter with the fellow?" he wondered, and, shaking his head, decided that the story about the alcohol having been put into the poor chap's blood-surrogate must be true. "Touched his brain, I suppose."

He put away the *soma* bottle, and taking out a packet of sex-hormone chewing-gum, stuffed a plug into his cheek and walked slowly away towards the hangars, ruminating.

Henry Foster had had his machine wheeled out of its lock-up and, when Lenina arrived, was already seated in the cockpit, waiting.

"Four minutes late," was all his comment, as she climbed in beside him. He started the engines and threw the helicopter screws into gear. The machine shot vertically into the air. Henry accelerated; the humming of the propeller shrilled from hornet to wasp, from wasp to mosquito; the speedometer showed that they were rising at the best part of two kilometres a minute. London diminished beneath them. The huge table-topped buildings were no more, in a few seconds, than a bed of geometrical mushrooms sprouting from the green of park and garden. In the midst of them, thin-stalked, a taller, slenderer fungus, the Charing-T Tower lifted towards the sky a disk of shining concrete.

Like the vague torsos of fabulous athletes, huge fleshy clouds lolled on the blue air above their heads. Out of one of them suddenly dropped a small scarlet insect, buzzing as it fell.

"There's the Red Rocket," said Henry, "just come in from New York." Looking at his watch, "Seven minutes behind time," he added, and shook his head. "These Atlantic services—they're really scandalously unpunctual."

He took his foot off the accelerator. The huming of the screws overhead dropped an octave and a half, back through wasp and hornet to bumble bee, to cockchafer, to stage-beetle. The upward rush of the machine slackened off; a moment later they were hanging motionless in the air. Henry pushed at a lever; there was a click. Slowly at first, then faster and faster, till it was a circular mist before their eyes, the propeller in front of them began to revolve. The wind of a horizontal speed whistled ever more shrilly in the stays. Henry kept his eye on the revolution-counter; when the needle touched the twelve hundred mark, he threw the helicopter screws out of gear. The machine had enough forward momentum to be able to fly on its planes.

Lenina looked down through the window in the floor between her feet. They were flying over the six kilometre zone of park-land that separated Central London from its first ring of satellite suburbs. The green was maggoty with fore-shortened life. Forests of Centrifugal Bumble-puppy towers gleamed between the trees. Near Shepherd's Bush two thousand Beta-Minus mixed doubles were playing Riemann-surface tennis. A double row of Escalator Fives Courts lined the main road from Notting Hill to Willesden. In the Ealing stadium a Delta gynmastic display and community sing was in progress.

"What a hideous colour khaki is," remarked Lenina, voicing the hyp-nopædic prejudices of her caste.

The buildings of the Hounslow Feely Studio covered seven and a half hectares. Near them a black and khaki army of labourers was busy revitri-fying the surface of the Great West Road. One of the huge travelling cru-cibles was being tapped as they flew over. The molten stone poured out in a stream of dazzling incandescence across the road; the asbestos rollers came and went; at the tail of an insulated watering cart the steam rose in white clouds.

At Brentford the Television Corporation's factory was like a small town.

"They must be changing the shift," said Lenina.

Like aphides and ants, the leaf-green Gamma girls, the black Semi-Morons swarmed round the entrances, or stood in queues to take their places in the monorail tram-cars. Mulberry-coloured Beta-Minuses came and went among the crowd. The roof of the main building was alive with the alighting and departure of helicopters.

"My word," said Lenina, "I'm glad I'm not a Gamma."

Ten minutes later they were at Stoke Poges and had started their first round of Obstacle Golf.

With eyes for the most part downcast and, if ever they lighted on a fellow creature, at once and furtively averted, Bernard hastened across the roof. He was like a man pursued, but pursued by enemies he does not wish to see, lest they should seem more hostile even than he had supposed, and he himself be made to feel guiltier and even more help-lessly alone.

"That horrible Benito Hoover!" And yet the man had meant well enough. Which only made it, in a way, much worse. Those who meant well behaved in the same way as those who meant badly. Even Lenina was making him suffer. He remembered those weeks of timid indecision, dur-ing which he had looked and longed and despaired of ever having the courage to ask her. Dared he face the risk of being humiliated by a con-temptuous refusal? But if she were to say yes, what rapture! Well, now she had said it and he was still wretched—wretched that she should have thought it such a perfect afternoon for Obstacle Golf, that she should have trotted away to join Henry Foster, that she should have found him funny for not wanting to talk of their most private affairs in public. Wretched, in a word, because she had behaved as any healthy and virtu-ous English girl ought to behave and not in some other, abnormal, extraor-dinary way.

He opened the door of his lock-up and called to a lounging couple of

Delta-Minus attendants to come and push his machine out on to the roof. The hangars were staffed by a single Bokanovsky Group, and the men were twins, identically small, black and hideous. Bernard gave his orders in the sharp, rather arrogant and even offensive tone of one who does not feel himself too secure in his superiority. To have dealings with members of the lower castes was always, for Bernard, a most distressing experience. For whatever the cause (and the current gossip about the alcohol in his blood-surrogate may very likely—for accidents will happen—have been true) Bernard's physique was hardly better than that of the average Gamma. He stood eight centimetres short of the standard Alpha height and was slender in proportion. Contact with members of the lower castes always reminded him painfully of this physical inadequacy. "I am I, and wish I wasn't"; his self-consciousness was acute and distressing. Each time he found himself looking on the level, instead of downward, into a Delta's face, he felt humiliated. Would the creature treat him with the respect due to his caste? The question haunted him. Not without reason. For Gammas, Deltas and Epsilons had been to some extent conditioned to associate corporeal mass with social superiority. Indeed, a faint hypnopædic prejudice in favour of size was universal. Hence the laughter of the women to whom he made proposals, the practical joking of his equals among the men. The mockery made him feel an outsider; and feeling an outsider he behaved like one, which increased the prejudice against him and intensified the contempt and hostility aroused by his physical defects. Which in turn increased his sense of being alien and alone. A chronic fear of being slighted made him avoid his equals, made him stand, where his inferiors were concerned, self-consciously on his dignity. How bitterly he envied men like Henry Foster and Benito Hoover! Men who never had to shout at an Epsilon to get an order obeyed; men who took their position for granted; men who moved through the caste system as a fish through the water—so utterly at home as to be unaware either of themselves or of the beneficent and comfortable element in which they had their being.

Slackly, it seemed to him, and with reluctance, the twin attendants wheeled his plane out on the roof.

"Hurry up!" said Bernard irritably. One of them glanced at him. Was that a kind of bestial derision that he detected in those blank grey eyes? "Hurry up!" he shouted more loudly, and there was an ugly rasp in his voice.

He climbed into the plane and, a minute later, was flying southwards, towards the river.

The various Bureaux of Propaganda and the College of Emotional Engineering were housed in a single sixty-story building in Fleet Street. In the basement and on the lower floors were the presses and offices of the three great London newspapers—*The Hourly Radio*, an upper-caste sheet, the pale green *Gamma Gazette*, and, on khaki paper and in words exclusively of one syllable, *The Delta Mirror*. Then came the Bureaux of Propaganda by Television, by Feeling Picture, and by Synthetic Voice and Music respectively—twenty-two floors of them. Above were the research laboratories and the padded rooms in which the Sound-Track Writers and Synthetic Composers did their delicate work. The top eighteen floors were occupied by the College of Emotional Engineering.

Bernard landed on the roof of Propaganda House and stepped out.

"Ring down to Mr. Helmholtz Watson," he ordered the Gamma-Plus porter, "and tell him that Mr. Bernard Marx is waiting for him on the roof."

He sat down and lit a cigarette.

Helmholtz Watson was writing when the message came down.

"Tell him I'm coming at once," he said and hung up the receiver. Then, turning to his secretary, "I'll leave you to put my things away," he went on in the same official and impersonal tone; and, ignoring her lustrous smile, got up and walked briskly to the door.

He was a powerfully built man, deep-chested, broad-shouldered, massive, and yet quick in his movements, springy and agile. The round strong pillar of his neck supported a beautifully shaped head. His hair was dark and curly, his features strongly marked. In a forcible emphatic way, he was handsome and looked, as his secretary was never tired of repeating, every centimetre an Alpha-Plus. By profession he was a lecturer at the College of Emotional Engineering (Department of Writing) and in the intervals of his educational activities, a working Emotional Engineer. He wrote regularly for *The Hourly Radio*, composed feely scenarios, and had the happiest knack for slogans and hypnopædic rhymes.

"Able," was the verdict of his superiors. "Perhaps," (and they would shake their heads, would significantly lower their voices) "a little *too* able."

Yes, a little too able; they were right. A mental excess had produced in Helmholtz Watson effects very similar to those which, in Bernard Marx, were the result of a physical defect. Too little bone and brawn had isolated Bernard from his fellow men, and the sense of this apartness, being, by all the current standards, a mental excess, became in its turn a cause of wider separation. That which had made Helmholtz so uncomfortably aware of being himself and all alone was too much ability. What the two men shared was the knowledge that they were individuals. But whereas the physically defective Bernard had suffered all his life from the consciousness of being separate, it was only quite recently that, grown aware of his mental excess, Helmholtz Watson had also become aware of his difference from the people who surrounded him. This Escalator-Squash champion, this indefatigable lover (it was said that he had had six hun-

dred and forty different girls in under four years), this admirable committee man and best mixer had realized quite suddenly that sport, women,
communal activities were only, so far as he was concerned, second bests.
Really, and at the bottom, he was interested in something else. But in
what? In what? That was the problem which Bernard had come to discuss
with him—or rather, since it was always Helmholtz who did all the talking, to listen to his friend discussing, yet once more.

Three charming girls from the Bureau of Propaganda by Synthetic
Voice waylaid him as he stepped out of the lift.

"Oh, Helmholtz, darling, *do* come and have a picnic supper with us on
Exmoor." They clung round him imploringly.

He shook his head, he pushed his way through them. "No, no."

"We're not inviting any other man."

But Helmholtz remained unshaken even by this delightful promise.
"No," he repeated, "I'm busy." And he held resolutely on his course.
The girls trailed after him. It was not till he had actually climbed into
Bernard's plane and slammed the door that they gave up pursuit. Not
without reproaches.

"These women!" he said, as the machine rose into the air. "These
women!" And he shook his head, he frowned. "Too awful," Bernard hypocritically agreed, wishing, as he spoke the words, that he could have as
many girls as Helmholtz did, and with as little trouble. He was seized
with a sudden urgent need to boast. "I'm taking Lenina Crowne to New
Mexico with me," he said in a tone as casual as he could make it.

"Are you?" said Helmholtz, with a total absence of interest. Then
after a little pause, "This last week or two," he went on, "I've been cutting
all my committees and all my girls. You can't imagine what a hullabaloo
they've been making about it at the College. Still, it's been worth it, I
think. The effects . . ." He hesitated. "Well, they're odd, they're very
odd."

A physical shortcoming could produce a kind of mental excess. The
process, it seemed, was reversible. Mental excess could produce, for its
own purposes, the voluntary blindness and deafness of deliberate solitude,
the artificial impotence of asceticism.

The rest of the short flight was accomplished in silence. When they
had arrived and were comfortably stretched out on the pneumatic sofas
in Bernard's room, Helmholtz began again.

Speaking very slowly, "Did you ever feel," he asked, "as though you
had something inside you that was only waiting for you to give it a chance
to come out? Some sort of extra power that you aren't using—you know,
like all the water that goes down the falls instead of through the turbines?" He looked at Bernard questioningly.

"You mean all the emotions one might be feeling if things were different?"

Helmholtz shook his head. "Not quite. I'm thinking of a queer feeling I sometimes get, a feeling that I've got something important to say and the power to say it—only I don't know what it is, and I can't make any use of the power. If there was some different way of writing . . . Or else something else to write about . . ." He was silent; then, "You see," he went on at last, "I'm pretty good at inventing phrases—you know, the sort of words that suddenly make you jump, almost as though you'd sat on a pin, they seem so new and exciting even though they're about something hypnopædically obvious. But that doesn't seem enough. It's not enough for the phrases to be good; what you make with them ought to be good too."

"But your things are good, Helmholtz."

"Oh, as far as they go." Helmholtz shrugged his shoulders. "But they go such a little way. They aren't important enough, somehow. I feel I could do something much more important. Yes, and more intense, more violent. But what? What is there more important to say? And how can one be violent about the sort of things one's expected to write about? Words can be like X-rays, if you use them properly—they'll go through anything. You read and you're pierced. That's one of the things I try to teach my students—how to write piercingly. But what on earth's the good of being pierced by an article about a Community Sing, or the latest improvement in scent organs? Besides, can you make words really piercing—you know, like the very hardest X-rays—when you're writing about that sort of thing? Can you say something about nothing? That's what it finally boils down to. I try and I try . . ."

"Hush!" said Bernard suddenly, and lifted a warning finger; they listened. "I believe there's somebody at the door," he whispered.

Helmholtz got up, tiptoed across the room, and with a sharp quick movement flung the door wide open. There was, of course, nobody there.

"I'm sorry," said Bernard, feeling and looking uncomfortably foolish. "I suppose I've got things on my nerves a bit. When people are suspicious with you, you start being suspicious with them."

He passed his hand across his eyes, he sighed, his voice became plaintive. He was justifying himself. "If you knew what I'd had to put up with recently," he said almost tearfully—and the uprush of his self-pity was like a fountain suddenly released. "If you only knew!"

Helmholtz Watson listened with a certain sense of discomfort. "Poor little Bernard!" he said to himself. But at the same time he felt rather ashamed for his friend. He wished Bernard would show a little more pride.

CHAPTER V: By eight o'clock the light was failing. The loud speakers in the tower of the Stoke Poges Club House began, in a more than human tenor, to announce the closing of the courses. Lenina and Henry abandoned their game and walked back towards the Club. From the grounds of the Internal and External Secretion Trust came the lowing of those thousands of cattle which provided, with their hormones and their milk, the raw materials for the great factory at Farnham Royal.

An incessant buzzing of helicopters filled the twilight. Every two and a half minutes a bell and the screech of whistles announced the departure of one of the light monorail trains which carried the lower caste golfers back from their separate course to the metropolis.

Lenina and Henry climbed into their machine and started off. At eight hundred feet Henry slowed down the helicopter screws, and they hung for a minute or two poised above the fading landscape. The forest of Burnham Beeches stretched like a great pool of darkness towards the bright shore of the western sky. Crimson at the horizon, the last of the sunset faded, through orange, upwards into yellow and a pale watery green. Northwards, beyond and above the trees, the Internal and External Secretions factory glared with a fierce electric brilliance from every window of its twenty stories. Beneath them lay the buildings of the Golf Club— the huge Lower Caste barracks and, on the other side of a dividing wall, the smaller houses reserved for Alpha and Beta members. The approaches to the monorail station were black with the ant-like pullulation of lower-caste activity. From under the glass vault a lighted train shot out into the open. Following its southeasterly course across the dark plain their eyes were drawn to the majestic buildings of the Slough Crematorium. For the safety of night-flying planes, its four tall chimneys were flood-lighted and tipped with crimson danger signals. It was a landmark.

"Why do the smoke-stacks have those things like balconies round them?" enquired Lenina.

"Phosphorus recovery," explained Henry telegraphically. "On their way up the chimney the gases go through four separate treatments. P_2O_5 used to go right out of circulation every time they cremated some one. Now they recover over ninety-eight per cent. of it. More than a kilo and a half per adult corpse. Which makes the best part of four hundred tons of phosphorus every year from England alone." Henry spoke with a happy pride, rejoicing whole-heartedly in the achievement, as though it had been his own. "Fine to think we can go on being socially useful even after we're dead. Making plants grow."

Lenina, meanwhile, had turned her eyes away and was looking perpendicularly downwards at the monorail station. "Fine," she agreed. "But queer that Alphas and Betas won't make any more plants grow than those nasty little Gammas and Deltas and Epsilons down there."

"All men are physico-chemically equal," said Henry sententiously. "Besides, even Epsilons perform indispensable services."

"Even an Epsilon . . ." Lenina suddenly remembered an occasion when, as a little girl at school, she had woken up in the middle of the night and become aware, for the first time, of the whispering that had haunted all her sleeps. She saw again the beam of moonlight, the row of small white beds; heard once more the soft, soft voice that said (the words were there, unforgotten, unforgettable after so many night-long repetitions): "Every one works for every one else. We can't do without any one. Even Epsilons are useful. We couldn't do without Epsilons. Every one works for every one else. We can't do without any one . . ." Lenina remembered her first shock of fear and surprise; her speculations through half a wakeful hour; and then, under the influence of those endless repetitions, the gradual soothing of her mind, the soothing, the smoothing, the stealthy creeping of sleep. . . .

"I suppose Epsilons don't really mind being Epsilons," she said aloud.

"Of course they don't. How can they? They don't know what it's like being anything else. We'd mind, of course. But then we've been differently conditioned. Besides, we start with a different heredity."

"I'm glad I'm not an Epsilon," said Lenina, with conviction.

"And if you were an Epsilon," said Henry, "your conditioning would have made you no less thankful that you weren't a Beta or an Alpha." He put his forward propeller into gear and headed the machine towards London. Behind them, in the west, the crimson and orange were almost faded; a dark bank of cloud had crept into the zenith. As they flew over the Crematorium, the plane shot upwards on the column of hot air rising from the chimneys, only to fall as suddenly when it passed into the descending chill beyond.

"What a marvellous switchback!" Lenina laughed delightedly.

But Henry's tone was almost, for a moment, melancholy. "Do you know what that switchback was?" he said. "It was some human being finally and definitely disappearing. Going up in a squirt of hot gas. It would be curious to know who it was—a man or a woman, an Alpha or an Epsilon. . . ." He sighed. Then, in a resolutely cheerful voice, "Anyhow," he concluded, "there's one thing we can be certain of; whoever he may have been, he was happy when he was alive. Everybody's happy now."

"Yes, everybody's happy now," echoed Lenina. They had heard the words repeated a hundred and fifty times every night for twelve years.

Landing on the roof of Henry's forty-story apartment house in Westminster, they went straight down to the dining-hall. There, in a loud and cheerful company, they ate an excellent meal. *Soma* was served with the coffee. Lenina took two half-gramme tablets and Henry three. At twenty past nine they walked across the street to the newly opened Westminster Abbey Cabaret. It was a night almost without clouds, moonless and starry; but of this on the whole depressing fact Lenina and Henry were fortunately unaware. The electric sky-signs effectively shut off the outer darkness. "CALVIN STOPES AND HIS SIXTEEN SEXOPHONISTS." From the façade of the new Abbey the giant letters invitingly glared. "LONDON'S FINEST SCENT AND COLOUR ORGAN. ALL THE LATEST SYNTHETIC MUSIC."

They entered. The air seemed hot and somehow breathless with the scent of ambergris and sandalwood. On the domed ceiling of the hall, the colour organ had momentarily painted a tropical sunset. The Sixteen Sexophonists were playing an old favourite: "There ain't no Bottle in all the world like that dear little Bottle of mine." Four hundred couples were five-stepping round the polished floor. Lenina and Henry were soon the four hundred and first. The sexophones wailed like melodious cats under the moon, moaned in the alto and tenor registers as though the little death were upon them. Rich with a wealth of harmonics, their tremulous chorus mounted towards a climax, louder and ever louder—until at last, with a wave of his hand, the conductor let loose the final shattering note of ether-music and blew the sixteen merely human blowers clean out of existence. Thunder in A flat major. And then, in all but silence, in all but darkness, there followed a gradual deturgescence, a *diminuendo* sliding gradually, through quarter tones, down, down to a faintly whispered dominant chord that lingered on (while the five-four rhythms still pulsed below) charging the darkened seconds with an intense expectancy. And at last expectancy was fulfilled. There was a sudden explosive sunrise, and simultaneously, the Sixteen burst into song:

> *"Bottle of mine, it's you I've always wanted!*
> *Bottle of mine, why was I ever decanted?*
> *Skies are blue inside of you,*
> *The weather's always fine;*
> *For*
> *There ain't no Bottle in all the world*
> *Like that dear little Bottle of mine."*

Five-stepping with the other four hundred round and round Westminster Abbey, Lenina and Henry were yet dancing in another world— the warm, the richly coloured, the infinitely friendly world of *soma*-holiday. How kind, how good-looking, how delightfully amusing every one was! "Bottle of mine, it's you I've always wanted . . ." But Lenina and Henry had what they wanted . . . They were inside, here and now— safely inside with the fine weather, the perennially blue sky. And when, exhausted, the Sixteen had laid by their sexophones and the Synthetic Music apparatus was producing the very latest in slow Malthusian Blues, they might have been twin embryos gently rocking together on the waves of a bottled ocean of blood-surrogate.

"Good-night, dear friends. Good-night, dear friends." The loud speakers veiled their commands in a genial and musical politeness. "Good-night, dear friends. . . ."

Obediently, with all the others, Lenina and Henry left the building. The depressing stars had travelled quite some way across the heavens. But though the separating screen of the sky-signs had now to a great extent dissolved, the two young people still retained their happy ignorance of the night. . . .

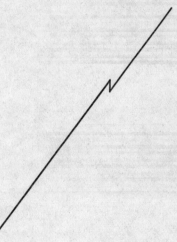

worlds
in conflict

the invasion from mars

by H. G. WELLS

SUNDAY, OCTOBER 30, 1938

ANNOUNCER: The Columbia Broadcasting System and its affiliated stations present Orson Welles and the Mercury Theatre on the Air in *War of the Worlds* by H. G. Wells.

THEME

ANNOUNCER: Ladies and gentlemen: the director of the Mercury Theatre and star of these broadcasts, Orson Welles. . . .

ORSON WELLES: We know now that in the early years of the twentieth century this world was being watched closely by intelligences greater than man's and yet as mortal as his own. We know now that as human beings busied themselves about their various concerns they were scrutinized and studied, perhaps almost as narrowly as a man with a microscope might scrutinize the transient creatures that swarm and multiply in a drop of water. With infinite complacence people went to and fro over the earth about their little affairs, serene in the assurance of their dominion over this small spinning fragment of solar driftwood which by chance or design man has inherited out of the dark mystery of Time and Space. Yet across an immense ethereal gulf, minds that are to our minds as ours are to the beasts in the jungle, intellects vast, cool and unsympathetic regarded

Invasion from Mars, *by Howard Koch* (*the Orson Welles broadcast of H. G. Well's "The War of the Worlds."*) *Copyright, 1940, by Princeton University Press. By arrangement with Monica McCall.*

this earth with envious eyes and slowly and surely drew their plans against us. In the thirty-ninth year of the twentieth century came the great disillusionment.

It was near the end of October. Business was better. The war scare was over. More men were back at work. Sales were picking up. On this particular evening, October 30, the Crossley service estimated that thirty-two million people were listening in on radios.

ANNOUNCER TWO: . . . for the next twenty-four hours not much change in temperature. A slight atmospheric disturbance of undetermined origin is reported over Nova Scotia, causing a low pressure area to move down rather rapidly over the northeastern states, bringing a forecast of rain, accompanied by winds of light gale force. Maximum temperature 66; minimum 48. This weather report comes to you from the Government Weather Bureau.

. . . We now take you to the Meridian Room in the Hotel Park Plaza in downtown New York, where you will be entertained by the music of Ramon Raquello and his orchestra.
(*Spanish theme song . . . fades*)

ANNOUNCER THREE: Good evening, ladies and gentlemen. From the Meridian Room in the Park Plaza in New York City, we bring you the music of Ramon Raquello and his orchestra. With a touch of the Spanish, Ramon Raquello leads off with "La Cumparsita."
(*piece starts playing*)

ANNOUNCER TWO: Ladies and gentlemen, we interrupt our program of dance music to bring you a special bulletin from the Intercontinental Radio News. At twenty minutes before eight, central time, Professor Farrell of the Mount Jennings Observatory, Chicago, Illinois, reports observing several explosions of incandescent gas, occurring at regular intervals on the planet Mars.

The spectroscope indicates the gas to be hydrogen and moving towards the earth with enormous velocity. Professor Pierson of the observatory at Princeton confirms Farrell's observation, and describes the phenomenon as (QUOTE) like a jet of blue flame shot from a gun. (UNQUOTE.) We now return you to the music of Ramon Raquello, playing for you in the Meridian Room of the Park Plaza Hotel, situated in downtown New York.
(*music plays for a few moments until piece ends. . . . sound of applause*)

Now a tune that never loses favor, the ever-popular "Star Dust." Ramon Raquello and his orchestra. . . .
(*music*)

ANNOUNCER TWO: Ladies and gentlemen, following on the news given in our bulletin a moment ago, the Government Meteorological Bureau has requested the large observatories of the country to keep an astronomical watch on any further disturbances occurring on the planet Mars. Due to the unusual nature of this occurrence, we have arranged an interview with the noted Astronomer, Professor Pierson, who will give us his views on this event. In a few moments we will take you to the Princeton Observatory at Princeton, New Jersey. We return you until then to the music of Ramon Raquello and his orchestra.

(*music . . .*)

ANNOUNCER TWO: We are ready now to take you to the Princeton Observatory at Princeton where Carl Phillips, our commentator, will interview Professor Richard Pierson, famous astronomer. We take you now to Princeton, New Jersey.

(*echo chamber*)

PHILLIPS: Good evening, ladies and gentlemen. This is Carl Phillips, speaking to you from the observatory at Princeton. I am standing in a large semicircular room, pitch black except for an oblong split in the ceiling. Through this opening I can see a sprinkling of stars that cast a kind of frosty glow over the intricate mechanism of the huge telescope. The ticking sound you hear is the vibration of the clockwork. Professor Pierson stands directly above me on a small platform, peering through the giant lens. I ask you to be patient, ladies and gentlemen, during any delay that may arise during our interview. Beside his ceaseless watch of the heavens, Professor Pierson may be interrupted by telephone or other communications. During this period he is in constant touch with the astronomical centers of the world. . . . Professor, may I begin our questions?

PIERSON: At any time, Mr. Phillips.

PHILLIPS: Professor, would you please tell our radio audience exactly what you see as you observe the planet Mars through your telescope?

PIERSON: Nothing unusual at the moment, Mr. Phillips. A red disk swimming in a blue sea. Transverse stripes across the disk. Quite distinct now because Mars happens to be at the point nearest the earth . . . in opposition, as we call it.

PHILLIPS: In your opinion, what do these transverse stripes signify, Professor Pierson?

PIERSON: Not canals, I can assure you, Mr. Phillips, although that's the popular conjecture of those who imagine Mars to be inhabited. From a scientific viewpoint the stripes are merely the result of atmospheric conditions peculiar to the planet. .

PHILLIPS: Then you're quite convinced as a scientist that living intelligence as we know it does not exist on Mars?

PIERSON: I should say the chances against it are a thousand to one.

PHILLIPS: And yet how do you account for these gas eruptions occurring on the surface of the planet at regular intervals?

PIERSON: Mr. Phillips, I cannot account for it.

PHILLIPS: By the way, Professor, for the benefit of our listeners, how far is Mars from the earth?

PIERSON: Approximately forty million miles.

PHILLIPS: Well, that seems a safe enough distance.

PHILLIPS: Just a moment, ladies and gentlemen, someone has just handed Professor Pierson a message. While he reads it, let me remind you that we are speaking to you from the observatory in Princeton, New Jersey, where we are interviewing the world-famous astronomer, Professor Pierson. . . . One moment, please. Professor Pierson has passed me a message which he has just received. . . . Professor, may I read the message to the listening audience?

PIERSON: Certainly, Mr. Phillips.

PHILLIPS: Ladies and gentlemen, I shall read you a wire addressed to Professor Pierson from Dr. Gray of the National History Museum, New York. "9:15 p.m. eastern standard time. Seismograph registered shock of almost earthquake intensity occurring within a radius of twenty miles of Princeton. Please investigate. Signed, Lloyd Gray, Chief of Astronomical Division." . . . Professor Pierson, could this occurrence possibly have something to do with the disturbances observed on the planet Mars?

PIERSON: Hardly, Mr. Phillips. This is probably a meteorite of unusual size and its arrival at this particular time is merely a coincidence. However, we shall conduct a search, as soon as daylight permits.

PHILLIPS: Thank you, Professor. Ladies and gentlemen, for the past ten minutes we've been speaking to you from the observatory at Princeton, bringing you a special interview with Professor Pierson, noted astronomer. This is Carl Phillips speaking. We now return you to our New York studio.

(fade in piano playing)

ANNOUNCER TWO: Ladies and gentlemen, here is the latest bulletin from the Intercontinental Radio News. Toronto, Canada: Professor Morse of

Macmillan University reports observing a total of three explosions on the planet Mars, between the hours of 7:45 p.m. and 9:20 p.m., eastern standard time. This confirms earlier reports received from American observatories. Now, nearer home, comes a special announcement from Trenton, New Jersey. It is reported that at 8:50 p.m. a huge, flaming object, believed to be a meteorite, fell on a farm in the neighborhood of Grovers Mill, New Jersey, twenty-two miles from Trenton. The flash in the sky was visible within a radius of several hundred miles and the noise of the impact was heard as far north as Elizabeth.

We have dispatched a special mobile unit to the scene, and will have our commentator, Mr. Phillips, give you a word description as soon as he can reach there from Princeton. In the meantime, we take you to the Hotel Martinet in Brooklyn, where Bobby Millette and his orchestra are offering a program of dance music.

(*swing band for 20 seconds . . . then cut*)

ANNOUNCER TWO: We take you now to Grovers Mill, New Jersey.
(*crowd noises . . . police sirens*)

PHILLIPS: Ladies and gentlemen, this is Carl Phillips again, at the Wilmuth farm, Grovers Mill, New Jersey. Professor Pierson and myself made the eleven miles from Princeton in ten minutes. Well, I . . . I hardly know where to begin, to paint for you a word picture of the strange scene before my eyes, like something out of a modern Arabian Nights. Well, I just got here. I haven't had a chance to look around yet. I guess that's *it.* Yes, I guess that's the . . . *thing,* directly in front of me, half buried in a vast pit. Must have struck with terrific force. The ground is covered with splinters of a tree it must have struck on its way down. What I can see of the . . . object itself doesn't look very much like a meteor, at least not the meteors I've seen. It looks more like a huge cylinder. It has a diameter of . . . what would you say, Professor Pierson?

PIERSON (*off*): About thirty yards.

PHILLIPS: About thirty yards. . . . The metal on the sheath is . . . well, I've never seen anything like it. The color is sort of yellowish-white. Curious spectators now are pressing close to the object in spite of the efforts of the police to keep them back. They're getting in front of my line of vision. Would you mind standing on one side, please?

POLICEMAN: One side, there, one side.

PHILLIPS: While the policemen are pushing the crowd back, here's Mr. Wilmuth, owner of the farm here. He may have some interesting facts to add. . . . Mr. Wilmuth, would you please tell the radio audience as much as you remember of this rather unusual visitor that dropped in your backyard? Step closer, please. Ladies and gentlemen, this is Mr. Wilmuth.

WILMUTH: I was listenin' to the radio.

PHILLIPS: Closer and louder, please.

WILMUTH: Pardon me!

PHILLIPS: Louder, please, and closer.

WILMUTH: Yes, sir—while I was listening to the radio and kinda drowsin', that Professor fellow was talkin' about Mars, so I was half dozin' and half . . .

PHILLIPS: Yes, Mr. Wilmuth. Then what happened?

WILMUTH: As I was sayin', I was listenin' to the radio kinda half-ways . . .

PHILLIPS: Yes, Mr. Wilmuth, and then you saw something?

WILMUTH: Not first off. I heard something.

PHILLIPS: And what did you hear?

WILMUTH: A hissing sound. Like this: sssssssssss . . . kinda like a fourt' of July rocket.

PHILLIPS: Then what?

WILMUTH: Turned my head out the window and would have swore I was to sleep and dreamin'.

PHILLIPS: Yes?

WILMUTH: I seen a kinda greenish streak and then zingo! Somethin' smacked the ground. Knocked me clear out of my chair!

PHILLIPS: Well, were you frightened, Mr. Wilmuth?

WILMUTH: Well, I–I ain't quite sure. I reckon I–I was kinda riled.

PHILLIPS: Thank you, Mr. Wilmuth. Thank you.

WILMUTH: Want me to tell you some more?

PHILLIPS: No. . . . That's quite all right, that's plenty.

PHILLIPS: Ladies and gentlemen, you've just heard Mr. Wilmuth, owner of the farm where this thing has fallen. I wish I could convey the atmosphere . . . the background of this . . . fantastic scene. Hundreds of cars are parked in a field in back of us. Police are trying to rope off the roadway leading into the farm. But it's no use. They're breaking right through. Their headlights throw an enormous spot on the pit where the object's half-buried. Some of the more daring souls are venturing near the edge. Their silhouettes stand out against the metal sheen.

(*faint humming sound*)

One man wants to touch the thing . . . he's having an argument with a policeman. The policeman wins. . . . Now, ladies and gentlemen, there's something I haven't mentioned in all this excitement, but it's becoming more distinct. Perhaps you've caught it already on your radio. Listen: (*long pause*) . . . Do you hear it? It's a curious humming sound that seems to come from inside the object. I'll move the microphone nearer. Here. (*Pause*) Now we're not more than twenty-five feet away. Can you hear it now? Oh, Professor Pierson!

PIERSON: Yes, Mr. Phillips?

PHILLIPS: Can you tell us the meaning of that scraping noise inside the thing?

PIERSON: Possibly the unequal cooling of its surface.

PHILLIPS: Do you still think it's a meteor, Professor?

PIERSON: I don't know what to think. The metal casing is definitely extra-terrestrial . . . not found on this earth. Friction with the earth's atmosphere usually tears holes in a meteorite. This thing is smooth and, as you can see, of cylindrical shape.

PHILLIPS: Just a minute! Something's happening! Ladies and gentlemen, this is terrific! This end of the thing is beginning to flake off! The top is beginning to rotate like a screw! The thing must be hollow!

VOICES

She's a movin'!
Look, the darn thing's unscrewing!
Keep back, there! Keep back, I tell you.
Maybe there's men in it trying to escape!
It's red hot, they'll burn to a cinder!
Keep back there! Keep those idiots back!
(*suddenly the clanking sound of a huge piece of falling metal*)

VOICES

She's off! The top's loose!
Look out there! Stand back!

Ladies and gentlemen, this is the most terrifying thing I have ever witnessed. . . . Wait a minute! Someone's *crawling out of the hollow top.* Someone or . . . something. I can see peering out of that black hole two luminous disks . . . are they eyes? It might be a face. It might be. . . . (*shout of awe from the crowd*)

Good heavens, something's wriggling out of the shadow like a grey snake. Now it's another one, and another. They look like tentacles to me. There, I can see the thing's body. It's large as a bear and it glistens like wet leather. But that face. It . . . it's indescribable. I can hardly force myself to keep looking at it. The eyes are black and gleam like a serpent. The mouth is V-shaped with saliva dripping from its rimless lips that seem to quiver and pulsate. The monster or whatever it is can hardly move. It seems weighed down by . . . possibly gravity or something. The thing's raising up. The crowd falls back. They've seen enough. This is the most extraordinary experience. I can't find words. . . . I'm pulling this microphone with me as I talk. I'll have to stop the description until I've taken a new position. Hold on, will you please, I'll be back in a minute. (*fade into piano*)

ANNOUNCER TWO: We are bringing you an eyewitness account of what's happening on the Wilmuth farm, Grovers Mill, New Jersey.
(*more piano*)
We now return you to Carl Phillips at Grovers Mill.

PHILLIPS: Ladies and gentlemen (Am I on?). Ladies and gentlemen, here I am, back of a stone wall that adjoins Mr. Wilmuth's garden. From here I get a sweep of the whole scene. I'll give you every detail as long as I can talk. As long as I can see. More state police have arrived. They're drawing up a cordon in front of the pit, about thirty of them. No need to push the crowd back now. They're willing to keep their distance. The captain is conferring with someone. We can't quite see who. Oh yes, I believe it's Professor Pierson. Yes, it is. Now they've parted. The professor moves around one side, studying the object, while the captain and two policemen advance with something in their hands. I can see it now. It's a white handkerchief tied to a pole . . . a flag of truce. If those creatures know what that means . . . what anything means! . . . *Wait!* Something's happening!
(*hissing sound followed by a humming that increases in intensity*)

A humped shape is rising out of the pit. I can make out a small beam of light against a mirror. What's that? There's a jet of flame springing from that mirror, and it leaps right at the advancing men. It strikes them head on! Good Lord, they're turning into flame!
(*screams and unearthly shrieks*)

Now the whole field's caught fire. (*explosion*) The woods . . . the barns . . . the gas tanks of automobiles . . . it's spreading everywhere. It's coming this way. About twenty yards to my right. . . .
(*crash of microphone . . . then dead silence . . .*)

ANNOUNCER TWO: Ladies and gentlemen, due to circumstances beyond our control, we are unable to continue the broadcast from Grovers Mill. Evidently there's some difficulty with our field transmission. However, we will return to that point at the earliest opportunity. In the meantime, we have a late bulletin from San Diego, California. Professor Indellkoffer, speaking at a dinner of the California Astronomical Society, expressed the opinion that the explosions on Mars are undoubtedly nothing more than severe volcanic disturbances on the surface of the planet. We continue now with our piano interlude.
(*piano . . . then cut*)

Ladies and gentlemen, I have just been handed a message that came in from Grovers Mill by telephone. Just a moment. At least forty people, including six State Troopers lie dead in a field east of the village of Grovers Mill, their bodies burned and distorted beyond all possible recognition. The next voice you hear will be that of Brigadier General Montgomery Smith, commander of the State Militia at Trenton, New Jersey.

SMITH: I have been requested by the governor of New Jersey to place the counties of Mercer and Middlesex as far west as Princeton, and east to Jamesburg, under martial law. No one will be permitted to enter this area except by special pass issued by state or military authorities. Four companies of State Militia are proceeding from Trenton to Grovers Mill, and will aid in the evacuation of homes within the range of military operations. Thank you.

ANNOUNCER: You have just been listening to General Montgomery Smith commanding the State Militia at Trenton. In the meantime, further details of the catastrophe at Grovers Mill are coming in. The strange creatures after unleashing their deadly assault, crawled back in their pit and made no attempt to prevent the efforts of the firemen to recover the bodies and extinguish the fire. Combined fire departments of Mercer County are fighting the flames which menace the entire countryside.

We have been unable to establish any contact with our mobile unit at Grovers Mill, but we hope to be able to return you there at the earliest possible moment. In the meantime we take you—uh, just one moment please.
(*long pause*) (*whisper*)

Ladies and gentlemen, I have just been informed that we have finally established communication with an eyewitness of the tragedy. Professor Pierson has been located at a farmhouse near Grovers Mill where he has established an emergency observation post. As a scientist, he will give you his explanation of the calamity. The next voice you hear will be that of Professor Pierson, brought to you by direct wire. Professor Pierson.

PIERSON: Of the creatures in the rocket cylinder at Grovers Mill, I can give you no authoritative information—either as to their nature, their origin, or their purposes here on earth. Of their destructive instrument I might venture some conjectural explanation. For want of a better term, I shall refer to the mysterious weapon as a heat-ray. It's all too evident that these creatures have scientific knowledge far in advance of our own. It is my guess that in some way they are able to generate an intense heat in a chamber of practically absolute nonconductivity. This intense heat they project in a parallel beam against any object they choose, by means of a polished parabolic mirror of unknown composition, much as the mirror of a lighthouse projects a beam of light. That is my conjecture of the origin of the heat-ray. . . .

ANNOUNCER TWO: Thank you, Professor Pierson. Ladies and gentlemen, here is a bulletin from Trenton. It is a brief statement informing us that the charred body of Carl Phillips has been identified in a Trenton Hospital. Now here's another bulletin from Washington, D.C.

Office of the director of the National Red Cross reports ten units of Red Cross emergency workers have been assigned to the headquarters of the State Militia stationed outside of Grovers Mill, New Jersey. Here's a bulletin from State Police, Princeton Junction: The fires at Grovers Mill and vicinity now under control. Scouts report all quiet in the pit, and no sign of life appearing from the mouth of the cylinder. . . . And now, ladies and gentlemen, we have a special statement from Mr. Harry Mc-Donald, vice-president in charge of operations.

MCDONALD: We have received a request from the militia at Trenton to place at their disposal our entire broadcasting facilities. In view of the gravity of the situation, and believing that radio has a definite responsibility to serve in the public interest at all times, we are turning over our facilities to the State Militia at Trenton.

ANNOUNCER: We take you now to the field headquarters of the State Militia near Grovers Mill, New Jersey.

CAPTAIN: This is Captain Lansing of the Signal Corps, attached to the State Militia now engaged in military operations in the vicinity of Grovers Mill. Situation arising from the reported presence of certain individuals of unidentified nature, is now under complete control.

The cylindrical object which lies in a pit directly below our position is surrounded on all sides by eight battalions of infantry, without heavy fieldpieces, but adequately armed with rifles and machine guns. All cause for alarm, if such cause ever existed, is now entirely unjustified. The things, whatever they are, do not even venture to poke their heads above the pit. I can see their hiding place plainly in the glare of the searchlights here. With all their reported resources, these creatures can scarcely stand up against heavy machine-gun fire. Anyway, it's an interesting outing for the troops. I can make out their khaki uniforms, crossing back and forth in front of the lights. It looks almost like a real war. There appears to be some slight smoke in the woods bordering the Millstone River. Probably fire started by campers. Well, we ought to see some action soon. One of the companies is deploying on the left flank. A quick thrust and it will all be over. Now wait a minute! I see something on top of the cylinder. No, it's nothing but a shadow. Now the troops are on the edge of the Wilmuth farm. Seven thousand armed men closing in on an old metal tube. Wait, that wasn't a shadow! It's something moving . . . solid metal . . . kind of a shield-like affair rising up out of the cylinder. . . . It's going higher and higher. Why, it's standing on legs . . . actually rearing up on a sort of metal framework. Now it's reaching above the trees and the searchlights are on it! Hold on!

ANNOUNCER TWO: Ladies and gentlemen, I have a grave announcement to make. Incredible as it may seem, both the observations of science and the evidence of our eyes lead to the inescapable assumption that those strange beings who landed in the Jersey farmlands tonight are the vanguard of an invading army from the planet Mars. The battle which took place tonight at Grovers Mill has ended in one of the most startling defeats ever suffered by an army in modern times; seven thousand men armed with rifles and machine guns pitted against a single fighting machine of the invaders from Mars. One hundred and twenty known survivors. The rest strewn over the battle area from Grovers Mill to Plainsboro crushed and trampled to death under the metal feet of the monster, or burned to cinders by its heat-ray. The monster is now in control of the middle section of New Jersey and has effectively cut the state through its center. Communication lines are down from Pennsylvania to the Atlantic Ocean. Railroad tracks are torn and service from New York to Philadelphia discontinued except routing some of the trains through Allentown and Phoenixville. Highways to the north, south, and west are clogged with frantic human traffic. Police and army reserves are unable to control the mad flight. By morning the fugitives will have swelled Philadelphia, Camden and Trenton, it is estimated, to twice their normal population.

At this time martial law prevails throughout New Jersey and eastern Pennsylvania. We take you now to Washington for a special broadcast on the National Emergency . . . the Secretary of the Interior. . . .

SECRETARY: Citizens of the nation: I shall not try to conceal the gravity of the situation that confronts the country, nor the concern of your government in protecting the lives and property of its people. However, I wish to impress upon you—private citizens and public officials, all of you—the urgent need of calm and resourceful action. Fortunately, this formidable enemy is still confined to a comparatively small area, and we may place our faith in the military forces to keep them there. In the meantime placing our faith in God we must continue the performance of our duties each and everyone of us, so that we may confront this destructive adversary with a nation united, courageous, and consecrated to the preservation of human supremacy on this earth. I thank you.

ANNOUNCER: You have just heard the Secretary of the Interior speaking from Washington. Bulletins too numerous to read are piling up in the studio here. We are informed that the central portion of New Jersey is blacked out from radio communication due to the effect of the heat-ray upon power lines and electrical equipment. Here is a special bulletin from New York. Cables received from English, French, German scientific bodies offering assistance. Astronomers report continued gas outbursts at regular intervals on planet Mars. Majority voice opinion that enemy will be reinforced by additional rocket machines. Attempts made to locate Professor Pierson of Princeton, who has observed Martians at close range. It is feared he was lost in recent battle. LANGHAM FIELD, VIRGINIA: Scouting planes report three Martian machines visible above tree tops, moving north towards Somerville with population fleeing ahead of them. Heat-ray not in use: although advancing at express-train speed, invaders pick their way carefully. They seem to be making conscious effort to avoid destruction of cities and countryside. However, they stop to uproot power lines, bridges, and railroad tracks. Their apparent objective is to crush resistance, paralyze communication, and disorganize human society.

Here is a bulletin from BASKING RIDGE, NEW JERSEY: Coon hunters have stumbled on a second cylinder similar to the first embedded in the great swamp twenty miles south of Morristown. U.S. Army fieldpieces are proceeding from Newark to blow up second invading unit before cylinder can be opened and the fighting machine rigged. They are taking up position in the—— foothills of Watchung Mountains. Another bulletin from LANGHAM FIELD, VIRGINIA: Scouting planes report enemy machines, now three in number, increasing speed northward kicking over houses and trees in their evident haste to form a conjunction with their allies south of Morristown. Machines also sighted by telephone operator east of Middlesex within ten miles of Plainfield. Here's a bulletin from WINSTON FIELD, LONG ISLAND: Fleet of army bombers carrying heavy explosives flying north in pursuit of enemy. Scouting planes act as guides. They keep speeding enemy in sight. Just a moment please. Ladies and gentlemen, we've run special wires to the artillery line in adjacent villages to give you direct reports in the zone of the advancing enemy. First we take you to the battery of the 22nd Field Artillery, located in the Watchung Mountains.

OFFICER: Range 32 meters.

GUNNER: Thirty-two meters.

OFFICER: Projection, 39 degrees.

GUNNER: Thirty-nine degrees.

OFFICER: Fire! (*boom of heavy gun . . . pause*)

OBSERVER: One hundred and forty yards to the right, sir.

OFFICER: Shift range . . . 31 meters.

GUNNER: Thirty-one meters.

OFFICER: Projection . . . 37 degrees.

GUNNER: Thirty-seven degrees.

OFFICER: Fire! (*boom of heavy gun . . . pause*)

OBSERVER: A hit, sir! We got the tripod of one of them. They've stopped. The others are trying to repair it.

OFFICER: Quick, get the range! Shift 50 30 meters.

GUNNER: Thirty meters.

OFFICER: Projection . . . 27 degrees.

GUNNER: Twenty-seven degrees.

OFFICER: Fire! (*Boom of heavy gun . . . Pause*)

OBSERVER: Can't see the shell land, sir. They're letting off a smoke.

OFFICER: What is it?

OBSERVER: A black smoke, sir. Moving this way. Lying close to the ground. It's moving fast.

OFFICER: Put on gas masks. (*Pause*) Get ready to fire. Shift to 24 meters.

GUNNER: Twenty-four meters.

OFFICER: Projection, 24 degrees.

GUNNER: Twenty-four degrees.

OFFICER: Fire! (*Boom*)

OBSERVER: Still can't see, sir. The smoke's coming nearer.

OFFICER: Get the range. (*Coughs*)

OBSERVER: Twenty-three meters. (*Coughs*)

OFFICER: Twenty-three meters. (*Coughs*)

GUNNER: Twenty-three meters. (*Coughs*)

OBSERVER: Projection 22 degrees. (*Coughing*)

OFFICER: Twenty-two degrees. (*Fade in coughing*)
(*Fading in . . . Sound of airplane motor*)

COMMANDER: Army bombing plane, V-8-43 off Bayonne, New Jersey, Lieutenant Voght, commanding eight bombers. Reporting to Commander Fairfax, Langham Field. . . . This is Voght, reporting to Commander Fairfax, Langham Field. . . . Enemy tripod machines now in sight. Reinforced by three machines from the Morristown cylinder. Six altogether. One machine partially crippled. Believed hit by shell from army gun in Watchung Mountains. Guns now appear silent. A heavy black fog hanging close to the earth . . . of extreme density, nature unknown. No sign of heat-ray. Enemy now turns east, crossing Passaic River into the Jersey marshes. Another straddles the Pulaski Skyway. Evident objective is New York City. They're pushing down a high tension power station. The machines are close together now, and we're ready to attack. Planes circling, ready to strike. A thousand yards and we'll be over the first—800 yards . . . 600 . . . 400 . . . 200. . . . There they go! The giant arm raised. . . . Green flash! They're spraying us with flame! Two thousand feet. Engines are giving out. No chance to release bombs. Only one thing left . . . drop on them, plane and all. We're diving on the first one. Now the engine's gone! Eight. . . .

OPERATOR ONE: This is Bayonne, New Jersey, calling Langham Field. . . .

This is Bayonne, New Jersey, calling Langham Field. . . .

Come in, please. . . . Come in, please. . . .

OPERATOR TWO: This is Langham Field . . . go ahead. . . .

OPERATOR ONE: Eight army bombers in engagement with enemy tripod machines over Jersey flats. Engines incapacitated by heat-ray. All crashed. One enemy machine destroyed. Enemy now discharging heavy black smoke in direction of—

OPERATOR THREE: This is Newark, New Jersey. . . .
This is Newark, New Jersey. . . .
Warning! Poisonous black smoke pouring in from Jersey marshes. Reaches South Street. Gas masks useless. Urge population to move into open spaces . . . automobiles use routes 7, 23, 24. . . . Avoid congested areas. Smoke now spreading over Raymond Boulevard. . . .

OPERATOR FOUR: 2X2L . . . calling CQ. . . .
2X2 L. . . calling CQ. . . .
2X2L . . . calling CQ. . . .
2X2L . . . calling 8X3R. . . .
Come in, please. . . .

OPERATOR FIVE: This is 8X3R . . . coming back at 2X2L.

OPERATOR FOUR: How's reception? How's reception? K, please. Where are you, 8X3R?
What's the matter? Where are you?
(*Bells ringing over city gradually diminishing*)

ANNOUNCER: I'm speaking from the roof of Broadcasting Building, New York City. The bells you hear are ringing to warn the people to evacuate the city as the Martians approach. Estimated in last two hours three million people have moved out along the roads to the north, Hutchison River Parkway still kept open for motor traffic. Avoid bridges to Long Island . . . hopelessly jammed. All communication with Jersey shore closed ten minutes ago. No more defenses. Our army wiped out . . . artillery, air force, everything wiped out. This may be the last broadcast. We'll stay here to the end. . . . People are holding service below us . . . in the cathedral.
(*Voices singing hymn*)
Now I look down the harbor. All manner of boats, overloaded with fleeing population, pulling out from docks.
(*Sound of boat whistles*)
Streets are all jammed. Noise in crowds like New Year's Eve in city. Wait a minute. . . . Enemy now in sight above the Palisades. Five great machines. First one is crossing river. I can see it from here, wading the

Hudson like a man wading through a brook. . . . A bulletin's handed me.
. . . Martian cylinders are falling all over the country. One outside
Buffalo, one in Chicago, St. Louis . . . seem to be timed and spaced.
. . . Now the first machine reaches the shore. He stands watching, looking
over the city. His steel, cowlish head is even with the skyscrapers. He
waits for the others. They rise like a line of new towers on the city's
west side. . . . Now they're lifting their metal hands. This is the end
now. Smoke comes out . . . black smoke, drifting over the city. People
in the streets see it now. They're running towards the East River . . .
thousands of them, dropping in like rats. Now the smoke's spreading
faster. It's reached Times Square. People trying to run away from it, but
it's no use. They're falling like flies. Now the smoke's crossing Sixth Avenue . . . Fifth Avenue . . . 100 yards away . . . it's 50 feet. . . .

OPERATOR FOUR: 2X2L calling CQ. . . .
   2X2L calling CQ. . . .
   2X2L calling CQ. . . . New York.
   Isn't there anyone on the air?
   Isn't there anyone. . . .
   2X2L——

(*Middle break*)

ANNOUNCER: You are listening to a CBS presentation of Orson Welles
and the Mercury Theatre on the Air in an original dramatization of *War
of the Worlds* by H. G. Wells. The performance will continue after a
brief intermission.
    This is the COLUMBIA . . . BROADCASTING SYSTEM (*Fade theme 10
seconds*) WABC—NEW YORK.
(*Entire break 20 seconds*)

ANNOUNCER: *War of the Worlds* by H. G. Wells, starring Orson Welles
and the Mercury Theatre on the Air. . . .
(*Music*)

PIERSON: As I set down these notes on paper, I'm obsessed by the thought
that I may be the last living man on earth. I have been hiding in this
empty house near Grovers Mill—a small island of daylight cut off by the
black smoke from the rest of the world. All that happened before the
arrival of these monstrous creatures in the world now seems part of another life . . . a life that has no continuity with the present, furtive existence of the lonely derelict who pencils these words on the back of some
astronomical notes bearing the signature of Richard Pierson. I look down
at my blackened hands, my torn shoes, my tattered clothes, and I try to
connect them with a professor who lives at Princeton, and who on the

night of October 20, glimpsed through his telescope an orange splash of light on a distant planet. My wife, my colleagues, my students, my books, my observatory, my . . . my world . . . where are they? Did they ever exist? Am I Richard Pierson? What day is it? Do days exist without calendars? Does time pass when there are no human hands left to wind the clocks? . . . In writing down my daily life I tell myself I shall pre-serve human history between the dark covers of this little book that was meant to record the movements of the stars. . . . But to write I must live, and to live I must eat. . . . I find mouldy bread in the kitchen, and an orange not too spoiled to swallow. I keep watch at the window. From time to time I catch sight of a Martian above the black smoke.

The smoke still holds the house in its black coil. . . . But at length there is a hissing sound and suddenly I see a Martian mounted on his machine, spraying the air with a jet of steam, as if to dissipate the smoke. I watch in a corner as his huge metal legs nearly brush against the house. Exhausted by terror, I fall asleep. . . . It's morning. Sun streams in the window. The black cloud of gas has lifted, and the scorched meadows to the north look as though a black snow storm had passed over them. I venture from the house. I make my way to a road. No traffic. Here and there a wrecked car, baggage overturned, a blackened skeleton. I push on north. For some reason I feel safer trailing these monsters than running away from them. And I keep a careful watch. I have seen the Martians feed. Should one of their machines appear over the top of trees, I am ready to fling myself flat on the earth. I come to a chestnut tree. October, chestnuts are ripe. I fill my pockets. I must keep alive. Two days I wander in a vague northerly direction through a desolate world. Finally I notice a living creature . . . a small red squirrel in a beech tree. I stare at him, and wonder. He stares back at me. I believe at that moment the animal and I shared the same emotion . . . the joy of finding another living being. . . . I push on north. I find dead cows in a brackish field. Beyond, the charred ruins of a dairy. The silo remains standing guard over the waste land like a lighthouse deserted by the sea. Astride the silo perches a weathercock. The arrow points north.

Next day I came to a city vaguely familiar in its contours, yet its build-ings strangely dwarfed and levelled off, as if a giant had sliced off its highest towers with a capricious sweep of his hand. I reached the out-skirts. I found Newark, undemolished, but humbled by some whim of the advancing Martians. Presently, with an odd feeling of being watched, I caught sight of something crouching in a doorway. I made a step towards it, and it rose up and became a man—a man, armed with a large knife.

STRANGER: Stop. . . . Where did you come from?

PIERSON: I come from . . . many places. A long time ago from Princeton.

STRANGER: Princeton, huh? That's near Grovers Mill!

PIERSON: Yes.

STRANGER: Grovers Mill. . . . (*Laughs as at a great joke*). . . . There's no food here. This is my country . . . all this end of town down to the river. There's only food for one. . . . Which way are you going?

PIERSON: I don't know. I guess I'm looking for—for people.

STRANGER: (*Nervously*) What was that? Did you hear something just then?

PIERSON: Only a bird (*Marvels*). . . . A live bird!

STRANGER: You get to know that birds have shadows these days. . . . Say, we're in the open here. Let's crawl into this doorway and talk.

PIERSON: Have you seen any Martians?

STRANGER: They've gone over to New York. At night the sky is alive with their lights. Just as if people were still living in it. By daylight you can't see them. Five days ago a couple of them carried something big across the flats from the airport. I believe they're learning how to fly.

PIERSON: Fly!

STRANGER: Yeah, fly.

PIERSON: Then it's all over with humanity. Stranger, there's still you and I. Two of us left.

STRANGER: They got themselves in solid; they wrecked the greatest country in the world. Those green stars, they're probably falling somewhere every night. They've only lost one machine. There isn't anything to do. We're done. We're licked.

PIERSON: Where were *you*? You're in a uniform.

STRANGER: What's left of it. I was in the militia—national guard. . . . That's good! Wasn't any war any more than there's war between men and ants.

PIERSON: And we're eatable ants. I found that out. . . . What will they do to us?

STRANGER: I've thought it all out. Right now we're caught as we're wanted. The Martian only has to go a few miles to get a crowd on the run. But they won't keep doing that. They'll begin catching us systematic like—keeping the best and storing us in cages and things. They haven't begun on us yet!

PIERSON: Not begun!

STRANGER: Not begun. All that's happened so far is because we don't have sense enough to keep quiet . . . bothering them with guns and such stuff and losing our heads and rushing off in crowds. Now instead of our rushing around blind we've got to fix ourselves up according to the way things are now. Cities, nations, civilization, progress. . . .

PIERSON: But if that's so, what is there to live for?

STRANGER: There won't be any more concerts for a million years or so, and no nice little dinners at restaurants. If it's amusement you're after, I guess the game's up.

PIERSON: And what is there left?

STRANGER: Life . . . that's what! I want to live. And so do you! We're not going to be exterminated. And I don't mean to be caught, either, and tamed, and fattened, and bred like an ox.

PIERSON: What are you going to do?

STRANGER: I'm going on . . . right under their feet. I gotta plan. We men as men are finished. We don't know enough. We gotta learn plenty before we've got a chance. And we've got to live and keep free while we learn. I've thought it all out, see.

PIERSON: Tell me the rest.

STRANGER: Well, it isn't all of us that are made for wild beasts, and that's what it's got to be. That's why I watched you. All these little office workers that used to live in these houses—they'd be no good. They haven't any stuff to 'em. They just used to run off to work. I've seen hundreds of 'em, running wild to catch their commuters' train in the morning for fear that they'd get canned if they didn't; running back at night afraid they won't be in time for dinner. Lives insured and a little invested in case of accidents. And on Sundays, worried about the hereafter. The Martians will be a godsend for those guys. Nice roomy cages, good food, careful breeding, no worries. After a week or so chasing about the fields on empty stomachs they'll come and be glad to be caught.

PIERSON: You've thought it all out, haven't you?

STRANGER: You bet I have! And that isn't all. These Martians will make pets of some of them, train 'em to do tricks. Who knows? Get sentimental over the pet boy who grew up and had to be killed. And some, maybe, they'll train to hunt us.

PIERSON: No, that's impossible. No human being. . . .

STRANGER: Yes they will. There's men who'll do it gladly. If one of them ever comes after *me*. . . .

PIERSON: In the meantime, you and I and others like us . . . where are we to live when the Martians own the earth?

STRANGER: I've got it all figured out. We'll live under ground. I've been thinking about the sewers. Under New York are miles and miles of 'em. The main ones are big enough for anybody. Then there's cellars, vaults, underground storerooms, railway tunnels, subways. You begin to see, eh? And we'll get a bunch of strong men together. No weak ones, that rubbish, out.

PIERSON: And you meant me to go?

STRANGER: Well, I gave you a chance didn't I?

PIERSON: We won't quarrel about that. Go on.

STRANGER: And we've got to make safe places for us to stay in, see, and get all the books we can—science books. That's where men like you come in, see? We'll raid the museums, we'll even spy on the Martians. It may not be so much we have to learn before—just imagine this: four or five of their own fighting machines suddenly start off—heat-rays right and left and not a Martian in 'em. Not a Martian in 'em! But *men*—men who have learned the way how. It may even be in our time. Gee! Imagine having one of them lovely things with its heat-ray wide and free! We'd turn it on Martians, we'd turn it on men. We'd bring everybody down to their knees.

PIERSON: That's your plan?

STRANGER: You and me and a few more of us we'd own the world.

PIERSON: I see.

STRANGER: Say, what's the matter? Where are you going?

PIERSON: Not to *your* world. . . . Good-bye, Stranger. . . .

PIERSON: After parting with the artilleryman, I came at last to the Holland Tunnel. I entered that silent tube anxious to know the fate of the great city on the other side of the Hudson. Cautiously I came out of the tunnel and made my way up Canal Street.

I reached Fourteenth Street, and there again were black powder and several bodies, and an evil ominous smell from the gratings of the cellars of some of the houses. I wandered up through the thirties and forties; I stood alone on Times Square. I caught sight of a lean dog running down Seventh Avenue with a piece of dark brown meat in his jaws, and a pack of starving mongrels at his heels. He made a wide circle around me, as though he feared I might prove a fresh competitor. I walked up Broadway in the direction of that strange powder—past silent shop windows, displaying their mute wares to empty sidewalks—past the Capitol Theatre, silent, dark—past a shooting gallery, where a row of empty guns faced an arrested line of wooden ducks. Near Columbus Circle I noticed models of 1939 motor cars in the show rooms facing empty streets. From over the top of the General Motors Building, I watched a flock of black birds circling in the sky. I hurried on. Suddenly I caught sight of the hood of a Martian machine, standing somewhere in Central Park, gleaming in the late afternoon sun. An insane idea! I rushed recklessly across Columbus Circle and into the Park. I climbed a small hill above the pond at Sixtieth Street. From there I could see, standing in a silent row along the Mall, nineteen of those great metal Titans, their cowls empty, their steel arms hanging listlessly by their sides. I looked in vain for the monsters that inhabit those machines.

Suddenly, my eyes were attracted to the immense flock of black birds that hovered directly below me. They circled to the ground, and there before my eyes, stark and silent, lay the Martians, with the hungry birds pecking and tearing brown shreds of flesh from their dead bodies. Later when their bodies were examined in laboratories, it was found that they were killed by the putrefactive and disease bacteria against which their systems were unprepared . . . slain after all man's defenses had failed, by the humblest thing that God in His wisdom put upon this earth.

Before the cylinder fell there was a general persuasion that through all the deep of space no life existed beyond the petty surface of our minute sphere. Now we see further. Dim and wonderful is the vision I have conjured up in my mind of life spreading slowly from this little seed-bed of the solar system throughout the inanimate vastness of sidereal space. But that is a remote dream. It may be, that the destruction of the Martians is only a reprieve. To them, and not to us, is the future ordained perhaps.

Strange it now seems to sit in my peaceful study at Princeton writing down this last chapter of the record begun at a deserted farm in Grovers Mill. Strange to see from my window the university spires dim and blue through an April haze. Strange to watch children playing in the streets. Strange to see young people strolling on the green, where the new spring grass heals the last black scars of a bruised earth. Strange to watch the

sight-seers enter the museum where the dissembled parts of a Martian machine are kept on public view. Strange when I recall the time when I first saw it, bright and clean-cut, hard and silent, under the dawn of that last great day.
(*Music*)

This is Orson Welles, ladies and gentlemen, out of character to assure you that the *War of the Worlds* has no further significance than as the holiday offering it was intended to be. The Mercury Theatre's own radio version of dressing up in a sheet and jumping out of a bush and saying Boo! Starting now, we couldn't soap all your windows and steal all your garden gates, by tomorrow night . . . so we did the next best thing. We annihilated the world before your very ears, and utterly destroyed the Columbia Broadcasting System. You will be relieved, I hope, to learn that we didn't mean it, and that both institutions are still open for business. So good-bye everybody, and remember, please, for the next day or so, the terrible lesson you learned tonight. That grinning, glowing, globular invader of your living-room is an inhabitant of the pumpkin patch, and if your doorbell rings and nobody's there, that was no Martian . . . it's Hallowe'en.
(*Music*)

ANNOUNCER: Tonight the Columbia Broadcasting System, and its affiliated stations coast-to-coast, has brought you *War of The Worlds* by H. G. Wells . . . the seventeenth in its weekly series of dramatic broadcasts featuring Orson Welles and the Mercury Theatre on the Air.

edison's conquest of mars

by GARRETT P. SERVISS

"LET US GO TO MARS" It is impossible that the stupendous events which followed the disastrous invasion of the earth by the Martians should go without record, and circumstances having placed the facts at my disposal, I deem it a duty, both to posterity and to those who were witnesses of and participants in the avenging counterstroke that the earth dealt back at its ruthless enemy in the heavens, to write down the story in a connected form.

The Martians had nearly all perished, not through our puny efforts, but in consequence of disease, and the few survivors fled in one of their projectile cars, inflicting their cruelest blow in the act of departure.

They possessed a mysterious explosive, of unimaginable puissance, with whose aid they set their car in motion for Mars from a point in Bergen County, N. J., just back of the Palisades.

The force of the explosion may be imagined when it is recollected that they had to give the car a velocity of more than seven miles per second in order to overcome the attraction of the earth and the resistance of the atmosphere.

The shock destroyed all of New York that had not already fallen a prey, and all the buildings yet standing in the surrounding towns and cities fell in one far-circling ruin.

The Palisades tumbled in vast sheets, starting a tidal wave in the Hudson that drowned the opposite shore.

The victims of this ferocious explosion were numbered by tens of thousands, and the shock, transmitted through the rocky frame of the globe, was recorded by seismographic pendulums in England and on the Continent of Europe.

The terrible results achieved by the invaders had produced everywhere a mingled feeling of consternation and hopelessness. The devastation was widespread. The death-dealing engines which the Martians had brought with them had proved irresistible and the inhabitants of the earth possessed nothing capable of contending against them. There had been no protection for the great cities; no protection even for the open country. Everything had gone down before the savage onslaught of those merciless invaders from space. Savage ruins covered the sites of many formerly flourishing towns and villages, and the broken walls of great cities stared at the heavens like the exhumed skeletons of Pompeii. The awful agencies had extirpated pastures and meadows and dried up the very springs of fertility in the earth where they had touched it. In some parts of the devastated lands pestilence broke out; elsewhere there was famine. Despondency black as night brooded over some of the fairest portions of the globe.

Yet all had not been destroyed, because all had not been reached by the withering hand of the destroyer. The Martians had not had time to complete their work before they themselves fell a prey to the diseases that carried them off at the very culmination of their triumph.

From those lands which had, fortunately, escaped invasion, relief was sent to the sufferers. The outburst of pity and of charity exceeded anything that the world had known. Differences of race and religion were swallowed up in the universal sympathy which was felt for those who had suffered so terribly from an evil that was as unexpected as it was unimaginable in its enormity.

But the worst was not yet. More dreadful than the actual suffering and the scenes of death and devastation which overspread the afflicted lands was the profound mental and moral depression that followed. This was shared even by those who had not seen the Martians and had not witnessed the destructive effects of the frightful engines of war that they had imported for the conquest of the earth. All mankind was sunk deep in this universal despair, and it became tenfold blacker when the astronomers announced from their observatories that strange lights were visible, moving and flashing upon the red surface of the Planet of War. These mysterious appearances could only be interpreted in the light of past experience to mean that the Martians were preparing for another invasion of the earth, and who could doubt that with the invincible powers of destruction at their command they would this time make their work complete and final?

This startling announcement was the more pitiable in its effects because it served to unnerve and discourage those few of stouter hearts and more hopeful temperaments who had already begun the labor of restoration and reconstruction amid the embers of their desolated homes. In

New York this feeling of hope and confidence, this determination to rise against disaster and to wipe out the evidences of its dreadful presence as quickly as possible, had especially manifested itself. Already a company had been formed and a large amount of capital subscribed for the reconstruction of the destroyed bridges over the East River. Already architects were busily at work planning new twenty-story hotels and apartment houses; new churches and new cathedrals on a grander scale than before.

Amid this stir of renewed life came the fatal news that Mars was undoubtedly preparing to deal us a death blow. The sudden revulsion of feeling flitted like the shadow of an eclipse over the earth. The scenes that followed were indescribable. Men lost their reason. The faint-hearted ended the suspense with self-destruction, the stout-hearted remained steadfast, but without hope and knowing not what to do.

But there was a gleam of hope of which the general public as yet knew nothing. It was due to a few dauntless men of science, conspicuous among whom were Lord Kelvin, the great English savant; Herr Roentgen, the discoverer of the famous X-ray, and especially Thomas A. Edison, the American genius of science. These men and a few others had examined with the utmost care the engines of war, the flying machines, the generators of mysterious destructive forces that the Martians had produced, with the object of discovering, if possible, the sources of their power.

Suddenly from Mr. Edison's laboratory at Orange flashed the startling intelligence that he had not only discovered the manner in which the invaders had been able to produce the mighty energies which they employed with such terrible effect, but that, going further, he had found a way to overcome them.

The glad news was quickly circulated throughout the civilized world. Luckily the Atlantic cables had not been destroyed by the Martians, so that communication between the Eastern and Western continents was uninterrupted. It was a proud day for America. Even while the Martians had been upon the earth, carrying everything before them, demonstrating to the confusion of the most optimistic that there was no possibility of standing against them, a feeling—a confidence had manifested itself in France, to a minor extent in England, and particularly in Russia, that the Americans might discover means to meet and master the invaders.

Now, it seemed, this hope and expectation was to be realized. Too late, it is true, in a certain sense, but not too late to meet the new invasion which the astronomers had announced was impending. The effect was as wonderful and indescribable as that of the despondency which but a little while before had overspread the world. One could almost hear the universal sigh of relief which went up from humanity. To relief succeeded confidence—so quickly does the human spirit recover like an elastic spring, when pressure is released.

"Let them come," was the almost joyous cry. "We shall be ready for them now. The Americans have solved the problem. Edison has placed the means of victory within our power."

Looking back upon that time now, I recall, with a thrill, the pride that stirred me at the thought that, after all, the inhabitants of the earth were a match for those terrible men from Mars, despite all the advantage which they had gained from their millions of years of prior civilization and science.

As good fortunes, like bad, never come singly, the news of Mr. Edison's discovery was quickly followed by additional glad tidings from that laboratory of marvels in the lap of the Orange mountains. During their career of conquest the Martians had astonished the inhabitants of the earth no less with their flying machines—which nagivated our atmosphere as easily as they had that of their native planet—than with their more destructive inventions. These flying machines in themselves had given them an enormous advantage in the contest. High above the desolation that they had caused to reign on the surface of the earth, and, out of the range of our guns, they had hung safe in the upper air. From the clouds they had dropped death upon the earth.

· Now, rumor declared that Mr. Edison had invented and perfected a flying machine much more complete and manageable than those of the Martians had been. Wonderful stories quickly found their way into the newspapers concerning what Mr. Edison had already accomplished with the aid of his model electrical balloon. His laboratory was carefully guarded against the invasion of the curious, because he rightly felt that a premature announcement, which should promise more than could actually be fulfilled, would, at this critical juncture, plunge mankind back again into the gulf of despair, out of which it had just begun to emerge.

Nevertheless, inklings of the truth leaked out. The flying machine had been seen by many persons hovering by night high above the Orange hills and disappearing in the faint starlight as if it had gone away into the depths of space, out of which it would re-emerge before the morning light had streaked the east, and be seen settling down again within the walls that surrounded the laboratory of the great inventor. At length the rumor, gradually deepening into a conviction, spread that Edison himself, accompanied by a few scientific friends, had made an experimental trip to the moon. At a time when the spirit of mankind was less profoundly stirred, such a story would have been received with complete incredulity, but now, rising on the wings of the new hope that was buoying up the earth, this extraordinary rumor became a day star of truth to the nations.

And it was true. I had myself been one of the occupants of the car of the flying Ship of Space on that night when it silently left the earth, and rising out of the great shadow of the globe, sped on to the moon. We had landed upon the scarred and desolate face of the earth's satellite, and but that there are greater and more interesting events, the telling of which must not be delayed, I should undertake to describe the particulars of this first visit of men to another world.

But, as I have already intimated, this was only an experimental trip. By visiting this little nearby island in the ocean of space, Mr. Edison simply wished to demonstrate the practicability of his invention, and to convince, first of all, himself and his scientific friends that it was possible for men—mortal men—to quit and to revisit the earth at their will. That aim this experimental trip triumphantly attained.

It would carry me into technical details that would hardly interest the reader to describe the mechanism of Mr. Edison's flying machine. Let it suffice to say that it depended upon the principle of electrical attraction and repulsion. By means of a most ingenious and complicated construction he had mastered the problem of how to produce, in a limited space, electricity of any desired potential and of any polarity, and that without danger to the experimenter or to the material experimented upon. It is gravitation, as everybody knows, that makes man a prisoner on the earth. If he could overcome or neutralize gravitation, he could float away, a free creature of interstellar space. Mr. Edison in his invention had pitted electricity against gravitation. Nature, in fact, had done the same thing long before. Every astronomer knew it, but none had been able to imitate or to reproduce this miracle of nature. When a comet approaches the sun, the orbit in which it travels indicates that it is moving under the impulse of the sun's gravitation. It is in reality falling in a great parabolic or elliptical curve through space. But, while a comet approaches the sun it begins to display—stretching out for millions, and sometimes hundreds of millions of miles on the side away from the sun—an immense luminous train called its tail. This train extends back into that part of space from which the comet is moving. Thus the sun at one and the same time is drawing the comet toward itself and driving off from the comet in an opposite direction minute particles or atoms which, instead of obeying the gravitational force, are plainly compelled to disobey it. That this energy, which the sun exercises against its own gravitation, is electrical in its nature, hardly anybody will doubt. The head of the comet being comparatively heavy and massive, falls on toward the sun, despite the electrical repulsion. But the atoms which form the tail, being almost without weight, yield to the electrical rather than to the gravitational influence, and so fly away from the sun.

Now, what Mr. Edison had done was, in effect, to create an electrified particle which might be compared to one of the atoms composing the tail of a comet, although in reality it was a kind of car, of metal, weighing some hundreds of pounds and capable of bearing some thousands of pounds with it in its flight. By producing, with the aid of the electrical generator contained in this car, an enormous charge of electricity, Mr. Edison was able to counterbalance, and a trifle more than counterbalance, the attraction of the earth, and thus cause the car to fly off from the earth as an electrified pithball flies from the prime conductor.

As we sat in the brilliantly lighted chamber that formed the interior of the car, and where stores of compressed air had been provided together with chemical apparatus, by means of which fresh supplies of oxygen and nitrogen might be obtained for our consumption during the flight through space, Mr. Edison touched a polished button, thus causing the generation of the required electrical charge on the exterior of the car, and immediately we began to rise.

The moment and direction of our flight had been so timed and prearranged, that the original impulse would carry us straight toward the moon.

When we fell within the sphere of attraction of that orb it only became necessary to so manipulate the electrical charge upon our car as nearly, but not quite, to counterbalance the effect of the moon's attraction in order that we might gradually approach it and with an easy motion, settle, without shock, upon its surface.

We did not remain to examine the wonders of the moon, although we could not fail to observe many curious things therein. Having demonstrated the fact that we could not only leave the earth, but could journey through space and safely land upon the surface of another planet, Mr. Edison's immediate purpose was fulfilled, and we hastened back to the earth, employing in leaving the moon and landing again upon our own planet the same means of control over the electrical attraction and repulsion between the respective planets and our car which I have already described.

When actual experiment had thus demonstrated the practicability of the invention, Mr. Edison no longer withheld the news of what he had been doing from the world. The telegraph lines and the ocean cables labored with the messages that in endless succession, and burdened with an infinity of detail, were sent all over the earth. Everywhere the utmost enthusiasm was aroused.

"Let the Martians come," was the cry. "If necessary, we can quit the earth as the Athenians fled from Athens before the advancing host of Xerxes, and like them, take refuge upon our ships—these new ships of space, with which American inventiveness has furnished us."

And then, like a flash, some genius struck out an idea that fired the world.

"Why should we wait? Why should we run the risk of having our cities destroyed and our lands desolated a second time? Let us go to Mars. We have the means. Let us beard the lion in his den. Let us ourselves turn conquerors and take possession of that detestable planet, and if necessary, destroy it in order to relieve the earth of this perpetual threat which now hangs over us like the sword of Damocles."

THE DISINTEGRATOR This enthusiasm would have had but little justification had Mr. Edison done nothing more than invent a machine which could navigate the atmosphere and the regions of interplanetary space.

He had, however, and this fact was generally known, although the details had not yet leaked out—invented also machines of war intended to meet the utmost that the Martians could do for either offence or defence in the struggle which was now about to ensue.

Acting upon the hint which had been conveyed from various investigations in the domain of physics, and concentrating upon the problem all those unmatched powers of intellect which distinguished him, the great inventor had succeeded in producing a little implement which one could carry in his hand, but which was more powerful than any battleship that ever floated. The details of its mechanism could not be easily explained, without the use of tedious technicalities and the employment of terms, diagrams and mathematical statements, all of which would lie outside the scope of this narrative. But the principle of the thing was simple enough. It was upon the great scientific doctrine, which we have since seen so completely and brilliantly developed, of the law of harmonic vibrations, extending from atoms and molecules at one end of the series up to the worlds and suns at the other end, that Mr. Edison based his invention.

Every kind of substance has its own vibratory rhythm. That of iron differs from that of pine wood. The atoms of gold do not vibrate in the same time or through the same range as those of lead, and so on for all known substances, and all the chemical elements. So, on a larger scale, every massive body has its period of vibration. A great suspension bridge vibrates, under the impulse of forces that are applied to it, in long periods. No company of soldiers ever crosses such a bridge without breaking step. If they tramped together, and were followed by other companies keeping the same time with their feet, after a while the vibrations of the bridge would become so great and destructive that it would fall in pieces. So any structure, if its vibration rate is known, could easily be destroyed by a force applied to it in such a way that it should simply increase the swing of those vibrations up to the point of destruction.

Now Mr. Edison had been able to ascertain the vibratory swing of many well-known substances, and to produce, by means of the instrument which he had contrived, pulsations in the ether which were completely under his control, and which could be made long or short, quick or slow, at his will. He could run through the whole gamut from the slow vibrations of sound in air up to the four hundred and twenty-five millions of millions of vibrations per second of the ultra red rays.

Having obtained an instrument of such power, it only remained to concentrate its energy upon a given object in order that the atoms composing that object should be set into violent undulation, sufficient to burst it asunder and to scatter its molecules broadcast. This the inventor effected by the simplest means in the world—simply a parabolic reflector by which the destructive waves could be sent like a beam of light, but invisible, in any direction and focused upon any desired point.

I had the good fortune to be present when this powerful engine of destruction was submitted to its first test. We had gone upon the roof of Mr. Edison's laboratory and the inventor held the little instrument, with its attached mirror, in his hand. We looked about for some object on which to try its powers. On a bare limb of a tree not far away, for it was late in fall, sat a disconsolate crow.

"Good," said Mr. Edison, "that will do." He touched a button at the side of the instrument and a soft, whirring noise was heard.

"Feathers," said Mr. Edison, "have a vibration period of three hundred and eighty-six million per second."

He adjusted the index as he spoke. Then, through a sighting tube, he aimed at the bird.

"Now watch," he said.

Another soft whirr in the instrument, a momentary flash of light close around it, and, behold, the crow had turned from black to white!

"Its feathers are gone," said the inventor; "they have been dissipated into their constituent atoms. Now, we will finish the crow."

Instantly there was another adjustment of the index, another outshooting of vibratory force, a rapid up and down motion of the index to include a certain range of vibrations, and the crow itself was gone—vanished in empty space! There was the bare twig on which a moment before it had stood. Behind, in the sky, was the white cloud against which its black form had been sharply outlined, but there was no more crow.

"That looks bad for the Martians, doesn't it?" said the Wizard. "I have ascertained the vibration rate of all the materials of which their war engines, whose remains we have collected together, are composed. They can be shattered into nothingness in the fraction of a second. Even if the vibration period were not known, it could quickly be hit upon by simply running through the gamut."

"Hurrah!" cried one of the onlookers. "We have met the Martians and they are ours."

Such in brief was the first of the contrivances which Mr. Edison invented for the apporaching war with Mars. . . .

TO CONQUER ANOTHER WORLD   It is not necessary for me to describe the manner in which Mr. Edison performed his tremendous task. He was as good as his word, and within six months from the first stroke of the hammer, a hundred electrical ships, each provided with a full battery of disintegrators, were floating in the air above the harbor and the partially rebuilt city of New York.

It was a wonderful scene. The polished sides of the huge floating cars sparkled in the sunlight, and, as they slowly rose and fell, and swung this way and that, upon the tides of the air, as if held by invisible cables, the brilliant pennons streaming from their peaks waved up and down like the wings of an assemblage of gigantic humming birds.

Not knowing whether the atmosphere of Mars would prove suitable to be breathed by inhabitants of the earth, Mr. Edison had made provision, by means of an abundance of glass-protected openings, to permit the inmates of the electrical ships to survey their surroundings without quitting the interior. It was possible by properly selecting the rate of undulation, to pass the vibratory impulse from the disintegrators through the glass windows of a car without damage to the glass itself. The windows were so arranged that the disintegrators could sweep around the car on all sides, and could also be directed above or below, as necessity might dictate.

To overcome the destructive forces employed by the Martians no satisfactory plan had yet been devised, because there was no means to experiment with them. The production of those forces was still the secret of our enemies. But Mr. Edison had no doubt that if we could not resist their efforts we might at least be able to avoid them by the rapidity of our motions. As he pointed out, the war machines which the Martians had employed in their invasion of the earth, were really very awkward and unmanageable affairs. Mr. Edison's electrical ships, on the other hand, were marvels of speed and of manageability. They could dart about, turn, reverse their course, rise, fall, with the quickness and ease of a fish in the water. Mr. Edison calculated that even if mysterious bolts should fall upon our ships we could diminish their power to cause injury by our rapid evolutions.

We might be deceived in our expectations, and might have overestimated our powers, but at any rate we must take our chances and try.

A multitude, exceeding even that which had assembled during the great congress in Washington, now thronged New York and its neighborhood to witness the mustering and the departure of the ships bound for Mars.

Nothing further had been heard of the mysterious phenomenon reported from the observatories six months before, and which at the time was believed to indicate the departure of another expedition from Mars for the invasion of the earth. If the Martians had set out to attack us they had evidently gone astray; or, perhaps, it was some other world that they were aiming at this time.

The expedition had, of course, profoundly stirred the interest of the scientific world, and representatives of every branch of science, from all the civilized nations, urged their claims to places in the ships. Mr. Edison was compelled, from lack of room, to refuse transportation to more than one in a thousand of those who now, on the plea that they might be able to bring back something of advantage to science, wished to embark for Mars.

On the model of the celebrated corps of literary and scientific men which Napoleon carried with him in his invasion of Egypt, Mr. Edison selected a company of the foremost astronomers, archaeologists, anthropologists, botanists, bacteriologists, chemists, physicists, mathematicians, mechanics, meteorologists and experts in mining, metallurgy and every other branch of practical science, as well as artists and photographers. It was but reasonable to believe that in another world, and a world so much older than the earth as Mars was, these men would be able to gather materials in comparison with which the discoveries made among the ruins of ancient empires in Egypt and Babylonia would be insignificant indeed.

It was a wonderful undertaking and a strange spectacle. There was a feeling of uncertainty which awed the vast multitude whose eyes were upturned to the ships. The expedition was not large, considering the gigantic character of the undertaking. Each of the electrical ships carried about twenty men, together with an abundant supply of compressed provisions, compressed air, scientific apparatus and so on. In all, there were about 2,000 men, who were going to conquer, if they could, another world!

But though few in numbers, they represented the flower of the earth, the culmination of the genius of the planet. The greatest leaders in science, both theoretical and practical, were there. It was the evolution of the earth against the evolution of Mars. It was a planet in the heyday of its strength matched against an aged and decrepit world which, nevertheless, in consequence of its long ages of existence, had acquired an experience which made it a most dangerous foe. On both sides there was desperation. The earth was desperate because it foresaw destruction unless it could first destroy its enemy. Mars was desperate because nature was gradually depriving it of the means of supporting life, and its teeming population was compelled to swarm like the inmates of an overcrowded hive of bees, and find new homes elsewhere. In this respect the situation on Mars, as we were well aware, resembled what had already been known upon the earth, where the older nations overflowing with population had sought new lands in which to settle, and for that purpose had driven out the native inhabitants, whenever those natives had proven unable to resist the invasion.

No man could foresee the issue of what we were about to undertake, but the tremendous powers which the disintegrators had exhibited and the marvelous efficiency of the electrical ships bred almost universal confidence that we should be successful.

The car in which Mr. Edison travelled was, of course, the flagship of the squadron, and I had the good fortune to be included among its inmates. Here, besides several leading men of science from our own country, were Lord Kelvin, Lord Rayleigh, Professor Roentgen, Dr. Moissan—the man who first made artificial diamonds—and several others whose fame had encircled the world. Each of these men cherished hopes of wonderful discoveries, along his line of investigation, to be made in Mars.

An elaborate system of signals had, of course, to be devised for the control of the squadron. These signals consisted of brilliant electric lights displayed at night and so controlled that by their means long sentences and directions could be easily and quickly transmitted.

Once out of the shadow of the earth we should have no more clouds and no more night until we arrived at Mars. In open space the sun would be continually shining. It would be perpetual day for us, except as, by artificial means, we furnished ourselves with darkness for the purpose of promoting sleep. In this region of perpetual day, then, the signals were also to be transmitted by flashes of light from mirrors reflecting the rays of the sun.

Yet this perpetual day would be also, in one sense, a perpetual night. There would be no more blue sky for us, because without an atmosphere the sunlight could not be diffused. Objects would be illuminated only on the side toward the sun. Anything that screened off the direct rays of sunlight would produce absolute darkness behind it. There would be no graduation of shadow. The sky would be as black as ink on all sides.

While it was the intention to remain as much as possible within the cars, yet since it was probable that necessity would arise for occasionally quitting the interior of the electrical ships, Mr. Edison had provided for this emergency by inventing an air-tight dress constructed somewhat after the manner of a diver's suit, but of much lighter material. Each ship was provided with several of these suits, by wearing which one could venture outside the ship even when it was beyond the atmosphere of the earth.

Provision had been made to meet the terrific cold which we knew would be encountered the moment we had passed beyond the atmosphere—that awful absolute zero which men had measured by anticipation, but never yet experienced—by a simple system of producing within the air-tight suits a temperature sufficiently elevated to counteract the effects of the frigidity without. By means of long, flexible tubes, air could be continually supplied to the wearers of the suits, and by an ingenious contrivance a store of compressed air sufficient to last for several hours was provided for each suit, so that in case of necessity the wearer could throw off the tubes connecting him with the air tanks in the car. Another object which had been kept in view in the preparation of these suits was the possible exploration of an airless planet, such as the moon.

The necessity of some contrivance by means of which we should be enabled to converse with one another while outside the cars in open space, or when in an airless world, like the moon, where there would be no medium by which the waves of sound could be conveyed as they are in the atmosphere of the earth, had been foreseen by our great inventor, and he had not found it difficult to contrive suitable devices for meeting the emergency.

Inside the headpiece of each of the electrical suits was the mouthpiece of a telephone. This was connected to a wire which, when not in use, could be conveniently coiled upon the arm of the wearer. Near the ears, similarly connected with wires, were telephonic receivers.

When two persons wearing the air-tight dresses wished to converse with one another it was only necessary for them to connect themselves by the wires, and conversation could then be easily carried on.

Careful calculations of the precise distance of Mars from the earth at the time when the expedition was to start had been made by a large number of experts in mathematical astronomy. But it was not Mr. Edison's intention to go direct to Mars. With the exception of the first electrical ship, which he had completed, none had yet been tried in a long voyage. It was desirable that the qualities of each of the ships should first be carefully tested, and for this reason the leader of the expedition determined that the moon should be the first port of space at which the squadron would call.

It chanced that the moon was so situated at this time as to be nearly in a line between the earth and Mars, which latter was in opposition to the sun, and consequently as favorably situated as possible for the purposes of the voyage. What would be, then, for 99 out of the 100 ships of the squadron, a trial trip would at the same time be a step of a quarter of a million of miles gained in the direction of our journey, and so no time would be wasted.

The departure from the earth was arranged to occur precisely at midnight. The moon near the full was hanging high over head, and a marvelous spectacle was presented to the eyes of those below as the great squadron of floating ships, with their insignia lights ablaze, cast loose and began slowly to move away on their adventurous and unprecedented expedition into the great unknown. A tremendous cheer, billowing up from the throats of millions of excited men and women, seemed to rend the curtain of the night, and made the airships tremble with the atmospheric vibrations that were set in motion.

Instantly magnificent fireworks were displayed in honor of our departure. Rockets by hundreds of thousands shot heaven-ward, and then burst in constellations of fiery drops. The sudden illumination thus produced, overspreading hundreds of square miles of the surface of the earth with a light almost like that of day, must certainly have been visible to the inhabitants of Mars, if they were watching us at the time. They might, or might not, correctly interpret its significance; but, at any rate, we did not care. We were off, and were confident that we could meet our enemy on his own ground before he could attack us again.

And now, as we slowly rose higher, a marvelous scene was disclosed. At first the earth beneath us, buried as it was in night, resembled the hollow of a vast cup of ebony blackness, in the center of which, like the molten lava run together at the bottom of a volcanic crater, shone the light of the illuminations around New York. But when we got beyond the atmosphere, and the earth still continued to recede below us, its aspect changed. The cup-shaped appearance was gone, and it began to round out beneath our eyes in the form of a vast globe—an enormous ball mysteriously suspended under us, glimmering over most of its surface, with the faint illumination of the moon, and showing toward its eastern edge the oncoming light of the rising sun.

When we were still further away, having slightly varied our course so that the sun was once more entirely hidden behind the center of the earth, we saw its atmosphere completely illuminated, all around it, with prismatic lights, like a gigantic rainbow in the form of a ring.

Another shift in our course rapidly carried us out of the shadow of the earth and into that all pervading sunshine. Then the great planet beneath us hung unspeakable in its beauty. The outlines of several of the continents were clearly discernible on its surface, streaked and spotted with delicate shades of varying color, and the sunlight flashed and glowed in long lanes across the convex surface of the oceans. Parallel with the Equator and along the regions of the ever blowing trade winds, were vast belts of clouds, gorgeous with crimson and purple as the sunlight fell upon them. Immense expanses of snow and ice lay like a glittering garment upon both land and sea around the North Pole.

As we gazed upon this magnificent spectacle, our hearts bounded within us. This was our earth—this was the planet we were going to defend—our home in the trackless wilderness of space. And it seemed to us indeed a home for which we might gladly expend our last breath. A new determination to conquer or die sprang up in our hearts, and I saw Lord Kelvin, after gazing at the beauteous scene which the earth presented through his eyeglass, turn about and peer in the direction in which we knew that Mars lay, with a sudden frown that caused the glass to lose its grip and fall dangling from its string upon his breast. Even Mr. Edison seemed moved.

"I am glad I thought of the disintegrator," he said. "I shouldn't like to see that world down there laid waste again."

"And it won't be," said Professor Sylvanus P. Thompson, gripping the handle of an electric machine, "not if we can help it."

THE FOOTPRINT ON THE MOON   To prevent accidents, it had been arranged that the ships should keep a considerable distance apart. Some of them gradually drifted away, until, on account of the neutral tint of their sides, they were swallowed up in the abyss of space. Still it was possible to know where every member of the squadron was through the constant interchange of signals. These, as I have explained, were effected by means of mirrors flashing back the light of the sun.

But, although it was now unceasing day for us, yet, there being no atmosphere to diffuse the sun's light, the stars were visible to us just as at night upon the earth, and they shone with extraordinary splendor against the intense black background of the firmament. The lights of some of the more distant ships of our squadron were not brighter than the stars in whose neighborhood they seemed to be. In some cases it was only possible to distinguish between the light of a ship and that of a star by the fact that the former was continually flashing while the star was steady in its radiance.

The most uncanny effect was produced by the absence of atmosphere around us. Inside the car, where there was air, the sunlight, streaming through one or more of the windows, was diffused and produced ordinary daylight.

But when we ventured outside we could only see things by halves. The side of the car that the sun's rays touched was visible, the other side was invisible, the light from the stars not making it bright enough to affect the eye in contrast with the sun-illumined half.

As I held up my arm before my eyes, half of it seemed to be shaved off lengthwise; a companion on the deck of the ship looked like half a man. So the other electrical ships near us appeared as half ships, only the illumined sides being visible.

We had now gotten so far away that the earth had taken on the appearance of a heavenly body like the moon. Its colors had become all blended into a golden-reddish hue, which overspread nearly its entire surface, except at the poles, where there were broad patches of white. It was marvelous to look at this huge orb behind us, while far beyond it shone the blazing sun like an enormous star in the blackest of nights. In the opposite direction appeared the silver orb of the moon, and scattered all around were millions of brilliant stars, amid which, like fireflies, flashed and sparkled the signal lights of the squadron.

A danger that might easily have been anticipated, that perhaps had been anticipated, but against which it had been difficult, if not impossible, to provide, presently manifested itself.

Looking out of a window toward the right, I suddenly noticed the lights of a distant ship darting about in a curious curve. Instantly afterward, another member of the squadron, nearer by, behaved in the same inexplicable manner. Then two or three of the floating cars seemed to be violently drawn from their courses and hurried rapidly in the direction of the flagship. Immediately I perceived a small object, luridly flaming, which seemed to move with immense speed in our direction.

The truth instantly flashed upon my mind, and I shouted to the other occupants of the car:

"A meteor!"

And such indeed it was. We had met this mysterious wanderer in space at a moment when we were moving in a direction at right angles to the path it was pursuing around the sun. Small as it was, and its diameter probably did not exceed a single foot, it was yet an independent little world, and as such a member of the solar system. Its distance from the sun being so near that of the earth, I knew that its velocity, assuming it to be travelling in a nearly circular orbit, must be about eighteen miles in a second. With this velocity, then, it plunged like a projectile shot by some mysterious enemy in space directly through our squadron. It had come and was gone before one could utter a sentence of three words. Its appearance, and the effect it had produced upon the ships in whose neighborhood it passed, indicated that it bore an intense and tremendous charge of electricity. How it had become thus charged I cannot pretend to say. I simply record the fact. And this charge, it was evident, was opposite in polarity to that which the ships of the squadron bore. It therefore exerted an attractive influence upon them and thus drew them after it.

I had just time to think how lucky it was that the meteor did not strike any of us, when, glancing at a ship just ahead, I perceived that an accident had occurred. The ship swayed violently from its course, dazzling flashes played around it, and two or three of the men forming its crew appeared for an instant on its exterior, wildly gesticulating, but almost instantly falling prone.

It was evident at a glance that the car had been struck by the meteor. How serious the damage might be we could not instantly determine. The course of our ship was immediately altered, the electric polarity was changed and we rapidly approached the disabled car.

The men who had fallen lay upon its surface. One of the heavy circular glasses covering a window had been smashed to atoms. Through this the meteor had passed, killing two or three men who stood in its course. Then it had crashed through the opposite side of the car, and, passing on, had disappeared into space. The store of air contained in the car had immediately rushed out through the openings, and when two or three of us, having donned our air-tight suits as quickly as possible, entered the wrecked car we found all its inmates stretched upon the floor in a condition of asphyxiation. They, as well as those who lay upon the exterior, were immediately removed to the flagship, restoratives were applied, and, fortunately, our aid had come so promptly that the lives of all of them were saved. But life had fled from the mangled bodies of those who had stood directly in the path of the fearful projectile.

This strange accident had been witnessed by several of the members of the fleet, and they quickly drew together, in order to inquire for the particulars. As the flagship was now overcrowded by the addition of so many men to its crew, Mr. Edison had them distributed among the other cars. Fortunately it happened that the disintegrators contained in the wrecked car were not injured. Mr. Edison thought that it would be possible to repair the car itself, and for that purpose he had it attached to the flagship in order that it might be carried on as far as the moon. The bodies of the dead were transported with it, as it was determined, instead of committing them to the fearful deep of space, where they would have wandered forever, or else have fallen like meteors upon the earth, to give them interment in the lunar soil.

As we now rapidly approached the moon the change which the appearance of its surface underwent was no less wonderful than that which the surface of the earth had presented in the reverse order while we were receding from it. From a pale silver orb, shining with comparative faintness among the stars, it slowly assumed the appearance of a vast mountainous desert. As we drew nearer its colors became more pronounced; the great flat regions appeared darker; the mountain peaks shone more brilliantly. The huge chasms seemed bottomless and blacker than midnight. Gradually separate mountains appeared. What seemed like expanses of snow and immense glaciers streaming down their sides sparkled with great brilliancy in the perpendicular rays of the sun. Our motion had now assumed the aspect of falling. We seemed to be dropping from an immeasurable height, and with an inconceivable velocity, straight down upon those giant peaks.

Here and there curious lights glowed upon the mysterious surface of the moon. Where the edge of the moon cut the sky behind it, it was broken and jagged with mountain masses. Vast crater rings overspread its surface, and in some of these I imagined I could perceive a lurid illumination coming out of their deepest cavities, and the curling of mephitic vapors around their terrible jaws.

We were approaching that part of the moon which is known to the astronomers as the Bay of Rainbows. Here a huge semi-circular region, as smooth almost as the surface of a prairie, lay beneath our eyes, stretching southward into a vast ocean-like expanse, while on the north it was enclosed by an enormous range of mountain cliffs, rising perpendicularly to a height of many thousands of feet, and rent and gashed in every direction by forces which seemed at some remote period to have labored at tearing this little world in pieces.

It was a fearful spectacle; a dead and mangled world, too dreadful to look upon. The idea of the death of the moon was, of course, not a new one to many of us. We had long been aware that the earth's satellite was a body which had passed beyond the stage of life, if indeed it had ever been a life supporting globe; but none of us were prepared for the terrible spectacle which now smote our eyes.

At each end of the semi-circular ridge that encloses the Bay of Rainbows there is a lofty promontory. That at the northwestern extremity had long been known to the astronomers under the name of Cape Laplace. The other promontory, at the southeastern termination, is called Cape Heraclides. It was toward the latter that we were approaching, and by interchange of signals all the members of the squadron had been informed that Cape Heraclides was to be our rendezvous upon the moon.

I may say that I had been somewhat familiar with the scenery of this part of the lunar world, for I had often studied it from the earth with a telescope, and I had thought that if there was any part of the moon where one might, with fair expectation of success, look for inhabitants, or if not inhabitants, at least for relics of life no longer existent there, this would surely be the place. It was, therefore, with no small degree of curiosity, notwithstanding the unexpectedly frightful and repulsive appearance that the surface of the moon presented, that I now saw myself rapidly approaching the region concerning whose secrets my imagination had so often busied itself. When Mr. Edison and I had paid our previous trip to the moon on our first experimental trip of the electrical ship we had landed at a point on its surface remote from this, and, as I have before explained, we then made no effort to investigate its secrets. But now it was to be different, and we were at length to see something of the wonders of the moon.

I had often on the earth drawn a smile from my friends by showing them Cape Heraclides with a telescope, and calling their attention to the fact that the outline of the peak terminating the cape was such as to present a remarkable resemblance to a human face, unmistakably a feminine countenance, seen in profile, and possessing no small degree of beauty. To my astonishment, this curious human semblance still remained when we had approached so close to the moon that the mountains forming the cape filled nearly the whole field of view of the window from which I was watching it. The resemblance, indeed, was most startling.

"Can this indeed be Diana herself?" I said half-aloud, but instantly afterward I was laughing at my fancy, for Mr. Edison had overheard me and exclaimed, "Where is she?"

"Who?"

"Diana."

"Why, there," I said, pointing to the moon. But lo! the appearance was gone even while I spoke. A swift change had taken place in the line of sight by which we were viewing it, and the likeness had disappeared in consequence.

A few moments later my astonishment was revived, but the cause this time was a very different one. We had been dropping rapidly toward the mountains, and the electrician in charge of the car was swiftly and constantly changing his potential, and, like a pilot who feels his way into an unknown harbor, endeavoring to approach the moon in such a manner that no hidden peril should surprise us. As we thus approached I suddenly perceived, crowning the very apex of the lofty peak near the termination of the cape, the ruins of what appeared to be an ancient watch tower. It was evidently composed of Cyclopean blocks larger than any that I had ever seen even among the ruins of Greece, Egypt and Asia Minor.

Here, then, was visible proof that the moon had been inhabited, although probably it was not inhabited now. I cannot describe the exultant feeling which took possession of me at this discovery. It settled so much that learned men had been disputing about for centuries.

"What will they say," I exclaimed, "when I show them a photograph of that?"

Below the peak, stretching far to right and left, lay a barren beach which had evidently once been washed by sea waves, because it was marked by long curved ridges such as the advancing and retiring tide leaves upon the shore of the ocean.

This beach sloped rapidly outward and downward toward a profound abyss, which had once, evidently, been the bed of a sea, but which now appeared to us simply as the empty, yawning shell of an ocean that had long vanished.

It was with no small difficulty, and only after the expenditure of considerable time, that all the floating ships of the squadron were gradually brought to rest on this lone mountain top of the moon. In accordance with my request, Mr. Edison had the flagship moored in the interior of the great ruined watch tower that I have described. The other ships rested upon the slope of the mountain around us.

Although time pressed, for we knew that the safety of the earth depended upon our promptness in attacking Mars, yet it was determined to remain here at least two or three days in order that the wrecked car might be repaired. It was found also that the passage of the highly electrified meteor had disarranged the electrical machinery in some of the other cars, so that there were many repairs to be made besides those needed to restore the wreck.

Moreover, we must bury our unfortunate companions who had been killed by the meteor. This, in fact, was the first work that we performed. Strange was the sight, and stranger our feelings, as here on the surface of a world distant from the earth, and on soil which had never before been pressed by the foot of man, we performed that last ceremony of respect which mortals pay to mortality. In the ancient beach at the foot of the peak we made a deep opening, and there covered forever the faces of our friends, leaving them to sleep among the ruins of empires, and among the graves of races which had vanished probably ages before Adam and Eve appeared in Paradise.

While the repairs were being made several scientific expeditions were sent out in various directions across the moon. One went westward to investigate the great ring of Plato, and the lunar Alps. Another crossed the ancient Sea of Showers toward the inner Appenines.

One started to explore the immense Crater of Copernicus, which, yawning fifty miles across, presents a wonderful appearance even from the distance of the earth. The ship in which I, myself, had the good fortune to embark, was bound for the mysterious inner mountain Aristarchus.

Before these expeditions started, a careful exploration had been made in the neighborhood of Cape Heraclides. But, except that the broken walls of the watch tower on the peak, composed of blocks of enormous size, had evidently been the work of creatures endowed with human intelligence, no remains were found indicating the former presence of inhabitants upon this part of the moon.

But along the shore of the old sea, just where the so-called Bay of Rainbows separates itself from the abyss of the Sea of Showers, there were found some stratified rocks in which the fascinated eyes of the explorer beheld the clear imprint of a gigantic human foot, measuring five feet in length from toe to heel.

The most minute search failed to reveal another trace of the presence of the ancient giant, who had left the impress of his foot in the wet sands of the beach here so many millions of years ago that even the imagination of the geologists shrank from the task of attempting to fix the precise period.

Around this gigantic footprint gathered most of the scientific members of the expedition, wearing their oddly shaped air-tight suits, connected with telephonic wires, and the spectacle, but for the impressiveness of the discovery, would have been laughable in the extreme. Bending over the mark in the rock, nodding their heads together, pointing with their awkwardly accoutred arms, they looked like an assemblage of antidiluvian monsters collected around their prey. Their disappointment over the fact that no other marks of anything resembling human habitation could be discovered was very great.

Still this footprint in itself was quite sufficient, as they all declared, to settle the question of the former habitation of the moon, and it would serve for the production of many a learned volume after their return to earth, even if no further discoveries should be made in other parts of the lunar world.

It was the hope of making such other discoveries that led to the dispatch of the other various expeditions which I have already named. I was chosen to accompany the car that was going to Aristarchus, because, as every one who had viewed the moon from the earth was aware, there was something very mysterious about that mountain. I knew that it was a crater nearly thirty miles in diameter and very deep, although its floor was plainly visible.

What rendered it remarkable was the fact that the floor and the walls of the crater, particularly on the inner side, glowed with a marvelous brightness which rendered them almost blinding when viewed with a powerful telescope.

So bright were they, indeed, that the eye was unable to see many of the details which the telescope would have made visible but for the flood of light which poured from the mountains. Sir William Hershel had been so completely misled by this appearance that he supposed he was watching a lunar volcano in eruption.

It had always been a difficult question what caused the extraordinary luminosity of Aristarchus. No end of hypothesis had been invented to account for it. Now I was to assist in settling these questions forever.

From Cape Heraclides to Aristarchus the distance in air line was something over 300 miles. Our course lay across the northeastern part of the Sea of Showers, with enormous cliffs, mountain masses and peaks shining on the right, while in the other direction the view was bounded by the distant range of the lunar Appenines, some of whose towering peaks, when viewed from our immense elevation, appeared as sharp as the Swiss Matterhorn.

When we had arrived within about a hundred miles of our destination, we found ourselves floating directly over the so-called Harbinger Mountains. The serrated peaks of Aristarchus then appeared ahead of us, fairly blazing in the sunshine.

It seemed as if a gigantic string of diamonds, every one as great as a mountain peak, had been cast down upon the barren surface of the moon and left to waste their brilliance upon the desert air of this abandoned world.

As we rapidly approached, the dazzling splendor of the mountain became almost unbearable to our eyes, and we were compelled to resort to the device, practised by all climbers of lofty mountains where the glare of sunlight on snow surfaces is liable to cause temporary blindness, of protecting our eyes with neutral-tinted glasses.

Professor Moissan, the great French chemist and maker of artificial diamonds, fairly danced with delight.

"Voila! Voila! Voila!" was all that he could say.

When we were comparatively near, the mountain no longer seemed to glow with a uniform radiance, evenly distributed over its entire surface, but now innumerable points of light, all as bright as so many little suns, blazed away at us. It was evident that we had before us a mountain composed of, or at least covered with, crystals.

Without stopping to alight on the outer slopes of the great ring-shaped range of peaks which composed Aristarchus, we sailed over their rim and looked down into the interior. Here the splendor of the crystals was greater than on the outer slopes, and the broad floor of the crater, thousands of feet beneath us, shone and sparkled with overwhelming radiance, as if it were an immense bin of diamonds, while a peak in the center flamed like a stupendous tiara incrusted with selected gems.

Eager to see what these crystals were, the car was now allowed rapidly to drop into the interior of the crater. With great caution we brought it to rest upon the blazing ground, for the sharp edges of the crystals would certainly have torn the metallic sides of the car if it had come into violent contact with them.

Donning our air-tight suits and stepping carefully out upon this wonderful footing we attempted to detach some of the crystals. Many of them were firmly fastened, but a few—some of astonishing size—were readily loosened.

A moment's inspection showed that we had stumbled upon the most marvelous work of the forces of crystallization that human eyes had ever rested upon. Some time in the past history of the moon there had been an enormous outflow of molten material from the crater. This had overspread the walls and partially filled up the interior, and later its surface had flowered into gems, as thick as blossoms in a bed of pansies.

The whole mass flashed prismatic rays of indescribable beauty and intensity. We gazed at first speechless with amazement.

"It cannot be, surely it cannot be," said Professor Moissan at length.

"But it is," said another member of the party.

"Are these diamonds?" asked a third.

"I cannot yet tell," replied the Professor. "They have the brilliancy of diamonds, but they may be something else."

"Moon jewels," suggested a third.

"And worth untold millions, whatever they are," remarked another. These magnificent crystals, some of which appeared to be almost flawless, varied in size from the dimensions of a hazelnut to geometrical solids several inches in diameter. We carefully selected as many as it was convenient to carry and placed them in the car for future examination. We had solved another long standing lunar problem and had, perhaps, opened up an inexhaustible future mine of wealth which might eventually go far toward reimbursing the earth for the damage which it had suffered from the invasion of the Martians.

On returning to Cape Heraclides we found that the other expeditions had arrived at the rendezvous ahead of us. Their members had wonderful stories to tell of what they had seen, but nothing caused quite so much astonishment as that which we had to tell and to show.

The party which had gone to visit Plato and the lunar Alps brought back, however, information which, in a scientific sense, was no less interesting than what we had been able to gather.

They had found within this curious ring of Plato, which is a circle of mountains sixty miles in diameter, enclosing a level plain remarkably smooth over most of its surface, unmistakable evidences of former habitation. A gigantic city had evidently at one time existed near the center of this great plain. The outlines of its walls and the foundation marks of some of its immense buildings were plainly made out, and elaborate plans of this vanished capitol of the moon were prepared by several members of the party.

One of them was fortunate enough to discover an even more precious relic of the ancient lunarians. It was a piece of petrified skullbone, representing but a small portion of the head to which it had belonged, but yet sufficient to enable the anthropologists, who immediately fell to examining it, to draw ideal representations of the head as it must have been in life—the head of a giant of enormous size, which, if it had possessed a highly organized brain, of proportionate magnitude, must have given to its possessor intellectual powers immensely greater than any of the descendants of Adam have ever been endowed with.

Indeed, one of the professors was certain that some little concretions found on the interior of the piece of skull were petrified portions of the brain matter itself, and he set to work with the microscope to examine its organic quality.

In the meantime, the repairs to the electrical ships had been completed, and, although these discoveries on the moon had created a most profound sensation among the members of the expedition, and aroused an almost irresistible desire to continue the explorations thus happily begun, yet everybody knew that these things were aside from the main purpose in view, and that we should be false to our duty in wasting a moment more upon the moon than was absolutely necessary to put the ships in proper condition to proceed on their warlike voyage.

Everything being prepared then, we left the moon with great regret, just forty-eight hours after we had landed upon its surface, carrying with us a determination to revisit it and to learn more of its wonderful secrets in case we should survive the dangers which we were now going to face.

THE MONSTERS ON THE ASTEROID   A day or two after leaving the moon, we had another adventure with a wandering inhabitant of space which brought us into far greater peril than had our encounter with the meteor.

The airships had been partitioned off so that a portion of the interior could be darkened in order to serve as a sleeping chamber, wherein, according to the regulations prescribed by the commander of the squadron each member of the expedition in his turn passed eight out of every twenty-four hours—sleeping if he could, if not, meditating in a more or less dazed way, upon the wonderful things that he was seeing and doing —things far more incredible than the creations of a dream.

One morning, if I may call by the name morning the time of my periodical emergence from the darkened chamber, glancing from one of the windows, I was startled to see in the black sky a brilliant comet.

No periodical comet, as I knew, was at this time approaching the neighborhood of the sun, and no stranger of that kind had been detected from the observatories making its way sunward before we left the earth. Here, however, was unmistakably a comet rushing toward the sun, flinging out a great gleaming tail behind it and so close to us that I wondered to see it remaining almost motionless in the sky. This phemomenon was soon explained to me, and the explanation was of a most disquieting character.

The stranger had already been perceived, not only from the flagship, but from the other members of the squadron, and, as I now learned, efforts had been made to get out of the neighborhood, but for some reason the electrical apparatus did not work perfectly—some mysterious disturbing force acting upon it—and so it had been found impossible to avoid an encounter with the comet, not an actual coming into contact with it, but a falling into the sphere of its influence.

In fact, I was informed that for several hours the squadron had been dragging along in the wake of a comet, very much as boats are sometimes towed off by a wounded whale. Every effort had been made to so adjust the electric charge upon the ships that they would be repelled from the cometic mass, but, owing apparently to electric changes affecting the clashing mass of meteoric bodies which constituted the head of the comet, we found it impossible to escape from its influence.

At one instant the ships would be repelled; immediately afterward they would be attracted again, and thus they were dragged hither and thither, but never able to break from the invisible leash which the comet had cast upon them. The latter was moving with enormous velocity toward the sun, and, consequently, we were being carried back again, away from the object of our expedition, with a fair prospect of being dissipated in blazing vapors when the comet had dragged us, unwilling prisoners, into the immediate neighborhood of the solar furnace.

Even the most cool-headed lost his self control in this terrible emergency. Every kind of devise that experience or the imagination could suggest was tried, but nothing would do. Still on we rushed with the electrified atoms composing the tail of the comet swinging to and fro over the members of the squadron, as they shifted their position, like the plume of smoke from a gigantic steamer, drifting over the sea birds that follow in its course.

Was this to end it all, then? Was this the fate that Providence had in store for us? Were the hopes of the earth thus to perish? Was the expedition to be wrecked and its fate to remain for ever unknown to the planet from which it had set forth? And was our beloved globe, which had seemed so fair to us when we last looked upon it nearby, and in whose defense we had resolved to spend our last breath, to be left helpless and at the mercy of its implacable foe in the sky?

At length we gave ourselves up for lost. There seemed to be no possible way to free ourselves from the baleful grip of this terrible and unlooked-for enemy.

As the comet approached the sun its electrical energy rapidly increased, and watching it with telescopes, for we could not withdraw our fascinated eyes from it, we could clearly behold the fearful things that went on in its nucleus.

This consisted of an immense number of separate meteors of no very great size individually, but which were in constant motion among one another, darting to and fro, clashing and smashing together, while fountains of blazing metallic particles and hot mineral vapours poured out in every direction.

As I watched it, unable to withdraw my eyes, I saw imaginary forms revealing themselves amid the flaming meteors. They seemed like creatures in agony, tossing their arms, bewailing in their attitudes the awful fate that had overtaken them, and fairly chilling my blood with the pantomime of torture which they exhibited. I thought of an old superstition which I had often heard about the earth, and exclaimed:

"Yes, surely, this is a flying hell!"

As the electric activity of the comet increased, its continued changes of potential and polarity became more frequent, and the electrical ships darted about with even greater confusion than before. Occasionally one of them, seized with a sudden impulse, would spring forward toward the nucleus of the comet with a sudden access of velocity that would fling every one of its crew from his feet, and all would lie sprawling on the floor of the car while it rushed, as it seemed, to inevitable and instant destruction.

Then, either through the frantic efforts of the electrician struggling with the controller or through another change in the polarity of the comet, the ship would be saved on the very brink of ruin and stagger away out of immediate danger.

Thus the captured squadron was swept, swaying and darting hither and thither, but never able to get sufficiently far from the comet to break the bond of its fatal attraction.

So great was our excitement and so complete our absorption in the fearful peril that we had not noticed the precise direction in which the comet was carrying us. It was enough to know that the goal of the journey was the furnace of the sun. But presently someone in the flagship recalled us to a more accurate sense of our situation in space by exclaiming:

"Why, there is the earth!"

And there, indeed, it was, its great globe rolling under our eyes, with the contrasted colors of the continents and clouds and the watery gleam of the oceans spread beneath us.

"We're going to strike it!" exclaimed somebody. "The comet is going to dash us into the earth."

Such a collision at first seemed inevitable, but presently it was noticed that the direction of the comet's motion was such that while it might graze the earth it would not actually strike it.

And so, like a swarm of giant insects circling about an electric light from whose magic influence they could not escape, our ships went on, to be whipped against the earth in passing and then to continue their swift journey to destruction.

"Thank God, this saves us," suddenly cried Mr. Edison.

"What—what?"

"Why, the earth, of course. Do you not see that as the comet sweeps close to the great planet the superior attraction of the latter will snatch us from its grasp, and that thus we shall be able to escape."

And it was indeed as Mr. Edison had predicted. In a blaze of falling meteors the comet swept the outer limits of the earth's atmosphere and passed on, while the swaying ships, having been instructed by signals what to do, desperately applied their electrical machinery to reverse the attraction and threw themselves into the arms of their mother earth.

In another instant we were all free, settling down through the quiet atmosphere with the Atlantic Ocean sparkling in the morning sun far below.

We looked at one another in amazement. So this was the end of our voyage! This was the completion of our warlike enterprise. We had started out to conquer a world, and we had come back ignominiously dragged in the train of a comet.

The earth which we were going to defend and protect had herself turned protector, and reaching out her strong arm had snatched her foolish children from the destruction which they had invited.

It would be impossible to describe the chagrin of every member of the expedition.

The electric ships rapidly assembled and hovered high in the air, while their commanders consulted about what should be done. A universal feeling of shame almost drove them to a decision not to land upon the surface of the planet, and if possible not to let its inhabitants know what had occurred.

But it was too late for that. Looking carefully beneath us, we saw that fate had brought us back to our very starting point, and signals displayed in the neighborhood of New York indicated that we had already been recognized. There was nothing for us then but to drop down and explain the situation.

I shall not delay my narrative by undertaking to describe the astonishment and the disappointment of the inhabitants of the earth when, within a fortnight from our departure, they saw us back again, with no laurels of victory crowning our brows.

At first they had hoped that we were returning in triumph, and we were overwhelmed with questions the moment we had dropped within speaking distance.

"Have you whipped them?"

"How many are lost?"

"Is there any more danger?"

"Faix, have ye got one of thim men from Mars?"

But their rejoicing and their facetiousness were turned into wailing when the truth was imparted.

We made a short story of it, for we had not the heart to go into details. We told of our unfortunate comrades whom we had buried upon the moon, and there was one gleam of satisfaction when we exhibited the wonderful crystals we had collected in the crater of Aristarchus.

Mr. Edison determined to stop only long enough to test the electrical machinery of the cars, which had been more or less seriously deranged during our wild chase after the comet, and then to start straight back for Mars—this time on a through trip.

The astronomers, who had been watching Mars, since our departure, with their telescopes, reported that mysterious lights continued to be visible, but that nothing indicating the starting of another expedition for the earth had been seen.

Within twenty-four hours we were ready for our second start.

The moon was now no longer in a position to help us on our way. It had moved out of line between Mars and the earth.

High above us, in the center of the heavens, glowed the red planet which was the goal of our journey.

The needed computations of velocity and direction of flight having been repeated, and the ships being all in readiness, we started direct for Mars.

An enormous charge of electricity was imparted to each member of the squadron so that when we reached the upper limits of the atmosphere, where the ships could move swiftly without danger of being consumed by the heat developed by the friction of their passage through the air, a very great initial velocity could be imparted.

Once started off by this tremendous electrical kick, and with no atmosphere to resist our motion, we should be able to retain the same velocity, barring incidental encounters, until we arrived near the surface of Mars.

When we were free of the atmosphere, and the ships were moving away from the earth, with the highest velocity which we were able to impart to them, observations on the stars were made in order to determine the rate of our speed.

This was found to be ten miles in a second, or 864,000 miles in a day, a very much greater speed than that with which we had travelled on starting to touch at the moon. Supposing this velocity to remain uniform, and, with no known resistance, it might reasonably be expected to do so, we should arrive at Mars in a little less than forty-two days, the distance of the planet from the earth being at this time, about thirty-six million miles.

Nothing occurred for many days to interrupt our journey. We became accustomed to our strange surroundings, and many entertainments were provided to while away the time. The astronomers in the expedition found plenty of occupation in studying the aspects of the stars and the other heavenly bodies from their new point of view.

At the expiration of about thirty-five days we had drawn so near to Mars that with our telescopes, which, though small, were of immense power, we could discern upon its surface features and details which no one had been able to glimpse from the earth.

As the surface of this world, that we were approaching as a tiger hunter draws near the jungle, gradually unfolded itself to our inspection, there was hardly one of us willing to devote to sleep or idleness the prescribed eight hours that had been fixed as the time during which each member of the expedition must remain in the darkened chamber. We were too eager to watch for every new revelation upon Mars.

But something was in store that we had not expected. We were to meet the Martians before arriving at the world in which they dwelt.

Among the stars which shone in that quarter of the heavens where Mars appeared as the master orb, there was one lying directly in our path which, to our astonishment, altered from the aspect of a star, underwent a gradual magnification, and soon presented itself in the form of a little planet.

"It is an asteroid," said somebody.

"Yes, evidently; but how does it come inside the orbit of Mars?"

"Oh, there are several asteroids," said one of the astronomers, "which travel inside the orbit of Mars, along a part of their course, and, for aught we can tell, there may be many which have not yet been caught sight of from the earth, that are nearer to the sun than Mars is."

"This must be one of them."

"Manifestly so."

As we drew nearer the mysterious little planet revealed itself to us as a perfectly formed globe not more than five miles in diameter.

"What is that upon it?" asked Lord Kelvin, squinting intently at the little world through his glass. "As I live, it moves."

"Yes, yes!" exclaimed several others, "there are inhabitants upon it, but what giants!"

"What monsters!"

"Don't you see?" exclaimed an excited savant. "They are the Martians!"

The startling truth burst upon the minds of all. Here upon this little planetoid were several of the gigantic inhabitants of the world that we were going to attack. There was more than one man in the flagship who recognized them well, and who shuddered at the recognition, instinctively recalling the recent terrible experience of the earth.

Was this an outpost of the warlike Mars?

Around these monstrous enemies we saw several of their engines of war. Some of these appeared to have been wrecked, but at least one, as far as we could see, was still in a proper condition for use.

How had these creatures got there?

"Why, that is easy enough to account for," I said, as a sudden recollection flashed into my mind. "Don't you remember the report of the astronomers more than six months ago, at the end of the conference in Washington, that something would seem to indicate the departure of a new expedition from Mars had been noticed by them? We have heard nothing of that expedition since. We know that it did not reach the earth. It must have fallen foul of this asteroid, run upon this rock in the ocean of space and been wrecked here."

"We've got 'em, then," shouted our electric steersman, who had been a workman in Mr. Edison's laboratory and had unlimited confidence in his chief.

The electrical ships were immediately instructed by signal to slow down, an operation that was easily effected through the electrical repulsion of the asteroid.

The nearer we got the more terrifying was the appearance of the gigantic creatures who were riding upon the little world before us like castaway sailors upon a block of ice. Like men, and yet not like men, combining the human and the beast in their appearance, it required a steady nerve to look at them. If we had not known their malignity and their power to work evil, it would have been different, but in our eyes their moral character shone through their physical aspect and thus rendered them more terrible than they would otherwise have been.

When we first saw them their appearance was most forlorn, and their attitudes indicated only despair and desperation, but as they caught sight of us their malign power of intellect instantly penetrated the mystery, and they recognized us for what we were.

Their despair immediately gave place to reawakened malevolence. On the instant they were astir, with such heart-chilling movements as those that characterize a venomous serpent preparing to strike.

Not imagining that they would be in a position to make serious resistance, we had been somewhat incautious in approaching.

Suddenly there was a quicker movement than usual among the Martians, a swift adjustment of that one of their engines of war which, as already noticed, seemed to be practically uninjured, then there darted from it and alighted upon one of the foremost ships, a dazzling lightning stroke a mile in length, at whose touch the metallic sides of the car curled and withered and, licked for a moment by what seemed lambent flames, collasped into a mere cinder.

For an instant not a word was spoken, so sudden and unexpected was the blow.

We knew that every soul in the stricken car had perished.

"Back! Back!" was the signal instantly flashed from the flagship, and reversing their polarities the members of the squadron sprang away from the little planet as rapidly as the electrical impulse could drive them.

But before we were out of reach a second flaming tongue of death shot from the fearful engine, and another of our ships, with all its crew, was destroyed.

It was an inauspicious beginning for us. Two of our electrical ships, with their entire crews, had been wiped out of existence, and this appalling blow had been dealt by a few stranded and disabled enemies floating on an asteroid.

What hope would there be for us when we came to encounter the millions of Mars itself on their own ground and prepared for war?

However, it would not do to despond. We had been incautious, and we should take good care not to commit the same fault again.

The first thing to do was to avenge the death of our comrades. The question whether we were able to meet these Martians and overcome them might as well be settled right here and now. They had proved what they could do, even when disabled and at a disadvantage. Now it was our turn.

A PLANET OF GOLD   The squadron had been rapidly withdrawn to a very considerable distance from the asteroid. The range of the mysterious artillery employed by the Martians was unknown to us. We did not even know the limit of the effective range of our own disintegrators. If it should prove that the Martians were able to deal their strokes at a distance greater than any we could reach, then they would of course have an insuperable advantage.

On the other hand, if it should turn out that our range was greater than theirs, the advantage would be on our side. Or—which was perhaps most probable—there might be practically no difference in the effective range of the engines.

Anyhow, we were going to find out how the case stood, and that without delay.

Everything being in readiness, the disintegrators all in working order, and the men who were able to handle them, most of whom were experienced marksmen, chosen from among the officers of the regular army of the United States, and accustomed to the straight shooting and the sure hits of the West, standing at their posts, the squadron again advanced.

In order to distract the attention of the Martians, the electrical ships had been distributed over a wide space. Some dropped straight down toward the asteroid; others approached it by flank attack, from this side and that. The flagship moved straight in toward the point where the first disaster occurred. Its intrepid commander felt that his post should be that of the greatest danger, and where the severest blows would be given and received.

The approach of the ships was made with great caution. Watching the Martians with our telescopes we could clearly see that they were disconcerted by the scattered order of our attack. Even if all of their engines of war had been in proper condition for use it would have been impossible for them to meet the simultaneous assault of so many enemies dropping down upon them from the sky.

But they were made of fighting mettle, as we knew from old experience. It was no question of surrender. They did not know how to surrender, and we did not know how to demand their surrender. Besides, the destruction of the two electrical ships with the forty men, many of whom bore names widely known upon the earth, had excited a kind of fury among the members of the squadron which called for vengeance.

Suddenly a repetition of the quick movement by the Martians, which had been the forerunner of the former coup, was observed; again a blinding flash burst from their war engines and instantaneously a shiver ran through the frame of the flagship; the air within quivered with strange pulsations and seemed suddenly to have assumed the temperature of a blast furnace.

We all gasped for breath. Our throats and lungs seemed scorched in the act of breathing. Some fell unconscious upon the floor. The marksmen, carrying the disintegrators ready for use, staggered, and one of them dropped his instrument.

But we had not been destroyed like our comrades before us. In a moment the wave of heat passed; those who had fallen recovered from their momentary stupor and staggered to their feet.

The electrical steersman stood hesitating at his post.

"Move on," said Mr. Edison sternly, his features set with determination and his eyes afire.

"We are still beyond their effective range. Let us get closer in order to make sure work when we strike."

The ship moved on. One could hear the heartbeats of its inmates. The other members of the squadron, thinking for the moment that disaster had overtaken the flagship, had paused and seemed to be meditating flight.

"Signal them to move on," said Mr. Edison.

The signal was given, and the circle of electrical ships closed in upon the asteroid.

In the meantime Mr. Edison had been donning his airtight suit. Before we could clearly comprehend his intention he had passed through the double trapped door which gave access to the exterior of the car without permitting the loss of air, and was standing upon what served as the deck of the ship.

In his hand he carried a disintegrator. With a quick motion he sighted it.

As quickly as possible I sprang to his side. I was just in time to note the familiar blue gleam about the instrument, which indicated that its terrific energies were at work. The whirring sound was absent, because here, in open space, where there was no atmosphere, there could be no sound.

My eyes were fixed upon the Martian's engine, which had just dealt us a staggering, but not fatal, blow, and particularly I noticed a polished knob projecting from it which seemed to have been the focus from which its destructive bolt emanated.

A moment later the knob disappeared. The irresistible vibrations darted from the electrical disintegrator and had fallen upon it and instantaneously shattered it into atoms.

"That fixes them," said Mr. Edison, turning to me with a smile.

And indeed it did fix them. We had most effectually spiked their gun. It would deal no more death blows.

The doings of the flagship had been closely watched throughout the squadron. The effect of its blow had been evident to all, and a moment later we saw, on some of the nearer ships, men dressed in their air suits, appearing upon the deck, swinging their arms and sending forth soundless cheers into empty space.

The stroke that we had dealt was taken by several of the electrical ships as a signal for a common assault, and we saw two of the Martians fall beside the ruins of their engine, their heads having been blown from their bodies.

"Signal them to stop firing," commanded Mr. Edison. "We have got them down, and we are not going to murder them without necessity."

"Besides," he added, "I want to capture some of them alive."

The signal was given as he had ordered. The flagship then alone dropped slowly toward the place on the asteroid where the prostrate Martians were.

As we got near them a terrible scene unfolded itself to our eyes. There had evidently been not more than a half dozen of the monsters in the beginning. Two of these were stretched headless upon the ground. Three others had suffered horrible injuries where the invisible vibratory beams from the disintegrators had grazed them, and they could not long survive. One only remained apparently uninjured.

It is impossible for me to describe the appearance of this creature in terms that would be readily understood. Was he like a man? Yes and no. He possessed many human characteristics, but they were exaggerated and monstrous in scale and detail. His head was of enormous size, and his huge projecting eyes gleamed with a strange fire of intelligence. His face was like a caricature, but not one to make the beholder laugh. Drawing himself up, he towered to a height of at least fifteen feet.

But let the reader not suppose from this inadequate description that the Martians stirred in the beholder precisely the sensation that would be caused by the sight of a gorilla, or other repulsive inhabitant of our terrestrial jungles, suddenly confronting him in its native wilds.

With all his horrible characteristics, and all his suggestions of beast and monster, nevertheless the Martian produced the impression of being a person and not a mere animal.

I have already referred to the enormous size of his head, and to the fact that his countenance bore considerable resemblance to that of a man. There was something in his face that sent a shiver through the soul of the beholder. One could feel in looking upon it that here was intellect, intelligence developed to the highest degree, but in the direction of evil instead of good.

The sensations of one who had stood face to face with Satan, when he was driven from the battlements of heaven by the swords of his fellow archangels, and had beheld him transformed from Lucifer, the Son of the Morning, into the Prince of Night and Hell, might not have been unlike those which we now experienced as we gazed upon this dreadful personage, who seemed to combine the intellectual powers of a man, raised to their highest pitch, with some of the physical features of a beast, and all the moral depravity of a fiend.

The appearance of the Martian was indeed so threatening and repellent that we paused at the height of fifty feet above the ground, hesitating to approach nearer. A grin of rage and hate overspread his face. If he had been a man I should say he shook his fist at us. What he did was to express in even more telling pantomime his hatred and defiance, and his determination to grind us to shreds if he could once get us within his clutches.

Mr. Edison and I still stood upon the deck of the ship, where several others had gathered around us. The atmosphere of the little asteroid was so rare that it practically amounted to nothing, and we could not possibly have survived if we had not continued to wear our airtight suits. How the Martians contrived to live here was a mystery to us. It was another of their secrets which we were yet to learn.

Mr. Edison retained his disintegrator in his hand.

"Kill him," said someone. "He is too horrible to live."

"If we do not kill him we shall never be able to land upon the asteroid," said another.

"No," said Mr. Edison. "I shall not kill him. We have got another use for him. Tom," he continued, turning to one of his assistants, whom he had brought from his laboratory, "bring me the anaesthetic."

This was something entirely new to nearly all the members of the expedition. Mr. Edison, however, had confided to me before we left the earth the fact that he had invented a little instrument by means of which a bubble, strongly charged with a powerful anaesthetic agent, could be driven to a considerable distance into the face of an enemy, where exploding without other damage, it would instantly put him to sleep.

When Tom had placed the instrument in his hands Mr. Edison ordered the electrical ship to forge slightly ahead and drop a little lower toward the Martian, who, with watchful eyes and threatening gestures, noted our approach in the attitude of a wild beast on the spring. Suddenly Mr. Edison discharged from the instrument in his hand a little gaseous globe, which glittered like a ball of tangled rainbows in the sunshine, and darted with astonishing velocity straight into the upturned face of the Martian. It burst as it touched and the monster fell back senseless upon the ground.

"You have killed him!" exclaimed all.

"No," said Mr. Edison. "He is not dead, only asleep. Now we shall drop down and bind him tight before he can awake."

When we came to bind our prisoner with strong ropes we were more than ever impressed with his gigantic stature and strength. Evidently in single combat with equal weapons he would have been a match for twenty of us.

All that I had read of giants had failed to produce upon my mind the impression of enormous size and tremendous physical energy which the sleeping body of this immense Martian produced. He had fallen on his back, and was in a most profound slumber. All his features were relaxed, and yet even in that condition there was a devilishness about him that made the beholders instinctively shudder.

So powerful was the effect of the anaesthetic which Mr. Edison had discharged into his face that he remained perfectly unconscious while we turned him half over in order the more securely to bind his muscular limbs.

In the meantime the other electrical ships approached, and several of them made a landing upon the asteroid. Everybody was eager to see this wonderful little world, which, as I have already remarked, was only five miles in diameter. . . .

The asteroid being a body of some mass was, of course, able to impart to us a measurable degree of weight. Being five miles in diameter, on the assumption that its mean density was the same as that of the earth, the weight of bodies on its surface should have borne the same ratio to their weight upon the earth that the radius of the asteroid bore to the radius of the earth; in other words, as 1 to 1,600.

Having made this mental calculation, I knew that my weight, being 150 pounds on the earth, should on this asteroid be an ounce and a half.

Curious to see whether fact would bear out theory, I had myself weighed with a spring balance. Mr. Edison, Lord Kelvin and the other distinguished scientists stood by watching the operation with great interest.

To our complete surprise, my weight instead of coming out an ounce and a half, as it should have done, on the supposition that the mean density of the asteroid resembled that of the earth—a very liberal supposition on the side of the asteroid, by the way—actually came out five ounces and a quarter!

"What in the world makes me so heavy?" I asked.

"Yes, indeed, what an elephant you have become," said Mr. Edison.

Lord Kelvin screwed his eyeglass in his eye, and carefully inspected the balance.

"It's quite right," he said. "You do indeed weigh five ounces and a quarter. Too much; altogether too much," he added. "You shouldn't do it, you know."

"Perhaps the fault is in the asteroid," suggested Professor Sylvanus P. Thompson.

"Quite so," exclaimed Lord Kelvin, a look of sudden comprehension overspreading his features. "No doubt it is the internal constitution of the asteroid which is the cause of the anomaly. We must look into that. Let me see? This gentleman's weight is three and one-half times as great as it ought to be. What element is there whose density exceeds the mean density of the earth in about that proportion?"

"Gold," exclaimed one of the party.

For a moment we were startled beyond expression. The truth had flashed upon us.

This must be a golden planet—this little asteroid. If it were not composed internally of gold it could never have made me weigh three times more than I ought to weigh.

"But where is the gold?" cried one.

"Covered up, of course," said Lord Kelvin. "Buried in star dust. This asteroid could not have continued to travel for millions of years through legions of space strewn with meteoric particles without becoming covered with the inevitable dust and grime of such a journey. We must dig now, and then doubtless we shall find the metal."

This hint was instantly acted upon. Something that would serve as a spade was seized by one of the men, and in a few minutes a hole had been dug in the comparatively light soil of the asteroid.

I shall never forget the sight, nor the exclamations of wonder that broke forth from all of us standing around, when the yellow gleam of the precious metal appeared under the "star dust." Collected in huge masses it reflected the light of the sun from its hiding place.

Evidently the planet was not a solid ball of gold, formed like a bullet run in a mold, but was composed of nuggets of various sizes, which had come together here under the influence of their mutual gravitation, and formed a little metallic planet.

Judging by the test of weight which we had already tried, and which had led to the discovery of the gold, the composition of the asteroid must be the same to its very center.

In an assemblage of famous scientific men such as this the discovery, of course, immediately led to questions as to the origin of this incredible phenomenon.

How did these masses of gold come together? How did it chance that, with the exception of the thin crust of the asteroid, nearly all its substance was composed of the precious metal?

One asserted that it was quite impossible that there should be so much gold at so great a distance from the sun.

"It is the general law," he said, "that the planets increase in density towards the sun. There is every reason to think that the inner planets possess the greater amount of dense elements, while the outer ones are comparatively light."

But another referred to the old theory that there was once in this part of the solar system a planet which had been burst in pieces by some mysterious explosion, the fragments forming what we know as the asteroids. In his opinion, this planet might have contained a large quantity of gold, and in the course of ages the gold, having, in consequence of its superior atomic weight, not been so widely scattered by the explosion as some of the other elements of the planet, had collected itself together in this body.

But I observed that Lord Kelvin and the other more distinguished men of science said nothing during this discussion. The truly learned man is the truly wise man. They were not going to set up the theories without sufficient facts to sustain them. The one fact that the gold was here was all they had at present. Until they could learn more they were not prepared to theorize as to how the gold got there.

And in truth, it must be confessed, the greater number of us really cared less for the explanation of the wonderful fact than we did for the fact itself.

Gold is a thing which may make its appearance anywhere and at any time without offering any excuses or explanations.

"Phew! Won't we be rich?" exclaimed a voice.

"How are we going to dig it and get it back to earth?" asked another.

"Carry it in your pockets," said one.

"No need of staking claims here," remarked another. "There is enough for everybody."

Mr. Edison suddenly turned the current of talk.

"What do you suppose those Martians were doing here?"

"Why, they were wrecked here."

"Not a bit of it," said Mr. Edison. "According to your own showing they could not have been wrecked here. This planet hasn't gravitation enough to wreck them by a fall, and besides I have been looking at their machines and I know there has been a fight."

"A fight?" exclaimed several, pricking up their ears.

"Yes," said Mr. Edison. "Those machines bear the marks of the lightning of the Martians. They have been disabled, but they are made of some metal or some alloy of metals unknown to me, and consequently they have withstood the destructive force applied to them, as our electric ships were unable to withstand it. It is perfectly plain to me that they have been disabled in a battle. The Martians must have been fighting among themselves."

"About the gold!" exclaimed one.

"Of course. What else was there to fight about?"

At this instant one of our men came running from a considerable distance, waving his arms excitedly, but unable to give voice to his story, in the inappreciable atmosphere of the asteroid, until he had come up and made telephonic connection with us.

"There are a lot of dead Martians over there," he said. "They've been cleaning one another out."

"That's it," said Mr. Edison. "I knew it when I saw the condition of those machines."

"Then this is not a wrecked expedition, directed against the earth?"

"Not at all."

"This must be the great gold mine of Mars," said the president of an Australian mining company, opening both his eyes and his mouth as he spoke.

"Yes, evidently that's it. Here's where they come to get their wealth."

"And this," I said, "must be their harvest time. You notice that this asteroid, being several million miles nearer to the sun than Mars is, must have an appreciably shorter period of revolution. When it is in conjunction with Mars, or nearly so, as it is at present, the distance between the two is not very great, whereas when it is in the opposite part of its orbit they are separated by an enormous gap in space and the sun is between them.

"Manifestly in the latter case it would be perilous if not entirely impossible for the Martians to visit the golden asteroid, but when it is near Mars, as it is at present, and as it must be periodically for several years at a time, then is their opportunity.

"With their projectile cars sent forth with the aid of the mysterious explosives which they possess, it is easy for them under such circumstances, to make visits to the asteroid.

"Having obtained all the gold they need or all that they can carry, a comparatively slight impulse given to their car, the direction of which is carefully calculated, will carry them back again to Mars."

"If that's so," exclaimed a voice, "we had better look out for ourselves! We have got into a very hornet's nest! If this is the place where the Martians come to dig gold, and if this is the height of their season, as you say, they are not likely to leave us here long undisturbed."

"These fellows must have been pirates that they had the fight with," said another.

"But what's become of the regulars, then?"

"Gone back to Mars for help, probably, and they'll be here again pretty quick, I am afraid!"

Considerable alarm was caused by this view of the case, and orders were sent to several of the electrical ships to cruise out to a safe distance in the direction of Mars and keep a sharp outlook for the approach of enemies.

Meanwhile our prisoner awoke. He turned his eyes upon those standing about him, without any appearance of fear, but rather with a look of contempt, like that which Gulliver must have felt for the Lilliputians who had bound him under similar circumstances.

There were both hatred and defiance in his glance. He attempted to free himself, and the ropes strained with the tremendous pressure that he put upon them, but he could not break loose.

Satisfied that the Martian was safely bound, we left him where he lay, and, while awaiting news from the ships which had been sent to reconnoitre, continued the exploration of the little planet.

At a point nearly opposite to that where we had landed we came upon the mine which the Martians had been working. They had removed the thin coating of soil, laying bare the rich stores of gold beneath, and large quantities of the latter had been removed. Some of it was so solidly packed that the strokes of the instruments by means of which they had detached it were visible like the streaks left by a knife cutting cheese.

The more we saw of this golden planet the greater became our astonishment. What the Martians had removed was a mere nothing in comparison with the entire bulk of the asteroid. Had the celestial mine been easier to reach, perhaps they would have removed more, or, possibly, their political economists perfectly understood the necessity of properly controlling the amount of precious metal in circulation. Very likely, we thought, the mining operations were under government control in Mars and it might be that the majority of the people there knew nothing of this store of wealth floating in the firmament. That would account for the battle with the supposed pirates, who, no doubt had organized a secret expedition to the asteroid and had been caught red-handed at the mine.

There were many detached masses of gold scattered about, and some of the men, on picking them up, exclaimed with astonishment at their lack of weight, forgetting for the moment that the same law which caused their own bodies to weigh so little must necessarily affect everything else in a like degree.

A mass of gold that on the earth no man would have been able to lift could here be tossed about like a hollow rubber ball.

While we were examining the mine, one of the men left to guard the Martian came running to inform us that the latter evidently wished to make some communication. Mr. Edison and the others hurried to the side of the prisoner. He still lay on his back, from which position he was not able to move, notwithstanding all his efforts. But by the motion of his eyes, aided by the pantomime with his fingers, he made us understand that there was something in a metallic box fastened at his side which he wished to reach.

With some difficulty we succeeded in opening the box and in it there appeared a number of bright red pellets, as large as an ordinary egg.

When the Martians saw these in our hands he gave us to understand by the motion of his lips that he wished to swallow one of them. A pellet was accordingly placed in his mouth, and he instantly and with great eagerness swallowed it.

While trying to communicate his wishes to us, the prisoner had seemed to be in no little distress. He exhibited spasmodic movements which led some of the bystanders to think that he was on the point of dying, but within a few seconds after he had swallowed the pellet he appeared to be completely restored. All evidence of distress vanished, and a look of content came over his ugly face.

"It must be a powerful medicine," said one of the bystanders. "I wonder what it is?"

"I will explain to you my notion," said Professor Moissan, the great French chemist. "I think it was a pill of the air, which he has taken."

"What do you mean by that?"

"My meaning is," said Professor Moissan, "that the Martian must have, for that he may live, the nitrogen and the oxygen. These can he not obtain here, where there is not the atmosphere. Therefore must he get them in some other manner. This has he managed to do by combining in these pills the oxygen and the nitrogen in the proportions which make atmospheric air. Doubtless upon Mars there are the very great chemists. They have discovered how this may be done. When the Martian has swallowed his little pill, the oxygen and the nitrogen are rendered to his blood as if he had breathed them, and so he can live with that air which has been distributed to him with the aid of his stomach in place of his lungs."

If Monsieur Moissan's explanation was not correct, at any rate it seemed the only one which would fit the facts before us. Certainly the Martian could not breathe where there was practically no air, yet just as certainly after he had swallowed his pill he seemed as comfortable as any of us.

Suddenly, while we were gathered around the prisoner, and interested in this fresh evidence of the wonderful ingenuity of the Martians, and of their control over the processes of nature, one of the electrical ships that had been sent off in the direction of Mars was seen rapidly returning and displaying signals.

It reported that the Martians were coming!

"THE MARTIANS ARE COMING!" The alarm was spread instantly among those upon the planet and through the remainder of the fleet.

One of the men from the returning electrical ship dropped down upon the asteroid and gave a more detailed account of what they had seen.

His ship had been the one which had gone to the greatest distance, in the direction of Mars. While cruising there, with all eyes intent, they had suddenly perceived a glittering object moving from the direction of the ruddy planet, and manifestly approaching them. A little inspection with the telescope had shown them that it was one of the projectile cars used by the Martians.

Our ship had ventured so far from the asteroid that for a moment it seemed doubtful whether it would be able to return in time to give warning, because the electrical influence of the asteroid was comparatively slight at such a distance, and, after they had reversed their polarity, and applied their intensifier, so as to make that influence effective, their motion was at first exceedingly slow.

Fortunately after a time they got under way with sufficient velocity to bring them back to us before the approaching Martians could overtake them.

The latter were not moving with great velocity, having evidently projected themselves from Mars with only just sufficient force to throw them within the feeble sphere of gravitation of the asteroid, so that they should very gently land upon its surface.

Indeed, looking out behind the electrical ship which had brought us the warning, we immediately saw the projectile of the Martians approaching. It sparkled like a star in the black sky as the sunlight fell upon it.

The ships of the squadron whose crews had not landed upon the planet were signaled to prepare for action, while those who were upon the asteroid made ready for battle there. A number of disintegrators were trained upon the approaching Martians, but Mr. Edison gave strict orders that no attempt should be made to discharge the vibratory force at random.

"They do not know that we are here," he said, "and I am convinced that they are unable to control their motions as we can do with our electrical ships. They depend simply upon the force of gravitation. Having passed the limit of the attraction of Mars, they have now fallen within the attraction of the asteroid, and they must slowly sink to its surface.

"Having, as I am convinced, no means of producing or controlling electrical attraction and repulsion, they cannot stop themselves, but must come down upon the asteroid. Having got here, they could never get away again, except as we know the survivors got away from earth, by propelling their projectile against gravitation with the aid of an explosive.

"Therefore, to a certain extent they will be at our mercy. Let us allow them quietly to land upon the planet, and then I think, if it becomes necessary, we can master them."

Notwithstanding Mr. Edison's reassuring words and manner, the company upon the asteroid experienced a dreadful suspense while the projectile which seemed very formidable as it drew near, sank with a slow and graceful motion toward the surface of the ground. Evidently it was about to land very near the spot where we stood awaiting it.

Its inmates had apparently just caught sight of us. They evinced signs of astonishment, and seemed at a loss exactly what to do. We could see projecting from the fore part of their car at least two of the polished knobs, whose fearful use and power we well comprehended.

Several of our men cried out to Mr. Edison in an extremity of terror: "Why do you not destroy them? Be quick, or we shall all perish."

"No," said Mr. Edison, "there is no danger. You can see that they are not prepared. They will not attempt to attack us until they have made their landing."

And Mr. Edison was right. With gradually accelerated velocity, and yet very, very slowly in comparison with the speed they would have exhibited in falling upon such a planet as the earth, the Martians and their car came down to the ground.

We stood at a distance of perhaps three hundred feet from the point where they touched the asteroid. Instantly a dozen of the giants sprang from the car and gazed about for a moment with a look of intense surprise. At first it was doubtful whether they meant to attack us at all.

We stood on our guard, several carrying disintegrators in our hands, while a score more of these terrible engines were turned upon the Martians from the electrical ships which hovered near.

Suddenly he who seemed to be the leader of the Martians began to speak to them in pantomime, using his fingers after the manner in which they are used for conversation by deaf and dumb people.

Of course, we did not know what he was saying, but his meaning became perfectly evident a minute later. Clearly they did not comprehend the powers of the insignificant looking strangers with whom they had to deal. Instead of turning their destructive engines on us, they advanced on a run, with the evident purpose of making us prisoners or crushing us by main force.

The soft whirr of the disintegrator in the hands of Mr. Edison standing near me came to my ears through the telephonic wire. He quickly swept the concentrating mirror a little up and down, and instantly the foremost Martian vanished! Part of some metallic dress that he wore fell upon the ground where he had stood, its vibratory rate not having been included in the range imparted to the disintegrator.

His followers paused for a moment, amazed, stared about as if looking for their leader, and then hurried back to their projectile and disappeared within it.

"Now we've got business on our hands," said Mr. Edison. "Look out for yourselves."

As he spoke, I saw the death-dealing knob of the war engine contained in the car of the Martians moving around toward us. In another instant it would have launched its destroying bolt.

Before that could occur, however, it had been dissipated into space by a vibratory stream from a disintegrator.

But we were not to get the victory quite so easily. There was another of the war engines in the car, and before we could concentrate our fire upon it, its awful flash shot forth, and a dozen of our comrades perished before our eyes.

"Quick! Quick!" shouted Mr. Edison to one of his electrical experts standing near. "There is something the matter with this disintegrator, and I cannot make it work. Aim at the knob, and don't miss it."

But the aim was not well taken, and the vibratory force fell upon a portion of the car at a considerable distance from the knob, making a great breach, but leaving the engine uninjured.

A section of the side of the car had been destroyed, and the vibratory energy had spread no further. To have attempted to sweep the car from end to end would have been futile, because the period of action of the disintegrators during each discharge did not exceed one second, and distributing the energy over so great a space would have seriously weakened its power to shatter apart the atoms of the resisting substance. The disintegrators were like firearms, in that after each discharge they must be readjusted before they could be used again.

Through the breach we saw the Martians inside making desperate efforts to train their engine upon us, for after their first disastrous stroke we had rapidly shifted our position. Swiftly the polished knob, which gleamed like an evil eye, moved round to sweep over us. Instinctively, though incautiously, we had collected in a group.

A single discharge would sweep us all into eternity.

"Will no one fire upon them?" exclaimed Mr. Edison, struggling with the disintegrator in his hands which still refused to work.

At this fearful moment I glanced around upon our company, and was astonished at the spectacle. In the presence of the danger many of them had lost all self-command. A half dozen had dropped their disintegrators upon the ground. Others stood as if frozen fast in their tracks. The expert electrician, whose poor aim had had such disastrous results, held in his hand an instrument which was in perfect condition, yet with mouth agape, he stood trembling like a captured bird.

It was a disgraceful exhibition. Mr. Edison, however, had not lost his head. Again and again he sighted at the dreadful knob with his disintegrator, but the vibratory force refused to respond.

The means of safety were in our hands, and yet through a combination of ill luck and paralyzing terror, we seemed unable to use them.

In a second more it would be all over with us.

The suspense in reality lasted only during the twinkling of an eye, though it seemed ages long.

Unable to endure it, I sharply struck the shoulder of the paralyzed electrician. To have attempted to seize the disintegrator from his hands would have been a fatal waste of time. Luckily the blow either roused him from his stupor or caused an instinctive movement of his hand that set the little engine in operation.

I am sure he took no aim, but providentially the vibratory force fell upon the desired point, and the knob disappeared.

We were saved!

Instantly half a dozen rushed toward the car of the Martians. We bitterly repented their haste; they did not live to repent.

Unknown to us the Martians carried hand engines, capable of launching bolts of death of the same character as those which emanated from the knobs of their larger machines. With these they fired, so to speak, through the breach in their car, and four of our men who were rushing upon them fell in heaps of cinders. The effect of the terrible fire was like that which the most powerful strokes of lightning occasionally produce on earth.

The destruction of the threatening knob had instantaneously relieved the pressure upon the terror-stricken nerves of our company, and they had all regained their composure and self-command. But this new and unexpected disaster, following so close upon the fear which had recently overpowered them, produced a second panic, the effect of which was not to stiffen them in their tracks as before, but to send them scurrying in every direction in search of hiding places.

And now a most curious effect of the smallness of the planet we were on began to play a conspicious part in our adventures. Standing on a globe only five miles in diameter was like being on the summit of a mountain whose sides sloped rapidly off in every direction, disappearing in the black sky on all sides, as if it were some stupendous peak rising out of an unfathomable abyss.

In consequence of the quick rounding off of the sides of this globe, the line of the horizon was close at hand, and by running a distance of less that 250 yards the fugitives disappeared down the sides of the asteroid, and behind the horizon, even from the elevation of about fifteen feet from which the Martians were able to watch them. From our sight they disappeared much sooner.

The slight attraction of the planet and their consequent almost entire lack of weight enabled the men to run with immense speed. The result, as I have subsequently learned, was that after they had disappeared from our view they quitted the planet entirely, the force being sufficient to partially free them from its gravitation, so that they sailed out into space, whirling helplessly end over end, until the elliptical orbits in which they travelled eventually brought them back again to the planet on the side nearly opposite to that from which they had departed.

But several of us, with Mr. Edison, stood fast, watching for an opportunity to get the Martians within range of the disintegrators. Luckily we were enabled, by shifting our position a little to the left, to get out of the line of sight of our enemies concealed in the car.

"If we cannot catch sight of them," said Mr. Edison, "we shall have to riddle the car on the chance of hitting them."

"It will be like firing into a bush to kill a hidden bear," said one of the party.

But help came from a quarter which was unexpected to us, although it should not have been so. Several of the electric ships had been hovering above us during the fight, their commanders being apparently uncertain how to act—fearful, perhaps, of injuring us in the attempt to smite our enemy.

But now the situation apparently lightened for them. They saw that we were at an immense disadvantage, and several of them immediately turned their batteries upon the car of the Martians.

They riddled it far more quickly and effectively than we could have done. Every stroke of the vibratory emanation made a gap in the side of the car, and we could perceive from the commotion within that our enemies were being rapidly massacred in their fortification.

So overwhelming was the force and the advantage of the ships that in a little while it was all over. Mr. Edison signaled them to stop firing because it was plain that all resistance had ceased and probably not one of the Martians remained alive.

We now approached the car, which had been transpierced in every direction, and whose remaining portions were glowing with heat in consequence of the spreading of the atomic vibrations. Immediately we discovered that all our anticipations were correct and that all of our enemies had perished.

The effect of the disintegrators upon them had been awful—too repulsive, indeed, to be described in detail. Some of the bodies had evidently entirely vanished; only certain metal articles which they had worn remaining, as in the case of the first Martian killed, to indicate that such beings had ever existed. The nature of the metal composing these articles was unknown to us. Evidently its vibratory rhythm did not correspond with any included in the ordinary range of the disintegrators.

Some of the giants had been only partially destroyed, the vibratory current having grazed them, in such a manner that the shattering undulations had not acted upon the entire body.

One thing that lends a peculiar horror to a terrestrial battlefield was absent; there was no bloodshed. The vibratory energy, not only completely destroyed whatever it fell upon but it seared the veins and arteries of the dismembered bodies so that there was no sanguinary exhibition connected with its murderous work.

All this time the shackled Martian had lain on his back where we had left him bound. What his feeling must have been may be imagined. At times, I caught a glimpse of his eyes, wildly rolling and exhibiting, when he saw that the victory was in our hands, the first indications of fear and terror shaking his soul that had yet appeared.

"That fellow is afraid at last," I said to Mr. Edison.

"Well, I should think he ought to be afraid," was the reply.

"So he ought, but if I am not mistaken this fear of his may be the beginning of a new discovery for us."

"How so?" asked Mr. Edison.

"In this way. When once he fears our power, and perceives that there would be no hope of contending against us, even if he were at liberty, he will respect us. This change in his mental attitude may tend to make him communicative. I do not see why we should despair of learning his language from him, and having done that, he will serve as our guide and interpreter, and will be of incalculable advantage to us when we have arrived at Mars."

"Capital! Capital!" said Mr. Edison. "We must concentrate the linguistic genius of our company upon that problem at once." . . .

JOURNEY'S END "All aboard!" was the signal, and the squadron having assembled under the lead of the flagship, we started again for Mars.

This time, as it proved, there was to be no further interruption, and when next we paused it was in the presence of the world inhabited by our enemies, and facing their frowning batteries.

We did not find it so easy to start from the asteroid as it had been to start from the earth; that is to say, we could not so readily generate a very high velocity.

In consequence of the comparatively small size of the asteroid, its electric influence was very much less than that of the earth, and notwithstanding the appliances which we possessed for intensifying the electrical effect, it was not possible to produce a sufficient repulsion to start us off for Mars with anything like the impulse which we had received from the earth on our original departure.

The utmost velocity that we could generate did not exceed three miles in a second, and to get this required our utmost efforts. In fact, it had not seemed possible that we should attain even so great a speed as that. It was far more than we could have expected, and even Mr. Edison was surprised, as well as greatly gratified, when he found that we were moving with the velocity that I have named.

We were still about 6,000,000 miles from Mars, so that, traveling three miles in a second, we should require at least twenty-three days to reach the immediate neighborhood of the planet.

Meanwhile we had plenty of occupation to make the time pass quickly. Our prisoner was transported along with us, and we now began our attempts to ascertain what his language was, and, if possible, to master it ourselves.

Before quitting the asteroid we had found that it was necessary for him to swallow one of his "air pills," as Professor Moissan had called them, at least three times in the course of every twenty-four hours. One of us supplied him regularly and I thought I could detect evidences of a certain degree of gratitude in his expression. This was encouraging, because it gave additional promise of the possibility of our being able to communicate with him in some more effective way than by mere signs. But once inside the car, where we had a supply of air kept at the ordinary pressure experienced on the earth, he could breathe like the rest of us.

The best linguists in the expedition, as Mr. Edison had suggested, were now assembled in the flagship, where the prisoner was, and they set to work to devise some means of ascertaining the manner in which he was accustomed to express his thoughts. We had not heard him speak, because until we carried him into our car there was no atmosphere capable of conveying any sounds he might attempt to utter.

It seemed a fair assumption that the language of the Martians would be scientific in its structure. We had so much evidence of the practical bent of their minds, and of the immense progress which they had made in the direction of the scientific conquest of nature, that it was not to be supposed their medium of communication with one another would be lacking in clearness, or would possess any of the puzzling and unnecessary ambiguities that characterized the languages spoken on the earth.

"We shall not find them making he's and she's of stones, sticks and other inanimate objects," said one of the American linguists. "They must certainly have gotten rid of all that nonsense long ago."

"Ah," said a French Professor from the Sorbonne, one of the makers of the never-to-be-finished dictionary. "It will be like the language of my country. Transparent, similar to the diamond, and sparkling as is the fountain."

"I think," said a German enthusiast, "that it will be a universal language, the Volapuk of Mars, spoken by all the inhabitants of that planet."

"But all these speculations," broke in Mr. Edison, "do not help you much. Why not begin in a practical manner by finding out what the Martian calls himself, for instance."

This seemed a good suggestion, and accordingly several of the bystanders began an expressive pantomime, intended to indicate to the giant, who was following all their motions with his eyes, that they wished to know by what name he called himself. Pointing their fingers to their own breast they repeated, one after the other, the word "man."

If our prisoner had been a stupid savage, of course any such attempt as this to make him understand would have been idle. But it must be remembered that we were dealing with a personage who had presumably inherited from hundreds of generations the results of a civilization, and an intellectual advance, measured by the constant progress of millions of years.

Accordingly we were not very much astonished, when, after a few repetitions of the experiment, the Martian—one of whose arms had been partially released from its bonds in order to give him a little freedom of motion—imitated the action of his interrogators by pressing his finger over his heart.

Then, opening his mouth, he gave utterance to a sound which shook the air of the car like the hoarse roar of a lion. He seemed himself surprised by the noise he made, for he had not been used to speak in so dense an atmosphere.

Our ears were deafened and confused, and we recoiled in astonishment, not to say, half in terror.

With an ugly grin distorting his face as if he enjoyed our discomfiture, the Martian repeated the motion and the sound.

"R-r-r-r-r-h!"

It was not articulate to our ears and not to be represented by any combination of letters.

"Faith," exclaimed a Dublin University professor, "if that's what they call themselves, how shall we ever translate their names when we come to write the history of the conquest?"

"Whist, mon," replied a professor from the University of Aberdeen, "let us whip the gillravaging villains first, and then we can describe them by any intitulation that may suit our deesposition."

The beginning of our linguistic conquest was certainly not promising, at least if measured by our acquirement of words, but from another point of view it was very gratifying, inasmuch as it was plain that the Martian understood what we were trying to do, and was, for the present, at least, disposed to aid us.

These efforts to learn the language of Mars were renewed and repeated every few hours, all the experience, learning and genius of the squadron being concentrated upon the work, and the result was that in the course of a few days we had actually succeeded in learning a dozen or more of the Martian's words and were able to make him understand us when we pronounced them, as well as to understand him when our ears had become accustomed to the growling of his voice.

Finally, one day the prisoner, who seemed to be in an unusually cheerful frame of mind, indicated that he carried in his breast some object which he wished us to see.

With our assistance he pulled out a book!

Actually, it was a book, not very unlike the books which we have upon the earth, but printed, of course, in characters that were entirely strange and unknown to us. Yet these characters evidently gave expression to a highly intellectual language. All those who were standing by at the moment uttered a shout of wonder and of delight, and the cry of "a book! a book!" ran around the circle, and the good news was even promptly communicated to some of the neighboring electric ships of the squadron. Several other learned men were summoned in haste from them to examine our new treasure.

The Martian, whose good nature had manifestly been growing day after day, watched our inspection of his book with evidences of great interest, not unmingled with amusement. Finally he beckoned the holder of the book to his side, and placing his broad finger upon one of the huge letters —if letters they were, for they more nearly resembled the characters employed by the Chinese printer—he uttered a sound which we, of course, took to be a word, but which was different from any we had yet heard. Then he pointed to one after another of us standing around.

"Ah," explained everybody, the truth being apparent, "that is the word by which the Martians designate us. They have a name, then, for the inhabitants of the earth."

"Or, perhaps, it is rather the name for the earth itself," said one.

But this could not, of course, be at once determined. Anyhow, the word, whatever its precise meaning might be, had now been added to our vocabulary, although as yet our organs of speech proved unable to reproduce it in a recognizable form.

This promising and unexpected discovery of the Martian's book lent added enthusiasm to those who were engaged in the work of trying to master the language of our prisoner, and the progress that they made in the course of the next few days was truly astonishing. If the prisoner had been unwilling to aid them, of course, it would have been impossible to proceed, but, fortunately for us, he seemed more and more to enter into the spirit of the undertaking, and actually to enjoy it himself. So bright and quick was his understanding that he was even able to indicate to us methods of mastering his language that would otherwise, probably, never have occurred to our minds.

In fact, in a very short time he had turned teacher and all these learned men, pressing around him with eager attention, had become his pupils.

I cannot undertake to say precisely how much of the Martian language had been acquired by the chief linguists of the expedition before the time when we arrived so near to Mars that it became necessary for most of us to abandon our studies in order to make ready for the more serious business which now confronted us.

But, at any rate, the acquisition was so considerable as to allow of the interchange of ordinary ideas with our prisoner, and there was no longer any doubt that he would be able to give us much information when we landed on his native planet.

At the end of twenty-three days as measured by terrestrial time, since our departure from the asteroid, we arrived in the sky of Mars.

For a long time the ruddy planet had been growing larger and more formidable, gradually turning from a huge star into a great red moon, and then expanding more and more until it began to shut out from sight the constellations behind it. The curious markings on its surface, which from the earth can only be dimly glimpsed with a powerful telescope, began to reveal themselves clearly to our naked eyes.

I have related how even before we had reached the asteroid, Mars began to present a most imposing appearance as we saw it with our telescopes. Now, however, that it was close at hand, the naked eye view of

the planet was more wonderful than anything we had been able to see
with telescopes when at a greater distance.

We were approaching the southern hemisphere of Mars in about latitude 45 degrees south. It was near the time of the vernal equinox in that
hemisphere of the planet, and under the stimulating influence of the
spring sun, rising higher and higher every day, some such awakening of
life and activity upon its surface as occurs on the earth under similar
circumstances was evidently going on.

Around the South Pole were spread immense fields of snow and ice,
gleaming with great brilliance. Cutting deep into the borders of these
ice-fields, we could see broad channels of open water, indicating the rapid
breaking of the grip of the frost.

Almost directly beneath us was a broad oval region, light red in color,
to which terrestrial astronomers had given the name of Hellas. Toward
the south, between Hellas and the borders of the polar ice, was a great
belt of darkness that astronomers had always been inclined to regard as
a sea. Looking toward the north, we could perceive the immense red expanses of the continent of Mars, with the long curved line of the Syrtis
Major, or "The Hour-glass Sea," sweeping through the midst of them
toward the north until it disappeared under the horizon.

Crossing and recrossing the red continent, in every direction, were the
canals of Schiaparelli.

Plentifully sprinkled over the surface we could see brilliant points,
some of dazzling brightness, outshining the daylight. There were also an
astonishing variety in the colors of the broad expanses beneath us. Activity, vivacity and beauty, such as we were utterly unprepared to behold,
expressed their presence on all sides.

The excitement on the flagship and among the other members of the
squadron was immense. It was certainly a thrilling scene. Here, right under
our feet, lay the world we had come to do battle with. Its appearances,
while recalling in some of their broader aspects those which it had presented when viewed from our observatories, were far more strange, complex and wonderful than any astronomer had ever dreamed. Suppose all
of our anticipations about Mars should prove to have been wrong, after
all?

There could be no longer any question that it was a world which, if
not absolutely teeming with inhabitants, like a gigantic ant-hill, at any
rate bore on every side the marks of their presence and of their incredible
undertakings and achievements.

Here and there clouds of smoke arose and spread slowly through the
atmosphere beneath us. Floating higher above the surface of the planet
were clouds of vapor, assuming the familiar forms of stratus and cumu-
lus with which we were acquainted upon the earth.

These clouds, however, seemed upon the whole to be much less dense than those to which we were accustomed at home. They had, too, a peculiar iridescent beauty as if there was something in their composition or their texture which split up the chromatic elements of the sunlight and thus produced internal rainbow effects that caused some of the heavier cloud masses to resemble immense collections of opals, alive with the play of ever-changing colors and magically suspended above the planet.

As we continued to study the phenomena that was gradually unfolded beneath us we thought we could detect in many places evidences of the existence of strong fortifications. The planet of war appeared to be prepared for the attacks of enemies. Since, as our own experience had shown, it sometimes waged war with distant planets, it was but natural that it should be found prepared to resist foes who might be disposed to revenge themselves for injuries suffered at its hands.

As had been expected, our prisoner now proved to be of very great assistance to us. Apparently he took a certain pride in exhibiting to strangers from a distant world the beauties and wonders of his own planet.

We could not understand by any means all that he said, but we could readily comprehend, from his gestures, and from the manner in which his features lighted up at the recognition of familiar scenes and objects, what his sentiments in regard to them were, and, in a general way, what part they played in the life of the planet.

He confirmed our opinion that certain of the works which we saw beneath us were fortifications, intended for the protection of the planet against invaders from outer space. A cunning and almost diabolical look came into his eyes as he pointed to one of these strongholds.

His confidence and his mocking looks were not reassuring to us. He knew what his planet was capable of, and we did not. He had seen, on the asteroid, the extent of our power, and while its display served to intimidate him there, yet now that he and we together were facing the world of his birth, his fear had evidently fallen from him, and he had the manner of one who feels that the shield of an all-powerful protector had been extended over him.

But it could not be long now before we could ascertain, by the irrevocable test of actual experience, whether the Martians possessed the power to annihilate us or not.

How shall I describe our feelings as we gazed at the scene spread beneath us? They were not quite the same as those of the discoverer of new lands upon the earth. This was a whole new world that we had discovered, and it was filled, as we could see, with inhabitants.

But that was not all. We had not come with peaceful intentions.

We were to make war on this new world. . . .

Our enemies, instead of being below us in the scale of intelligence were, we had every reason to believe, greatly our superiors. They had proved that they possessed a command over the powers of nature such as we, up to the time when Mr. Edison made his inventions, had not even dreamed that it was possible for us to obtain.

It was true that at present we appeared to have the advantage, both in our electrical ships and in our means of offense. The disintegrator was at least as powerful an engine of destruction as any that the Martians had yet shown that they possessed. It did not seem that in that respect they could possibly excel us.

During the brief war with the Martians upon the earth it had been gunpowder against a mysterious force as much stronger than gunpowder as the latter was superior to the bows and arrows that preceded it.

There had been no comparison whatever between the offensive means employed by the two parties in the struggle on the earth.

But the genius of one man had suddenly put us on the level of our enemies in regard to fighting capacity. . . .

The thing that gave us the most uneasiness was the fact that we did not yet know what powers the Martians might have in reserve. It was but natural to suppose that here, on their own ground, they would possess means of defense even more effective than the offensive engines they had employed in attacking enemies so many millions of miles from home.

It was important that we should waste no time, and it was equally important that we should select the most vulnerable point for attack. It was self-evident, therefore, that our first duty would be to reconnoiter the surface of the planet and determine its weakest point of defense.

At first Mr. Edison contemplated sending the various ships in different directions around the planet in order that the work of exploration might be quickly accomplished. But upon second thought it seemed wiser to keep the squadron together, thus diminishing the chance of disaster.

Besides, the commander wished to see with his own eyes the exact situation of the various parts of the planet, where it might appear advisable for us to begin our assault.

Thus far we had remained suspended at so great a height above the planet that we had hardly entered into the perceptible limits of its atmosphere and there was no evidence that we had been seen by the inhabitants of Mars; but before starting on our voyage of exploration it was determined to drop down closer to the surface in order that we might the more certainly identify the localities over which we passed.

This maneuver nearly got us into serious trouble.

When we had arrived within a distance of three miles from the surface of Mars we suddenly perceived approaching from the eastward a large airship which was navigating the Martian atmosphere at a height of perhaps half a mile above the ground.

This airship moved rapidly on to a point nearly beneath us, when it suddenly paused, reversed its course, and evidently made signals, the purpose of which was not at first evident to us.

But in a short time their meaning became perfectly plain, when we found ourselves surrounded by at least twenty similar aerostats approaching swiftly from different sides.

It was a great mystery to us where so many airships had been concealed previous to their sudden appearance in answer to the signals.

But the mystery was quickly solved when we saw detaching itself from the surface of the planet beneath us, where, while it remained immovable, its color had blended with that of the soil so as to render it invisible, another of the mysterious ships.

Then our startled eyes beheld on all sides these formidable-looking enemies rising from the ground beneath us like so many gigantic insects, disturbed by a sudden alarm.

In a short time the atmosphere a mile or two below us, and to a distance of perhaps twenty miles around in every direction, was alive with airships of various sizes, and some of most extraordinary forms, exchanging signals, rushing to and fro, but all finally concentrating beneath the place where our squadron was suspended.

We had poked the hornet's nest with a vengeance!

As yet there had been no sting, but we might quickly expect to feel it if we did not get out of range.

Quickly instructions were flashed to the squadrons to rise as rapidly as possible to a great height.

It was evident that this maneuver would save us from danger if it were quickly effected, because the airships of the Martians were simply airships and nothing more. They could only float in the atmosphere, and had no means of rising above it, or of navigating empty space.

To have turned our disintegrators upon them, and to have begun a battle then and there, would have been folly.

They overwhelmingly outnumbered us, the majority of them were yet at a considerable distance and we could not have done battle, even with our entire squadron acting together, with more than one-quarter of them simultaneously. In the meantime the others would have surrounded and might have destroyed us. We must first get some idea of the planet's means of defence before we ventured to assail it.

Having risen rapidly to a height of twenty-five or thirty miles, so that we could feel confident that our ships had vanished at least from the naked eye view of our enemies beneath, a brief consultation was held.

It was determined to adhere to our original program and to circumnavigate Mars in every direction before proceeding to open the war.

The overwhelming forces shown by the enemy had intimidated even some of the most courageous of our men, but still it was universally felt that it would not do to retreat without a blow struck.

The more we saw of the power of the Martians, the more we became convinced that there would be no hope for the earth, if these enemies ever again effected a landing upon its surface, the more especially since our squadron contained nearly all of the earth's force that would be effective in such a contest.

With Mr. Edison and the other men of science away, they would not be able at home to construct such engines as we possessed, or to manage them even if they were constructed.

Our planet had staked everything on a single throw.

These considerations again steeled our hearts, and made us bear up as bravely as possible in the face of the terrible odds that confronted us.

Turning the noses of our electrical ships toward the west, we began our circumnavigation.

THE GREAT SMOKE BARRIER   At first we rose to a still greater height, in order more effectually to escape the watchful eyes of our enemies, and then, after having moved rapidly several hundred miles toward the west, we dropped down again within easy eyeshot of the surface of the planet, and commenced our inspection.

When we originally reached Mars, as I have related, it was at a point in its southern hemisphere, in latitude 45 degrees south, and longitude 75 degrees east, that we first closely approached its surface. Underneath us was the land called "Hellas," and it was over this land of Hellas that the Martian air fleet had suddenly made its appearance.

Our westward motion, while at a great height above the planet, had brought us over another oval-shaped land called "Noachia," surrounded by the dark ocean, the "Mare Erytræum." Now approaching nearer the surface our course was changed so as to carry us toward the equator of Mars.

We passed over the curious half-drowned continent known to terrestrial astronomers as the Region of Deucalion, then across another sea, or gulf, until we found ourselves floating at a height of perhaps five miles, above a great continental land, at least three thousand miles broad from east to west, and which I immediately recognized as that to which astronomers had given the various names of "Aeria," "Edom," "Arabia," and "Eden."

Here the spectacle became of breathless interest.

"Wonderful! Wonderful!"

"Who could have believed it!"

Such were the exclamations heard on all sides.

When at first we were suspended above Hellas, looking toward the north, the northeast and the northwest, we had seen at a distance some of these great red regions, and had perceived the curious network of canals by which they were intersected. But that was a far-off and imperfect view.

Now, when we were near at hand and straight above one of these singular lands, the magnificence of the panorama surpassed belief.

From the earth about a dozen of the principal canals crossing the continent beneath us had been perceived, but we saw hundreds, nay thousands of them!

It was a double system, intended both for irrigation and for protection, and far more marvelous in its completeness than the boldest speculative minds among our astronomers had ever dared to imagine.

"Ha! that's what I always said," exclaimed a veteran from one of our great observatories. "Mars is red because its soil and vegetation are red."

And certainly appearances indicated that he was right.

There were no green trees, and there was no green grass. Both were red, not of a uniform red tint, but presenting an immense variety of shades which produced a most brilliant effect, fairly dazzling our eyes.

But what trees! And what grass! And what flowers!

Our telescopes showed that even the smaller trees must be 200 or 300 feet in height, and there were forests of giants, whose average height was evidently at least 1,000 feet.

"That's all right," exclaimed the enthusiast I have just quoted. "I knew it would be so. The trees are big for the same reason that the men are, because the planet is small, and they can grow big without becoming too heavy to stand."

Flashing in the sun on all sides were the roofs of metallic buildings, which were evidently the only kind of edifices which Mars possessed. At any rate, if stone or wood were employed in their construction both were completely covered with metallic plates.

This added immensely to the warlike aspect of the planet. For warlike it was. Everywhere we recognized fortified stations, glittering with an array of the polished knobs of the lightning machines, such as we had seen in the land of Hellas.

From the land of Edom, directly over the equator of the planet, we turned our faces westward, and, skirting the Mare Erytræum, arrived above the place where the broad canal known as the Indus empties into the sea.

Before us, and stretching away to the northwest, now lay the Continent of Chryse, a vast red land, oval in outline, and surrounded and crossed by innumerable canals. Chryse was not less than 1,600 miles across and it, too, evidently swarmed with giant inhabitants.

But the shadow of night lay upon the greater portion of the land of

Chryse. In our rapid motion westward we had outstripped the sun and had now arrived at a point where day and night met upon the surface of the planet beneath us.

Behind all was brilliant with sunshine, but before us the face of Mars gradually disappeared in the deepening gloom. Through the darkness, far away, we could behold magnificent beams of electric light darting across the curtain of night, and evidently serving to illuminate towns and cities that lay beneath.

We pushed on into the night for two or three hundred miles over that part of the continent of Chryse whose inhabitants were doubtless enjoying the deep sleep that accompanies the dark hours immediately preceding the dawn. Still everywhere splendid clusters of light lay like fallen constellations upon the ground, indicating the sites of great towns, which, like those of the earth never sleep.

But this scene, although weird and beautiful, could give us little of the kind of information of which we were in search.

Accordingly it was resolved to turn back eastward until we had arrived in the twilight space separating day and night, and then hover over the planet at that point, allowing it to turn beneath us so that, as we looked down, we should see in succession the entire circuit of the globe of Mars while it rolled under our eyes.

The rotation of Mars on its axis is performed in a period very little longer than the earth's rotation, so that the length of the day and night in the world of Mars is only some forty minutes longer than their length upon the earth.

In thus remaining suspended over the planet, on the line of daybreak, so to speak, we believed that we should be peculiarly safe from detection by the eyes of the inhabitants. Even astronomers are not likely to be wide awake just at the peep of dawn. Almost all of the inhabitants, we confidently believed, would still be sound asleep upon that part of the planet passing directly beneath us, and those who were awake would not be likely to watch for unexpected appearances in the sky.

Besides, our height was so great that notwithstanding the numbers of the squadron, we could not easily be seen from the surface of the planet, and if seen at all we might be mistaken for high-flying birds.

Here we remained then through the entire course of twenty-four hours and saw in succession as they passed from night into day beneath our feet the land of Chryse, the great continent of Tharsis, the curious region of intersecting canals which puzzled astronomers on the earth had named the "Gordian Knot." The continental lands of Memnonia, Amozonia and Aeolia, the mysterious center where hundreds of vast canals came together from every direction, called the Triviun Charontis; the vast circle of Elysium, a thousand miles across, and completely surrounded by a broad green canal; the continent of Libya, which, as I remembered, had been half covered by a tremendous inundation whose effects were visible from the earth in 1889, and finally the long, dark sea of the Syrtis Major, lying directly south of the land of Hellas.

The excitement and interest which we all experienced were so great that not one of us took a wink of sleep during the entire twenty-four hours of our marvelous watch.

There are one or two things of special interest amid the multitude of wonderful observations that we made which I must mention here on account of their connection with the important events that followed soon after.

Just west of the land of Chryse we saw the smaller land of Ophir, in the midst of which is a singular spot called the Juventæ Fons, and this Fountain of Youth, as our astronomers, by a sort of prophetic inspiration, had named it, proved later to be one of the most incredible marvels on the planet of Mars.

Further to the west, and north from the great continent of Tharsis, we beheld the immense oval-shaped land of Thaumasia containing in its center the celebrated "Lake of the Sun," a circular body of water not less than five hundred miles in diameter, with dozens of great canals running away from it like the spokes of a wheel in every direction, thus connecting it with the ocean which surrounds it on the south and east, and with the still larger canals that encircle it toward the north and west.

This Lake of the Sun came to play a great part in our subsequent adventures. It was evident to us from the beginning that it was the chief center of population on the planet. It lies in latitude 25 degrees south and longitude about 90 degrees west.

Having completed the circuit of the Martian globe, we were moved by the same feeling which every discoverer of new lands experiences, and immediately returned to our original place above the land of Hellas, because since that was the first part of Mars which we had seen, we felt a greater degree of familiarity with it than with any portion of the planet, and there, in a certain sense, we felt "at home."

But, as it proved, our enemies were on the watch for us there. We had almost forgotten them, so absorbed were we by the great spectacles that had been unrolling themselves beneath our feet.

We ought, of course, to have been a little more cautious in approaching the place where they first caught sight of us, since we might have known that they would remain on the watch near that spot.

But at any rate they had seen us, and it was now too late to think of taking them again by surprise.

They on their part had a surprise in store for us, which was greater than any we had yet experienced.

We saw their ships assembling once more far down in the atmosphere beneath us, and we thought we could detect evidences of something unusual going on upon the surface of the planet.

Suddenly from the ships, and from various points on the ground beneath, there rose high in the air, and carried by invisible currents in every direction, immense volumes of black smoke, or vapor, which blotted out of sight everything below them!

South, north, west and east, the curtain of blackness rapidly spread, until the whole face of the planet as far as our eyes could reach, and the airships thronging under us, were all concealed from sight!

Mars had played the game of the cuttlefish, which when pursued by its enemies darkens the water behind it by a sudden outgush of inky fluid and thus escapes the eye of its foe.

The eyes of man had never beheld such a spectacle!

Where a few minutes before the sunny face of a beautiful and populous planet had been shining beneath us, there was now to be seen nothing but black, billowing clouds, swelling up everywhere like the mouse-colored smoke that pours from a great transatlantic liner when fresh coal has just been heaped upon her fires.

In some places the smoke spouted upward in huge jets to the height of several miles; elsewhere it eddied in vast whirlpools of inky blackness.

Not a glimpse of the hidden world beneath us was anywhere to be seen.

Mars had put on its war mask, and fearful indeed was the aspect of it!

After the first pause of surprise the squadron quickly backed away into the sky, rising rapidly, because, from one of the swirling eddies beneath us the smoke began suddenly to pile itself up in an enormous aerial mountain, whose peaks shot higher and higher, with apparently increasing velocity, until they seemed about to engulf us with their tumbling ebon masses.

Unaware what the nature of this mysterious smoke might be, and fearing that it was something more than a shield for the planet, and might be destructive to life, we fled before it, as before the onward sweep of a pestilence.

Directly underneath the flagship, one of the aspiring smoke peaks grew with most portentous swiftness, and, notwithstanding all our efforts, in a little while it had enveloped us. . . .

"This spoils our plans," said the commander. "There is no use of remaining here for the present; let us see how far this thing extends."

At first we rose straight away to a height of 200 or 300 miles, thus passing entirely beyond the sensible limits of the atmosphere, and far above the highest point that the smoke could reach.

From this commanding point of view our line of sight extended to an immense distance over the surface of Mars in all directions. Everywhere the same appearance; the whole planet was evidently covered with the smoke.

A complete telegraphic system evidently connected all the strategic points upon Mars, so that, at a signal from the central station, the wonderful curtain could be instantaneously drawn over the entire face of the planet.

In order to make certain that no part of Mars remained uncovered, we dropped down again nearer to the upper level of the smoke clouds, and then completely circumnavigated the planet. It was thought possible that on the night side no smoke would be found and that it would be practicable for us to make a descent there.

But when we had arrived on that side of Mars which was turned away from the sun, we no longer saw beneath us, as we had done on our previous visit to the night hemisphere of the planet, brilliant groups and clusters of electric lights beneath us. All was dark.

In fact, so completely did the great shell of smoke conceal the planet that the place occupied by the latter seemed to be simply a vast black hole in the firmament.

The sun was hidden behind it, and so dense was the smoke that even the solar rays were unable to penetrate it, and consequently there was no atmospheric halo visible around the concealed planet.

All the sky around was filled with stars, but their countless host suddenly disappeared when our eyes turned in the direction of Mars. The great black globe blotted them out without being visible itself.

"Apparently we can do nothing here," said Mr. Edison. "Let us return to the daylight side."

When we had arrived near the point where we had been when the wonderful phenomenon first made its appearance, we paused, and then, at the suggestion of one of the chemists, dropped close to the surface of the smoke curtain which had now settled down into comparative quiescence, in order that we might examine it a little more critically.

The flagship was driven into the smoke cloud so deeply that for a minute we were again enveloped in night. A quantity of the smoke was entrapped in a glass jar.

Rising again into the sunlight, the chemists began an examination of the constitution of the smoke. They were unable to determine its precise character, but they found that its density was astonishingly slight. This accounted for the rapidity with which it had risen, and the great height which it had attained in the comparatively light atmosphere of Mars.

"It is evident," said one of the chemists, "that this smoke does not extend down to the surface of the planet. From what the astronomers say as to the density of the air on Mars, it is probable that a clear space of at least a mile in height exists between the surface of Mars and the lower limit of the smoke curtain. Just how deep the latter is we can only determine by experiment, but it would not be surprising if the thickness of this great blanket which Mars has thrown around itself should prove to be a quarter or half a mile."

"Anyhow," said one of the United States army officers, "they have dodged out of sight, and I don't see why we should not dodge in and get at them. If there is clear air under the smoke, as you think, why couldn't the ships dart down through the curtain and come to a close tackle with the Martians?"

"It would not do at all," said the commander. "We might simply run ourselves into an ambush. No; we must stay outside, and if possible fight them from here."

"They can't keep this thing up forever," said the officer. "Perhaps the smoke will clear off after a while, and then we will have a chance."

"Not much hope of that, I'm afraid," said the chemist who had originally spoken. "This smoke could remain floating in the atmosphere for weeks, and the only wonder to me is how they ever expect to get rid of it, when they think their enemies have gone and they want some sunshine again."

"All that is mere speculation," said Mr. Edison; "let us get at something practical. We must do one of two things; either attack them shielded as they are, or wait until the smoke has cleared away. The only other alternative, that of plunging blindly down through the curtain is at present not to be thought of."

"I am afraid we couldn't stand a very long siege ourselves," suddenly remarked the chief commissary of the expedition, who was one of the members of the flagship's company.

"What do you mean by that?" asked Mr. Edison sharply, turning to him.

"Well, sir, you see," said the commissary, stammering, "our provisions wouldn't hold out."

"Wouldn't hold out?" exclaimed Mr. Edison, in astonishment, "why we have compressed and prepared provisions enough to last this squadron for three years."

"We had, sir, when we left the earth," said the commissary, in apparent distress, "but I am sorry to say that something has happened."

"Something has happened! Explain yourself!"

"I don't know what it is, but on inspecting some of the compressed stores, a short time ago, I found that a large number of them were destroyed, whether through leakage of air, or what, I am unable to say. I sent to inquire as to the condition of the stores in the other ships in the squadron and I found that a similar condition of things prevailed there.

"The fact is," continued the commissary, "we have only provisions enough, in proper condition, for about ten days' consumption."

"After that we shall have to forage on the country, then," said the army officer.

"Why did you not report this before?" demanded Mr. Edison.

"Because, sir," was the reply, "the discovery was not made until after we arrived close to Mars, and since then there has been so much excitement that I have hardly had time to make an investigation and find out what the precise condition of affairs is; besides, I thought we should land upon the planet and then we would be able to renew our supplies."

I closely watched Mr. Edison's expression in order to see how this most alarming news would affect him. Although he fully comprehended its fearful significance, he did not lose his self-command.

"Well, well," he said, "then it will become necessary for us to act quickly. Evidently we cannot wait for the smoke to clear off, even if there was any hope of its clearing. We must get down on Mars now, having conquered it first if possible, but anyway we must get down there, in order to avoid starvation."

"It is very lucky," he continued, "that we have ten days' supply left. A great deal can be done in ten days."

A few hours after this the commander called me aside, and said:

"I have thought it all out. I am going to reconstruct some of our disintegrators, so as to increase their range and their power. Then I am going to have some of the astronomers of the expedition locate for me the most vulnerable points upon the planet, where the population is densest and a hard blow would have the most effect, and I am going to pound away at them, through the smoke, and see whether we cannot draw them out of their shell."

With his expert assistants Mr. Edison set to work at once to transform a number of the disintegrators into still more formidable engines of the same description. One of these new weapons having been distributed to each of the members of the squadron, the next problem was to decide where to strike.

When we first examined the surface of the planet it will be remembered that we had regarded the Lake of the Sun and its environs as being the very focus of the planet. While it might also be a strong point of defence, yet an effective blow struck there would go to the enemy's heart and be more likely to bring the Martians promptly to terms than anything else.

The first thing, then, was to locate the Lake of the Sun on the smoke hidden surface of the planet beneath us. This was a problem that the astronomers could readily solve.

Fortunately, in the flagship itself there was one of the star-gazing gentlemen who had made a specialty of the study of Mars. That planet, as I have already explained, was now in opposition to the earth. The astronomer had records in his pocket which enabled him, by a brief calculation, to say just when the Lake of the Sun would be on the meridian of Mars as seen from the earth. Our chronometers still kept terrestrial time; we knew the exact number of days and hours that had elapsed since we had departed, and so it was possible by placing ourselves in a line between the earth and Mars to be practically in the situation of an astronomer in his observatory at home.

Then it was only necessary to wait for the hour when the Lake of the Sun would be upon the meridian of Mars in order to be certain what was the true direction of the latter from the flagship.

Having thus located the heart of our foe behind its shield of darkness, we prepared to strike.

"I have ascertained," said Mr. Edison, "the vibration period of the smoke, so that it will be easy for us to shatter it into invisible atoms. You will see that every stroke of the disintegrators will open a hole through the black curtain. If their field of destruction could be made wide enough, we might in that manner clear away the entire covering of smoke, but all that we shall really be able to do will be to puncture it with holes, which will, perhaps, enable us to catch glimpses of the surface beneath. In that manner we may be able more effectually to concentrate our fire upon the most vulnerable points."

Everything being prepared, and the entire squadron having assembled to watch the effect of the opening blow and be ready to follow it up, Mr. Edison himself poised one of the new disintegrators, which was too large to be carried in the hand, and, following the direction indicated by the calculations of the astronomers, launched the vibratory discharge into the ocean of blackness beneath.

Instantly there opened beneath us a huge well-shaped hole from which the black clouds rolled violently back in every direction.

Through this opening we saw the gleam of brilliant lights beneath. We had made a hit.

"It's the Lake of the Sun!" shouted the astronomer who furnished the calculation by means of which its position had been discovered.

And, indeed, it was the Lake of the Sun. While the opening in the clouds made by the discharge was not wide, yet it sufficed to give us a view of a portion of the curving shore of the lake, which was ablaze with electric lights.

Whether our shot had done any damage, beyond making the circular opening in the cloud curtain, we could not tell, for almost immediately the surrounding black smoke masses billowed in to fill up the hole.

But in the brief glimpse we had caught sight of two or three large airships hovering in space above that part of the Lake of the Sun and its bordering city which we had beheld. It seemed to me in the brief glance I had that one ship had been touched by the discharge and was wandering in an erratic manner. But the clouds closed in so rapidly that I could not be certain.

Anyhow, we had demonstrated one thing, and that was that we could penetrate the cloud shield and reach the Martians in their hiding place.

It had been prearranged that the first discharge from the flagship should be a signal for the concentration of the fire of all the other ships upon the same spot.

A little hesitation, however, occurred, and a half a minute had elapsed before the disintegrators from the other members of the squadron were got into play.

Then, suddenly we saw an immense commotion in the cloud beneath us. It seemed to be beaten and hurried in every direction and punctured like a sieve with nearly a hundred great circular holes. Through these gaps we could see clearly a large region of the planet's surface, with many airships floating above it and the blaze of innumerable electric lights illuminating it. The Martians had created an artificial day under the curtain.

This time there was no question that the blow had been effective. Four or five of the airships, partially destroyed, tumbled headlong toward the ground, while even from our great distance there was unmistakable evidence that fearful execution had been done among the crowded structures along the shore of the lake.

As each of our ships possessed but one of the new disintegrators, and since a minute or so was required to adjust them for a fresh discharge, we remained for a little while inactive after delivering the blow. Meanwhile the cloud curtain, though rent to shreds by the concentrated discharge of the disintegrators, quickly became a uniform black sheet again, hiding everything.

We had just had time to congratulate ourselves on the successful opening of our bombardment, and the disintegrator of the flagship was poised for another discharge, when suddenly out of the black expanse beneath, quivered immense electric beams, clear cut and straight as bars of steel, but dazzling our eyes with unendurable brilliance.

It was the reply of the Martians to our attack.

Three or four of the electrical ships were seriously damaged, and one, close beside the flagship, changed color, withered and collapsed, with the same sickening phenomena that had made our hearts shudder when the first disaster of this kind occurred during our brief battle over the asteroid.

Another score of our comrades were gone, and yet we had hardly begun the fight.

Glancing at the other ships which had been injured, I saw that the damage to them was not so serious, although they were evidently *hors de combat* for the present.

Our fighting blood was now boiling and we did not stop long to count our losses.

"Into the smoke!" was the signal, and the ninety and more electric ships which still remained in condition for action immediately shot downward.

THE EARTH GIRL   It was a wild plunge. We kept off the decks while rushing through the blinding smoke, but the instant we emerged below, where we found ourselves still a mile above the ground, we were out again, ready to strike.

I have simply a confused recollection of flashing lights beneath, and a great, dark arch of clouds above, out of which our ships seemed dropping on all sides, and then the fray burst on and around us, and no man could see or notice anything except by half-comprehended glances.

Almost in an instant, it seemed, a swarm of airships surrounded us, while from what, for lack of a more descriptive name, I shall call the forts about the Lake of the Sun, leaped tongues of electric fire, before which some of our ships were driven like bits of flaming paper in a high wind, gleaming for a moment, then curling up and gone forever!

It was an awful sight; but the battle fever was raging within us, and we, on our part, were not idle.

Every man carried a disintegrator, and these hand instruments, together with those of heavier caliber on the ship poured their resistless vibrations in every direction through the quivering air.

The airships of the Martians were destroyed by the score, and yet they flocked upon us thicker and faster.

We dropped lower and our blows fell upon the forts, and upon the widespread city bordering the Lake of the Sun. We almost entirely silenced the fire of one of the forts; but there were forty more in full action within reach of our eyes!

Some of the metallic buildings were partly unroofed by the disintegrators and some had their walls riddled and fell with thundering crashes, whose sound rose to our ears above the hellish din of battle. I caught glimpses of giant forms struggling in the ruins and rushing wildly through the streets, but there was no time to see anything clearly.

Our flagship seemed charmed. A crowd of airships hung upon it like a swarm of angry bees, and, at times, one could not see for the lightning strokes—yet we escaped destruction, while ourselves dealing death on every hand.

It was a glorious fight, but it was not war; no, it was not war. We really had no more chance of ultimate success amid that multitude of enemies than a prisoner running the gauntlet in a crowd of savages has of escape.

A conviction of the hopelessness of the contest finally forced itself upon our minds, and the shattered squadron, which had kept well together amid the storm of death, was signaled to retreat.

Shaking off their pursuers, as a hunted bear shakes off the dogs, sixty of the electrical ships rose up through the clouds where more than ninety had gone down!

Madly we rushed upward through the vast curtain and continued our flight to a great elevation, far beyond the reach of the awful artillery of the enemy.

Looking back it seemed the very mouth of hell from which we had escaped.

The Martians did not for an instant cease their fire, even when we were far beyond their reach. With furious persistence they blazed away through the cloud curtain, and the vivid spikes of lightning shuddered so swiftly on one another's track that they were like a flaming halo of electric lances around the frowning helmet of the War Planet.

But after a while they stopped their terrific sparring, and once more the immense globe assumed the appearance of a vast ball of black smoke still widely agitated by the recent disturbance, but exhibiting no opening through which we could discern what was going on beneath.

Evidently the Martians believed they had finished us.

At no time since the beginning of our adventure had it appeared to me quite so hopeless, reckless and mad as it seemed at present.

We had suffered fearful losses, and yet what had we accomplished? We had won two fights on the asteroid, it is true, but then we had overwhelming numbers on our side.

Now we were facing millions on their own ground, and our very first assault had resulted in a disastrous repulse, with the loss of at least thirty electric ships and 600 men!

Evidently we could not endure this sort of thing. We must find some other means of assailing Mars or else give up the attempt.

But the latter was not to be thought. It was no mere question of self-pride, however, and no consideration of the tremendous interests at stake, which would compel us to continue our apparently vain attempt.

Our provisions could last only a few days longer. The supply would not carry us one-quarter of the way back to earth, and we must therefore remain here and literally conquer or die.

In this extremity a consultation of the principal officers was called upon the deck of the flagship.

Here the suggestion was made that we should attempt to effect by strategy what we had failed to do by force.

An old army officer who had served in many wars against the cunning Indians of the West, Colonel Alonzo Jefferson Smith, was the author of this suggestion.

"Let us circumvent them," he said. "We can do it in this way. The chances are that all of the available fighting force of the planet Mars is now concentrated on this side and in the neighbourhood of The Lake of the Sun.

"Possibly, by some kind of X-ray business, they can only see us dimly through the clouds, and if we get a little further away they will not be able to see us at all.

"Now, I suggest that a certain number of the electrical ships be withdrawn from the squadron to a great distance, while the remainder stay here; or, better still, approach to a point just beyond the reach of those streaks of lightning, and begin a bombardment of the clouds without paying any attention to whether the strokes reach through the clouds and do any damage or not.

"This will induce the Martians to believe that we are determined to press our attack at this point.

"In the meantime, while these ships are raising a hulabaloo on this side of the planet, and drawing their fire, as much as possible, without running into any actual danger, let the others which have been selected for the purpose, sail rapidly around to the other side of Mars and take them in the rear."

It was not perfectly clear what Colonel Smith intended to do after the landing had been effected in the rear of the Martians, but still there seemed a good deal to be said for his suggestion, and it would, at any rate, if carried out, enable us to learn something about the condition of things on the planet, and perhaps furnish us with a hint as to how we could best proceed in the further prosecution of the siege.

Accordingly it was resolved that about twenty ships should be told off for this movement, and Colonel Smith himself was placed in command.

At my desire I accompanied the new commander in his flagship.

Rising to a considerable elevation in order that there might be no risk of being seen, we began our flank movement while the remaining ships, in accordance with the understanding, dropped nearer the curtain of cloud and commenced a bombardment with the disintegrators, which caused a tremendous commotion in the clouds, opening vast gaps in them, and occasionally revealing a glimpse of the electric lights on the planet, although it was evident that the vibratory currents did not reach the ground. The Martians immediately replied to this renewed attack, and again the cloud-covered globe bristled with lightning, which flashed so fiercely out of the blackness below that the stoutest hearts among us quailed, although we were situated well beyond the danger.

But this sublime spectacle rapidly vanished from our eyes when, having attained a proper elevation, we began our course toward the opposite hemisphere of the planet.

We guided our flight by the stars, and from our knowledge of the rotation period of Mars, and the position which the principal points on its surface must occupy at certain hours, we were able to tell what part of the planet lay beneath us.

Having completed our semi-circuit we found ourselves on the night side of Mars, and determined to lose no time in executing our coup. But it was deemed best that an exploration should first be made by a single electrical ship, and Colonel Smith naturally wished to undertake the adventure with his own vessel.

We dropped rapidly through the black cloud curtain, which proved to be at least half a mile in thickness, and then suddenly emerged, as if suspended at the apex of an enormous dome, arching above the surface of the planet a mile beneath us, which sparkled on all sides with innumerable lights.

These lights were so numerous and so brilliant as to produce a faint imitation of daylight, even at our immense height above the ground, and the dome of cloud out of which we had emerged assumed a soft fawn color which produced an indescribably beautiful effect.

For a moment we recoiled from our undertaking, and arrested the motion of the electric ship.

But on closely examining the surface beneath us we found that there was a broad region, where comparatively few bright lights were to be seen. From my knowledge of the geography of Mars I knew that this was a part of the Land of Ausonia, situated a few hundred miles northeast of Hellas, where we had first seen the planet.

Evidently it was not so thickly populated as some of the other parts of Mars, and its comparative darkness was an attraction to us. We determined to aproach within a few hundred feet of the ground with the electric ship, and then, in case no enemies appeared, to visit the soil itself.

"Perhaps we shall see or hear something that will be of use to us," said Colonel Smith, "and for the purposes of this first reconnoissance it is better that we should be few in number. The other ships will await our return, and at any rate we shall not be gone long."

As our car approached the ground we found ourselves near the tops of some lofty trees.

"This will do," said Colonel Smith to the electrical steersman, "Stay right here."

He and I then lowered ourselves into the branches of the trees, each carrying a small disintegrator, and cautiously clambered down to the ground.

We believed we were the first of the descendants of Adam to set foot on the planet of Mars.

At first we suffered somewhat from the effects of the rare atmosphere. It was so lacking in density that it resembled the air on the summits of the loftiest terrestrial mountains.

Having reached the foot of the tree in safety, we lay down for a moment on the ground to recover ourselves and to become accustomed to our new surroundings.

A thrill, born half of wonder, half of incredulity, ran through me at the touch of the soil of Mars. Here was I, actually on that planet, which had seemed so far away, so inaccessible, and so full of mysteries when viewed from the earth. And yet, surrounding me, were things—gigantic, it is true—but still resembling and recalling the familiar sights of my own world.

After a little while our lungs became accustomed to the rarity of the atmosphere and we experienced a certain stimulation in breathing.

We then got upon our feet and stepped out from under the shadow of the gigantic tree. High above we could faintly see our electrical ship, gently swaying in the air close to the tree top.

There were no electric lights in our immediate neighborhood, but we noticed that the whole surface of the planet around us was gleaming with them, producing an effect like the glow of a great city seen from a distance at night. The glare was faintly reflected from the vast dome of clouds above, producing the general impression of a moonlight night upon the earth.

It was a wonderfully quiet and beautiful spot where we had come down. The air had a delicate feel and a bracing temperature, while a soft breeze soughed through the leaves of the tree above our heads.

Not far away was the bank of a canal, bordered by a magnificent avenue shaded by a double row of immense umbrageous trees.

We approached the canal, and, getting upon the road, turned to the left to make an exploration in that direction. The shadow of the trees falling upon the roadway produced a dense gloom, in the midst of which we felt that we should be safe, unless the Martians had eyes like those of cats.

As we pushed along, our hearts, I confess, beating a little quickly, a shadow stirred in front of us.

Something darker than the night itself approached.

As it drew near it assumed the appearance of an enormous dog, as tall as an ox, which ran swiftly our way with a threatening motion of its head. But before it could even utter a snarl, the whirr of Colonel Smith's disintegrator was heard and the creature vanished in the shadow.

"Gracious, did you ever see such a beast?" said the Colonel. "Why he was as big as a grizzly."

"The people he belonged to must be near by," I said. "Very likely he was a watch on guard."

"But I see no signs of a habitation."

"True, but you observe there is a thick hedge on the side of the road opposite the canal. If we get through that perhaps we shall catch sight of something."

Cautiously we pushed our way through the hedge, which was composed of shrubs as large as small trees, and very thick at the bottom, and, having traversed it, found ourselves in a great meadow-like expanse which might have been a lawn. At a considerable distance, in the midst of a clump of trees, a large building towered skyward, its walls of some red metal, gleaming like polished copper in the soft light that fell from the cloud dome.

There were no lights around the building itself, and we saw nothing corresponding to windows on that side which faced us, but toward the right a door was evidently open, and out of this streamed a brilliant shaft of illumination, which lay bright upon the lawn, then crossed the highway through an opening in the hedge, and gleamed on the water of the canal beyond.

Where we stood the ground had evidently been recently cleared, and there was no obstruction, but as we crept closer to the house—for our curiosity had now become irresistible—we found ourselves crawling through grass so tall that if we had stood erect it would have risen well above our heads.

"This affords good protection," said Colonel Smith, recalling his adventures on the western plains. "We can get close in to the Indians— I beg pardon, I mean the Martians—without being seen."

Heavens, what an adventure was this! To be crawling about in the night on the face of another world and venturing, perhaps, into the jaws of a danger which human experience could not measure!

But on we went, and in a little while we had emerged from the tall grass and were somewhat startled by the discovery that we had got close to the wall of the building.

Carefully we crept around to the open door.

As we neared it we suddenly stopped as if we had been stricken with instantaneous paralysis.

Out of the door floated, on the soft night air, the sweetest music to which I have ever listened.

It carried me back in an instant to my own world. It was the music of the earth. It was the melodious expression of a human soul. It thrilled us both to the heart's core.

"My God!" exclaimed Colonel Smith. "What can that be? Are we dreaming, or where in heaven's name are we?"

Still the enchanting harmony floated out upon the air.

What the instrument was I could not tell, but the sound seemed more nearly to resemble that of a violin than anything else of which I could think.

When we first heard it the strains were gentle, sweet, caressing and full of an infinite depth of feeling, but in a little while its tone changed, and it became a magnificent march, throbbing upon the air in stirring notes that set our hearts beating in unison with its stride and inspiring in us a courage that we had not felt before.

Then it drifted into a wild fantasia, still inexpressibly sweet, and from that changed again into a requiem or lament, whose mellifluous tide of harmony swept our thoughts back again to the earth.

"I can endure this no longer," I said. "I must see who it is that makes that music. It is the product of a human heart and must come from the touch of human fingers."

We carefully shifted our position until we stood in the blaze of light that poured out of the door.

The doorway was an immense arched opening, magnificently ornamented, rising to a height of, I should say, not less than twenty or twenty-five feet and broad in proportion. The door itself stood widely open and it, together with all of its fittings and surroundings, was composed of the same beautiful red metal.

Stepping out a little way into the light I could see within the door an immense apartment, glittering on all sides with metallic ornaments and gems and lighted from the center by a great chandelier of electric candles.

In the middle of the great floor, holding the instrument delicately poised, and still awaking its ravishing voice, stood a figure, the sight of which almost stopped my breath.

It was a slender sylph of a girl!

A girl of my own race; a human being here upon the planet Mars!

Her hair was loosely coiled and she was attired in graceful white drapery.

"By God!" cried Colonel Smith, "she's human!"

RETREAT TO DEIMOS   Still the bewildering strains of the music came to our ears, and yet we stood there unperceived, though in the full glare of the chandelier.

The girl's face was presented in profile. It was exquisite in beauty, pale, delicate with a certain pleading sadness which stirred us to the heart.

An element of romance and a touch of personal interest such as we had not looked for suddenly entered into our adventure.

Colonel Smith's mind still ran back to the perils of the plains.

"She is a prisoner," he said, "and by the Seven Devils of Dona Ana we'll not leave her here. But where are the hellhounds themselves?"

Our attention had been so absorbed by the sight of the girl that we had scarcely thought of looking to see if there was any one else in the room.

Glancing beyond her, I now perceived sitting in richly decorated chairs three or four gigantic Martians. They were listening to the music as if charmed.

The whole story told itself. This girl, if not their slave, was at any rate under their control, and she was furnishing entertainment for them by her musical skill. The fact that they could find pleasure in music so beautiful was, perhaps, an indication that they were not really as savage as they seemed.

Yet our hearts went out to the girl, and were turned against them with an uncontrollable hatred.

They were of the same remorseless race with those who had so lately lain waste our fair earth and who would have completed its destruction had not Providence interfered in our behalf.

Singularly enough, although we stood full in the light, they had not yet seen us.

Suddenly the girl, moved by what impulse I know not, turned her face in our direction. Her eyes fell upon us. She paused abruptly in her playing, and her instrument dropped to the floor. Then she uttered a cry, and with extended arms ran toward us.

But when she was near she stopped abruptly, the glad look fading from her face, and started back with terror-stricken eyes, as if, after all, she had found us not what she expected.

Then for an instant she looked more intently at us, her countenance cleared once more, and, overcome by some strange emotion, her eyes filled with tears, and, drawing a little nearer, she stretched forth her hands to us appealingly.

Meanwhile the Martians had started to their feet. They looked down upon us in astonishment. We were like pygmies to them; like little gnomes which had sprung out of the ground at their feet.

One of the giants seized some kind of a weapon and started forward with a threatening gesture.

The girl sprang to my side and grasped my arm with a cry of fear.

This seemed to throw the Martian into a sudden frenzy, and he raised his arms to strike.

But the disintegrator was in my hand.

My rage was equal to his.

I felt the concentrated vengeance of the earth quivering through me as I pressed the button of the disintegrator and, sweeping it rapidly up and down, saw the gigantic form that confronted me melt into nothingness.

There were three other giants in the room, and they had been on the point of following up the attack of their comrade. But when he disappeared from before their eyes, they paused, staring in amazement at the place where, but a moment before, he had stood, but where now only the metal weapon he had wielded lay on the floor.

At first they started back, and seemed on the point of fleeing; then, with a second glance, perceiving again how small and insignificant we were, all three together advanced upon us.

The girl sank trembling on her knees.

In the meantime I had readjusted my disintegrator for another discharge, and Colonel Smith stood by me with the light of battle upon his face.

"Sweep the discharge across the three," I exclaimed. "Otherwise there will be one left and before we can fire again he will crush us."

The whirr of the two instruments sounded simultaneously, and with a quick horizontal motion we swept the lines of force around in such a manner that all three of the Martians were caught by the vibratory streams and actually cut in two.

Long gaps were opened in the wall of the room behind them, where the destroying currents had passed, for with wrathful fierceness, we had run the vibrations through half a gamut on the index.

The victory was ours. There were no other enemies, that we could see, in the house.

Yet at any moment others might make their appearance, and what more we did must be done quickly.

The girl evidently was as much amazed as the Martians had been by the effects which we had produced. Still she was not terrified, and continued to cling to us and glance beseechingly into our faces, expressing in her every look and gesture the fact that she knew we were of her own race.

But clearly she could not speak our tongue, for the words she uttered were unintelligible.

Colonel Smith, whose long experience in Indian warfare had made him intensely practical, did not lose his military instincts, even in the midst of events so strange.

"It occurs to me," he said, "that we have got a chance at the enemies' supplies. Suppose we begin foraging right here. Let's see if this girl can't show us the commissary department."

He immediately began to make signs to the girl to indicate that he was hungry.

A look of comprehension flitted over her features, and, seizing our hands, she led us into an adjoining apartment, and pointed to a number of metallic boxes.

One of these she opened, taking out of it a kind of cake, which she placed between her teeth, breaking off a very small portion and then handing it to us, motioning that we should eat, but at the same time showing us that we ought to take only a small quantity.

"Thank God! It's compressed food," said Colonel Smith. "I thought these Martians with their wonderful civilization would be up to that. And it's mighty lucky for us, because, without overburdening ourselves, if we can find one or two more caches like this we shall be able to re-provision the entire fleet. But we must get reinforcements before we can take possession of the fodder."

Accordingly we hurried out into the night, passed into the roadway, and, taking the girl with us, ran as rapidly as possible to the foot of the tree where we had made our descent. Then we signalled to the electric ship to drop down to the level of the ground.

This was quickly done, the girl was taken aboard, and a dozen men, under our guidance, hastened back to the house, where we loaded ourselves with the compressed provisions and conveyed them to the ship.

On this second trip to the mysterious house we had discovered another apartment containing a very large number of the metallic boxes, filled with compressed food.

"By Jove, it is a storehouse," said Colonel Smith. "We must get more force and carry it all off. Gracious, but this is a lucky night. We can reprovision the whole fleet from this room."

"I thought it singular," I said, "that with the exception of the girl whom we have rescued no women were seen in the house. Evidently the lights over yonder indicate the location of a considerable town, and it is quite probable that this building, without windows, and so strongly constructed, is the common storehouse, where the provisions for the town are kept. The fellows we killed must have been the watchmen in charge of the storehouse, and they were treating themselves to a little music from the slave girl when we happened to come upon them."

With the utmost haste several of the other electrical ships, waiting above the cloud curtain, were summoned to descend, and, with more than a hundred men, we returned to the building, and this time almost entirely exhausted its stores, each man carrying as much as he could stagger under.

Fortunately our proceedings had been conducted without much noise, and the storehouse being situated at a considerable distance from other buildings, none of the Martians, except those who would never tell the story, had known of our arrival or of our doings on the planet.

"Now, we'll return and surprise Edison with the news," said Colonel Smith.

Our ship was the last to pass up through the clouds, and it was a strange sight to watch the others as one after another they rose toward the great dome, entered it, though from below it resembled a solid vault of grayish-pink marble, and disappeared.

We quickly followed them, and having penetrated the enormous curtain, were considerably surprised on emerging at the other side to find that the sun was shining brilliantly upon us. It will be remembered that it was night on this side of Mars when we went down, but our adventure had occupied several hours, and now Mars had so turned upon its axis that the portion of its surface over which we were had come around into the sunlight.

We knew that the squadron which we had left beseiging the Lake of the Sun must also have been carried around in a similar manner, passing into the night while the side of the planet where we were was emerging into day.

Our shortest way back would be by traveling westward, because then we should be moving in a direction opposite to that in which the planet rotated, and the main squadron, sharing that rotation, would be continually moving in our direction.

But to travel westward was to penetrate once more into the night side of the planet.

The prows, if I may so call them, of our ships were accordingly turned in the direction of the vast shadow which Mars was invisibly projecting into space behind it, and on entering that shadow the sun disappeared from our eyes, and once more the huge hidden globe beneath us became a black chasm among the stars.

Now that we were in the neighborhood of a globe capable of imparting considerable weight to all things under the influence of its attraction that peculiar condition which I have before described as existing in the midst of space, where there was neither up nor down for us, had ceased. Here where we had weight "up" and "down" had resumed their old meanings. "Down" was toward the center of Mars, and "up" was away from that center.

Standing on the deck, and looking overhead as we swiftly ploughed our smooth way at a great height through the now imperceptible atmosphere of the planet, I saw the two moons of Mars meeting in the sky exactly above us.

Before our arrival at Mars, there had been considerable discussion among the learned men as to the advisability of touching at one of their moons, and when the discovery was made that our provisions were nearly exhausted, it had been suggested that the Martian satellites might furnish us with an additional supply.

But it had appeared a sufficient reply to this suggestion that the moons of Mars are both insignificant bodies, not much larger than the asteroid we had fallen in with, and that there could not possibly be any form of vegetation or other edible products upon them.

This view having prevailed, we had ceased to take an interest in the satellites, further than to regard them as objects of great curiosity on account of their motions.

The nearer of these moons, Phobos, is only 3,700 miles from the surface of Mars, and we watched it traveling around the planet three times in the course of every day. The more distant one, Deimos, 12,500 miles away, required considerably more than one day to make its circuit.

It now happened that the two had come into conjunction, as I have said, just over our heads, and, throwing myself down on my back on the deck of the electrical ship, for a long time I watched the race between the two satellites, until Phobos, rapidly gaining upon the other, had left its rival far behind.

Suddenly Colonel Smith, who took very little interest in these astronomical curiosities, touched me, and pointing ahead, said:

"There they are."

I looked, and sure enough there were the signal lights of the principal squadron, and as we gazed we occasionally saw, darting up from the vast cloud mass beneath, an electric bayonet, fiercely thrust into the sky, which showed that the siege was still actively going on, and that the Martians were jabbing away at their invisible enemies outside the curtain.

In a short time the two fleets had joined, and Colonel Smith and I immediately transferred ourselves to the flagship.

"Well, what have you done?" asked Mr. Edison, while others crowded around with eager attention.

"If we have not captured their provision train," said Colonel Smith, "we have done something just about as good. We have foraged on the country, and have collected a supply that I reckon will last this fleet for at least a month."

"What's that? What's that?"

"It's just what I say," and Colonel Smith brought out of his pocket one of the square cakes of compressed food. "Set your teeth in that, and see what you think of it, but don't take too much, for it's powerful strong."

"I say," he continued, "we have got enough of that stuff to last us all for a month, but we've done more than that; we have got a surprise for you that will make you open your eyes. Just wait a minute."

Colonel Smith made a signal to the electrical ship which we had just quitted to draw near. It came alongside, so that one could step from its deck onto the flagship. Colonel Smith disappeared for a minute in the interior of his ship, then re-emerged, leading the girl whom we had found upon the planet.

"Take her inside, quick," he said, "for she is not used to this thin air."

In fact, we were at so great an elevation that the rarity of the atmosphere now compelled us all to wear our airtight suits, and the girl, not being thus attired, would have fallen unconscious on the deck if we had not instantly removed her to the interior of the car.

There she quickly recovered from the effects of the deprivation of air and looked about her, pale, astonished, but yet apparently without fear.

Every motion of this girl convinced me that she not only recognized us as members of her own race, but that she felt that her only hope lay in our aid. Therefore, strange as we were to her in many respects, nevertheless she did not think that she was in danger while among us.

The circumstances under which we had found her were quickly explained. Her beauty, her strange fate and the impenetrable mystery which surrounded her excited universal admiration and wonder.

"How did she get on Mars?" was the question that everybody asked, and that nobody could answer.

But while all were crowding around and overwhelming the poor girl with their staring, suddenly she burst into tears, and then, with arms outstretched in the same appealing manner which had so stirred our sympathies when we first saw her in the house of the Martians, she broke forth in a wild recitation, which was half a song and half a wail.

As she went on I noticed that a learned professor of languages from the University of Heidelberg was listening to her with intense attention. Several times he appeared to be on the point of breaking in with an exclamation. I could plainly see that he was becoming more and more excited as the words poured from the girl's lips. Occasionally he nodded and muttered, smiling to himself.

Her song finished, the girl sank half-exhausted upon the floor. She was lifted and placed in a reclining position at the side of the car.

Then the Heidelberg professor stepped to the center of the car, in the sight of all, and in a most impressive manner said:

"Gentlemen, our sister.

"I have her tongue recognized! The language that she speaks, the roots of the great Indo-European, or Aryan stock, contains.

"This girl, gentlemen, to the oldest family of the human race belongs. Her language every tongue that now upon the earth is spoken antedates. Convinced am I that it that great original speech is from which have all the languages of the civilized world sprung.

"How she here came, so many millions of miles from the earth, a great mystery is. But it shall be penetrated, and it is from her own lips that we shall the truth learn, because not difficult to us shall it be the language that she speaks to acquire since to our own it is akin."

This announcement of the Heidelberg professor stirred us all most profoundly. It not only deepened our interest in the beautiful girl whom we had rescued, but, in a dim way, it gave us reason to hope that we should yet discover some means of mastering the Martians by dealing them a blow from within.

It had been expected, the reader will remember, that the Martian whom we had made prisoner on the asteroid, might be of use to us in a similar way, and for that reason great efforts had been made to acquire his language, and considerable progress had been effected in that direction.

But from the moment of our arrival at Mars itself, and especially after the battles began, the prisoner had resumed his savage and uncommunicative disposition, and had seemed continually to be expecting that we would fall victims to the prowess of his fellow beings, and that he would be released. How an outlaw, such as he evidently was, who had been caught in the act of robbing the Martian gold mines, could expect to escape punishment on returning to his native planet it was difficult to see. Nevertheless, so strong are the ties of race we could plainly perceive that all his sympathies were for his own people.

In fact, in consequence of his surly manner, and his attempts to escape, he had been more strictly bound than before and to get him out of the way had been removed from the flagship, which was already overcrowded, and placed in one of the other electric ships, and this ship—as it happened —was one of those which were lost in the great battle beneath the clouds. So after all, the Martian had perished, by a vengeful stroke launched from his native globe.

But Providence had placed in our hands a far better interpreter than he could ever have been. This girl of our own race would need no urging, or coercion, on our part in order to induce her to reveal any secrets of the Martians that might be useful in our further proceedings.

But one thing was first necessary to be done.

We must learn to talk with her.

But for the discovery of the store of provisions it would have been impossible for us to spare the time needed to acquire the language of the girl, but now that we had been saved from the danger of starvation, we could prolong the siege for several weeks, employing the intervening time to the best advantage.

The terrible disaster which we had suffered in the great battle above the Lake of the Sun, wherein we had lost nearly a third of our entire force, had been quite sufficient to convince us that our only hope of victory lay in dealing the Martians some paralyzing stroke that at one blow would deprive them of the power of resistance. A victory that cost us the loss of a single ship would be too dearly purchased now.

How to deal that blow, and first of all, how to discover the means of dealing it, were at present the uppermost problems in our minds.

The only hope for us lay in the girl.

If, as there was every reason to believe, she was familiar with the ways and secrets of the Martians, then she might be able to direct our efforts in such a manner as to render them effective.

"We can spare two weeks for this," said Mr. Edison. "Can you fellows of many tongues learn to talk with the girl in that time?"

"We'll try it," said several.

"It shall we do," cried the Heidelberg professor more confidently.

"Then there is no use of staying here," continued the commander. "If we withdraw the Martians will think that we have given up. That will give us a better opportunity to strike effectively when we are again ready."

"Why not rendezvous at one of the moons?" said an astronomer. "Neither of the two moons is of much consequence, as far as size goes, but still it would serve as sort of an anchorage ground, and while there, if we were careful to keep on the side away from Mars, we should escape detection."

This suggestion was immediately accepted, and the squadron having been signaled to assemble quickly bore off in the direction of the more distant moon of Mars, Deimos. We knew that it was slightly smaller than Phobos, but its greater distance gave promise that it would better serve our purpose of temporary concealment. The moons of Mars, like the earth's moon, always kept the same face toward their master. By hiding behind Deimos we should escape the prying eyes of the Martians, even when they employed telescopes, and thus be able to remain comparatively close at hand, ready to pounce down upon them again, after we had obtained, as we now had good hope of doing, information that would make us masters of the situation.

THE FLOOD GATES OF MARS   It was a curious scene when the momentous interview which was to determine our fate and that of Mars began. Aina had been warned of what was coming. We in the flagship had all learned to speak her language with more or less ease, but it was deemed best that the Heidelberg professor, assisted by one of his colleagues, should act as interpreter.

The girl, flushed with excitement of the novel situation, fully appreciating the importance of what was about to occur, and looking more charming than before, stood at one side of the principal apartment. Directly facing her were the interpreters, and the rest of us, all with ears intent and eyes focused upon Aina, stood in a double row behind them. As heretofore, I am setting down her words translated into our own tongue, having taken only so much liberty as to connect the sentences into a stricter sequence than they had when falling from her lips in reply to the questions which were showered upon her.

"You will never be victorious," she said, "if you attack them openly as you have been doing. They are too strong and too numerous. They are well prepared for such attacks, because they have had to resist them before.

"They have waged war with the inhabitants of the asteroid Ceres, whose people are giants greater than themselves. Their enemies from Ceres have attacked them here. Hence these fortifications, with weapons pointing skyward, and the great air fleets which you have encountered."

"But there must be some point," said Mr. Edison, "where we can."

"Yes, yes," interrupted the girl quickly, "There is one blow you can deal them which they could not withstand."

"What is that?" eagerly inquired the commander.

"You can drown them out."

"How? With the canals?"

"Yes, I will explain to you. I have already told you, and, in fact, you must have seen for yourselves, that there are almost no mountains on Mars. A very learned man of my race used to say that the reason was because Mars is so very old a world that the mountains it once had have been almost completely leveled, and the entire surface of the planet had become a great plain. There are depressions, however, most of which are occupied by the seas. The greater part of the land lies below the level of the ocean. In order at the same time to irrigate the soil and make it fruitful, and to protect themselves from overflows by the ocean breaking in upon them, the Martians have constructed the immense and innumerable canals which you see running in all directions over the continents.

"There is one period in the year, and that period has now arrived when there is special danger of a great deluge. Most of the oceans of Mars lie in the southern hemisphere. When it is Summer in that hemisphere, the great masses of ice and snow collected around the south pole melt rapidly away.

"Yes, that is so," broke in one of the astronomers, who was listening attentively. "Many a time I have seen the vast snow fields around the southern pole of Mars completely disappear as the Summer sun rose high upon them."

"With the melting of these snows," continued Aina, "a rapid rise in the level of the water in the southern oceans occurs. On the side facing these oceans the continents of Mars are sufficiently elevated to prevent an overflow, but nearer the equator the level of the land sinks lower.

"With your telescopes you have no doubt noticed that there is a great bending sea connecting the oceans of the south with those of the north and running through the midst of the continents."

"Quite so," said the astronomer who had spoken before, "we call it the Syrtis Major."

"That long narrow sea," Aina went on, "forms a great channel through which the flood of waters caused by the melting of the southern polar snows flows swiftly toward the equator and then on toward the north until it reaches the sea basins which exist there. At that point it is rapidly turned into ice and snow, because, of course, while it is Summer in the southern hemisphere it is Winter in the northern.

"The Syrtis Major (I am giving our name to the channel of communication in place of that by which the girl called it) is like a great safety valve, which, by permitting the waters to flow northward, saves the continents from inundation.

"But when mid-Summer arrives, the snows around the pole, having been completely melted away, the flood ceases and the water begins to recede. At this time, but for a device which the Martians have employed, the canals connected with the oceans would run dry, and the vegetation left without moisture under the Summer sun, would quickly perish.

"To prevent this they have built a series of enormous gates extending completely across the Syrtis Major at its narrowest point (latitude 25 degrees south). These gates are all controlled by machinery collected at a single point on the shore of the strait. As soon as the flood in the Syrtis Major begins to recede, the gates are closed, and, the water being thus restrained, the irrigating canals are kept full long enough to mature the harvests."

"The clue! The clue at last!" exclaimed Mr. Edison. "That is the place where we shall nip them. If we can close those gates now at the moment of high tide we shall flood the country. Did you say," he continued, turning to Aina, "that the movement of the gates was all controlled from a single point?"

"Yes," said the girl. "There is a great building (power house) full of tremendous machinery which I once entered when my father was taken there by his master, and where I saw one Martian, by turning a little handle, cause the great line of gates, stretching a hundred miles across the sea, to slowly shut in, edge to edge, until the flow of the water toward the north had been stopped."

"How is the building protected?"

"So completely," said Aina, "that my only fear is that you may not be able to reach it. On account of the danger from their enemies on Ceres, the Martians have fortified it strongly on all sides, and have even surrounded it and covered it overhead with a great electrical network, to touch which would be instant death."

"Ah," said Mr. Edison, "they have got an electric shield, have they? Well, I think we shall be able to manage that."

"Anyhow," he continued, "we have got to get into that power house, and we have got to close those gates, and we must not lose much time in making up our minds how it is to be done. Evidently this is our only chance. We have not force enough to contend in open battle with the Martians, but if we can flood them out, and thereby render the engines contained in their fortifications useless, perhaps we shall be able to deal with the airships, which will be all the means of defense that will then remain to them."

This idea commended itself to all the leaders of the expedition. It was determined to make a reconnoissance at once.

But it would not do for us to approach the planet too hastily, and we certainly could not think of landing upon it in broad daylight. Still, as long as we were yet a considerable distance from Mars, we felt that we should be safe from observation because so much time had elapsed while we were hidden behind Deimos that the Martians had undoubtedly concluded that we were no longer in existence.

So we boldly quitted the little satellite with our entire squadron and once more rapidly approached the red planet of war. This time it was to be a death grapple and our chances of victory still seemed good.

As soon as we arrived so near the planet that there was danger of our being actually seen, we took pains to keep continually in the shadow of Mars, and, the more surely to conceal our presence, all lights upon the ships were extinguished. The precaution of the commander even went so far as to have the smooth metallic sides of the cars blackened over so that they should not reflect light, and thus become visible to the Martians as shining specks, moving suspiciously among the stars.

The precise location of the great power house on the shores of the

Syrtis Major having been carefully ascertained, the squadron dropped down one night into the upper limits of the Martian atmosphere, directly over the gulf.

Then a consultation was called on the flagship and a plan of campaign was quickly devised.

It was deemed wise that the attempt should be made with a single electric ship, but that the others should be kept hovering near, ready to respond on the instant to any signal for aid which might come from below. It was thought that, notwithstanding the wonderful defences, which, according to Aina's account surrounded the building, a small party would have a better chance of success than a large one.

Mr. Edison was certain that the electrical network which was described as covering the power house would not prove a serious obstruction to us, because by carefully sweeping the space where we intended to pass with the disintegrators before quitting the ship, the netting could be sufficiently cleared away to give us uninterrupted passage.

At first the intention was to have twenty men, each armed with two disintegrators (that being the largest number one person could carry to advantage) descend from the electrical ship and make the venture. But, after further discussion, this number was reduced; first to a dozen, and finally, to only four. These four consisted of Mr. Edison, Colonel Smith, Mr. Sydney Phillips and myself.

Both by her own request and because we could not help feeling that her knowledge of the locality would be indispensable to us, Aina was also included in our party, but not, of course, as a fighting member of it.

It was about an hour after midnight when the ship in which we were to make the venture parted from the remainder of the squadron and dropped cautiously down. The blaze of electric lights running away in various directions indicated the lines of innumerable canals with habitations crowded along their banks, which came to a focus at a point on the continent of Aeria, westward from the Syrtis Major.

We stopped the electrical ship at an elevation of perhaps three hundred feet above the vast roof of a structure which Aina assured us was the building of which we were in search.

Here we remained for a few minutes, cautiously reconnoitering. On that side of the power house which was opposite to the shore of the Syrtis Major there was a thick grove of trees, lighted beneath, as was apparent from the illumination which here and there streamed up through the cover of leaves, but, nevertheless, dark and gloomy above the tree tops.

"The electric network extends over the grove as well as over the building," said Aina.

This was lucky for us, because we wished to descend among the trees, and, by destroying part of the network over the tree tops, we could reach the shelter we desired and at the same time pass within the line of electric defenses.

With increased caution, and almost holding our breath lest we should make some noise that might reach the ears of the sentinels below, we caused the car to settle gently down until we caught sight of a metallic net stretched in the air between us and the trees.

After our first encounter with the Martians on the asteroid, where, as I have related, some metal which was included in their dress resisted the action of the disintegrators, Mr. Edison had readjusted the range of vibrations covered by the instruments, and since then we had found nothing that did not yield to them. Consequently, we had no fear that the metal of the network would not be destroyed.

There was danger, however, of arousing attention by shattering holes through the tree tops. This could be avoided by first carefully ascertaining how far away the network was and then with the adjustable mirrors attached to the disintegrators focusing the vibratory discharge at that distance.

So successful were we that we opened a considerable gap in the network without doing any perceptible damage to the trees beneath.

The ship was cautiously lowered through the opening and brought to rest among the upper branches of one of the tallest trees. Colonel Smith, Mr. Phillips, Mr. Edison and myself at once clambered out upon a strong limb.

For a moment I feared our arrival had been betrayed on account of the altogether too noisy contest that arose between Colonel Smith and Mr. Phillips as to which of them should assist Aina. To settle the dispute I took charge of her myself.

At length we were all safely in the tree.

Then followed the still more dangerous undertaking of descending from this great height to the ground. Fortunately, the branches were very close together and they extended down within a short distance of the soil. So the actual difficulties of the descent were not very great after all. The one thing that we had particularly to bear in mind was the absolute necessity of making no noise.

At length the descent was successfully accomplished, and we all five stood together in the shadow at the foot of the great tree. The grove was so thick around that while there was an abundance of electric lights among the trees, their illumination did not fall upon us where we stood.

Peering cautiously through the vistas in various directions, we ascertained our location with respect to the wall of the building. Like all the structures which we had seen on Mars, it was composed of polished red metal.

"Where is the entrance?" inquired Mr. Edison, in a whisper.

"Come softly this way, and look out for the sentinel," replied Aina.

Gripping our disintegrators firmly, and screwing up our courage, with noiseless steps we followed the girl among the shadows of the trees.

We had one very great advantage. The Martians had evidently placed so much confidence in the electric network which surrounded the power house that they never dreamed of enemies being able to penetrate it—at least, without giving warning of their coming.

But the hole which we had blown in this network with the disintegrators had been made noiselessly, and Mr. Edison believed, since no enemies had appeared, that our operations had not been betrayed by any automatic signal to watchers inside the building.

Consequently, we had every reason to think that we now stood within the line of defense, in which they reposed the greatest confidence, without their having the least suspicion of our presence.

Aina assured us that on the occasion of her former visit to the power house there had been but two sentinels on guard at the entrance. At the inner end of a long passage leading to the interior, she said, there were two more. Besides these there were three or four Martian engineers watching the machinery in the interior of the building. A number of airships were supposed to be on guard around the structure, but possibly their vigilance had been relaxed, because not long ago the Martians had sent an expedition against Ceres which had been so successful that the power of that planet to make any attack upon Mars had, for the present, been destroyed.

Supposing us to have been annihilated in the recent battle among the clouds, they would have no fear or cause for vigilance on our account.

The entrance to the great structure was low—at least, when measured by the stature of the Martians. Evidently the intention was that only one person at a time should find room to pass through it.

Drawing cautiously near, we discerned the outlines of two gigantic forms, standing in the darkness, one on either side of the door. Colonel Smith whispered to me:

"If you will take the fellow on the right, I will attend to the other one."

Adjusting our aim as carefully as was possible in the gloom, Colonel Smith and I simultaneously discharged our disintegrators, sweeping them rapidly up and down in the manner which had become familiar to us when endeavoring to destroy one of the gigantic Martians with a single stroke. And so successful were we that the two sentinels disappeared as if they were ghosts of the night.

Instantly we all hurried forward and entered the door. Before us extended a long, straight passage, brightly illuminated by a number of electric candles. Its polished sides gleamed with blood-red reflections, and the gallery terminated, at a distance of two or three hundred feet, with an opening into a large chamber beyond, on the further side of which we could see part of a gigantic and complicated mass of machinery.

Making as little noise as possible, we pushed ahead along the passage, but when we had arrived within the distance of a dozen paces from the inner end, we stopped, and Colonel Smith, getting down upon his knees, crept forward, until he had reached the inner end of the passage. There he peered cautiously around the edge into the chamber, and, turning his head a moment later, beckoned us to come forward. We crept to his side, and, looking out into the vast apartment, could perceive no enemies.

What had become of the sentinels supposed to stand at the inner end the passage we could not imagine. At any rate, they were not at their posts.

The chamber was an immense square room at least a hundred feet in height and 400 feet on a side, and almost filling the wall opposite to us was an intricate display of machinery, wheels, levers, rods and polished plates. This we had no doubt was one end of the engine which opened and shut the great gates that could dam an ocean.

"There is no one in sight," said Colonel Smith.

"Then we must act quickly," said Mr. Edison.

"Where," he said, turning to Aina, "is the handle by turning which you saw the Martian close the gates?"

Aina looked about in bewilderment. The mechanism before us was so complicated that even an expert mechanic would have been excusable for finding himself unable to understand it. There were scores of knobs and handles, all glistening in the electric light, any one of which, so far as the uninstructed could tell, might have been the master key that controlled the whole complex apparatus.

"Quick," said Mr. Edison, "where is it?"

The girl in her confusion ran this way and that, gazing hopelessly upon the machinery, but evidently utterly unable to help us.

To remain here inactive was not merely to invite destruction for ourselves, but was sure to bring certain failure upon the purpose of the expedition. All of us began instantly to look about in search of the proper handle, seizing every crank and wheel in sight and striving to turn it.

"Stop that!" shouted Mr. Edison, "you may set the whole thing wrong. Don't touch anything until we have found the right lever."

But to find that seemed to most of us now utterly beyond the power of man.

It was at this critical moment that the wonderful depth and reach of Mr. Edison's mechanical genius displayed itself. He stepped back, ran his eyes quickly over the whole immense mass of wheels, handles, bolts, bars and levers, paused for an instant, as if making up his mind, then said decidedly, "There it is," and stepping quickly forward, selected a small wheel amid a dozen others, all furnished at the circumference with handles like those of a pilot's wheel, and giving it a quick wrench, turned it half-way around.

At this instant, a startling shout fell upon our ears. There was a thunderous clatter behind us, and, turning, we saw three gigantic Martians rushing forward.

VENGEANCE IS OURS "Sweep them! Sweep them!" shouted Colonel Smith, as he brought his disintegrator to bear. Mr. Phillips and I instantly followed his example, and thus we swept the Martians into eternity, while Mr. Edison coolly continued his manipulations of the wheel.

The effect of what he was doing became apparent in less than half a minute. A shiver ran through the mass of machinery and shook the entire building.

"Look! Look!" cried Sydney Phillips, who had stepped a little apart from the others.

We all ran to his side and found ourselves in front of a great window which opened through the side of the engine, giving a view of what lay in front of it. There, gleaming in the electric lights, we saw Syrtis Major, its waters washing high against the walls of the vast power house. Running directly out from the shore, there was an immense metallic gate at least 400 yards in length and rising three hundred feet above the present level of the water.

This great gate was slowly swinging upon an invisible hinge in such a manner that in a few minutes it would evidently stand across the current of the Syrtis Major at right angles.

Beyond was a second gate, which was moving in the same manner. Further on was a third gate, and then another, and another, as far as the eye could reach, evidently extending in an unbroken series completely across the great strait.

As the gates, with accelerated motion when the current caught them, clanged together, we beheld a spectacle that almost stopped the beating of our hearts.

The great Syrtis seemed to gather itself for a moment, and then it leaped upon the obstruction and buried its waters into one vast foaming geyser that seemed to shoot a thousand feet skyward.

But the metal gates withstood the shock, though buried from our sight in the seething white mass, and the baffled waters instantly swirled around in ten thousand gigantic eddies, rising to the level of our window and beginning to inundate the power house before we fairly comprehended our peril.

"We have done the work," said Mr. Edison, smiling grimly. "Now we had better get out of this before the flood bursts upon us."

The warning came none too soon. It was necessary to act upon it at once if we would save our lives. Even before we could reach the entrance to the long passage through which we had come into the great engine room, the water had risen half-way to our knees. Colonel Smith, catching Aina under his arm, led the way. The roar of the maddened torrent behind deafened us.

As we ran through the passage the water followed us, with a wicked swishing sound, and within five seconds it was above our knees; in ten seconds up to our waists.

The great danger now was that we should be swept from our feet, and once down in that torrent there would have been little chance of our ever getting our heads above its level. Supporting ourselves as best we could with the aid of the walls, we partly ran, and were partly swept along, until when we reached the outer end of the passage and emerged into the open air, the flood was swirling about our shoulders.

Here there was an opportunity to clutch some of the ornamental work surrounding the doorway, and thus we managed to stay our mad progress, and gradually to work out of the current until we found that the water, having now an abundance of room to spread, had fallen again as low as our knees.

But suddenly we heard the thunder of the banks tumbling behind us, and to the right and left, the savage growl of the released water as it sprang through the breaches.

To my dying day, I think, I shall not forget the sight of a great fluid column that burst through the dike at the edge of the grove of trees, and, by the tremendous impetus of its rush, seemed turned into a solid thing.

Like an enormous ram, it plowed the soil to a depth of twenty feet, uprooting acres of the immense trees like stubble turned over by the plowshare.

The uproar was so awful that for an instant the coolest of us lost our self-control. Yet we knew that we had not the fraction of a second to waste. The breaking of the banks had caused the water again rapidly to rise about us. In a little while it was once more as high as our waists.

In the excitement and confusion, deafened by the noise and blinded by the flying foam, we were in danger of becoming separated in the flood. We no longer knew certainly in what direction was the tree by whose aid we had ascended from the electrical ship. We pushed first one way and then another, staggering through the rushing waters in search of it. Finally we succeeded in locating it, and with all our strength hurried toward it.

Then there came a noise as if the globe of Mars had been split asunder, and another great head of water hurled itself down upon the soil before us, and, without taking time to spread, bored a vast cavity in the ground, and scooped out the whole of the grove before our eyes as easily as a gardener lifts a sod with his spade.

Our last hope was gone. For a moment the level of the water around us sank again, as it poured into the immense excavation where the grove had stood, but in an instant it was reinforced from all sides and began once more rapidly to rise.

We gave ourselves up for lost, and, indeed, there did not seem any possible hope of salvation.

Even in the extremity I saw Colonel Smith lifting the form of Aina, who had fainted, above the surface of the surging water, while Sydney Phillips stood by his side and aided him in supporting the unconscious girl.

"We stayed a little too long," was the only sound I heard from Mr. Edison.

The huge bulk of the power house partially protected us against the force of the current, and the water spun us around in great eddies. These swept us this way and that, but yet we managed to cling together, determined not to be separated in death if we could avoid it.

Suddenly a cry rang out directly above our heads:

"Jump for your lives, and be quick!"

At the same instant the ends of several ropes splashed into the water.

We glanced upward, and there, within three or four yards of our heads, hung the electrical ship, which we had left moored at the top of the tree.

Tom, the expert electrician from Mr. Edison's shop, who had remained in charge of the ship, had never once dreamed of such a thing as deserting us. The moment he saw the water bursting over the dam, and evidently flooding the building which we had entered, he cast off his moorings, as we subsequently learned, and hovered over the entrance to the power house, getting as low down as possible and keeping a sharp watch for us.

But most of the electric lights in the vicinity had been carried down by the first rush of water, and in the darkness he did not see us when we emerged from the entrance. It was only after the sweeping away of the grove of trees had allowed a flood of light to stream upon the scene from a cluster of electric lamps on a distant portion of the bank on the Syrtis that had not yet given way that he caught sight of us.

Immediately he began to shout to attract our attention, but in the awful uproar we could not hear him. Getting together all the ropes that he could lay his hands on, he steered the ship to a point directly over us, and then dropped down within a few yards of the boiling flood.

Now as he hung over our heads, and saw the water up to our very necks and still swiftly rising, he shouted again:

"Catch hold, for God's sake!"

The three men who were with him in the ship seconded his cries.

But by the time we had fairly grasped the ropes, so rapidly was the flood rising, we were already afloat. With the assistance of Tom and his men we were rapidly drawn up, and immediately Tom reversed the electric polarity, and the ship began to rise.

At that same instant, with a crash that shivered the air, the immense metallic power house gave way and was swept tumbling, like a hill torn loose from its base, over the very spot where a moment before we had stood. One second's hesitation on the part of Tom, and the electrical ship would have been battered into a shapeless wad of metal by the careening mass.

When we had attained a considerable height, so that we could see a great distance on either side, the spectacle became even more fearful than it was when we were close to the surface.

On all sides banks and dykes were going down; trees were being uprooted; buildings were tumbling, and the ocean was achieving that victory over the land which had long been its due, but which the ingenuity of the inhabitants of Mars had postponed for ages.

Far away we could see the front of the advancing wave crested with foam that sparkled in the electric lights, and as it swept on it changed the entire aspect of the planet—in front of it all life, behind it all death.

Eastward our view extended across the Syrtis Major toward the land of Libya and the region of Isidis. On that side also the dykes were giving way under the tremendous pressure, and the floods were rushing toward the sunrise, which had just begun to streak the eastern sky.

The continents that were being overwhelmed on the western side of the Syrtis were Meroc, Aeria, Arabia, Edom and Eden.

The water beneath us continually deepened. The current from the melting snows around the southern pole was at its strongest, and one could hardly have believed that any obstruction put in its path would have been able to arrest it and turn it into these two all-swallowing deluges, sweeping east and west. But, as we now perceived, the level of the land over a large part of its surface was hundreds of feet below the ocean, so that the latter, when once the barriers were broken, rushed into depressions that yawned to receive it.

The point where we had dealt our blow was far removed from the great capitol of Mars, around the Lake of the Sun, and we knew that we should have to wait for the floods to reach that point before the desired effect could be produced. By the nearest way, the water had at least 5,000 miles to travel. We estimated that its speed where we hung above it was as much as a hundred miles an hour. Even if that speed were maintained, more than two days and nights would be required for the floods to reach the Lake of the Sun.

But as the water rushed on it would break the banks of all the canals intersecting the country, and these, being also elevated above the surface, would add the impetus of their escaping waters to hasten the advance of the flood. We calculated, therefore, that about two days would suffice to place the planet at our mercy.

Halfway from the Syrtis Major to the Lake of the Sun another great connecting link between the Southern and Northern ocean basins, called on our maps of Mars the Indus, existed, and through this channel we knew that another great current must be setting from the south toward the north. The flood that we had started would reach and break the banks of the Indus within one day.

The flood traveling in the other direction, toward the east, would have considerably further to go before reaching the neighborhood of the Lake of the Sun. It, too, would involve hundreds of great canals as it advanced and would come plunging upon the Lake of the Sun and its surrounding forts and cities, probably about half a day later than the arrival of the deluge that traveled toward the west.

Now that we had let the awful destroyer loose we almost shrank from the thought of the consequences which we had produced. How many millions would perish as the result of our deed we could not even guess. Many of the victims, so far as we knew, might be entirely innocent of enmity toward us, or of the evil which had been done to our native planet. But this was a case in which the good—if they existed—must suffer with the bad on account of the wicked deeds of the latter.

I have already remarked that the continents of Mars were higher on their northern and southern borders where they faced the great oceans. These natural barriers bore to the main mass of land somewhat the relation of the edge of a shallow dish to its bottom. Their rise on the land side was too gradual to give them the appearance of hills, but on the side toward the sea they broke down in steep banks and cliffs several hundred feet in height. We guessed that it would be in the direction of these elevations that the inhabitants would flee, and those who had timely warning might thus be able to escape in case the flood did not—as it seemed possible it might in its first mad rush—overtop the highest elevations on Mars.

As day broke and the sun slowly rose upon the dreadful scene beneath us, we began to catch sight of some of the fleeing inhabitants. We had shifted the position of the fleet toward the south, and were now suspended above the southeastern corner of Aeria. Here a high bank of reddish rock confronted the sea, whose waters ran lashing and roaring along the bluffs to supply the rapid drought produced by the emptying of Syrtis Major. Along the shore there was a narrow line of land, hundreds of miles in length, but less than a quarter of a mile broad, which still rose slightly above the surface of the water, and this land of refuge was absolutely packed with the monstrous inhabitants of the planet who had fled hither on the first warning that the water was coming.

In some places it was so crowded that the later comers could not find standing ground on dry land, but were continually slipping back and falling into the water. It was an awful sight to look at them. It reminded me of pictures I had seen of the deluge in the days of Noah, when the waters had risen to the mountain tops, and men, women and children were fighting for a foothold upon the last dry spots the earth contained.

We were all moved by a desire to help our enemies, for we were overwhelmed with feelings of pity and remorse, but to aid them was now utterly beyond our power. The mighty floods were out, and the end was in the hands of God.

Fortunately, we had little time for these thoughts, because no sooner had the day begun to dawn around us than the airships of the Martians appeared. Evidently the people in them were dazed by the disaster and uncertain what to do. It is doubtful whether at first they comprehended the fact that we were the agents who had produced the cataclysm.

But as the morning advanced the airships came flocking in greater and greater numbers from every direction, many swooping down close to the flood in order to rescue those who were drowning. Hundreds gathered along the slip of land which was crowded as I have described, with refugees, while other hundreds rapidly assembled about us, evidently preparing for an attack.

We had learned in our previous contests with the airships of the Martians that our electrical ships had a great advantage over them, not merely in rapidity and facility of movement, but in the fact that our disintegrators could sweep in every direction, while it was only with much difficulty that the Martian airships could discharge their electrical strokes at an enemy poised directly above their heads.

Accordingly, orders were instantly flashed to all the squadrons to rise vertically to an elevation so great that the rarity of the atmosphere would prevent the airships from attaining the same level.

This maneuver was executed so quickly that the Martians were unable to deal us a blow before we were poised above them in such a position that they could not easily reach us. Still they did not mean to give up the conflict.

Presently we saw one of the largest of their ships maneuvering in a very peculiar manner, the purpose of which we did not at first comprehend. Its forward portion commenced slowly to rise, until it pointed upward like the nose of a fish approaching the surface of the water. The moment it was in this position, an electrical bolt was darted from its prow, and one of our ships received a shock which, although it did not prove fatal to the vessel itself, killed two or three men aboard it, disarranged its apparatus, and rendered it for the time being useless.

"Ah, that's their trick, is it?" said Mr. Edison. "We must look out for that. Whenever you see one of the airships beginning to stick its nose up after that fashion blaze away at it."

An order to this effect was transmitted throughout the squadron. At the same time several of the most powerful disintegrators were directed upon the ship which had executed the stratagem and, reduced to a wreck, it dropped, whirling like a broken kite until it fell into the flood beneath.

Still the Martian ships came flocking in ever greater numbers from all directions. They made desperate attempts to attain the level at which we hung above them. This was impossible, but many, getting an impetus by a swift run in the denser portion of the atmosphere beneath, succeeded in rising so high that they could discharge their electric artillery with considerable effect. Others, with more or less success, repeated the maneuver of the ship which had first attacked us, and thus the battle gradually became more general and more fierce, until, in the course of an hour or two, our squadron found itself engaged with probably a thousand airships, which blazed with incessant lightning strokes, and were able, all too frequently, to do us serious damage.

But on our part the battle was waged with a cool determination and a consciousness of insuperable advantage which boded ill for the enemy. Only three or four of our sixty electrical ships were seriously damaged, while the work of the disintegrators upon the crowded fleet that floated beneath us was terrible to look upon.

Our strokes fell thick and fast on all sides. It was like firing into a flock of birds that could not get away. Notwithstanding all their efforts they were practically at our mercy. Shattered into unrecognizable fragments, hundreds of the airships continually dropped from their great height to be swallowed up in the boiling waters.

Yet they were game to the last. They made every effort to get at us, and in their frenzy they seemed to discharge their bolts without much regard to whether friends or foes were injured. Our eyes were nearly blinded by the ceaseless glare beneath us, and the uproar was indescribable.

At length, after this fearful contest had lasted for at least three hours, it became evident that the strength of the enemy was rapidly weakening. Nearly the whole of their immense fleet of airships had been destroyed, or so far damaged that they were barely able to float. Just so long, however, as they showed signs of resistance we continued to pour our merciless fire upon them, and the signal to cease was not given until the airships, which had escaped serious damage began to flee in every direction.

"Thank God, the thing is over," said Mr. Edison. "We have got the victory at last, but how we shall make use of it is something that at present I do not see."

"But will they not renew the attack?" asked someone.

"I do not think they can," was the reply. "We have destroyed the very flower of their fleet."

"And better than that," said Colonel Smith, "we have destroyed their clan; we have made them afraid. Their discipline is gone."

But this was only the beginning of our victory. The floods below were achieving a still greater triumph, and now that we had conquered the airships we dropped within a few hundred feet of the surface of the water and then turned our faces westward in order to follow the advance of the deluge and see whether, as we hoped, it would overwhelm our enemies in the very center of their power.

In a little while we had overtaken the first wave, which was still devouring everything. We saw it bursting the banks of the canal, sweeping away forests of gigantic trees, and swallowing cities and villages, leaving nothing but a broad expanse of swirling and eddying waters, which, in consequence of the prevailing red hue of the vegetation and the soil, looked, as shuddering we gazed down upon it, like an ocean of blood flecked with foam and steaming with the escaping life of the planet from whose veins it gushed.

As we skirted the southern borders of the continent the same dreadful scenes which we had beheld on the coast of Aeria presented themselves. Crowds of refugees thronged the high borders of the land and struggled with one another for a foothold against the continually rising flood.

We saw, too, flitting in every direction, but rapidly fleeing before our approach, many airships, evidently crowded with Martians, but not armed either for offense or defense. These, of course, we did not disturb, for merciless as our proceedings seemed even to ourselves, we had no intention of making war upon the innocent, or upon those who had no means to resist. What we had done it had seemed to us necessary to do, but henceforth we were resolved to take no more lives if it could be avoided.

Thus, during the remainder of that day, all of the following night and all of the next day, we continued upon the heels of the advancing flood.

THE WOMAN FROM CERES   The second night we could perceive ahead of us the electric lights covering the land of Thaumasia, in the midst of which lay the Lake of the Sun. The flood would be upon it by daybreak, and, assuming that the demoralization produced by the news of the coming of the waters, which we were aware had hours before been flashed to the capitol of Mars, would prevent the Martians from effectively manning their forts, we thought it safe to hasten on with the flagship, and one or two others, in advance of the waters, and to hover over the Lake of the Sun, in the darkness, in order that we might watch the deluge perform its awful work in the morning.

Thaumasia, as we have before remarked, was a broad, oval-shaped land, about 1,800 miles across, having the Lake of the Sun exactly in its center. From this lake, which was four or five hundred miles in diameter, and circular in outline, many canals radiated, as straight as the spokes of a wheel, in every direction, and connected it with the surrounding seas.

Like all the other Martian continents, Thaumasia lay below the level of the sea, except toward the south, where it fronted the ocean.

Completely surrounding the lake was a great ring of cities constituting the capitol of Mars. Here the genius of the Martians had displayed itself to the full. The surrounding country was irrigated until it fairly bloomed with gigantic vegetation and flowers; the canals were carefully regulated with locks so that the supply of water was under complete control; the display of magnificent metallic buildings of all kinds and sizes produced a most dazzling effect, and the protection against enemies afforded by the innumerable fortifications surrounding the ringed city, and guarding the neighboring lands, seemed complete.

Suspended at a height of perhaps two miles from the surface, near the southern edge of the lake, we waited for the oncoming flood. With the dawn of day we began to perceive more clearly the effects which the news of the drowning of the planet had produced. It was evident that many of the inhabitants of the cities had already fled. Airships on which the fugitives hung as thick as swarms of bees were seen, elevated but a short distance above the ground, and making their way rapidly toward the south.

The Martians knew that their only hope of escape lay in reaching the high southern border of the land before the floods were upon them. But they must have known also that that narrow beach would not suffice to contain one in ten of those who sought refuge there. The density of the population around the Lake of the Sun seemed to us incredible. Again our hearts sank within us at the sight of the fearful destruction of life for which we were responsible. Yet we comforted ourselves with the reflection that it was unavoidable. As Colonel Smith put it:

"You couldn't trust these coyotes. The only thing to do was to drown them out. I am sorry for them, but I guess there will be as many left as will be good for us, anyhow."

We had not long to wait for the flood. As the dawn began to streak the east, we saw its awful crest moving out of the darkness, bursting across the canals and plowing its way into the direction of the crowded shores of the Lake of the Sun. The supply of water behind that great wave seemed inexhaustible. Five thousand miles it had traveled, and yet its power was as great as when it started from the Syrtis Major.

We caught sight of the oncoming water before it was visible to the Martians beneath us. But while it was yet many miles away, the roar of it reached them, and then arose a chorus of terrified cries, the effect of which, coming to our ears out of the half gloom of the morning, was most uncanny and horrible. Thousands upon thousands of the Martians still remained here to become victims of the deluge. Some, perhaps, had doubted the truth of the reports that the banks were down and the floods were out; others, for one reason or another had been unable to get away; others, like the inhabitants of Pompeii, had lingered too long, or had returned after beginning their flight to secure abandoned treasures, and now it was too late to get away.

With a roar that shook the planet the white wall rushed upon the great city beneath our feet, and in an instant it had been engulfed. On went the flood, swallowing up the Lake of the Sun itself, and in a little while, as far as our eyes could range, the land of Thaumasia had been turned into a raging sea.

We now turned our ships toward the southern border of the land, following the direction of the airships carrying the fugitives, a few of which were still navigating the atmosphere a mile beneath us. In their excitement and terror the Martians paid little attention to us, although, as the morning brightened, they must have been aware of our presence over their heads. But, apparently, they no longer thought of resistance; their only object was escape from the immediate and appalling danger.

When we had progressed to a point about halfway from the Lake of the Sun to the border of the sea, having dropped down within a few hundred feet of the surface, there suddenly appeared, in the midst of the raging waters, a sight so remarkable that at first I rubbed my eyes in astonishment, not crediting their report of what they beheld.

Standing on the apex of a sandy elevation, which still rose a few feet above the gathering flood, was a figure of a woman, as perfect in form and in classic beauty of feature as the Venus of Milo—a magnified human being not less than forty feet in height!

But for her swaying and the wild motions of her arms, we should have mistaken her for a marble statue.

Aina, who happened to be looking, instantly exclaimed:

"It is the woman from Ceres. She was taken prisoner by the Martians during their last invasion of that world, and since then has been a slave in the palace of the emperor."

Apparently her great stature had enabled her to escape, while her masters had been drowned. She had fled like the others, toward the south, but being finally surrounded by the rising waters, had taken refuge on the hillock of sand, where we saw her. This was fast giving way under the assault of the waves, and even while we watched the water rose to her knees.

"Drop lower," was the order of the electrical steersman of the flagship, and as quickly as possible we approached the place where the towering figure stood.

She had realized the hopelessness of her situation, and quickly ceased those appalling and despairing gestures, which had at first served to convince us that it was indeed a living being on whom we were looking.

There she stood, with a light, white garment thrown about her, erect, half-defiant, half-yielding to her fear, more graceful than any Greek statue, her arms outstretched, yet motionless, and her eyes upcast, as if praying to her God to protect her. Her hair, which shone like gold in the increasing light of day, streamed over her shoulders, and her great eyes were astare between terror and supplication. So wildly beautiful a sight not one of us had ever beheld.

For a moment sympathy was absorbed in admiration. Then:

"Save her! Save her!" was the cry that arose throughout the ship.

Ropes were instantly thrown out, and one or two men prepared to let themselves down in order better to aid her.

But when we were almost within reach, and so close that we could see the very expression of her eyes, which appeared to take no note of us, but to be fixed, with a faraway look upon something beyond human ken, suddenly the undermined bank on which she stood gave way, the blood-red flood swirled in from right to left, and then:

> The waters closed above her face
> With many a ring.

"If but for that woman's sake, I am sorry we drowned the planet," exclaimed Sydney Phillips. But a moment afterward I saw that he regretted what he had said, for Aina's eyes were fixed upon him. Perhaps, however, she did not understand his remark, and perhaps if she did it gave her no offence.

After this episode we pursued our way rapidly until we arrived at the shore of the Southern Ocean. There, as we had expected, was to be seen a narrow strip of land with the ocean on one side and the raging flood seeking to destroy it on the other. In some places it had already broken through, so that the ocean was flowing in to assist in the drowning of Thaumasia.

But some parts of the coast were evidently so elevated that no matter how high the flood might rise it would not completely cover them. Here the fugitives had gathered in dense throngs and above them hovered most of the airships, loaded down with others who were unable to find room upon the dry land.

On one of the loftiest and broadest of these elevations we noticed indications of military order in the alignment of the crowds and the shore all around was guarded by gigantic pickets, who mercilessly shoved back into the flood all the later comers, and thus prevented too great crowding upon the land. In the center of this elevation rose a palatial structure of red metal which Aina informed us was one of the residences of the Emperor, and we concluded that the monarch himself was now present there.

The absence of any signs of resistance on the part of the airships, and the complete drowning of all of the formidable fortifications on the surface of the planet, convinced us that all we had to do in order to complete our conquest was to get possession of the person of the chief ruler.

The fleet was, accordingly, concentrated, and we rapidly approached the great Martian palace. As we came down within a hundred feet of them and boldly made our way among their airships, which retreated at our approach, the Martians gazed at us with mingled fear and astonishment.

We were their conquerors and they knew it. We were coming to demand their surrender, and they evidently understood that also. As we approached the palace signals were made from it with brilliant colored banners which Aina informed us were intended as a token of truce.

"We shall have to go down and have a confab with them, I suppose," said Mr. Edison. "We can't kill them off now that they are helpless, but we must manage somehow to make them understand that unconditional surrender is their only chance."

"Let us take Aina with us," I suggested, "and since she can speak the language of the Martians we shall probably have no difficulty in arriving at an understanding."

Accordingly the flagship was carefully brought further down in front of the entrance to the palace, which had been kept clear by the Martian guards, and while the remainder of the squadron assembled within a few feet directly over our heads with the disintegrators turned upon the palace and the crowd below, Mr. Edison and myself, accompanied by Aina, stepped out upon the ground.

There was a forward movement in the immense crowd, but the guards sternly kept everybody back. A party of a dozen giants, preceded by one who seemed to be their commander, gorgeously attired in jewelled garments, advanced from the entrance of the palace to meet us. Aina addressed a few words to the leader, who replied sternly, and then, beckoning us to follow, retraced his steps into the palace.

Notwithstanding our confidence that all resistance had ceased, we did not deem it wise actually to venture into the lion's den without having taken every precaution against a surprise. Accordingly, before following the Martian into the palace, we had twenty of the electrical ships moored around it in such a position that they commanded not only the entrance but all of the principal windows, and then a party of forty picked men, each doubly armed with powerful disintegrators, were selected to attend us into the building. This party was placed under the command of Colonel Smith, and Sydney Phillips insisted on being a member of it.

In the meantime the Martian with his attendants who had first invited us to enter, finding that we did not follow him, had returned to the front of the palace. He saw the disposition that we had made of our forces, and instantly comprehended its significance, for his manner changed somewhat, and he seemed more desirous than before to conciliate us.

When he again beckoned us to enter, we unhesitatingly followed him, and passing through the magnificent entrance, found ourselves in a vast ante-chamber, adorned after the manner of the Martians in the most expensive manner. Thence we passed into a great circular apartment, with a dome painted in imitation of the sky, and so lofty that to our eyes it seemed like the firmament itself. Here we found ourselves approaching an elevated throne situated in the center of the apartment, while long rows of brilliantly armored guards flanked us on either side, and grouped around the throne, some standing and others reclining upon the flights of steps which appeared to be of solid gold, was an array of Martian women, beautifully and becomingly attired, all of whom greatly astonished us by the singular charm of their faces and bearing, so different from the aspect of most of the Martians whom we had encountered.

Despite their stature—for these women averaged twelve or thirteen feet in height—the beauty of their complexions—of a dark olive tint—was no less brilliant than that of the women of Italy or Spain.

At the top of the steps on a magnificent golden throne, sat the Emperor himself. There are some busts of Caracalla which I have seen that are almost as ugly as the face of the Martian ruler. He was of gigantic stature, larger than the majority of his subjects, and as near as I could judge must have been between fifteen and sixteen feet in height.

As I looked at him I understood a remark which had been made by Aina to the effect that the Martians were not all alike, and that the peculiarities of their minds were imprinted on their faces and expressed in their forms in a very wonderful, and sometimes terrible manner.

I had also learned from her that Mars was under a military government, and that the military class had absolute control of the planet. I was somewhat startled, then, in looking at the head and center of the great military system of Mars, to find in his appearance a striking conformation of the speculations of our terrestrial phrenologists. His broad, misshapen head bulged in those parts where they had placed the so-called organs of combativeness, destructiveness, etc.

Plainly, this was an effect of his training and education. His very brain had become a military engine; and the aspect of his face, the pitiless lines of his mouth and chin, the evil glare of his eyes, the attitude and carriage of his muscular body, all tended to complete the warlike ensemble.

He was magnificently dressed in some vesture that had the luster of a polished plate of gold, and the suppleness of velvet. As we approached he fixed his immense, deep-set eyes sternly upon our faces.

The contrast between his truly terrible countenance and the Eve-like features of the women which surrounded his throne was as great as if Satan after his fall had here re-enthroned himself in the midst of angels.

Mr. Edison, Colonel Smith, Sydney Phillips, Aina and myself advanced at the head of the procession, our guard following in close order behind us. It had been evident from the moment that we entered the palace that Aina was regarded with aversion by all of the Martians. Even the women about the throne gazed scowlingly at her as we drew near. Apparently, the bitterness of feeling which had led to the massacre of all of her race had not yet vanished. And, indeed, since the fact that she remained alive could have been known only to the Martian who had abducted her and to his immediate companions, her reappearance with us must have been a great surprise to all those who now looked upon her.

It was clear to me that the feeling aroused by her appearance was every moment becoming more intense. Still, the thought of a violent outbreak did not occur to me, because our recent triumph had seemed so complete that I believed the Martians would be awed by our presence, and would not undertake actually to injure the girl.

I think we all had the same impression, but as the event proved, we were mistaken.

Suddenly one of the gigantic guards, as if actuated by a fit of ungovernable hatred, lifted his foot and kicked Aina. With a loud shriek she fell to the floor.

The blow was so unexpected that for a second we all stood riveted to the spot. Then I saw Colonel Smith's face turn livid, and at the same instant heard the whirr of his disintegrator, while Sydney Phillips, forgetting the deadly instrument he carried in his hand, sprung madly toward the brute who had kicked Aina, as if he intended to throttle him, colossus that he was.

But Colonel Smith's aim, though instantaneously taken, as he had been accustomed to shoot on the plains, was true, and Phillips, plunging madly forward, seemed wreathed in a faint blue mist—all that the disintegrator had left of the gigantic Martian.

Who could adequately describe the scene that followed?

I remember that the Martian emperor sprang to his feet, looking tenfold more terrible than before. I remember that there instantly burst from the line of guards on either side crinkling beams of death-fire that seemed to sear the eyeballs. I saw a half a dozen of our men fall in heaps of ashes, and even at that terrible moment I had time to wonder that a single one of us remained alive.

Rather by instinct than in consequence of any order given, we formed ourselves in a hollow square, with Aina lying apparently lifeless in the center, and then with gritted teeth we did our work.

The lines of guards melted before the disintegrators like rows of snow men before a licking flame.

The discharge of the lightning engines in the hands of the Martians in that confined space made an uproar so tremendous that it seemed to pass the bounds of human sense.

More of our men fell before their awful fire, and for the second time since our arrival on this deadful planet of war our annihilation seemed inevitable.

But in a moment the whole scene changed. Suddenly there was a discharge into the room which I knew came from one of the disintegrators of the electrical ships. It swept through the crowded throng like a destroying blast. Instantly from another side, swished a second discharge, no less destructive, and this was quickly followed by a third.

Our ships were firing through the windows.

Almost at the same moment I saw the flagship, which had been moored in the air close to the entrance and floating only three or four feet above the ground, pushing its way through the gigantic doorway from the anteroom, with its great disintegrators pointed upon the crowd like the muzzles of a cruiser's guns.

And now the Martians saw that the contest was hopeless for them, and their mad struggle to get out of the range of the disintegrators and to escape from the death chamber was more appalling to look upon than anything that had yet occurred.

It was a panic of giants. They trod one another underfoot; they yelled and screamed in their terror; they tore each other with their claw-like fingers. They no longer thought of resistance. The battle spirit had been blown out of them by a breath of terror that shivered their marrow.

Still the pitiless disintegrators played upon them until Mr. Edison, making himself heard, now that the thunder of their engines had ceased to reverberate through the chamber, commanded that our fire should cease.

In the meantime the armed Martians outside the palace, hearing the uproar within, seeing our men pouring their fire through the windows, and supposing that we were guilty at once of treachery and assassination, had attempted an attack upon the electrical ships stationed round the building. But fortunately they had none of their larger engines at hand, and with their hand arms alone they had not been able to stand up against the disintegrators. They were blown away before the withering fire of the ships by the hundreds until, fleeing from destruction, they rushed madly, driving their unarmed companions before them into the seething waters of the flood close at hand.

THE FEARFUL OATHS OF COLONEL SMITH   Through all this terrible contest the emperor of the Martians had remained standing upon his throne, gazing at the awful spectacle, and not moving from the spot. Neither he nor the frightened women gathered upon the steps of the throne had been injured by the disintegrators. Their immunity was due to the fact that the position and elevation of the throne were such that it was not within the range of fire of the electrical ships which had poured their vibratory discharges through the windows, and we inside had only directed our fire toward the warriors who had attacked us.

Now that the struggle was over we turned our attention to Aina. Fortunately the girl had not been seriously injured and she was quickly restored to consciousness. Had she been killed, we would have been practically helpless in attempting further negotiations, because the knowledge which we had acquired of the language of the Martians from the prisoner captured on the golden asteroid, was not sufficient to meet the requirements of the occasion.

When the Martian monarch saw that we ceased the work of death, he sank upon his throne. There he remained, leaning his chin upon his two hands and staring straight before him like that terrible doomed creature who fascinates the eyes of every beholder standing in the Sistine Chapel and gazing at Michael Angelo's dreadful painting of "The Last Judgement."

This wicked Martian also felt that he was in the grasp of pitiless and irresistible fate, and that a punishment too well deserved, and from which there was no possible escape, now confronted him.

There he remained in a hopelessness which almost compelled our sympathy, until Aina had so far recovered that she was once more able to act as our interpreter. Then we made short work of the negotiations. Speaking through Aina, the commander said:

"You know who we are. We have come from the earth, which, by your command, was laid waste. Our commission was not revenge, but self-protection. What we have done has been accomplished with that in view. You have just witnessed an example of our power, the exercise of which was not dictated by our wish, but compelled by the attack wantonly made upon a helpless member of our own race under our protection.

"We have laid waste your planet, but it is simply a just retribution for what you did with ours. We are prepared to complete the destruction, leaving not a living being in this world of yours, or to grant you peace, at your choice. Our condition of peace is simply this: All resistance must cease absolutely."

"Quite right," broke in Colonel Smith; "let the scorpion pull out his sting or we shall do it for him."

"Nothing that we could do now," continued the commander, "would in my opinion save you from ultimate destruction. The forces of nature which we have been compelled to let loose upon you will complete their own victory. But we do not wish, unnecessarily, to stain our hands further with your blood. We shall leave you in possession of your lives. Preserve them if you can. But, in case the flood recedes before you have all perished from starvation, remember that you here take an oath, solemnly binding yourself and your descendants forever never again to make war upon the earth."

"That's really the best we can do," said Mr. Edison, turning to us. "We can't possibly murder these people in cold blood. The probability is that the flood has hopelessly ruined all their engines of war. I do not believe that there is one chance in ten that the waters will drain off in time to enable them to get at their stores of provisions before they have perished from starvation."

"It is my opinion," said Lord Kelvin, who had joined us (his pair of disintegrators hanging by his side, attached to a strap running over the back of his neck, very much as a farmer sometimes carries his big mittens), "it is my opinion that the flood will recede more rapidly than you think, and that the majority of these people will survive. But I quite agree with your merciful view of the matter. We must be guilty of no wanton destruction. Probably more than nine-tenths of the inhabitants of Mars have perished in the deluge. Even if all the others survived ages would elapse before they could regain the power to injure us."

I need not describe in detail how our propositions were received by the Martian monarch. He knew, and his advisors, some of whom he had called in consultation, also knew, that everything was in our hands to do as we pleased. They readily agreed, therefore, that they would make no more resistance and that we and our electrical ships should be undisturbed while we remained upon Mars. The monarch took the oath prescribed after the manner of his race; thus the business was completed. But through it all there had been a shadow of a sneer on the emperor's face which I did not like. But I said nothing.

And now we began to think of our return home, and of the pleasure we should have in recounting our adventures to our friends on the earth, who undoubtedly were eagerly awaiting news from us. We knew that they had been watching Mars with powerful telescopes, and we were also eager to learn how much they had seen and how much they had been able to guess of our proceedings.

But a day or two at least would be required to overhaul the electrical ships and examine the state of our provisions. Those which we had brought from the earth, it will be remembered, had been spoiled and we had been compelled to replace them from the compressed provisions found in the Martians' storehouse. This compressed food had proved not only exceedingly agreeable to the taste, but very nourishing, and all of us had grown extremely fond of it. A new supply, however, would be needed in order to carry us back to the earth. At least sixty days would be required for the homeward journey, because we could hardly expect to start from Mars with the same initial velocity which we had been able to generate on leaving home.

In considering the matter of provisioning the fleet it finally became necessary to take an account of our losses. This was a thing that we had all shrunk from, because they had seemed to us almost too terrible to be borne. But now the facts had to be faced. Out of the one hundred ships, carrying something more than two thousand souls, with which we had quitted the earth, there remained only fifty-five ships and 1085 men! All the others had been lost in our terrible encounters with the Martians, and particularly in our first disastrous battle beneath the clouds.

Among the lost were many men whose names were famous upon the earth, and whose deaths would be widely deplored when the news of it was received upon their native planet. Fortunately this number did not include any of those whom I have had occasion to mention in the course of this narrative. The venerable Lord Kelvin, who, notwithstanding his age, and his pacific disposition, proper to a man of science, had behaved with the courage and coolness of a veteran in every crisis; Monsieur Moissan, the eminent chemist; Professor Sylvanus P. Thompson, and the Heidelberg professor, to whom we all felt under special obligations because he had opened to our comprehension the charming lips of Aina—all these had survived, and were about to return with us to the earth.

It seemed to some of us almost heartless to deprive the Martians who still remained alive of any of the provisions which they themselves would require to tide them over the long period which must elapse before the recession of the flood should enable them to discover the sites of their ruined homes, and to find the means of sustenance. But necessity was now our only law. We learned from Aina that there must be stores of provisions in the neighborhood of the palace, because it was the custom of the Martians to lay up such stores during the harvest time in each Martian year in order to provide against the contingency of an extraordinary drought.

It was not with very good grace that the Martian emperor acceded to our demands that one of the storehouses should be opened, but resistance was useless and of course we had our way.

The supplies of water which we brought from the earth, owing to a peculiar process invented by Monsieur Moissan, had been kept in exceedingly good condition, but they were now running low and it became necessary to replenish them also. This was easily done from the Southern Ocean, for on Mars, since the levelling of the continental elevations, brought about many years ago, there is comparatively little salinity in the sea waters.

While these preparations were going on Lord Kelvin and the other men of science entered with the utmost eagerness upon those studies, the prosecution of which had been the principal inducement leading them to embark on the expedition. But, almost all of the face of the planet being covered with the flood, there was comparatively little that they could do. Much, however, could be learned with the aid of Aina from the Martians, now crowded on the land above the palace.

The results of these discoveries will in due time appear, fully elaborated in learned and authoritative treatises prepared by these servants themselves. I shall only call attention to one, which seemed to me very remarkable. I have already said that there were astonishing differences in the personal appearance of the Martians evidently arising from differences of character and education, which had impressed themselves in the physical aspect of the individuals. We now learned that these differences were more completely the result of education than we had at first supposed.

Looking about among the Martians by whom we were surrounded, it soon became easy for us to tell who were the soldiers and who were the civilians, simply by the appearance of their bodies, and particularly of their heads. All members of the military class resembled, to a greater or less extent, the monarch himself, in that those parts of their skulls which our phrenologists had designated as the bumps of destructiveness, combativeness and so on were enormously and disproportionately developed.

And all this, we were assured, was completely under the control of the Martians themselves. They had learned, or invented, methods by which the brain itself could be manipulated, so to speak, and any desired portions of it could be especially developed, while other parts of it were left to their normal growth. The consequence was that in the Martian schools and colleges there was no teaching in our sense of the word. It was all brain culture.

A Martian youth selected to be a soldier had his fighting faculties especially developed, together with those parts of the brain which impart courage and steadiness of nerve. He who was intended for scientific investigation had his brain developed into a mathematical machine, or an instrument of observation. Poets and literary men had their heads bulging with the imaginative faculties. The heads of the inventors were developed into a still different shape.

"And so," said Aina, translating for us the words of a professor in the Imperial University of Mars, from whom we derived the greater part of our information on this subject, "the Martian boys do not study a subject; they do not have to learn it, but, when their brains have been sufficiently developed in the proper direction, they comprehend it instantly, by a kind of divine instinct."

But among the women of Mars, we saw none of these curious, and to our eyes, monstrous differences of development. While the men received, in addition to their special education, a broad general culture also, with the women there was no special education. It was all general in its character, yet thorough enough in that way. The consequence was that only female brains upon Mars were entirely well balanced. This was the reason why we invariably found the Martian women to be remarkably charming creatures, with none of those physical exaggerations and uncouth developments which disfigured their masculine companions.

All the books of the Martians, we ascertained, were books of history and of poetry. For scientific treatises they had no need, because, as I have explained, when the brains of those intended for scientific pursuits had been developed in the proper way the knowledge of nature's laws came to them without effort, as a spring bubbles from the rocks.

One word of explanation may be needed concerning the failure of the Martians, with all their marvelous powers, to invent electrical ships like those of Mr. Edison's and engines of destruction comparable with our disintegrators. This failure was simply due to the fact that on Mars there did not exist the peculiar metals by the combination of which Mr. Edison had been able to effect his wonders. The theory involved by our inventions was perfectly understood by them and had they possessed the means, doubtless they would have been able to carry it into practice even more effectively than we had done.

After two or three days all the preparations having been completed the signal was given for our departure. The men of science were still unwilling to leave this strange world, but Mr. Edison decided we could linger no longer.

At the moment of starting a most tragic event occurred. Our fleet was assembled around the palace, and the signal was given to rise slowly to a considerable height before imparting a great velocity to the electrical ships. As we slowly rose we saw the immense crowd of giants beneath us, with upturned faces, watching our departure. The Martian monarch and all his suite had come out upon the terrace of the palace to look at us. At a moment when he probably supposed himself to be unwatched he shook his fist at the retreating fleet. My eyes and those of several others in the flagship chanced to be fixed upon him. Just as he made the gesture one of the women of his suite, in her eagerness to watch us, apparently lost her balance and stumbled against him. Without a moment's hesitation, with a tremendous blow, he felled her like an ox at his feet.

A fearful oath broke from the lips of Colonel Smith, who was one of those looking on. It chanced that he stood near the principal disintegrator of the flagship. Before anybody could interfere he had sighted and discharged it. The entire force of the terrible engine, almost capable of destroying a fort, fell upon the Martian emperor and not merely blew him into a cloud of atoms but opened a great cavity in the ground on the spot where he had stood.

A shout arose from the Martians, but they were too much astounded at what had occurred to make any hostile demonstrations, and, anyhow, they knew well that they were completely at our mercy.

Mr. Edison was on the point of rebuking Colonel Smith for what he had done, but Aina interposed.

"I am glad it was done," said she "for now only can you be safe. That monster was more directly responsible than any other inhabitant of Mars for all the wickedness of which they have been guilty.

"The expedition against the earth was inspired solely by him. There is a tradition among the Martians—which my people, however, could never credit—that he possessed a kind of immortality. They declared that it was he who led the former expedition against the earth when my ancestors were brought away prisoners from their happy home, and that it was his image which they had set up in stone in the midst of the Land of Sand. He prolonged his existence, according to this legend, by drinking the waters of a wonderful fountain, the secret of whose precise location was known to him alone but which was situated at that point where in your maps of Mars the name of the Fons Juventae occurs. He was personified wickedness, that I know; and he never would have kept his oath if power had returned to him again to injure the earth. In destroying him, you have made your victory secure."

THE GREAT OVATION   When at length we once more saw our native planet, with its well-remembered features of land and sea, rolling beneath our eyes, the feeling of joy that came over us transcended all powers of expression.

In order that all the nations which had united in sending out the expedition should have visual evidence of its triumphal return, it was decided to make the entire circuit of the earth before seeking our starting point and disembarking. Brief accounts in all known languages, telling the story of what we had done was accordingly prepared, and then we dropped down through the air until again we saw the well-loved blue dome over our heads, and found ourselves suspended directly above the white-topped cone of Fujiyama, the sacred mountain of Japan. Shifting our position toward the northeast, we hung above the city of Tokyo and dropped down into the crowds which had assembled to watch us, the prepared accounts of our journey, which, the moment they had been read and comprehended, led to such an outburst of rejoicing as it would be quite impossible to describe.

One of the ships containing the Japanese members of the expedition, dropped to the ground, and we left them in the midst of their rejoicing countrymen. Before we started—and we remained but a short time suspended above the Japanese capitol—millions had assembled to greet us with their cheers.

We now repeated what we had done during our first examination of the surface of Mars. We simply remained suspended in the atmosphere, allowing the earth to turn beneath us. As Japan receded in the distance we found China beginning to appear. Shifting our position a little toward the south, we again came to rest over the city of Pekin, where once more we parted with some of our companions, and where the outburst of universal rejoicing was repeated.

From Asia, crossing the Caspian Sea, we passed over Russia, visiting in turn Moscow and St. Petersburg.

Still the great globe rolled steadily beneath, and still we kept the sun with us. Now Germany appeared, and now Italy, and then France, and England, as we shifted our position, first north then south, in order to give all the world the opportunity to see that its warriors had returned victorious from its far conquest. And in each country as it passed beneath our feet, we left some of the comrades who had shared our perils and our adventures.

At length the Atlantic had rolled away under us, and we saw the spires of the new New York.

The news of our coming had been flashed ahead from Europe and our countrymen were prepared to welcome us. We had originally started, it will be remembered, at midnight, and now again as we approached the new capitol of the world the curtain of night was just beginning to be drawn over it. But our signal lights were ablaze, and through these they were aware of our approach.

Again the air was filled with bursting rockets and shaken with the roar of cannon, and with volleying cheers, poured from millions of throats, as we came to rest directly above the city.

Three days after the landing of the fleet, and when the first enthusiasm of our reception had a little passed, I received a beautifully engraved card inviting me to be present in Trinity Church at the wedding of Aina and Sydney Phillips.

When I arrived at the church, which had been splendidly decorated, I found there Mr. Edison, Lord Kelvin, and all the other members of the crew of the flagship, and, considerably to my surprise, Colonel Smith, appropriately attired, and with a grace for the possession of which I had not given him credit, gave away the beautiful bride.

But Alonzo Jefferson Smith was a man and a soldier, every inch of him.

"I asked her for myself," he whispered to me after the ceremony, swallowing a great lump in his throat, "but she has had the desire of her heart. I am going back to the plains. I can get a command again, and I still know how to fight."

And thus was united, for all future time, the first stem of the Aryan race, which had been long lost, but not destroyed, with the latest offspring of that great family, and the link which had served to bring them together was the faraway planet of Mars.

the martians

by OLAF STAPLEDON

1. THE FIRST MARTIAN INVASION Upon the foot-hills of the new and titanic mountains that were once the Hindu Kush, were many holiday centres, whence the young men and women of Asia were wont to seek Alpine dangers and hardships for their souls' refreshment. It was in this district, and shortly after a summer dawn, that the Martians were first seen by men. Early walkers noticed that the sky had an unaccountably greenish tinge, and that the climbing sun, though free from cloud, was wan. Observers were presently surprised to see the green concentrate itself into a thousand tiny cloudlets, with clear blue between. Field-glasses revealed within each fleck of green some faint hint of a ruddy nucleus, and shifting strands of an infra-red colour, which would have been invisible to the earlier human race. These extraordinary specks of cloud were all of about the same size, the largest of them appearing smaller than the moon's disk; but in form they varied greatly, and were seen to be changing their shapes more rapidly than the natural cirrus which they slightly resembled. In fact, though there was much that was cloudlike in their form and motion, there was also something definite about them, both in their features and behaviour, which suggested life. Indeed they were strongly reminiscent of primitive amœboid organisms seen through a microscope.

The whole sky was strewn with them, here and there in concentrations of unbroken green, elsewhere more sparsely. And they were observed to be moving. A general drift of the whole celestial population was setting

First published in 1930 by Methuen & Co., Ltd., London, England. Reprinted by permission of the publishers and Mrs. Olaf Stapledon.

toward one of the snowy peaks that dominated the landscape. Presently the foremost individuals reached the mountain's crest, and were seen to be creeping down the rock-face with a very slow amœboid action.

Meanwhile a couple of aeroplanes, electrically driven, had climbed the sky to investigate the strange phenomenon at close quarters. They passed among the drifting cloudlets, and actually through many of them, without hindrance, and almost without being obscured from view.

On the mountain a vast swarm of the cloudlets was collecting, and creeping down the precipices and snow-fields into a high glacier valley. At a certain point, where the glacier dropped steeply to a lower level, the advance guard slowed down and stopped, while hosts of their fellows continued to pack in on them from behind. In half an hour the whole sky was once more clear, save for normal clouds; but upon the glacier lay what might almost have been an exceptionally dark solid-looking thunder-cloud, save for its green tinge and seething motion. For some minutes this strange object was seen to concentrate itself into a somewhat smaller bulk and become darker. Then it moved forward again, and passed over the cliffy end of the glacier into the pine-clad valley. An intervening ridge now hid it from its first observers.

Lower down the valley there was a village. Many of the inhabitants, when they saw the mysterious dense fume advancing upon them, took to their mechanical vehicles and fled; but some waited out of curiosity. They were swallowed up in a murky olive-brown fog, shot here and there with queer shimmering streaks of a ruddier tint. Presently there was complete darkness. Artificial lights were blotted out almost at arm's length. Breathing became difficult. Throats and lungs were irritated. Every one was seized with a violent attack of sneezing and coughing. The cloud streamed through the village, and seemed to exercise irregular pressures upon objects, not always in the general direction of movement but sometimes in the opposite direction, as though it were getting a purchase upon human bodies and walls, and actually elbowing its way along. Within a few minutes the fog lightened; and presently it left the village behind it, save for a few strands and whiffs of its smoke-like substance, which had become entangled in side-streets and isolated. Very soon, however, these seemed to get themselves clear and hurry to overtake the main body.

When the gasping villagers had somewhat recovered, they sent a radio message to the little town lower down the valley, urging temporary evacuation. The message was not broadcast, but transmitted on a slender beam of rays. It so happened that the beam had to be directed through the noxious matter itself. While the message was being given, the cloud's progress ceased, and its outlines became vague and ragged. Fragments of it actually drifted away on the winds and dissipated themselves. Almost as soon as the message was completed, the cloud began to define itself again, and lay for a quarter of an hour at rest. A dozen bold young men from the town now approached the dark mass out of curiosity. No sooner did they come face to face with it, round a bend in the valley, than the cloud rapidly contracted, till it was no bigger than a house. Looking now something between a dense, opaque fume and an actual jelly, it lay still until the party had ventured within a few yards. Evidently their courage failed, for they were seen to turn. But before they had retreated three paces, a long proboscis shot out of the main mass with the speed of a chameleon's tongue, and enveloped them. Slowly it withdrew; but the young men had been gathered in with it. The cloud, or jelly, churned itself violently for some seconds, then ejected the bodies in a single chewed lump.

The murderous thing now elbowed itself along the road toward the town, leaned against the first house, crushed it, and proceeded to wander hither and thither, pushing everything down before it, as though it were a lava-stream. The inhabitants took to their heels, but several were licked up and slaughtered.

Powerful beam radiation was now poured into the cloud from all the neighbouring installations. Its destructive activity slackened, and once more it began to disintegrate and expand. Presently it streamed upwards as a huge column of smoke; and, at a great altitude, it dissipated itself again into a swarm of the original green cloudlets, noticeably reduced in numbers. These again faded into a uniform greenish tinge, which gradually vanished.

Thus ended the first invasion of the Earth from Mars.

2. LIFE ON MARS   Our concern is with humanity, and with the Martians only in relation to men. But in order to understand the tragic intercourse of the two planets, it is necessary to glance at conditions on Mars, and conceive something of those fantastically different yet fundamentally similar beings, who were now seeking to possess man's home.

To describe the biology, psychology and history of a whole world in a few pages is as difficult as it would be to give the Martians themselves in the same compass a true idea of man. Encyclopædias, libraries, would be needed in either case. Yet, somehow, I must contrive to suggest the alien sufferings and delights, and the many aeons of struggle, which went to the making of these strange nonhuman intelligences, in some ways so inferior yet in others definitely superior to the human species which they encountered.

Mars was a world whose mass was about one-tenth that of the earth. Gravity therefore had played a less tyrannical part in Martian than in terrestrial history. The weakness of Martian gravity combined with the paucity of the planet's air envelope to make the general atmospheric pressure far lighter than on earth. Oxygen was far less plentiful. Water also was comparatively rare. There were no oceans or seas, but only shallow lakes and marshes, many of which dried up in summer. The climate of the planet was in general very dry, and yet very cold. Being without cloud, it was perennially bright with the feeble rays of a distant sun.

Earlier in the history of Mars, when there were more air, more water, and a higher temperature from internal heat, life had appeared in the coastal waters of the seas, and evolution had proceeded in much the same manner as on earth. Primitive life was differentiated into the fundamental animal and vegetable types. Multicellular structures appeared, and specialized themselves in diverse manners to suit diverse environments. A great variety of plant forms clothed the lands, often with forests of gigantic and slender-stemmed plumes. Mollusc-like and insect-like animals crept or swam, or shot themselves hither and thither in fantastic jumps. Huge spidery creatures of a type not wholly unlike crustaceans, or gigantic grasshoppers, bounded after their prey, and developed a versatility and cunning which enabled them to dominate the planet almost as, at a much later date, early man was to dominate the terrestrial wild.

But meanwhile a rapid loss of atmosphere, and especially of water-vapor, was changing Martian conditions beyond the limits of adaptability of this early fauna and flora. At the same time a very different kind of vital organization was beginning to profit by the change. On Mars, as on the Earth, life had arisen from one of many "subvital" forms. The new type of life on Mars evolved from another of these subvital kinds of molecular organization, one which had hitherto failed to evolve at all, and had played an insignificant part, save occasionally as a rare virus in the respiratory organs of animals. These fundamental subvital units of organization were ultra-microscopic, and indeed far smaller than the terrestrial bacteria, or even the terrestrial viruses. They originally occurred in the marshy ponds, which dried up every spring, and became depressions of baked mud and dust. Certain of their species, borne into the air upon dust particles, developed an extremely dry habit of life. They maintained themselves by absorbing chemicals from the wind-borne dust, and a very slight amount of moisture from the air. Also they absorbed sunlight by a photo-synthesis almost identical with that of the plants.

To this extent they were similar to the other living things, but they had also certain capacities which the other stock had lost at the very outset of its evolutionary career. Terrestrial organisms, and Martian organisms of the terrestrial type, maintained themselves as vital unities by means of nervous systems, or other forms of material contact between parts. In the most developed forms, an immensely complicated neural "telephone" system connected every part of the body with a vast central exchange, the

brain. Thus on the earth a single organism was without exception a continuous system of matter, which maintained a certain constancy of form.
But from the distinctively Martian subvital unit there evolved at length a
very different kind of complex organism, in which material contact of
parts was not necessary either to coordination of behaviour or unity of consciousness. These ends were achieved upon a very different physical basis.
The ultra-microscopic subvital members were sensitive to all kinds of
etherial vibrations, directly sensitive, in a manner impossible to terrestrial
life; and they could also initiate vibrations. Upon this basis Martian life
developed at length the capacity of maintaining vital organization as a
single conscious individual without continuity of living matter. Thus the
typical Martian organism was a cloudlet, a group of free-moving members
dominated by a "group-mind." But in one species individuality came to
inhere, for certain purposes, not in distinct cloudlets only, but in a great
fluid system of cloudlets. Such was the single-minded Martian host which
invaded the Earth.

The Martian organism depended, so to speak, not on "telephone"
wires, but on an immense crowd of mobile "wireless stations," transmitting and receiving different wave-lengths according to their function.
The radiation of a single unit was of course very feeble; but a great system
of units could maintain contact with its wandering parts over a considerable distance.

One other important characteristic distinguished the dominant form of
life on Mars. Just as a cell, in the terrestrial form of life, has often the
power of altering its shape (whence the whole mechanism of muscular
activity), so in the Martian form the free-floating ultra-microscopic unit
might be specialized for generating around itself a magnetic field, and so
either repelling or attracting its neighbours. Thus a system of materially
disconnected units had a certain cohesion. Its consistency was something
between a smoke-cloud and a very tenuous jelly. It had a definite, though
ever-changing contour and resistant surface. By massed mutual repulsions
of its constituent units it could exercise pressure on surrounding objects;
and in its most concentrated form the Martian cloud-jelly could bring to
bear immense forces which could also be controlled for very delicate
manipulation. Magnetic forces were also responsible for the mollusc-like
motion of the cloud as a whole over the ground, and again for the transport
of lifeless material and living units from region to region within the cloud.

The magnetic field of repulsion and attraction generated by a subvital
unit was much more restricted than its field of "wireless" communication.
Similarly with organized systems of units. Thus each of the cloudlets
which the Second Men saw in their sky was an independent motor unit;
but also it was in a kind of "telepathic" communication with all its fellows. Indeed in every public enterprise, such as the terrestrial campaigns,

almost perfect unity of consciousness was maintained within the limits of a huge field of radiation. Yet only when the whole population concentrated itself into a small and relatively dense cloud-jelly, did it become a single magnetic motor unit. The Martians, it should be noted, had three possible forms, or formations, namely: first, an "open order" of independent and very tenuous cloudlets in "telepathic" communication, and often in strict unity as a group mind; second, a more concentrated and less vulnerable corporate cloud; and third, an extremely concentrated and formidable cloud-jelly.

Save for these very remarkable characteristics, there was no really fundamental difference between the distinctively Martian and the distinctively terrestrial forms of life. The chemical basis of the former was somewhat more complicated than that of the latter; and selenium played a part in it, to which nothing corresponded in terrestrial life. The Martian organism, moreover, was unique in that it fulfilled within itself the functions of both animal and vegetable. But, save for these peculiarities, the two types of life were biochemically much the same. Both needed material from the ground, both needed sunlight. Each lived in the chemical changes occurring in its own "flesh." Each, of course, tended to maintain itself as an organic unity. There was a certain difference, indeed, in respect of reproduction; for the Martian subvital units retained the power of growth and sub-division. Thus the birth of a Martian cloud arose from the sub-division of myriads of units within the parent cloud, followed by their ejection as a new individual. And, as the units were highly specialized for different functions, representatives of many types had to pass into the new cloud.

In the earliest stages of evolution on Mars the units had become independent of each other as soon as they parted in reproduction. But later the hitherto useless and rudimentary power of emitting radiation was specialized, so that, after reproduction, free individuals came to maintain radiant contact with one another, and to behave with ever-increasing coordination. Still later, these organized groups themselves maintained radiant contact with groups of their offspring, thus constituting larger individuals with specialized members. With each advance in complexity the sphere of radiant influence increased; until, at the zenith of Martian evolution, the whole planet (save for the remaining animal and vegetable representatives of the other and unsuccessful kind of life) constituted sometimes a single biological and psychological individual. But this occurred as a rule only in respect of matters which concerned the species as a whole. At most times the Martian individual was a cloudlet, such as those which first astonished the Second Men. But in great public crises each cloudlet would suddenly wake up to find himself the mind of the whole race, sensing through many individuals, and interpreting his sensations in the light of the experience of the whole race.

The life which dominated Mars was thus something between an extremely well-disciplined army of specialized units, and a body possessed by one mind. Like an army, it could take any form without destroying its organic unity. Like an army it was sometimes a crowd of free-wandering units, yet at other times also it disposed itself in very special orders to fulfil special functions. Like an army it was composed of free, experiencing individuals who voluntarily submitted themselves to discipline. On the other hand, unlike an army, it woke occasionally into unified consciousness.

The same fluctuation between individuality and multiplicity which characterized the race as a whole, characterized also each of the cloudlets themselves. Each was sometimes an individual, sometimes a swarm of more primitive individuals. But while the race rather seldom rose to full individuality, the cloudlets declined from it only in very special circumstances. Each cloudlet was an organization of specialized groups formed of minor specialized groups, which in turn were composed of the fundamental specialized varieties of subvital units. Each free-roving group of free-roving units constituted a special organ, fulfilling some particular function in the whole. Thus some were specialized for attraction and repulsion, some for chemical operations, some for storing the sun's energy, some for emitting radiation, some for absorbing and storing water, some for special sensitivities, such as awareness of mechanical pressure and vibration, or temperature changes, or light rays. Others again were specialized to fulfil the function of the brain of man; but in a peculiar manner. The whole volume of the cloudlet vibrated with innumerable "wireless" messages in very many wave-lengths from the different "organs." It was the function of the "brain" units to receive, and correlate, and interpret these messages in the light of past experience, and to initiate responses in the wave-lengths appropriate to the organs concerned.

All these subvital units, save a few types that were too highly specialized, were capable of independent life as air-borne bacteria or viruses. And whenever they lost touch with the radiation of the whole system, they continued to live their own simple lives until they were once more controlled. All were free-floating units, but normally they were under the influence of the cloudlet's system of electro-magnetic fields, and were directed hither and thither for their special functions. And under this influence some of them might be held rigidly in position in relation to one another. Such was the case of the organs of sight. In early stages of evolution, some of the units had specialized for carrying minute globules of water. Later, much larger droplets were carried, millions of units holding between them a still microscopic globule of life's most precious fluid. Ultimately this function was turned to good account in vision. Aqueous lenses as large as the eye of an ox, were supported by a scaffolding of units; while, at focal length from the lens, a rigid retina of units was held in position. Thus the Martian could produce eyes of every variety whenever he wanted them, and telescopes and microscopes too. This production and manipulation of visual organs was of course largely subconscious, like the focussing mechanism in man. But latterly the Martians had greatly increased their conscious control of physiological processes; and it was this achievement which facilitated their remarkable optical triumphs.

One other physiological function we must note before considering the Martian psychology. The fully evolved, but as yet uncivilized, Martian had long ago ceased to depend for his chemicals on wind-borne volcanic dust. Instead, he rested at night on the ground, like a knee-high mist on terrestrial meadows, and projected specialized tubular groups of units into the soil, like rootlets. Part of the day also had to be occupied in this manner. Somewhat later this process was supplemented by devouring the declining plant-life of the planet. But the final civilized Martians had greatly improved their methods of exploiting the ground and the sunlight, both by mechanical means and by artificial specialization of their own organs. Even so, however, as their activities increased, these vegetable functions became an ever more serious problem for them. They practised agriculture; but only a very small area of the arid planet could be induced to bear. It was terrestrial water and terrestrial vegetation that finally determined them to make the great voyage.

3. THE MARTIAN MIND   The Martian mind was of a very different type from the terrestrial,—different, yet at bottom identical. In so strange a body, the mind was inevitably equipped with alien cravings, and alien manners of apprehending its environment. And with so different a history, it was confused by prejudices very unlike those of man. Yet it was none the less mind, concerned in the last resort with the maintenance and advancement of life, and the exercise of vital capacities. Fundamentally the Martian was like all other living beings, in that he delighted in the free working of his body and his mind. Yet superficially, he was as unlike man in mind as in body.

The most distinctive feature of the Martian, compared with man, was that his individuality was both far more liable to disruption, and at the same time immeasurably more capable of direct participation in the minds of other individuals. The human mind in its solid body maintained its unity and its dominance over its members in all normal circumstances. Only in disease was man liable to mental or physical dissociation. On the other hand, he was incapable of direct contact with other individuals, and the emergence of a "super-mind" in a group of individuals was quite impossible. The Martian cloudlet, however, though he fell to pieces physically, and also mentally, far more readily than a man, might also at any moment wake up to be the intelligent mind of his race, might begin to perceive with the sense-organs of all other individuals, and experience thoughts and desires which were, so to speak, the resultant of all individual thoughts and desires upon some matter of general interest. But unfortunately, as I shall tell, the common mind of the Martians never woke into any order of mentality higher than that of the individual.

These differences between the Martian and the human psyche entailed characteristic advantages and disadvantages. The Martian, immune from man's inveterate selfishness and spiritual isolation from his fellows, lacked the mental coherence, the concentrated attention and far-reaching analysis and synthesis, and again the vivid self-consciousness and relentless self-criticism, which even the First Men, at their best, had attained in some degree, and which in the Second Men were still more developed. The Martians, moreover, were hampered by being almost identical in character. They possessed perfect harmony; but only through being almost wholly in temperamental unison. They were all hobbled by their sameness to one another. They were without that rich diversity of personal character, which enabled the human spirit to cover so wide a field of mentality. This infinite variety of human nature entailed, indeed, endless wasteful and cruel personal conflicts in the first, and even to some extent in the second, species of man; but also it enabled every individual of developed sympathy to enrich his spirit by intercourse with individuals whose temperament, thought and ideals differed from his own. And while the Martians were little troubled by internecine strife and the passion of hate, they were also almost wholly devoid of the passion of love. The Martian individual could admire, and be utterly faithful to, the object of his loyalty; but his admiration was given, not to concrete and uniquely charactered persons of the same order as himself, but at best to the vaguely conceived "spirit of the race." Individuals like himself he regarded merely as instruments or organs of the "super-mind."

This would not have been amiss, had the mind of the race, into which he so frequently awoke under the influence of the general radiation, been indeed a mind of higher rank than his own. But it was not. It was but a pooling of the percipience and thought and will of the cloudlets. Thus it was that the superb loyalty of the Martians was squandered upon something which was not greater than themselves in mental calibre, but only in mere bulk.

The Martian cloudlet, like the human animal, had a complex instinctive nature. By night and day, respectively, he was impelled to perform the vegetative functions of absorbing chemicals from the ground and energy from the sunlight. Air and water he also craved, though he dealt with them, of course, in his own manner. He had also his own characteristic instinctive impulses to move his "body," both for locomotion and manipulation. Martian civilization provided an outlet for these cravings, both in the practice of agriculture and in intricate and wonderfully beautiful cloud-dances and gymnastics. For these perfectly supple beings rejoiced in executing aerial evolutions, flinging out wild rhythmical streamers, intertwining with one another in spirals, concentrating into opaque spheres, cubes, cones, and all sorts of fantastical volumes. Many of these movements and shapes had intense emotional significance for them in relation to the operations of their life, and were executed with a religious fervour and solemnity.

The Martian had also his impulses of fear and pugnacity. In the remote past these had often been directed against hostile members of his own species; but since the race had become unified, they found exercise only upon other types of life and upon inanimate nature. Instinctive gregariousness was, of course, extremely developed in the Martian at the expense of instinctive self-assertion. Sexuality the Martian had not; there were no partners in reproduction. But his impulse to merge physically and mentally with other individuals, and wake up as the super-mind, had in it much that was characteristic of sex in man. Parental impulses, of a kind, he knew; but they were scarcely worthy of the name. He cared only to eject excessive living matter from his system, and to keep *en rapport* with the new individual thus formed, as he would with any other individual. He knew no more of the human devotion to children as budding personalities than of the subtle intercourse of male and female temperaments. By the time of the first invasion, however, reproduction had been greatly restricted; for the planet was fully populated, and each individual cloudlet was potentially immortal. Among the Martians there was no "natural death," no spontaneous death through mere senility. Normally the cloudlet's members kept themselves in repair indefinitely by the reproduction of their constituent units. Diseases, indeed, were often fatal. And chief among them was a plague, corresponding to terrestrial cancer, in which the subvital units lost their sensitivity to radiation, so that they proceeded to live as primitive organisms and reproduced without restraint. As they also became parasitic on the unaffected units, the cloudlet inevitably died.

Like the higher kinds of terrestrial mammal, the Martians had strong impulses of curiosity. Having also many practical needs to fulfil as a result of their civilization, and being extremely well equipped by nature for physical experiment and microscopy, they had gone far in the natural sciences. In physics, astronomy, chemistry and even in the chemistry of life, man had nothing to teach them.

The vast corpus of Martian knowledge had taken many thousands of years to grow. All its stages, and its current achievements were recorded on immense scrolls of paper made from vegetable pulp, and stored in libraries of stone. For the Martians, curiously enough, had become great masons, and had covered much of their planet with buildings of feathery and toppling design, such as would have been quite impossible on earth. They had no need of buildings for habitation, save in the arctic regions; but as workshops, granaries, and store rooms of all sorts, buildings had become very necessary to the Martians. Moreover these extremely tenuous creatures took a peculiar joy in manipulating solids. Even their most utilitarian architecture blossomed with a sort of gothic or arabesque ornateness and fantasy, wherein the ethereal seemed to torture the substance of solid rocks into its own likeness.

At the time of the invasion, the Martians were still advancing intellectually; and, indeed, it was through an achievement in theoretical physics that they were able to leave their planet. They had long known that minute particles at the upper limit of the atmosphere might be borne into space by the pressure of the sun's rays at dawn and sunset. And at length they discovered how to use this pressure as the wind is used in sailing. Dissipating themselves into their ultra-microscopic units, they contrived to get a purchase on the gravitational fields of the solar system, as a boat's keel and rudder get a purchase on the water. Thus they were able to tack across to the earth as an armada of ultra-microscopic vessels. Arrived in the terrestrial sky, they re-formed themselves as cloudlets, swam through the dense air to the alpine summit, and climbed downwards, as a swimmer may climb down a ladder under water.

This achievement involved very intricate calculations and chemical inventions, especially for the preservation of life in transit and on an alien planet. It could never have been done save by beings with far-reaching and accurate knowledge of the physical world. But though in respect of "natural knowledge" the Martians were so well advanced, they were extremely backward in all those spheres which may be called "spiritual knowledge." They had little understanding of their own mentality, and less of the place of mind in the cosmos. Though in a sense a highly intelligent species, they were at the same time wholly lacking in philosophical interest. They scarcely conceived, still less tackled, the problems which even the First Men had faced so often, though so vainly. For the Martians there was no mystery in the distinction between reality and appearance or in the relation of the one and the many, or in the status of good and evil. Nor were they ever critical of their own ideals. They aimed wholeheartedly at the advancement of the Martian super-individual. But what should constitute individuality, and its advancement, they never seriously considered. And the idea that they were under obligation also toward beings not included in the Martian system of radiation, proved wholly beyond them. For, though so clever, they were the most naïve of self-deceivers, and had no insight to see what it is that is truly desirable.

4. DELUSIONS OF THE MARTIANS To understand how the Martians tricked themselves, and how they were finally undone by their own insane will, we must glance at their history.

The civilized Martians constituted the sole remaining variety of a species. That species itself, in the remote past, had competed with, and exterminated, many other species of the same general type. Aided by the changing climate, it had also exterminated almost all the species of the more terrestrial kind of fauna, and had thereby much reduced the vegetation which it was subsequently to need and foster so carefully. This victory of the species had been due partly to its versatility and intelligence, partly to a remarkable zest in ferocity, partly to its unique powers of radiation and sensitivity to radiation, which enabled it to act with a co-ordination impossible even to the most gregarious of animals. But, as with other species in biological history, the capacity by which it triumphed became at length a source of weakness. When the species reached a stage corresponding to primitive human culture, one of its races, achieving a still higher degree of radiant intercourse and physical unity, was able to behave as a single vital unit; and so it succeeded in exterminating all its rivals. Racial conflict had persisted for many thousands of years, but as soon as the favoured race had developed this almost absolute solidarity of will, its victory was sweeping, and was clinched by joyous massacre of the enemy.

But ever afterwards the Martians suffered from the psychological effects of their victory at the close of the epoch of racial wars. The extreme brutality with which the other races had been exterminated conflicted with the generous impulses which civilization had begun to foster, and left a scar upon the conscience of the victors. In self-defence they persuaded themselves that since they were so much more admirable than the rest, the extermination was actually a sacred duty. And their unique value, they said, consisted in their unique radiational development. Hence arose a gravely insincere tradition and culture, which finally ruined the species. They had long believed that the physical basis of consciousness must necessarily be a system of units directly sensitive to ethereal vibrations, and that organisms dependent on the physical contact of their parts were too gross to have any experience whatever. After the age of the racial massacres they sought to persuade themselves that the excellence, or ethical worth, of any organism depended upon the degree of complexity and unity of its radiation. Century by century they strengthened their faith in this vulgar doctrine, and developed also a system of quite irrational delusions and obsessions based upon an obsessive and passionate lust in radiation.

It would take too long to tell of all these subsidiary fantasies, and of the ingenious ways in which they were reconciled with the main body of sane knowledge. But one at least must be mentioned, because of the part it played in the struggle with man. The Martians knew, of course, that "solid matter" was solid by virtue of the interlocking of the minute electro-magnetic systems called atoms. Now rigidity had for them somewhat the same significance and prestige that air, breath, spirit, had for early man. It was in the quasi-solid form that Martians were physically most potent; and the maintenance of this form was exhausting and difficult. These facts combined in the Martian consciousness with the knowledge that rigidity was after all the outcome of interlocked electro-magnetic systems. Rigidity was thus endowed with a peculiar sanctity. The superstition was gradually consolidated, by a series of psychological accidents, into a fanatical admiration of all very rigid materials, but especially of hard crystals, and above all of diamonds. For diamonds were extravagantly resistant; and at the same time, as the Martians themselves put it, diamonds were superb jugglers with the ethereal radiation called light. Every diamond was therefore a supreme embodiment of the tense energy and eternal equilibrium of the cosmos, and must be treated with reverence. In Mars, all known diamonds were exposed to sunlight on the pinnacles of sacred buildings; and the thought that on the neighbour planet might be diamonds which were not properly treated, was one motive of the invasion.

Thus did the Martian mind, unwittingly side-tracked from its true development, fall sick, and strive ever more fanatically toward mere phantoms of its goal. In the early stages of the disorder, radiation was merely regarded as an infallible *sign* of mentality, and radiative complexity was taken as an infallible *measure*, merely, of spiritual worth. But little by little, radiation and mentality failed to be distinguished, and radiative organization was actually mistaken for spiritual worth.

In this obsession the Martians resembled somewhat the First Men during their degenerate phase of servitude to the idea of movement; but with a difference. For the Martian intelligence was still active, though its products were severely censored in the name of the "spirit of the race." Every Martian was a case of dual personality. Not merely was he sometimes a private consciousness, sometimes the consciousness of the race, but further, even as a private individual he was in a manner divided against himself. Though his practical allegiance to the super-individual was absolute, so that he condemned or ignored all thoughts and impulses that could not be assimilated to the public consciousness, he did in fact have such thoughts and impulses, as it were in the deepest recesses of his being. He very seldom noticed that he was having them, and whenever he did notice it, he was shocked and terrified; yet he did have them. They constituted an intermittent, sometimes almost a continuous, critical commentary on all his more reputable experience.

This was the great tragedy of the spirit on Mars. The Martians were in many ways extremely well equipped for mental progress and for true spiritual adventure, but through a trick of fortune which had persuaded them to prize above all else unity and uniformity, they were driven to thwart their own struggling spirits at every turn.

Far from being superior to the private mind, the public mind which obsessed every Martian was in many ways actually inferior. It had come into dominance in a crisis which demanded severe military co-ordination; and though, since that remote age, it had made great intellectual progress, it remained at heart a military mind. Its disposition was something between that of a field-marshal and the God of the ancient Hebrews. A certain English philosopher once described and praised the fictitious corporate personality of the state, and named it "Leviathan." The Martian super-individual was Leviathan endowed with consciousness. In this consciousness there was nothing but what was easily assimilated and in accord with tradition. Thus the public mind was always intellectually and culturally behind the times. Only in respect of practical social organization did it keep abreast of its own individuals. Intellectual progress had always been initiated by private individuals, and had only penetrated the public mind when the mass of individuals had been privately infected by intercourse with the pioneers. The public consciousness itself initiated progress only in the sphere of social, military, and economic organization.

The novel circumstances which were encountered on the earth put the mentality of the Martians to a supreme test. For the unique enterprise of tackling a new world demanded the extremes of both public and private activity, and so led to agonizing conflicts within each private mind. For, while the undertaking was essentially social and even military, and necessitated very strict co-ordination and unity of action, the extreme novelty of the new environment demanded all the resources of the untrammelled private consciousness. Moreover the Martians encountered much on the earth which made nonsense of their fundamental assumptions. And in their brightest moments of private consciousness they sometimes recognized this fact.

EARTH AND MARS

1. THE SECOND MEN AT BAY   Such were the beings that invaded the earth when the Second Men were gathering their strength for a great venture in artificial evolution. The motives of the invasion were both economic and religious. The Martians sought water and vegetable matter; but they came also in a crusading spirit, to "liberate" the terrestrial diamonds.

Conditions on the earth were very unfavourable to the invaders. Excessive gravitation troubled them less than might have been expected. Only in their most concentrated form did they find it oppressive. More harmful was the density of the terrestrial atmosphere, which constricted the tenuous animate cloudlets very painfully, hindering their vital processes, and deadening all their movements. In their native atmosphere they swam hither and thither with ease and considerable speed; but the treacly air of the earth hampered them as a bird's wings are hampered under water. Moreover, owing to their extreme buoyancy as individual cloudlets, they were scarcely able to dive down so far as the mountain-tops. Excessive oxygen was also a source of distress; it tended to put them into a violent fever, which they had only been able to guard against very imperfectly. Even more damaging was the excessive moisture of the atmosphere, both through its solvent effect upon certain factors in the subvital units, and because heavy rain interfered with the physiological processes of the cloudlets and washed many of their materials to the ground.

The invaders had also to cope with the tissue of "radio" messages that constantly enveloped the planet, and tended to interfere with their own organic systems of radiation. They were prepared for this to some extent; but "beam wireless" at close range surprised, bewildered, tortured, and finally routed them; so that they fled back to Mars, leaving many of their number disintegrated in the terrestrial air.

But the pioneering army (or individual, for throughout the adventure it maintained unity of consciousness) had much to report at home. As was expected, there was rich vegetation, and water was even too abundant. There were solid animals, of the type of the prehistoric Martian fauna, but mostly two-legged and erect. Experiment had shown that these creatures died when they were pulled to pieces, and that though the sun's rays affected them by setting up chemical action in their visual organs, they had no really direct sensitivity to radiation. Obviously, therefore, they must be unconscious. On the other hand, the terrestrial atmosphere was permanently alive with radiation of a violent and incoherent type. It was still uncertain whether these crude ethereal agitations were natural phenomena, mere careless offshoots of the cosmic mind, or whether they were emitted by a terrestrial organism. There was reason to suppose this last to be the case, and that the solid organisms were used by some hidden terrestrial intelligence as instruments; for there were buildings, and many of the bipeds were found within the buildings. Moreover, the sudden violent concentration of beam radiation upon the Martian cloud suggested purposeful and hostile behaviour. Punitive action had therefore been taken, and many buildings and bipeds had been destroyed. The physical basis of such a terrestrial intelligence was still to be discovered. It was certainly not in the terrestrial clouds, for these had turned out to be insensitive to radiation. Anyhow, it was obviously an intelligence of very low order, for its radiation was scarcely at all systematic, and was indeed excessively crude. One or two unfortunate diamonds had been found in a building. There was no sign that they were properly venerated.

The Terrestrials, on their side, were left in complete bewilderment by the extraordinary events of that day. Some had jokingly suggested that since the strange substance had behaved in a manner obviously vindictive, it must have been alive and conscious; but no one took the suggestion seriously. Clearly, however, the thing had been dissipated by beam radiation. That at least was an important piece of practical knowledge. But theoretical knowledge about the real nature of the clouds, and their place in the order of the universe, was for the present wholly lacking. To a race of strong cognitive interest and splendid scientific achievement, this ignorance was violently disturbing. It seemed to shake the foundations of the great structure of knowledge. Many frankly hoped, in spite of the loss of life in the first invasion, that there would soon be another opportunity for studying these amazing objects, which were not quite gaseous and not quite solid, not (apparently) organic, yet capable of behaving in a manner suggestive of life. An opportunity was soon afforded.

Some years after the first invasion the Martians appeared again, and in far greater force. This time, moreover, they were almost immune from man's offensive radiation. Operating simultaneously from all the alpine regions of the earth, they began to dry up the great rivers at their sources; and, venturing further afield, they spread over jungle and agricultural land, and stripped off every leaf. Valley after valley was devastated as though by endless swarms of locusts, so that in whole countries there was not a green blade left. The booty was carried off to Mars. Myriads of the subvital units, specialized for transport of water and food materials, were loaded each with a few molecules of the treasure, and dispatched to the home planet. The traffic continued indefinitely. Meanwhile the main body of the Martians proceeded to explore and loot. They were irresistible. For the absorption of water and leafage, they spread over the countryside as an impalpable mist which man had no means to dispel. For the destruction of civilization, they became armies of gigantic cloud-jellies, far bigger than the brute which had formed itself during the earlier invasion. Cities were knocked down and flattened, human beings masticated into pulp. Man tried weapon after weapon in vain.

Presently the Martians discovered the sources of terrestrial radiation in the innumerable wireless transmitting stations. Here at last was the physical basis of the terrestrial intelligence! But what a lowly creature! What a caricature of life! Obviously in respect of complexity and delicacy of organization these wretched immobile systems of glass, metal and vegetable compounds were not to be compared with the Martian cloud. Their only feat seemed to be that they had managed to get control of the unconscious bipeds who tended them.

In the course of their explorations the Martians also discovered a few more diamonds. The second human species had outgrown the barbaric lust for jewellery; but they recognized the beauty of gems and precious metals, and used them as badges of office. Unfortunately, the Martians, in sacking a town, came upon a woman who was wearing a large diamond between her breasts; for she was mayor of the town, and in charge of the evacuation. That the sacred stone should be used thus, apparently for the mere indentification of cattle, shocked the invaders even more than the discovery of fragments of diamonds in certain cutting-instruments. The war now began to be waged with all the heroism and brutality of a crusade. Long after a rich booty of water and vegetable matter had been secured, long after the Terrestrials had developed an effective means of attack, and were slaughtering the Martian clouds with high-tension electricity in the form of artificial lightning flashes, the misguided fanatics stayed on to rescue the diamonds and carry them away to the mountain tops, where, years afterwards, climbers discovered them, arranged along the rock-edges in glittering files, like seabird's eggs. Thither the dying remnant of the Martian host had transported them with its last strength, scorning to save itself before the diamonds were borne into the pure mountain air, to be lodged with dignity. When the Second Men learned of this great hoard of diamonds, they began to be seriously persuaded that they had been dealing, not with a freak of physical nature, nor yet (as some said) with swarms of bacteria, but with organisms of a higher order. For how could the jewels have been singled out, freed from their metallic settings, and so carefully regimented on the rocks, save by conscious purpose? The murderous clouds must have had at least the pilfering mentality of jackdaws, since evidently they had been fascinated by the treasure. But the very action which revealed their consciousness suggested also that they were no more intelligent than the merely instinctive animals. There was no opportunity of correcting this error, since all the clouds had been destroyed.

The struggle had lasted only a few months. Its material effects on Man were serious but not insurmountable. Its immediate psychological effect was invigorating. The Second Men had long been accustomed to a security and prosperity that were almost utopian. Suddenly they were overwhelmed by a calamity which was quite unintelligible in terms of their own systematic knowledge. Their predecessors, in such a situation, would have behaved with their own characteristic vacillation between the human and the subhuman. They would have contracted a fever of romantic loyalty, and have performed many random acts of secretly self-regarding self-sacrifice. They would have sought profit out of the public disaster, and howled at all who were more fortunate than themselves. They would have cursed their gods, and looked for more useful ones. But also, in an incoherent manner, they would sometimes have behaved reasonably, and would even have risen now and again to the standards of the Second Men. Wholly unused to large-scale human bloodshed, these more developed beings suffered an agony of pity for their mangled fellows. But they said nothing about their pity, and scarcely noticed their own generous grief; for they were busy with the work of rescue. Suddenly confronted with the need of extreme loyalty and courage, they exulted in complying, and experienced that added keenness of spirit which comes when danger is well faced. But it did not occur to them that they were bearing themselves heroically; for they thought they were merely behaving reasonably, showing common sense. And if any one failed in a tight place, they did not call him coward, but gave him a drug to clear his head; or, if that failed, they put him under a doctor. No doubt, among the First Men such a policy would not have been justified, for those bewildered beings had not the clear and commanding vision which kept all sane members of the second species constant in loyalty.

The immediate psychological effect of the disaster was that it afforded this very noble race healthful exercise for its great reserves of loyalty and heroism. Quite apart from this immediate invigoration, however, the first agony, and those many others which were to follow, influenced the Second Men for good and ill in a train of effects which may be called spiritual. They had long known very well that the universe was one in which there could be not only private but also great public tragedies; and their philosophy did not seek to conceal this fact. Private tragedy they were able to face with a bland fortitude, and even an ecstasy of acceptance, such as the earlier species had but rarely attained. Public tragedy, even world-tragedy, they declared should be faced in the same spirit. But to know world-tragedy in the abstract, is very different from the direct acquaintance with it. And now the Second Men, even while they held their attention earnestly fixed upon the practical work of defence, were determined to absorb this tragedy into the very depths of their being, to scrutinize it fearlessly, savour it, digest it, so that its fierce potency should henceforth be added to them. Therefore they did not curse their gods, nor supplicate them. They said to themselves, "Thus, and thus, and thus, is the world. Seeing the depth we shall see also the height; and we shall praise both."

But their schooling was yet scarcely begun. The Martian invaders were all dead, but their subvital units were dispersed over the planet as a virulent ultra-microscopic dust. For, though as members of the living cloud they could enter the human body without doing permanent harm, now that they were freed from their functions within the higher organic system, they became a predatory virus. Breathed into man's lungs, they soon adapted themselves to the new environment, and threw his tissues into disorder. Each cell that they entered overthrew its own constitution, like a state which the enemy has successfully infected with lethal propaganda through a mere handful of agents. Thus, though man was temporarily victor over the Martian super-individual, his own vital units were poisoned and destroyed by the subvital remains of his dead enemy. A race whose physique had been as utopian as its body politic was reduced to timid invalidity. And it was left in possession of a devastated planet. The loss of water proved negligible; but the destruction of vegetation in all the war areas produced for a while a world famine such as the Second Men had never known. And the material fabric of civilization had been so broken that many decades would have to be spent in rebuilding it.

But the physical damage proved far less serious than the physiological. Earnest research discovered, indeed, a means of checking the infection; and, after a few years of rigorous purging, the atmosphere and man's flesh were clean once more. But the generations that had been stricken never recovered; their tissues had been too seriously corroded. Little by little, of course, there arose a fresh population of undamaged men and women. But it was a small population; for the fertility of the stricken had been much reduced. Thus the earth was now occupied by a small number of healthy persons below middle age and a very large number of ageing invalids. For many years these cripples had contrived to carry on the work of the world in spite of their frailty, but gradually they began to fail both in endurance and competence. For they were rapidly losing their grip on life, and sinking into a long-drawn-out senility, from which the Second Men had never before suffered; and at the same time the young, forced to take up work for which they were not yet equipped, committed all manner of blunders and crudities of which their elders would never have been guilty. But such was the general standard of mentality in the second human species, that what might have been an occasion for recrimination produced an unparalleled example of human loyalty at its best. The stricken generations decided almost unanimously that whenever an individual was declared by his generation to have outlived his competence, he should commit suicide. The younger generations, partly through affection, partly through dread of their own incompetence, were at first earnestly opposed to this policy. "Our elders," one young man said, "may have declined in vigour, but they are still beloved, and still wise. We dare not carry on without them." But the elders maintained their point. Many members of the rising generation were no longer juveniles. And, if the body politic was to survive the economic crisis, it must now ruthlessly cut out all its damaged tissues. Accordingly the decision was carried out. One by one, as occasion demanded, the stricken "chose the peace of annihilation," leaving a scanty, inexperienced, but vigorous, population to rebuild what had been destroyed.

Four centuries passed, and then again the Martian clouds appeared in the sky. Once more devastation and slaughter. Once more a complete failure of the two mentalities to conceive one another. Once more the Martians were destroyed. Once more the pulmonary plague, the slow purging, a crippled population, and generous suicide.

Again, and again they appeared, at irregular intervals for fifty thousand years. On each occasion the Martians came irresistibly fortified against whatever weapon humanity had last used against them. And so, by degrees, men began to recognize that the enemy was no merely instinctive brute, but intelligent. They therefore made attempts to get in touch with these alien minds, and make overtures for a peaceful settlement. But since obviously the negotiations had to be performed by human beings, and since the Martians always regarded human beings as the mere cattle of the terrestrial intelligence, the envoys were always either ignored or destroyed.

During each invasion the Martians contrived to dispatch a considerable bulk of water to Mars. And every time, not satisfied with this material gain, they stayed too long crusading, until man had found a weapon to circumvent their new defences; and then they were routed. After each invasion man's recovery was slower and less complete, while Mars, in spite of the loss of a large proportion of its population, was in the long run invigorated with the extra water.

2. THE RUIN OF TWO WORLDS   Rather more than fifty thousand years after their first appearance, the Martians secured a permanent footing on the Antarctic table-land and over-ran Australasia and South Africa. For many centuries they remained in possession of a large part of the earth's

surface, practising a kind of agriculture, studying terrestrial conditions, and spending much energy on the "liberation" of diamonds.

During the considerable period before their settlement their mentality had scarcely changed; but actual habitation of the earth now began to undermine their self-complacency and their unity. It was borne in upon certain exploring Martians that the terrestrial bipeds, though insensitive to radiation, were actually the intelligences of the planet. At first this fact was studiously shunned, but little by little it gripped the attention of all terrestrial Martians. At the same time they began to realize that the whole work of research into terrestrial conditions, and even the social construction of their colony, depended, not on the public mind, but on private individuals, acting in their private capacity. The colonial super-individual inspired only the diamond crusade, and the attempt to extirpate the terrestrial intelligence, or radiation. These various novel acts of insight woke the Martian colonists from an age-long dream. They saw that their revered super-individual was scarcely more than the least common measure of themselves, a bundle of atavistic fantasies and cravings, knit into one mind and gifted with a certain practical cunning. A rapid and bewildering spiritual renascence now came over the whole Martian colony. The central doctrine of it was that what was valuable in the Martian species was not radiation but mentality. These two utterly different things had been confused, and even identified, since the dawn of Martian civilization. At last they were clearly distinguished. A fumbling but sincere study of mind now began; and distinction was even made between the humbler and loftier mental activities.

There is no telling whither this renascence might have led, had it run its course. Possibly in time the Martians might have recognized worth even in minds other than Martian minds. But such a leap was at first far beyond them. Though they now understood that human animals were conscious and intelligent, they regarded them with no sympathy, rather indeed, with increased hostility. They still rendered allegiance to the Martian race, or brotherhood, just because it was in a sense one flesh, and, indeed, one mind. For they were concerned not to abolish but to recreate the public mind of the colony, and even that of Mars itself.

But the colonial public mind still largely dominated them in their more somnolent periods, and actually sent some of those who, in their private phases, were revolutionaries across to Mars for help against the revolutionary movement. The home planet was quite untouched by the new ideas. Its citizens co-operated whole-heartedly in an attempt to bring the colonists to their senses. But in vain. The colonial public mind itself changed its character as the centuries passed, until it became seriously alienated from Martian orthodoxy. Presently, indeed, it began to undergo a very strange and thorough metamorphosis, from which, conceivably, it might have emerged as the noblest inhabitant of the solar system. Little by little it fell into a kind of hypnotic trance. That is to say, it ceased to possess the attention of its private members, yet remained as a unity of their subconscious, or un-noticed mentality. Radiational unity of the colony was maintained, but only in this subconscious manner; and it was at that depth that the great metamorphosis began to take place under the fertilizing influence of the new ideas; which, so to speak, were generated in the tempest of the fully conscious mental revolution, and kept on spreading down into the oceanic depth of the subconsciousness. Such a condition was likely to produce in time the emergence of a qualitatively new and finer mentality, and to waken at last into a fully conscious super-individual of higher order than its own members. But meanwhile this trance of the public consciousness incapacitated the colony for that prompt and co-ordinated action which had been the most successful faculty of Martian life. The public mind of the home planet easily destroyed its disorderly offspring, and set about re-colonizing the earth.

Several times during the next three hundred thousand years this process repeated itself. The changeless and terribly efficient super-individual of Mars extirpated its own offspring on the earth, before it could emerge from the chrysalis. And the tragedy might have been repeated indefinitely, but for certain changes that took place in humanity.

The first few centuries after the foundation of the Martian colony had been spent in ceaseless war. But at last, with terribly reduced resources, the Second Men had reconciled themselves to the fact that they must live in the same world with their mysterious enemy. Moreover, constant observation of the Martians began to restore somewhat man's shattered self-confidence. For during the fifty thousand years before the Martian colony was founded his opinion of himself had been undermined. He had formerly been used to regarding himself as the sun's ablest child. Then suddenly a stupendous new phenomenon had defeated his intelligence. Slowly he had learned that he was at grips with a determined and versatile rival, and that this rival hailed from a despised planet. Slowly he had been forced to suspect that he himself was outclassed, outshone, by a race whose very physique was incomprehensible to man. But after the Martians had established a permanent colony, human scientists began to discover the real physiological nature of the Martian organism, and were comforted to find that it did not make nonsense of human science. Man also learned that the Martians, though very able in certain spheres, were not really of a high mental type. These discoveries restored human self-confidence. Man settled down to make the best of the situation. Impassable barriers of high-power electric current were devised to keep the Martians out of human territory, and men began patiently to rebuild their ruined home as best they could. At first there was little respite from the crusading zeal of the Martians, but in the second millennium this began to abate, and the two races left one another alone, save for occasional revivals of Martian fervour. Human civilization was at last reconstructed and consolidated, though upon a modest scale. Once more, though interrupted now and again by decades of agony, human beings lived in peace and relative prosperity. Life was somewhat harder than formerly, and the physique of the race was definitely less reliable than of old; but men and women still enjoyed conditions which most nations of the earlier species would have envied. The age of ceaseless personal sacrifice in service of the stricken community had ended at last. Once more a wonderful diversity of untrammelled personalities was put forth. Once more the minds of men and women were devoted without hindrance to the joy of skilled work, and all the subtleties of personal intercourse. Once more the passionate interest in one's fellows, which had for so long been hushed under the all-dominating public calamity, refreshed and enlarged the mind. Once more there was music, sweet and backward-hearkening towards a golden past. Once more a wealth of literature, and of the visual arts. Once more intellectual exploration into the nature of the physical world and the potentiality of mind. And once more the religious experience, which had for so long been coarsened and obscured by all the violent distractions and inevitable self-deceptions of war, seemed to be refining itself under the influence of reawakened culture.

In such circumstances the earlier and less sensitive human species might well have prospered indefinitely. Not so the Second Men. For their very refinement of sensibility made them incapable of shunning an ever-present conviction that in spite of all their prosperity they were undermined. Though superficially they seemed to be making a slow but heroic recovery they were at the same time suffering from a still slower and far more profound spiritual decline. Generation succeeded generation. Society became almost perfected, within its limited territory and its limitations of material wealth. The capacities of personality were developed with extreme subtlety and richness. At last the race proposed to itself once more its ancient project of re-making human nature upon a loftier plane. But somehow it had no longer the courage and self-respect for such work. And so, though there was much talk, nothing was done. Epoch succeeded epoch, and everything human remained apparently the same. Like a twig that has been broken but not broken off, man settled down to retain his life and culture, but could make no progress.

It is almost impossible to describe in a few words the subtle malady of the spirit that was undermining the Second Men. To say that they were suffering from an inferiority complex, would not be wholly false, but it would be a misleading vulgarization of the truth. To say that they had lost faith, both in themselves and in the universe, would be almost as inadequate. Crudely stated, their trouble was that, as a species, they had attempted a certain spiritual feat beyond the scope of their still-primitive nature. Spiritually they had over-reached themselves, broken every muscle (so to speak) and incapacitated themselves for any further effort. For they had determined to see their own racial tragedy as a thing of beauty, and they had failed. It was the obscure sense of this defeat that had poisoned them, for, being in many respects a very noble species, they could not simply turn their backs upon their failure and pursue the old way of life with the accustomed zest and thoroughness.

During the earliest Martian raids, the spiritual leaders of humanity had preached that the disaster must be an occasion for a supreme religious experience. While striving mightily to save their civilization, men must yet (so it was said) learn not merely to endure, but to admire, even the sternest issue. "Thus and thus is the world. Seeing the depth, we shall see also the height, and praise both." The whole population had accepted this advice. At first they had seemed to succeed. Many noble literary expressions were given forth, which seemed to define and elaborate, and even actually to create in men's hearts, this supreme experience. But as the centuries passed and the disasters were repeated, men began to fear that their forefathers had deceived themselves. Those remote generations had earnestly longed to feel the racial tragedy as a factor in the cosmic beauty; and at last they had persuaded themselves that this experience had actually befallen them. But their descendants were slowly coming to suspect that no such experience had ever occurred, that it would never occur to any man, and that there was in fact no such cosmic beauty to be experienced. The First Men would probably, in such a situation, have swung violently either into spiritual nihilism, or else into some comforting religious myth. At any rate, they were of too coarse-grained a nature to be ruined by a trouble so impalpable. Not so the Second Men. For they realized all too clearly that they were faced with the supreme crux of existence. And so, age after age the generations clung desperately to the hope that, if only they could endure a little longer, the light would break in on them. Even after the Martian colony had been three times established and destroyed by the orthodox race in Mars, the supreme preoccupation of the human species was with this religious crux. But afterwards, and very gradually, they lost heart. For it was borne in on them that either they themselves were by nature too obtuse to perceive this ultimate excellence of things (an excellence which they had strong reason to believe in intellectually, although they could not actually experience it), or the human race had utterly deceived itself, and the course of cosmic events after all was not significant, but a meaningless rigmarole.

It was this dilemma that poisoned them. Had they been still physically in their prime, they might have found fortitude to accept it, and proceed to the patient exfoliation of such very real excellencies as they were still capable of creating. But they had lost the vitality which alone could perform such acts of spiritual abnegation. All the wealth of personality, all the intricacies of personal relationship, all the complex enterprise of a very great community, all art, all intellectual research, had lost their savour. It is remarkable that a purely religious disaster should have warped even the delight of lovers in one another's bodies, actually taken the flavour out of food, and drawn a veil between the sun-bather and the sun. But individuals of this species, unlike their predecessors, were so closely integrated, that none of their functions could remain healthy while the highest was disordered. Moreover, the general slight failure of physique, which was the legacy of age-long war, had resulted in a recurrence of those shattering brain disorders which had dogged the earliest races of their species. The very horror of the prospect of racial insanity increased their aberration from reasonableness. Little by little, shocking perversions of desire began to terrify them. Masochistic and sadistic orgies alternated with phases of extravagant and ghastly revelry. Acts of treason against the community, hitherto almost unknown, at last necessitated a strict police system. Local groups organized predatory raids against one another. Nations appeared, and all the phobias that make up nationalism.

The Martian colonists, when they observed man's disorganization, prepared, at the instigation of the home planet, a very great offensive. It so happened that at this time the colony was going through its phase of enlightenment, which had always hitherto been followed sooner or later by chastisement from Mars. Many individuals were at the moment actually toying with the idea of seeking harmony with man, rather than war. But the public mind of Mars, outraged by this treason, sought to overwhelm it by instituting a new crusade. Man's disunion offered a great opportunity.

The first attack produced a remarkable change in the human race. Their madness seemed suddenly to leave them. Within a few weeks the national governments had surrendered their sovereignty to a central authority. Disorders, debauchery, perversions, wholly ceased. The treachery and self-seeking and corruption, which had by now been customary for many centuries, suddenly gave place to universal and perfect devotion to the social cause. The species was apparently once more in its right mind. Everywhere, in spite of the war's horrors, there was gay brotherliness, combined with a heroism, which clothed itself in an odd extravagance of jocularity.

The war went ill for man. The general mood changed to cold resolution. And still victory was with the Martians. Under the influence of the huge fanatical armies which were poured in from the home planet, the colonists had shed their tentative pacifism, and sought to vindicate their loyalty by ruthlessness. In reply the human race deserted its sanity, and succumbed to an uncontrollable lust for destruction. It was at this stage that a human bacteriologist announced that he had bred a virus of peculiar deadliness and transmissibility, with which it would be possible to infect the enemy, but at the cost of annihilating also the human race. It is significant of the insane condition of the human population at this time that, when these facts were announced and broadcast, there was no discussion of the desirability of using this weapon. It was immediately put in action, the whole human race applauding.

Within a few months the Martian colony had vanished, their home planet itself had received the infection, and its population was already aware that nothing could save it. Man's constitution was tougher than that of the animate clouds, and he appeared to be doomed to a somewhat more lingering death. He made no effort to save himself, either from the disease which he himself had propagated, or from the pulmonary plague which was caused by the disintegrated substance of the dead Martian colony. All the public processes of civilization began to fall to pieces; for the community was paralysed by disillusion, and by the expectation of death. Like a bee-hive that has no queen, the whole population of the earth sank into apathy. Men and women stayed in their homes, idling, eating whatever food they could procure, sleeping far into the mornings, and, when at last they rose, listlessly avoiding one another. Only the children could still be gay, and even they were oppressed by their elders' gloom. Meanwhile the disease was spreading. Household after household was stricken, and was left unaided by its neighbours. But the pain in each individual's flesh was strangely numbed by his more poignant distress in the spiritual defeat of the race. For such was the high development of this species, that even physical agony could not distract it from the racial failure. No one wanted to save himself; and each knew that his neighbours desired not his aid. Only the children, when the disease crippled them, were plunged into agony and terror. Tenderly, yet listlessly, their elders would then give them the last sleep. Meanwhile the unburied dead spread corruption among the dying. Cities fell still and silent. The corn was not harvested.

adventures
in time

the time machine

by H. G. WELLS

The Time Traveller (for so it will be convenient to speak of him) was expounding a recondite matter to us. His grey eyes shone and twinkled, and his usually pale face was flushed and animated. The fire burned brightly, and the soft radiance of the incandescent lights in the lilies of silver caught the bubbles that flashed and passed in our glasses. Our chairs, being his patents, embraced and caressed us rather than submitted to be sat upon, and there was that luxurious after-dinner atmosphere when thought runs gracefully free of the trammels of precision. And he put it to us in this way—marking the points with a lean forefinger—as we sat and lazily admired his earnestness over this new paradox (as we thought it) and his fecundity.

"You must follow me carefully. I shall have to controvert one or two ideas that are almost universally accepted. The geometry, for instance, they taught you at school is founded on a misconception."

"Is not that rather a large thing to expect us to begin upon?" said Filby, an argumentative person with red hair.

"I do not mean to ask you to accept anything without reasonable ground for it. You will soon admit as much as I need from you. You know of course that a mathematical line, a line of thickness *nil*, has no real existence. They taught you that? Neither has a mathematical plane. These things are mere abstractions."

"That is all right," said the Psychologist.

"Nor, having only length, breadth, and thickness, can a cube have a real existence."

Reprinted by permission of William Heinemann, Ltd., London, England.

"There I object," said Filby. "Of course a solid body may exist. All real things——"

"So most people think. But wait a moment. Can an *instantaneous* cube exist?"

"Don't follow you," said Filby.

"Can a cube that does not last for any time at all have a real existence?"

Filby became pensive. "Clearly," the Time Traveller proceeded, "any real body must have extension in *four* directions: it must have Length, Breadth, Thickness, and—Duration. But through a natural infirmity of the flesh, which I will explain to you in a moment, we incline to overlook this fact. There are really four dimensions, three which we call the three planes of Space, and a fourth, Time. There is, however, a tendency to draw an unreal distinction between the former three dimensions and the latter, because it happens that our consciousness moves intermittently in one direction along the latter from the beginning to the end of our lives."

"That," said a very young man, making spasmodic efforts to relight his cigar over the lamp; "that . . . very clear indeed."

"Now, it is very remarkable that this is so extensively overlooked," continued the Time Traveller, with a slight accession of cheerfulness. "Really this is what is meant by the Fourth Dimension, though some people who talk about the Fourth Dimension do not know they mean it. It is only another way of looking at Time. *There is no difference between Time and any of the three dimensions of Space except that our consciousness moves along it.* But some foolish people have got hold of the wrong side of that idea. You have all heard what they have to say about this Fourth Dimension?"

"*I* have not," said the Provincial Mayor.

"It is simply this. That Space, as our mathematicians have it, is spoken of as having three dimensions, which one may call Length, Breadth, and Thickness, and is always definable by reference to three planes, each at right angles to the others. But some philosophical people have been asking why *three* dimensions particularly—why not another direction at right angles to the other three?—and have even tried to construct a Four-Dimensional geometry. Professor Simon Newcomb was expounding this to the New York Mathematical Society only a month or so ago. You know how on a flat surface, which has only two dimensions, we can represent a figure of a three-dimensional solid, and similarly they think that by models of three dimensions they could represent one of four—if they could master the perspective of the thing. See?"

"I think so," murmured the Provincial Mayor; and, knitting his brows, he lapsed into an introspective state, his lips moving as one who repeats mystic words. "Yes, I think I see it now," he said after some time, brightening in a quite transitory manner.

"Well, I do not mind telling you I have been at work upon this geometry of Four Dimensions for some time. Some of my results are curious. For instance, here is a portrait of a man at eight years old, another at fifteen, another at seventeen, another at twenty-three, and so on. All these are evidently sections, as it were, Three-Dimensional representations of his Four-Dimensioned being, which is a fixed and unalterable thing.

"Scientific people," proceeded the Time Traveller, after the pause required for the proper assimilation of this, "know very well that Time is only a kind of Space. Here is a popular scientific diagram, a weather record. This line I trace with my fingers shows the movement of the barometer. Yesterday it was so high, yesterday night it fell, then this morning it rose again, and so gently upward to here. Surely the mercury did not trace this line in any of the dimensions of Space generally recognised? But certainly it traced such a line, and that line, therefore, we must conclude was along the Time-Dimension."

"But," said the Medical Man, staring hard at a coal in the fire, "if Time is really only a fourth dimension of Space, why is it, and why has it always been, regarded as something different? And why cannot we move in Time as we move about in the other dimensions of Space?"

The Time Traveller smiled. "Are you so sure we can move freely in Space? Right and left we can go, backward and forward freely enough, and men always have done so. I admit we move freely in two dimensions. But how about up and down? Gravitation limits us there."

"Not exactly," said the Medical Man. "There are balloons."

"But before the balloons, save for spasmodic jumping and the inequalities of the surface, man had no freedom of vertical movement."

"Still they could move a little up and down," said the Medical Man.

"Easier, far easier down than up."

"And you cannot move at all in Time, you cannot get away from the present moment."

"My dear sir, that is just where you are wrong. That is just where the whole world has gone wrong. We are always getting away from the present moment. Our mental existences, which are immaterial and have no dimensions, are passing along the Time-Dimension with a uniform velocity from the cradle to the grave. Just as we should travel *down* if we began our existence fifty miles above the earth's surface."

"But the great difficulty is this," interrupted the Psychologist. "You *can* move about in all directions of Space, but you cannot move about in Time."

"That is the germ of my great discovery. But you are wrong to say that we cannot move about in Time. For instance, if I am recalling an incident very vividly I go back to the instant of its occurrence: I become absent-minded, as you say. I jump back for a moment. Of course we have no means of staying back for any length of Time, any more than a savage or an animal has of staying six feet above the ground. But a civilised man is better off than the savage in this respect. He can go up against gravitation in a balloon, and why should he not hope that ultimately he may be able to stop or accelerate his drift along the Time-Dimension, or even turn about and travel the other way?"

"Oh, *this*," began Filby, "is all——"

"Why not?" said the Time Traveller.

"It's against reason," said Filby.

"What reason?" said the Time Traveller.

"You can show black is white by argument," said Filby, "but you will never convince me."

"Possibly not," said the Time Traveller. "But now you begin to see the object of my investigations into the geometry of Four Dimensions. Long ago I had a vague inkling of a machine——"

"To travel through Time!" exclaimed the Very Young Man.

"That shall travel indifferently in any direction of Space and Time, as the driver determines."

Filby contented himself with laughter.

"But I have experimental verification," said the Time Traveller.

"It would be remarkably convenient for the historian," the Psychologist suggested. "One might travel back and verify the accepted account of the Battle of Hastings, for instance!"

"Don't you think you would attract attention?" said the Medical Man. "Our ancestors had no great tolerance for anachronisms."

"One might get one's Greek from the very lips of Homer and Plato," the Very Young Man thought.

"In which case they would certainly plough you for the Little-go. The German scholars have improved Greek so much."

"Then there is the future," said the Very Young Man. "Just think! One might invest all one's money, leave it to accumulate at interest, and hurry on ahead!"

"To discover a society," said I, "erected on a strictly communistic basis."

"Of all the wild extravagant theories!" began the Psychologist.

"Yes, so it seemed to me, and so I never talked of it until——"

"Experimental verification!" cried I. "You are going to verify *that?*"

"The experiment!" cried Filby, who was getting brain-weary.

"Let's see your experiment anyhow," said the Psychologist, "though it's all humbug, you know."

The Time Traveller smiled round at us. Then, still smiling faintly, and with his hands deep in his trousers pockets, he walked slowly out of the room, and we heard his slippers shuffling down the long passage to his laboratory.

The Psychologist looked at us. "I wonder what he's got?"

"Some sleight-of-hand trick or other," said the Medical Man, and Filby tried to tell us about a conjurer he had seen at Burslem; but before he had finished his preface the Time Traveller came back, and Filby's anecdote collapsed.

The thing the Time Traveller held in his hand was a glittering metallic framework, scarcely larger than a small clock, and very delicately made. There was ivory in it, and some transparent crystalline substance. And now I must be explicit, for this that follows—unless his explanation is to be accepted—is an absolutely unaccountable thing. He took one of the small octagonal tables that were scattered about the room, and set it in front of the fire, with two legs on the hearth rug. On this table he placed the mechanism. Then he drew up a chair, and sat down. The only other object on the table was a small shaded lamp, the bright light of which fell full upon the model. There were also perhaps a dozen candles about, two in brass candlesticks upon the mantel and several in sconces, so that the room was brilliantly illuminated. I sat in a low armchair nearest the fire, and I drew this forward so as to be almost between the Time Traveller and the fireplace. Filby sat behind him, looking over his shoulder. The Medical Man and the Provincial Mayor watched him in profile from the right, the Psychologist from the left. The Very Young Man stood behind the Psychologist. We were all on the alert. It appears incredible to me that any kind of trick, however subtly conceived and however adroitly done, could have been played upon us under these conditions.

The Time Traveller looked at us, and then at the mechanism. "Well?" said the Psychologist.

"This little affair," said the Time Traveller, resting his elbows upon the table and pressing his hands together above the apparatus, "is only a model. It is my plan for a machine to travel through time. You will notice that it looks singularly askew, and that there is an odd twinkling appearance about this bar, as though it was in some way unreal." He pointed to the part with his finger. "Also, here is one little white lever, and here is another."

The Medical Man got up out of his chair and peered into the thing. "It's beautifully made," he said.

"It took two years to make," retorted the Time Traveller. Then, when we had all imitated the action of the Medical Man, he said: "Now I want you clearly to understand that this lever, being pressed over, sends the machine gliding into the future, and this other reverses the motion. This saddle represents the seat of a time traveller. Presently I am going to press the lever, and off the machine will go. It will vanish, pass into future Time, and disappear. Have a good look at the thing. Look at the table too, and satisfy yourselves there is no trickery. I don't want to waste this model, and then be told I'm a quack."

There was a minute's pause perhaps. The Psychologist seemed about to speak to me, but changed his mind. Then the Time Traveller put forth his finger towards the lever. "No," he said suddenly. "Lend me your hand." And turning to the Psychologist, he took that individual's hand in his own and told him to put out his forefinger. So that it was the Psychologist himself who sent forth the model Time Machine on its interminable voyage. We all saw the lever turn. I am absolutely certain there was no trickery. There was a breath of wind, and the lamp flame jumped. One of the candles on the mantel was blown out, and the little machine suddenly swung round, became indistinct, was seen as a ghost for a second perhaps, as an eddy of faintly glittering brass and ivory; and it was gone—vanished! Save for the lamp the table was bare.

Every one was silent for a minute. Then Filby said he was damned.

The Psychologist recovered from his stupor, and suddenly looked under the table. At that the Time Traveller laughed cheerfully. "Well?" he said, with a reminiscence of the Psychologist. Then, getting up, he went to the tobacco jar on the mantel, and with his back to us began to fill his pipe.

We stared at each other. "Look here," said the Medical Man, "are you in earnest about this? Do you seriously believe that that machine has travelled into time?"

"Certainly," said the Time Traveller, stooping to light a spill at the fire. Then he turned, lighting his pipe, to look at the Psychologist's face. (The Psychologist, to show that he was not unhinged, helped himself to a cigar and tried to light it uncut.) "What is more, I have a big machine nearly finished in there"—he indicated the laboratory—"and when that is put together I mean to have a journey on my own account."

"You mean to say that that machine has travelled into the future?" said Filby.

"Into the future or the past—I don't, for certain, know which."

After an interval the Psychologist had an inspiration. "It must have gone into the past if it has gone anywhere," he said.

"Why?" said the Time Traveller.

"Because I presume that it has not moved in space, and if it travelled into the future it would still be here all this time, since it must have travelled through this time."

"But," said I, "if it travelled into the past it would have been visible when we came first into this room; and last Thursday when we were here; and the Thursday before that; and so forth!"

"Serious objections," remarked the Provincial Mayor, with an air of impartiality, turning towards the Time Traveller.

"Not a bit," said the Time Traveller, and, to the Psychologist: "You think. *You* can explain that. It's presentation below the threshold, you know, diluted presentation."

"Of course," said the Psychologist, and reassured us. "That's a simple point of psychology. I should have thought of it. It's plain enough, and helps the paradox delightfully. We cannot see it, nor can we appreciate this machine, any more than we can the spoke of a wheel spinning, or a bullet flying through the air. If it is travelling through time fifty times or a hundred times faster than we are, if it gets through a minute while we get through a second, the impression it creates will of course be only one-fiftieth or one-hundredth of what it would make if it were not travelling in time. That's plain enough." He passed his hand through the space in which the machine had been. "You see?" he said, laughing.

We sat and stared at the vacant table for a minute or so. Then the Time Traveller asked us what we thought of it all.

"It sounds plausible enough to-night," said the Medical Man; "but wait until to-morrow. Wait for the common sense of the morning."

"Would you like to see the Time Machine itself?" asked the Time Traveller. And therewith, taking the lamp in his hand, he led the way down the long, draughty corridor to his laboratory. I remember vividly the flickering light, his queer, broad head in silhouette, the dance of the shadows, how we all followed him, puzzled but incredulous, and how there in the laboratory we beheld a larger edition of the little mechanism which we had seen vanish from before our eyes. Parts were of nickel, parts of ivory, parts had certainly been filed or sawn out of rock crystal. The thing was generally complete, but the twisted crystalline bars lay unfinished upon the bench beside some sheets of drawings, and I took one up for a better look at it. Quartz it seemed to be.

"Look here," said the Medical Man, "are you perfectly serious? Or is this a trick—like that ghost you showed us last Christmas?"

"Upon that machine," said the Time Traveller, holding the lamp aloft, "I intend to explore time. Is that plain? I was never more serious in my life."

None of us quite knew how to take it.

I caught Filby's eye over the shoulder of the Medical Man, and he winked at me solemnly.

CHAPTER II: I think that at that time none of us quite believed in the Time Machine. The fact is, the Time Traveller was one of those men who are too clever to be believed: you never felt that you saw all round him; you always suspected some subtle reserve, some ingenuity in ambush, behind his lucid frankness. Had Filby shown the model and explained the matter in the Time Traveller's words, we should have shown *him* far less scepticism. For we should have perceived his motives: a pork butcher could understand Filby. But the Time Traveller had more than a touch of whim among his elements, and we distrusted him. Things that would have made the fame of a less clever man seemed tricks in his hands. It is a mistake to do things too easily. The serious people who took him seriously never felt quite sure of his deportment: they were somehow aware that trusting their reputations for judgment with him was like furnishing a nursery with egg-shell china. So I don't think any of us said very much about time travelling in the interval between that Thursday and the next, though its odd potentialities ran, no doubt, in most of our minds: its plausibility, that is, its practical incredibleness, the curious possibilities of anachronism and of utter confusion it suggested. For my own part, I was particularly preoccupied with the trick of the model. That I remember discussing with the Medical Man, whom I met on Friday at the Linnæan. He said he had seen a similar thing at Tübingen, and laid considerable stress on the blowing out of the candle. But how the trick was done he could not explain.

The next Thursday I went again to Richmond—I suppose I was one of the Time Traveller's most constant guests—and arriving late, found four or five men already assembled in his drawing-room. The Medical Man was standing before the fire with a sheet of paper in one hand and his watch in the other. I looked round for the Time Traveller, and—"It's half-past seven now," said the Medical Man. "I suppose we'd better have dinner?"

"Where's ——?" said I, naming our host.

"You've just come? It's rather odd. He's unavoidably detained. He asks me in this note to lead off with dinner at seven if he's not back. Says he'll explain when he comes."

"It seems a pity to let the dinner spoil," said the Editor of a well-known daily paper; and thereupon the Doctor rang the bell.

The Psychologist was the only person besides the Doctor and myself who had attended the previous dinner. The other men were Blank, the Editor afore-mentioned, a certain journalist, and another—a quiet, shy man with a beard—whom I didn't know, and who, as far as my observation went, never opened his mouth all the evening. There was some speculation at the dinner table about the Time Traveller's absence, and I suggested time travelling, in a half-jocular spirit. The Editor wanted that explained to him, and the Psychologist volunteered a wooden account of the "ingenious paradox and trick" we had witnessed that day week. He was in the midst of his exposition when the door from the corridor opened slowly and without noise. I was facing the door, and saw it first. "Hallo!" I said. "At last!" And the door opened wider, and the Time Traveller stood before us. I gave a cry of surprise. "Good heavens! man, what's the matter?" cried the Medical Man, who saw him next. And the whole tableful turned towards the door.

He was in an amazing plight. His coat was dusty and dirty and smeared with green down the sleeves; his hair disordered, and as it seemed to me greyer—either with dust and dirt or because its colour had actually faded. His face was ghastly pale; his chin had a brown cut on it—a cut half healed; his expression was haggard and drawn, as by intense suffering. For a moment he hesitated in the doorway, as if he had been dazzled by the light. Then he came into the room. He walked with just such a limp as I have seen in footsore tramps. We stared at him in silence, expecting him to speak.

He said not a word, but came painfully to the table, and made a motion towards the wine. The Editor filled a glass of champagne, and pushed it towards him. He drained it, and it seemed to do him good: for he looked round the table, and the ghost of his old smile flickered across his face. "What on earth have you been up to, man?" said the Doctor. The Time Traveller did not seem to hear. "Don't let me disturb you," he said, with a certain faltering articulation. "I'm all right." He stopped, held out his glass for more, and took it off at a draught. "That's good," he said. His eyes grew brighter, and a faint colour came into his cheeks. His glance flickered over our faces with a certain dull approval, and then went round the warm and comfortable room. Then he spoke again, still as it were feeling his way among his words. "I'm going to wash and dress, and then I'll come down and explain things. . . . Save me some of that mutton. I'm starving for a bit of meat."

He looked across at the Editor, who was a rare visitor, and hoped he was all right. The Editor began a question. "Tell you presently," said the Time Traveller. "I'm—funny! Be all right in a minute."

He put down his glass, and walked towards the staircase door. Again I remarked his lameness and the soft padding sound of his footfall, and standing up in my place, I saw his feet as he went out. He had nothing on them but a pair of tattered, bloodstained socks. Then the door closed upon him. I had half a mind to follow, till I remembered how he detested any fuss about himself. For a minute, perhaps, my mind was wool gathering. Then, "Remarkable Behaviour of an Eminent Scientist," I heard the Editor say, thinking (after his wont) in head-lines. And this brought my attention back to the bright dinner table.

"What's the game?" said the Journalist. "Has he been doing the Amateur Cadger? I don't follow." I met the eye of the Psychologist, and read my own interpretation in his face. I thought of the Time Traveller limping painfully upstairs. I don't think any one else had noticed his lameness.

The first to recover completely from this surprise was the Medical Man, who rang the bell—the Time Traveller hated to have servants waiting at dinner—for a hot plate. At that the Editor turned to his knife and fork with a grunt, and the Silent Man followed suit. The dinner was resumed. Conversation was exclamatory for a little while, with gaps of wonderment; and then the Editor got fervent in his curiosity. "Does our friend eke out his modest income with a crossing or has he his Nebuchadnezzar phases?" he inquired. "I feel assured it's this business of the Time Machine," I said, and took up the Psychologist's account of our previous meeting. The new guests were frankly incredulous. The Editor raised objections. "What *was* this time travelling? A man couldn't cover himself with dust by rolling in a paradox, could he?" And then, as the idea came home to him, he resorted to caricature. Hadn't they any clothes-brushes in the Future? The Journalist, too, would not believe at any price, and joined the Editor in the easy work of heaping ridicule on the whole thing. They were both the new kind of journalist—very joyous, irreverent young men. "Our Special Correspondent in the Day after To-morrow reports," the Journalist was saying—or rather shouting—when the Time Traveller came back. He was dressed in ordinary evening clothes, and nothing save his haggard look remained of the change that had startled me.

"I say," said the Editor hilariously, "these chaps here say you have been travelling into the middle of next week!! Tell us all about little Rosebery, will you? What will you take for the lot?"

The Time Traveller came to the place reserved for him without a word. He smiled quietly, in his old way. "Where's my mutton?" he said. "What a treat it is to stick a fork into meat again!"

"Story!" cried the Editor.

"Story be damned!" said the Time Traveller. "I want something to eat. I won't say a word until I get some peptone into my arteries. Thanks. And the salt."

"One word," said I. "Have you been time travelling?"

"Yes," said the Time Traveller, with his mouth full, nodding his head.

"I'd give a shilling a line for a verbatim note," said the Editor. The Time Traveller pushed his glass towards the Silent Man and rang it with his finger nail; at which the Silent Man, who had been staring at his face, started convulsively, and poured him wine. The rest of the dinner was uncomfortable. For my own part, sudden questions kept on rising to my lips, and I dare say it was the same with the others. The Journalist tried to relieve the tension by telling anecdotes of Hettie Potter. The Time Traveller devoted his attention to his dinner, and displayed the appetite of a tramp. The Medical Man smoked a cigarette, and watched the Time

Traveller through his eyelashes. The Silent Man seemed even more clumsy than usual, and drank champagne with regularity and determination out of sheer nervousness. At last the Time Traveller pushed his plate away, and looked around us. "I suppose I must apologise," he said. "I was simply starving. I've had a most amazing time." He reached out his hand for a cigar, and cut the end. "But come into the smoking-room. It's too long a story to tell over greasy plates." And ringing the bell in passing, he led the way into the adjoining room.

"You have told Blank, and Dash, and Chose about the machine?" he said to me, leaning back in his easy chair and naming the three new guests.

"But the thing's a mere paradox," said the Editor.

"I can't argue to-night. I don't mind telling you the story, but I can't argue. I will," he went on, "tell you the story of what has happened to me, if you like, but you must refrain from interruptions. I want to tell it. Badly. Most of it will sound like lying. So be it! It's true—every word of it, all the same. I was in my laboratory at four o'clock, and since then . . . I've lived eight days . . . such days as no human being ever lived before! I'm nearly worn out, but I shan't sleep till I've told this thing over to you. Then I shall go to bed. But no interruptions! Is it agreed?"

"Agreed," said the Editor, and the rest of us echoed "Agreed." And with that the Time Traveller began his story as I have set it forth. He sat back in his chair at first, and spoke like a weary man. Afterwards he got more animated. In writing it down I feel with only too much keenness the inadequacy of pen and ink—and, above all, my own inadequacy—to express its quality. You read, I will suppose, attentively enough; but you cannot see the speaker's white, sincere face in the bright circle of the little lamp, nor hear the intonation of his voice. You cannot know how his expression followed the turns of his story! Most of us hearers were in shadow, for the candles in the smoking-room had not been lighted, and only the face of the Journalist and the legs of the Silent Man from the knees downward were illuminated. At first we glanced now and again at each other. After a time we ceased to do that, and looked only at the Time Traveller's face.

CHAPTER III: "I told some of you last Thursday of the principles of the Time Machine, and showed you the actual thing itself, incomplete in the workshop. There it is now, a little travel-worn, truly; and one of the ivory bars is cracked, and a brass rail bent; but the rest of it's sound enough. I expected to finish it on Friday; but on Friday, when the putting together was nearly done, I found that one of the nickel bars was exactly one inch too short, and this I had to get remade; so that the thing was not complete until this morning. It was at ten o'clock to-day that the first of all Time Machines began its career. I gave it a last tap, tried all the screws again, put one more drop of oil on the quartz rod, and sat myself in the saddle. I suppose a suicide who holds a pistol to his skull feels much the same wonder at what will come next as I felt then. I took the starting lever in one hand and the stopping one in the other, pressed the first, and almost immediately the second. I seemed to reel; I felt a nightmare sensation of falling; and, looking round, I saw the laboratory exactly as before. Had anything happened? For a moment I suspected that my intellect had tricked me. Then I noted the clock. A moment before, as it seemed, it had stood at a minute or so past ten; now it was nearly half-past three!

"I drew a breath, set my teeth, gripped the starting lever with both hands, and went off with a thud. The laboratory got hazy and went dark. Mrs. Watchett came in and walked, apparently without seeing me, towards the garden door. I suppose it took her a minute or so to traverse the place, but to me she seemed to shoot across the room like a rocket. I pressed the lever over to its extreme position. The night came like the turning out of a lamp, and in another moment came to-morrow. The laboratory grew faint and hazy, then fainter and ever fainter. To-morrow night came black, then day again, night again, day again, faster and faster still. An eddying murmur filled my ears, and a strange, dumb confusedness descended on my mind.

"I am afraid I cannot convey the peculiar sensations of time travelling. They are excessively unpleasant. There is a feeling exactly like that one has upon a switchback—of a helpless headlong motion! I felt the same horrible anticipation, too, of an imminent smash. As I put on pace, night followed day like the flapping of a black wing. The dim suggestion of the laboratory seemed presently to fall away from me, and I saw the sun hopping swiftly across the sky, leaping it every minute, and every minute marking a day. I supposed the laboratory had been destroyed and I had come into the open air. I had a dim impression of scaffolding, but I was already going too fast to be conscious of any moving things. The slowest snail that ever crawled dashed by too fast for me. The twinkling succession of darkness and light was excessively painful to the eye. Then, in the intermittent darknesses, I saw the moon spinning swiftly through her quarters from new to full, and had a faint glimpse of the circling stars. Presently, as I went on, still gaining velocity, the palpitation of night and day merged into one continuous greyness; the sky took on a wonderful deepness of blue, a splendid luminous colour like that of early twilight; the jerking sun became a streak of fire, a brilliant arch, in space; the moon a fainter fluctuating band; and I could see nothing of the stars, save now and then a brighter circle flickering in the blue.

"The landscape was misty and vague. I was still on the hillside upon which this house now stands, and the shoulder rose above me grey and dim. I saw trees growing and changing like puffs of vapour, now brown, now green; they grew, spread, shivered, and passed away. I saw huge buildings rise up faint and fair, and pass like dreams. The whole surface of the earth seemed changed—melting and flowing under my eyes. The little hands upon the dials that registered my speed raced round faster and faster. Presently I noted that the sun belt swayed up and down, from solstice to solstice, in a minute or less, and that consequently my pace was over a year a minute; and minute by minute the white snow flashed across the world, and vanished, and was followed by the bright, brief green of spring.

"The unpleasant sensations of the start were less poignant now. They merged at last into a kind of hysterical exhilaration. I remarked indeed a clumsy swaying of the machine for which I was unable to account. But my mind was too confused to attend to it, so with a kind of madness growing upon me, I flung myself into futurity. At first I scarce thought of stopping, scarce thought of anything but these new sensations. But presently a fresh series of impressions grew up in my mind—a certain curiosity and therewith a certain dread—until at last they took complete possession of me. What strange developments of humanity, what wonderful advances upon our rudimentary civilisation, I thought, might not appear when I came to look nearly into the dim elusive world that raced and fluctuated before my eyes! I saw great and splendid architecture rising about me, more massive than any buildings of our own time, and yet, as it seemed, built of glimmer and mist. I saw a richer green flow up the hillside, and remain there without any wintry intermission. Even through the veil of my confusion the earth seemed very fair. And so my mind came round to the business of stopping.

"The peculiar risk lay in the possibility of my finding some substance in the space which I, or the machine, occupied. So long as I travelled at a high velocity through time, this scarcely mattered; I was, so to speak, attenuated—was slipping like a vapour through the interstices of intervening substances! But to come to a stop involved the jamming of myself, molecule by molecule, into whatever lay in my way; meant bringing my atoms into such intimate contact with those of the obstacle that a profound chemical reaction—possibly a far-reaching explosion—would result, and blow myself and my apparatus out of all possible dimensions—into the Unknown. This possibility had occurred to me again and again while I was making the machine; but then I had cheerfully accepted it as an unavoidable risk—one of the risks a man has got to take! Now the risk was inevitable, I no longer saw it in the same cheerful light. The fact is that, insensibly, the absolute strangeness of everything, the sickly jarring and swaying of the machine, above all, the feeling of prolonged falling, had absolutely upset my nerve. I told myself that I could never stop, and with a gust of petulance I resolved to stop forthwith. Like an impatient fool, I lugged over the lever, and incontinently the thing went reeling over, and I was flung headlong through the air.

"There was the sound of a clap of thunder in my ears. I may have been stunned for a moment. A pitiless hail was hissing round me, and I was sitting on soft turf in front of the overset machine. Everything still seemed grey, but presently I remarked that the confusion in my ears was gone. I looked round me. I was on what seemed to be a little lawn in a garden, surrounded by rhododendron bushes, and I noticed that their mauve and purple blossoms were dropping in a shower under the beating of the hailstones. The rebounding, dancing hail hung in a cloud over the machine, and drove along the ground like smoke. In a moment I was wet to the skin. 'Fine hospitality,' said I, 'to a man who has travelled innumerable years to see you.'

"Presently I thought what a fool I was to get wet. I stood up and looked round me. A colossal figure, carved apparently in some white stone, loomed indistinctly beyond the rhododendrons through the hazy downpour. But all else of the world was invisible.

"My sensations would be hard to describe. As the columns of hail grew thinner, I saw the white figure more distinctly. It was very large, for a silver birch-tree touched its shoulder. It was of white marble, in shape something like a winged sphinx, but the wings, instead of being carried vertically at the sides, were spread so that it seemed to hover. The pedestal, it appeared to me, was of bronze, and was thick with verdigris. It chanced that the face was towards me; the sightless eyes seemed to watch me; there was the faint shadow of a smile on the lips. It was greatly weather-worn, and that imparted an unpleasant suggestion of disease. I stood looking at it for a little space—half a minute, perhaps, or half an hour. It seemed to advance and to recede as the hail drove before it denser or thinner. At last I tore my eyes from it for a moment, and saw that the hail curtain had worn threadbare, and that the sky was lightening with the promise of the sun.

"I looked up again at the crouching white shape, and the full temerity of my voyage came suddenly upon me. What might appear when that hazy curtain was altogether withdrawn? What might not have happened to men? What if cruelty had grown into a common passion? What if in this interval the race had lost its manliness, and had developed into something inhuman, unsympathetic, and overwhelmingly powerful? I might seem some old-world savage animal, only the more dreadful and disgusting for our common likeness—a foul creature to be incontinently slain.

"Already I saw other vast shapes—huge buildings with intricate parapets and tall columns, with a wooded hillside dimly creeping in upon me through the lessening storm. I was seized with a panic fear. I turned frantically to the Time Machine, and strove hard to readjust it. As I did so the shafts of the sun smote through the thunderstorm. The grey downpour was swept aside and vanished like the trailing garments of a ghost. Above me, in the intense blue of the summer sky, some faint brown shreds of cloud whirled into nothingness. The great buildings about me stood out clear and distinct, shining with the wet of the thunderstorm, and picked out in white by the unmelted hailstones piled along their courses. I felt naked in a strange world. I felt as perhaps a bird may feel in the clear air, knowing the hawk wins above and will swoop. My fear grew to frenzy. I took a breathing space, set my teeth, and again grappled fiercely, wrist and knee, with the machine. It gave under my desperate onset and turned over. It struck my chin violently. One hand on the saddle, the other on the lever, I stood panting heavily in attitude to mount again.

"But with this recovery of a prompt retreat my courage recovered. I looked more curiously and less fearfully at this world of the remote future. In a circular opening, high up in the wall of the nearer house, I saw a group of figures clad in rich soft robes. They had seen me, and their faces were directed towards me.

"Then I heard voices approaching me. Coming through the bushes by the White Sphinx were the heads and shoulders of men running. One of these emerged in a pathway leading straight to the little lawn upon which I stood with my machine. He was a slight creature—perhaps four feet high—clad in a purple tunic, girdled at the waist with a leather belt. Sandals or buskins—I could not clearly distinguish which—were on his feet; his legs were bare to the knees, and his head was bare. Noticing that, I noticed for the first time how warm the air was.

"He struck me as being a very beautiful and graceful creature, but indescribably frail. His flushed face reminded me of the more beautiful kind of consumptive—that hectic beauty of which we used to hear so much. At the sight of him I suddenly regained confidence. I took my hands from the machine.

CHAPTER IV: "In another moment we were standing face to face, I and this fragile thing out of futurity. He came straight up to me and laughed into my eyes. The absence from his bearing of any sign of fear struck me at once. Then he turned to the two others who were following him and spoke to them in a strange and very sweet and liquid tongue.

"There were others coming, and presently a little group of perhaps eight or ten of these exquisite creatures were about me. One of them addressed me. It came into my head, oddly enough, that my voice was too harsh and deep for them. So I shook my head, and, pointing to my ears, shook it again. He came a step forward, hesitated, and then touched my hand. Then I felt other soft little tentacles upon my back and shoulders. They wanted to make sure I was real. There was nothing in this at all alarming. Indeed, there was something in these pretty little people that inspired confidence—a graceful gentleness, a certain childlike ease. And besides, they looked so frail that I could fancy myself flinging the whole dozen of them about like nine-pins. But I made a sudden motion to warn them when I saw their little pink hands feeling at the Time Machine. Happily then, when it was not too late, I thought of a danger I had hitherto forgotten, and reaching over the bars of the machine I unscrewed the little levers that would set it in motion, and put these in my pocket. Then I turned again to see what I could do in the way of communication.

"And then, looking more nearly into their features, I saw some further peculiarities in their Dresden-china type of prettiness. Their hair, which was uniformly curly, came to a sharp end at the neck and cheek; there was not the faintest suggestion of it on the face, and their ears were singularly minute. The mouths were small, with bright red, rather thin lips, and the little chins ran to a point. The eyes were large and mild; and—this may seem egotism on my part—I fancied even then that there was a certain lack of the interest I might have expected in them.

"As they made no effort to communicate with me, but simply stood round me smiling and speaking in soft cooing notes to each other, I began the conversation. I pointed to the Time Machine and to myself. Then hesitating for a moment how to express time, I pointed to the sun. At once a quaintly pretty little figure in chequered purple and white followed my gesture, and then astonished me by imitating the sound of thunder.

"For a moment I was staggered, though the import of his gesture was plain enough. The question had come into my mind abruptly: were these creatures fools? You may hardly understand how it took me. You see I had always anticipated that the people of the year Eight Hundred and Two Thousand odd would be incredibly in front of us in knowledge, art, everything. Then one of them suddenly asked me a question that showed him to be on the intellectual level of one of our five-year-old children —asked me, in fact, if I had come from the sun in a thunderstorm! It let loose the judgment I had suspended upon their clothes, their frail light limbs, and fragile features. A flow of disappointment rushed across my mind. For a moment I felt that I had built the Time Machine in vain.

"I nodded, pointed to the sun, and gave them such a vivid rendering of a thunderclap as startled them. They all withdrew a pace or so and bowed. Then came one laughing towards me, carrying a chain of beautiful flowers altogether new to me, and put it about my neck. The idea was received with melodious applause; and presently they were all running to and fro for flowers, and laughingly flinging them upon me until I was almost smothered with blossom. You who have never seen the like can scarcely imagine what delicate and wonderful flowers countless years of culture had created. Then someone suggested that their plaything should be exhibited in the nearest building, and so I was led past the sphinx of white marble, which had seemed to watch me all the while with a smile at my astonishment, towards a vast grey edifice of fretted stone. As I went with them the memory of my confident anticipations of a profoundly grave and intellectual posterity came, with irresistible merriment, to my mind.

"The building had a huge entry, and was altogether of colossal dimensions. I was naturally most occupied with the growing crowd of little people, and with the big open portals that yawned before me shadowy and mysterious. My general impression of the world I saw over their heads was of a tangled waste of beautiful bushes and flowers, a long-neglected and yet weedless garden. I saw a number of tall spikes of strange white flowers, measuring a foot perhaps across the spread of the waxen petals. They grew scattered, as if wild, among the variegated shrubs, but, as I say, I did not examine them closely at this time. The Time Machine was left deserted on the turf among the rhododendrons.

"The arch of the doorway was richly carved, but naturally I did not observe the carving very narrowly, though I fancied I saw suggestions of old Phœnician decorations as I passed through, and it struck me that they were very badly broken and weather-worn. Several more brightly clad people met me in the doorway, and so we entered, I, dressed in dingy nineteenth-century garments, looking grotesque enough, garlanded with flowers, and surrounded by an eddying mass of bright, soft-coloured robes and shining white limbs, in a melodious whirl of laughter and laughing speech.

"The big doorway opened into a proportionately great hall hung with brown. The roof was in shadow, and the windows, partially glazed with coloured glass and partially unglazed, admitted a tempered light. The floor was made up of huge blocks of some very hard white metal, not plates nor slabs,—blocks, and it was so much worn, as I judged by the going to and fro of past generations, as to be deeply channelled along the more frequented ways. Transverse to the length were innumerable tables made of slabs of polished stone, raised perhaps a foot from the floor, and upon these were heaps of fruits. Some I recognised as a kind of hypertrophied raspberry and orange, but for the most part they were strange.

"Between the tables was scattered a great number of cushions. Upon these my conductors seated themselves, signing for me to do likewise. With a pretty absence of ceremony they began to eat the fruit with their hands, flinging peel and stalks and so forth into the round openings in the sides of the tables. I was not loth to follow their example, for I felt thirsty and hungry. As I did so I surveyed the hall at my leisure.

"And perhaps the thing that struck me most was its dilapidated look. The stained-glass windows, which displayed only a geometrical pattern, were broken in many places, and the curtains that hung across the lower end were thick with dust. And it caught my eye that the corner of the marble table near me was fractured. Nevertheless, the general effect was extremely rich and picturesque. There were, perhaps, a couple of hundred people dining in the hall, and most of them, seated as near to me as they could come, were watching me with interest, their little eyes shining over the fruit they were eating. All were clad in the same soft, and yet strong, silky material.

"Fruit, by the bye, was all their diet. These people of the remote future were strict vegetarians, and while I was with them, in spite of some carnal cravings, I had to be frugivorous also. Indeed, I found afterwards that horses, cattle, sheep, dogs, had followed the Ichthyosaurus into extinction. But the fruits were very delightful; one, in particular, that seemed to be in season all the time I was there—a floury thing in a three-sided husk—was especially good, and I made it my staple. At first I was puzzled by all these strange fruits, and by the strange flowers I saw, but later I began to perceive their import.

"However, I am telling you of my fruit dinner in the distant future now. So soon as my appetite was a little checked, I determined to make a resolute attempt to learn the speech of these new men of mine. Clearly that was the next thing to do. The fruits seemed a convenient thing to begin upon, and holding one of these up I began a series of interrogative sounds and gestures. I had some considerable difficulty in conveying my meaning. At first my efforts met with a stare of surprise or inextinguishable laughter, but presently a fair-haired little creature seemed to grasp my intention and repeated a name. They had to chatter and explain the business at great length to each other, and my first attempts to make the exquisite little sounds of their language caused an immense amount of amusement. However, I felt like a schoolmaster amidst children, and persisted, and presently I had a score of noun substantives at least at my command; and then I got to demonstrative pronouns, and even the verb 'to eat.' But it was slow work, and the little people soon tired and wanted to get away from my interrogations, so I determined, rather of necessity, to let them give their lessons in little doses when they felt inclined. And very little doses I found they were before long, for I never met people more indolent or more easily fatigued.

"A queer thing I soon discovered about my little hosts, and that was their lack of interest. They would come to me with eager cries of astonishment, like children, but like children they would soon stop examining me and wander away after some other toy. The dinner and my conversational beginnings ended, I noted for the first time that almost all those who had surrounded me at first were gone. It is odd, too, how speedily I came to disregard these little people. I went out through the portal into the sunlit world again so soon as my hunger was satisfied. I was continually meeting more of these men of the future, who would follow me a little distance, chatter and laugh about me, and, having smiled and gesticulated in a friendly way, leave me again to my own devices.

"The calm of evening was upon the world as I emerged from the great hall, and the scene was lit by the warm glow of the setting sun. At first things were very confusing. Everything was so entirely different from the world I had known—even the flowers. The big building I had left was situate on the slope of a broad river valley, but the Thames had shifted perhaps a mile from its present position. I resolved to mount to the summit of a crest, perhaps a mile and a half away, from which I could get a wider view of this our planet in the year Eight Hundred and Two Thousand Seven Hundred and One A.D. For that, I should explain, was the date the little dials of my machine recorded.

"As I walked I was watchful for every impression that could possibly help to explain the condition of ruinous splendour in which I found the world—for ruinous it was. A little way up the hill, for instance, was a great heap of granite, bound together by masses of aluminium, a vast labyrinth of precipitous walls and crumbled heaps, amidst which were thick heaps of very beautiful pagoda-like plants—nettles possibly—but wonderfully tinted with brown about the leaves, and incapable of stinging. It was evidently the derelict remains of some vast structure, to what end built I could not determine. It was here that I was destined, at a later date, to have a very strange experience—the first intimation of a still stranger discovery—but of that I will speak in its proper place.

"Looking round with a sudden thought, from a terrace on which I rested for a while, I realised that there were no small houses to be seen. Apparently the single house, and possibly even the household, had vanished. Here and there among the greenery were palace-like buildings, but the house and the cottage, which form such characteristic features of our own English landscape, had disappeared.

" 'Communism,' said I to myself.

"And on the heels of that came another thought. I looked at the half-dozen little figures that were following me. Then, in a flash, I perceived that all had the same form of costume, the same soft hairless visage, and the same girlish rotundity of limb. It may seem strange, perhaps, that I had not noticed this before. But everything was so strange. Now, I saw the fact plainly enough. In costume, and in all the differences of texture and bearing that now mark off the sexes from each other, these people of the future were alike. And the children seemed to my eyes to be but the miniatures of their parents. I judged, then, that the children of that time were extremely precocious, physically at least, and I found afterwards abundant verification of my opinion.

"Seeing the ease and security in which these people were living, I felt that this close resemblance of the sexes was after all what one would expect; for the strength of a man and the softness of a woman, the institution of the family, and the differentiation of occupations are mere militant necessities of an age of physical force. Where population is balanced and abundant, much child-bearing becomes an evil rather than a blessing to the State; where violence comes but rarely and offspring are secure, there is less necessity—indeed there is no necessity—for an efficient family, and the specialisation of the sexes with reference to their children's needs disappears. We see some beginnings of this even in our own time, and in this future age it was complete. This, I must remind you, was my speculation at the time. Later, I was to appreciate how far it fell short of the reality.

"While I was musing upon these things, my attention was attracted by a pretty little structure, like a well under a cupola. I thought in a transitory way of the oddness of wells still existing, and then resumed the thread of my speculations. There were no large buildings towards the top of the hill, and as my walking powers were evidently miraculous, I was presently left alone for the first time. With a strange sense of freedom and adventure I pushed on up to the crest.

"There I found a seat of some yellow metal that I did not recognise, corroded in places with a kind of pinkish rust and half smothered in soft moss, the arm rests cast and filed into the resemblance of griffins' heads. I sat down on it, and I surveyed the broad view of our old world under the sunset of that long day. It was as sweet and fair a view as I have ever seen. The sun had already gone below the horizon and the west was flaming gold, touched with some horizontal bars of purple and crimson. Below was the valley of the Thames, in which the river lay like a band of burnished steel. I have already spoken of the great palaces dotted about among the variegated greenery, some in ruins and some still occupied. Here and there rose a white or silvery figure in the waste garden of the earth, here and there came the sharp vertical line of some cupola or obelisk. There were no hedges, no signs of proprietary rights, no evidences of agriculture; the whole earth had become a garden.

"So watching, I began to put my interpretation upon the things I had seen, and as it shaped itself to me that evening, my interpretation was something in this way. (Afterwards I found I had got only a half-truth —or only a glimpse of one facet of the truth.)

"It seemed to me that I had happened upon humanity upon the wane. The ruddy sunset set me thinking of the sunset of mankind. For the first time I began to realise an odd consequence of the social effort in which we are at present engaged. And yet, come to think, it is a logical consequence enough. Strength is the outcome of need; security sets a premium on feebleness. The work of ameliorating the conditions of life—the true civilising process that makes life more and more secure—had gone steadily on to a climax. One triumph of a united humanity over Nature had followed another. Things that are now mere dreams had become projects deliberately put in hand and carried forward. And the harvest was what I saw!

"After all, the sanitation and the agriculture of to-day are still in the rudimentary stage. The science of our time has attacked but a little department of the field of human disease, but, even so, it spreads its operations very steadily and persistently. Our agriculture and horticulture destroy a weed just here and there and cultivate perhaps a score or so of wholesome plants, leaving the greater number to fight out a balance as they can. We improve our favourite plants and animals—and how few they are—gradually by selective breeding; now a new and better peach, now a seedless grape, now a sweeter and larger flower, now a more convenient breed of cattle. We improve them gradually, because our ideals are vague and tentative, and our knowledge is very limited; because Nature, too, is shy and slow in our clumsy hands. Some day all this will be better organised, and still better. That is the drift of the current in spite of the eddies. The whole world will be intelligent, educated, and coöperating; things will move faster and faster towards the subjugation of Nature. In the end, wisely and carefully we shall readjust the balance of animal and vegetable life to suit our human needs.

"This adjustment, I say, must have been done, and done well; done indeed for all Time, in the space of Time across which my machine had leaped. The air was free from gnats, the earth from weeds or fungi; everywhere were fruits and sweet and delightful flowers; brilliant butterflies flew hither and thither. The ideal of preventive medicine was attained. Diseases had been stamped out. I saw no evidence of any contagious diseases during all my stay. And I shall have to tell you later that even the processes of putrefaction and decay had been profoundly affected by these changes.

"Social triumphs, too, had been effected. I saw mankind housed in splendid shelters, gloriously clothed, and as yet I had found them engaged in no toil. There were no signs of struggle, neither social nor economical struggle. The shop, the advertisement, traffic, all that commerce which constitutes the body of our world, was gone. It was natural on that golden evening that I should jump at the idea of a social paradise. The difficulty of increasing population had been met, I guessed, and population had ceased to increase.

"But with this change in condition come inevitably adaptations to the change. What, unless biological science is a mass of errors, is the cause of human intelligence and vigour? Hardship and freedom: conditions under which the active, strong, and subtle survive and the weaker go to the wall; conditions that put a premium upon the loyal alliance of capable men, upon self-restraint, patience, and decision. And the institution of the family, and the emotions that arise therein, the fierce jealousy, the tenderness for offspring, parental self-devotion, all found their justification and support in the imminent dangers of the young. Now, where are these imminent dangers? There is a sentiment arising, and it will grow, against connubial jealousy, against fierce maternity, against passion of all sorts; unnecessary things now, and things that make us uncomfortable, savage survivals, discords in a refined and pleasant life.

"I thought of the physical slightness of the people, their lack of intelligence, and those big abundant ruins, and it strengthened my belief in a perfect conquest of Nature. For after the battle comes Quiet. Humanity has been strong, energetic, and intelligent, and had used all its abundant vitality to alter the conditions under which it lived. And now came the reaction of the altered conditions.

"Under the new conditions of perfect comfort and security that restless energy, that with us is strength, would become weakness. Even in our own time certain tendencies and desires, once necessary to survival, are a constant source of failure. Physical courage and the love of battle, for instance, are no great help—may even be hindrances—to a civilised man. And in a state of physical balance and security, power, intellectual as well as physical, would be out of place. For countless years I judged there had been no danger of war or solitary violence, no danger from wild beasts, no wasting disease to require strength of constitution, no need of toil. For such a life, what we should call the weak are as well equipped as the strong, are indeed no longer weak. Better equipped indeed they are, for the strong would be fretted by an energy for which there was no outlet. No doubt the exquisite beauty of the buildings I saw was the outcome of the last surgings of the now purposeless energy of mankind before it settled down into perfect harmony with the conditions under which it lived—the flourish of that triumph which began the last great peace. This has ever been the fate of energy in security; it takes to art and to eroticism, and then come languor and decay.

"Even this artistic impetus would at last die away—had almost died in the Time I saw. To adorn themselves with flowers, to dance, to sing in the sunlight; so much was left of the artistic spirit, and no more. Even that would fade in the end into a contented inactivity. We are kept keen on the grindstone of pain and necessity, and, it seemed to me, that here was that hateful grindstone broken at last!

"As I stood there in the gathering dark I thought that in this simple explanation I had mastered the problem of the world—mastered the whole secret of these delicious people. Possibly the checks they had devised for the increase of population had succeeded too well, and their numbers had rather diminished than kept stationary. That would account for the abandoned ruins. Very simple was my explanation, and plausible enough —as most wrong theories are!

CHAPTER V: "As I stood there musing over this too perfect triumph of man, the full moon, yellow and gibbous, came up out of an overflow of silver light in the northeast. The bright little figures ceased to move about below, a noiseless owl flitted by, and I shivered with the chill of the night. I determined to descend and find where I could sleep.

"I looked for the building I knew. Then my eye travelled along to the figure of the White Sphinx upon the pedestal of bronze, growing distinct as the light of the rising moon grew brighter. I could see the silver birch against it. There was the tangle of rhododendron bushes, black in the pale light, and there was the little lawn. I looked at the lawn again. A queer doubt chilled my complacency. 'No,' said I stoutly to myself, 'that was not the lawn.'

"But it was the lawn. For the white leprous face of the sphinx was towards it. Can you imagine what I felt as this conviction came home to me? But you cannot. The Time Machine was gone!

"At once, like a lash across the face, came the possibility of losing my own age, of being left helpless in this strange new world. The bare thought of it was an actual physical sensation. I could feel it grip me at the throat and stop my breathing. In another moment I was in a passion of fear and running with great leaping strides down the slope. Once I fell headlong and cut my face; I lost no time in stanching the blood, but jumped up and ran on, with a warm trickle down my cheek and chin. All the time I ran I was saying to myself, 'They have moved it a little, pushed it under the bushes out of the way.' Nevertheless, I ran with all my might. All the time, with the certainty that sometimes comes with excessive dread, I knew that such assurance was folly, knew instinctively that the machine was removed out of my reach. My breath came with pain. I suppose I covered the whole distance from the hill crest to the little lawn, two miles, perhaps, in ten minutes. And I am not a young man. I cursed aloud, as I ran, at my confident folly in leaving the machine, wasting good breath thereby. I cried aloud, and none answered. Not a creature seemed to be stirring in that moonlit world.

"When I reached the lawn my worst fears were realised. Not a trace of the thing was to be seen. I felt faint and cold when I faced the empty space among the black tangle of bushes. I ran round it furiously, as if the thing might be hidden in a corner, and then stopped abruptly, with my hands clutching my hair. Above me towered the sphinx, upon the bronze pedestal, white, shining, leprous, in the light of the rising moon. It seemed to smile in mockery of my dismay.

"I might have consoled myself by imagining the little people had put the mechanism in some shelter for me, had I not felt assured of their physical and intellectual inadequacy. That is what dismayed me: the sense of some hitherto unsuspected power, through whose intervention my invention had vanished. Yet, of one thing I felt assured: unless some other age had produced its exact duplicate, the machine could not have moved in time. The attachment of the levers—I will show you the method later—prevented any one from tampering with it in that way when they were removed. It had moved, and was hid, only in space. But then, where could it be?

"I think I must have had a kind of frenzy. I remember running violently in and out among the moonlit bushes all round the sphinx, and startling some white animal that, in the dim light, I took for a small deer. I remember, too, late that night, beating the bushes with my clenched fists until my knuckles were gashed and bleeding from the broken twigs. Then, sobbing and raving in my anguish of mind, I went down to the great building of stone. The big hall was dark, silent, and deserted. I slipped on the uneven floor, and fell over one of the malachite tables, almost breaking my shin. I lit a match and went on past the dusty curtains, of which I have told you.

"There I found a second great hall covered with cushions, upon which, perhaps, a score or so of the little people were sleeping. I have no doubt they found my second appearance strange enough, coming suddenly out of the quiet darkness with inarticulate noises and the splutter and flare of a match. For they had forgotten about matches. 'Where is my Time Machine?' I began, bawling like an angry child, laying hands upon them and shaking them up together. It must have been very queer to them. Some laughed, most of them looked sorely frightened. When I saw them standing round me, it came into my head that I was doing as foolish a thing as it was possible for me to do under the circumstances, in trying to revive the sensation of fear. For, reasoning from their daylight behaviour, I thought that fear must be forgotten.

"Abruptly, I dashed down the match, and, knocking one of the people over in my course, went blundering across the big dining-hall again, out under the moonlight. I heard cries of terror and their little feet running and stumbling this way and that. I do not remember all I did as the moon crept up the sky. I suppose it was the unexpected nature of my loss that maddened me. I felt hopelessly cut off from my own kind—a strange animal in an unknown world. I must have raved to and fro, screaming and crying upon God and Fate. I have a memory of horrible fatigue, as the long night of despair wore away; of looking in this impossible place and that; of groping among moonlit ruins and touching strange creatures in the black shadows; at last, of lying on the ground near the sphinx and weeping with absolute wretchedness. I had nothing left but misery. Then I slept, and when I woke again it was full day, and a couple of sparrows were hopping round me on the turf within reach of my arm.

"I sat up in the freshness of the morning, trying to remember how I had got there, and why I had such a profound sense of desertion and despair. Then things came clear in my mind. With the plain, reasonable daylight, I could look my circumstances fairly in the face. I saw the wild folly of my frenzy overnight, and I could reason with myself. 'Suppose the worst?' I said. 'Suppose the machine altogether lost—perhaps destroyed? It behoves me to be calm and patient, to learn the way of the people, to get a clear idea of the method of my loss, and the means of getting materials and tools; so that in the end, perhaps, I may make another.' That would be my only hope, a poor hope perhaps, but better than despair. And, after all, it was a beautiful and curious world.

"But probably the machine had only been taken away. Still, I must be calm and patient, find its hiding place, and recover it by force or cunning. And with that I scrambled to my feet and looked about me, wondering where I could bathe. I felt weary, stiff, and travel-soiled. The freshness of the morning made me desire an equal freshness. I had exhausted my emotion. Indeed, as I went about my business, I found myself wondering at my intense excitement overnight. I made a careful examination of the ground about the little lawn. I wasted some time in futile questionings, conveyed, as well as I was able, to such of the little people as came by. They all failed to understand my gestures; some were simply stolid, some thought it was a jest and laughed at me. I had the hardest task in the world to keep my hands off their pretty laughing faces. It was a foolish impulse, but the devil begotten of fear and blind anger was ill curbed and still eager to take advantage of my perplexity. The turf gave better counsel. I found a groove ripped in it, about midway between the pedestal of the sphinx and the marks of my feet where, on arrival, I had struggled with the overturned machine. There were other signs of removal about, with queer narrow footprints like those I could imagine made by a sloth. This directed my closer attention to the pedestal. It was, as I think I have said, of bronze. It was not a mere block, but highly decorated with deep framed panels on either side. I went and rapped at these. The pedestal was hollow. Examining the panels with care I found them discontinuous with the frames. There were no handles or keyholes, but possibly the panels, if they were doors, as I supposed, opened from within. One thing was clear enough to my mind. It took no very great mental effort to infer that my Time Machine was inside that pedestal. But how it got there was a different problem.

"I saw the heads of two orange-clad people coming through the bushes and under some blossom-covered apple-trees towards me. I turned smiling to them and beckoned them to me. They came, and then, pointing to the bronze pedestal, I tried to intimate my wish to open it. But at my first gesture towards this they behaved very oddly. I don't know how to convey their expression to you. Suppose you were to use a grossly improper gesture to a delicate-minded woman—it is how she would look. They went off as if they had received the last possible insult. I tried a sweet-looking little chap in white next, with exactly the same result. Somehow, his manner made me feel ashamed of myself. But, as you know, I wanted the Time Machine, and I tried him once more. As he turned off, like the others, my temper got the better of me. In three strides I was after him, had him by the loose part of his robe round the neck, and began dragging him towards the sphinx. Then I saw the horror and repugnance of his face, and all of a sudden I let him go.

"But I was not beaten yet. I banged with my fist at the bronze panels. I thought I heard something stir inside—to be explicit, I thought I heard a sound like a chuckle—but I must have been mistaken. Then I got a big pebble from the river, and came and hammered till I had flattened a coil in the decorations, and the verdigris came off in powdery flakes. The delicate little people must have heard me hammering in gusty outbreaks a mile away on either hand, but nothing came of it. I saw a crowd of them upon the slopes, looking furtively at me. At last, hot and tired, I sat down to watch the place. But I was too restless to watch long; I am too Occidental for a long vigil. I could work at a problem for years, but to wait inactive for twenty-four hours—that is another matter.

"I got up after a time, and began walking aimlessly through the bushes towards the hill again. 'Patience,' said I to myself. 'If you want your machine again you must leave that sphinx alone. If they mean to take your machine away, it's little good your wrecking their bronze panels, and if they don't, you will get it back as soon as you can ask for it. To sit among all these unknown things before a puzzle like that is hopeless. That way lies monomania. Face this world. Learn its ways, watch it, be careful of too hasty guesses at its meaning. In the end you will find clues to it all.' Then suddenly the humour of the situation came into my mind: the thought of the years I had spent in study and toil to get into the future age, and now my passion of anxiety to get out of it. I had made myself the most complicated and the most hopeless trap that ever a man devised. Although it was at my own expense, I could not help myself. I laughed aloud.

"Going through the big palace, it seemed to me that the little people avoided me. It may have been my fancy, or it may have had something to do with my hammering at the gates of bronze. Yet I felt tolerably sure of the avoidance. I was careful, however, to show no concern and to abstain from any pursuit of them, and in the course of a day or two things got back to the old footing. I made what progress I could in the language, and in addition I pushed my explorations here and there. Either I missed some subtle point, or their language was excessively simple—almost exclusively composed of concrete substantives and verbs. There seemed to be few, if any, abstract terms, or little use of figurative language. Their sentences were usually simple and of two words, and I failed to convey or understand any but the simplest propositions. I determined to put the thought of my Time Machine and the mystery of the bronze doors under the sphinx as much as possible in a corner of memory, until my growing knowledge would lead me back to them in a natural way. Yet a certain feeling, you may understand, tethered me in a circle of a few miles round the point of my arrival.

"So far as I could see, all the world displayed the same exuberant richness as the Thames valley. From every hill I climbed I saw the same abundance of splendid buildings, endlessly varied in material and style, the same clustering thickets of evergreens, the same blossom-laden trees and tree-ferns. Here and there water shone like silver, and beyond, the land rose into blue undulating hills, and so faded into the serenity of the sky. A peculiar feature, which presently attracted my attention, was the presence of certain circular wells, several, as it seemed to me, of a very great depth. One lay by the path up the hill, which I had followed during my first walk. Like the others, it was rimmed with bronze, curiously wrought, and protected by a little cupola from the rain. Sitting by the side of these wells, and peering down into the shafted darkness, I could see no gleam of water, nor could I start any reflection with a lighted match. But in all of them I heard a certain sound: a thud—thud—thud, like the beating of some big engine; and I discovered, from the flaring of my matches, that a steady current of air set down the shafts. Further, I threw a scrap of paper into the throat of one, and, instead of fluttering slowly down, it was at once sucked swiftly out of sight.

"After a time, too, I came to connect these wells with tall towers standing here and there upon the slopes; for above them there was often just such a flicker in the air as one sees on a hot day above a sun-scorched beach. Putting things together, I reached a strong suggestion of an extensive system of subterranean ventilation, whose true import it was difficult to imagine. I was at first inclined to associate it with the sanitary apparatus of these people. It was an obvious conclusion, but it was absolutely wrong.

"And here I must admit that I learned very little of drains and bells and modes of conveyance, and the like conveniences during my time in this real future. In some of these visions of Utopias and coming times which I have read, there is a vast amount of detail about building, and social arrangements, and so forth. But while such details are easy enough to obtain when the whole world is contained in one's imagination, they are altogether inaccessible to a real traveller amid such realities as I found here. Conceive the tale of London which a negro, fresh from Central Africa, would take back to his tribe! What would he know of railway companies, of social movements, of telephone and telegraph wires, of the Parcels Delivery Company, and postal orders and the like? Yet we, at least, should be willing enough to explain these things to him! And even of what he knew, how much could he make his untravelled friend either apprehend or believe? Then, think how narrow the gap between a negro and a white man of our own times, and how wide the interval between myself and these of the Golden Age! I was sensible of much which was unseen, and which contributed to my comfort; but save for a general impression of automatic organisation, I fear I can convey very little of the difference to your mind.

"In the matter of sepulture, for instance, I could see no signs of crematoria nor anything suggestive of tombs. But it occurred to me that, possibly, there might be cemeteries (or crematoria) somewhere beyond the range of my explorings. This, again, was a question I deliberately put to myself, and my curiosity was at first entirely defeated upon the point. The thing puzzled me, and I was led to make a further remark, which puzzled me still more: that aged and infirm among this people there were none.

"I must confess that my satisfaction with my first theories of an automatic civilisation and a decadent humanity did not long endure. Yet I could think of no other. Let me put my difficulties. The several big palaces I had explored were mere living places, great dining-halls and sleeping apartments. I could find no machinery, no appliances of any kind. Yet these people were clothed in pleasant fabrics that must at times need renewal, and their sandals, though undecorated, were fairly complex specimens of metalwork. Somehow such things must be made. And the little people displayed no vestige of a creative tendency. There were no shops, no workshops, no sign of importations among them. They spent all their time in playing gently, in bathing in the river, in making love in a half-playful fashion, in eating fruit and sleeping. I could not see how things were kept going.

"Then, again, about the Time Machine: something, I knew not what, had taken it into the hollow pedestal of the White Sphinx. *Why?* For the life of me I could not imagine. Those waterless wells, too, those flickering pillars. I felt I lacked a clue. I felt—how shall I put it? Suppose you found an inscription, with sentences here and there in excellent plain English, and interpolated therewith, others made up of words, of letters even, absolutely unknown to you? Well, on the third day of my visit, that was how the world of Eight Hundred and Two Thousand Seven Hundred and One presented itself to me!

"That day, too, I made a friend—of a sort. It happened that, as I was watching some of the little people bathing in a shallow, one of them was seized with cramp and began drifting downstream. The main current ran rather swiftly, but not too strongly for even a moderate swimmer. It will give you an idea, therefore, of the strange deficiency in these creatures, when I tell you that none made the slightest attempt to rescue the weakly crying little thing which was drowning before their eyes. When I realised this, I hurriedly slipped off my clothes, and, wading in at a point lower down, I caught the poor mite and drew her safe to land. A little rubbing of the limbs soon brought her round, and I had the satisfaction of seeing she was all right before I left her. I had got to such a low estimate of her kind that I did not expect any gratitude from her. In that, however, I was wrong.

"This happened in the morning. In the afternoon I met my little woman, as I believe it was, as I was returning towards my centre from an exploration, and she received me with cries of delight and presented me with a big garland of flowers—evidently made for me and me alone. The thing took my imagination. Very possibly I had been feeling desolate. At any rate I did my best to display my appreciation of the gift. We were soon seated together in a little stone arbour, engaged in conversation, chiefly of smiles. The creature's friendliness affected me exactly as a child's might have done. We passed each other flowers, and she kissed my hands. I did the same to hers. Then I tried talk, and found that her name was Weena, which, though I don't know what it meant, somehow seemed appropriate enough. That was the beginning of a queer friendship which lasted a week, and ended—as I will tell you!

"She was exactly like a child. She wanted to be with me always. She tried to follow me everywhere, and my next journey out and about it went to my heart to tire her down, and leave her at last, exhausted and calling after me rather plaintively. But the problems of the world had to be mastered. I had not, I said to myself, come into the future to carry on a miniature flirtation. Yet her distress when I left her was very great, her expostulations at the parting were sometimes frantic, and I think, altogether, I had as much trouble as comfort from her devotion. Nevertheless she was, somehow, a very great comfort. I thought it was mere childish affection that made her cling to me. Until it was too late, I did not clearly know what I had inflicted upon her when I left her. Nor until it was too late did I clearly understand what she was to me. For, by merely seeming fond of me, and showing in her weak, futile way that she cared for me, the little doll of a creature presently gave my return to the neighbourhood of the White Sphinx almost the feeling of coming home; and I would watch for her tiny figure of white and gold so soon as I came over the hill.

"It was from her, too, that I learned that fear had not yet left the world. She was fearless enough in the daylight, and she had the oddest confidence in me; for once, in a foolish moment, I made threatening grimaces at her, and she simply laughed at them. But she dreaded the dark, dreaded shadows, dreaded black things. Darkness to her was the one thing dreadful. It was a singularly passionate emotion, and it set me thinking and observing. I discovered then, among other things, that these little people gathered into the great houses after dark, and slept in droves. To enter upon them without a light was to put them into a tumult of apprehension. I never found one out of doors, or one sleeping alone within doors, after dark. Yet I was still such a blockhead that I missed the lesson of that fear, and in spite of Weena's distress I insisted upon sleeping away from these slumbering multitudes.

"It troubled her greatly, but in the end her odd affection for me triumphed, and for five of the nights of our acquaintance, including the last night of all, she slept with her head pillowed on my arm. But my story slips away from me as I speak of her. It must have been the night before her rescue that I was awakened about dawn. I had been restless, dreaming most disagreeably that I was drowned, and that sea-anemones were feeling over my face with their soft palps. I woke with a start, and with an odd fancy that some greyish animal had just rushed out of the chamber. I tried to get to sleep again, but I felt restless and uncomfortable. It was that dim grey hour when things are just creeping out of darkness, when everything is colourless and clear cut, and yet unreal. I got up, and went down into the great hall, and so out upon the flagstones in front of the palace. I thought I would make a virtue of necessity, and see the sunrise.

"The moon was setting, and the dying moonlight and the first pallor of dawn were mingled in a ghastly half-light. The bushes were inky black, the ground a sombre grey, the sky colourless and cheerless. And up the hill I thought I could see ghosts. Three several times, as I scanned the slope, I saw white figures. Twice I fancied I saw a solitary white, ape-like creature running rather quickly up the hill, and once near the ruins I saw a leash of them carrying some dark body. They moved hastily. I did not see what became of them. It seemed that they vanished among the bushes. The dawn was still indistinct, you must understand. I was feeling that chill, uncertain, early-morning feeling you may have known. I doubted my eyes.

"As the eastern sky grew brighter, and the light of the day came on and its vivid colouring returned upon the world once more, I scanned the view keenly. But I saw no vestige of my white figures. They were mere creatures of the half-light. 'They must have been ghosts,' I said; 'I wonder whence they dated.' For a queer notion of Grant Allen's came into my head, and amused me. If each generation die and leave ghosts, he argued, the world at last will get overcrowded with them. On that theory they would have grown innumerable some Eight Hundred Thousand Years hence, and it was no great wonder to see four at once. But the jest was unsatisfying, and I was thinking of these figures all the morning, until Weena's rescue drove them out of my head. I associated them in some indefinite way with the white animal I had startled in my first passionate search for the Time Machine. But Weena was a pleasant substitute. Yet all the same, they were soon destined to take far deadlier possession of my mind.

"I think I have said how much hotter than our own was the weather of this Golden Age. I cannot account for it. It may be that the sun was hotter, or the earth nearer the sun. It is usual to assume that the sun will go on cooling steadily in the future. But people, unfamiliar with such speculations as those of the younger Darwin, forget that the planets must ultimately fall back one by one into the parent body. As these catastrophes occur, the sun will blaze with renewed energy; and it may be that some inner planet had suffered this fate. Whatever the reason, the fact remains that the sun was very much hotter than we know it.

"Well, one very hot morning—my fourth, I think—as I was seeking shelter from the heat and glare in a colossal ruin near the great house where I slept and fed, there happened this strange thing: Clambering among these heaps of masonry, I found a narrow gallery, whose end and side windows were blocked by fallen masses of stone. By contrast with the brilliancy outside, it seemed at first impenetrably dark to me. I entered it groping, for the change from light to blackness made spots of colour swim before me. Suddenly I halted spellbound. A pair of eyes, luminous by reflection against the daylight without, was watching me out of the darkness.

"The old instinctive dread of wild beasts came upon me. I clenched my hands and steadfastly looked into the glaring eyeballs. I was afraid to turn. Then the thought of the absolute security in which humanity appeared to be living came to my mind. And then I remembered that strange terror of the dark. Overcoming my fear to some extent, I advanced a step and spoke. I will admit that my voice was harsh and ill-controlled. I put out my hand and touched something soft. At once the eyes darted sideways, and something white ran past me. I turned with my heart in my mouth, and saw a queer little ape-like figure, its head held down in a peculiar manner, running across the sunlit space behind me. It blundered against a block of granite, staggered aside, and in a moment was hidden in a black shadow beneath another pile of ruined masonry.

"My impression of it is, of course, imperfect; but I know it was a dull white, and had strange large greyish-red eyes; also that there was flaxen hair on its head and down its back. But, as I say, it went too fast for me to see distinctly. I cannot even say whether it ran on all-fours, or only with its forearms held very low. After an instant's pause I followed it into the second heap of ruins. I could not find it at first; but, after a time in the profound obscurity, I came upon one of those round well-like openings of which I have told you, half closed by a fallen pillar. A sudden thought came to me. Could this Thing have vanished down the shaft? I lit a match, and, looking down, I saw a small, white, moving creature, with large bright eyes which regarded me steadfastly as it retreated. It made me shudder. It was so like a human spider! It was clambering down the wall, and now I saw for the first time a number of metal foot and hand rests forming a kind of ladder down the shaft. Then the light burned my fingers and fell out of my hand, going out as it dropped, and when I had lit another the little monster had disappeared.

"I do not know how long I sat peering down that well. It was not for some time that I could succeed in persuading myself that the thing I had seen was human. But, gradually, the truth dawned on me: that Man had not remained one species, but had differentiated into two distinct animals: that my graceful children of the Upper World were not the sole descendants of our generation, but that this bleached, obscene, nocturnal Thing, which had flashed before me, was also heir to all the ages.

"I thought of the flickering pillars and of my theory of an underground ventilation. I began to suspect their true import. And what, I wondered, was this Lemur doing in my scheme of a perfectly balanced organisation? How was it related to the indolent serenity of the beautiful Upper-worlders? And what was hidden down there at the foot of that shaft? I sat upon the edge of the well telling myself that, at any rate, there was nothing to fear, and that there I must descend for the solution of my difficulties. And withal I was absolutely afraid to go! As I hesitated, two of the beautiful upper-world people came running in their amorous sport across the daylight into the shadow. The male pursued the female, flinging flowers at her as he ran.

"They seemed distressed to find me, my arm against the overturned pillar, peering down the well. Apparently it was considered bad form to remark these apertures; for when I pointed to this one, and tried to frame a question about it in their tongue, they were still more visibly distressed and turned away. But they were interested by my matches, and I struck some to amuse them. I tried them again about the well, and again I failed. So presently I left them, meaning to go back to Weena, and see what I could get from her. But my mind was already in revolution; my guesses and impressions were slipping and sliding to a new adjustment. I had now a clue to the import of these wells, to the ventilating towers, to the mystery of the ghosts; to say nothing of a hint at the meaning of the bronze gates and the fate of the Time Machine! And very vaguely there came a suggestion towards the solution of the economic problem that had puzzled me.

"Here was the new view. Plainly, this second species of Man was subterranean. There were three circumstances in particular which made me think that its rare emergence above ground was the outcome of a long-continued underground habit. In the first place, there was the bleached look common in most animals that live largely in the dark—the white fish of the Kentucky caves, for instance. Then, those large eyes, with that capacity for reflecting light, are common features of nocturnal things—witness the owl and the cat. And last of all, that evident confusion in the sunshine, that hasty yet fumbling and awkward flight towards dark shadow, and that peculiar carriage of the head while in the light—all reinforced the theory of an extreme sensitiveness of the retina.

"Beneath my feet, then, the earth must be tunnelled enormously, and these tunnellings were the habitat of the new race. The presence of ventilating-shafts and wells along the hill slopes—everywhere, in fact, except along the river valley—showed how universal were its ramifications. What so natural, then, as to assume that it was in this artificial underworld that such work as was necessary to the comfort of the daylight race was done? The notion was so plausible that I at once accepted it, and went on to assume the how of this splitting of the human species. I dare say you will anticipate the shape of my theory; though, for myself, I very soon felt that it fell far short of the truth.

"At first, proceeding from the problems of our own age, it seemed clear as daylight to me that the gradual widening of the present merely temporary and social difference between the Capitalist and the Labourer was the key to the whole position. No doubt it will seem grotesque enough to you—and wildly incredible!—and yet even now there are existing circumstances to point that way. There is a tendency to utilise underground

space for the less ornamental purposes of civilisation; there is the Metro-
politan Railway in London, for instance, there are new electric railways,
there are subways, there are underground workrooms and restaurants,
and they increase and multiply. Evidently, I thought, this tendency had
increased till Industry had gradually lost its birthright in the sky. I mean
that it had gone deeper and deeper into larger and ever larger underground factories, spending a still-increasing amount of its time therein,
till, in the end—! Even now, does not an East-end worker live in such
artificial conditions as practically to be cut off from the natural surface
of the earth?

"Again, the exclusive tendency of richer people—due, no doubt, to the
increasing refinement of their education, and the widening gulf between
them and the rude violence of the poor—is already leading to the closing,
in their interest, of considerable portions of the surface of the land.
About London, for instance, perhaps half the prettier country is shut in
against intrusion. And this same widening gulf—which is due to the
length and expense of the higher educational process and the increased
facilities for and temptations towards refined habits on the part of the
rich—will make that exchange between class and class, that promotion by
intermarriage which at present retards the splitting of our species along
lines of social stratification, less and less frequent. So, in the end, above
ground you must have the Haves, pursuing pleasure and comfort, and
beauty, and below ground the Have-nots, the Workers getting continually adapted to the conditions of their labour. Once they were there, they
would no doubt have to pay rent, and not a little of it, for the ventilation
of their caverns; and if they refused, they would starve or be suffocated
for arrears. Such of them as were so constituted as to be miserable and
rebellious would die; and, in the end, the balance being permanent, the
survivors would become as well adapted to the conditions of underground
life, and as happy in their way, as the Upper-world people were to theirs.
As it seemed to me, the refined beauty and the etiolated pallor followed
naturally enough.

"The great triumph of Humanity I had dreamed of took a different
shape in my mind. It had been no such triumph of moral education and
general coöperation as I had imagined. Instead, I saw a real aristocracy,
armed with a perfected science and working to a logical conclusion the
industrial system of to-day. Its triumph had not been simply a triumph
over Nature, but a triumph over Nature and the fellow-man. This, I
must warn you, was my theory at the time. I had no convenient cicerone
in the pattern of the Utopian books. My explanation may be absolutely
wrong. I still think it is the most plausible one. But even on this supposition the balanced civilisation that was at last attained must have long
since passed its zenith, and was now far fallen into decay. The too-perfect

security of the Upper-worlders had led them to a slow movement of degeneration, to a general dwindling in size, strength, and intelligence. That I could see clearly enough already. What had happened to the Undergrounders I did not yet suspect; but from what I had seen of the Morlocks —that, by the bye, was the name by which these creatures were called—I could imagine that the modification of the human type was even far more profound than among the 'Eloi,' the beautiful race that I already knew.

"Then came troublesome doubts. Why had the Morlocks taken my Time Machine? For I felt sure it was they who had taken it. Why, too, if the Eloi were masters, could they not restore the machine to me? And why were they so terribly afraid of the dark? I proceeded, as I have said, to question Weena about this Underworld, but here again I was disappointed. At first she would not understand my questions, and presently she refused to answer them. She shivered as though the topic was unendurable. And when I pressed her, perhaps a little harshly, she burst into tears. They were the only tears, except my own, I ever saw in that Golden Age. When I saw them I ceased abruptly to trouble about the Morlocks, and was only concerned in banishing these signs of the human inheritance from Weena's eyes. And very soon she was smiling and clapping her hands, while I solemnly burned a match.

CHAPTER VI: "It may seem odd to you, but it was two days before I could follow up the new-found clue in what was manifestly the proper way. I felt a peculiar shrinking from those pallid bodies. They were just the half-bleached colour of the worms and things one sees preserved in spirit in a zoölogical museum. And they were filthily cold to the touch. Probably my shrinking was largely due to the sympathetic influence of the Eloi, whose disgust of the Morlocks I now began to appreciate.

"The next night I did not sleep well. Probably my health was a little disordered. I was oppressed with perplexity and doubt. Once or twice I had a feeling of intense fear for which I could perceive no definite reason. I remember creeping noiselessly into the great hall where the little people were sleeping in the moonlight—that night Weena was among them—and feeling reassured by their presence. It occurred to me even then, that in the course of a few days the moon must pass through its last quarter, and the nights grow dark, when the appearances of these unpleasant creatures from below, these whitened Lemurs, this new vermin that had replaced the old, might be more abundant. And on both these days I had the restless feeling of one who shirks an inevitable duty. I felt assured that the Time Machine was only to be recovered by boldly penetrating these underground mysteries. Yet I could not face the mystery. If only I had had a companion it would have been different. But I was so horribly alone, and even to clamber down into the darkness of the well appalled me. I don't know if you will understand my feeling, but I never felt quite safe at my back.

"It was this restlessness, this insecurity, perhaps, that drove me further and further afield in my exploring expeditions. Going to the south-westward towards the rising country that is now called Combe Wood, I observed far off, in the direction of nineteenth-century Banstead, a vast green structure, different in character from any I had hitherto seen. It was larger than the largest of the palaces or ruins I knew, and the façade had an Oriental look: the face of it having the lustre, as well as the pale-green tint, a kind of bluish-green, of a certain type of Chinese porcelain. This difference in aspect suggested a difference in use, and I was minded to push on and explore. But the day was growing late, and I had come upon the sight of the place after a long and tiring circuit; so I resolved to hold over the adventure for the following day, and I returned to the welcome and the caresses of little Weena. But next morning I perceived clearly enough that my curiosity regarding the Palace of Green Porcelain was a piece of self-deception, to enable me to shirk, by another day, an experience I dreaded. I resolved I would make the descent without further waste of time, and started out in the early morning towards a well near the ruins of granite and aluminium.

"Little Weena ran with me. She danced beside me to the well, but when she saw me lean over the mouth and look downward, she seemed strangely disconcerted. 'Good-bye, little Weena,' I said, kissing her; and then, putting her down, I began to feel over the parapet for the climbing hooks. Rather hastily, I may as well confess, for I feared my courage might leak away! At first she watched me in amazement. Then she gave a most piteous cry, and, running to me, she began to pull at me with her little hands. I think her opposition nerved me rather to proceed. I shook her off, perhaps a little roughly, and in another moment I was in the throat of the well. I saw her agonised face over the parapet, and smiled to reassure her. Then I had to look down at the unstable hooks to which I clung.

"I had to clamber down a shaft of perhaps two hundred yards. The descent was effected by means of metallic bars projecting from the sides of the well, and these being adapted to the needs of a creature much smaller and lighter than myself, I was speedily cramped and fatigued by the descent. And not simply fatigued! One of the bars bent suddenly under my weight, and almost swung me off into the blackness beneath. For a moment I hung by one hand, and after that experience I did not dare to rest again. Though my arms and back were presently acutely painful, I went on clambering down the sheer descent with as quick a motion as possible. Glancing upward, I saw the aperture, a small blue disk, in which a star was visible, while little Weena's head showed as a round black projection. The thudding sound of a machine below grew louder and more oppressive. Everything save that little disk above was profoundly dark, and when I looked up again Weena had disappeared.

"I was in an agony of discomfort. I had some thought of trying to go up the shaft again, and leave the Underworld alone. But even while I turned this over in my mind I continued to descend. At last, with intense relief, I saw dimly coming up, a foot to the right of me, a slender loophole in the wall. Swinging myself in, I found it was the aperture of a narrow horizontal tunnel in which I could lie down and rest. It was not too soon. My arms ached, my back was cramped, and I was trembling with the prolonged terror of a fall. Besides this, the unbroken darkness had had a distressing effect upon my eyes. The air was full of the throb and hum of machinery pumping air down the shaft.

"I do not know how long I lay. I was roused by a soft hand touching my face. Starting up in the darkness I snatched at my matches and, hastily striking one, I saw three stooping white creatures similar to the one I had seen above ground in the ruin, hastily retreating before the light. Living, as they did, in what appeared to me impenetrable darkness, their eyes were abnormally large and sensitive, just as are the pupils of the abysmal fishes, and they reflected the light in the same way. I have no doubt they could see me in that rayless obscurity, and they did not seem to have any fear of me apart from the light. But, so soon as I struck a match in order to see them, they fled incontinently, vanishing into dark gutters and tunnels, from which their eyes glared at me in the strangest fashion.

"I tried to call to them, but the language they had was apparently different from that of the Overworld people; so that I was needs left to my own unaided efforts, and the thought of flight before exploration was even then in my mind. But I said to myself, 'You are in for it now,' and, feeling my way along the tunnel, I found the noise of machinery grow louder. Presently the walls fell away from me, and I came to a large open space, and, striking another match, saw that I had entered a vast arched cavern, which stretched into utter darkness beyond the range of my light. The view I had of it was as much as one could see in the burning of a match.

"Necessarily my memory is vague. Great shapes like big machines rose out of the dimness, and cast grotesque black shadows, in which dim spectral Morlocks sheltered from the glare. The place, by the bye, was very stuffy and oppressive, and the faint halitus of freshly shed blood was in the air. Some way down the central vista was a little table of white metal, laid with what seemed a meal. The Morlocks at any rate were carnivorous! Even at the time, I remember wondering what large animal could have survived to furnish the red joint I saw. It was all very indistinct: the heavy smell, the big unmeaning shapes, the obscene figures lurking in the shadows, and only waiting for the darkness to come at me again! Then the match burned down, and stung my fingers, and fell, a wriggling red spot in the blackness.

"I have thought since how particularly ill equipped I was for such an experience. When I had started with the Time Machine, I had started with the absurd assumption that the men of the Future would certainly be infinitely ahead of ourselves in all their appliances. I had come without arms, without medicine, without anything to smoke—at times I missed tobacco frightfully—even without enough matches. If only I had thought of a Kodak! I could have flashed that glimpse of the underworld in a second, and examined it at leisure. But, as it was, I stood there with only the weapons and the powers that Nature had endowed me with—hands, feet, and teeth; these, and four safety-matches that still remained to me.

"I was afraid to push my way in among all this machinery in the dark, and it was only with my last glimpse of light I discovered that my store of matches had run low. It had never occurred to me until that moment that there was any need to economise them, and I had wasted almost half the box in astonishing the Upper-worlders, to whom fire was a novelty. Now, as I say, I had four left, and while I stood in the dark, a hand touched mine, lank fingers came feeling over my face, and I was sensible of a peculiar unpleasant odour. I fancied I heard the breathing of a crowd of those dreadful little beings about me. I felt the box of matches in my hand being gently disengaged, and other hands behind me plucking at my clothing. The sense of these unseen creatures examining me was indescribably unpleasant. The sudden realisation of my ignorance of their ways of thinking and doing came home to me very vividly in the darkness. I shouted at them as loudly as I could. They started away, and then I could feel them approaching me again. They clutched at me more boldly, whispering odd sounds to each other. I shivered violently, and shouted again —rather discordantly. This time they were not so seriously alarmed, and they made a queer laughing noise as they came back at me. I will confess I was horribly frightened. I determined to strike another match and escape under the protection of its glare. I did so, and eking out the flicker with a scrap of paper from my pocket, I made good my retreat to the narrow tunnel. But I had scarce entered this when my light was blown out, and in the blackness I could hear the Morlocks rustling like wind among leaves, and pattering like the rain, as they hurried after me.

"In a moment I was clutched by several hands, and there was no mistaking that they were trying to haul me back. I struck another light, and waved it in their dazzled faces. You can scarce imagine how nauseatingly inhuman they looked—those pale, chinless faces and great, lidless, pinkish-grey eyes!—as they stared in their blindness and bewilderment. But I did not stay to look, I promise you: I retreated again, and when my second match had ended, I struck my third. It had almost burned through when I reached the opening into the shaft. I lay down on the edge, for the throb of the great pump below made me giddy. Then I felt sideways for the projecting hooks, and, as I did so, my feet were grasped from behind, and I was violently tugged backward. I lit my last match . . . and it incontinently went out. But I had my hand on the climbing bars now, and, kicking violently, I disengaged myself from the clutches of the Morlocks and was speedily clambering up the shaft, while they stayed peering and blinking up at me: all but one little wretch who followed me for some way, and well-nigh secured my boot as a trophy.

"That climb seemed interminable to me. With the last twenty or thirty feet of it a deadly nausea came upon me. I had the greatest difficulty in keeping my hold. The last few yards was a frightful struggle against this faintness. Several times my head swam, and I felt all the sensations of falling. At last, however, I got over the well-mouth somehow, and staggered out of the ruin into the blinding sunlight. I fell upon my face. Even the soil smelt sweet and clean. Then I remember Weena kissing my hands and ears, and the voices of others among the Eloi. Then, for a time, I was insensible.

CHAPTER VII: "Now, indeed, I seemed in a worse case than before. Hitherto, except during my night's anguish at the loss of the Time Machine, I had felt a sustaining hope of ultimate escape, but that hope was staggered by these new discoveries. Hitherto I had merely thought myself impeded by the childish simplicity of the little people, and by some unknown forces which I had only to understand to overcome; but there was an altogether new element in the sickening quality of the Morlocks—a something inhuman and malign. Instinctively I loathed them. Before, I had felt as a man might feel who had fallen into a pit: my concern was with the pit and how to get out of it. Now I felt like a beast in a trap, whose enemy would come upon him soon.

"The enemy I dreaded may surprise you. It was the darkness of the new moon. Weena had put this into my head by some at first incomprehensible remarks about the Dark Nights. It was not now such a very difficult problem to guess what the coming Dark Nights might mean. The moon was on the wane: each night there was a longer interval of darkness. And I now understood to some slight degree at least the reason of the fear of the little Upper-world people for the dark. I wondered vaguely what foul villainy it might be that the Morlocks did under the new moon. I felt pretty sure now that my second hypothesis was all wrong. The Upper-world people might once have been the favoured aristocracy, and the Morlocks their mechanical servants; but that had long since passed away. The two species that had resulted from the evolution of man were sliding down towards, or had already arrived at, an altogether new relationship. The Eloi, like the Carlovingian kings, had decayed to a mere beautiful futility. They still possessed the earth on sufferance: since the Morlocks, subterranean for innumerable generations, had come at last to find the daylit surface intolerable. And the Morlocks made their garments, I inferred, and maintained them in their habitual needs, perhaps through the survival of an old habit of service. They did it as a standing horse paws with his foot, or as a man enjoys killing animals in sport: because ancient and departed necessities had impressed it on the organism. But, clearly, the old order was already in part reversed. The Nemesis of the delicate ones was creeping on apace. Ages ago, thousands of generations ago, man had thrust his brother man out of the ease and the sunshine. And now that brother was coming back—changed! Already the Eloi had begun to learn one old lesson anew. They were becoming reacquainted with Fear. And suddenly there came into my head the memory of the meat I had seen in the Under-world. It seemed odd how it floated into my mind: not stirred up as it were by the current of my meditations, but coming in almost like a question from outside. I tried to recall the form of it. I had a vague sense of something familiar, but I could not tell what it was at the time.

"Still, however helpless the little people in the presence of their mysterious Fear, I was differently constituted. I came out of this age of ours, this ripe prime of the human race, when Fear does not paralyse and mystery has lost its terrors. I at least would defend myself. Without further delay I determined to make myself arms and a fastness where I might sleep. With that refuge as a base, I could face this strange world with some of that confidence I had lost in realising to what creatures night by night I lay exposed. I felt I could never sleep again until my bed was secure from them. I shuddered with horror to think how they must already have examined me.

"I wandered during the afternoon along the valley of the Thames, but found nothing that commended itself to my mind as inaccessible. All the buildings and trees seemed easily practicable to such dexterous climbers as the Morlocks, to judge by their wells, must be. Then the tall pinnacles of the Palace of Green Porcelain and the polished gleam of its walls came back to my memory; and in the evening, taking Weena like a child upon my shoulder, I went up the hills towards the south-west. The distance, I had reckoned, was seven or eight miles, but it must have been nearer eighteen. I had first seen the place on a moist afternoon when distances are deceptively diminished. In addition, the heel of one of my shoes was loose, and a nail was working through the sole—they were comfortable old shoes I wore about indoors—so that I was lame. And it was already long past sunset when I came in sight of the palace, silhouetted black against the pale yellow of the sky.

"Weena had been hugely delighted when I began to carry her, but after a time she desired me to let her down, and ran along by the side of me, occasionally darting off on either hand to pick flowers to stick in my pockets. My pockets had always puzzled Weena, but at the last she had concluded that they were an eccentric kind of vase for floral decoration. At least she utilised them for that purpose. And that reminds me! In changing my jacket I found . . ."

The Time Traveller paused, put his hand into his pocket, and silently placed two withered flowers, not unlike very large white mallows, upon the little table. Then he resumed his narrative.

"As the hush of evening crept over the world and we proceeded over the hill crest towards Wimbledon, Weena grew tired and wanted to return to the house of grey stone. But I pointed out the distant pinnacles of the Palace of Green Porcelain to her, and contrived to make her understand that we were seeking a refuge there from her Fear. You know that great pause that comes upon things before the dusk? Even the breeze stops in the trees. To me there is always an air of expectation about that evening stillness. The sky was clear, remote, and empty save for a few horizontal bars far down in the sunset. Well, that night the expectation took the colour of my fears. In that darkling calm my senses seemed preternaturally sharpened. I fancied I could even feel the hollowness of the ground beneath my feet: could, indeed, almost see through it the Morlocks on their ant-hill going hither and thither and waiting for the dark. In my excitement I fancied that they would receive my invasion of their burrows as a declaration of war. And why had they taken my Time Machine?

"So we went on in the quiet, and the twilight deepened into night. The clear blue of the distance faded, and one star after another came out. The ground grew dim and the trees black. Weena's fears and her fatigue grew upon her. I took her in my arms and talked to her and caressed her. Then, as the darkness grew deeper, she put her arms round my neck, and, closing her eyes, tightly pressed her face against my shoulder. So we went down a long slope into a valley, and there in the dimness I almost walked into a little river. This I waded, and went up the opposite side of the valley, past a number of sleeping houses, and by a statue—a Faun, or some such figure, *minus* the head. Here too were acacias. So far I had seen nothing of the Morlocks, but it was yet early in the night, and the darker hours before the old moon rose were still to come.

"From the brow of the next hill I saw a thick wood spreading wide and black before me. I hesitated at this. I could see no end to it, either to the right or the left. Feeling tired—my feet, in particular, were very sore—I carefully lowered Weena from my shoulder as I halted, and sat down upon the turf. I could no longer see the Palace of Green Porcelain, and I was in doubt of my direction. I looked into the thickness of the wood and thought of what it might hide. Under that dense tangle of branches one would be out of sight of the stars. Even were there no other lurking danger—a danger I did not care to let my imagination loose upon—there would still be all the roots to stumble over and the tree-boles to strike against.

"I was very tired, too, after the excitements of the day; so I decided that I would not face it, but would pass the night upon the open hill.

"Weena, I was glad to find, was fast asleep. I carefully wrapped her in my jacket, and sat down beside her to wait for the moonrise. The hillside was quiet and deserted, but from the black of the wood there came now and then a stir of living things. Above me shone the stars, for the night was very clear. I felt a certain sense of friendly comfort in their twinkling. All the old constellations had gone from the sky, however: that slow movement which is imperceptible in a hundred human lifetimes, had long since rearranged them in unfamiliar groupings. But the Milky Way, it seemed to me, was still the same tattered streamer of star-dust as of yore. Southward (as I judged it) was a very bright red star that was new to me; it was even more splendid than our own green Sirius. And amid all these scintillating points of light one bright planet shone kindly and steadily like the face of an old friend.

"Looking at these stars suddenly dwarfed my own troubles and all the gravities of terrestrial life. I thought of their unfathomable distance, and the slow inevitable drift of their movements out of the unknown past into the unknown future. I thought of the great precessional cycle that the pole of the earth describes. Only forty times had that silent revolution occurred during all the years that I had traversed. And during these few revolutions all the activity, all the traditions, the complex organisations, the nations, languages, literatures, aspirations, even the mere memory of Man as I knew him, had been swept out of existence. Instead were these frail creatures who had forgotten their high ancestry, and the white Things of which I went in terror. Then I thought of the Great Fear that was between the two species, and for the first time, with a sudden shiver, came the clear knowledge of what the meat I had seen might be. Yet it was too horrible! I looked at little Weena sleeping beside me, her face white and starlike under the stars, and forthwith dismissed the thought.

"Through that long night I held my mind off the Morlocks as well as I could, and whiled away the time by trying to fancy I could find signs of the old constellations in the new confusion. The sky kept very clear, except for a hazy cloud or so. No doubt I dozed at times. Then, as my vigil wore on, came a faintness in the eastward sky, like the reflection of some colourless fire, and the old moon rose, thin and peaked and white. And close behind, and overtaking it, and overflowing it, the dawn came, pale at first, and then growing pink and warm. No Morlocks had approached us. Indeed, I had seen none upon the hill that night. And in the confidence of renewed day it almost seemed to me that my fear had been unreasonable. I stood up and found my foot with the loose heel swollen at the ankle and painful under the heel; so I sat down again, took off my shoes, and flung them away.

"I awakened Weena, and we went down into the wood, now green and pleasant instead of black and forbidding. We found some fruit wherewith to break our fast. We soon met others of the dainty ones, laughing and dancing in the sunlight as though there was no such thing in Nature as the night. And then I thought once more of the meat that I had seen. I felt assured now of what it was, and from the bottom of my heart I pitied this last feeble rill from the great flood of humanity. Clearly, at some time in the Long-Ago of human decay the Morlocks' food had run short. Possibly they had lived on rats and suchlike vermin. Even now man is far less discriminating and exclusive in his food than he was—far less than any monkey. His prejudice against human flesh is no deep-seated instinct. And so these inhuman sons of men——! I tried to look at the thing in a scientific spirit. After all, they were less human and more remote than our cannibal ancestors of three or four thousand years ago. And the intelligence that would have made this state of things a torment had gone. Why should I trouble myself? These Eloi were mere fatted cattle, which the ant-like Morlocks preserved and preyed upon—probably saw to the breeding of. And there was Weena dancing at my side!

"Then I tried to preserve myself from the horror that was coming upon me, by regarding it as a rigorous punishment of human selfishness. Man had been content to live in ease and delight upon the labours of his fellow man, had taken Necessity as his watchword and excuse, and in the fulness of time Necessity had come home to him. I even tried a Carlyle-like scorn of this wretched aristocracy in decay. But this attitude of mind was impossible. However great their intellectual degradation, the Eloi had kept too much of the human form not to claim my sympathy, and to make me perforce a sharer in their degradation and their Fear.

"I had at that time very vague ideas as to the course I should pursue. My first was to secure some safe place of refuge, and to make myself such arms of metal or stone as I could contrive. That necessity was immediate.

In the next place, I hoped to procure some means of fire, so that I should have the weapon of a torch at hand, for nothing, I knew, would be more efficient against these Morlocks. Then I wanted to arrange some contrivance to break open the doors of bronze under the White Sphinx. I had in mind a battering-ram. I had a persuasion that if I could enter those doors and carry a blaze of light before me I should discover the Time Machine and escape. I could not imagine the Morlocks were strong enough to move it far away. Weena I had resolved to bring with me to our own time. And turning such schemes over in my mind I pursued our way towards the building which my fancy had chosen as our dwelling.

CHAPTER VIII: "I found the Palace of Green Porcelain, when we approached it about noon, deserted and falling into ruin. Only ragged vestiges of glass remained in its windows, and great sheets of the green facing had fallen away from the corroded metallic framework. It lay very high upon a turfy down, and looking north-eastward before I entered it, I was surprised to see a large estuary, or even creek, where I judged Wandsworth and Battersea must once have been. I thought then—though I never followed up the thought—of what might have happened, or might be happening, to the living things in the sea.

"The material of the Palace proved on examination to be indeed porcelain, and along the face of it I saw an inscription in some unknown character. I thought, rather foolishly, that Weena might help me to interpret this, but I only learned that the bare idea of writing had never entered her head. She always seemed to me, I fancy, more human than she was, perhaps because her affection was so human.

"Within the big valves of the door—which were open and broken—we found, instead of the customary hall, a long gallery lit by many side windows. At the first glance I was reminded of a museum. The tiled floor was thick with dust, and a remarkable array of miscellaneous objects was shrouded in the same grey covering. Then I perceived, standing strange and gaunt in the centre of the hall, what was clearly the lower part of a huge skeleton. I recognised by the oblique feet that it was some extinct creature after the fashion of the Megatherium. The skull and the upper bones lay beside it in the thick dust, and in one place, where rain-water had dropped through a leak in the roof, the thing itself had been worn away. Further in the gallery was the huge skeleton barrel of a Brontosaurus. My museum hypothesis was confirmed. Going towards the side I found what appeared to be sloping shelves, and, clearing away the thick dust, I found the old familiar glass cases of our own time. But they must have been air-tight to judge from the fair preservation of some of their contents.

"Clearly we stood among the ruins of some latter-day South Kensington! Here, apparently, was the Palæontological Section, and a very splendid array of fossils it must have been, though the inevitable process of decay that had been staved off for a time, and had, through the extinction of bacteria and fungi, lost ninety-nine hundredths of its force, was, nevertheless, with extreme sureness if with extreme slowness at work again upon all its treasures. Here and there I found traces of the little people in the shape of rare fossils broken to pieces or threaded in strings upon reeds. And the cases had in some instances been bodily removed—by the Morlocks as I judged. The place was very silent. The thick dust deadened our footsteps. Weena, who had been rolling a sea-urchin down the sloping glass of a case, presently came, as I stared about me, and very quietly took my hand and stood beside me.

"And at first I was so much surprised by this ancient monument of an intellectual age, that I gave no thought to the possibilities it presented. Even my preoccupation about the Time Machine receded a little from my mind.

"To judge from the size of the place, this Palace of Green Porcelain had a great deal more in it than a Gallery of Palæontology; possibly historical galleries; it might be, even a library! To me, at least in my present circumstances, these would be vastly more interesting than this spectacle of old-time geology in decay. Exploring, I found another short gallery running transversely to the first. This appeared to be devoted to minerals, and the sight of a block of sulphur set my mind running on gunpowder. But I could find no saltpetre; indeed, no nitrates of any kind. Doubtless they had deliquesced ages ago. Yet the sulphur hung in my mind, and set up a train of thinking. As for the rest of the contents of that gallery, though on the whole they were the best preserved of all I saw, I had little interest. I am no specialist in mineralogy, and I went on down a very ruinous aisle running parallel to the first hall I had entered. Apparently this section had been devoted to natural history, but everything had long since passed out of recognition. A few shrivelled and blackened vestiges of what had once been stuffed animals, desiccated mummies in jars that had once held spirit, a brown dust of departed plants; that was all! I was sorry for that, because I should have been glad to trace the patent readjustments by which the conquest of animated nature had been attained. Then we came to a gallery of simply colossal proportions, but singularly ill-lit, the floor of it running downward at a slight angle from the end at which I entered. At intervals white globes hung from the ceiling—many of them cracked and smashed—which suggested that originally the place had been artificially lit. Here I was more in my element, for rising on either side of me were the huge bulks of big machines, all greatly corroded and many broken down, but some still fairly complete. You know I have a certain weakness for mechanism, and I was inclined to linger among these; the more so as for the most part they had the interest of puzzles, and I could make only the vaguest guesses at what they were for. I fancied that if I could solve their puzzles I should find myself in possession of powers that might be of use against the Morlocks.

"Suddenly Weena came very close to my side. So suddenly that she startled me. Had it not been for her I do not think I should have noticed that the floor of the gallery sloped at all.* The end I had come in at was quite above ground, and was lit by rare slit-like windows. As you went down the length, the ground came up against these windows, until at last there was a pit like the 'area' of a London house before each, and only a narrow line of daylight at the top. I went slowly along, puzzling about the machines, and had been too intent upon them to notice the gradual diminution of the light, until Weena's increasing apprehensions drew my attention. Then I saw that the gallery ran down at last into a thick darkness. I hesitated, and then, as I looked round me, I saw that the dust was less abundant and its surface less even. Further away towards the dimness, it appeared to be broken by a number of small narrow footprints. My sense of the immediate presence of the Morlocks revived at that. I felt that I was wasting my time in this academic examination of machinery. I called to mind that it was already far advanced in the afternoon, and that I had still no weapon, no refuge, and no means of making a fire. And then down in the remote blackness of the gallery I heard a peculiar pattering, and the same odd noises I had heard down the well.

"I took Weena's hand. Then, struck with a sudden idea, I left her and turned to a machine from which projected a lever not unlike those in a signal-box. Clambering upon the stand, and grasping this lever in my hands, I put all my weight upon it sideways. Suddenly Weena, deserted in the central aisle, began to whimper. I had judged the strength of the lever pretty correctly, for it snapped after a minute's strain, and I rejoined her with a mace in my hand more than sufficient, I judged, for any Morlock skull I might encounter. And I longed very much to kill a Morlock or so. Very inhuman, you may think, to want to go killing one's own descendants! But it was impossible, somehow, to feel any humanity in the things. Only my disinclination to leave Weena, and a persuasion that if I began to slake my thirst for murder my Time Machine might suffer, restrained me from going straight down the gallery and killing the brutes I heard.

"Well, mace in one hand and Weena in the other, I went out of that gallery and into another and still larger one, which at the first glance re-

* It may be, of course, that the floor did not slope, but that the museum was built into the side of a hill.—Ed.

minded me of a military chapel hung with tattered flags. The brown and charred rags that hung from the sides of it, I presently recognised as the decaying vestiges of books. They had long since dropped to pieces, and every semblance of print had left them. But here and there were warped boards and cracked metallic clasps that told the tale well enough. Had I been a literary man I might, perhaps, have moralised upon the futility of all ambition. But as it was, the thing that struck me with keenest force was the enormous waste of labour to which this sombre wilderness of rotting paper testified. At the time I will confess that I thought chiefly of the *Philosophical Transactions* and my own seventeen papers upon physical optics.

"Then, going up a broad staircase, we came to what may once have been a gallery of technical chemistry. And here I had not a little hope of useful discoveries. Except at one end where the roof had collapsed, this gallery was well preserved. I went eagerly to every unbroken case. And at last, in one of the really air-tight cases, I found a box of matches. Very eagerly I tried them. They were perfectly good. They were not even damp. I turned to Weena. 'Dance,' I cried to her in her own tongue. For now I had a weapon indeed against the horrible creatures we feared. And so, in that derelict museum, upon the thick soft carpeting of dust, to Weena's huge delight, I solemnly performed a kind of composite dance, whistling *The Land of the Leal* as cheerfully as I could. In part it was a modest *cancan*, in part a step-dance, in part a skirt-dance (so far as my tail-coat permitted), and in part original. For I am naturally inventive, as you know.

"Now, I still think that for this box of matches to have escaped the wear of time for immemorial years was a most strange, as for me it was a most fortunate thing. Yet, oddly enough, I found a far unlikelier substance, and that was camphor. I found it in a sealed jar, that by chance, I suppose, had been really hermetically sealed. I fancied at first that it was paraffin wax, and smashed the glass accordingly. But the odour of camphor was unmistakable. In the universal decay this volatile substance had chanced to survive, perhaps through many thousands of centuries. It reminded me of a sepia painting I had once seen done from the ink of a fossil Belemnite that must have perished and become fossilised millions of years ago. I was about to throw it away, but I remembered that it was inflammable and burned with a good bright flame—was, in fact, an excellent candle—and I put it in my pocket. I found no explosives, however, nor any means of breaking down the bronze doors. As yet my iron crowbar was the most helpful thing I had chanced upon. Nevertheless I left that gallery greatly elated.

"I cannot tell you all the story of that long afternoon. It would require a great effort of memory to recall my explorations in at all the proper order. I remember a long gallery of rusting stands of arms, and how I hesitated between my crowbar and a hatchet or a sword. I could not carry both, however, and my bar of iron promised best against the bronze gates. There were numbers of guns, pistols, and rifles. The most were masses of rust, but many were of some new metal, and still fairly sound. But any cartridges or powder there may once have been had rotted into dust. One corner I saw was charred and shattered; perhaps, I thought, by an explosion among the specimens. In another place was a vast array of idols—Polynesian, Mexican, Grecian, Phœnician, every country on earth I should think. And here, yielding to an irresistible impulse, I wrote my name upon the nose of a steatite monster from South America that particularly took my fancy.

"As the evening drew on, my interest waned. I went through gallery after gallery, dusty, silent, often ruinous, the exhibits sometimes mere heaps of rust and lignite, sometimes fresher. In one place I suddenly found myself near the model of a tin-mine, and then by the merest accident I discovered, in an air-tight case, two dynamite cartridges! I shouted 'Eureka!' and smashed the case with joy. Then came a doubt. I hesitated. Then, selecting a little side gallery, I made my essay. I never felt such a disappointment as I did in waiting five, ten, fifteen minutes for an explosion that never came. Of course the things were dummies, as I might have guessed from their presence. I really believe that, had they not been so, I should have rushed off incontinently and blown Sphinx, bronze doors, and (as it proved) my chances of finding the Time Machine, all together into non-existence.

"It was after that, I think, that we came to a little open court within the palace. It was turfed, and had three fruit trees. So we rested and refreshed ourselves. Towards sunset I began to consider our position. Night was creeping upon us, and my inaccessible hiding place had still to be found. But that troubled me very little now. I had in my possession a thing that was, perhaps, the best of all defences against the Morlocks—I had matches! I had the camphor in my pocket, too, if a blaze were needed. It seemed to me that the best thing we could do would be to pass the night in the open, protected by a fire. In the morning there was the getting of the Time Machine. Towards that, as yet, I had only my iron mace. But now, with my growing knowledge, I felt very differently towards those bronze doors. Up to this, I had refrained from forcing them, largely because of the mystery on the other side. They had never impressed me as being very strong, and I hoped to find my bar of iron not altogether inadequate for the work.

CHAPTER IX: "We emerged from the palace while the sun was still in part above the horizon. I was determined to reach the White Sphinx early the next morning, and ere the dusk I purposed pushing through the woods that had stopped me on the previous journey. My plan was to go as far as possible that night, and then, building a fire, to sleep in the protection of its glare. Accordingly, as we went along I gathered any sticks or dried grass I saw, and presently had my arms full of such litter. Thus loaded, our progress was slower than I had anticipated, and besides Weena was tired. And I began to suffer from sleepiness too; so that it was full night before we reached the wood. Upon the shrubby hill of its edge Weena would have stopped, fearing the darkness before us; but a singular sense of impending calamity, that should indeed have served me as a warning, drove me onward. I had been without sleep for a night and two days, and I was feverish and irritable. I felt sleep coming upon me, and the Morlocks with it.

"While we hesitated, among the black bushes behind us, and dim against their blackness, I saw three crouching figures. There was scrub and long grass all about us, and I did not feel safe from their insidious approach. The forest, I calculated, was rather less than a mile across. If we could get through it to the bare hillside, there, as it seemed to me, was an altogether safer resting-place; I thought that with my matches and my camphor I could contrive to keep my path illuminated through the woods. Yet it was evident that if I was to flourish matches with my hands I should have to abandon my firewood; so, rather reluctantly, I put it down. And then it came into my head that I would amaze our friends behind by lighting it. I was to discover the atrocious folly of this proceeding, but it came to my mind as an ingenious move for covering our retreat.

"I don't know if you have ever thought what a rare thing flame must be in the absence of man and in a temperate climate. The sun's heat is rarely strong enough to burn, even when it is focussed by dewdrops, as is sometimes the case in more tropical districts. Lightning may blast and blacken, but it rarely gives rise to widespread fire. Decaying vegetation may occasionally smoulder with the heat of its fermentation, but this rarely results in flame. In this decadence, too, the art of fire-making had been forgotten on the earth. The red tongues that went licking up my heap of wood were an altogether new and strange thing to Weena.

"She wanted to run to it and play with it. I believe she would have cast herself into it had I not restrained her. But I caught her up, and, in spite of her struggles, plunged boldly before me into the wood. For a little way the glare of my fire lit the path. Looking back presently, I could see, through the crowded stems, that from my heap of sticks the blaze had spread to some bushes adjacent, and a curved line of fire was creeping up the grass of the hill. I laughed at that, and turned again to the dark trees before me. It was very black, and Weena clung to me convulsively, but there was still, as my eyes grew accustomed to the darkness, sufficient light for me to avoid the stems. Overhead it was simply black, except where a gap of remote blue sky shone down upon us here and there. I struck none of my matches because I had no hand free. Upon my left arm I carried my little one, in my right hand I had my iron bar.

"For some way I heard nothing but the crackling twigs under my feet, the faint rustle of the breeze above, and my own breathing and the throb of the blood-vessels in my ears. Then I seemed to know of a pattering about me. I pushed on grimly. The pattering grew more distinct, and then I caught the same queer sounds and voices I had heard in the Underworld. There were evidently several of the Morlocks, and they were closing in upon me. Indeed, in another minute I felt a tug at my coat, then something at my arm. And Weena shivered violently, and became quite still.

"It was time for a match. But to get one I must put her down. I did so, and, as I fumbled with my pocket, a struggle began in the darkness about my knees, perfectly silent on her part and with the same peculiar cooing sounds from the Morlocks. Soft little hands, too, were creeping over my coat and back, touching even my neck. Then the match scratched and fizzed. I held it flaring, and saw the white backs of the Morlocks in flight amid the trees. I hastily took a lump of camphor from my pocket, and prepared to light it as soon as the match should wane. Then I looked at Weena. She was lying clutching my feet and quite motionless, with her face to the ground. With a sudden fright I stooped to her. She seemed scarcely to breathe. I lit the block of camphor and flung it to the ground, and as it split and flared up and drove back the Morlocks and the shadows, I knelt down and lifted her. The wood behind seemed full of the stir and murmur of a great company!

"She seemed to have fainted. I put her carefully upon my shoulder and rose to push on, and then there came a horrible realisation. In manœuvring with my matches and Weena, I had turned myself about several times, and now I had not the faintest idea in what direction lay my path. For all I knew, I might be facing back towards the Palace of Green Porcelain. I found myself in a cold sweat. I had to think rapidly what to do. I determined to build a fire and encamp where we were. I put Weena, still motionless, down upon a turfy bole, and very hastily, as my first lump of camphor waned, I began collecting sticks and leaves. Here and there out of the darkness round me the Morlocks' eyes shone like carbuncles.

"The camphor flickered and went out. I lit a match, and as I did so, two white forms that had been approaching Weena dashed hastily away. One was so blinded by the light that he came straight for me, and I felt his bones grind under the blow of my fist. He gave a whoop of dismay, staggered a little way, and fell down. I lit another piece of camphor, and went on gathering my bonfire. Presently I noticed how dry was some of the foliage above me, for since my arrival on the Time Machine, a matter of a week, no rain had fallen. So, instead of casting about among the trees for fallen twigs, I began leaping up and dragging down branches. Very soon I had a choking smoky fire of green wood and dry sticks, and could economise my camphor. Then I turned to where Weena lay beside my iron mace. I tried what I could to revive her, but she lay like one dead. I could not even satisfy myself whether or not she breathed.

"Now, the smoke of the fire beat over towards me, and it must have made me heavy of a sudden. Moreover, the vapour of camphor was in the air. My fire would not need replenishing for an hour or so. I felt very weary after my exertion, and sat down. The wood, too, was full of a slumbrous murmur that I did not understand. I seemed just to nod and open my eyes. But all was dark, and the Morlocks had their hands upon me. Flinging off their clinging fingers I hastily felt in my pocket for the matchbox, and—it had gone! Then they gripped and closed with me, again. In a moment I knew what had happened. I had slept, and my fire had gone out, and the bitterness of death came over my soul. The forest seemed full of the smell of burning wood. I was caught by the neck, by the hair, by the arms, and pulled down. It was indescribably horrible in the darkness to feel all these soft creatures heaped upon me. I felt as if I was in a monstrous spider's web. I was overpowered, and went down. I felt little teeth nipping at my neck. I rolled over, and as I did so my hand came against my iron lever. It gave me strength. I struggled up, shaking the human rats from me, and, holding the bar short, I thrust where I judged their faces might be. I could feel the succulent giving of flesh and bone under my blows, and for a moment I was free.

"The strange exultation that so often seems to accompany hard fighting came upon me. I knew that both I and Weena were lost, but I determined to make the Morlocks pay for their meat. I stood with my back to a tree, swinging the iron bar before me. The whole wood was full of the stir and cries of them. A minute passed. Their voices seemed to rise to a higher pitch of excitement, and their movements grew faster. Yet none came within reach. I stood glaring at the blackness. Then suddenly came hope. What if the Morlocks were afraid? And close on the heels of that came a strange thing. The darkness seemed to grow luminous. Very dimly I began to see the Morlocks about me—three battered at my feet—and then I recognised, with incredulous surprise, that the others were running, in an incessant stream, as it seemed, from behind me, and away through the wood in front. And their backs seemed no longer white, but reddish. As I stood agape, I saw a little red spark go drifting across a gap of starlight between the branches, and vanish. And at that I understood the smell of burning wood, the slumbrous murmur that was growing now into a gusty roar, the red glow, and the Morlocks' flight.

"Stepping out from behind my tree and looking back, I saw, through the black pillars of the nearer trees, the flames of the burning forest. It was my first fire coming after me. With that I looked for Weena, but she was gone. The hissing and crackling behind me, the explosive thud as each fresh tree burst into flame, left little time for reflection. My iron bar still gripped, I followed in the Morlocks' path. It was a close race. Once the flames crept forward so swiftly on my right as I ran that I was outflanked and had to strike off to the left. But at last I emerged upon a small open space, and as I did so, a Morlock came blundering towards me, and past me, and went on straight into the fire!

"And now I was to see the most weird and horrible thing, I think, of all that I beheld in that future age. This whole space was as bright as day with the reflection of the fire. In the centre was a hillock or tumulus, surmounted by a scorched hawthorn. Beyond this was another arm of the burning forest, with yellow tongues already writhing from it, completely encircling the space with a fence of fire. Upon the hillside were some thirty or forty Morlocks, dazzled by the light and heat, and blundering hither and thither against each other in their bewilderment. At first I did not realise their blindness, and struck furiously at them with my bar, in a frenzy of fear, as they approached me, killing one and crippling several more. But when I had watched the gestures of one of them groping under the hawthorn against the red sky, and heard their moans, I was assured of their absolute helplessness and misery in the glare, and I struck no more of them.

"Yet every now and then one would come straight towards me, setting loose a quivering horror that made me quick to elude him. At one time the flames died down somewhat, and I feared the foul creatures would presently be able to see me. I was even thinking of beginning the fight by killing some of them before this should happen; but the fire burst out again brightly, and I stayed my hand. I walked about the hill among them and avoided them, looking for some trace of Weena. But Weena was gone.

"At last I sat down on the summit of the hillock, and watched this strange incredible company of blind things groping to and fro, and making uncanny noises to each other, as the glare of the fire beat on them. The coiling uprush of smoke streamed across the sky, and through the rare tatters of that red canopy, remote as though they belonged to another universe, shone the little stars. Two or three Morlocks came blundering into me, and I drove them off with blows of my fists, trembling as I did so.

"For the most part of that night I was persuaded it was a nightmare. I bit myself and screamed in a passionate desire to awake. I beat the ground with my hands, and got up and sat down again, and wandered here and there, and again sat down. Then I would fall to rubbing my eyes and calling upon God to let me awake. Thrice I saw Morlocks put their heads down in a kind of agony and rush into the flames. But, at last, above the subsiding red of the fire, above the streaming masses of black smoke and the whitening and blackening tree stumps, and the diminishing numbers of these dim creatures, came the white light of the day.

"I searched again for traces of Weena, but there were none. It was plain that they had left her poor little body in the forest. I cannot describe how it relieved me to think that it had escaped the awful fate to which it seemed destined. As I thought of that, I was almost moved to begin a massacre of the helpless abominations about me, but I contained myself. The hillock, as I have said, was a kind of island in the forest. From its summit I could now make out through a haze of smoke the Palace of Green Porcelain, and from that I could get my bearings for the White Sphinx. And so, leaving the remnant of these damned souls still going hither and thither and moaning, as the day grew clearer, I tied some grass about my feet and limped on across smoking ashes and among black stems, that still pulsated internally with fire, towards the hiding place of the Time Machine. I walked slowly, for I was almost exhausted, as well as lame, and I felt the intensest wretchedness for the horrible death of little Weena. It seemed an overwhelming calamity. Now, in this old familiar room, it is more like the sorrow of a dream than an actual loss. But that morning it left me absolutely lonely again—terribly alone. I began to think of this house of mine, of this fireside, of some of you, and with such thoughts came a longing that was pain.

"But, as I walked over the smoking ashes under the bright morning sky, I made a discovery. In my trouser pocket were still some loose matches. The box must have leaked before it was lost.

CHAPTER X: "About eight or nine in the morning I came to the same seat of yellow metal from which I had viewed the world upon the evening of my arrival. I thought of my hasty conclusions upon that evening and could not refrain from laughing bitterly at my confidence. Here was the same beautiful scene, the same abundant foliage, the same splendid palaces and magnificent ruins, the same silver river running between its fertile banks. The gay robes of the beautiful people moved hither and thither among the trees. Some were bathing in exactly the place where I had saved Weena, and that suddenly gave me a keen stab of pain. And like blots upon the landscape rose the cupolas above the ways to the Under-world. I understood now what all the beauty of the Over-world people covered. Very pleasant was their day, as pleasant as the day of the cattle in the field. Like the cattle, they knew of no enemies and provided against no needs. And their end was the same.

"I grieved to think how brief the dream of the human intellect had been. It had committed suicide. It had set itself steadfastly towards com-fort and ease, a balanced society with security and permanency as its watchword, it had attained its hopes—to come to this at last. Once, life and property must have reached almost absolute safety. The rich had been assured of his wealth and comfort, the toiler assured of his life and work. No doubt in that perfect world there had been no unemployed problem, no social question left unsolved. And a great quiet had followed.

"It is a law of Nature we overlook, that intellectual versatility is the compensation for change, danger, and trouble. An animal perfectly in harmony with its environment is a perfect mechanism. Nature never appeals to intelligence until habit and instinct are useless. There is no intelligence where there is no change and no need of change. Only those animals partake of intelligence that have to meet a huge variety of needs and dangers.

"So, as I see it, the Upper-world man had drifted towards his feeble prettiness, and the Under-world to mere mechanical industry. But that perfect state had lacked one thing even for mechanical perfection—absolute permanency. Apparently, as time went on, the feeding of the Un-der-world, however it was effected, had become disjointed. Mother Neces-sity, who had been staved off for a few thousand years, came back again, and she began below. The Under-world being in contact with machinery, which, however perfect, still needs some little thought outside habit, had probably retained perforce rather more initiative, if less of every other human character, than the Upper. And when other meat failed them, they turned to what old habit had hitherto forbidden. So I say I saw it in my last view of the world of Eight Hundred and Two Thousand Seven Hundred and One. It may be as wrong an explanation as mortal wit could invent. It is how the thing shaped itself to me, and as that I give it to you.

"After the fatigues, excitements, and terrors of the past days, and in spite of my grief, this seat and the tranquil view and the warm sunlight were very pleasant. I was very tired and sleepy, and soon my theorising passed into dozing. Catching myself at that, I took my own hint, and spreading myself out upon the turf I had a long and refreshing sleep.

"I awoke a little before sunsetting. I now felt safe against being caught napping by the Morlocks, and, stretching myself, I came on down the hill towards the White Sphinx. I had my crowbar in one hand, and the other hand played with the matches in my pocket.

"And now came a most unexpected thing. As I approached the pedestal of the sphinx I found the bronze valves were open. They had slid down into grooves.

"At that I stopped short before them, hesitating to enter.

"Within was a small apartment, and on a raised place in the corner of this was the Time Machine. I had the small levers in my pocket. So here, after all my elaborate preparations for the siege of the White Sphinx, was a meek surrender. I threw my iron bar away, almost sorry not to use it.

"A sudden thought came into my head as I stooped towards the portal. For once, at least, I grasped the mental operations of the Morlocks. Suppressing a strong inclination to laugh, I stepped through the bronze frame and up to the Time Machine. I was surprised to find it had been carefully oiled and cleaned. I have suspected since that the Morlocks had even partially taken it to pieces while trying in their dim way to grasp its purpose.

"Now as I stood and examined it, finding a pleasure in the mere touch of the contrivance, the thing I had expected happened. The bronze panels suddenly slid up and struck the frame with a clang. I was in the dark—trapped. So the Morlocks thought. At that I chuckled gleefully.

"I could already hear their murmuring laughter as they came towards me. Very calmly I tried to strike the match. I had only to fix on the levers and depart then like a ghost. But I had overlooked one little thing. The matches were of that abominable kind that light only on the box.

"You may imagine how all my calm vanished. The little brutes were close upon me. One touched me. I made a sweeping blow in the dark at them with the levers, and began to scramble into the saddle of the machine. Then came one hand upon me and then another. Then I had simply to fight against their persistent fingers for my levers, and at the same time feel for the studs over which these fitted. Once, indeed, they almost got away from me. As it slipped from my hand, I had to butt in the dark with my head—I could hear the Morlock's skull ring—to recover it. It was a nearer thing than the fight in the forest, I think, this last scramble.

"But at last the lever was fixed and pulled over. The clinging hands slipped from me. The darkness presently fell from my eyes. I found myself in the same grey light and tumult I have already described.

CHAPTER XI: "I have already told you of the sickness and confusion that comes with time travelling. And this time I was not seated properly in the saddle, but sideways and in an unstable fashion. For an indefinite time I clung to the machine as it swayed and vibrated, quite unheeding how I went, and when I brought myself to look at the dials again I was amazed to find where I had arrived. One dial records days, another thousands of days, another millions of days, and another thousands of millions. Now, instead of reversing the levers, I had pulled them over so as to go forward with them, and when I came to look at these indicators I found that the thousands hand was sweeping round as fast as the seconds hand of a watch—into futurity.

"As I drove on, a peculiar change crept over the appearance of things. The palpitating greyness grew darker; then—though I was still travelling with prodigious velocity—the blinking succession of day and night, which was usually indicative of a slower pace, returned, and grew more and more marked. This puzzled me very much at first. The alternations of night and day grew slower and slower, and so did the passage of the sun across the sky, until they seemed to stretch through centuries. At last a steady twilight brooded over the earth, a twilight only broken now and then when a comet glared across the darkling sky. The band of light that had indicated the sun had long since disappeared; for the sun had ceased to set—it simply rose and fell in the west, and grew ever broader and more red. All trace of the moon had vanished. The circling of the stars, growing slower and slower, had given place to creeping points of light. At last, some time before I stopped, the sun, red and very large, halted motionless upon the horizon, a vast dome glowing with a dull heat, and now and then suffering a momentary extinction. At one time it had for a little while glowed more brilliantly again, but it speedily reverted to its sullen red heat. I perceived by this slowing down of its rising and setting that the work of the tidal drag was done. The earth had come to rest with one face to the sun, even as in our own time the moon faces the earth. Very cautiously, for I remembered my former headlong fall, I began to reverse my motion. Slower and slower went the circling hands until the thousands one seemed motionless and the daily one was no longer a mere mist upon its scale. Still slower, until the dim outlines of a desolate beach grew visible.

"I stopped very gently and sat upon the Time Machine, looking round. The sky was no longer blue. North-eastward it was inky black, and out of the blackness shone brightly and steadily the pale white stars. Overhead it was a deep Indian red and starless, and south-eastward it grew brighter to a glowing scarlet where, cut by the horizon, lay the huge hull of the sun, red and motionless. The rocks about me were of a harsh reddish colour, and all the trace of life that I could see at first was the intensely green vegetation that covered every projecting point on their south-eastern face. It was the same rich green that one sees on forest moss or on the lichen in caves: plants which like these grow in a perpetual twilight.

"The machine was standing on a sloping beach. The sea stretched away to the south-west, to rise into a sharp bright horizon against the wan sky. There were no breakers and no waves, for not a breath of wind was stirring. Only a slight oily swell rose and fell like a gentle breathing, and showed that the eternal sea was still moving and living. And along the margin where the water sometimes broke was a thick incrustation of salt—pink under the lurid sky. There was a sense of oppression in my head, and I noticed that I was breathing very fast. The sensation reminded me of my only experience of mountaineering, and from that I judged the air to be more rarefied than it is now.

"Far away up the desolate slope I heard a harsh scream, and saw a thing like a huge white butterfly go slanting and fluttering up into the sky and, circling, disappear over some low hillocks beyond. The sound of its voice was so dismal that I shivered and seated myself more firmly upon the machine. Looking round me again, I saw that, quite near, what I had taken to be a reddish mass of rock was moving slowly towards me. Then I saw the thing was really a monstrous crab-like creature. Can you imagine a crab as large as yonder table, with its many legs moving slowly and uncertainly, its big claws swaying, its long antennæ, like carters' whips, waving and feeling, and its stalked eyes gleaming at you on either side of its metallic front? Its back was corrugated and ornamented with ungainly bosses, and a greenish incrustation blotched it here and there. I could see the many palps of its complicated mouth flickering and feeling as it moved.

"As I stared at this sinister apparition crawling towards me, I felt a tickling on my cheek as though a fly had lighted there. I tried to brush it away with my hand, but in a moment it returned, and almost immediately came another by my ear. I struck at this, and caught something threadlike. It was drawn swiftly out of my hand. With a frightful qualm, I turned, and saw that I had grasped the antenna of another monster crab that stood just behind me. Its evil eyes were wriggling on their stalks, its mouth was all alive with appetite, and its vast ungainly claws, smeared with an algal slime, were descending upon me. In a moment my hand was on the lever, and I had placed a month between myself and these monsters. But I was still on the same beach, and I saw them distinctly now as soon as I stopped. Dozens of them seemed to be crawling here and there, in the sombre light, among the foliated sheets of intense green.

"I cannot convey the sense of abominable desolation that hung over the world. The red eastern sky, the northward blackness, the salt Dead Sea, the stony beach crawling with these foul, slow-stirring monsters, the uniform poisonous-looking green of the lichenous plants, the thin air that hurts one's lungs; all contributed to an appalling effect. I moved on a hundred years, and there was the same red sun—a little larger, a little duller—the same dying sea, the same chill air, and the same crowd of earthly crustacea creeping in and out among the green weed and the red rocks. And in the westward sky I saw a curved pale line like a vast new moon.

"So I travelled, stopping ever and again, in great strides of a thousand years or more, drawn on by the mystery of the earth's fate, watching with a strange fascination the sun grow larger and duller in the westward sky, and the life of the old earth ebb away. At last, more than thirty million years hence, the huge red-hot dome of the sun had come to obscure nearly a tenth part of the darkling heavens. Then I stopped once more, for the crawling multitude of crabs had disappeared, and the red beach, save for its livid green liverworts and lichens, seemed lifeless. And now it was flecked with white. A bitter cold assailed me. Rare white flakes ever and again came eddying down. To the north-eastward, the glare of snow lay under the starlight of the sable sky, and I could see an undulating crest of hillocks pinkish white. There were fringes of ice along the sea margin, with drifting masses further out; but the main expanse of that salt ocean, all bloody under the eternal sunset, was still unfrozen.

"I looked about me to see if any traces of animal life remained. A certain indefinable apprehension still kept me in the saddle of the machine. But I saw nothing moving, in earth or sky or sea. The green slime on the rocks alone testified that life was not extinct. A shallow sand-bank had appeared in the sea and the water had receded from the beach. I fancied I saw some black object flopping about upon this bank, but it became motionless as I looked at it, and I judged that my eye had been deceived, and that the black object was merely a rock. The stars in the sky were intensely bright and seemed to me to twinkle very little.

"Suddenly I noticed that the circular westward outline of the sun had changed; that a concavity, a bay, had appeared in the curve. I saw this grow larger. For a minute perhaps I stared aghast at this blackness that was creeping over the day, and then I realised that an eclipse was beginning. Either the moon or the planet Mercury was passing across the sun's disk. Naturally, at first I took it to be the moon, but there is much to incline me to believe that what I really saw was the transit of an inner planet passing very near to the earth.

"The darkness grew apace; a cold wind began to blow in freshening gusts from the east, and the showering white flakes in the air increased in number. From the edge of the sea came a ripple and whisper. Beyond these lifeless sounds the world was silent. Silent? It would be hard to convey the stillness of it. All the sounds of man, the bleating of sheep, the cries of birds, the hum of insects, the stir that makes the background of our lives—all that was over. As the darkness thickened, the eddying flakes grew more abundant, dancing before my eyes; and the cold of the air more intense. At last, one by one, swiftly, one after the other, the white peaks of the distant hills vanished into blackness. The breeze rose to a moaning wind. I saw the black central shadow of the eclipse sweeping towards me. In another moment the pale stars alone were visible. All else was rayless obscurity. The sky was absolutely black.

"A horror of this great darkness came on me. The cold, that smote to my marrow, and the pain I felt in breathing, overcame me. I shivered, and a deadly nausea seized me. Then like a red-hot bow in the sky appeared the edge of the sun. I got off the machine to recover myself. I felt giddy and incapable of facing the return journey. As I stood sick and confused I saw again the moving thing upon the shoal—there was no mistake now that it was a moving thing—against the red water of the sea. It was a round thing, the size of a football perhaps, or, it may be, bigger, and tentacles trailed down from it; it seemed black against the weltering blood-red water, and it was hopping fitfully about. Then I felt I was fainting. But a terrible dread of lying helpless in that remote and awful twilight sustained me while I clambered upon the saddle.

CHAPTER XII: "So I came back. For a long time I must have been insensible upon the machine. The blinking succession of the days and nights was resumed, the sun got golden again, the sky blue. I breathed with greater freedom. The fluctuating contours of the land ebbed and flowed. The hands spun backward upon the dials. At last I saw again the dim shadows of houses, the evidences of decadent humanity. These, too, changed and passed, and others came. Presently, when the millions dial was at zero, I slackened speed. I began to recognise our own petty and familiar architecture, the thousands hand ran back to the starting-point, the night and day flapped slower and slower. Then the old walls of the laboratory came round me. Very gently, now, I slowed the mechanism down.

"I saw one little thing that seemed odd to me. I think I have told you that when I set out, before my velocity became very high, Mrs. Watchett had walked across the room, travelling, as it seemed to me, like a rocket. As I returned, I passed again across that minute when she traversed the laboratory. But now her every motion appeared to be the exact inversion of her previous ones. The door at the lower end opened, and she glided quietly up the laboratory, back foremost, and disappeared behind the door by which she had previously entered. Just before that I seemed to see Hillyer for a moment; but he passed like a flash.

"Then I stopped the machine, and saw about me again the old familiar laboratory, my tools, my appliances just as I had left them. I got off the thing very shakily, and sat down upon my bench. For several minutes I trembled violently. Then I became calmer. Around me was my old workshop again, exactly as it had been. I might have slept there, and the whole thing have been a dream.

"And yet, not exactly! The thing had started from the south-east corner of the laboratory. It had come to rest again in the north-west, against the wall where you saw it. That gives you the exact distance from my little lawn to the pedestal of the White Sphinx, into which the Morlocks had carried my machine.

"For a time my brain went stagnant. Presently I got up and came through the passage here, limping, because my heel was still painful, and feeling sorely begrimed. I saw the *Pall Mall Gazette* on the table by the door. I found the date was indeed to-day, and looking at the timepiece, saw the hour was almost eight o'clock. I heard your voices and the clatter of plates. I hesitated—I felt so sick and weak. Then I sniffed good wholesome meat, and opened the door on you. You know the rest. I washed, and dined, and now I am telling you the story.

"I know," he said, after a pause, "that all this will be absolutely incredible to you. To me the one incredible thing is that I am here to-night in this old familiar room looking into your friendly faces and telling you these strange adventures."

He looked at the Medical Man. "No. I cannot expect you to believe it. Take it as a lie—or a prophecy. Say I dreamed it in the workshop. Consider I have been speculating upon the destinies of our race until I have hatched this fiction. Treat my assertion of its truth as a mere stroke of art to enhance its interest. And taking it as a story, what do you think of it?"

He took up his pipe, and began, in his old accustomed manner, to tap with it nervously upon the bars of the grate. There was a momentary stillness. Then chairs began to creak and shoes to scrape upon the carpet. I took my eyes off the Time Traveller's face, and looked round at his audience. They were in the dark, and little spots of colour swam before them. The Medical Man seemed absorbed in the contemplation of our host. The Editor was looking hard at the end of his cigar—the sixth. The Journalist fumbled for his watch. The others, as far as I remember, were motionless.

The Editor stood up with a sigh. "What a pity it is you're not a writer of stories!" he said, putting his hand on the Time Traveller's shoulder.

"You don't believe it?"

"Well——"

"I thought not."

The Time Traveller turned to us. "Where are the matches?" he said. He lit one and spoke over his pipe, puffing. "To tell you the truth . . . I hardly believe it myself. . . . And yet . . ."

His eye fell with a mute inquiry upon the withered white flowers upon the little table. Then he turned over the hand holding his pipe, and I saw he was looking at some half-healed scars on his knuckles.

The Medical Man rose, came to the lamp, and examined the flowers. "The gynæceum's odd," he said. The Psychologist leant forward to see, holding out his hand for a specimen.

"I'm hanged if it isn't a quarter to one," said the Journalist. "How shall we get home?"

"Plenty of cabs at the station," said the Psychologist.

"It's a curious thing," said the Medical Man; "but I certainly don't know the natural order of these flowers. May I have them?"

The Time Traveller hesitated. Then suddenly: "Certainly not."

"Where did you really get them?" said the Medical Man.

The Time Traveller put his hand to his head. He spoke like one who was trying to keep hold of an idea that eluded him. "They were put into my pocket by Weena, when I travelled into Time." He stared round the room. "I'm damned if it isn't all going. This room and you and the atmosphere of every day are too much for my memory. Did I ever make a Time Machine, or a model of a Time Machine? Or is it all only a dream? They say life is a dream, a precious poor dream at times—but I can't stand another that won't fit. It's madness. And where did the dream come from? . . . I must look at that machine. If there *is* one!"

He caught up the lamp swiftly, and carried it, flaring red, through the door into the corridor. We followed him. There in the flickering light of the lamp was the machine sure enough, squat, ugly, and askew; a thing of brass, ebony, ivory, and translucent glimmering quartz. Solid to the touch—for I put out my hand and felt the rail of it—and with brown spots and smears upon the ivory, and bits of grass and moss upon the lower parts, and one rail bent awry.

The Time Traveller put the lamp down on the bench, and ran his hand along the damaged rail. "It's all right now," he said. "The story I told you was true. I'm sorry to have brought you out here in the cold." He took up the lamp, and, in an absolute silence, we returned to the smoking-room.

He came into the hall with us and helped the Editor on with his coat. The Medical Man looked into his face and, with a certain hesitation, told him he was suffering from overwork, at which he laughed hugely. I remember him standing in the open doorway, bawling good-night.

I shared a cab with the Editor. He thought the tale a "gaudy lie." For my own part I was unable to come to a conclusion. The story was so fantastic and incredible, the telling so credible and sober. I lay awake most of the night thinking about it. I determined to go next day and see the Time Traveller again. I was told he was in the laboratory, and being on easy terms in the house, I went up to him. The laboratory, however, was empty. I stared for a minute at the Time Machine and put out my hand and touched the lever. At that the squat, substantial-looking mass swayed like a bough shaken by the wind. Its instability startled me extremely, and I had a queer reminiscence of the childish days when I used to be forbidden to meddle. I came back through the corridor. The Time Traveller met me in the smoking-room. He was coming from the house. He had a small camera under one arm and a knapsack under the other. He laughed when he saw me, and gave me an elbow to shake. "I'm frightfully busy," said he, "with that thing in there."

"But is it not some hoax?" I said. "Do you really travel through time?"

"Really and truly I do." And he looked frankly into my eyes. He hesitated. His eye wandered about the room. "I only want half an hour," he said, "I know why you came, and it's awfully good of you. There's some magazines here. If you'll stop to lunch I'll prove you this time travelling up to the hilt, specimen and all. If you'll forgive my leaving you now?"

I consented, hardly comprehending then the full import of his words, and he nodded and went on down the corridor. I heard the door of the laboratory slam, seated myself in a chair, and took up a daily paper. What was he going to do before lunch-time? Then suddenly I was reminded by an advertisement that I had promised to meet Richardson, the publisher, at two. I looked at my watch, and saw that I could barely save that engagement. I got up and went down the passage to tell the Time Traveller.

As I took hold of the handle of the door I heard an exclamation, oddly truncated at the end, and a click and a thud. A gust of air whirled round me as I opened the door, and from within came the sound of broken glass falling on the floor. The Time Traveller was not there. I seemed to see a ghostly, indistinct figure sitting in a whirling mass of black and brass for a moment—a figure so transparent that the bench behind with its sheets of drawings was absolutely distinct; but this phantasm vanished as I rubbed my eyes. The Time Machine had gone. Save for a subsiding stir of dust, the further end of the laboratory was empty. A pane of the skylight had, apparently, just been blown in.

I felt an unreasonable amazement. I knew that something strange had happened, and for the moment could not distinguish what the strange thing might be. As I stood staring, the door into the garden opened, and the man-servant appeared.

We looked at each other. Then ideas began to come. "Has Mr. —— gone out that way?" said I.

"No, sir. No one has come out this way. I was expecting to find him here."

At that I understood. At the risk of disappointing Richardson I stayed on, waiting for the Time Traveller; waiting for the second, perhaps still stranger story, and the specimens and photographs he would bring with him. But I am beginning now to fear that I must wait a lifetime. The Time Traveller vanished three years ago. And, as everybody knows now, he has never returned.

EPILOGUE: One cannot choose but wonder. Will he ever return? It may be that he swept back into the past, and fell among the blood-drinking, hairy savages of the Age of Unpolished Stone; into the abysses of the Cretaceous Sea; or among the grotesque saurians, the huge reptilian brutes of the Jurassic times. He may even now—if I may use the phrase—be wandering on some plesiosaurus-haunted Oolitic coral reef, or beside the lonely saline lakes of the Triassic Age. Or did he go forward, into one of the nearer ages, in which men are still men, but with the riddles of our own time answered and its wearisome problems solved? Into the manhood of the race: for I, for my own part, cannot think that these latter days of weak experiment, fragmentary theory, and mutual discord are indeed man's culminating time! I say, for my own part. He, I know—for the question had been discussed among us long before the Time Machine was made—thought but cheerlessly of the Advancement of Mankind, and saw in the growing pile of civilisation only a foolish heaping that must inevitably fall back upon and destroy its makers in the end. If that is so, it remains for us to live as though it were not so. But to me the future is still black and blank—is a vast ignorance, lit at a few casual places by the memory of his story. And I have by me, for my comfort, two strange white flowers—shrivelled now, and brown and flat and brittle—to witness that even when mind and strength had gone, gratitude and a mutual tenderness still lived on in the heart of man.

the curious case
of benjamin button

by F. SCOTT FITZGERALD

As long ago as 1860 it was the proper thing to be born at home. At present, so I am told, the high gods of medicine have decreed that the first cries of the young shall be uttered upon the anesthetic air of a hospital, preferably a fashionable one. So young Mr. and Mrs. Roger Button were fifty years ahead of style when they decided, one day in the summer of 1860, that their first baby should be born in a hospital. Whether this anachronism had any bearing upon the astonishing history I am about to set down will never be known.

I shall tell you what occurred, and let you judge for yourself.

The Roger Buttons held an enviable position, both social and financial, in ante-bellum Baltimore. They were related to the This Family and the That Family, which, as every Southerner knew, entitled them to membership in that enormous peerage which largely populated the Confederacy. This was their first experience with the charming old custom of having babies—Mr. Button was naturally nervous. He hoped it would be a boy so that he could be sent to Yale College in Connecticut, at which institution Mr. Button himself had been known for four years by the somewhat obvious nickname of "Cuff."

On the September morning consecrated to the enormous event he arose nervously at six o'clock, dressed himself, adjusted an impeccable stock, and hurried forth through the streets of Baltimore to the hospital, to determine whether the darkness of the night had borne in new life upon its bosom.

When he was approximately a hundred yards from the Maryland Private Hospital for Ladies and Gentlemen he saw Doctor Keene, the family physician, descending the front steps, rubbing his hands together with a washing movement—as all doctors are required to do by the unwritten ethics of their profession.

Mr. Roger Button, the president of Roger Button & Co., Wholesale Hardware, began to run toward Doctor Keene with much less dignity than was expected from a Southern gentleman of that picturesque period. "Doctor Keene!" he called. "Oh, Doctor Keene!"

The doctor heard him, faced around, and stood waiting, a curious expression settling on his harsh, medicinal face as Mr. Button drew near.

"What happened?" demanded Mr. Button, as he came up in a gasping rush. "What was it? How is she? A boy? Who is it? What——"

"Talk sense!" said Doctor Keene sharply. He appeared somewhat irritated.

"Is the child born?" begged Mr. Button.

Doctor Keene frowned. "Why, yes, I suppose so—after a fashion." Again he threw a curious glance at Mr. Button.

"Is my wife all right?"

"Yes."

"Is it a boy or a girl?"

"Here now!" cried Doctor Keene in a perfect passion of irritation, "I'll ask you to go and see for yourself. Outrageous!" He snapped the last word out in almost one syllable, then he turned away muttering: "Do you imagine a case like this will help my professional reputation? One more would ruin me—ruin anybody."

"What's the matter?" demanded Mr. Button, appalled. "Triplets?"

"No, not triplets!" answered the doctor cuttingly. "What's more, you can go and see for yourself. And get another doctor. I brought you into the world, young man, and I've been physician to your family for forty years, but I'm through with you! I don't want to see you or any of your relatives ever again! Good-by!"

Then he turned sharply, and without another word climbed into his phaeton, which was waiting at the curbstone, and drove severely away.

Mr. Button stood there upon the sidewalk, stupefied and trembling from head to foot. What horrible mishap had occurred? He had suddenly lost all desire to go into the Maryland Private Hospital for Ladies and Gentlemen—it was with the greatest difficulty that, a moment later, he forced himself to mount the steps and enter the front door.

A nurse was sitting behind a desk in the opaque gloom of the hall. Swallowing his shame, Mr. Button approached her.

"Good morning," she remarked, looking at him pleasantly.

"Good morning. I—I am Mr. Button."

At this a look of utter terror spread itself over the girl's face. She rose to her feet and seemed about to fly from the hall, restraining herself only with the most apparent difficulty.

"I want to see my child," said Mr. Button.

The nurse gave a little scream. "Oh—of course!" she cried hysterically. "Upstairs. Right upstairs. Go—*up!*"

She pointed the direction, and Mr. Button, bathed in a cool perspiration, turned falteringly, and began to mount to the second floor. In the upper hall he addressed another nurse who approached him, basin in hand. "I'm Mr. Button," he managed to articulate. "I want to see my——"

Clank! The basin clattered to the floor and rolled in the direction of the stairs. Clank! Clank! It began a methodical descent as if sharing in the general terror which this gentleman provoked.

"I want to see my child!" Mr. Button almost shrieked. He was on the verge of collapse.

Clank! The basin had reached the first floor. The nurse regained control of herself, and threw Mr. Button a look of hearty contempt.

"All *right*, Mr. Button," she agreed in a hushed voice. "Very *well!* But if you *knew* what state it's put us all in this morning! It's perfectly outrageous! The hospital will never have the ghost of a reputation after——"

"Hurry!" he cried hoarsely, "I can't stand this!"

"Come this way, then, Mr. Button."

He dragged himself after her. At the end of a long hall they reached a room from which proceeded a variety of howls—indeed, a room which, in later parlance, would have been known as the "crying-room." They entered. Ranged around the walls were half a dozen white-enameled rolling cribs, each with a tag tied at the head.

"Well," gasped Mr. Button, "which is mine?"

"There!" said the nurse.

Mr. Button's eyes followed her pointing finger, and this is what he saw. Wrapped in a voluminous white blanket, and partially crammed into one of the cribs, there sat an old man apparently about seventy years of age. His sparse hair was almost white, and from his chin dripped a long smoke-colored beard, which waved absurdly back and forth, fanned by the breeze coming in at the window. He looked up at Mr. Button with dim, faded eyes in which lurked a puzzled question.

"Am I mad?" thundered Mr. Button, his terror resolving into rage. "Is this some ghastly hospital joke?"

"It doesn't seem like a joke to us," replied the nurse severely. "And I don't know whether you're mad or not—but that is most certainly your child."

The cool perspiration redoubled on Mr. Button's forehead. He closed his eyes, and then, opening them, looked again. There was no mistake—he was gazing at a man of threescore and ten—a *baby* of threescore and ten, a baby whose feet hung over the sides of the crib in which it was reposing.

The old man looked placidly from one to the other for a moment, and then suddenly spoke in a cracked and ancient voice. "Are you my father?" he demanded.

Mr. Button and the nurse started violently.

"Because if you are," went on the old man querulously, "I wish you'd get me out of this place—or, at least, get them to put a comfortable rocker in here."

"Where in God's name did you come from? Who are you?" burst out Mr. Button frantically.

"I can't tell you *exactly* who I am," replied the querulous whine, "because I've only been born a few hours—but my last name is certainly Button."

"You lie! You're an impostor!"

The old man turned wearily to the nurse. "Nice way to welcome a newborn child," he complained in a weak voice. "Tell him he's wrong, why don't you?"

"You're wrong, Mr. Button," said the nurse severely. "This is your child, and you'll have to make the best of it. We're going to ask you to take him home with you as soon as possible—some time today."

"Home?" repeated Mr. Button incredulously.

"Yes, we can't have him here. We really can't, you know."

"I'm glad of it," whined the old man. "This is a fine place to keep a youngster of quiet tastes. With all this yelling and howling, I haven't been able to get a wink of sleep. I asked for something to eat"—here his voice rose to a shrill note of protest—"and they brought me a bottle of milk!"

Mr. Button sank down upon a chair near his son and concealed his face in his hands. "My heavens!" he murmured, in an ecstasy of horror. "What will people say? What must I do?"

"You'll have to take him home," insisted the nurse—"immediately!"

A grotesque picture formed itself with dreadful clarity before the eyes of the tortured man—a picture of himself walking through the crowded streets of the city with this appalling apparition stalking by his side. "I can't. I can't," he moaned.

People would stop to speak to him, and what was he going to say? He would have to introduce this—this septuagenarian: "This is my son, born early this morning." And then the old man would gather his blanket around him and they would plod on, past the bustling stores, the slave market—

for a dark instant Mr. Button wished passionately that his son was black—past the luxurious houses of the residential district, past the home for the aged. . . .

"Come! Pull yourself together," commanded the nurse.

"See here," the old man announced suddenly, "if you think I'm going to walk home in this blanket, you're entirely mistaken."

"Babies always have blankets."

With a malicious crackle the old man held up a small white swaddling garment. "Look!" he quavered. "*This* is what they had ready for me."

"Babies always wear those," said the nurse primly.

"Well," said the old man, "this baby's not going to wear anything in about two minutes. This blanket itches. They might at least have given me a sheet."

"Keep it on! Keep it on!" said Mr. Button hurriedly. He turned to the nurse. "What'll I do?"

"Go downtown and buy your son some clothes."

Mr. Button's son's voice followed him down into the hall: "And a cane, father. I want to have a cane."

Mr. Button banged the outer door savagely. . . .

CHAPTER II: "Good morning," Mr. Button said, nervously, to the clerk in the Chesapeake Dry Goods Company. "I want to buy some clothes for my child."

"How old is your child, sir?"

"About six hours," answered Mr. Button, without due consideration.

"Babies' supply department in the rear."

"Why, I don't think—I'm not sure that's what I want. It's—he's an unusually large-size child. Exceptionally—ah—large."

"They have the largest child's sizes."

"Where's the boys' department?" inquired Mr. Button, shifting his ground desperately. He felt that the clerk must surely scent his shameful secret.

"Right here."

"Well——" He hesitated. The notion of dressing his son in men's clothes was repugnant to him. If, say, he could only find a *very* large boy's suit, he might cut off that long and awful beard, dye the white hair brown, and thus manage to conceal the worst, and to retain something of his own self-respect—not to mention his position in Baltimore society.

But a frantic inspection of the boys' department revealed no suits to fit the newborn Button. He blamed the store, of course—in such cases it is the thing to blame the store.

"How old did you say that boy of yours was?" demanded the clerk curiously.

"He's—sixteen."

"Oh, I beg your pardon, I thought you said six *hours*. You'll find the youths' department in the next aisle."

Mr. Button turned miserably away. Then he stopped, brightened, and pointed his finger toward a dressed dummy in the window display. "There!" he exclaimed. "I'll take that suit, out there on the dummy."

The clerk stared. "Why," he protested, "that's not a child's suit. At least it *is*, but it's for fancy dress. You could wear it yourself!"

"Wrap it up," insisted his customer nervously. "That's what I want."

The astonished clerk obeyed.

Back at the hospital Mr. Button entered the nursery and almost threw the package at his son. "Here's your clothes," he snapped out.

The old man untied the package and viewed the contents with a quizzical eye.

"They look sort of funny to me," he complained. "I don't want to be made a monkey of——"

"You've made a monkey of me!" retorted Mr. Button fiercely. "Never you mind how funny you look. Put them on—or I'll—or I'll *spank* you." He swallowed uneasily at the penultimate word, feeling nevertheless that it was the proper thing to say.

"All right, father"—this with a grotesque simulation of filial respect—"you've lived longer; you know best. Just as you say."

As before, the sound of the word "father" caused Mr. Button to start violently.

"And hurry."

"I'm hurrying, father."

When his son was dressed Mr. Button regarded him with depression. The costume consisted of dotted socks, pink pants, and a belted blouse with a wide white collar. Over the latter waved the long whitish beard, drooping almost to the waist. The effect was not good.

"Wait!"

Mr. Button seized a hospital shears and with three quick snaps amputated a large section of the beard. But even with this improvement the ensemble fell far short of perfection. The remaining brush of scraggly hair, the watery eyes, the ancient teeth, seemed oddly out of tone with the gayety of the costume. Mr. Button, however, was obdurate—he held out his hand. "Come along!" he said sternly.

His son took the hand trustingly. "What are you going to call me, dad?" he quavered as they walked from the nursery—"just 'baby' for a while? till you think of a better name?"

Mr. Button grunted. "I don't know," he answered harshly. "I think we'll call you Methuselah."

CHAPTER III: Even after the new addition to the Button family had had his hair cut short and then dyed to a sparse unnatural black, had had his face shaved so close that it glistened, and had been attired in small-boy clothes made to order by a flabbergasted tailor, it was impossible for Mr. Button to ignore the fact that his son was a poor excuse for a first family baby. Despite his aged stoop, Benjamin Button—for it was by this name they called him instead of by the appropriate but invidious Methuselah—was five feet eight inches tall. His clothes did not conceal this, nor did the clipping and dyeing of his eyebrows disguise the fact that the eyes underneath were faded and watery and tired. In fact, the baby nurse who had been engaged in advance left the house after one look, in a state of considerable indignation.

But Mr. Button persisted in his unwavering purpose. Benjamin was a baby, and a baby he should remain. At first he declared that if Benjamin didn't like warm milk he could go without food altogether, but he was finally prevailed upon to allow his son bread and butter, and even oatmeal by way of a compromise. One day he brought home a rattle and, giving it to Benjamin, insisted in no uncertain terms that he should "play with it," whereupon the old man took it with a weary expression and could be heard jingling it obediently at intervals throughout the day.

There can be no doubt, though, that the rattle bored him, and that he found other and more soothing amusements when he was left alone. For instance, Mr. Button discovered one day that during the preceding week he had smoked more cigars than ever before—a phenomenon which was explained a few days later when, entering the nursery unexpectedly, he found the room full of faint blue haze and Benjamin, with a guilty expression on his face, trying to conceal the butt of a dark Havana. This, of course, called for a severe spanking, but Mr. Button found that he could not bring himself to administer it. He merely warned his son that he would "stunt his growth."

Nevertheless he persisted in his attitude. He brought home lead soldiers, he brought toy trains, he brought large pleasant animals made of cotton, and, to perfect the illusion which he was creating—for himself at least—he passionately demanded of the clerk in the toy store whether "the paint would come off the pink duck if the baby put it in his mouth." But, despite all his father's efforts, Benjamin refused to be interested. He would steal down the back stairs and return to the nursery with a volume of the "Encyclopædia Britannica," over which he would pore through an afternoon, while his cotton cows and his Noah's ark were left neglected on the floor. Against such a stubbornness Mr. Button's efforts were of little avail.

The sensation created in Baltimore was, at first, prodigious. What the mishap would have cost the Buttons and their kinsfolk socially cannot be determined, for the outbreak of the Civil War drew the city's attention to other things. A few people who were unfailingly polite racked their brains for compliments to give to the parents—and finally hit upon the ingenious device of declaring that the baby resembled his grandfather, a fact which, due to the standard state of decay common to all men of seventy, could not be denied. Mr. and Mrs. Roger Button were not pleased, and Benjamin's grandfather was furiously insulted.

Benjamin, once he left the hospital, took life as he found it. Several small boys were brought to see him, and he spent a stiff-jointed afternoon trying to work up an interest in tops and marbles—he even managed, quite accidentally, to break a kitchen window with a stone from a slingshot, a feat which secretly delighted his father.

Thereafter Benjamin contrived to break something every day, but he did these things only because they were expected of him, and because he was by nature obliging.

When his grandfather's initial antagonism wore off, Benjamin and that gentleman took enormous pleasure in one another's company. They would sit for hours, these two so far apart in age and experience, and, like old cronies, discuss with tireless monotony the slow events of the day. Benjamin felt more at ease in his grandfather's presence than in his parents'—they seemed always somewhat in awe of him and, despite the dictatorial authority they exercised over him, frequently addressed him as "Mr."

He was as puzzled as anyone else at the apparently advanced age of his mind and body at birth. He read up on it in the medical journal, but found that no such case had been previously recorded. At his father's urging he made an honest attempt to play with other boys, and frequently he joined in the milder games—football shook him up too much, and he feared that in case of a fracture his ancient bones would refuse to knit.

When he was five he was sent to kindergarten, where he was initiated into the art of pasting green paper on orange paper, of weaving colored maps and manufacturing eternal cardboard necklaces. He was inclined to drowse off to sleep in the middle of these tasks, a habit which both irritated and frightened his young teacher. To his relief she complained to his parents, and he was removed from the school. The Roger Buttons told their friends that they felt he was too young.

By the time he was twelve years old his parents had grown used to him. Indeed, so strong is the force of custom that they no longer felt that he was different from any other child—except when some curious anomaly reminded them of the fact. But one day a few weeks after his twelfth birthday, while looking in the mirror, Benjamin made, or thought he made, an astonishing discovery. Did his eyes deceive him, or had his hair turned in the dozen years of his life from white to iron-gray under its concealing dye? Was the network of wrinkles on his face becoming less pronounced? Was his skin healthier and firmer, with even a touch of ruddy winter color? He could not tell. He knew that he no longer stooped and that his physical condition had improved since the early days of his life.

"Can it be——?" he thought to himself, or rather, scarcely dared to think.

He went to his father. "I am grown," he announced determinedly. "I want to put on long trousers."

His father hesitated. "Well," he said finally, "I don't know. Fourteen is the age for putting on long trousers—and you are only twelve."

"But you'll have to admit," protested Benjamin, "that I'm big for my age."

His father looked at him with illusory speculation. "Oh, I'm not so sure of that," he said. "I was as big as you, when I was twelve."

This was not true—it was all part of Roger Button's silent agreement with himself to believe in his son's normality.

Finally a compromise was reached. Benjamin was to continue to dye his hair. He was to make a better attempt to play with boys of his own age. He was not to wear his spectacles or carry a cane in the street. In return for these concessions he was allowed his first suit of long trousers. . . .

CHAPTER IV: Of the life of Benjamin Button between his twelfth and twenty-first year I intend to say little. Suffice to record that they were years of normal ungrowth. When Benjamin was eighteen he was erect as a man of fifty; he had more hair and it was of a dark gray; his step was firm, his voice had lost its cracked quaver and descended to a healthy baritone. So his father sent him up to Connecticut to take examinations for entrance to Yale College. Benjamin passed his examination and became a member of the freshman class.

On the third day following his matriculation he received a notification from Mr. Hart, the college registrar, to call at his office and arrange his schedule. Benjamin, glancing in the mirror, decided that his hair needed a new application of its brown dye, but an anxious inspection of his bureau drawer disclosed that the dye bottle was not there. Then he remembered—he had emptied it the day before and thrown it away.

He was in a dilemma. He was due at the registrar's in five minutes. There seemed to be no help for it—he must go as he was. He did.

"Good morning," said the registrar politely. "You've come to inquire about your son."

"Why, as a matter of fact, my name's Button——" began Benjamin, but Mr. Hart cut him off.

"I'm very glad to meet you, Mr. Button. I'm expecting your son here any minute."

"That's me!" burst out Benjamin. "I'm a freshman."

"What!"

"I'm a freshman."

"Surely you're joking."

"Not at all."

The registrar frowned and glanced at a card before him. "Why, I have Mr. Benjamin Button's age down here as eighteen."

"That's my age," asserted Benjamin, flushing slightly.

The registrar eyed him wearily. "Now surely, Mr. Button, you don't expect me to believe that."

Benjamin smiled wearily. "I am eighteen," he repeated.

The registrar pointed sternly to the door. "Get out," he said. "Get out of college and get out of town. You are a dangerous lunatic."

"I am eighteen."

Mr. Hart opened the door. "The idea!" he shouted. "A man of your age trying to enter here as a freshman. Eighteen years old, are you? Well, I'll give you eighteen minutes to get out of town."

Benjamin walked with dignity from the room, and half a dozen undergraduates, who were waiting in the hall, followed him curiously with their eyes. When he had gone a little way he turned around, faced the infuriated registrar, who was still standing in the doorway, and repeated in a firm voice: "I am eighteen years old."

To a chorus of titters which went up from the group of undergraduates, Benjamin walked away.

But he was not fated to escape so easily. On his melancholy walk to the railroad station he found that he was being followed by a group, then by a swarm, and finally by a dense mass of undergraduates. The word had gone around that a lunatic had passed the entrance examinations for Yale and attempted to palm himself off as a youth of eighteen. A fever of excitement permeated the college. Men ran hatless out of classes, the football team abandoned its practice and joined the mob, professors' wives, with bonnets awry and bustles out of position, ran shouting after the procession, from which proceeded a continual succession of remarks aimed at the tender sensibilities of Benjamin Button.

"He must be the Wandering Jew!"

"He ought to go to prep school at his age!"

"Look at the infant prodigy!"

"He thought this was the old men's home."

"Go up to Harvard!"

Benjamin increased his gait, and soon he was running. He would show them! He *would* go to Harvard, and then they would regret these ill-considered taunts!

Safely on board the train for Baltimore, he put his head from the window. "You'll regret this!" he shouted.

"Ha-ha!" the undergraduates laughed. "Ha-ha-ha!" It was the biggest mistake that Yale College had ever made. . . .

CHAPTER V: In 1880 Benjamin Button was twenty years old, and he signalized his birthday by going to work for his father in Roger Button & Co., Wholesale Hardware. It was in that same year that he began "going out socially"—that is, his father insisted on taking him to several fashionable dances. Roger Button was now fifty, and he and his son were more and more companionable—in fact, since Benjamin had ceased to dye his hair (which was still grayish) they appeared about the same age, and could have passed for brothers.

One night in August they got into the phaeton attired in their full-dress suits and drove out to a dance at the Shevlins' country house, situated just outside of Baltimore. It was a gorgeous evening. A full moon drenched the road to the lustreless color of platinum, and late-blooming harvest flowers breathed into the motionless air aromas that were like low, half-heard laughter. The open country, carpeted for rods around with bright wheat, was translucent as in the day. It was almost impossible not to be affected by the sheer beauty of the sky—almost.

"There's a great future in the dry-goods business," Roger Button was saying. He was not a spiritual man—his esthetic sense was rudimentary.

"Old fellows like me can't learn new tricks," he observed profoundly. "It's you youngsters with energy and vitality that have the great future before you."

Far up the road the lights of the Shevlins' country house drifted into view, and presently there was a sighing sound that crept persistently toward them—it might have been the fine plaint of violins or the rustle of the silver wheat under the moon.

They pulled up behind a handsome brougham whose passengers were disembarking at the door. A lady got out, then an elderly gentleman, then another young lady, beautiful as sin. Benjamin started; an almost chemical change seemed to dissolve and recompose the very elements of his body. A rigor passed over him, blood rose into his cheeks, his forehead, and there was a steady thumping in his ears. It was first love.

The girl was slender and frail, with hair that was ashen under the moon and honey-colored under the sputtering gas lamps of the porch. Over her shoulders was thrown a Spanish mantilla of softest yellow, butterflied in black; her feet were glittering buttons at the hem of her bustled dress.

Roger Button leaned over to his son. "That," he said, "is young Hildegarde Moncrief, the daughter of General Moncrief."

Benjamin nodded coldly. "Pretty little thing," he said indifferently. But when the negro boy had led the buggy away, he added: "Dad, you might introduce me to her."

They approached a group of which Miss Moncrief was the centre. Reared in the old tradition, she curtsied low before Benjamin. Yes, he might have a dance. He thanked her and walked away—staggered away.

The interval until the time for his turn should arrive dragged itself out interminably. He stood close to the wall, silent, inscrutable, watching with murderous eyes the young bloods of Baltimore as they eddied around Hildegarde Moncrief, passionate admiration in their faces. How obnoxious they seemed to Benjamin; how intolerably rosy! Their curling brown whiskers aroused in him a feeling equivalent to indigestion.

But when his own time came, and he drifted with her out upon the changing floor to the music of the latest waltz from Paris, his jealousies and anxieties melted from him like a mantle of snow. Blind with enchantment, he felt that life was just beginning.

"You and your brother got here just as we did, didn't you?" asked Hildegarde, looking up at him with eyes that were like bright blue enamel.

Benjamin hesitated. If she took him for his father's brother, would it be best to enlighten her? He remembered his experience at Yale, so he decided against it. It would be rude to contradict a lady; it would be criminal to mar this exquisite occasion with the grotesque story of his origin. Later, perhaps. So he nodded, smiled, listened, was happy.

"I like men of your age," Hildegarde told him. "Young boys are so idiotic. They tell me how much champagne they drink at college, and how much money they lose playing cards. Men of your age know how to appreciate women."

Benjamin felt himself on the verge of a proposal—with an effort he choked back the impulse.

"You're just the romantic age," she continued—"fifty. Twenty-five is too worldly-wise; thirty is apt to be pale from overwork; forty is the age of long stories that take a whole cigar to tell; sixty is—oh, sixty is too near seventy; but fifty is the mellow age. I love fifty."

Fifty seemed to Benjamin a glorious age. He longed passionately to be fifty.

"I've always said," went on Hildegarde, "that I'd rather marry a man of fifty and be taken care of than marry a man of thirty and take care of *him*."

For Benjamin the rest of the evening was bathed in a honey-colored mist. Hildegarde gave him two more dances, and they discovered that they were marvellously in accord on all the questions of the day. She was to go driving with him on the following Sunday, and then they would discuss all these questions further.

Going home in the phaeton just before the crack of dawn, when the first bees were humming and the fading moon glimmered in the cool dew, Benjamin knew vaguely that his father was discussing wholesale hardware.

". . . And what do you think should merit our biggest attention after hammers and nails?" the elder Button was saying.

"Love," replied Benjamin absent-mindedly.

"Lugs?" exclaimed Roger Button. "Why, I've just covered the question of lugs."

Benjamin regarded him with dazed eyes just as the eastern sky was suddenly cracked with light, and an oriole yawned piercingly in the quickening trees. . . .

CHAPTER VI: When, six months later, the engagement of Miss Hildegarde Moncrief to Mr. Benjamin Button was made known (I say "made known," for General Moncrief declared he would rather fall upon his sword than announce it), the excitement in Baltimore society reached a feverish pitch. The almost forgotten story of Benjamin's birth was remembered and sent out upon the winds of scandal in picaresque and incredible forms. It was said that Benjamin was really the father of Roger Button, that he was his brother who had been in prison for forty years, that he was John Wilkes Booth in disguise—and, finally, that he had two small conical horns sprouting from his head.

The Sunday supplements of the New York papers played up the case with fascinating sketches which showed the head of Benjamin Button attached to a fish, to a snake, and, finally, to a body of solid brass. He became known, journalistically, as the Mystery Man of Maryland. But the true story, as is usually the case, had a very small circulation.

However, everyone agreed with General Moncrief that it was "criminal" for a lovely girl who could have married any beau in Baltimore to throw herself into the arms of a man who was assuredly fifty. In vain Mr.

Roger Button published his son's birth certificate in large type in the Baltimore *Blaze*. No one believed it. You had only to look at Benjamin and see.

On the part of the two people most concerned there was no wavering. So many of the stories about her fiancé were false that Hildegarde refused stubbornly to believe even the true one. In vain General Moncrief pointed out to her the high mortality among men of fifty—or, at least, among men who looked fifty; in vain he told her of the instability of the wholesale hardware business. Hildegarde had chosen to marry for mellowness—and marry she did. . . .

CHAPTER VII: In one particular, at least, the friends of Hildegarde Moncrief were mistaken. The wholesale hardware business prospered amazingly. In the fifteen years between Benjamin Button's marriage in 1880 and his father's retirement in 1895, the family fortune was doubled—and this was due largely to the younger member of the firm.

Needless to say, Baltimore eventually received the couple to its bosom. Even old General Moncrief became reconciled to his son-in-law when Benjamin gave him the money to bring out his "History of the Civil War" in twenty volumes, which had been refused by nine prominent publishers.

In Benjamin himself fifteen years had wrought many changes. It seemed to him that the blood flowed with new vigor through his veins. It began to be a pleasure to rise in the morning, to walk with an active step along the busy, sunny street, to work untiringly with his shipments of hammers and his cargoes of nails. It was in 1890 that he executed his famous business coup: he brought up the suggestion that *all nails used in nailing up the boxes in which nails are shipped are the property of the shippee*, a proposal which became a statute, was approved by Chief Justice Fossile, and saved Roger Button and Company, Wholesale Hardware, more than *six hundred nails every year*.

In addition, Benjamin discovered that he was becoming more and more attracted by the gay side of life. It was typical of his growing enthusiasm for pleasure that he was the first man in the city of Baltimore to own and run an automobile. Meeting him on the street, his contemporaries would stare enviously at the picture he made of health and vitality.

"He seems to grow younger every year," they would remark. And if old Roger Button, now sixty-five years old, had failed at first to give a proper welcome to his son he atoned at last by bestowing on him what amounted to adulation.

And here we come to an unpleasant subject which it will be well to pass over as quickly as possible. There was only one thing that worried Benjamin Button: his wife had ceased to attract him.

At that time Hildegarde was a woman of thirty-five, with a son, Roscoe, fourteen years old. In the early days of their marriage Benjamin had worshiped her. But, as the years passed, her honey-colored hair became an unexciting brown, the blue enamel of her eyes assumed the aspect of cheap crockery—moreover, and most of all, she had become too settled in her ways, too placid, too content, too anemic in her excitements, and too sober in her taste. As a bride it had been she who had "dragged" Benjamin to dances and dinners—now conditions were reversed. She went out socially with him, but without enthusiasm, devoured already by that eternal inertia which comes to live with each of us one day and stays with us to the end.

Benjamin's discontent waxed stronger. At the outbreak of the Spanish-American War in 1898 his home had for him so little charm that he decided to join the army. With his business influence he obtained a commission as captain, and proved so adaptable to the work that he was made a major, and finally a lieutenant-colonel just in time to participate in the celebrated charge up San Juan Hill. He was slightly wounded, and received a medal.

Benjamin had become so attached to the activity and excitement of army life that he regretted to give it up, but his business required attention, so he resigned his commission and came home. He was met at the station by a brass band and escorted to his house.

CHAPTER VIII: Hildegarde, waving a large silk flag, greeted him on the porch, and even as he kissed her he felt with a sinking of the heart that these three years had taken their toll. She was a woman of forty now, with a faint skirmish line of gray hairs in her head. The sight depressed him.

Up in his room he saw his reflection in the familiar mirror—he went closer and examined his own face with anxiety, comparing it after a moment with a photograph of himself in uniform taken just before the war. "Good Lord!" he said aloud. The process was continuing. There was no doubt of it—he looked now like a man of thirty. Instead of being delighted, he was uneasy—he was growing younger. He had hitherto hoped that once he reached a bodily age equivalent to his age in years, the grotesque phenomenon which had marked his birth would cease to function. He shuddered. His destiny seemed to him awful, incredible.

When he came downstairs Hildegarde was waiting for him. She appeared annoyed, and he wondered if she had at last discovered that there was something amiss. It was with an effort to relieve the tension between them that he broached the matter at dinner in what he considered a delicate way.

"Well," he remarked lightly, "everybody says I look younger than ever."

Hildegarde regarded him with scorn. She sniffed. "Do you think it's anything to boast about?"

"I'm not boasting," he asserted uncomfortably.

She sniffed again. "The idea," she said, and after a moment: "I should think you'd have enough pride to stop it."

"How can I?" he demanded.

"I'm not going to argue with you," she retorted. "But there's a right way of doing things and a wrong way. If you've made up your mind to be different from everybody else, I don't suppose I can stop you, but I really don't think it's very considerate."

"But, Hildegarde, I can't help it."

"You can too. You're simply stubborn. You think you don't want to be like anyone else. You always have been that way, and you always will be. But just think how it would be if everyone else looked at things as you do—what would the world be like?"

As this was an inane and unanswerable argument Benjamin made no reply, and from that time on a chasm began to widen between them. He wondered what possible fascination she had ever exercised over him.

To add to the breach, he found, as the new century gathered headway, that his thirst for gayety grew stronger. Never a party of any kind in the city of Baltimore but he was there, dancing with the prettiest of the young married women, chatting with the most popular of the débutantes, and finding their company charming, while his wife, a dowager of evil omen, sat among the chaperons, now in haughty disapproval, and now following him with solemn, puzzled, and reproachful eyes.

"Look!" people would remark. "What a pity! A young fellow that age tied to a woman of forty-five. He must be twenty years younger than his wife." They had forgotten—as people inevitably forget—that back in 1880 their mammas and papas had also remarked about this same ill-matched pair.

Benjamin's growing unhappiness at home was compensated for by his many new interests. He took up golf and made a great success of it. He went in for dancing: in 1906 he was an expert at "The Boston," and in 1908 he was considered proficient at the "Maxixe," while in 1909 his "Castle Walk" was the envy of every young man in town.

His social activities, of course, interfered to some extent with his business, but then he had worked hard at wholesale hardware for twenty-five years and felt that he could soon hand it on to his son, Roscoe, who had recently graduated from Harvard.

He and his son were, in fact, often mistaken for each other. This pleased Benjamin—he soon forgot the insidious fear which had come over him on his return from the Spanish-American War, and grew to take a naïve pleasure in his appearance. There was only one fly in the delicious ointment—he hated to appear in public with his wife. Hildegarde was almost fifty, and the sight of her made him feel absurd. . . .

CHAPTER IX: One September day in 1910—a few years after Roger Button & Co., Wholesale Hardware, had been handed over to young Roscoe Button—a man, apparently about twenty years old, entered himself as a freshman at Harvard University in Cambridge. He did not make the mistake of announcing that he would never see fifty again nor did he mention the fact that his son had been graduated from the same institution ten years before.

He was admitted, and almost immediately attained a prominent position in the class, partly because he seemed a little older than the other freshmen, whose average age was about eighteen.

But his success was largely due to the fact that in the football game with Yale he played so brilliantly, with so much dash and with such a cold, remorseless anger that he scored seven touchdowns and fourteen field goals for Harvard, and caused one entire eleven of Yale men to be carried singly from the field, unconscious. He was the most celebrated man in college.

Strange to say, in his third or junior year he was scarcely able to "make" the team. The coaches said that he had lost weight, and it seemed to the more observant among them that he was not quite as tall as before. He made no touchdowns—indeed, he was retained on the team chiefly in hope that his enormous reputation would bring terror and disorganization to the Yale team.

In his senior year he did not make the team at all. He had grown so slight and frail that one day he was taken by some sophomores for a freshman, an incident which humiliated him terribly. He became known as something of a prodigy—a senior who was surely no more than sixteen—and he was often shocked at the worldliness of some of his classmates. His studies seemed harder to him—he felt that they were too advanced. He had heard his classmates speak of St. Midas', the famous preparatory school, at which so many of them had prepared for college, and he determined after his graduation to enter himself at St. Midas', where the sheltered life among boys his own size would be more congenial to him.

Upon his graduation in 1914 he went home to Baltimore with his Harvard diploma in his pocket. Hildegarde was now residing in Italy, so

Benjamin went to live with his son, Roscoe. But though he was welcomed in a general way, there was obviously no heartiness in Roscoe's feeling toward him—there was even perceptible a tendency on his son's part to think that Benjamin, as he moped about the house in adolescent mooniness, was somewhat in the way. Roscoe was married now and prominent in Baltimore life, and he wanted no scandal to creep out in connection with his family.

Benjamin, no longer persona grata with the débutantes and younger college set, found himself left much alone, except for the companionship of three or four fifteen-year-old boys in the neighborhood. His idea of going to St. Midas' school recurred to him.

"Say," he said to Roscoe one day, "I've told you over and over that I want to go to prep school."

"Well, go, then," replied Roscoe shortly. The matter was distasteful to him, and he wished to avoid a discussion.

"I can't go alone," said Benjamin helplessly. "You'll have to enter me and take me up there."

"I haven't got time," declared Roscoe abruptly. His eyes narrowed and he looked uneasily at his father. "As a matter of fact," he added, "you'd better not go on with this business much longer. You better pull up short. You better—you better"—he paused and his face crimsoned as he sought for words—"you better turn right around and start back the other way. This has gone too far to be a joke. It isn't funny any longer. You—you behave yourself!"

Benjamin looked at him, on the verge of tears.

"And another thing," continued Roscoe, "when visitors are in the house I want you to call me 'Uncle'—not 'Roscoe,' but 'Uncle,' do you understand? It looks absurd for a boy of fifteen to call me by my first name. Perhaps you'd better call me 'Uncle' *all* the time, so you'll get used to it."

With a harsh look at his father, Roscoe turned away. . . .

CHAPTER X: At the termination of this interview, Benjamin wandered dismally upstairs and stared at himself in the mirror. He had not shaved for three months, but he could find nothing on his face but a faint white down with which it seemed unnecessary to meddle. When he had first come home from Harvard, Roscoe had approached him with the proposition that he should wear eyeglasses and imitation whiskers glued to his cheeks, and it had seemed for a moment that the farce of his early years was to be repeated. But whiskers had itched and made him ashamed. He wept and Roscoe had reluctantly relented.

Benjamin opened a book of boys' stories, "The Boy Scouts in Bimini

Bay," and began to read. But he found himself thinking persistently about the war. America had joined the Allied cause during the preceding month, and Benjamin wanted to enlist, but, alas, sixteen was the minimum age, and he did not look that old. His true age, which was fifty-seven, would have disqualified him, anyway.

There was a knock at his door, and the butler appeared with a letter bearing a large official legend in the corner and addressed to Mr. Benjamin Button. Benjamin tore it open eagerly, and read the enclosure with delight. It informed him that many reserve officers who had served in the Spanish-American War were being called back into service with a higher rank, and it enclosed his commission as brigadier-general in the United States Army with orders to report immediately.

Benjamin jumped to his feet fairly quivering with enthusiasm. This was what he had wanted. He seized his cap and ten minutes later he had entered a large tailoring establishment on Charles Street, and asked in his uncertain treble to be measured for a uniform.

"Want to play soldier, sonny?" demanded a clerk, casually.

Benjamin flushed. "Say! Never mind what I want!" he retorted angrily. "My name's Button and I live on Mt. Vernon Place, so you know I'm good for it."

"Well," admitted the clerk, hesitatingly, "if you're not, I guess your daddy is, all right."

Benjamin was measured, and a week later his uniform was completed. He had difficulty in obtaining the proper general's insignia because the dealer kept insisting to Benjamin that a nice Y. W. C. A. badge would look just as well and be much more fun to play with.

Saying nothing to Roscoe, he left the house one night and proceeded by train to Camp Mosby, in South Carolina, where he was to command an infantry brigade. On a sultry April day he approached the entrance to the camp, paid off the taxicab which had brought him from the station, and turned to the sentry on guard:

"Get someone to handle my luggage!" he said briskly.

The sentry eyed him reproachfully. "Say," he remarked, "where you goin' with the general's duds, sonny?"

Benjamin, veteran of the Spanish-American War, whirled upon him with fire in his eye, but with, alas, a changing treble voice.

"Come to attention!" he tried to thunder; he paused for breath—then suddenly he saw the sentry snap his heels together and bring his rifle to the present. Benjamin concealed a smile of gratification, but when he glanced around, his smile faded. It was not he who had inspired obedience, but an imposing artillery colonel who was approaching on horseback.

"Colonel!" called Benjamin shrilly.

The colonel came up, drew rein, and looked coolly down at him with a twinkle in his eyes. "Whose little boy are you?" he demanded kindly.

"I'll soon darn well show you whose little boy I am!" retorted Benjamin in a ferocious voice. "Get down off that horse!"

The colonel roared with laughter.

"You want him, eh, general?"

"Here!" cried Benjamin desperately. "Read this." And he thrust his commission toward the colonel.

The colonel read it, his eyes popping from their sockets.

"Where'd you get this?" he demanded, slipping the document into his own pocket.

"I got it from the Government, as you'll soon find out!"

"You come along with me," said the colonel with a peculiar look. "We'll go up to headquarters and talk this over. Come along."

The colonel turned and began walking his horse in the direction of headquarters. There was nothing for Benjamin to do but follow with as much dignity as possible—meanwhile promising himself a stern revenge.

But this revenge did not materialize. Two days later, however, his son Roscoe materialized from Baltimore, hot and cross from a hasty trip, and escorted the weeping general, *sans* uniform, back to his home.

CHAPTER XI: In 1920 Roscoe Button's first child was born. During the attendant festivities, however, no one thought it "the thing" to mention that the little grubby boy, apparently about ten years of age, who played around the house with lead soldiers and a miniature circus was the new baby's own grandfather.

No one disliked the little boy whose fresh, cheerful face was crossed with just a hint of sadness, but to Roscoe Button his presence was a source of torment. In the idiom of his generation, Roscoe did not consider the matter "efficient." It seemed to him that his father, in refusing to look sixty, had not behaved like a "red-blooded he-man"—this was Roscoe's favorite expression—but in a curious and perverse manner. Indeed, to think about the matter for as much as a half hour drove him to the edge of insanity. Roscoe believed that "live wires" should keep young, but carrying it out on such a scale was—was—was inefficient. And there Roscoe rested.

Five years later Roscoe's little boy had grown old enough to play childish games with little Benjamin under the supervision of the same nurse. Roscoe took them both to kindergarten on the same day and Benjamin found that playing with little strips of colored paper, making mats and chains and curious and beautiful designs, was the most fascinating game in the world. Once he was bad and had to stand in the corner—then he cried—but for the most part there were gay hours in the cheerful room, with the sunlight coming in the windows and Miss Bailey's kind hand resting for a moment now and then in his tousled hair.

Roscoe's son moved up into the first grade after a year, but Benjamin stayed on in the kindergarten. He was very happy. Sometimes when other tots talked about what they would do when they grew up a shadow would cross his little face as if in a dim, childish way he realized that those were things in which he was never to share.

The days flowed on in monotonous content. He went back a third year to the kindergarten, but he was too little now to understand what the bright shining strips of paper were for. He cried because the other boys were bigger than he and he was afraid of them. The teacher talked to him, but though he tried to understand he could not understand at all.

He was taken from the kindergarten. His nurse, Nana, in her starched gingham dress, became the centre of his tiny world. On bright days they walked in the park; Nana would point at a great gray monster and say "elephant," and Benjamin would say it after her, and when he was being undressed for bed that night he would say it over and over aloud to her: "Elyphant, elyphant, elyphant." Sometimes Nana let him jump on the bed, which was fun, because if you sat down exactly right it would bounce you up on your feet again, and if you said "Ah" for a long time while you jumped you got a very pleasing broken vocal effect.

He loved to take a big cane from the hatrack and go around hitting chairs and tables with it and saying: "Fight, fight, fight." When there were people there the old ladies would cluck at him, which interested him, and the young ladies would try to kiss him, which he submitted to with mild boredom. And when the long day was done at five o'clock he would go upstairs with Nana and be fed oatmeal and nice soft mushy foods with a spoon.

There were no troublesome memories in his childish sleep; no token came to him of his brave days at college, of the glittering years when he flustered the hearts of many girls. There were only the white, safe walls of his crib and Nana and a man who came to see him sometimes, and a great big orange ball that Nana pointed at just before his twilight bed hour and called "sun." When the sun went his eyes were sleepy—there were no dreams, no dreams to haunt him.

The past—the wild charge at the head of his men up San Juan Hill; the first years of his marriage when he worked late into the summer dusk down in the busy city for young Hildegarde whom he loved; the days before that when he sat smoking far into the night in the gloomy old Button house on Monroe Street with his grandfather—all these had faded like unsubstantial dreams from his mind as though they had never been.

He did not remember. He did not remember clearly whether the milk was warm or cool at his last feeding or how the days passed—there was only his crib and Nana's familiar presence. And then he remembered nothing. When he was hungry he cried—that was all. Through the noons and nights he breathed and over him there were soft mumblings and murmurings that he scarcely heard, and faintly differentiated smells, and light and darkness.

Then it was all dark, and his white crib and the dim faces that moved above him, and the warm sweet aroma of the milk, faded out altogether from his mind.

the rat

by S. FOWLER WRIGHT

Dr. Merson looked at the dying rat, and decided that, should he delay his experiment longer, it would be dead before morning.

He had nursed it now for nearly six months, and it had been very old and blind when he had bought it.

He had told Briggs that he would give him £5 for the oldest rat in Belsham, and the ratcatcher had earned his money.

It had surprised him, when he had first approached the subject, to realize how difficult it would be to find an animal that was really old and feeble. He had to observe that Nature does not encourage the prolongation of pain and weariness: when youth goes, life very quickly follows.

But he knew that, in the course of their age-long warfare with the human race, the rats had arrived at some social organization, and had adopted some of our practices, and in particular, that when a disease of blindness (to which they are very liable) attacks them, they may be nursed and fed by members of their family, so that life is prolonged to an age which would otherwise be impossible.

So he had asked for an aged rat, and had watched its vitality recede, till now it was too weak to crawl toward the tempting food that was offered.

. . . It was so dull with age that it did not flinch when the needle pricked it.

The next morning it was not dead. It lay sleeping; old, and blind and decrepit. It was not pleasant to look at, but it may have been less feeble than the night before—and the food had been eaten.

Dr. Merson, observing this, became aware that his heart was beating fast, with a sudden excitement, of which he had not supposed himself to be capable.

When he looked at it again at midday, and observed that it was feebly attending to a neglected toilet, he did a thing which was less wise than his usual custom.

Mrs. Merson disliked his experiments, and his own habits of professional reticence disinclined him from speech which had no immediate purpose. But this was a discovery of such momentous consequence that he was impelled to share it.

"You mean that no one need ever die?" she asked incredulously. She was not greatly impressed, even if she took it with any seriousness. She was a healthy young woman, utterly without imagination, and the cook had given notice an hour ago.

"Yes, it might mean that—or nearly—unless by accident.—You see," he continued, to an auditor who scarcely heard him, "it isn't really new. We've known for a long time that youth would continue if the cells of which the body is built have the right stimuli; but it's been difficult to find what they are. Some of the lower forms of life never die, as it is. The old ones break apart, and each section acquires a new impetus of growth from the shock of that division. But in the higher animals there is a change in the substance or activities of the cells as the years pass, the nature of which has been difficult to ascertain, though its results have been evident. . . ."

He stopped, as he became aware that Mrs. Merson had ceased to listen. She regarded the sleeping rat with disfavour.

"I shouldn't think anything wants to live when it's that old," she said, with decision. She had the impatience of healthy youth for all signs of decrepitude. They seemed stupid.

She heard the voice of the butcher at the back door, and her mind reverted to matters of greater urgency. She went back to the kitchen.

The rat improved very slowly. Its appetite increased. It moved more briskly. It gained weight. It gave more attention to its toilet. It became wilder, and more alert to the sounds around it. Finally, its sight returned.

The process was not rapid, but continuous. At the end of three months from when it had received the injection (which had not been repeated) it showed the bodily activity and physique of a young rat.

Dr. Merson did not mention it again to his wife, nor did he seek another confidant. He became thoughtful, and, at times, appeared to be

suffering from acute depression. His patients complained, and his practice suffered.

The fact is that he was beginning to fear the consequences of his discovery.

At first, it had seemed simple—and stupendous. He was about to benefit his race, as no man had done before him. Had he not found a way by
which death itself was defeated? He saw that it would change the whole
face of the earth. Old age would become an obscene tradition. Disease
would be powerless to overcome the new vitality which he had discovered.
Men would no longer die as their minds approached the threshold of
wisdom.

He thought of his own patients. There was Mrs. Corner who would
be dead of tuberculosis within a year, unless he should use his new power
for her rescue—Minnie Corner, with three young children, fighting her
hopeless battle, always "a little better to-day," when he called to watch
the slow relentless progress of a disease that he could not conquer. He
would be very glad to give her health. Having it in his power, it was a
clear and simple duty, as her doctor, to do it. But (so far as he could
suppose) he would do more than that. He would give her an approximation to immortality. Not absolute immortality. Her body would still be
liable to be damaged or destroyed by violence. Certainly, it would have
no power to survive the planet on which it lived. It would be liable to
drowning, or suffocation. But it would no longer be in subjection to the
treachery of time. Fed, and guarded from violence, it would not age nor
decay. There was something odd in imagining Minnie Corner immortal.
But there was nothing repellent. He supposed it would mean treating her
children in the same way. They would be annoyed if they observed themselves growing old and feeble, while their mother remained young. It
would confuse the relationship. Neither would she thank him for such
a tableau. He knew Mrs. Corner well enough to realize that there would
be no rest for him till he had conferred the same boon upon her household
that he should give to her. Well, why not?

About two of the children there would be no difficulty. But he disliked
Peter. He disliked Peter intensely. He could not endure the thought of
an immortal Peter. It wasn't the club-foot, though it did seem a pity
that it should become an abiding feature of a world grown static: it was
certain qualities of meanness and cruelty which the boy had shown from
infancy, which his mother had lamented, but which she had been powerless to influence.

According to the law of Nature which now prevailed, Peter would grow
old, and in due course he would die, and his unpleasant characteristics
would perish with him. He might have children, but these children would
be different from himself, whether better or worse, and, in due course,

they would have still different children, the race repeating itself with an unending variety.

Somehow, this seemed a better prospect than that of an enduring Peter.

Yet he could not imagine an arrangement being smoothly made by which Peter would be consigned to an exceptional mortality. However carefully his moral and physical inferiorities, and the importance of his early elimination, might be explained to him, Dr. Merson felt sure that he would resent it furiously. He imagined a violent assault upon his own person by an adult and desperate Peter to whom he was refusing the boon of immortality. Even a murderous assault. . . .

His mind was diverted to observe that murder would become a more serious crime than it now is—the risk of being murdered a more dreadful probability. Indeed, all physical risks would be taken at an almost infinitely greater price, and—presumably—with a corresponding reluctance. . . .

It was a relief to abandon these speculations to the task of lancing a boil on the neck of the landlord of the *Spotted Cow*.

The weeks went on, and the rat continued, and even increased, its youthful vigour. Its eyes were bright. Its coat was smooth and glossy. Its movements were lithe and swift. It was fierce, and watchful for a chance of biting. Once its teeth met in the sleeve of Dr. Merson's coat, and the incident led him to wonder whether its new vitality could be communicated by the medium of a bite. He was aware that the thought gave him a sensation of peril escaped, and he realized that he was already regarding his discovery with apprehension rather than pleasure. Certainly, he had no wish to have its benefits thrust upon him before he had deliberated more fully on their ultimate consequences.

Also, the rat was disconcertingly watchful for a chance of escaping from its confinement. Once it actually got its head through the closing door, and it needed a sharp blow to induce it to abandon the hope of freedom. Dr. Merson had an actual nightmare as the result of imagining that it had escaped, and that his invention were destroyed or forgotten, so that the world would pass at last to the dominion of a continually-increasing army of immortal rats.

After that incident, Dr. Merson became careful to lock the door of the laboratory, in which the rat was confined, and to keep the key in his pocket. Considering the possibilities which might follow, should it be accidentally let loose, he realized how little he yet knew of the nature of his discovery. He could not even say whether the vitality it conferred would be passed on to succeeding generations. He imagined some prolific and noxious insect, inoculated to immortality, and still exercising a blind fecundity. It might become uncontrollable, and destroy everything before it. That would be a weird ending to created life on this abortive planet, which must already be a joke to all surrounding intelligences.

Yet the idea was more than remotely possible. He imagined his discovery made public, and its advantages become the common property of mankind, and then some super-criminal threatening his race with the results of such an inoculation of some hostile vermin unless they should do his pleasure eternally.

Day by day his mind renewed its efforts to probe the consequences of his discovery, and retired bewildered, as it encountered some new problem, or some obvious result which he had not previously contemplated.

. . . He saw that the human race would become static. Not in brain, perhaps, but, at least, in body. That alone must make profound differences, produce profound cleavages. The ugly and deformed must remain so to all eternity. Perhaps, with an increased vitality: but vitality would not alter structure.

. . . There might be an agitation to eliminate the obviously unfit in brain or body, and to replace them with healthier children. But who would decide? Would those who were judged inferior be content to be sacrificed? He imagined fierce and ruthless wars of extermination. Suppose, again, that the white races should attempt to confine his discovery to their own use. He imagined the black and yellow races attacking them with a mad ferocity to force the priceless secret from them. Would the white races yield, or would they risk their potentially immortal bodies in such a conflict? If they should yield, would not the latent animosities of race and race still remain, to break out into wars, which, under such conditions, must result in servitude or extermination?

. . . He saw that, in the absence of widespread war, the world would soon reach a maximum population, and that their children must cease . . . or, perhaps, an occasional child might be permitted to replace an accidental death . . . or a large number of children to replace the wastage of war. Would the race remain capable of these occasional fertilities? Or would it arrive at a position at which its numbers would be reduced (however slowly) by occasional misadventure, and these reductions would be irreplaceable?

. . . Or, if children remained a potential possibility, would not the desire for them become at times irresistible with at least many of the unoccupied women? Might they not welcome a war which would throw upon them the duty of replacement?

He was aroused from these visions by the consciousness that he was by Mrs. Empsey's bedside.

It was some years since Mrs. Empsey had walked across her bedroom floor. Her daughter, Ada, waited on her without complaint, and earned a little money by sewing and taking care of the neighbours' children.

It was many years since Joe Horton had asked for any rent for the cottage. They had a few shillings weekly from the parish. So they lived.

Dr. Merson had not sent in a bill for ten years past. He never thought of doing so. He had fought as hard for Mrs. Empsey's life as for that of his wealthiest patient. It was all in the day's work.

But he had not been able to cure her. Indeed, he had not hoped to do so. Even now, he was not certain that her damaged interior could be reconstructed, though he could give her a new vitality. But he hoped, even for that. Anyway, she would be about again, and Ada could marry the booking clerk at Belsham station, who had waited long enough. They were both over thirty. Here was one of the first places to which his discovery would bring a joy almost beyond imagination. Mrs. Empsey had always clung to life with a desperate cowardice. But even here he would do nothing—would say nothing—too hastily. The whole prospect was too stupendous.

He checked himself in writing a prescription which would have placed his patient beyond the power of any drug to revive her. . . . That was another thought. . . . The power of poisons would continue. . . . If the certainty of death were removed, would the dread of such contingencies be increased until life became an intolerable care to avoid them? Only experience could resolve that problem.

Out of much confusion of speculation, a thought came in the end, clearly born out of chaos. If he were right that his discovery could give perpetual youth to mankind, it could only mean that a limited number of people would live long, where, otherwise, a larger number of people would have lived for a shorter time. Putting aside all theories of future life, all the speculations or dogmatisms of religion, its only result could be to make the single life longer, and the individual lives less numerous. Finally, therefore, it could only be advantageous if it resulted in higher and happier conditions of life than those which were prevailing around him. It would abolish children. It would abolish age. It would make youth perpetual. Youth was the desire of all men. Those who were young desired to retain it. Those who were old would give anything they had to recover it. So much was clear—if he were only sure. Aiming to abolish age, might it not be found—and perhaps too late—that it was youth that had left the world?

By all outward evidences, the rat had regained its youth. Why should he doubt that it was the perpetuity of youth which he would offer to a grateful world? Perhaps he vexed himself because his own mind was too small to understand the greatness of his own discovery?

Yet, could youth be perpetual? Youth was not only of the body, it was of the spirit. He did not know. . . . As a doctor, he was pre-disposed to consider the physical as dominant. But the freshness of youth—?

He considered another possibility. Perhaps age would come, though more gradually, as the spirit tired. Then the body might be periodically inoculated to a new youth, as he had done to the rat, with all the joy of a returning spring-time. "If youth but knew—" How many men had wasted youth, and longed for its return in vain, when they had gained the experience which would have valued it more highly, and used it differently! To unite the experience of age with youth's vitality!—and then he saw his delusion . . . the joy of youth is not of experience but of inexperience. It is because the adventure is new: the path untrodden.

He considered himself. He did not feel old. He was forty-three. He knew that he must appear old to the young people around him. If he were unmarried, and should he ask a young girl to share his life, she might make it a jest to her companions.

But he had a good constitution, and he had lived temperately. His body was still strong and vigorous. Yet he had not the outlook of youth. He realized that his youth would not return, though twenty years should be taken from the age of his body.

With a sudden clarity he realized that, to regain his youth, it was not so much a new body which would be needed; that which he had would serve his purpose well enough, could it only throw off the appearances of thinning hair and growing corpulence, which disguised it from the youth around it; it was a new youth of the soul, and intervening Lethe, which would be needed.—He had made no discovery in that direction. Physically, youth might continue, but, as the centuries passed—and the millenniums—

He made efforts to regain the standpoint of his own youth, that he might explore its differences. He became absent-minded in reminiscence. . . . He used to write poetry then. He had not done anything quite so foolish for many years. All the same, he had done it rather well. The only weak point was that the poems were usually left unfinished. It was so much easier to get the first lines. The memories of youth moved him to the old impulse. With a sudden keen recovery of emotion he remembered his first meeting with Mollie. . . . The picnic under the trees. . . . The first shy kiss on her shoulder. . . . That was before he had gone to college. . . . He had always been loyal to her, and she to him. . . . He was not of the shallower sort of those that change lightly. . . . He loved her now, as he had loved her then—But oh! the world between . . .

> It takes a life to learn
> That none may steer his course to shear
> The trail of light astern

That was well expressed. He would have written those lines down twenty years ago. He would have intended to make them into a complete poem. But he knew better now. He knew that they would never be finished. He knew so much about himself, and others. He even knew his own weaknesses.

That was the trouble. The inexperience of youth was something which could never be recovered, and the experience of age was no substitute. He realized that to abolish age is to abolish youth also.

Seeing this, his mind started itself with a further possibility—might it be equally true to say that to abolish death would be to abolish life? In a moment's vision he saw life and death in a conflict from which each wins recurrent victory: he saw them interdependent, and this strife as the condition on which they both existed. . . . He imagined his discovery applied to the vegetable world. An oak-tree in perpetual vigour —Would there be no place left for fruit-time and harvest? For the young growths of spring?—There was the question of food—Corn must still be grown for food, and mown down in due season—Or perhaps there might be developed roots of a continuing vigour? But the question of food was not merely a human one. All life grew by feeding upon the life around it.

This was fundamental. It had an aspect of cruel rapacity, seeming inconsistent with the idea of a beneficent God. Yet, if there be mortality at all, there can be no better end to the outworn or defeated body than to support the vigour of a new life. . . . His mind stopped, bewildered once again before the stupendous nature of the change which his discovery must bring to the earth's economy.

Perhaps the question was too great for one man to face. Would it not be well to announce his discovery, and for some small committee of selected men to consider whether it should be used? . . . But he knew that there would be no such question in the minds of men. They might doubt its advantages for other men, for alien races, for animal or vegetable creations, but for themselves there would be no doubt at all.

It was true that he might withhold the discovery itself, and merely announce that he possessed it, but even that announcement (if it were believed) might arouse an excitement that he could not estimate. . . . He imagined himself mobbed, beaten, even tortured, till he consented to reveal it to a frantic world. . . .

Pacing the laboratory restlessly, distracted with such thoughts as these, afraid to meet the reproaches of his wife, who could not understand why he was changed and ageing so rapidly, so that he had acquired a habit of remaining there till it should be time to go out on his daily round, he regarded the rat, now running up the bars of its cage in a restless and tireless activity, with sudden hatred. He would kill the loathsome thing, and forget the horror he had discovered. Perhaps he might enjoy life once again. . . .

He looked at his watch, and was startled to see that it was half an hour after the usual time at which he set out on his daily round—and he had a consultation with Sir William Brett at 10:30 . . . he went out hurriedly.

School was just commencing that morning when Peter Corner left it. He owed his freedom to his ability to take unscrupulous advantage of the caprice of circumstance, and the credulity of his fellows. His two sisters had colds, and his mother had kept them home. Had he reported to his schoolmistress that his mother suspected measles he would have incurred the risk of ultimate retribution, which he was always adroit to avoid. Instead of that, he made the remark to Jessie Phipson, who could be relied upon to report it promptly. Challenged on the point, he strenuously denied the truth of the suggestion. His mother had never said so. He had told Jessie that they had not got measles *nor* scarlet fever. The mistress did not know what to believe, and sent him home till she could obtain more reliable information. He had expected that. His expression was almost good-tempered as he dragged his club-foot toward Dr. Merson's surgery. His sisters usually called for his mother's medicine, but as they had not come to school today the duty fell to him. He did not like going there. He hated Dr. Merson. He hated his eyes, which seemed to see through him without effort, and then to look elsewhere, as though he were not worth seeing. But he had got to go to-day, and he had a hopeful idea this morning. He did not expect to get the medicine before noon. He knew that the doctor was not at home during the mornings. But he could not be blamed for calling on his way home.

He found the surgery door unlocked, as it was sometimes left when Dr. Merson was absent. He had expected that. He knew when and whether most of the doors in Belsham were locked or open. He did not often make use of this knowledge. His physical deformity, and the practical difficulties of secreting or disposing of illicit gains, had withheld him from active dishonesties. But in his waking dreams (for he had them, as much as more attractive children) he was most often a cat burglar of superhuman audacities.

Had he rung the surgery bell, the maid would have come, or the doctor's wife, but he turned the handle without haste or hesitation, and stood quietly inside, in an attitude of respectful waiting, till he was reassured of the surrounding silence. Then he passed through to the passage. He could not move very quietly, but a sound of crockery in the distant kitchen reassured him, and—beyond his hopes—the key was in the door on the other side of the passage.

Dr. Merson did not often experiment with living animals, but it was generally known that he held a vivisection certificate. It was the dream of Peter's life to enter that room, and see the horrors which he vaguely imagined to be concealed behind the frosted glass that could be seen sideways from the road, if you forced your face sufficiently far between the palings.

Now the door was not even locked, though the key was in it. Peter opened it quietly, entered, and closed it behind him.

Dr. Merson had not gone far when he was vexed by a doubt as to whether he had locked the door. He was almost sure that he had—yes, he was quite sure—but he felt vaguely uneasy. He felt for the key in its usual pocket, but it was not there. He felt in his other pockets, with the same result. He must have left it in the door. He felt sure now that he had turned the key, but had not removed it. That was what had made his mind uneasy. Really, it didn't matter. No one of his household would enter the room under such circumstances. Certainly Mollie wouldn't. She hated the room, and never entered it except to seek him. More certainly still, the maid would not venture. She would not enter to dust it. Not that he wanted her to. Women are a curse where a man works. But he knew her feeling. It was, in fact, her talk in the village which was mainly responsible for the fact that Peter Corner was now inside the room. But Dr. Merson didn't know that. He only thought that if the women of his household found the door locked and the key outside they would know that he couldn't be in, and would be unlikely to enter. But was he sure that he had locked it?

Probably he wouldn't have turned back, being so late already, had he not discovered, to his added annoyance, that he had left behind some clinical notes which he should require at the consultation for which he was late already.

He went back hastily. On the way, he made a resolution that he would kill the rat that night, and destroy the serum he had invented. He perceived with a sudden clarity, that the world's Creator might understand His job better than a local practitioner in Belsham village. The relief that the decision gave him confirmed its wisdom. He was in better spirits than he had been for many weeks as he passed through the surgery, and crossed the passage to the room beyond.

Sir William Brett waited for over half an hour at the house of the patient for the benefit of whose health, and relief of whose pocket, the consultation had been arranged. Then he rang up Dr. Merson's house for an explanation. He received a reply (after some delay) that the doctor had been seized with a sudden indisposition, and greatly regretted that the appointment must be deferred until the following day.

The inquest on the body of Peter Corner had been adjourned by a coroner who had known Dr. Merson sufficiently well to regard it as incredible that he should have committed a crime so strange and so inex-plicable. He hoped that the doctor might be found, or that his voluntary return would furnish some satisfactory explanation. But the police had not been retarded by any similar hesitation. Within twenty-four hours of the doctor's disappearance the dismembered body of Peter Corner had been discovered, and the facts that he could not be found, and that he had drawn nearly four hundred pounds (practically the whole of his available balance), from his bank in Treasury notes on the previous day, had enabled them to obtain a warrant for his arrest without difficulty. . . . But the warrant had not been executed.

Dr. Merson had walked to the station quite openly. He had chatted with casual acquaintances on the platform. He had even got into a compartment containing others who knew him. He had travelled to London, saying that he was in search of certain surgical instruments which he required to renew, and had disappeared absolutely.

It was agreed that he had been in particularly good spirits. Indeed—and this was one of the minor mysteries of the case—there had been a noticeable change in his demeanour from the morning when Peter had been seen to enter the door of his surgery. Everyone noticed the change. It was as though a load of fear or trouble had been suddenly lifted from him.

Mrs. Merson—who had insisted on giving evidence in spite of the coroner's warning—had confirmed this. She had entered the witness-box to urge her conviction, against the weight of overwhelming evidence, that he had not murdered Peter at all, and to assert that he had himself been living in dread of some mysterious enemy who must be responsible both for the fate of Peter, and for her husband's disappearance.

Her evidence, given with the convincing simplicity of an unimaginative mind, had impressed its hearers with her sincerity, and increased the sympathy with which she was regarded, but it could not shake the weight of evidence which placed the crime upon the shoulders of the absent doctor.

It was recognized by the police that the doctor could not have known that Peter would be released from school that morning, but their theory was that he had met the boy by chance in the street, and had recognized an unexpected opportunity for the commission of a crime which had been designed within his mind previously. He had told the boy to go to the surgery, and await his return. He had followed immediately, by a different route, entered the surgery unobserved, and promptly disposed of his unsuspecting victim. His household admitted that they had not known that he was at home till the telephone inquiry from Sir William Brett had caused them to seek him, and he had then replied, through a half-opened door, that he was unwell, and the appointment must be deferred to the following day.

He had callously proceeded to the dissection of his victim's body, and it was only when the police had traced the missing boy to his own door, and the inquiries had become too close and pointed for his comfort, that he had decided to bolt, without delaying for the added risk of attempting the destruction or removal of the dismembered corpse.

Such was the theory of the police, and while it failed to offer the explanation of any adequate motive for a deed so ghastly, and a risk so great, and while there was nothing in the doctor's previous record to support the suggestion of criminality at once so gross and so reckless, yet it had the advantage of meeting the admitted facts more plausibly than appeared otherwise possible, and even those who were least willing to believe that the doctor could have been guilty of such a murder were unable to put forward any reasonable supposition which could explain the presence of the boy's remains on his premises, and his subsequent flight and silence.

It was now two months since Dr. Merson had alighted at Paddington, and been seen to make a leisurely descent of the stairs to the Underground station which adjoins that terminus. Doubtless, the police would continue their inquiries, and the public would continue to keep them occupied with abortive "clues," but the coroner could see no reason for adjourning the inquest further, nor means of avoiding the obvious verdict which the jury would be expected to render. It would place him under the painful necessity of issuing a warrant against an old friend, of whose guilt his own mind was not easily convinced, but it would be of no practical importance, in view of the magistrate's warrant on which the police were already acting. (The time had not arrived at which this duplication of procedure was reformed in practice.)

He had no further evidence to bring forward, except that of Sir Lionel Tipshift, the Home Office expert, who had conducted the *post-mortem* on the dismembered body, and who would give his opinion upon the cause of death with the air of Olympic impartiality on which the police had relied so often for the hanging of suspected persons.

The coroner's Court was small, and crowded. It was a rainy day, and the atmosphere within the court was one of depression, and of damp umbrellas. The room was plainly furnished, with a table for the legal profession, an arm-chair for the coroner, a partitioned corner for the jury, and some benches for the use of the waiting witnesses, and the general public. It was clean, and its windows were wide and high. Yet it had an aspect of invincible grime, as though it were washed incessantly and vainly to remove an ingrained dirt, against which no physical assault could be directed successfully.

Mrs. Merson sat on the front bench, looking grave, but not acutely miserable. Her husband's cousin, Mr. Reginald Merson, sat beside her. This gentleman (of whose existence she had not known previously), had arrived from the Argentine about six weeks after Dr. Merson had disappeared. He had made a casual call upon a cousin whom he had not seen for over twenty years, and finding himself in the midst of circumstances so strange and tragic, and having time at his disposal, he had offered such help as he could give to his cousin's wife by remaining until the inquest should be over. He had declined her invitation to reside in the house, preferring to take a room at the *Spotted Cow*, but this discretion had not prevented some unkindly gossip, which had attributed Mrs. Merson's equanimity to the very opportune companionship which he was able to offer.

On this point, gossip was not entirely wrong; but the emotions of the doctor's wife, being beyond her own analysis, were not likely to be understood by the observation of strangers. She had not wavered in her loyalty to her absent husband, nor had her affection lessened. She held a matter-of-course opinion that he had not murdered anyone; she was quite sure that he was not dead; and she was equally sure that he would return at his own time, and deal with the situation with his usual efficiency. She had decided that the whole trouble was the work of some enmity, as to the nature of which, as was natural in the case of one who was destitute of normal imagination, her imaginations were very wild indeed. Mr. Reginald Merson attracted and sometimes bewildered her by a likeness, not so much to her husband as she had last seen him, as to that which had been at the time of their engagement, and during the first years of her married life. His voice, though stronger in tone, was curiously similar; his hair, though abundant, whereas her husband had become partially bald, was of the same colour and quality—or, perhaps, very slightly darker. His features were alike, except for the short hair on the upper lip, and even that was a reminder of how her husband once had worn it. He was slow and guarded in speech, but, even so, he would let fall remarks at times which showed a puzzling familiarity with the past events of the household.

She did not disguise from herself that his presence gave her confidence, though there was mystery even in that, for he never spoke with any conviction of the doctor's innocence, nor suggested that he might return and vindicate his reputation, and any plans he might casually indicate for her future appeared to assume that the doctor's disappearance was to be accepted as final.

Inspector Clawson, who was in charge of the case, had not overlooked the strangeness of the arrival of this young man, and his curiosity had been increased when he had failed to trace the name of Merson on the passenger lists of any recently-arriving liners. He did not see how Mr. Reginald Merson could be associated with the crime, in the absence of any evidence that he had been in the neighbourhood when it was committed, but he felt that he was a source from which valuable information might be obtained, who might very probably be aware of the place in which the doctor was hiding, and might very possibly be induced to speak if the penalties which are incurred by an accessory after the fact were judiciously indicated.

He had him watched, and discovered nothing. He appeared to have no acquaintances, except Mrs. Merson. He wrote no letters. He received none. The Inspector decided to interview him.

Mr. Reginald received him genially. He alluded to the murder at once, and condoled with him on his failure to make any arrest. The position seemed to amuse him. The Inspector could not see the joke, and did not like the tone he adopted. He asserted, with a confidence that he did not feel, that he expected that an arrest would soon be made. "Scotland Yard," he asserted, lying with the boldness of exasperation, "always gets its man in the end."

Mr. Reginald suggested humourously that he might himself be the doctor in disguise. Would the Inspector like to arrest him? The Inspector would have liked to do so very well, had a sufficient pretext arisen. He had already considered the possibility which was now suggested in an obvious mockery. The appearance of this mysterious cousin, at such a time, and of so vague an origin, would have attracted the notice of the dullest detective of fiction, and Inspector Clawson was a very capable officer.

But his judgment was too sound to lead him into an error so obvious. He knew how much may be done by disguise, and he knew its limitations. He had never seen Dr. Merson, but he had examined some recent photographs. He knew his age. He had discussed his appearance with local members of the force, who had seen him daily.

Between the suddenly-disappearing doctor and the suddenly-arriving cousin there were more than the usual cousinly resemblances. But the differences were beyond the possibilities of disguise or explanation. A bald man cannot disguise himself with a thick crop of natural hair. A man of a growing rotundity cannot disguise himself in a few weeks by the production of a slim and obviously youthful figure. A man of forty-five cannot disguise himself into an appearance of half his age which will deceive the hostile eyes of a detective who is standing two feet away in the open street, when the morning is sunny.

Inspector Clawson only remarked that it was a fine day.

That was yesterday. In the Coroner's Court this morning the Inspector's eyes were still drawn in the same direction. He was not greatly interested in the evidence of Sir Lionel Tipshift. For one reason, he knew what it was to be, and for another, he had no respect for the expert witness. He is useful to impress juries, but the police and lawyers knew that another can always be procured to contradict him. Sir Lionel Tipshift was a tame expert, regularly hired by the Crown. The nature of his evidence could be relied upon as certainly as that a prosecuting counsel would not point out the probable innocence of the prisoner against whom his brief was drawn.

So the Inspector's attention wandered while Sir Lionel, with a manner suggesting that he was slightly bored by his own infallibility, gave the result of his *post-mortem* examination. The body, he assured the Court, had been disjointed after death—probably several hours later—by someone with considerable knowledge of anatomy. The internal organs had been preserved, and (with some technical qualifications) were healthy. There was no trace of poison. There were marks of violence upon the body, including certain bruises on the legs, which must have been caused before death, by some blunt instrument. (That was correct. They had been inflicted by Bunny Simpson's boot in the school playground on the afternoon before Peter's existence had abruptly terminated.)

The listeners were hypnotized by the coldly decisive voice to the belief that additional and important evidence had been given. The coroner only, being accustomed to analyse evidence, was conscious that nothing had been added to that which was already known, or could have been reasonably deduced from admitted circumstances, and he was about to address a final word to the jury, when Mr. Reginald Merson rose, and asked, in a deferential but self-possessed manner, if, as the nearest male relative of the absent doctor, whose reputation was so much concerned, the unfortunate death having taken place on his premises, he might ask Sir Lionel Tipshift a few questions upon the evidence he had given.

The coroner hesitated. A coroner's inquiry is somewhat less formal than are the proceedings in the criminal courts. Possibly the fact that all coroners do not belong to the legal profession (many are doctors) may have produced a less rigid etiquette for preventing oral intercourse of any kind except through the medium of a paid lawyer. But it is not usual for a witness to be examined in such a manner. He was about to say that he would himself put any inquiry which he might approve, if Mr. Merson would let him know what was in his mind, when that gentleman, taking his pause of hesitation for consent, addressed a question to Sir Lionel which was sufficiently unexpected to cause him to remain silent to await the answer.

"Can you tell me if any other body was discovered in the laboratory, besides that of Peter Corner?"

Sir Lionel, who had already moved some paces from the witness-stand, turned back, as he answered with a dry precision.

"There were no other human remains. Dr. Merson appears to have been engaged in the dissection of a recently-killed rat, on the last occasion on which he occupied the laboratory."

"Does not the fact that he could have been so occupied, at such a time, with the boy's body upon his hands, suggest that there must have been some connection between the two?" Mr. Reginald asked, but the coroner interposed before Sir Lionel could answer.

"If you have any information which may be of assistance to this inquiry, Mr. Merson, I must ask you to take the oath, and offer your evidence in the usual way; it cannot be given in the form of suggestions to another witness."

Mr. Merson did not appear either disconcerted or annoyed by this rebuke. He answered easily. He apologized for his ignorance of the correct procedure. He regretted that he was not in a position to accept the coroner's offer. It had only occurred to him—and he submitted the suggestion with diffidence—that the doctor might have suddenly returned, having remembered, after starting out, that he had not locked the room in accordance with his usual practice, and found the boy trespassing within it. Suppose that the rat had been inoculated with some new and dreadful disease, and the boy had interfered with it, and had been bitten, so that he would be certain to contract it, and would not only die himself, but might give it to others, would it not become a natural thing—even a duty —however unlawful—to take any steps, at whatever personal risk, to prevent such consequences?

The Court listened in a tense silence to this unexpected theory, but Sir Lionel, though he had not been addressed, gave a reply which disposed of its probability, the coroner silently allowing his interposition, with respect which was usually accorded to his name and title.

"The rat was not diseased. It was a remarkably fine specimen. Indeed, it was the finest and healthiest that I have ever seen. There were remarkable signs of vitality in every organ."

"Then, if it were so exceptional in its physical development, might it not have sprung at the boy's throat, when he opened the door of its cage —which would be about at the same level—and inflicted a serious or even a fatal wound?"

Sir Lionel, who was seldom disinclined to the sound of his own voice, was about to answer, but his opinion on this point will never be known, for this time the coroner interposed too quickly.

"I don't think, Mr. Merson, that anything can be gained by pursuing hypothetical improbabilities. Such explanations, if put forward at all, should have come from Dr. Merson himself, or from some regularly-appointed advocate on his behalf. I am not aware that you have any claim to represent him at all, beyond that of an alleged relationship, and even that has not been sworn to. Dr. Merson is absent. He went away voluntarily, leaving the body of this unhappy boy on his premises, at a time when he knew that inquiries were turning in his direction. I am afraid that the jury will draw their own conclusions." He paused a moment, and then commenced a brief and lucid charge to the jury, from which a verdict of wilful murder against the absent doctor might be confidently expected.

Mr. Reginald Merson turned to the woman beside him, and said something in a low voice, on which she smiled, and rose with him. Evidently they did not propose to wait to hear the verdict given. The ease and confidence of his own demeanour appeared to have infected his companion, and she passed out somewhat briskly and buoyantly as one who leaves an unpleasant incident with finality.

As they went down the steps which led to the street, Inspector Clawson touched Mr. Merson's arm, and he turned politely.

"I should just like to ask," said the Inspector, "how you came to know that the boy opened the cage."

Mr. Merson appeared amused. "I dreamt it on Monday night, Inspector. . . . I'm rather good at dreams," he added pleasantly.

The Inspector's hand was in his pocket. His fingers closed upon the warrant which he was carrying. If only he had the courage to make the arrest to which his instinct urged him! It might make—or break—him. He became aware that Mr. Merson was speaking to him again, and in a voice of banter. "It's no good, Inspector. You won't get a word more. The voluntary statement's played out. . . . It's no use worrying," he said kindly, "you'd better go home, and forget it."

The Inspector felt that the advice was sound, though he did not like it. He thought of his wife and children and of the comfortable pension which waits the later years of frequently-promoted officers, who do not make mistakes which arouse adverse newspaper comment. He turned sadly away.

Dr. Merson walked home very happily, beside a wife who did not know him. He was very fond of Mollie. He wondered (as he had done before) if the time had come to show her the birth-mark on his left arm. He wondered whether it would be expedient to use the hypodermic syringe which was in his right-hand pocket, which would restore her youth, and give her the vitality which he was already experiencing. He liked her very well as she was, but he did not doubt that he should like her quite as well if she were looking twenty years younger. But he was not quite clear as to the pretext on which he should make the injection. Not quite clear, either, that it would be morally defensible to do it without explaining its results beforehand. He felt that to convince her of the actual truth would not be the easiest of mental enterprises. But he felt also that, if she should be led to share his experiences, she would admit his identity more readily than would be otherwise probable.

Still, there was no hurry. There might even be advantages in delay. He imagined Inspector Clawson studying the metamorphosis of the wife of the missing doctor. It would be amusing. It could hardly be dangerous. Still, it was a needless risk. There was no hurry.

Yes—he would come in to tea.

beyond time

and space

the damned thing

by AMBROSE BIERCE

CHAPTER I: ONE DOES NOT ALWAYS EAT WHAT IS ON THE TABLE By the light of a tallow candle which had been placed on one end of a rough table a man was reading something written in a book. It was an old account book, greatly worn; and the writing was not, apparently, very legible, for the man sometimes held the page close to the flame of the candle to get a stronger light on it. The shadow of the book would then throw into obscurity a half of the room, darkening a number of faces and figures; for besides the reader, eight other men were present. Seven of them sat against the rough log walls, silent, motionless, and the room being small, not very far from the table. By extending an arm anyone of them could have touched the eighth man, who lay on the table, face upward, partly covered by a sheet, his arms at his sides. He was dead.

The man with the book was not reading aloud, and no one spoke; all seemed to be waiting for something to occur; the dead man only was without expectation. From the blank darkness outside came in, through the aperture that served for a window, all the ever unfamiliar noises of night in the wilderness—the long nameless note of a distant coyote; the stilly pulsing thrill of tireless insects in trees; strange cries of night birds, so different from those of the birds of day; the drone of great blundering beetles, and all that mysterious chorus of small sounds that seem always to have been but half heard when they have suddenly ceased, as if conscious of an indiscretion. But nothing of all this was noted in that company; its members were not overmuch addicted to idle interest in matters of no practical importance; that was obvious in every line of their rugged faces—obvious even in the dim light of the single candle. They were evidently men of the vicinity—farmers and woodsmen.

The person reading was a trifle different; one would have said of him that he was of the world, worldly, albeit there was that in his attire which attested a certain fellowship with the organisms of his environment. His coat would hardly have passed muster in San Francisco; his foot-gear was not of urban origin, and the hat that lay by him on the floor (he was the only one uncovered) was such that if one had considered it as an article of mere personal adornment he would have missed its meaning. In countenance the man was rather prepossessing, with just a hint of stern-ness; though that he may have assumed or cultivated, as appropriate to one in authority. For he was a coroner. It was by virtue of his office that he had possession of the book in which he was reading; it had been found among the dead man's effects—in his cabin, where the inquest was now taking place.

When the coroner had finished reading he put the book into his breast pocket. At that moment the door was pushed open and a young man entered. He, clearly, was not of mountain birth and breeding: he was clad as those who dwell in cities. His clothing was dusty, however, as from travel. He had, in fact, been riding hard to attend the inquest.

The coroner nodded; no one else greeted him.

"We have waited for you," said the coroner. "It is necessary to have done with this business to-night."

The young man smiled. "I am sorry to have kept you," he said. "I went away, not to evade your summons, but to post to my newspaper an account of what I suppose I am called back to relate."

The coroner smiled.

"The account that you posted to your newspaper," he said, "differs, probably, from that which you will give here under oath."

"That," replied the other, rather hotly and with a visible flush, "is as you please. I used manifold paper and have a copy of what I sent. It was not written as news, for it is incredible, but as fiction. It may go as a part of my testimony under oath."

"But you say it is incredible."

"That is nothing to you, sir, if I also swear that it is true."

The coroner was silent for a time, his eyes upon the floor. The men about the sides of the cabin talked in whispers, but seldom withdrew their gaze from the face of the corpse. Presently the coroner lifted his eyes and said: "We will resume the inquest."

The men removed their hats. The witness was sworn.

"What is your name?" the coroner asked.

"William Harker."

"Age?"

"Twenty-seven."

"You knew the deceased, Hugh Morgan?"

"Yes."

"You were with him when he died?"

"Near him."

"How did that happen—your presence, I mean?"

"I was visiting him at this place to shoot and fish. A part of my purpose, however, was to study him and his odd, solitary way of life. He seemed a good model for a character in fiction. I sometimes write stories."

"I sometimes read them."

"Thank you."

"Stories in general—not yours."

Some of the jurors laughed. Against a sombre background humour shows high lights. Soldiers in the intervals of battle laugh easily, and a jest in the death chamber conquers by surprise.

"Relate the circumstances of this man's death," said the coroner. "You may use any notes or memoranda that you please."

The witness understood. Pulling a manuscript from his breast pocket he held it near the candle and turning the leaves until he found the passage that he wanted began to read.

CHAPTER II: WHAT MAY HAPPEN IN A FIELD OF WILD OATS ". . . The sun had hardly risen when we left the house. We were looking for quail, each with a shotgun, but we had only one dog. Morgan said that our best ground was beyond a certain ridge that he pointed out, and we crossed it by a trail through the *chaparral*. On the other side was comparatively level ground, thickly covered with wild oats. As we emerged from the *chaparral* Morgan was but a few yards in advance. Suddenly we heard, at a little distance to our right and partly in front, a noise as of some animal thrashing about in the bushes, which we could see were violently agitated.

" 'We've started a deer,' I said. 'I wish we had brought a rifle.'

"Morgan, who had stopped and was intently watching the agitated *chaparral*, said nothing, but had cocked both barrels of his gun and was holding it in readiness to aim. I thought him a trifle excited, which surprised me, for he had a reputation for exceptional coolness, even in moments of sudden and imminent peril.

" 'Oh, come,' I said. 'You are not going to fill up a deer with quail-shot, are you?'

"Still he did not reply; but catching a sight of his face as he turned it slightly toward me I was struck by the intensity of his look. Then I understood that we had serious business in hand, and my first conjecture was that we had 'jumped' a grizzly. I advanced to Morgan's side, cocking my piece as I moved.

"The bushes were now quiet and the sounds had ceased, but Morgan was as attentive to the place as before.

" 'What is it? What the devil is it?' I asked.

" 'That Damned Thing!' he replied, without turning his head. His voice was husky and unnatural. He trembled visibly.

"I was about to speak further, when I observed the wild oats near the place of the disturbance moving in the most inexplicable way. I can hardly describe it. It seemed as if stirred by a streak of wind, which not only bent it, but pressed it down—crushed it so that it did not rise; and this movement was slowly prolonging itself directly toward us.

"Nothing that I had ever seen had affected me so strangely as this unfamiliar and unaccountable phenomenon, yet I am unable to recall any sense of fear. I remember—and tell it here because, singularly enough, I recollected it then—that once in looking carelessly out of an open window I momentarily mistook a small tree close at hand for one of a group of larger trees at a little distance away. It looked the same size as the others, but being more distinctly and sharply defined in mass and detail seemed out of harmony with them. It was a mere falsification of the law of aerial perspective, but it startled, almost terrified me. We so rely upon the orderly operation of familiar natural laws that any seeming suspension of them is noted as a menace to our safety, a warning of unthinkable calamity. So now the apparently causeless movement of the herbage and the slow, undeviating approach of the line of disturbance were distinctly disquieting. My companion appeared actually frightened, and I could hardly credit my senses when I saw him suddenly throw his gun to his shoulder and fire both barrels at the agitated grain! Before the smoke of the discharge had cleared away I heard a loud savage cry—a scream like that of a wild animal—and flinging his gun upon the ground Morgan sprang away and ran swiftly from the spot. At the same instant I was thrown violently to the ground by the impact of something unseen in the smoke—some soft, heavy substance that seemed thrown against me with great force.

"Before I could get upon my feet and recover my gun, which seemed to have been struck from my hands, I heard Morgan crying out as if in mortal agony, and mingling with his cries were such hoarse, savage sounds as one hears from fighting dogs. Inexpressibly terrified, I struggled to my feet and looked in the direction of Morgan's retreat; and may Heaven in mercy spare me from another sight like that! At a distance of less than thirty yards was my friend, down upon one knee, his head thrown back at a frightful angle, hatless, his long hair in disorder and his whole body in violent movement from side to side, backward and forward. His right arm was lifted and seemed to lack the hand—at least, I could see none. The other arm was invisible. At times, as my memory now reports this extraordinary scene, I could discern but a part of his body; it was as if he had been partly blotted out—I cannot otherwise express it—then a shifting of his position would bring it all into view again.

"All this must have occurred within a few seconds, yet in that time Morgan assumed all the postures of a determined wrestler vanquished by superior weight and strength. I saw nothing but him, and him not always distinctly. During the entire incident his shouts and curses were heard, as if through an enveloping uproar of such sounds of rage and fury as I had never heard from the throat of man or brute!

"For a moment only I stood irresolute, then throwing down my gun I ran forward to my friend's assistance. I had a vague belief that he was suffering from a fit, or some form of convulsion. Before I could reach his side he was down and quiet. All sounds had ceased, but with a feeling of such terror as even these awful events had not inspired I now saw again the mysterious movement of the wild oats, prolonging itself from the trampled area about the prostrate man toward the edge of a wood. It was only when it had reached the wood that I was able to withdraw my eyes and look at my companion. He was dead."

CHAPTER III: A MAN THOUGH NAKED MAY BE IN RAGS The coroner rose from his seat and stood beside the dead man. Lifting an edge of the sheet he pulled it away, exposing the entire body, altogether naked and showing in the candle-light a clay-like yellow. It had, however, broad maculations of bluish black, obviously caused by extravasated blood from contusions. The chest and sides looked as if they had been beaten with a bludgeon. There were dreadful lacerations; the skin was torn in strips and shreds.

The coroner moved round to the end of the table and undid a silk handkerchief which had been passed under the chin and knotted on the top of the head. When the handkerchief was drawn away it exposed what had been the throat. Some of the jurors who had risen to get a better view repented their curiosity and turned away their faces. Witness Harker went to the open window and leaned out across the sill, faint and sick. Dropping the handkerchief upon the dead man's neck the coroner stepped to an angle of the room and from a pile of clothing produced one garment after another, each of which he held up a moment for inspection. All were torn, and stiff with blood. The jurors did not make a closer inspection. They seemed rather uninterested. They had, in truth, seen all this before; the only thing that was new to them being Harker's testimony.

"Gentlemen," the coroner said, "we have no more evidence, I think. Your duty has been already explained to you; if there is nothing you wish to ask you may go outside and consider your verdict."

The foreman rose—a tall, bearded man of sixty, coarsely clad.

"I should like to ask one question, Mr. Coroner," he said. "What asylum did this yer last witness escape from?"

"Mr. Harker," said the coroner gravely and tranquilly, "from what asylum did you last escape?"

Harker flushed crimson again, but said nothing, and the seven jurors rose and solemnly filed out of the cabin.

"If you have done insulting me, sir," said Harker, as soon as he and the officer were left alone with the dead man, "I suppose I am at liberty to go?"

"Yes."

Harker started to leave, but paused, with his hand on the door latch. The habit of his profession was strong in him—stronger than his sense of personal dignity. He turned about and said:

"The book that you have there—I recognize it as Morgan's diary. You seemed greatly interested in it; you read in it while I was testifying. May I see it? The public would like——"

"The book will cut no figure in this matter," replied the official, slipping it into his coat pocket; "all the entries in it were made before the writer's death."

As Harker passed out of the house the jury re-entered and stood about the table, on which the now covered corpse showed under the sheet with sharp definition. The foreman seated himself near the candle, produced from his breast pocket a pencil and scrap of paper and wrote rather laboriously the following verdict, which with various degrees of effort all signed:

"We, the jury, do find that the remains come to their death at the hands of a mountain lion, but some of us thinks, all the same, they had fits."

CHAPTER IV: AN EXPLANATION FROM THE TOMB   In the diary of the late Hugh Morgan are certain interesting entries having, possibly, a scientific value as suggestions. At the inquest upon his body the book was not put in evidence; possibly the coroner thought it not worth while to confuse the jury. The date of the first of the entries mentioned cannot be ascertained; the upper part of the leaf is torn away; the part of the entry remaining follows:

". . . would run in a half-circle, keeping his head turned always toward the centre, and again he would stand still, barking furiously. At last he ran away into the brush as fast as he could go. I thought at first that he had gone mad, but on returning to the house found no other alteration in his manner than what was obviously due to fear of punishment.

"Can a dog see with his nose? Do odours impress some cerebral centre with images of the thing that emitted them? . . .

"Sept. 2.—Looking at the stars last night as they rose above the crest of the ridge east of the house, I observed them successively disappear—from left to right. Each was eclipsed but an instant, and only a few at the same time, but along the entire length of the ridge all that were within a degree or two of the crest were blotted out. It was as if something had passed along between me and them; but I could not see it, and the stars were not thick enough to define its outline. Ugh! don't like this.". . .

Several weeks' entries are missing, three leaves being torn from the book.

"*Sept.* 27.—It has been about here again—I find evidences of its presence every day. I watched again all last night in the same cover, gun in hand, double-charged with buckshot. In the morning the fresh foot-prints were there, as before. Yet I would have sworn that I did not sleep —indeed, I hardly sleep at all. It is terrible, insupportable! If these amazing experiences are real I shall go mad; if they are fanciful I am mad already.

"*Oct.* 3.—I shall not go—it shall not drive me away. No, this is *my* house, *my* land. God hates a coward. . . .

"*Oct.* 5.—I can stand it no longer; I have invited Harker to pass a few weeks with me—he has a level head. I can judge from his manner if he thinks me mad.

"*Oct.* 7.—I have the solution of the mystery; it came to me last night— suddenly, as by revelation. How simple—how terribly simple!

"There are sounds that we cannot hear. At either end of the scale are notes that stir no chord of that imperfect instrument, the human ear. They are too high or too grave. I have observed a flock of blackbirds occupying an entire tree-top—the tops of several trees—and all in full song. Suddenly—in a moment—at absolutely the same instant—all spring into the air and fly away. How? They could not all see one another—whole tree-tops intervened. At no point could a leader have been visible to all. There must have been a signal of warning or command, high and shrill above the din, but by me unheard. I have observed, too, the same simultaneous flight when all were silent, among not only blackbirds, but other birds—quail, for example, widely separated by bushes—even on opposite sides of a hill.

"It is known to seamen that a school of whales basking or sporting on the surface of the ocean, miles apart, with the convexity of the earth between, will sometimes dive at the same instant—all gone out of sight in a moment. The signal has been sounded—too grave for the ear of the sailor at the masthead and his comrades on the deck—who nevertheless feel its vibrations in the ship as the stones of a cathedral are stirred by the bass of the organ.

"As with sounds, so with colours. At each end of the solar spectrum the chemist can detect the presence of what are known as 'actinic' rays. They represent colours—integral colours in the composition of light—which we are unable to discern. The human eye is an imperfect instrument; its range is but a few octaves of the real 'chromatic scale.' I am not mad; there are colours that we cannot see.

"And, God help me! the Damned Thing is of such a colour!"

mr. strenberry's tale

by J. B. PRIESTLEY

"And thank you," said the landlady, with the mechanical cheerfulness of her kind. She pushed across the counter one shilling and four coppers, which all contrived to get wet on the journey. "Yes, it's quiet enough. Sort of weather to bring them in too, though it's a bit early yet for our lot. Who's in the Private Bar?" She craned her fat little neck, peered across the other side, and then returned, looking very confidential. "Only one. But he's one of our reg'lars. A bit too reg'lar, if you ask me, Mr. Strenberry is."

I put down my glass, and glanced out, through the open door. All I could see was a piece of wet road. The rain was falling now with that precision which suggests it will go on for ever. It was darker too. "And who is Mr. Strenberry?" I enquired, merely for want of something better to do. It did not matter to me who Mr. Strenberry was.

The landlady leaned forward a little. "He's the schoolmaster from down the road," she replied, in a delighted whisper. "Been here—oh, lemme see—it must be four years, might be five. Came from London here. Yes, that's where he came from, London. Sydenham, near the Crystal Palace, that's his home. I know because he's told me so himself, and I've a sister that's lived near there these twenty years."

I said nothing. There did not seem to be anything to say. The fact that the local schoolmaster came from Sydenham left me as uninterested as it found me. So I merely nodded, took another sip, and filled a pipe.

The landlady glanced at me with a faint reproach in her silly prominent eyes. "And he's queer is Mr. Strenberry," she added, with something like defiance. "Oh yes, he's queer enough. Clever, y'know—in a sort of way, book-learning and all that, if you follow my meanin'—but, well—he's queer."

"In what way is he queer?" It was the least I could do.

She put her hand up to her mouth. "His wife left him. That's about two years ago. Took their little boy with her too. Gone to stay with relations, it was given out, but we all knew. She left him all right. Just walked out one fine morning and the little boy with her. Nice little boy, too, he was. He lives alone now, Mr. Strenberry. And a nice mess, too, I'll be bound. Just look at his clothes. He won't be schoolmastering here much longer neither. He's been given a few warnings, that I do know. And you can't blame 'em, can you?"

I replied, with the melancholy resignation that was expected of me, that I could not blame them. Clearly, Mr. Strenberry, with his nice mess, his clothes, his general queerness, would not do.

The landlady shook her head and tightened her lips. "It's the same old trouble now. Taking too much. I don't say getting drunk—because, as far as I can see, he doesn't—but still, taking too much, too reg'lar with it. A lot o' people, temperancers and that sort," she went on, bitterly, "think we want to push it down customers' throats. All lies. I never knew anybody that kept a decent house that didn't want people to go steady with it. I've dropped a few hints to Mr. Strenberry, but he takes no notice. And what can you do? If he's quiet, behaves himself, and wants it, he's got to have it, hasn't he? We can't stop him. However, I don't want to say too much. And anyhow it isn't just what he takes that makes him queer. It's the way he goes on, and what he says—when he feels like saying anything, and that's not often."

"You mean, he talks queerly?" I said, casually. Perhaps a man of ideas, Mr. Strenberry.

"He might go a week, he might go a fortnight, and not a word—except 'Good evening' or 'Thank you,' for he's always the gentleman in here, I must say—will you get out of him. Some of the lively ones try to draw him out a bit, pull his leg as you might say—but not a word. Then, all of a sudden, he'll let himself go, talk your head off. And you never heard such stuff. I don't say I've heard much of it myself because I haven't the time to listen to it and I can't be bothered with it, but some of the other customers have told me. If you ask me, it's a bit of a shame, the way they go on, because it's getting to be a case of——" And here she tapped her forehead significantly. "Mind you, it may have been his queerness that started all his troubles, his wife leaving him and all that. There's several that knows him better than I do will tell you that. Brought it all on himself, they say. But it does seem a pity, doesn't it?"

She looked at me mournfully for about a second and a half, then became brisk and cheerful again. "He's in there now," she added, and bustled away to the other side of the bar, where two carters were demanding half-pints.

I went to the outer door and stood there a moment, watching the persistent rain. It looked as if I should not be able to make a move for at least half an hour. So I ordered another drink and asked the landlady to serve it in the Private Bar, where Mr. Strenberry was hiding his queerness. Then I followed her and took a seat near the window, only a few feet away from Mr. Strenberry.

He was sitting there behind a nearly empty glass, with an unlighted stump of cigarette drooping from a corner of his mouth. Everything about him was drooping. He was a tall, slack, straggling sort of fellow; his thin greying hair fell forward in front; his nose was long, with something pendulous about its reddened tip; his moustache drooped wearily; and even his chin fell away, as if in despair. His eye had that boiled look common to all persevering topers.

"Miserable day," I told him.

"It is," he said. "Rotten day." He had a high-pitched but slightly husky voice, and I imagined that its characteristic tone would probably be querulous.

There was silence then, or at least nothing but the sound of the rain outside and the murmur of voices from the bar. I stared at the Highlanders and the hunting men who, from various parts of the room, invited you to try somebody's whisky and somebody else's port.

"Got a match?" said Mr. Strenberry, after fumbling in his pockets.

I handed him my matchbox and took the opportunity of moving a little nearer. It was obvious that that stump of cigarette would not last him more than half a minute, so I offered him my cigarette case too.

"Very quiet in here," I remarked.

"For once," he replied, a kind of weak sneer lighting up his face. "Lucky for us too. There are more fools in this town than in most, and they all come in here. Lot of loud-mouthed idiots. I won't talk to 'em, won't waste my breath on 'em. They think there's something wrong with me here. They *would*." He carefully drained his glass, set it down, then pushed it away.

I hastened to finish my glass of bitter. Then I made a pretence of examining the weather. "Looks as if I shall have to keep under cover for another quarter of an hour or so," I said carelessly. "I'm going to have another drink. Won't you join me?"

After a little vague humming and spluttering, he said he would, and thanked me. He asked for a double whisky and a small soda.

"And so you find the people here very stupid?" I said, after we had taken toll of our fresh supply of drink. "They often are in these small towns."

"All idiots," he muttered. "Not a man with an educated mind amongst them. But then—education! It's a farce, that's all it is, a farce. I come in here—I must go somewhere, you know—and I sit in a corner and say nothing. I know what they're beginning to think. Oh, I've seen them—nudging, you know, giving each other the wink. I don't care. One time I would have cared. Now I don't. It doesn't matter. Nothing matters, really."

I objected mildly to this pessimism.

"I know," he went on, looking at me sombrely. "You needn't tell me. I can see you're an intelligent man, so it's different. But you can't argue with me, and I'll tell you why. You see, you don't know what I know. Oh, I don't care if they do think I'm queer. I *am* queer. And so would you be if you'd seen what I've seen. They wouldn't because they wouldn't have the sense. . . ." His voice trailed away. He shrugged his thin sloping shoulders. His face took on a certain obstinate look that you often see on the faces of weak men. Evidently he thought he had said too much.

I was curious now. "I don't see what you mean," I began. "No doubt you've had unpleasant experiences, but then most of us have at some time or other." I looked at him expectantly.

"I don't mean that," he said, raising his voice and adding a touch of scorn. "This is different. You wouldn't understand, unless I told you it all. Even then you mightn't. It's difficult. Oh, what's the use!" He finished his whisky in one quick gulp.

"Well, I wish you'd tell me."

Doubtfully, mournfully, he examined my face, then he stared about the room, pulling his straggling and drooping moustache. "Could I have another cigarette?" he asked, finally. When he had lit it, he blew out a cloud of smoke, then looked at me again.

"I've seen something nobody else has seen," said Mr. Strenberry. "I've seen the end of it all, all this," he waved a hand and gave a bitter little laugh, "building houses, factories, education, public health, churches, drinking in pubs, getting children, walking in fields, everything, every mortal blessed thing. That's what I've seen, a glimpse anyhow. Finish! Finish! The End!"

"It sounds like doomsday," I told him.

"And that's what it was," cried Mr. Strenberry, his face lighting up strangely. "Anyhow, that's what it amounted to. I can't think about anything else. And you couldn't either, if you'd been there. I've gone back to it, thought about it, thought round and round it, oh, thousands of times! Do you know Opperton Heath? You do? Well, that's where it happened, nearly three years ago. That's all, three years ago. I'd gone up there for a walk and to have a look at the birds. I used to be very interested in birds—my God, I've dropped that now—and there are one or two rare kinds up on the Heath there. You know what it's like—lonely. I hadn't met a soul all afternoon. That's the worst of it. If there'd only been somebody else there——"

He broke off, took up his smouldering cigarette, put it down again and stared in front of him. I kept quiet, afraid that a chance word might suddenly shut him up altogether.

"It was a warm afternoon," he said, beginning again as abruptly as he had stopped, "and I was lying on the grass, smoking. I remember I was wondering whether to hurry back and get home in time for tea or to stay where I was and not bother about tea. And I wish to God I'd decided to go back, before it happened. But I didn't. There I was, warm, a bit drowsy, just looking at the Heath. Not a soul in sight. Very quiet. If I could write poetry, I'd write a poem about the Heath as I saw it then, before the thing happened. It's all I would write too. The last five minutes there." He broke off again, and I believe there were tears in his eyes. He looked a figure of maudlin self-pity, but nevertheless it may have been the lost peace and beauty of the world that conjured up those tears. I did not know then. I do not know now.

"Then I saw something," said Mr. Strenberry. "It was a sort of disturbance in the air, not fifty yards from where I was. I didn't take much notice at first, because you get that flickering on a warm day up there. But this went on. I can't describe it properly, not to make you see it. But in a minute or two, you couldn't help noticing it. Like a thin revolving column of air. A waterspout made of air, if you see what I mean? And there was something dark, something solid, in the centre of it. I thought it must have something to do with a meteor. I got up and went closer, cautiously, you know, taking no chances. It didn't seem to be affecting anything else. There was no wind or anything. Everything was as quiet as it was before. But this column of air was more definite now, though I can't exactly explain how it came to look so definite. But you knew it was there all right, like seeing one piece of glass against another piece. Only there was movement in this, and faster than the fastest piece of machinery you ever set eyes on. And that dark thing in the centre was solider every second. I went closer still. And then the movement inside the column—like a glassy sort of pillar it was, though that doesn't quite give you the idea—stopped, though there was still a flickering and whirling on the outside. I could see that dark thing plainly now. It was a man—a sort of man."

Mr. Strenberry shut his eyes, put his hands up to them, and leaned forward on his elbows. In the quiet that followed, I could hear two fellows laughing in the bar outside. They were shouting something about a litter of pigs.

"He was a lightish greeny-blue in colour, this man," Mr. Strenberry continued, "and the same all over. He'd no clothes on, but I got the idea that he'd a very tough skin, leathery, y'know. It shone a bit too. He'd no hair on him at all, and didn't look as if he'd shaved it all off but as if he'd never had any. He was bigger than me, bigger than you, but no giant. I should say he was about the size and figure of one of your big heavyweight boxers—except for his head. He'd a tremendous head—and of course as bald as an egg—and a wonderful face. I can see it now. It was flattish, like some of the faces of the Egyptian statues in the British Museum, but what you noticed the minute you saw it, were the eyes. They were more like a beautiful woman's eyes than a man's, very big and soft, y'know, but bigger and softer than any woman's eyes—and such a colour, a kind of dark purple. Full of intelligence too. Blazing with it, I knew that at once. In fact, I could see that this man was as far above me as I am above a Hottentot. More highly developed, y'know. I'm not saying this because of what I learned afterwards. I saw it at once. You couldn't mistake it. This greeny-blue hairless man knew a million things we'd never heard of, and you could see it in his eyes. Well, there he was, and he stared at me and I stared at him."

"Go on," I said, for Mr. Strenberry had stopped and was now busy staring at me.

"This is the part you've got to try and understand," he cried, excitedly. "You see, this queer revolving cylinder of air was between us, and if it had been glass two feet thick it couldn't have separated us any better. I couldn't get at him. I don't say I tried very hard at first; I was too surprised and frightened. But I did try to get nearer after a minute or two, but I couldn't, and I can't possibly explain to you—no, not if I tried for a week—how I was stopped. Call it a transparent wall, if you like, but that doesn't give you the idea of it. Anyhow, it doesn't matter about me. The point is, he couldn't get out, and he obviously knew more about it than I did and he was trying desperately hard. He'd got some sort of little instrument in each hand—I could see them flash—and he kept bringing these together. He was terribly agitated. But he couldn't get out. He'd stopped the inside of this column revolving, as I said, but apparently he couldn't stop the outside, which was whirling and whirling just as fast as ever.

"I've asked myself thousands of times," Mr. Strenberry went on, more reflectively now, "what would have happened if he had got out. Would he have ruled the whole world, knowing so much more than we do? Or would these fools have shoved him into a cage, made a show of him, and finally killed him? Though I don't imagine they could have done that, not with this man. And then again, could he have existed at all once he had got out? I don't mean just microbes and things, though they might easily have killed him off, because I don't suppose his body knew anything about such a germ-ridden atmosphere as ours. No, I don't mean that. This is the point. If he'd got out, really burst into this twentieth-century world, he might have stopped existing at all, just vanished into nothing, because after all this twentieth-century isn't just a date, it's also a condition, a state of things, and—you see—it doesn't include him. Though, of course, in a sense it does—or it did—because there he was, on the Heath that day."

"I'm afraid I don't follow all this," I said. "But go on, perhaps it will become clearer."

Mr. Strenberry leaned forward and fixed me with his little boiled eyes. "Don't you see, this man had come from the future? Fellows like H. G. Wells have always been writing about us taking a jump into the future, to have a look at our distant descendants, but of course we don't. We can't; we don't know enough. But what about them, taking a jump into the past, to have a look at *us?* That's far more likely, when you come to think of it. But I don't mean that is what this man was doing. He was trying to do more than that. If you ask me, they'd often taken a peep at us, and at our great-great-grandparents, and for that matter at our great-great-grandchildren too. But he wasn't just doing that. He was trying to get out, to escape from his own time altogether."

I drew in a long breath, then blew it out again, slowly.

"Don't you think I'm merely guessing that," cried Mr. Strenberry, "because I'm not. I *know.* And I know because he told me. I don't mean to say we talked. As a matter of fact, I did try shouting at him—asking him who he was and where he'd come from, and all that—but I don't think he heard me, and if he did, he certainly didn't understand. But don't make any mistake—he saw me all right. He looked at me just as I looked at him. He made a sign or two, and might have made more if he hadn't been so busy with those instruments and so desperately agitated. He didn't shout at me, never opened his lips. But he *thought* at me. That's the only way I can describe it. Messages from him arrived in my head, and turned themselves into my own words, and even little pictures. And it was horrible—horrible, I tell you. Everything was finished, and he was trying to escape. The only way he could do it was to try and jump back into the past, out of the way. There wasn't much of the world left, fit to live in. Just one biggish island, not belonging to any of the continents we know—they'd all gone, long ago. I don't know the date. That never came through, and if it had, I don't suppose it would have told me much. But it was a long time ahead—perhaps twenty thousand years, perhaps fifty thousand, perhaps more—I don't know. What I do know is that this man wasn't anybody very important, just a sort of minor assistant in some kind of laboratory where they specialized in time experiments, quite a low-class fellow among his own kind, though he would have seemed a demigod to me and you. And I knew that while he was so terrified that he was frantic in his attempt to escape, at the same time he was ashamed of himself, too—felt he was a kind of dodger, you see. But even then, what was happening was so ghastly that he'd never hesitated at all. He had run to the laboratory or whatever it was, and just had time to jump back through the ages. He was in terror. He didn't show it as we might, but I tell you—his mind was *screaming*. Some place—a city, I think it was—had been entirely destroyed and everything else was going too, everything that had once been human. No words came into my mind to describe what it was that was destroying everything and terrifying him. Perhaps I hadn't any words that would fit in. All I got were some little pictures, very blurred, just like bits of a nightmare. There were great black things rolling about, just wiping everything out. Not like anything you've ever seen. You couldn't give them a shape."

Here Mr. Strenberry leaned further forward still, grasped my coat-sleeve, and lowered his voice.

"They weren't beasts or huge insects even," he whispered. "They weren't anything you could put a name to. I don't believe they belonged to this world at all. And something he thought rather suggested that too. They came from some other place, from another planet perhaps. Don't you see, it was all finished here. They were blotting it out, great rolling black things—oh, horrible! Just imagine what he felt, this man, who had just managed to escape from them, but now couldn't get out, into this world and time of ours. Because he couldn't, that was the awful thing. He tried and tried, but it couldn't be done. And he hadn't long to try either, I knew that. Because of what was happening at the other end, you see. I tell you, I stood there, looking at him, with his thoughts buzzing round my own head, and the sweat was streaming down my face. I was terrified too, in a panic. And then he was in an agony of fear, and so was I. It was all up. The inside of that column of air began revolving again, just as it had done when it first came, and then I couldn't see him distinctly. Only his eyes. Just those eyes, staring out of the swirl. And then, I saw something. I swear I did. Something black. Just a glimpse. That's all. A bit of one of those things, getting hold of him—the last man left. That's what it must have been, though how I came to see it, I don't quite know, but I've worked it out this way and that way, and it seems to me——"

"A-ha, who have we here?" cried a loud, cheerful voice. "How's things, Mr. Strenberry?"

Two red-faced men had just entered the room. They grinned at my companion, then winked at one another.

"A nasty day, Mr. Strenberry," said the other fellow. "What do you say?"

Mr. Strenberry, who appeared to have crumpled up at their approach, merely muttered something in reply. Then, giving me a hasty glance, in which shame and despair and scorn were mingled, he suddenly rose and shuffled out of the room.

The two newcomers looked at one another, laughed, and then settled into their corner. The landlady appeared with their drinks. I stood up and looked out of the window. The downpour had dwindled to a few scattered drops, brightening in the sunlight.

"I seen you talking to Mr. Strenberry," the landlady said to me. "Least, I seen him talking to you. Got him going, too, you did. He's a queer one, isn't he? Didn't I tell you he was a queer one? Telling you one of his tales, I'll be bound. Take no notice of him, mister. You can't believe a single word he says. We found that out long since. That's why he doesn't want to talk to us any more. He knows we've got a pinch of salt ready, Mr. Strenberry does."